ISBN 978-0-276-44276-6

www.readersdigest.co.uk

The Reader's Digest Association Limited, 11 Westferry Circus, Canary Wharf, London E14 4HE

# of love & life

Three novels selected and condensed
by **Reader's Digest**

The Reader's Digest Association Limited, London

# CONTENTS

# An Offer You Can't Refuse

Jill Mansell

Lola Malone is seventeen years old and truly, madly, deeply in love with Dougie Tennant. And even though he is about to leave for Edinburgh University, the pair are determined not to let their love die. If the separation becomes unbearable, then Lola will just move to Edinburgh to be with Dougie.

The young lovers have it all worked out—but Dougie's over-protective mother has other ideas . . .

# Chapter 1
## Ten Years Ago

THERE ARE SOME PLACES where you might expect to bump into your boyfriend's ultra-posh mother. At a Buckingham Palace garden party perhaps, or Glyndebourne, or turning her nose up at Ferrero Rochers at some foreign ambassador's cocktail party. And then there are other places you wouldn't expect to bump into her *at all*.

Like the Cod Almighty at the dodgier end of Tooting High Street.

'Blimey, it's Dougie's mum.' Instinctively wiping her hands on her green nylon overall and curbing the urge to curtsy—because Dougie's mum was *that* posh—Lola said brightly, 'Hello, Mrs Tennant, how lovely to see you!'

And how typical that she should turn up two minutes before closing, when all they had left to offer her was a tired-looking saveloy and a couple of overlooked fish cakes.

'Hello, Lola. I wondered if we could have a chat.' Even for a visit to a fish-and-chip shop, Dougie's mother's make-up was immaculate, her hair swept into a Princess Michael of Kent chignon.

'Oh, right. Absolutely. I'm just finishing here.' Lola glanced across at Alf, who made good-humoured off-you-go gestures. 'We close at half past two. So you don't want anything to take away?'

Was that a shudder? Mrs Tennant shook her head and said with a flicker of amusement, 'I don't think so, do you?'

Having retrieved her shoulder bag from the back room and shrugged off her nylon overall, Lola ducked under the swing-top counter and took the king-sized portion of chips Alf had wrapped up for her.

'Bye, Alf. See you tomorrow.'

'I can drop you home if you like,' said Dougie's mother.

Lola beamed; free chips *and* a lift home in a brand-new Jaguar. This was definitely her lucky day.

Outside on the pavement it was stiflingly hot and muggy. Inside the Jaguar the cool air smelt deliciously of leather and Chanel No. 19.

Lola balanced the steaming parcel of chips in her lap. Her stomach was rumbling but she heroically resisted the temptation to open them. 'So why did you want to see me? Is this about Dougie's birthday?'

'No. It's about you and Dougie. I want you to stop seeing him.'

Lola blinked. 'Excuse me?'

'I'd like you to end your relationship with my son.'

This couldn't be happening. Her shoulders stiffening in disbelief, Lola watched as Dougie's mother drove along, as calm and unconcerned as if they were discussing nothing more taxing than the weather.

'*Why?*'

'He's eighteen years old.'

'Nearly nineteen.'

'He's eighteen now,' Mrs Tennant repeated firmly, 'and on his way to university. He *is* going to university.'

'I know.' Bewildered, Lola said, 'I'm not stopping him. We're going to see each other whenever we can, take it in turns to do the journey. I'll catch the coach up to Edinburgh every other weekend, and Dougie's going to drive down here when it's his turn, then—'

'No, no, no, I'm sorry but this isn't the kind of relationship Doug needs right now. He told me last night that he was having second thoughts about going to university. He wants to stay here. And that's all down to you, my girl. But I won't stand by and let you ruin his life.'

'Honestly, I'm not ruining his life. I want the best for Dougie, just like you do. We love each other! I've already told him, if we miss each other too much I'll move up to Edinburgh and we'll live together!'

'Oh, yes, he mentioned that too. And the next thing we know, you'd be feeling left out because he'd have all his university friends while you're stuck working in some fish-and-chip shop. So to regain his attention you'd accidentally get yourself pregnant. No, I'm sorry, I simply can't allow this to happen. It's best to make the break now.'

Who did this woman think she was?

'But I don't want to.' Lola's breathing was fast and shallow. 'And you can't force me to do it.'

'No, I can't force you. But I can do my best to persuade you.'

'I won't be persuaded. I love Dougie. With all my heart.'

'Ten thousand pounds, take it or leave it.'

'*What?*'

'That's what I'm offering. Think it over. How much do you earn in that fish-and-chip shop?' Dougie's mother raised a perfectly plucked eyebrow. 'No more than five pounds an hour, I'm sure.'

Four pounds actually. But it was still a mean dig; working at the Cod Almighty was only a temporary thing while she applied for jobs that would make more use of her qualifications.

'If I took your money, what kind of a person would that make me?'

'Oh, I don't know. The sensible kind, perhaps?'

Lola was so angry she could barely speak; her fingernails sank through the now-soggy chip paper, filling the air-conditioned interior of the car with the sharp smell of vinegar.

'How do you think Dougie's going to feel when he hears what you've said to me today?'

'Well, I should imagine he'd be very annoyed with me. If you told him.' Mrs Tennant paused for effect. 'But do yourself a favour, Lola. Give yourself time to think this through, because ten thousand pounds is a lot of money. When you've made your mind up, give me a ring when you know Dougie isn't at home. And I'll write out the cheque.'

'You can stop the car. I'll walk the rest of the way.' No longer willing to remain in her boyfriend's mother's plush Jag, Lola jabbed a finger to indicate that she should pull in at the bus-stop ahead.

'Sure? OK then.'

Lola paused with her hand on the passenger door handle and looked at Dougie's mother in her crisp white linen shirt and royal chignon. 'Can I ask you something?'

'Feel free.'

'Why don't you approve of me?'

'You risk ruining my son's future.' Mrs Tennant didn't hesitate.

'We love each other. We could be happy for the rest of our lives.'

'No you *couldn't*, Lola. Do you really not understand what I'm trying to explain here? You're too brash and noisy, you have no class, you're not good enough for Dougie. And'—the older woman paused, her gaze lingering significantly over Lola's low-cut red vest top and short denim skirt complete with grease stain—'you dress like a cheap tart.'

'Can I ask you something else?' said Lola. 'How are you going to feel when Dougie refuses to ever speak to you again?'

And, heroically resisting the urge to tear open the parcel of chips and fling them in Dougie's mother's face, she climbed out of the car.

**B**ack at home in Streatham—a far more modest house than Dougie's, which his mother would surely sneer at—Lola paced the small living room like a caged animal and went over everything that had happened.

OK, *now* what was she supposed to do? Dougie was currently up in Edinburgh for a few days, sorting out where he was going to be living come October and acquainting himself with the city that was due to be his home for the next three years. Doubtless Mrs Tennant had planned it this way with her usual meticulous attention to detail. Her own mother and stepfather were both out at work. Bloody, bloody woman—how *dare* she do this to her? What a *witch*.

Deliberately not changing out of her 'low-cut' top and 'far-too-short' denim skirt, Lola left the house. If she didn't talk to someone about the situation, she would burst.

'Ten thousand pounds,' said Jeannie.

'Yes.'

'I mean, ten thousand *pounds*.'

'So?' Lola banged down her Coke. 'It doesn't matter how much it is. She can't go around doing stuff like that. It's just sick.'

They were in McDonald's. Jeannie noisily slurped her own Coke through two straws. 'Can I say something?'

'Can I stop you?'

'OK, you say it's a sick thing to do. And you're going to say no. But what if Dougie comes back from Edinburgh on Friday and tells you he's met someone else? What if he tells you you're dumped?'

'Dougie wouldn't do that.'

'He *might*,' said Jeannie. 'OK, maybe not this week, but sooner or later the chances are that you two will break up. You're seventeen years old. How many seventeen-year-olds spend the rest of their lives with their first love? And if Dougie *is* the one who finishes it, you can't go running to his mother crying that you've changed your mind and can you have the money now, please? Because it'll be too late by then.' Mock sorrowfully, Jeannie clutched her chest. 'Heartbroken. No more Dougie Tennant *and* no ten thousand pounds.'

So that was the advice from a so-called friend. Well, what else should she have expected from someone like Jeannie, whose parents had fought an epic divorce battle and left her with a jaundiced view of relationships? Jeannie now despised her mother's new husband and was escaping all the hassle at home by moving to Majorca. The plan was to work in a bar, dance on the beach and generally have the time of her life.

The memory of Dougie's mother haunted Lola all the way home, that patrician face and disparaging voice letting her know in no uncertain terms why she was nowhere near good enough for her precious son.

Lola pictured the smirk on that face if Jeannie's cheery prediction were to come true. Then again, imagine how she'd react if she and Dougie defied her and got married! Ha, wouldn't *that* be fabulous?

Except . . . except . . . I'm seventeen, I don't want to get married just to spite someone. I'm too *young*.

Back home again, Lola was overcome by an overwhelming urge to speak to Dougie. When she heard his voice she would decide what to do. God, how would he feel when he found out?

Dougie was staying in a bed and breakfast in Edinburgh. The number was on the pad next to the phone in the narrow hallway. Dialling it, Lola checked her watch; it was five o'clock. He should be there now, back from his visit to the university campus . . .

'No, dear, I'm afraid you've missed him,' the landlady of the B&B told her. 'They came back an hour ago, Dougie changed and then they were off. Said they were going to check out the pubs on Rose Street!'

'Oh.' Lola's heart sank; she'd so wanted to hear his voice. 'Who was he with?'

'I didn't catch their names. Another boy and two girls . . . I'll tell him you rang, shall I? Although goodness knows what time he'll be back . . .'

Hanging up, Lola heard Jeannie's words again. It wasn't that she was overwhelmed with jealousy that Dougie had gone out for the evening with a group of new friends, two of whom happened to be female. It was just the realisation that this was the first of many hundreds of nights when she would be apart from him and—

Lola started as a floorboard creaked overhead; she'd thought the house was empty.

She called out, 'Hello?'

No reply.

'Mum?' Lola frowned. 'Dad?'

Still nothing. Had the floorboard just creaked on its own or was someone up there? Taking an umbrella as a precaution, Lola made her way upstairs.

What she saw when she pushed open the white-painted door of her parents' bedroom shocked her to the core.

'**D**ad?' Lola's stomach clenched in fear. Something was horribly, horribly wrong. Her stepfather—the only father she'd ever known, the man she loved with all her heart—was packing a case.

'Go downstairs.' He turned his back on her, barely able to speak.

Lola was shaking. 'Dad, what is it?'

'Please, just leave me alone.'

'No! I won't! Tell me what's wrong.' Dropping the umbrella, she cried, 'Why are you packing? Are you ill? Are you going to hospital?'

Grief-stricken, he shook his head. 'I'm not ill, not in that way. Lola, this is nothing to do with you . . .'

'Daddy, *tell* me,' Lola whispered in desperation, tears in her eyes.

Covering his face, he sank onto the bed. 'Oh, Lola, I'm sorry.'

She had never been so frightened. 'I'm going to phone Mum.'

'No, you mustn't.'

'Are you having an affair? Is that why you're packing? Don't you want to live with us any more?'

Another shake of the head. 'It's nothing like that.'

'So tell me what it *is* then.' Lola's voice wavered; they were both crying now. 'You have to, because I'm scared!'

Twenty minutes later she knew everything. Unbelievable though it seemed, Alex had been gambling and they'd never even suspected it. Through his twice-weekly visits to a snooker club he had been introduced to a crowd of card players and gradually, without even realising it, he'd found himself being sucked in. They had all met regularly at a house in Bermondsey to play poker and at first Alex had done pretty well. Now, he suspected that this had been the plan all along. Then the tide had turned, he had begun to lose and when the losses had mounted up to a worrying degree, Alex had confided to the genial group that he needed time to pay back what he owed them. It was at this point that the genial group had stopped being genial and had begun to threaten him. Realising he was in way over his head, Alex had concentrated all his energies on winning back all the money he'd lost. Since his bank manager wouldn't have appreciated this as a sensible business plan, he'd borrowed the money from the friend who'd introduced him to the poker group in the first place.

A week later he'd lost it all.

The following night, as he was leaving the garage where he worked as a mechanic, he was stopped by two heavies in a van who explained in graphic detail what they would do to him if he didn't repay every penny he owed by this time next week.

This time next week was now tomorrow and desperate times called for desperate measures. Sick with shame and in fear for his life, Alex had decided to disappear. It was the only answer; he couldn't admit to Blythe what he'd done. She and Lola meant everything to him. If Lola had arrived home half an hour later he would have been gone for good.

'I wish you had,' he said heavily. 'You told us you were going shopping in Oxford Street this afternoon. I thought I was safe here.'

Shopping in Oxford Street. She'd completely forgotten about that after Dougie's mother had dropped her bombshell.

Lola, her face wet with tears, said, 'But I didn't, and now I know.'

'I still have to go. I can't face your mother,' said Alex in desperation. 'Oh God, how could I have been so *stupid* . . .'

Hugging him tightly, Lola already knew she had no choice. Her biological father, an American, had done a bunk the moment he'd found out that Blythe was pregnant. But it hadn't mattered because Alex had come along two years later. He loved Lola as if she were his own daughter. He had made her boiled eggs with toast soldiers, he'd taught her to ride a bike, he had driven her all the way to Birmingham to see a boy band who were playing at the NEC. His love for her was unconditional . . .

Dry-eyed—this was too important for tears—Lola said, 'I can get the money for you.'

'Sweetheart, you can't. It's fifteen thousand pounds.'

Her stomach in knots, Lola didn't allow herself to think of the repercussions. 'I can get you most of it.'

And when Alex shook his head in disbelief she told him how.

When she'd finished he shook his head with even more vehemence. 'No, no, I can't let you do that. No way in the world, *absolutely not.*'

But what was the alternative? For him to disappear? For her to lose the only father she had ever known? For her mother's world to be shattered?

'Listen to me.' Although her own heart felt as if it were breaking in two, Lola played her trump card. 'Mum would never need to know.'

'Lola. How nice to see you again.' Adele Tennant opened her front door and stepped to one side. 'Come on in.'

Following her across the echoing, high-ceilinged hall, Lola felt sick but grimly determined.

'I'm glad you've seen sense.' Adele sat down at the desk in her study and reached for her chequebook. Next to her, morning sunlight bounced off the glass on a silver photo frame. Shifting position to avoid the glare, Lola saw that it was a photograph of Adele and her children, Dougie on the left and Sally on the right. The photo had been taken a couple of years ago while they were on holiday somewhere unbelievably exotic, with palm trees and an ocean the colour of lapis lazuli. Dougie, tanned and grinning, was looking heartbreakingly gorgeous. Sally, the older sister Lola had never met, was blonde and pretty in a flamingo-pink sarong. Now twenty-six and engaged to an Irish landowner, she was living with him in the Wicklow Mountains. Dougie adored his sister and Lola had been looking forward to getting to know her.

Her throat tightened. That wouldn't be happening now.

'You won't regret this.' Adele crisply uncapped a fat black fountain pen and hovered the glinting nib above the cheque.

'Hang on a minute.' Lola briefly closed her eyes, wondering if she could do this. Yes, she could. 'Ten thousand isn't enough.'

'I beg your pardon?'

'It isn't enough. I need fifteen. Then I'll never see Dougie again.'

'The cheek of you!'

Lola's mouth was bone-dry. 'Otherwise I'll move up to Edinburgh.'

Adele shot her a look of utter loathing. Frankly, Lola didn't blame her. 'You are beyond the pale.'

Lola felt sicker than ever. 'I need the money.'

'Eleven thousand,' Adele retaliated. 'And that's it.'

'Fourteen,' said Lola.

'Twelve.'

'Thirteen.'

'Twelve and a half.'

'Done.' That was it, she'd haggled her way up to twelve and a half thousand pounds. As far as Dougie's mother was concerned, she was now officially despicable beyond belief. But it was enough to get Alex out of trouble; his boss at the garage was able to advance him the rest.

'I hope you're proud of yourself.' Adele dismissively wrote out the newly agreed sum.

'I'm not. I just need the money.'

'And hallelujah for that.' Adele, for whom twelve and a half thousand wasn't that much money at all, smiled her chilly, unamused smile. 'So what are you going to be spending it on?'

As she said it, her gaze slid disparagingly over Lola in her turquoise vest, jeans and flip-flops.

It was all over now. No more Dougie. She no longer had to try to impress his mother. 'Moving abroad,' said Lola. 'New bikinis. Silicone implants. Isn't that what you'd expect?'

'It's your money now. I don't care what you do with it, so long as you keep out of my son's life.' Adele paused. 'Will you tell him about this?'

'No.' Lola shook her head and took the cheque which Alex would pay into his account this morning. He had arranged an overdraft to cover the days before it cleared. In exchange she handed over to Adele the hardest letter she'd ever had to write. 'I'm just going to finish with him. You can give him this when he gets home. I'll be out of the country by then.'

'Delighted to hear it. Dougie will be over you in no time, but I agree it's best to put some distance between you. Well, I'll show you out.' Adele rose to her feet and ushered Lola back through the house to the front door. 'Goodbye, Lola.'

This was it, this was really it. Lola's throat swelled up and for a moment she considered ripping the cheque into tiny pieces.

It was what she wanted to do. But then what would happen to Alex?

'I do love Dougie.' Her voice cracked; she still couldn't imagine living without him. 'I really, really do.'

Opening the door with a flourish, Adele said cheerfully, 'But you love money more.'

The moment he arrived home three days later, Dougie had only one thing on his mind.

'Hi, Mum, you OK?' He dumped his rucksack in the hall and kissed Adele on the cheek. 'Just going to shoot over to Lola's.'

Adele hugged her clever, handsome son, the light of her life. 'Actually there's a letter here for you from Lola.'

Now, as Dougie scanned the contents and she saw the colour drain from his face, Adele knew she'd been right to do as she had. At his age it was ridiculous to have let himself get so involved with any girl, let alone one as unequal socially as Lola Malone.

'What does it say?'

'Nothing.' Pain mingled with disbelief in Dougie's dark eyes as he crumpled the letter in his fist and headed upstairs.

Adele didn't want to see him hurt, but it was for his own good. Calling up after Dougie she said, 'Sweetheart, is everything all right?'

He turned abruptly. 'No, but it will be.' Filled with resolve, Dougie nodded and said, 'I'm going to my room, then I'm going out. And, yes, everything *will* be all right.'

But it wasn't, thank God. Lola had kept her part of the bargain. The moment Dougie left the house, Adele infiltrated his room and found the crumpled-up note under the bed.

> *Dear Dougie,*
>
> *Sorry to do it like this, but it's easier than face to face. It's over, Dougie, I don't want to see you any more. We've had fun and I don't regret our relationship but my feelings for you have changed recently. I don't want to move up to Edinburgh with you, it's not my kind of place, and the thought of all that travelling up to see you is just too much. It'd never work out—we both know that, deep down. So I've decided to go abroad, somewhere hot and sunny. Don't bother trying to contact me because I've made up my mind. You'll find someone else in no time, and so will I.*
>
> *Have a good life, Dougie.*
>
> *Lola x*

Adele nodded approvingly, crumpled the note back up again and replaced it under the bed.

Good girl. She couldn't have put it better herself.

'She's gone, love. I'm so sorry. You know what Lola's like once she makes up her mind about something—whoosh, off like a rocket.'

Dougie couldn't believe it. Lola *had* left. Struggling to retain his composure, he swallowed the golf ball in his throat. 'Did she say why?'

'Not really.' Blythe shrugged helplessly, as baffled as he was. 'Just said she fancied a change. Her friend Jeannie was moving to Majorca, they met up for a chat and the next day Lola announced that she was going out there with Jeannie. To *live*. Well, we were shocked! And I did ask her if she'd thought things through, what with you two having been so close, but there was no stopping her.'

'Do you have a phone number for her? An address?'

'Sorry, love, I can't do that. She doesn't want you to contact her. I think she just feels you have your own lives to lead.' Lola's mum struggled to console him.

As if anything could. Dougie raked his fingers through his hair in desperation. 'Is she seeing someone else?'

'No.' Vigorously Blythe shook her head. 'Definitely not that.'

He didn't know if that made things better or worse. Being dumped in favour of someone else was one thing, but being dumped in favour of no one at all was an even bigger kick in the teeth. Controlling his voice with difficulty, Dougie said, 'Can you do me a favour? Just tell her that if she changes her mind, she knows where I am.'

## Chapter 2
### Seven Years Ago

'OH, LOLA, LOOK at you.' Squeezing her tightly, Blythe slipped instantly into mother-hen mode. 'It's February. You'll catch your death of cold!'

'Mum, I'm twenty, you're not allowed to nag me any more.' But secretly Lola enjoyed it. Hugging her mother in return, she then teasingly lifted the hem of her top to show off her toffee-brown Majorcan tan.

'You'll be frostbitten once we get outside.' Taking one of Lola's bags, Blythe began threading her way through the crowded airport to the exit. 'Are you sure you don't want to pull a jumper out?'

'Quite sure. What's the point of being browner than anyone else and covering it all up with a jumper? And I'm starving. Are we going straight home or shall I pick up a burger here?'

'No burgers today. We're eating out. Alex is treating us to lunch,' said Blythe. 'He's booked a table at Emerson's in Piccadilly.'

'Whoo-hoo, lunch at Emerson's. There's posh,' Lola marvelled. 'What have we done to deserve this?'

Blythe gave her arm a squeeze. 'No special reason, love. It's just wonderful to have you back.'

Her mother had been lying. There was a special reason. Alex waited until they'd chosen their food before ordering a bottle of champagne.

'I'm out of the business,' he said as the waiter brought the bottle to the table.

'Oh no.' Lola's heart sank. Following her departure from home three years ago, Alex had given up gambling, just like that. He had given up visiting his snooker club too. Instead he had stayed at home, becoming more and more interested in the business opportunities being offered up by the fast-expanding Internet. When he'd come up with a germ of an idea for a Web-based hotel-booking service, Lola had listened politely without really understanding how it might work.

But Alex had persisted, eventually setting up a company and working on it in his spare time. Then last year he'd given up his job at the garage in order to devote more hours to it. Lola had been under the impression that things were going rather well.

Oh God . . . she hoped he hadn't slipped and gone back to gambling.

'So.' Here came the sick feeling of dread again. 'What went wrong?'

Alex's eyes crinkled at the corners. 'Nothing went wrong. It was too much for me to handle. I'd have needed to take on staff, find proper offices . . . I couldn't deal with everything myself.'

Lola nodded. 'Mum said you were working all hours.'

'I never imagined it would take off like that. It was incredible, but it was scary. Then another company approached me,' Alex explained. 'They offered to buy me out.'

'Oh! Well, that must have been a relief.'

'It is a relief.' Alex gravely nodded in agreement and raised his fizzing glass. 'So here's to us.'

'To us.' Lola enthusiastically clinked glasses with them both and took a big gulp of delicious icy-cold champagne.

'By the way,' said Alex, 'I sold the business for one point six million.'

Luckily the champagne had already disappeared down her throat, otherwise she'd have sprayed it across the table like a garden sprinkler.

'Are you *serious*?'

'It's true!' Blythe's eyes danced. 'You don't know how hard it's been for me not to tell you. I nearly blurted it out at the airport!'

'My God,' Lola breathed.

'And this is for you.' Alex took a folded cheque from his inside pocket and passed it across the table.

'My *God*.' Lola's hands began to tremble as she counted the noughts, then recounted them. Her mother had never found out about the traumatic events of three years ago, which made it all the more difficult to say what she wanted to say. But Alex, although he hadn't needed to, was paying her back many, many times over.

Finally, unsteadily, Lola said, 'Alex, you don't need to do this.'

Their eyes met. He smiled. 'You're my daughter. Why wouldn't I? Now you can afford to move out of that poky little rented apartment of yours and buy yourself a villa up in the hills.'

Unable to contain herself, Lola jumped up out of her chair and threw her arms round him. Never mind a villa up in the hills; now she could afford to move back to London and buy herself somewhere to live here.

'*Lola*.' Appalled by the attention she was receiving, Blythe frantically attempted to tug down her daughter's short skirt. 'Stand up straight, for heaven's sake. Everyone's looking at your pants!'

There was always something deliciously disorientating about emerging from a dark, candlelit restaurant at three thirty in the afternoon and discovering that it was still daylight outside, albeit grey city daylight.

Like a human magnet Lola found herself being drawn irresistibly in the direction of the biggest, sparkliest shops.

'We'll leave you to it.' Her mother and Alex couldn't be persuaded to join her. 'Don't spend too much.'

When they'd headed back to the car, Lola threaded her way through the narrow backstreets of Piccadilly until she reached Regent Street. Oh, yes, here they were, the department stores she'd missed so much.

Better still, here was Kingsley's.

Lola paused at the entrance, savouring the moment. Department stores were fabulous but they still came second to bookshops in her heart. Alcudia in Majorca had many things going for it but the sad collection of battered English-language paperbacks on the carousels in the beachfront souvenir shops wasn't one of them. She craved a proper bookshop like an addict craves a fix. There really wasn't much that could beat that gorgeous new-book smell, touching the covers and turning the pages of a book whose pages had never been turned before.

And if it was weird to feel like that, well, she just didn't care. Some people were obsessed with shoes and loved them with a passion. Shoes were fine but you couldn't stay up all night reading one, could you?

Anyway, it was freezing out here on the pavement. With a shiver of anticipation Lola plunged into the welcoming warmth of Kingsley's.

Oh, look at the piles of delicious hardbacks with glossy covers, crying out to be bought and devoured. Lola ran her fingers over them, prolonging the moment and not realising she had a dopey smile on her face until another customer caught her eye and smiled back.

'Sorry.' Several glasses of champagne over lunch had loosened her tongue. 'I live in Majorca, so it's been a while since I saw so many books.'

The man's ears glowed pink. 'Lucky you. Whereabouts in Majorca?'

'Alcudia, up on the north side of the island.'

'I know Alcudia!' the man blurted out. 'I go there with my mother every year. We stay in an apartment in the old town. What a coincidence!'

Hmm, not *that* much of one, seeing as a zillion holidaymakers invaded Alcudia each year, but Lola was touched by his enthusiasm. 'Well, I work in a restaurant down by the harbour. So if you fancy some great seafood next time you're there, you'll have to drop by for a meal.'

'That sounds most enjoyable.' He hesitated. 'Unless . . . um, are you very expensive?'

'Not expensive at all,' Lola assured him with a smile. 'And you can ask for anything you like. You'll have a great time, I promise.'

'Where exactly are you?' the man said eagerly.

Flipping open her silver handbag, Lola fished out one of the restaurant's business cards and handed it over.

'Excuse me,' barked a voice behind them, 'that's *quite* enough. I'm going to have to ask you to leave.'

Bemused, Lola turned and saw that she was being addressed by a grey-haired female member of staff who was aquiver with disapproval.

'I'm sorry, are you speaking to me?'

'Ha, don't give *me* any of your smart talk. Come on, off you go, leave our customers alone.' The woman pointed to the door like a traffic cop. 'Out, out. We don't need your sort in here, plying your filthy trade.'

'Plying my *trade*?' Lola's eyebrows shot up. 'What are you talking about? I'm not a prostitute!'

'Don't argue with me, young lady. I heard what you were saying to that gentleman. Look at you!' The woman jabbed an accusing finger at Lola's skimpy white top, abbreviated lime-green skirt and long bare legs. 'It's perfectly clear what you are!'

Oh, for crying out loud.

'I live in Majorca! I just flew back today! I didn't know it was going to be this cold here! Tell her what we were talking about,' Lola demanded, but it was too late. Mortified, the man had scurried out of the shop.

'And you can get out too, before I call the police.' The woman wore a look of triumph.

Walking out now wasn't an option; it simply wasn't in Lola's nature.

The woman, she now saw from the name badge, was called Pat.

'I came in here to buy books and I'll leave when I've bought them.' Refusing to be intimidated, Lola said coolly, 'But before I go, I'll be having a word with your manager, Pat.'

Fifteen minutes later she made her way to the till with an armful of books, aware that word of her set-to with Pat had spread around the store. Pat was no longer anywhere in sight. The young lad on the till rang up Lola's purchases and did his best not to look at her legs.

'Could I speak to the manager, please?' said Lola.

He nodded, picked up the phone and muttered a few words into it. Lola waited.

Finally a door at the back opened and a woman in her forties emerged. She approached Lola and said, 'I'm so sorry about Pat, she's just been telling me what happened and I'd like to apologise on behalf of Kingsley's. The thing is, Pat's retiring in six weeks and if you make a formal complaint it'll spoil everything for her.'

'I—'

'And I probably shouldn't be telling you this but she does have a bit of a bee in her bonnet about, um, working girls.' Lowering her voice to a whisper the woman said, 'Her husband, you see, ran off with one. So that's why she overreacted. I'm really, really sorry. I've had a talk with her and she'll never do it again.'

'Well, good,' said Lola. 'I'm happy to hear that.'

'So does that mean you won't make an official complaint?'

'No, I won't.'

'Oh, thank you *so much*.' She clasped Lola's hand in gratitude. 'Poor old Pat. I'm sure you can understand why she got so upset—'

'I'm not a prostitute,' said Lola.

This stopped the manageress in her tracks.

'Oh!' Covering her surprise, the woman hastily backtracked. 'Of course you aren't! Heavens, of *course* I didn't think that!'

Lola grinned because an outfit that wouldn't merit a second glance in Alcudia clearly held other connotations in a London bookshop in chilly February. Maybe the time had come to start modifying her wardrobe.

'I think you did. Don't worry about it. And you haven't asked me yet why I wanted to see you.'

The woman looked flustered. 'Right. Sorry, I'm in a bit of a muddle now. So why did you want to see me?'

'This.' Lola tapped the sign on the counter, identical to the one she'd spotted in the window earlier. 'You have a vacancy for a sales assistant.'

'We do. To replace Pat when she leaves.'

'Do you need many qualifications for that?'

Better still, she hadn't fancied him one bit.

Gabriel Adams, with his floppy blond hair and lean slouchy body, had been twenty-nine when he'd moved into the flat across the landing from her. And this time *he* had been the one who'd knocked on Lola's door to invite her over for a drink on his roof terrace.

'I never even knew there was a roof terrace,' Lola said, marvelling at the view from the back of the house.

'It's a sun trap.' Gabe grinned at her. 'I think I'm going to like it here. Does this T-shirt make me look gay?'

Since it was a vibrant shade of lilac, clearly expensive and quite tight-fitting, Lola said, 'Well, a bit.'

'I know, it's too much. I'm super-tidy and a great cook. I can't wear this as well.' Pulling off the T-shirt to reveal an enviably tanned torso, Gabe held it towards her. 'Do you want it or shall I chuck it away?'

It wasn't just expensive, Lola discovered. It was Dolce & Gabbana. Liking her new neighbour even more she said, 'I'll have it. Are you sure?'

'Sure I'm sure. The colour'll suit you. Better than me chucking it in the back of a drawer and never wearing it again.'

Except it wasn't, because a week later, as she was on her way out one evening, Lola bumped into Gabe and his girlfriend on their way in. The girlfriend stopped dead in her tracks and said, 'What are you doing wearing my boyfriend's T-shirt?'

'Um . . . well, he g-gave it to . . .' Catching the look on Gabe's face, Lola amended hastily, 'I mean, he *lent* it to me.'

The girlfriend shot her a killer glare before swinging round to Gabe. 'I bought you that for your birthday!'

Gabe broke up with that particular girl shortly afterwards and Lola had been able to start wearing the T-shirt again. From then on a stream of girlfriends came and went, entranced by the fact that Gabe was a charming commitment-phobe. Each of them in turn was utterly convinced they would be the one to make him see the error of his ways.

Each of them, needless to say, was wrong.

Or had been, up until three months ago when Gabe had met an Australian backpacker called Jaydena on the last leg of her round-the-world trip. Jaydena had bucked the trend and been the one to leave Gabe, returning to Sydney when they'd only known each other for a couple of weeks and were still completely crazy about each other. Back in Australia, she emailed Gabe every day and he emailed her back. Within weeks she'd persuaded him to jack in his job and fly out to join her.

Lola was stunned when she heard. 'But . . . I might never see you again.' It was a daunting prospect; Gabe was such a huge part of her life. And not only for the fun times. When Alex had died five years ago—suddenly, and desperately unfairly, of a heart attack—Lola had been distraught. Gabe had been her rock.

'Hey, I'm not selling the flat, just renting it out for a year. After that I could be back.'

Lola knew she would miss him terribly but alarm bells were ringing for another, far less altruistic reason. 'Where are you going to find a new tenant? Through a lettings agency?'

'Ha!' Gabe gleefully prodded her in the ribs. 'So it's only yourself you're worried about, panicking about who your new neighbour might be.'

'No. Well, yes.'

'Already sorted. Marcus from work just split up with his wife. He's moving in.'

Oh. Lola relaxed, because she knew Marcus and he was all right, if a bit on the boring side and inclined to yabber on about motorbikes.

Ugh, it was raining harder than ever now. Wishing she was wearing flatter shoes, Lola hurried along the road with her jacket collar up, then turned left down the side street that was a short cut to the tube station. She winced as her left foot landed in a puddle and—

*'Get off me, get off! Noooo!'*

Lola's head jerked up, her heart thudding in her chest at the sight of the violent scene unfolding ahead of her. The woman's piercing screams filled the air as she was dragged out of the driver's seat of her car by two men who flung her roughly to the ground. One of them knelt over her, ripping at something on the woman's hand. When she struggled against him he hit her in the face and snarled, 'Shut *up.*'

But the woman let out another shriek of fright and he hit her again, harder this time, bouncing her head off the road. 'I said *shut* it. Now give me your rings.'

'No! *Owww.*' The woman groaned as he wrenched back her arm.

'Leave her alone!' bellowed Lola, punching 999 into her phone and gasping, 'Police, ambulance, Keveley Street.' Filled with a boiling rage, she kicked off her shoes and raced down the road to the car. 'Get off her!'

'Yeah, right.' The man sneered while his cohort revved the engine of the woman's car.

'Come on,' bellowed the cohort, 'hurry up, hurry up.'

'Stop it!' Lola grabbed hold of the attacker's greasy hair and yanked his head back hard. 'Leave her alone, I've called the police.'

'Let go of me,' roared the man, fighting to free himself.

'No, I won't.' Grappling with him on the ground, Lola smelt alcohol on his fetid breath and felt ice-cold rain seeping through her tights. The woman was lying on her side facing away from her, curled up and moaning with pain. The man swore again and twisted like an eel to escape but Lola had him now and she was damned if she'd let him go—

*Crrrackk!* An explosion of noise and pain filled Lola's head and she realised the other attacker had hit her from behind with some kind of weapon. Then everything went black and she slumped to the ground.

As if from a great distance Lola heard the screech of tyres as the car accelerated away. Close to, the woman groaned. Without opening her eyes, Lola stretched out an arm, encountered the woman's foot and clumsily patted it.

'S'OK, just hang on and the police'll be here.'

'Th-they tricked m-me, I th-thought someone was hurt . . . then when I stopped the c-c-car they d-dragged me out . . .'

'Hey, don't be upset. I can hear sirens, you're OK now.'

'I'm not OK, there's b-blood everywhere, he b-broke my n-nose.'

'Sshh, don't cry.' Lola forced down a rising swell of nausea. 'Here's the ambulance.'

The next twenty minutes were a confusing blur. Lola was dimly aware that she was having trouble answering the questions put to her by the paramedics and the police. She hoped they didn't think she was paralytic with drink. When requested to hold out an arm then touch her nose with her forefinger, Lola missed and almost took her eye out.

The other woman had already been whisked off to hospital in the first ambulance. When a second arrived in the narrow, suddenly busy street and a stretcher was brought out, Lola waved her hands and protested, 'No, no, I can't go to the party, I've got work tomorrow.'

'You need to be checked over, love. You were knocked out.'

'I know I'm a knockout.' Lola beamed up at the curiously attractive paramedic. 'You're gorgeous.' How on earth had she never found big double chins and enormous stomachs attractive before?

'**M**um, I'm fine. They've X-rayed my skull and checked me out all over. It was just a bash on the head.' Gingerly Lola leaned forward in bed to show her mother the egg-sized bump. 'They're discharging me later. They only kept me in overnight because I was knocked out for a few seconds and when I came round I was a bit muddled.'

'So I've just been hearing in the nurses' office,' said Blythe. 'Apparently you were hilarious, propositioning one of the poor ambulance men. I can't believe you did something so ridiculous.'

'It wasn't my fault! I was concussed!'

'I don't mean that. I'm talking about you launching yourself into a dangerous situation. You could have been killed.'

This had occurred to Lola too; at the time she'd simply acted on impulse although in retrospect it had been a bit of a reckless thing to do. 'But I wasn't. And I'm OK.' Apart from the blistering headache. 'Could you give work a ring and tell them I should be in tomorrow?'

'I most certainly will not. I'll tell them you might be in next week, depending on how you feel.'

'Mum! It's December! Everyone's rushed off their feet!'

'And you were knocked unconscious,' Blythe retorted. 'My God, for once in your life will you listen to me?'

A man who'd been walking up the ward stopped and said genially, 'It always pays to do as your mother tells you.'

He was in his sixties, well-spoken and smartly dressed in a suit. Was this her consultant? Lola sat up a bit straighter in bed and smiled, all ready to convince him that she was well enough to be allowed home.

'Miss Malone?'

'That's me.' Eagerly Lola nodded. To prove her brain was in working order, he'd probably ask her the kind of questions doctors used on old people when they wanted to find out if they were on the ball. OK, what was the capital of Australia? What was thirty-three times seven? Yeesh, don't let him ask her to name the Shadow Chancellor of the Exchequer.

'Hello.' He moved towards her, smiling and extending his hand.

'Hi!' Quick, was it Melbourne? Victoria? Lola's brain was racing. People always thought it was Sydney but she knew it definitely wasn't.

The man shook her hand warmly. 'It's very nice to meet you. I'm Philip Nicholson.'

Watching him turn to shake her mother's hand, Lola breathed in his expensive aftershave—*ooh, was it Perth?*

'I just had to come and see you,' he went on.

'Well, I suppose you couldn't avoid it. All part of the job description!' Lola beamed at him, aware that he was looking at her head. Touching the tender area she said, 'Bit of a bump, that's all. I'm absolutely fine. Except, can I just quickly tell you that I'm rubbish at capital cities?'

Philip Nicholson hesitated and glanced over at Blythe, who shrugged and looked baffled.

'I mean, some are all right, like Paris and Amsterdam and Madrid, they're easy. But in general I have to say that capitals aren't my strong point.' To be on the safe side she added, 'Neither's politics.'

Carefully Dr Nicholson said, 'That's not a problem. I won't ask any questions about either subject.'

'What a relief.' Lola relaxed back against her pillows. 'I'd hate to be kept in just because I couldn't name the leader of the Liberal Democrats.'

Dr Nicholson said, 'I'm sure that wouldn't happen.'

'Well, hopefully not, but sometimes you *do* know the answer and you just can't think of it—your mind goes completely blank.'

'Of course it does.' He nodded understandingly.

'Like, let's try it with you.' Lola waggled an index finger at him. 'Capital of Australia.'

Dr Nicholson hesitated. Blythe, never able to resist a quiz question, let out a squeak of excitement and raised her arm. Lola swung the pointing finger round and barked in Paxmanesque fashion, '*Yes*, Mum?'

'Sydney!'

'No it *isn't*.' Lola returned her attention to Dr Nicholson. 'Your turn.'

He was looking taken aback. Opening his mouth to reply, he—

'Melbourne!' squealed Blythe.

'Mum, control yourself. It's Dr Nicholson's turn.'

At this, his shoulders relaxed and his mouth began to twitch. 'It's Canberra. And I'm not Dr Nicholson, by the way.'

Bemused, Lola said, 'No?'

He smiled. 'Entirely my fault. I knew the police had told you our name last night and I assumed you'd remember. But you were concussed. I'm sorry, let's start again. My name's Philip Nicholson and I'm here to thank you from the bottom of my heart for coming to my wife's rescue. You did an incredibly brave thing and I can't begin to tell you how grateful we are.' His voice thickened with emotion. 'Those thugs could have killed her if you hadn't gone to help.'

Lola clapped her hand over her mouth. 'I thought you were my consultant, coming to check whether I was compos mentis.'

Philip Nicholson looked amused. 'I realise that now.'

'How's your wife this morning?' said Lola.

'Still shocked. Battered and bruised. Two broken fingers.' There was a hard edge to his voice now. 'Where they tried to wrench her rings off.'

'Did they get them?'

'No. Which is also thanks to you.' Philip Nicholson shook his head. 'My wife and I owe you so much.'

Lola squirmed, embarrassed. 'Anyone would have done the same.'

'No they wouldn't,' Blythe retorted. 'Most people—'

'Hello, hello! Morning, all!' A little man wearing a maroon corduroy jacket over a green hand-knitted sweater came bouncing up to them. Pumping Lola's hand and simultaneously pulling closed the curtains around the bed, he said, 'I'm Dr Palmer, your consultant. Let's just give you a quick once-over, shall we? If you two could leave us alone for ten minutes that'd be marvellous. I say, that's a fair-sized bump on your head. How are you feeling after your little adventure last night?'

'Great.' Lola watched as he began testing her reflexes, her eyes, her coordination. 'Are you going to be asking me questions?'

'Absolutely.'

She couldn't help feeling smug. 'The capital of Australia is Canberra.'

'Good grief, is it really? Always thought it was Sydney. Never been much good at capital cities. When I'm checking out my patients I prefer to ask them sums. What's twenty-seven times sixty-three?'

'Uh . . . um . . .' Lola began to panic; seven threes were—

'Only kidding.' Mr Palmer's eyes twinkled as he snatched up her notes. 'What day is it today?'

'Wednesday the 4th of December.' Phew, that was more like it.

'Cheers.' He wrote the date on a fresh page then added o/e NAD.

'What does NAD mean?' Lola peered at it. 'Please don't say Neurotic and Demented.'

The consultant chuckled. 'On examination, no abnormality detected.'

'So does that mean I can go home?'

'I think we can let you go.'

Beaming, Lola wiggled her feet. 'Yay.'

'This is fantastic. I feel like the Queen.' Being at home and having a fuss made of her was a huge novelty and Lola was relishing every minute. Once you'd been officially signed off work by the doctor, well, you may as well lie back and make the most of it. Friends called in, bringing chocolate croissants and gossip, and Blythe had come over yesterday and spring-cleaned—well, winter-cleaned—the flat.

Best of all, she had Gabe at her beck and call.

'You're a fraud.' He brought in the cheese-and-mushroom toasted sandwich he'd just made. 'You don't have to be in bed.'

'I know.' Lola happily patted her ultra-squishy goosedown duvet, all puffed up around her like a cloud. 'But I get more sympathy this way. Ooh.' She bit into the toasted sandwich and caught a string of melted cheese before it attached itself to her chin. '*Mmmmpphh*. Oh, Gabe, don't go to Australia. Stay here and make toasted sandwiches for me for ever.'

Gabe tweaked her toes. 'What did your last slave die of?'

'Nothing. I've never had a slave before, but now I know I want one.' At that moment the doorbell rang downstairs. 'Like when the doorbell rings,' said Lola. 'And someone else runs down to see who it is.'

'That'll be me, then.'

'Sorry, but I'm an invalid.' Lola shrugged regretfully.

He was back a couple of minutes later with a great armful of white roses tied with straw and swathed in cellophane. 'Flowers for the lady. From a *very* up-market florist. Here's the card.' Gabe tossed a peacock-blue envelope over to Lola.

'They're from Philip Nicholson. Mum must have given him my

address in hospital. He hopes I'm feeling better. His wife was discharged yesterday.' She paused, reading on. 'He's inviting me to a party at their house so I can meet her and they can thank me properly.'

'You can't go to a party. You're an invalid.'

'It's not until next Friday; that's seven days away. I'll be fine by then.' Lola showed Gabe the letter. 'He's even organised a car to come and pick me up on the night. Crikey, now I *really* feel like the Queen.'

Five days later Lola was back at work. She adored her job and she loved her customers but sometimes they were capable of testing her patience to the limit. Especially in the run-up to Christmas, when vast hordes of people who didn't venture into bookshops at any other time of year came pouring through the doors with a great Need to Buy coupled with Absolutely No Idea What.

'No, no, it's none of them.' The woman with the plastic rain hat protecting her hair—why? It wasn't raining today—rejected the array of books Lola had shown her.

'OK, well, that's everything we have in stock about insects. If you like, I can look on the computer and—'

'It's nothing like *any* of these,' the woman retorted. 'There's no pictures in the one I'm after.'

A book about insects containing no illustrations of insects. Hmm.

'And you can't remember who wrote it?'

The woman frowned. 'No. I thought you'd know that.'

She clearly felt badly let down by the incompetence of Kingsley's staff. 'I'm so sorry,' said Lola, 'I'm afraid we're not going to be able to—'

The woman said triumphantly, 'There's a pig in it!'

A pig. Right. A pig in a book about insects. *Zrrrrr*, went Lola's brain, assimilating this new and possibly deal-clinching clue. *Zzzzrrrrrrrr* . . .

'Is it *Lord of the Flies*?'

'Yes! That's the one!'

Lola almost laughed. But no. She was a professional. To the woman in the rain hat she said cheerfully, 'It's a novel by William Golding. Let me show you where to find it,' and led her off to the fiction section.

When she returned, one of the assistants, Cheryl, was waiting for her. 'Lola, there's a TV crew here. They're interviewing store managers about Christmas shopping and they wonder if you could spare them five minutes.'

Well, when you were having a good hair day it was a shame to waste it. Lola made her way over to the young male reporter waiting at the tills with a cameraman and his assistant. 'Hi, I'm Lola Malone, the manager. Where would you like to do this?'

## *Chapter 4*

THE PIECE AIRED on the local evening news two days later. It lasted less than ninety seconds and the reporter had asked some pretty inane questions but Lola, watching herself on TV as she set about her hair with curling tongs, felt she'd acquitted herself well enough.

'Well?' Lola turned to Gabe when the piece ended. 'Was I OK?'

Gabe was busy unwrapping a Twix bar. 'You answered his questions, you didn't burp or swear. That has to be good news. What time's this car coming?'

'Seven thirty. I feel quite jittery. What if it's embarrassing and I want to leave?'

'OK, you'll get there around eight. Leave your phone on and I'll ring you at nine,' said Gabe. 'If you're desperate to get away, tell them I'm your best friend and I've gone into labour.'

'My hero. The things you do for me. How am I going to manage without you when you're gone?' Lola hugged him then made a light-ning lunge for the Twix in his hand. She was fast, but not fast enough.

'I'm sure you'll cope.' Gabe broke off an inch and gave it to her. 'You'll soon find some other poor guy's Twix bars to pinch.'

**B**y seven fifteen Lola was ready to go and peering out of the window.

'Wouldn't it be great if they sent a stretch limo?'

Gabe looked horrified. 'Don't get your hopes up. From the sound of him, this guy has better taste than you. In fact,' Gabe went on as a throaty roar filled the street outside, 'that could be your lift now.'

It was Lola's turn to be appalled. Flinging the window open as the motorbike rumbled to a halt outside, she watched as the helmeted rider dismounted. Surely not. Oh God, her hair would be *wrecked* . . .

'Hi there, Lola.' Phew, panic over, it was only Marcus.

'Hi there, neighbour-to-be! Come on up,' said Lola. 'Gabe's in my flat.'

Upstairs in Lola's living room, clutching his helmet and looking sheepish, Marcus said, 'All right, mate? The thing is, I've got some good news and some bad news.'

'Go on, then,' prompted Gabe.

'Well, me and Carol are back together, she's giving me one last chance. So that's the good news.' An embarrassed grin spread across Marcus's shiny face. 'But that means I won't be moving in. Sorry, mate.'

Gabe shrugged, having already pretty much guessed what Marcus had come here to say. 'Well, I suppose I can't blame you. Bit short notice though, seeing as I'm off next week.'

The car, a gleaming black Mercedes, arrived at seven thirty on the dot. It wasn't a stretch limo, but it was the cleanest, most valeted car Lola had ever been in. She sat back as it purred along, feeling like royalty.

The house, when they reached it, was a huge, double-fronted Victorian affair in Barnes. There were plenty of cars in the driveway and discreet twinkling white Christmas lights studding the bay trees in square stone tubs that flanked the super-shiny dark blue front door.

Even the brass doorbell was classy. Lola clutched her Accessorize sequinned handbag to her side and took a couple of deep breaths. It wasn't like her to be on edge. How bizarre that attempting to beat up a couple of muggers hadn't been nerve-racking, yet this was.

Then the door opened and there was Mr Nicholson with his lovely welcoming smile, and she relaxed.

'Lola, you're here!' He gave her a kiss on each cheek. 'You look terrific.'

Compared with the last time he'd seen her, she supposed she must. Not having uncombed, blood-soaked hair was always a bonus.

'It's good to see you, Mr Nicholson.'

'Please call me Philip. Now, my wife doesn't know I've invited you. You're our surprise guest of honour.' His grey eyes sparkled as he led her across the wood-panelled hall to a door at the far end. 'I can't wait to see her reaction when she realises who you are.'

Philip Nicholson pushed open the door and drew Lola into a huge glittering drawing room full of people, all chattering away and smartly dressed. A thirty-something blonde in aquamarine touched his arm and raised her eyebrows questioningly; when he nodded, she grinned at Lola and whispered, 'Ooh, I'm so excited, this is going to be great!'

'My stepdaughter,' Philip murmured by way of explanation. Nodding again, this time in the direction of the fireplace, he added, 'That's my wife over there, in the orange frock.'

Orange, bless him. Only a man could call it that. The woman, standing with her back to them and talking to another couple, was slim and elegant in a devoré velvet dress in delectable shades of russet, bronze and apricot. Her hair was fashioned in a glamorous chignon and she was wearing pearls round her neck.

Then Philip said, 'Darling . . .' and she swivelled round to look at him. In an instant Lola was seventeen again.

Adele Tennant's gaze in turn fastened on Lola and she took a sharp audible intake of breath.

'My God, what's going on here?' Her voice icy with disbelief, she turned to Philip Nicholson. 'Are you mad, letting her into the house?'

Poor Philip, his shock was palpable. Lola, who was pretty stunned too, couldn't work out who she felt more sorry for, him or herself.

Adele's eyes narrowed suspiciously. 'How did you track me down? My God, you have a nerve. This is a *private party*—'

'Adele, stop it,' Philip intervened at last, raising his hands in horrified protest. 'This was meant to be a surprise. This is Lola Malone, she—'

'I know it's Lola Malone! I'm not senile, Philip! And if she's come here chasing after my son . . . well, she's got another think coming.'

Yeek, Dougie! As if she'd just been zapped with an electric cattle prod, Lola spun round; was he here in this room? No, no sign of him unless he'd gone bald or had a sex change.

'I'm so sorry.' Philip Nicholson shook his head at Lola by way of apology. 'This is all most unfortunate. Adele, will you stop interrupting and listen? I don't know what's gone on in the past but I invited Lola here tonight because she's the one who came to the rescue when you were mugged.' His voice breaking with emotion he said, 'She saved your *life*.'

And what's more, thought Lola, she's starting to wish she hadn't bothered. OK, mustn't say that. At least Philip's pronouncement had succeeded in shutting Adele up.

'I thought you'd like the opportunity to thank her in person.'

People were starting to notice now. The couple Adele had been talking to were avidly observing proceedings. The blonde who was Philip's stepdaughter—crikey, that meant she was Dougie's older sister—came over and said, puzzled, 'Mum? Is everything all right?'

'Fine.' Recovering herself, Adele managed the most frozen of smiles and looked directly at Lola. 'Well . . . what can I say? Thank you.'

'No problem.' What else could she say? *My pleasure?*

'It was such a brave thing you did,' exclaimed Dougie's sister. What was her name? Sally, that was it. 'I can't bear to think what might have happened to Mum if you hadn't dived in like that. You were amazing!'

Lola managed to maintain a suitably modest smile, while her memory busily rewound to that eventful night ten days ago. Euurrgh, she had patted Adele's foot.

Except she wasn't Adele Tennant any more.

'So you remarried,' said Lola, longing to ask about Doug and feeling her stomach clench just at the thought of him.

'Four years ago.' Adele was being forced to be polite now, in a through-gritted-teeth, I-really-wish-you-weren't-here kind of way.

'Congratulations.' Lola wondered what Philip, who was *lovely*, had done to deserve Cruella de Vil as a wife.

'Thank you. Well, it's . . . nice to see you again. Can we offer you a drink? Or,' Adele said hopefully, 'do you have to rush off?'

Rushing off suddenly seemed a highly desirable thing to do. Excellent idea. Lola looked at her watch and said, 'Actually, there is somewhere else I need to—'

'Here he is!' cried Sally, her face lighting up as she waved across the room to attract someone's attention. 'Yoohoo, we're over here! And what sort of time do you call this anyway? You're *late*.'

Lola didn't need to turn round. She knew who it was. Some inner certainty told her that Dougie had entered the drawing room; she could *feel* his presence behind her. All of a sudden she was no longer breathing.

Dougie. Doug. Whom she'd thought she'd never see again.

'Sorry, I was held up at a meeting. Hi, everyone. What have I missed?'

'**W**ell.' Winking at Lola, Sally spoke with relish. 'Philip invited along a surprise guest . . .'

Who turned out to be one very surprised guest. Lola dug her nails into her palms—*don't pass out*—and turned round to look at him.

'Hello, Dougie.'

For a split second their eyes locked and it was as if the last decade had never happened. Doug looked the same but taller, broader, *better*. He'd always had the looks, the ability to stop girls dead in their tracks, and now here he was, having that exact same effect.

Except it would be nice if he could be smiling, looking a bit less stony-faced than this. OK, maybe not very likely, but nice all the same.

'Lola.' Doug's shoulders stiffened as if she were a tax inspector. Taking care to keep his voice neutral he said, 'What brings you here?'

Oh God, this was awful, all the old tumultuous feelings were flooding back. She'd never been able to forget Dougie; he'd been her first love. What's more, seeing as it had never really happened again since, her One and Only.

'I did,' said Philip. 'Sorry, I hope this isn't awkward, but I had no idea you two knew each other. Anyway, surely that's irrelevant now.' He cast a warning glance at Adele with her mouth like a prune and rested a hand reassuringly on Lola's shoulder. 'Under the circumstances I'm sure we can put the past behind us. Doug, this is the young lady who came to your mother's rescue when she was attacked.'

Dougie's expression altered. 'God, really? That was *you*?'

'The police told me her name was Lauren something or other,' Adele said with a hint of accusation, as if Lola had done it on purpose.

'It is, but I've been called Lola since I was a baby. It was a nickname that just stuck.'

'Well, thanks for doing what you did.' There was a warmth in Dougie's eyes now, breaking through the initial wariness. 'From what I hear, you were pretty fantastic.'

Oh, I *was*. Shaking inwardly, Lola did her best to look fantastic but at the same time incredibly self-effacing. Dougie was gorgeous and now fate had brought them back together. The breakup had happened a decade ago; they'd practically been children then. Surely Doug would forgive her for chucking him. 'Well, when someone needs help you just go for it, you don't stop to wonder what—'

'Ooh, I've got it now!' Sally let out a mini-squeal of recognition and pointed excitedly at Lola. 'You're the one I never got to meet! You were going out with my little brother when I was living in Dublin with Tim the Tosser! Then you did a bunk and broke his heart!'

*Oh don't say that,* please *don't say that. I'm so sorry, I didn't want to do it,* Lola longed to blurt out. *It broke my heart too!*

Doug said drily, 'Thanks, Sal.'

'Oh, come on, it was years ago. And she did break your heart.' Sally gave him a jab in the ribs, visibly relishing his discomfort. 'You were a complete pain. All because you couldn't believe your girlfriend had given you the elbow and buggered off abroad.' She nudged Lola and added cheerfully, 'Did him the world of good, if you ask me.'

'That's funny,' said Doug, 'because I don't recall anyone asking you.'

'That's enough.' Adele intervened before the bickering could start. 'Doug, the Mastersons have to leave very soon but they really want to see you before they go.'

'I'll go and find them now. As soon as I've got myself a drink.' Evidently glad of the reprieve, Doug glanced at Lola and Sally, and said, 'Excuse me.'

They watched Doug cross the room with Adele, while Philip went in search of a waiter.

'That's one rattled brother,' Sally observed gleefully.

Guilt swirled up through Lola's stomach. 'Did I really break his heart?'

'Too right you did! Talk about miserable! Ooh, is that yours?'

Lola's phone was chirruping in her bag. She took it out and Gabe's name flashed up at her.

'Feel free.' Sally made encouraging answer-it gestures.

'Thanks. Sorry, I'll just take it outside for a minute.' Longing to confide in Gabe, Lola excused herself and escaped the party. She crossed the hall, quietly let herself out of the house—better safe than sorry—and answered the phone.

'I know, I'm early,' said Gabe. 'Couldn't wait. So how's it going? Are they showering you with diamonds?'

She grimaced in the darkness. 'More like bullets.'

'What? Why?'

'You won't believe what's happening here.' Lola kept walking to warm herself up, round the side of the house and along a narrow stone path leading beneath a hand-carved wooden pergola into a rose garden. 'The woman who was mugged only turns out to be the mother of an old boyfriend of mine. And she loathed me! You should have seen her face tonight when she found out I was the one who'd gone to help her!'

'So you're leaving? Do I feel a contraction coming on?'

'Hang on, don't start boiling kettles just yet. I *was* going to leave,' said Lola. 'And it went without saying that the Wicked Witch couldn't wait to be shot of me.' She paused, reliving the moment her stomach had done a Red Arrows swoop-and-dive. 'But then *he* turned up. Oh, Gabe, I can't describe how it felt. I thought I'd never see Dougie again, but now I have. And he's more gorgeous than ever. It's like a miracle. So I'm not going to leave now. I've got to talk to him properly, he's only just arrived and it's been a bit awkward so far. But . . . oh God, it's just so amazing seeing him again, I haven't been this excited since—'

'Hey, hey, calm down, do you not think you're getting a bit carried away? If this guy dumped you before, what makes you think he's going to be thrilled to see you again?'

'Gabe, you don't understand. He isn't *an* ex-boyfriend. He's *the* ex-boyfriend. Plus, he didn't dump me. I was the one who left him.' Lola swallowed. 'According to his sister I broke his heart.'

'And now you've taken one look at him and decided you want him back. Trust me,' said Gabe, 'that's a recipe for disaster.'

'For heaven's sake, will you stop lecturing me? This is my first love we're talking about here! We were crazy about each other. Dougie was about to start at Edinburgh University,' Lola paced up and down the flag-stoned path in an attempt to keep warm, 'and we planned to visit each other every weekend, but if that wasn't enough I was going to move up there to be with him. You have no idea how happy we were together.'

'So happy that you finished with him. That makes sense.'

'But that's just it, I didn't *want* to finish with him. His bloody mother made me do it!' Lola squeezed her eyes shut as the long-ago hideous encounter in Adele Tennant's car swam back into her brain. 'She hated me, thought I was a bad influence on her precious golden boy . . . she was terrified I'd put him off his studies.'

'So she asked you to stop seeing her son. Erm,' said Gabe, 'did it ever occur to you to say no?'

'She didn't ask me. She made me an offer I couldn't refuse.' Lola hated even thinking about that bit.

'You're not serious!' At last she had Gabe's full attention. 'You mean, like swimming with the fishes? She actually threatened you with a concrete overcoat and a trip to the bottom of the Thames?'

'Not that kind. She offered me money. I was seventeen years old.' There was a bitter taste in Lola's mouth now; no matter how compelling the reason, the fact remained that she had betrayed her boyfriend. 'And she offered me ten thousand pounds if I'd stop seeing Dougie.'

'Which you *took*?'

'Which I took.' It wasn't an action she was proud of, hence never having mentioned it to Gabe before. 'I didn't want to, but I had to.'

'Bloody hell! Ten *grand*. What did you spend it on?'

Lola hesitated, but it was no good; she couldn't tell him. Racked with remorse, Alex had begged her never to reveal their secret to another living soul and it was a promise she had to keep. Alex might be gone now but her mother must never find out what had happened. Choking up at the memory, she said, 'I just needed it. I—'

*Crackkk.*

She froze at the sound of a dry twig snapping underfoot behind her. Swinging round with her heart in her throat, Lola saw the tall figure just visible in the darkness at the entrance to the rose garden.

Not just any old tall figure either. That silhouette was instantly recognisable.

'Ten thousand pounds,' said a voice every bit as incredulous as Gabe's.

Oh God.

'I'll call you back.' Her hand suddenly trembling with more than cold, Lola ended the call and dropped the phone back into her bag.

'Ten thousand pounds,' Doug repeated, shaking his head.

Lola swallowed. 'Your mum was desperate to split us up.'

'I can't believe I'm hearing this.' He moved towards her. 'You wrote me a letter and left the country.'

'Because that's what she wanted me to do. Don't you see? All that stuff I said in the letter wasn't true!' Lola knew she had to make him understand. 'I still loved you! It broke my heart too, I was miserable for *months*.'

'Oh, don't give me that.' Doug's tone hardened. 'I've heard some lines in my time, but—'

'Dougie, I'm not lying! And I'm sorry, *so* sorry I hurt you. But it was your mother's idea—she was the one who offered me the money. And trust me, she *was* desperate,' Lola pleaded.

'Jesus! Did it not occur to you to tell me what was going on? Did you not think it might have been fair to ask me how *I* felt about it?'

'I was going to.' Lola's fists were clenched with frustration; not being able to tell him the truth meant he was always going to think she was a mercenary bitch. Helplessly she said, 'But you were moving up to Edinburgh, you'd have started socialising with all those girls up there.'

'*What?*'

'We were so young! What were the chances, realistically, of us staying together? I knew I loved you,' Lola rattled on in desperation, 'but what if I'd said no to the money then a few weeks later you'd met someone you liked more than me? How stupid would I have felt if you'd sent me a Dear John letter then?'

In the darkness Doug raised his hands. 'Fine. You did absolutely the right thing. Let's just forget it, shall we?'

Did he mean that? 'Let's.' Lola nodded eagerly, wondering if now might be a good moment for a lovely-to-see-you-again kiss. 'From now on all that stuff's behind us, right? We can start afresh.'

'Start afresh?' There was a smidgen of sarcasm in his voice. 'No need to go that far, surely. You'll be leaving soon enough.'

'I don't have to.' Hurrying after him as he abruptly turned and headed down the path leading back to the house, Lola said, 'Dougie, it's fantastic to see you again, we've got so much catching up to do.'

'Trust me, we haven't.'

'But I want to know what you've been doing!' Desperation made her reckless. 'And you came outside, so that means you wanted to talk to me.'

Dougie reached the front door and paused to look at her. 'I came outside for a cigarette.'

'You smoke now? You should give up,' said Lola.

A muscle twitched irritably in his jaw. 'I did give up. Six weeks ago.'

So her sudden reappearance had jolted him. Lola sniffed the air but could only detect cold earth and aftershave. 'I can't smell smoke.'

Dougie pulled a single cigarette and Bic lighter from his shirt pocket. 'I was about to light it when I heard you talking on the phone.'

'So you didn't smoke it, you listened to me instead. See? I'm coming in useful already.' Reaching out and snatching the cigarette from his hand, Lola snapped it in two and tossed it into a lavender bush.

Dougie heaved a sigh and pushed open the front door. 'If you hadn't been here I wouldn't have been tempted in the first place. If you want to do something really useful you'll leave.'

'There you are.' Adele, flinty-eyed, was standing in the hall with Sally beside her. 'We were wondering what had happened to you.'

'We've been catching up.' Dougie's tone was brusque. 'I've just been hearing about the ten thousand pounds you paid Lola to stop seeing me.'

Adele shot Lola a look capable of shrivelling grapes. 'So she told you, did she? Ten thousand pounds, is that what she said?'

Lola's heart sank like a dropped anchor.

'What's that supposed to mean?' Doug demanded.

'I offered ten thousand. But she demanded fifteen.' Adele shrugged elegantly. 'And then, when I refused, she started haggling.'

'I don't believe this. How much did you end up with?'

'Twelve and a half, but I *needed* that—'

'Stop.' Dougie held up his hands. 'I've heard enough. Now I definitely need a drink.' He turned and strode back into the drawing room.

Lola watched him go. It probably wasn't the moment to be thinking this, but he was even more irresistible when he was angry.

'Now see what you've done,' said Adele. 'Why don't you leave before you ruin the entire evening?'

'Look, I'm not as bad as you're making out. I only took that money because there was an emergency and I desperately needed it. I'm actually a really nice person. Can't we just forget about all that old stuff?'

Adele exhaled audibly. 'I'm grateful for what you did the other night, obviously. But I can't pretend I'm happy to see you again. Giving you the money was what I needed to do at the time, but I never wanted Doug to find out.'

'Trust me, neither did I. He overheard me on the phone and I really wish he hadn't. That's why I need to talk to him properly, to explain.'

'Well, let's just get through the rest of the evening without any more unpleasantness.' Adele shook her coiffured head as if dismissing the thought of it from her mind. Cracking a thin pseudo-smile she said, 'Shall we go through and join the others?'

'I'll follow in a minute, when I've just, um . . .' Lola pointed to the downstairs loo.

The cloakroom was small but stylish, all ivory marble and tasteful lighting. A bit too tasteful actually; Lola, touching up her make-up, had to lean right across the basin to get close enough to the mirror.

Lost in thought about Doug and how she might win him over against his better judgment, Lola jumped out of her skin when her phone suddenly rang. Losing her precarious balance, she put out a hand to stop herself and sent her make-up bag flying off the side of the basin.

'Noooo!' Lola let out a shriek of horror as the bag landed with a splosh in the toilet bowl. Not her make-up . . . oh God . . .

It was too late, the contents of her cosmetics bag were drowned. All her favourite things—lovely eyeshadows, bronzing powder, her three *very* best lipsticks—were sitting there submerged in the bottom of the loo. And to add insult to injury her bloody phone was still ringing.

'Gabe, I know you're trying to help, but *not now!*' Switching the phone off, Lola let out a groan of despair. 'Oh *hell . . .*'

Then she jumped again, because someone was tapping cautiously on the cloakroom door.

'Everything OK in there?' It was a worried female, possibly Sally.

'It's all right. I'm fine.'

'Lola? Is that you? What's happened?'

Seeing as it was Sally, Lola unlocked the door.

She didn't have to say a word.

'Oh no, poor *you!* Crikey, no wonder you let out a screech. I had my handbag stolen once.' Sally squeezed her arm in sympathy. 'I mean, having to replace my credit cards and stuff was a pain in the neck. But losing my make-up was just traumatic. When I found out my favourite mascara had been discontinued I practically had a nervous breakdown right there in Harvey Nicks.'

Despite everything, Lola grinned. Bracing herself, she bent down and gingerly picked the unzipped make-up bag out of the toilet bowl then dropped it—splat—into the waste bin beneath the basin. 'Typical that it had to happen before I had a chance to do my mouth.'

'You want to borrow lipstick? Come upstairs with me.'

Sally's bedroom was yellow and white and super-tidy. Sitting on the king-sized bed and gazing around, Lola said, 'This is a great room.'

'It'd be more great if it wasn't in my mother's house.' Sally grimaced. 'Not that I don't love her, but it's hardly ideal, is it? I'm thirty-six. I was living with my boyfriend in Wimbledon until a fortnight ago but we broke up so I moved in here temporarily.'

'What happened with you and the boyfriend?'

'Oh God, nightmare. I'm a walking disaster when it comes to men.' Sally shook her head. 'I paid for him to have his teeth bleached as a birthday present. Next thing I know, he's telling me he's seeing the dental nurse. What kind of colour are you after?'

'Something rusty-bronzy, if you've got it.'

'Rusty-bronzy, rusty-bronzy . . .' Sally was busily rummaging through the boxes on her dressing table.

'If you're looking for somewhere to live, my neighbour's off to Australia next week. He's letting out his flat in Notting Hill for a year.'

'Is he? I haven't been to Notting Hill for years. Oooh, I know the one you need . . .' Sally flitted out of the bedroom, returning moments later with a lipstick in a bullet-shaped gold case. 'Is this more you?'

Lola took it with relief. Versace, no less, and a gorgeous, distinctive shade of russet-red with a brownish-gold lustre. 'This is exactly me.' Peering into the dressing-table mirror, she applied it with a flourish and smacked her lips together. 'Perfect. Does Dougie have a girlfriend?'

'D'you know, I'm not sure. You know what men are like, they don't talk about that kind of stuff like we do.' Sally fluffed translucent powder onto her nose and said, 'Why? Do you still fancy him?'

Only an older sister could say it quite like that, as if it was on a par with fancying Quasimodo.

Lola said regretfully, 'He's gorgeous. We were so happy together once and I messed that up. I made a mistake but I didn't . . . I just couldn't . . .'

'Oh, please, I didn't mean to make you feel worse. You were only seventeen,' Sally exclaimed. 'We all make mistakes at that age. And, OK, Dougie was miserable but he recovered.'

Grateful for Sally's understanding, Lola managed a wobbly smile. 'Sorry, seeing him again like this has been a bit overwhelming. But who knows, maybe I can persuade him I'm irresistible and he'll forgive me . . .'

The bedroom door, which hadn't been shut, swung further open. 'Look,' Doug said curtly, 'I really wish I didn't have to keep overhearing this stuff, but Philip wants to make a speech and he asked me to round everyone up.'

'OK, we're done here.' Sally gaily flipped back her hair and headed for the door.

'And can I just say,' Doug fixed Lola with a steely knee-trembler of a gaze as she passed him in the doorway, 'don't waste your energy with the being irresistible bit, because I'm not interested.'

'You might change your mind,' Lola said bravely. 'I'm very lovable.'

'Not to me.'

'I could be. If you'd just give me a chance.'

'Lola, don't even bother to try. Let's just go downstairs and get this farce over with. The sooner it's done, the sooner you can go home.'

Everyone gathered in the drawing room for Philip's speech. It was sweet, if hard to believe, hearing this nice man speak so movingly about the happiness Adele had brought into his life. Everyone raised their glasses to her, then Philip went on to talk about Lola and her actions on the night of the mugging. He concluded by announcing that they were all indebted to her, and that from now on she was part of the family. Cue applause, a toast and a brittle hug from Adele.

Then the embarrassing bit was over and everyone went back to drinking and chatting among themselves. Everyone except Adele, who looked at Lola's mouth and said, 'What an extraordinary coincidence, you appear to use the same lipstick as me.'

'Sorry.' Lola couldn't believe she hadn't recognised it. 'I . . . um, lost mine and Sally offered to lend me one. I didn't realise it was yours.'

'You may as well take it with you when you leave.' Adele shuddered. 'It's not as if I'd use it again now.'

'Everything OK?' Doug joined them.

'Lola used my lipstick.' With an incredulous half-laugh Adele said, 'I must be old-fashioned. It just seems an incredibly brazen thing to do.'

Lola opened her mouth to protest but now Dougie was surveying her with equal distaste, as if she were Typhoid Mary going around spreading her vile germs on other people's lipsticks. There came a time when you simply had to accept that winning someone over wasn't an option.

When Lola's phone trilled for the third time that evening, Adele's mouth narrowed with fresh annoyance.

'Will you stop hanging up on me?' Gabe demanded. 'I just need to know if everything's going OK. A simple yes or no will—'

'Are you serious? The contractions are *how* far apart? Just stay calm,' said Lola. 'Boil the kettle and take deep breaths. I'm on my way.'

'**I** dreamt about him last night,' said Lola.

Cheryl was restocking the best-seller shelves at the front of the shop. Pausing to gaze at the book in her hand, she frowned and said, 'Dreamt about who? Harry Potter?'

'As if. I'm talking about Dougie, you dingbat.'

'Oh. You mean you're *still* talking about Dougie. Do the words "not a hope in hell" mean anything to you?'

'Don't be such a pessimist. I dreamt I was rowing a boat down Portobello Road and I lost one of my oars, but all of a sudden Dougie swam up to me and jumped into the boat.'

'And tipped you out?'

'And rescued me! He showed me the hidden switch that turned on the engine.' Lola felt herself growing misty-eyed. 'And the next thing I knew, we were whizzing along like something out of a James Bond film, and Dougie was sitting next to me with his leg pressing against mine.'

'Is this about to turn into one of those mucky dreams?'

'Sadly not. We didn't have time. My alarm went off.' Lola passed Cheryl a handful of Dan Browns; it was Monday afternoon, three days since the party, and Dougie had taken up permanent residence inside her head. It wasn't going to be easy, making someone love you again when they didn't even want to see you, but she'd never felt this way about anyone else; having him reappear in her life like this was just—

'By the way, someone's watching you,' said Cheryl.

'They are? Who?'

'That one over there by autobiographies. He's been looking over at you. *Really* looking.'

'Probably saw me on TV last week and now he's trying to pluck up the courage to ask for my autograph.' Lola prepared to smile in a cheery, down-to-earth fashion and prove that fame hadn't gone to her head—God, wouldn't it be fantastic if he really did ask?—but the man had turned away. Oh well. Ooh, unless he was a private detective hired by Dougie to find out if she was a nicer person now than she'd been ten years ago . . . he'd done his best to put her out of his mind but hadn't been able to . . . maybe he could forgive her after all . . .

'Are you daydreaming again? Tim's waving at you,' Cheryl pointed out. 'They're short-handed over at the pay desk.'

Ten minutes later, Lola's fan arrived at her till. He was in his mid-forties, with dark hair, and was wearing a striped mulberry-and-olive shirt with black trousers. Quite trendy for a man of his age. Nice grey eyes too.

'I've never read one of these before.' He passed over the book, a thriller by a prolific American author. 'Is he good?'

'Very. You won't be able to stop reading even when you want to.' Lola rang the book up, aware that the man was studying her name badge.

'Sorry.' He saw that she'd noticed. 'Nice name. Unusual.'

'Thanks.' She took his ten-pound note and scooped the change out of the till. 'There you go. Hope you enjoy it. Don't blame me if you get sacked for not being able to stay awake at work tomorrow.'

He smiled. 'And if I do enjoy it, I'll be back to buy another one.'

There was something about the way he was looking at her that made Lola wonder if this was how it felt to be famous. She said lightly, 'Do you recognise me?'

He looked startled. 'What?'

'I was interviewed on TV. I thought maybe you'd seen it.'

The man's expression cleared. 'No, I'm afraid I missed that. I just came in to buy a book.'

Damn, she wasn't famous after all. 'Sorry.'

'No problem.' He relaxed visibly. 'Were you good?'

'I was brilliant.' As Lola passed him the bag containing his thriller a thought struck her: *Why* was he now visibly relaxed? Innocently she said, 'Does anyone ever recognise you?'

'Excuse me?'

'I just wondered if people ever realised who you are.'

A pause. 'Why would they?'

'Maybe because they're very clever and they've worked it out.'

He looked at her. 'Worked what out?'

'That you're a private detective.'

'Me?' He pointed to his chest, shaking his head in amused disbelief. 'Is that what you think? I'm not a private detective.'

'Ah,' said Lola, 'but you would say that, wouldn't you?'

'I suppose so.' He tilted his head to one side. 'So *if* I was, which I promise I'm not, who would I be spying on?'

'Anyone in this shop.' Lola shrugged playfully. 'Me, perhaps.'

'You. And why would a private detective be tailing you?' Another brief pause. 'Are you in some kind of trouble?'

'Not at all.' She'd only said it on the spur of the moment—nothing ventured, nothing gained—but Lola knew now that this man was no more than a charming stranger, albeit a slightly bemused one, thanks to her interrogation. 'OK, you're not a private detective. I believe you.'

He nodded gravely. 'Thank you.'

Out of nowhere a queue for the tills had materialised. Lola said, 'Enjoy your book.'

# Chapter 5

WEREN'T TOASTABAGS the greatest invention in the whole world *ever*?

The toaster popped up and Lola hooked out the bag, tipping the gorgeous crispy toasted cheese-and-tomato sandwich onto a plate. Possibly her favourite food, and to think that when she'd first clapped eyes on a Toastabag she hadn't believed it could work, because how could a plasticky baggy-type thing go into an electric toaster and not melt?

OK, toasted sandwich: check.

DVD in DVD player: check. She'd treated herself to the latest release starring Tom Dutton, one of her favourite actors.

Box of tissues: check. When she'd dragged Gabe along to the cinema to see the film she'd honked like a big goose during the weepy bits.

Remote control for DVD player: check.

Remote control for TV . . . bum, where was it? Oh, under the sofa cushions. Check.

Now she was all ready to go . . .

The doorbell rang as she was about to take the first heavenly bite of toasted sandwich. Lola looked at her make-up-free reflection in the kitchen window, teamed with wet hair and lime-green towelling dressing gown, and really hoped Tom Dutton hadn't chosen this moment to pitch up on her doorstep.

She pressed the intercom. 'Yes?'

'Lola. It's me! Sally Tennant!'

Good grief. *Sally. Doug's sister.* As Lola pressed the buzzer, her stomach gave a little squiggle of excitement. 'Come on up.'

Sally, wrapped in a glamorous cream coat and black patent high-heeled boots, was looking glossy and stylish.

'Oh, sorry.' She pulled a face when she saw Lola's hair and dressing gown. 'Bad time?'

'Of course not. I can't believe you're here.' Lola ushered her into the living room, switched off the TV. 'Is this something to do with Doug?'

'Doug.' Sally looked blank. 'No. Haven't seen him. Why, have you?'

'No.' Lola swallowed her disappointment.

'I asked Philip for your address. I'm here about that flat you mentioned.'

The flat. Lola hadn't thought for a moment that Sally would take her up on the offer—she hadn't appeared to be listening.

'You're really interested? That's fantastic. Gabe's off to Australia tomorrow and he's out saying goodbyes tonight. But I've got a key.' Tightening the belt of her dressing gown, Lola said, 'You'll love it, I promise!'

'**G**abe? Can you hear me? I've just found someone for your flat . . . Remember I told you about Sally, Doug's sister? Well, she's here and she's had a look round, and it's just what—'

'What?' hissed Sally when Lola stopped abruptly and listened. 'Tell him he won't find a better tenant *anywhere.* Look, I can pay the deposit now . . . Lola, tell him how much I want this flat!'

Lola said slowly, 'Yes . . . OK, right . . . no . . . no, of course I understand.' She finished listening to Gabe then hung up.

'What?' wailed Sally. 'Why can't I have it? I want it!'

'It's not you. Gabe registered the flat with a lettings agency. He's signed a contract with them. And they rang him a couple of hours ago to tell him they were bringing a client round tonight. If this guy says he wants it, there's nothing we can do. He's got first refusal.'

'Oh.' Sally looked crestfallen. 'Well, maybe he won't like it.'

'Everyone likes Gabe's flat. Damn it,' Lola said frustratedly, 'I want you to be my neighbour, I don't want some smelly *boy* moving in . . .'

'What?' Sally eyed her with curiosity as Lola's voice trailed off.

'Gabe says they're due round at eight.' Lola checked her watch. 'I'm just wondering what time the corner shop shuts.'

**T**he corner shop was still open. If Sanjeev wondered why his best customer when it came to magazines, chocolate and ice cream was all of a sudden buying up cabbages, he didn't ask. By ten to eight the evil stench of boiled cabbage was thick in both Lola's flat and Gabe's. When the saucepans had been removed from Gabe's kitchen Lola found a music channel on the TV in her own flat and turned the volume up to maximum. Eminem blared out and Sally kicked off her shoes.

At three minutes past eight they heard the front door being opened downstairs, then two people entering Gabe's flat. Lola gave it a few seconds then crossed the landing and thumped on the door.

It was opened by a man in a suit. 'Yes?'

'Hi there, is he in?'

'Excuse me?'

'The Angel Gabriel.' Lola raised her voice to be heard above the sound of the music. 'Mr Let's-Complain-About-Everything.'

The letting agent said frostily, 'If you mean Mr Adams, he isn't here.'

'No? Best news I've heard all day.' Grinning at the potential tenant behind him—thirties, spectacles, accountanty-looking—Lola said, 'Well, can you just pass on a message from Lola and Sal across the hall, tell him we're having a few friends round tonight. They'll be turning up after the pub and we'd appreciate it if he didn't give us the usual grief, seeing as this time we're warning him in advance.'

'Maybe you could leave a note for Mr Adams.' The letting agent spoke brusquely, keen to close the door.

'Hang on.' The gawky accountant-type behind him raised his voice above the thudding hip-hop beat that was now making the floor vibrate. 'How often do you have parties?'

'Not often. Two or three times a week, that's all.'

'And the smell,' said the accountant. 'What is that?'

Lola shrugged. 'No idea. It comes and goes—something to do with the drains, I think.' She paused and said, 'Why do you want to know?'

'This flat's been registered with a lettings agency.' The accountant blinked rapidly. 'The owner's moving to Australia.'

'You're kidding. Hey, fantastic!' Hearing footsteps behind her, Lola turned and said to Sally, 'Hear that? Neddy No-Mates is off to Oz!'

'To get away from us?' All of a sudden nine months pregnant beneath her coat, Sally nodded approvingly. 'Cool. So does that mean you're going to be our new neighbour?'

'I, um . . .' Was that a glint of terror behind the geeky spectacles?

'Because if you ever fancy a spot of baby-sitting, I've got just the thing for you right here!' Sally gave her swollen stomach a pat. 'Whoo-hoo!' Eminem had given way to Snoop Dogg. Sally, clutching her stomach with one hand and waving the other in the air, executed some enthusiastic hip-hop-esque dance moves.

It was a sight to make a grown man nervous. Two grown men, in fact. The geek and the lettings agent edged away slowly. Lola, filled with admiration, prayed that Sally wouldn't attempt to shake her booty.

Imagine the embarrassment if her cushion fell out.

When the agent and the geek had left the building, Lola turned off the earsplitting music and threw open the windows in both flats to disperse the nostril-curling boiled-cabbage smell.

'Gosh, that was fun.' Sally pulled the balled-up velvet cushion out from under her coat and flung it onto the sofa. 'Think it'll do the trick?'

'It'd do the trick if I was the one looking for a flat.' Lola took a bottle of white wine from the fridge and poured out two glasses.

'Poor bloke, he did look a bit stunned. I suppose we just have to wait now. Should I be drinking that in my condition?'

'You could always have water instead.'

'Water? Yeurgh, nasty wet *watery* stuff. No thanks.'

Lola's phone rang ten minutes later and she leapt on it.

'What did you do?' Gabe came straight to the point.

Innocently Lola said, 'Sorry?'

'No, you're not. I've just had a call from the lettings agent,' said Gabe, 'telling me that in view of the Situation, I'm going to need to drop my rental price.'

'Oh, Gabe, that's *terrible*.'

'He also said getting rid of that putrid smell had to be a priority.'

'Oh dear.'

'So this friend of yours, this sister-of-Doug,' said Gabe. 'I'm assuming she's there with you now.'

Lola looked over at Sally. 'Might be.'

'And she wants my flat.'

'Definitely. More than anything.'

'What caused the smell?'

'Four big saucepans of boiled cabbage.'

'Here, give me the phone.' Reaching over, Sally grabbed it and said, 'Gabe? Hi, please let me be your new tenant! I'm super-housetrained, I promise. I'd really look after your flat and I'm completely trustworthy, I'll pay the full rent by direct debit and leave the deposit with Lola now, you won't regret it . . . what? Oh, OK.'

'What did he say?' demanded Lola when Sally put down the phone.

'That you and I deserve each other and he feels sorry for the baby.'

Since Sally was currently sitting on the sofa with one elbow digging into the abandoned velvet cushion, Lola felt quite sorry for it too. 'So that means . . .?'

Sally clinked her glass against Lola's. 'I can move in as soon as I like.'

'**O**h, I'm going to miss you *sooo* much.' Lola blinked and hiccupped; she hadn't expected to feel this emotional but actually saying goodbye to Gabe was hard.

'Hang on, you're strangling me.' He prised her off him. 'It's like being hugged by a giant koala.'

'That's to get you into practice. Oh bugger, what do I look like?'

'A panda in a pink dress.' Gabe watched her mopping up mascara. 'I can't believe you're crying. I'm only going for a year.'

'But what if you decide to stay there for good? I'll never see you again. You're my best male friend in the world and you're about to fly off to the other side of it. What if you and Jaydena get married and buy a house and settle down and have loads of Aussie kids?'

She expected Gabe to burst out laughing, but he didn't.

'If that happens, you can always come out and visit us.'

Oh God, he really meant it! He was that besotted with Jaydena.

Lola did her best to feel happy for him. She looked at her watch. 'I'm going to be late to work.'

'And my cab's due in ten minutes.' Gabe gave her a kiss and pushed her towards the door. 'Get yourself out of here. You've got your new friend Sally moving in tonight—you won't even notice I'm gone.'

'**Y**ou were right,' said the man who wasn't a private detective.

'Oh, hi.' Recognising him, Lola dumped the hardbacks she'd brought out from the stockroom and said cheerfully, 'Right about what?'

'Last night. I couldn't put that book down. I was awake till four this morning finishing it.' He shook his head in baffled disbelief. 'I didn't know reading could be like that, I had no idea.'

'Ah, but now you've seen the light.' Lola loved it when this happened; witnessing a conversion never failed to give her a thrill. 'You've become one of us. Welcome to our world; you're going to love it here.'

'I need another thriller and I don't know where to start.' The man was wearing a navy suit today. 'Can you recommend an author?'

Could she recommend an author? Ha, it was only the favourite bit of her job!

'You'd like this one.' Lola picked up a book with a gunmetal-grey cover. 'Or this.' Eagerly she reached across the table for another. 'When you've tried a few different authors we can work out which—'

'*Beano!*'

'Excuse me?' She turned to face the hatchet-faced woman who had just barked in her ear.

'I need a *Beano Annual* for my grandson!'

'Sorry,' the man in the suit shook his head apologetically and took the book with the grey cover from her. 'You're busy. Thanks for this. I'll let you know how I get on with it.'

'Come on, come on,' bellowed the woman. 'I haven't got all day!'

By the time Lola fought her way back through the crowds with the *Beano Annual*, the man in the suit was gone. The hatchet-faced woman didn't even say thank you. But then people like that never did.

Twenty minutes later Lola felt an index finger poking at her left shoulder blade. 'Excuse me, excuse me,' came an irritated female voice. 'I want the new book by that Dan Black.'

Lola turned. 'You mean Dan Brown.'

'Don't tell me what I mean, missy. I don't care what the man's name is, just get me the book.'

'I tell you what,' said Lola, 'why don't you get it yourself?'

Outraged, the woman sucked in her breath. 'You impertinent creature! I shall report you to the manager and have you sacked!'

'And I'll have you arrested for crimes against colour coordination. Because pink,' Lola curled her lip at the woman's fluffy scarf and padded jacket, 'does *not* go with orange.'

Then they realised they were being watched by a bemused elderly man clutching a biography of Churchill.

'It's all right.' Lola winked at him. 'She's my mother.'

'Hello, darling.' Blythe gave her a quick hug. 'Can't stop, I'm racing to finish my Christmas shopping then I've made an appointment to have my hair done. Just popped in to show you what I've bought for tonight. Tell me which outfit I should keep and I'll take the other one back.'

Lola didn't get her hopes up; being allowed to choose was Blythe's attempt at compromise. Blythe had as much fashion sense as a chicken, coupled with a hopeless predilection for mixing and matching things that Really Didn't Go. Somehow it hadn't seemed to matter when Alex had been alive—between them, they had regarded Blythe's manner of dressing as no more than an endearing quirk. But it was five years now since Alex had died and during the last eighteen months Blythe had tentatively begun dating again. Keen for her mother to make a good impression, Lola had attempted to steer her into more stylish waters.

But it had to be said, this was on a par with trying to knit feathers. Lola braced herself as her mother rummaged in a pink carrier bag and pulled out a silky beige top.

With purply-blue satin butterflies adorning each shoulder strap.

Lola bit her lip. 'Okaaay. Now the other one.'

'Ta-daaa!' Having stuffed beige'n'silky back into its bag, Blythe produced the second top and held it up against herself with a flourish, indicating that this, *this* one, was her favourite.

As if Lola couldn't have guessed. Top number two was brighter—a retina-searing geranium red—and much frillier, with jaunty layered sleeves, silver buttons down each side and a huge red-and-white fabric flower—bigger than a Crufts' rosette—at the base of the V neck.

'Hmm,' said Lola. 'Is this for when you run away to join the circus?'

'Don't be so cruel! It's beautiful!'

'Right, so what would you wear it with?'

Her mother looked hopeful, like a five-year-old attempting to spell her name. 'My blue paisley skirt?'

'No.'

'Green striped trousers?'

'No!'

'Oh. Well, how about the pink and gold—'

'*Noooo!*'

Blythe flung up her hands in defeat. 'You're so picky.'

'I'm not, I just don't want people pointing and saying, "There goes Coco the Clown". Mum, if you really want to keep the red top, wear it with your white skirt.'

'Except I can't, because it's got a big curry stain on the front. Ooh,' Blythe exclaimed, her eyes lighting up as inspiration struck, 'but I could snip the red flower off this top and Super Glue it to the skirt instead, that'd cover the mark! That's it, problem solved!'

Lola opened her mouth to protest but her mother was busily stuffing the tops back into their carriers, and saying, 'I must fly!'

'Where are you going tonight?'

'Oh, it's just our quiz team having a Christmas get-together. Malcolm's driving, so I can have a drink.'

Hardly the Oscars. Lola let it go. Trinny and Susannah would have a field-day with Malcolm, who was bearded and bearlike, with a penchant for baggy corduroys and zigzaggy patterned sweaters. Since Malcolm was to sartorial elegance what John Prescott was to ice dance, he was unlikely to object to an oversized flower attached to the front of a skirt.

But Malcolm wasn't what Lola had in mind for her mother. Sweet though he was in his bumbling, teddy-bear way, she had her sights set several notches higher than that. Because Blythe deserved the best.

The eye-watering, throat-tightening boiled-cabbage smell had gone, thank goodness. Loaded up like a donkey, Sally struggled through to the living room then dumped her belongings on the floor.

Excitement squiggled through her. This was it, her new home for the next twelve months. New flat, new resolutions, whole new life.

Chief resolution being: no more having her heart broken by

boyfriends who were nothing more than rotten no-good *hounds*.

Sally gazed around, taking in the unadorned cream walls, ivory rugs and pale minimalist modern furniture. What with the lack of clutter, it exuded an air of bachelor-about-town.

Oh well, soon sort that out.

'**H**ellooo?'

Sally was looping multicoloured fairy lights around the fireplace when the bell buzzed and she heard Lola's voice. Eagerly she rushed to open the door.

'Wow,' said Lola, gazing around the living room. 'This is . . . different.'

'Isn't it?' Sally beamed with pride. 'Nothing like a splash of colour to cheer a place up!'

The floor was littered with empty bags and cases, not to mention several packets of biscuits. There were bright paintings adorning Gabe's cool cream walls, with six . . . no, *seven* sets of fairy lights draped around the frames. The brushed-steel lampshade from the Conran shop had been taken down; in its place was a hot-pink chandelier. The ivory cushions on the sofa sported new fluffy orange covers. A sequinned pink-and-orange throw covered the seat below the window. And a fountain of fake sparkly flowers exploded out of a silver bowl on top of the TV.

'Good for you,' said Lola. 'If Gabe could see this, he'd have a fit.'

'Good job he's in Australia then.' Unperturbed, Sally pulled a swath of peacock feathers, awash with iridescent blue and green glitter, from one of the cases. 'Pass me that gold vase, over there, would you? At the weekend I'm going to paint my bedroom to match these.'

'Paint the bedroom?'

'It's too plain as it is. Like being in a prison cell. I'm here for a whole year,' said Sally. 'Anyway, it's only a couple of coats of paint. I'll slosh some cream over the walls the day before Gabe gets back.'

'Sorry. He's a bit fussy, that's all. He had the colour specially mixed.'

Sally's eyebrows shot up. '*This* colour? Are you serious?'

'I know, I know.' Lola raised her hands, disclaiming responsibility. 'He's just . . . particular.'

'Is he gay?'

'Trust me. Gabe's the opposite of gay.'

'He's also fifty zillion miles away. So what I think is, you don't mention to him that I'm repainting his flat, and neither will I.'

'Go on then.' Relenting, Lola opened her bag. 'I'll drink to that.'

'Oh my God, champagne!'

'Not quite. It was either one bottle of the proper stuff or two of pretend.' Lola held one bottle in each hand.

'And we wouldn't want to run out.' Seizing them, Sally said joyfully, 'Come on, let's pop these corks—whoops, don't step on the Garibaldis!'

'. . . **I** mean, I'm thirty-six years old and this is the first time I've been able to do out a room just the way I like. How crazy is that?'

By ten o'clock the first bottle had been upended into the waste bin (parrot-pink, trimmed with marabou) and the second was three-quarters empty. Sally was crosslegged on the rug (purple, speckled with biscuit crumbs), waving her glass dramatically as she ran through her life history. Lola frowned, puzzled by Sally's statement. 'What about when you were a teenager?'

'God, especially when I was a teenager! My mother sent the cleaner into my bedroom every morning to tidy everything up and make my bed.' Sally paused to scoop another biscuit from the packet on the floor next to her. 'I left home when I was eighteen but I've never lived on my own, it's always been either flat-sharing or moving in with boyfriends. Which means there's always been someone around to moan about my decorating plans. I've spent the last eighteen years having to compromise. Well, not any more.' Sally's exuberant gesture encompassed the room and caused the contents of her glass to spill in an arc across the rug. 'From now on I'm going to do what I want to do and no one's going to stop me. Bum, my glass is empty.'

'That would be because you just swung it upside-down.'

'Did I? Bum, now *this* is empty.'

Tipsily aghast, Sally gave the second bottle a shake. 'OK, don't panic, I've got a bottle of burgundy in the fridge—oh, my foot's gone to sleep.'

'Shall I get it?' Lola jumped up, because Sally's attempts to stand were of the Bambi-on-ice persuasion.

'Excellent plan.'

In the kitchen, Lola took out the chilled burgundy and rummaged through drawers in search of Gabe's corkscrew.

The doorbell rang and she heard Sally say perplexedly, 'Who can that be?' But she must have limped over to the intercom because twenty seconds later the door to the flat was opened and Sally exclaimed, 'I wasn't expecting you here tonight!'

Friend?

Mother? *Please no.*

Old boyfriend?

Lola's hands froze in mid-corkscrew search as she heard the visitor say, 'I know, but this was the only time I could bring the stuff over. I tried to call but your phone's switched off.'

Oh, that voice, it was like warm honey spreading through her veins.

Not one of Sally's old boyfriends then, thought Lola. One of mine!

'That would explain why George Clooney hasn't rung. Thanks, just dump the cases against the wall.' Bursting with pride Sally said, 'So what d'you think of my new flat?'

'It's like a cross between Santa's grotto and a Moroccan souk.'

'I know, isn't it fantastic?' Sally clapped her hands. 'I can't believe how gorgeous it looks!'

Doug said drily, 'I can't believe you're my sister.' Evidently spotting the empty wineglasses on the coffee table he added, 'Drinking for two now? Or has someone else been round?'

Sally giggled. 'Someone else is still round.'

OK, enough skulking in the kitchen. Lola stepped into the living room. 'Actually I wouldn't call myself round, more curvily girl-shaped.'

'Oh, for God's sake.' Dark eyes narrowing, Doug said impatiently, 'Not you again. What are you doing here?'

'Dougie, don't be so *rude*,' wailed Sally. 'Lola's my *friend*.'

'I'm more than her friend.' Lola flashed him a playful smile. 'I'm her next-door neighbour.'

Doug shook his head in disbelief. He looked over at his sister. 'You didn't mention this.'

'Of course I didn't. If I'd told you I was going to be moving in next door to Lola, you'd have tried to talk me out of it.'

'Damn right I would. And I'm not the only one.'

'Well, too bad. I don't care what Mum says—it's not my fault she doesn't like Lola. You and Mum should put all that old stuff behind you. This is my flat and I'm jolly well staying here.'

Overcome with gratitude, Lola longed to burst into applause, but the line of Dougie's jaw wasn't exactly forgiving. Instead she attempted to change the subject.

'Erm, I couldn't find the corkscrew.'

'OK, I think there's one in one of the cases in my bedroom. Hang on, I'll go and have a look.'

'You never know,' Doug said softly when Sally had left the room, 'play your cards right and you could land yourself another handy little windfall. My mother might be so keen to keep you away from Sal that she'd be prepared to pay you to move out.'

It hurt like a knife sliding in under her ribs. Lola said, 'Look, what do you want me to do? Fall on my knees and beg for forgiveness? I did a bad thing once and I'm sorry I hurt you, but I didn't have any choice.'

'Fine. Anyway, we're not going to argue about that again. I'm just here to drop off the rest of Sal's things. I'll fetch them from the car.'

'I'll help you.'

'No need.'

'I want to.' Lola followed him out into the hallway.

'I can manage.'

'But it's going to be easier if there's two of us.' She clattered down the stairs behind him. 'And I'm strong! Remember that time I beat you at arm-wrestling?'

Doug's shoulders stiffened. 'No.'

'Oh, come on. At Mandy Green's party. Her brother started this whole arm-wrestling competition out in the garden because he said no girl could beat a boy. But he was wrong,' Lola said proudly, 'because I did, I beat him and I beat *you*—'

'That's because I let you win,' Doug said curtly.

'What? You didn't!'

'Of course I did.' Doug yanked open the front door. 'Did you seriously think you were stronger than me?'

'But . . .' Lola had spent the last decade being proud of that achievement. And now Doug was shattering her illusions.

*Woooooop* went the dark green Mercedes on the other side of the road as Doug pointed a key at it.

'Right, you can carry the bags with the clothes in. They're not so heavy.' He opened the boot. 'I'll deal with the boxes of books.'

Books. If there was one thing Lola was the queen of, it was carrying piles of books.

Reaching past Doug she slammed the boot shut.

'Jesus!' He snatched his hand away in the nick of time.

'I don't believe you lost on purpose. I think that's just your excuse.' Pushing up the sleeve of her sweater to give her elbow some grip, Lola angled herself up against the corner of the car's boot and waggled her fingers. 'So we'll just find out, shall we? On your marks, get set . . .'

'I tell you what,' said Doug, 'why don't we just carry my sister's things into the flat?'

'Chicken.'

'Lola, let me open the boot.'

'Clucka-lucka-luck.'

He gave her a raised-eyebrow look. 'What?'

OK, if she hadn't been a teeny bit squiffy she possibly wouldn't have done that. 'It's my chicken impression.'

'Not exactly Rory Bremner, are you?'

She waggled her fingers once more. 'You're scared I'll win, aren't you?'

'I don't believe this.' Heaving a sigh, Doug pushed up the sleeve of his pale grey sweatshirt, assumed the position against the car and clasped Lola's right hand. Her heart lolloped as his warm fingers closed round hers. She could feel his breath on her face, smell the aftershave he was wearing, see the glint of stubble on his jaw, imagine the way his mouth would feel if she were to kiss him right now . . .

CLONCK went the back of her forearm against the Mercedes's boot.

'That's not fair,' Lola wailed. 'I wasn't ready.'

'Correction. You weren't strong enough.' He paused. 'What's up now?'

'Just looking at you.' She'd seen a lot of eyes in her life but none more beautiful than Dougie's.

'Well, stop it. I don't trust what's going on here. All of a sudden you're persuading my sister to move into the flat next to yours and I want to know why.'

'I didn't persuade her. It was her decision. But I'm glad she chose to,' said Lola. 'Because I like Sally. We get on well together. And I'd rather have her living next door than the geeky nerdy type who would have moved in if she hadn't come along in the nick of time.'

'Is that the only reason?'

'Of course!'

'Now why don't I believe you? Oh, yes, that's right, because you're a mercenary liar. Take these.' Having sprung open the boot once more, Doug dumped a huge pink canvas holdall in Lola's arms.

'How many times can I say I'm sorry?'

'Forget it. Not interested.' There was that muscle again, twitching away in his jaw as he hauled out two boxes of books. 'Just so long as you aren't still harbouring some kind of plan to persuade me to change my mind about you, because *that's* not going to happen.'

Honestly, whatever happened to forgive and forget?


## Chapter 6


'WHERE TO, MATE?'

'Airport,' said Gabe.

He sat back in the air-conditioned cab and didn't glance up at the window of Jaydena's apartment as the driver pulled away.

That was it then. How had he managed to get it so wrong?

'It's not your fault.' Tears had been streaming down Jaydena's face last night as she finally came clean. 'You're a fantastic guy, really you are.

And I'm so *sorry*, it's just that it never occurred to me that Paul would change his mind and want me back. But he's, like, the big love of my life. Oh, Gabe, I don't want to hurt you, but there's no other way.'

It was almost a relief figuring out why Jaydena had been as jumpy as a cat on a hot plate ever since he'd arrived last night.

On the other hand, discovering the truth still hurt like hell.

'You slept with me.' Gabe frowned. 'We had sex. If you and this guy are back together, why would you do that?'

'Because I felt so terrible,' Jaydena wailed. 'You flew all this *way*.'

He looked at her. 'And that was my consolation prize? Thanks a lot.'

'I already said I'm sorry!'

'Fine.' Gabe turned away; the last thing he was going to do was beg. 'You could have told me before I left London.'

'I couldn't. By the time Paul made up his mind, you were on the plane.'

It hadn't been the easiest of nights. Gabe had slept fitfully on the sofa in Jaydena's living room and been up by six. The sensible part of him felt that after coming all this way he should stay on in Australia, see the sights and generally make the trip worth while.

The other pissed-off part of him just wanted to put some serious distance between himself and Jaydena and head back home.

As the taxi made its way across Sydney towards the airport, he gazed out at the glittering ocean, the paintbox-blue sky and the scantily clad blondes on their way to the beach. Reaching over and unzipping the front compartment of his rucksack, Gabe pulled out his digital camera and began taking photographs out of the window.

'Good holiday, mate?'

It wasn't the taxi guy's fault that his life had just taken a nose dive. Snapping a picture of a girl in a raspberry-pink bikini cycling along with a terrier on a lead in tow, Gabe said, 'Great, thanks.'

'Ah, it's a beautiful place, mate. Nowhere else like it.' The driver nodded with pride, then pointed to the service station up ahead. 'OK if I pull in for a couple of minutes or are you in a rush to get there?'

'No rush at all.' The flight Gabe had booked last night wasn't leaving for another five hours; he'd just been keen to get out of the flat.

The man drove into the service station, parked up next to the car wash and disappeared inside the shop. Gabe, in the back of the cab, scrolled through the half-dozen or so photos he'd taken. He glanced up as a slender brunette emerged from another parked car and made her way round the corner of the building. For a split second Gabe thought she seemed familiar, before remembering he was in Sydney, Australia. It wasn't like bumping into someone you knew in the supermarket back home.

Moments later, his head jerked up again as another figure, male this time, emerged from a second car and headed in the same direction as the brunette.

Gabe frowned. Wasn't that . . .? No, it couldn't be.

But as the man moved out of sight, curiosity got the better of Gabe. Opening the rear door of the cab, he climbed out. Ninety degrees of heat hit him in the face. Mystified, Gabe reached the side of the whitewashed building and saw . . . blimey . . . that he hadn't been mistaken after all. Except no wonder he hadn't twigged at first; it wasn't every day you saw two members of Hollywood's A-list sneaking off down a narrow alley behind a service station in order to kiss each other senseless.

Click. Gabe hadn't even planned on taking their photo; somehow, the camera in his hand came up and there they were in the frame, so completely wrapped up in each other that they neither saw him nor heard the shutter close. Gabe took another photo, this time getting a clear shot of the girl's face. Then, realising what he was doing—God, what was he, some kind of snooper?—he turned and hurried back to the cab.

'All right there?' The taxi driver emerged from the shop with a bottle of iced water and a bag of toffees.

'Fine.'

'Off we go, then.'

As they waited to pull out onto the main road, the male half of the couple emerged from the alley. Tom Dutton, Oscar-winning actor. Simply because it would thrill Lola, who had dragged him along to the cinema last summer and noisily sobbed her way through the weepy that had been Tom Dutton's most recent film, Gabe raised his camera and took one last photo.

Personally he'd thought the film was crap.

Lola wasn't averse to a bit of untidiness but stepping into Gabe's flat was something of an eye-opener. The initial impression was of utter chaos, Selfridges Christmas department mixed with a charity shop the morning after an all-night party.

'Hi there, I was wondering if you had any black shoe polish—whoops.' Lola just managed to avoid stepping on a triangle of pepperoni pizza lying on a copy of Heat. Just as well Gabe wasn't here to see this.

'I do, I do!' Sally gaily dropped her apple core onto Gabe's formerly pristine glass-topped coffee table and pressed her fingers, psychic-style, to her temples. 'Hmm, shoe polishes, shoe polishes. They're here somewhere . . . Ooh, I know! On the windowsill in the kitchen!'

Where else? Following Sally into the kitchen, Lola saw a whole range of shoe polishes flung into a pink and gold flowerpot along with a Nicky Clarke hairspray, a bag of satsumas and a skipping rope.

'Brilliant. I'll only be a couple of seconds.' Holding her favourite black stilettos, Lola squeezed liquid polish onto the toes. Instant magic.

Surveying her in her dressing gown, Sally said, 'Off somewhere nice?'

'Wine bar in Soho. Works Christmas party.' Lola pulled a face. 'Fancy dress.'

'Ooh, I love fancy dress! What are you going as?'

'A Playboy Bunny. Don't laugh,' said Lola. 'Everyone had to put an idea into the hat and I drew the short straw. Tim from work has gone over to the fancy-dress hire place to pick everything up. He'll be here any minute with my costume.'

'At least it's sexy. I always wanted to be a Playboy Bunny when I grew up. But Mum said over her dead body. Oh well,' Sally said cheerfully, 'you'll have to come and give me a twirl before you leave.'

'**B**limey.' Coming face to face with Tim on her doorstep, lugging an enormous zip-up carrying case, Lola said, 'That can't all be for me.'

Her outfit was a skimpy affair, surely? Black satin swimsuit thing, white fluffy tail and a pair of ears. How much space could that take up?

'Been a bit of a mix-up.' Tim looked embarrassed.

'What kind of a mix-up?'

His cheeks flamed. 'When I ordered a Bunny outfit they thought I meant . . . well, a *bunny* bunny.'

'You mean . . .?' Oh God, let me see.' Lola unzipped the carrying case and was confronted by a full-size rabbit suit made of white nylon fur.

'Sorry,' Tim said miserably.

She pulled out the suit and gave herself a static shock. On the bright side, she wouldn't need to spend the evening holding her stomach in.

'You can swap costumes with me if you want to,' said Tim.

The 'if you want to' part didn't fill her with optimism. 'Why, what's yours?'

'Well, I *was* going to be a gladiator. Kind of like Russell Crowe. But the breastplate snapped and they couldn't let me have it.'

'So you're not a gladiator. Instead you're . . .?'

Tim mumbled, 'Barney the Dinosaur.'

'Thanks, but I'll stay with the rabbit. Purple was never my colour.'

'**Y**ou're all pink!' Cheryl, looking glamorous and suitably exotic in her hula skirt, danced up to Lola.

'Imagine how hot it feels being trapped inside an all-in-one bunny suit.' Lola reached for a bottle of ice-cold water. 'Then double it.'

'Couldn't you take the bunny suit off now?' Cheryl tilted her head sympathetically to one side.

'I could, if I'd thought to bring a change of clothes with me.' Lola couldn't believe it hadn't occurred to her. But beneath the nylon fur she was scantily clad and, jolly though the crowd at Bernini's were, she didn't feel they were ready to witness her in her pink and green polka-dotty knickers and matching balcony bra.

Mind you, it was a salutary experience dressing up like a rabbit. Until tonight she hadn't realised how nice it was to be paid attention by members of the opposite sex. Being eyed up was something she'd pretty much taken for granted.

'You know, I feel as if I'm wearing an invisibility cloak,' said Lola. 'Nobody's looking at me.'

'Oh, that's not true.' Cheryl pointed across the dance floor. 'Those people over there are looking at you.'

'They're laughing. That's different. They're pretending to clean their whiskers and lick their paws.' Lola took another swig of water.

'Hey, at least you aren't Barney the Dinosaur.'

Poor old Tim, his outfit was even hotter and heavier than her own. Lola watched him attempting to dance, wincing as his dinosaur tail swung lethally from side to side.

'I can see someone looking at you.' Cheryl gave her a nudge.

Lola didn't get her hopes up. 'Where?'

'Over there, just come in.' Cheryl nodded at the door. 'The one in the blue shirt, see him yet? He hasn't taken his eyes off you since he got here. Actually . . .' Her voice trailed off as she peered more closely at the new arrival. 'Where have I seen him before? Ooh, he's coming over!'

Lola surveyed him, glad she hadn't got her hopes up. 'He's one of our customers.'

'God, you're right, it is. Did we invite customers along tonight?'

'No.' Mystified, Lola watched the man who wasn't a private detective. When he reached them she noticed that the usual easy smile was tinged with something else, possibly nerves.

'Hi.' As she nodded in recognition, one of the bunny ears flopped down into her line of sight, which didn't help.

'Hi there. I wasn't sure at first if it was you.' The smile became a grin. 'Nice outfit.'

'Thanks.' Lola paused as Cheryl melted tactfully away into the crowd. 'So, is this a coincidence, you turning up here tonight?'

'No, it isn't. When I was in the shop the other day I heard your friend talking about the party here tonight.'

At least he was honest. 'So, are you a stalker?'

Another pause. Finally he shook his head. 'Not really. I mean, I sup-pose so, kind of. But for a reason. Not in a creepy way, I promise.'

That was the thing, he just didn't *seem* creepy.

'Look, is there anywhere we could talk?'

'About what?'

'Something important. Sorry, I know this place isn't ideal, but I didn't want to talk at the bookshop. There's a free table over there.' As he steered Lola gently towards it, he eyed the half-empty bottle of water in her hand. 'Can I get you another drink? Maybe a . . . carrot juice?'

Lola stopped, gave him a look.

He raised his hands. 'OK, sorry, sorry. I can't believe I said that.'

'I can't believe it either. So far this evening eleven people have asked me if I'd like a carrot juice. Eight have asked me if I'd like some lettuce. Honestly, this place is just one huge comedy club.'

'Sorry, I'm usually more original than that. Put it down to nerves.'

They reached the table. The man pulled out a chair for Lola then sat down himself.

'Why are you nervous?'

In the dim lighting his expression was unreadable. 'Twentieth of May?'

Something squeezed tight in Lola's chest. 'That's my birthday.'

He sat back, exhaled, pushed his fingers through his dark hair then half smiled. 'In that case you're definitely my daughter.'

The furry white nylon ear flopped once more over Lola's face. Little stars danced in her field of vision as she fumbled with the Velcro fastening her costume at the neck. But her fingers couldn't manage it and heat was spreading through her body. Finally she managed to say, 'Please, could you help me take my head off? I'm feeling a bit . . . um, faint.'

**O**ne minute you were in a wine bar more or less blending in with the twenty-two other people cavorting around in fancy dress, the next minute you were sitting in an all-night café with a mug of hot tea, attracting all manner of funny looks from everyone else in the place.

Lola still couldn't assimilate what had happened; her brain had stubbornly refused to believe what he was telling her. Apart from anything else, this man wasn't even American. Yet . . . why would he be here saying this if it weren't true?

'Sorry.' The man sitting opposite her said it for the third time. 'I knew it was going to be a shock but I couldn't think of any way of saying it that wouldn't be.'

'That's OK.' At least it was cooler in here. The urge to pass out had receded. 'You can't imagine how unexpected this is.'

He did that rueful semi-smile again. 'For me too.'

Lola sipped her tea, burning her mouth but appreciating the sugar rush. 'So you're . . . Steve?'

The semi-smile abruptly disappeared. 'No. That's not me.'

So. Not American, not called Steve. Something wasn't right here. But he seemed so genuine, so convinced . . .

'What's your name then?'

'Nick. Nick James.' Shaking his head, he said, 'I can't believe your mother didn't tell you that.'

'Tuh, that's nothing! She told me you were from New York.'

His eyebrows went up. 'What else did she say?'

'Oh God.' Lola almost dropped her cup. 'Your eyebrows. That's just how mine go when I'm surprised . . .' Tea slopped onto the table as her trembling increased. 'You've got my eyebrows!'

'Actually, you've got mine,' Nick James pointed out.

'That's incredible! And we have dark hair.'

'You have your mother's eyes and freckles.'

'But not her hair. Before you saw me, did you think I'd be a redhead?'

He shook his head. 'I knew you weren't. I visited you once, when you were a baby.'

Lola felt as if all the air had been squeezed from her lungs. 'You did?'

'Oh, yes. Briefly.' He smiled. 'You were beautiful. Seeing you for the first time . . . well, it was incredible.'

Her eyes abruptly filling with tears, Lola said, 'And then you buggered off again.' The tears took her by surprise and she brushed them away angrily; it wasn't as if she'd had a miserable life without—

'No, no. That's not what happened at all.' Horrified, Nick James said, 'Is that what you think, that I was the one who walked away? Because I didn't, I swear. I loved your mother and I wanted the three of us to be a family, more than anything. She was the one who wouldn't have it.'

'Hang on.' Lola stopped him, because there had to have been some kind of misunderstanding here. 'This is Blythe we're talking about?'

She had to double-check. Imagine if he sat back in dismay and said, 'No, not Blythe! I'm talking about Linda.'

And the eyebrows had just been an eerie coincidence.

But he didn't, he just nodded and said simply, 'Blythe Malone.'

'Anything to eat, love?' A waitress bustled over to their table.

'No, thanks.' There was so much to take in, not least the discovery that her own mother had lied to her.

'Sure? We've got a lovely lamb hotpot.'

'She'd rather have a plate of carrots.' One of the men at the next table chuckled and nudged his friend, who broke into a buck-toothed Bugs Bunny impression.

'Sorry.' Nick James looked at Lola. 'I should have found somewhere better than this.'

Offended, the waitress sniffed and said, 'Charmed, I'm sure,' and walked away.

'When I was little I always thought my dad was a film star,' said Lola, 'because the only Americans I knew were the ones I'd seen on TV.'

'And you got yourself an advertising exec instead. Bad luck.'

'That's OK. It's just weird, all these years imagining you being an American, *talking* like an American, and now having to lose that idea.'

'If I'd known, I'd have brushed up on my American accent.' He shrugged, half smiled. 'I can't imagine why Blythe told you that.'

Lola glanced at her handbag, lying on the chair next to her and containing her mobile. There was nothing to stop her calling her mother right now and demanding an explanation.

But she couldn't bring herself to do that.

'How did you find me?'

'The piece you did on the local news,' he admitted. 'When I said I hadn't seen it . . . well, that was a lie. I was flicking through the TV channels that evening and there you were, with your name up on the screen. Lola Malone. You were Lauren when you were born.'

'I know,' said Lola.

'Sorry, I meant I knew you as Lauren. But the day I came round to your mother's house when you were a baby, she handed you over to a friend and said, "Could you take Lola out into the garden?"'

'Our next-door neighbour's daughter couldn't say Lauren so she called me Lola. It stuck. Nobody calls me Lauren.'

He nodded. 'Well, anyway, I didn't know for sure if it was you, but it was an unusual name and you were the right age and colouring. So I had to come to the shop and see you.'

That was why he had engaged her in conversation.

'Hang on, so you didn't really like those books I recommended.' Lola's pride was wounded. 'You were just pretending.'

Nick smiled. 'I loved the books. I read them because you'd recommended them. Don't worry, I'm definitely converted.'

That made her feel better. Lola took another sip of tea. 'I can't believe I'm sitting here talking to you now. Wait till I tell Mum.'

A flicker of something crossed her father's—*her father's!*—face. 'How is Blythe?'

'She's great. Living in Streatham.'

'Married?'

'I had a fantastic stepdad. He died five years ago.'

Nick shook his head. 'I'm sorry.'

'But Mum's started dating again. I'm trying to do something about her clothes. Did she have really weird dress sense when you knew her?'

He looked amused. 'Oh, yes.'

'At least that's something I didn't inherit from her.' Lola patted her furry white nylon suit. 'I mean, I'd rather shoot myself than go out in public wearing something that people might laugh at.'

Nick nodded in agreement. 'Thank goodness for that. I have pretty high standards myself.'

He did, come to think of it. Each time she'd seen him he'd been wearing expensive clothes.

'So what happened?' she blurted out. 'I don't understand. Why did you and Mum break up?'

He paused. 'What did she tell you?'

'Well. A big lie, obviously. But the story was that she met an American guy called Steve when he was working over here one summer. She completely fell for him, discovered she was pregnant, told him she was pregnant and never saw him again. She told me she never regretted it, because she got me. Then when I was four years old she married Alex Pargeter, who was the best stepfather any girl could ask for.'

'Good.' Nick sounded as if he meant it. 'I'm glad.'

'But none of that stuff was true, was it? Your name isn't even Steve. So now it's your turn. I want to know what really happened.'

'What really happened.' Another pause. Finally, slowly, he said, 'What really happened is I went to prison.'

'It was my own stupid fault. There's no one else to blame. Everything would have been different if I hadn't messed up.'

Having left the café, they were now heading in the direction of Notting Hill. It was a frosty night and the pavement glittered under the street lamps but Lola was protected from the cold by her bunny suit. She was getting a bit fed up, though, with groups of Christmas revellers singing 'Bright Eyes' at her. Or bellowing out 'Run, rabbit, run, rabbit, run run run' while taking aim with an imaginary shotgun.

'Blythe knew nothing about it,' Nick went on. 'She was four months pregnant. We'd been together for almost a year by then. Obviously we hadn't planned on having a baby, but these things happen. We started looking around for a place to buy, so we could be together. That was an eye-opener, I can tell you. I was only twenty-one; there wasn't much we could afford. I felt such a failure. If only we had more money. Are you cold? Because if you're cold we can flag down a cab.'

'I'm fine.' Lola's breath was puffing out in front of her but the rest of her was warm. 'So what did you do, rob a bank?'

'I got involved with a friend of a friend who'd set up a cigarette and booze smuggling operation. Bringing the stuff over from the Continent, selling it on, easy profit.' Drily, Nick said, 'Until you get caught. Let me tell you, that wasn't the best day of my life.'

'You were arrested?'

He nodded. 'I was young and stupid, and I panicked. Blythe would have been distraught, so I couldn't bring myself to tell her. I appeared at the magistrate's court, still didn't tell her. Had to wait four months for the case to come up in the Crown Court. *Still* didn't tell her. Because I'd only been involved in the operation for a few weeks my solicitor said there was a chance I wouldn't go down and I clung on to that. I know it's crazy, but I thought maybe, just maybe, Blythe wouldn't need to know about any of it. That she'd never find out.'

Lola could kind of see the logic in this. 'Good plan.'

'It would have been if it had worked. Except it didn't.' Nick shrugged. 'The judge gave me eighteen months.'

'So how did Mum find out?'

'My cousin had to phone her. Can you imagine what that must have been like? She came to visit me in prison ten days later, said it was all over and she never wanted to see me again. I told her I'd only done it for her and the baby, but she wasn't going to change her mind. As far as she was concerned, I was a criminal and a liar, and that wasn't the kind of father she wanted for her child. It was pretty emotional. But she was eight months pregnant, so all I could do was apologise and agree with everything she said. That was the second-worst day of my life.' He paused. 'You were born a week later.'

Lola was beginning to understand why her mother had invented an alternative history.

'I served my time, behaved myself and got out of prison after nine months,' Nick went on. 'You and your mother were all I'd thought about. I was desperate to see you, and to make Blythe understand how sorry I was. I thought I might be able to persuade her to change her mind, give me another chance. So I came round to the house and that's when I saw you for the first time. You were beaming at me, with your hair in a funny little curly topknot and Ribena stains on your white T-shirt. But your mother wasn't open to persuasion, she said she'd never be able to trust me. She also said I'd put her through hell and if I really wanted to prove how sorry I was, the best thing I could do was disappear. And you know what?' As they stood waiting for the traffic lights to change, he gave Lola a sideways look. 'She meant it.'

The lights turned green and together they crossed the road. 'So that's what you did?' asked Lola.

'I didn't want to. But I felt I owed Blythe that much. So I said goodbye and left.' He waited. 'That was the worst day of my life.'

Crikey, this was emotional stuff.

'I keep feeling as if I'm listening to you talk about some television drama.' Lola shook her head in disbelief. 'Then it hits me all over again; this is actually about *me*.'

'Oi, you in the fur,' roared a bloke in a van. 'Fancy a jump?'

'My flat's down here.' Loftily ignoring the van driver, Lola turned left into Radley Road. 'I've still got loads more questions.'

'Fire away.'

'Have you been in trouble with the law since then?'

Nick shook his head. 'No, no. Apart from three points on my licence for speeding. I learned my lesson, Your Honour.'

'Are you married?'

Another shake. 'Not any more. Amicable divorce six years ago.'

'Any children?'

He broke into a smile. 'No other children. Just you.'

'Well, this is where I live.' She stopped outside number 73; they'd walked all the way from Soho.

'Nice place.'

'Thanks.' The events of the evening abruptly caught up with Lola; one minute she'd been strolling happily along, the next she was so bone tired all she wanted to do was lie down and sleep for a week. But this man—*her father*—had just spent the last hour walking her home . . .

'Right then, I'll be off.' Nick James watched her yawn like a hippo.

'I feel awful, not inviting you in for a coffee.'

'Hey, it's fine. I'll get a cab.' He raked his fingers through his hair. 'It's been a lot to take in.'

Lola nodded; gosh, and now she didn't know how to say goodbye. Was she supposed to hug him, kiss him, shake hands or what?

Nick James laughed gently and said, 'Tricky, isn't it?'

'Yes, it *is*.' Relieved that he understood, Lola watched him take out his wallet. 'Ooh, do I start getting pocket money?'

'I was thinking more of a business card.' He studied her face as he handed over his card. 'I don't want to put pressure on you, so from now on I'll leave it up to you to get in touch with me. That's if you decide you want to.' Turning, he began to walk back down the street.

**A**t four o'clock the following afternoon the taxi pulled into Radley Road. Gabe said, 'It's the blue and white house up there on the left.'

OK, he was back.

When the cab had disappeared he hauled his luggage up the steps and let himself in through the front door. Leaving the cases in the hall, he made his way upstairs and knocked on Lola's door.

No reply.

Well, it wasn't as if she was expecting him. As far as Lola was concerned he was still on the other side of the world.

Gabe crossed the landing and knocked on the door of his own flat.

The girl was out too. He knocked again to make extra sure. OK, it was his property and he had a right to enter it. Gabe twiddled the key ring around until he located the right key.

He fitted it into the lock, twisted it left and pushed open the door.

Jesus Christ! The place had been burgled! Stepping back in horror, Gabe surveyed the scene of devastation. Except if burglars had been here, wouldn't they have made off with that flat-screen TV? Or the expensive DVD recorder? Or that pile of money over there on the floor next to the plate of spaghetti bolognese?

What the hell *was* this? Gabe ventured further into the living room, treading a careful path between abandoned clothes, CDs, magazines, opened packets of biscuits and coffee mugs. Did the girl have some kind of stalker ex-boyfriend who'd been round to the house and trashed it?

But he knew that wasn't right either. The mess and devastation was too casual to have been done in anger. Squeezing his eyes tight shut then opening them again, Gabe realised with a sinking heart what kind of a tenant had moved into his home.

He'd been away for *four days*.

His beautiful flat, his pride and joy. The muscles in Gabe's temples went into spasm and his head began to ache. As if he didn't have enough to deal with right now.

Oh well, the sooner the girl was out of here, the better. Maybe it was just as well he'd come back.

That was when he heard the bang of the front door downstairs, followed by the sound of footsteps on the staircase. Was it Lola or the new girl, the Queen of Trash?

Gabe left the flat, closed the door behind him and waited on the landing to see which one of them it—

'Aaaarrrggh!' Lola let out a shriek of fright and almost lost her footing on the stairs.

'No, I'm not a ghost,' said Gabe. 'It's really me.'

Lola was clasping her chest now. 'But you're . . . what's going on?'

'Didn't work out.'

Her mouth dropped open. 'You changed your mind?'

'No.' Gabe briefly shook his head. 'She changed hers.'

Lola threw herself at him, knocking the air from his lungs. *Whoosh*, she was in his arms babbling, 'So you're back? That's fantastic! Is Jaydena mad? I can't believe it, I thought I was hallucinating! What a *cow*!'

This was why he loved Lola. 'I think so too. She got back with an ex.'

'Oh well, her loss.' Lola gave him another squeeze. 'Come in and tell me all about it. My God, you went all that way for nothing! Will you be able to get your job back? Where on earth are you going to *live*?'

'What are you talking about?' Following Lola, Gabe said, 'I'm back. I'll be living here, of course.'

'You mean in Sally's flat?'

'It's not her flat! It's mine! I'll explain to her that I need it now, give her a week's notice. *And* I've just been in there,' he said incredulously. 'Have you seen the state of the place?'

'She's not terribly tidy.'

'Not terribly tidy? That's like saying the Beckhams aren't terribly thrifty. She only moved in four days ago—imagine what it'd look like after four months! No,' Gabe shook his head, 'she has to go. As for a job, I've no idea. I haven't even thought about that yet. The last week hasn't exactly gone according to plan.' He took the can of lager Lola was offering him and pinged off the ring-pull.

'No wonder you're a bit grumpy,' Lola said sympathetically.

'I'm not *a bit grumpy*. I went to Australia, I came back again and I didn't even have time to get a suntan.' Exasperated, Gabe glugged down ice-cold lager before wiping his mouth with the back of his hand. 'Dammit, I'm *pissed off*.'

'OK, you choose. Now, do you want to carry on talking about Australia or shall we change the subject?'

He surveyed Lola, who was evidently dying to unleash some gossip. Nodding in realisation he said, 'Right, of course, you've seen that guy again. Doug, isn't it? Has he forgiven you yet?'

Lola's face fell at the mention of her first love. 'Not even slightly.' Then she brightened. 'But something else has happened. I've met another man.'

'And to think they call you fickle.' Gabe regarded her with affection, because it wasn't her fault his own life was crap. 'Go on. Who is he?'

'Actually,' Lola grimaced, 'this is the weird bit. He's my father.'

**A**t seven o'clock they heard the front door open and close, then the sound of someone climbing the stairs.

'Here's Sally.' Lola stayed sitting, not looking forward to the next bit.

'Right, I'll speak to her. The sooner this is sorted out, the better.' Gabe rose to his feet, ready to do battle with the bag lady who'd wrecked his flat.

Except the girl he came face to face with on the landing was no bag lady. This girl was tall and curvaceous in a red wraparound dress and an elegant cream coat. Her hair was baby-blonde and swingy, her eyes were the colour of chestnuts. Her mouth was curvy and painted red to match her dress. She was even wearing Jo Malone's Lime, Basil and Mandarin, which was Gabe's all-time favourite perfume.

She smiled at Gabe and, key poised, headed for the door of his flat.

Gabe cleared his throat. 'Are you Sally?'

She stopped, turned. 'Yes! And you must be a friend of Lola's.'

'I'm Gabe Adams.' God, it *was* her.

'Gabe?' Sally looked puzzled. 'But that's the name of the one who moved to Australia.'

'I didn't *move* to Australia, I *went* to Australia. But things didn't work out,' Gabe said evenly, 'so now I'm back. Look, I realise this is inconvenient, but if you could be out by the end of the week, that'd be great.'

She stared at him. 'Excuse me?'

How could any girl who lived in such abject squalor look like this? 'Well, you'll be moving back in with your mother.' Ha, lucky old *her*.

'I don't understand,' said Sally. 'I'm not going anywhere.'

'But you have to. Because it's my flat and I need it back.'

Her eyebrows furrowed. 'And I'm saying you can't *have* it back because the agreement was that I could live here for a year.'

'OK.' Gabe heaved a sigh; it had always been on the cards that she might decide to be difficult. 'I'm giving you official notice as of today. That's in the contract. You have one month to find somewhere else—'

'Hang on,' Sally interrupted. 'What contract?'

'The one you signed with the lettings agency.'

'I haven't signed any contract,' said Sally.

Behind him, Gabe heard Lola's door click open. He turned and said evenly, 'What's going on here? Why didn't she sign the contract?'

Lola could feel her heart clattering away in overdrive. She'd been hiding behind the door listening to their heated exchange. Now it was time to face the music. She said reluctantly, 'I cancelled the agency.'

'*Why?*'

'OK, the thing is, I was trying to *help*. You told me yourself that the lettings agency charges a fortune, so when Sally came along I thought I could save you a heap of money, which I *thought* you'd be happy about. Because I knew we could trust Sally. She gave me the deposit and the first month's rent in cash and I paid them into your account.'

'No problem, I'll give it straight back,' Gabe retorted.

'This isn't fair.' Sally's tone was heated. 'You're being unreasonable.'

'*Me?*' Gabe jabbed at his own chest and yelled, '*I'm* being unreasonable? What about the state of my flat? Would you say the carnage you've reduced it to is *reasonable?*'

Sally stared at him. 'How do you know what I've done to it?'

'Because I went in and had a look!'

She gasped. 'You can't just let yourself in whenever you like.'

'You can't stop me.' Gabe was really losing it now. 'It's my flat!'

'Which you rented to me. And I like living here.' Sally's eyes abruptly brimmed with tears. 'What's more, I'm not going to move out.'

'Oh, please.' Lola was by this stage feeling absolutely terrible. 'I'm sure we can arrange something. Who are you phoning? Not the police?'

Having pulled out her mobile, Sally was blindly jabbing at buttons. 'I'm getting Doug over here. He'll sort this out.'

Doug? *Yeek*, the very name was enough to set Lola's heart racing. Would Gabe and Sally think her shallow if she quickly washed her hair and redid her face before he turned up?

The answer to that was a resounding yes, but she'd gone ahead and done it anyway. When Doug arrived at her flat forty minutes later he surveyed the three of them and said levelly, 'What a mess.'

Lola really hoped he didn't mean her.

'You're telling me.' Gabe's tone was curt. 'Have you seen what your sister's done to my flat?'

'I can guess. She's not what you'd call tidy,' said Doug.

'*And* she's a liar.' Gabe turned to Sally and said accusingly, 'When we spoke on the phone, you told me you were super-housetrained.'

Sally rolled her eyes. 'It wasn't a lie. Just a little fib. It's not against the law to be untidy.'

Gabe addressed Doug. 'I just want her out.'

'I can see that,' said Doug. 'Right, tell me exactly what's going on.'

When they'd finished explaining the situation, Doug looked at Lola and said, 'So basically this is all your fault.'

'Oh, of course it is. I do my best to help people out and this is what happens, this is the thanks I get.'

'Legally,' Doug turned to the others, 'either of you can cause untold hassle to the other. If you ask me, that's a waste of everyone's time and money. Shall we go and take a look at the flat now?'

'Everyone put on their anti-contamination suits,' said Gabe.

Over in Gabe's formerly pristine living room, now awash with magazines and clothes and abandoned food and·make-up, Doug nodded sagely. 'Oh, yes, this is familiar.'

'What I don't understand'—Lola was puzzled—'is when I came to the house in Barnes, your bedroom was fine. Completely normal.'

'That's because I have a mother who has two cleaners who barge in and tidy my room every day. Which is why I was so keen to move out.'

Glaring at Gabe she added, 'And why I'm definitely not going back.'

'How many bedrooms here?' Doug was exploring the flat. 'Two?'

'I hope you're not thinking what I think you're thinking,' said Gabe.

Doug shrugged. 'Do you have any better ideas?'

'I have a very much better idea,' Gabe retorted. 'She's your sister. You can take her home with you.'

'Not a chance. Lola, could you have her?'

Sally complained. 'You're making me sound like a delinquent dog.'

'Trust me,' Gabe gestured around the room in disgust, 'a delinquent dog wouldn't make this much mess.'

'I would take her.' Keen though she was to scramble into Doug's good books, Lola couldn't quite bring herself to make the ultimate sacrifice and thankfully had a get-out clause. 'But I've only got the one bedroom.'

'Fine. So you two,' Doug turned back to Gabe and Sally, 'have a choice. You either hire yourselves a couple of solicitors to slug it out or you give flat-sharing a go for a couple of weeks.'

'I can't believe this is happening to me.' The stubble on Gabe's chin rasped as he rubbed his hands over his face. 'I'll end up strangling her, then I'll be arrested and slung in prison.' As he said the word prison, Gabe winced and looked apologetically at Lola. 'Sorry.'

'Right, decision time.' Doug pointed to Sally. 'Would you be willing to give it a try?'

Sally shrugged and said, 'I suppose I could give sharing a go for a couple of weeks.'

Doug swung back to Gabe. 'But you still want to stick with the legal route, or . . .?'

Gabe hesitated, then exhaled and threw up his hands. 'Oh, for God's sake. We'll try it, then. Seeing as I don't have any choice.'

'Good call,' said Doug.

'But only for a couple of weeks. Then she has to move out.'

'Agreed. And *you*,' he instructed Sally, 'behave yourself and put your clothes away once in a while.'

'Not once in a while!' Gabe exploded. 'All the time!'

'Oh, don't start,' Sally jeered. 'You sound like *such* an old woman.'

Doug forestalled their bickering. 'My work here is done.' His gaze fixed on Lola. 'You can show me out.'

Lola's breathing quickened; she so desperately wanted him to stop regarding her as the wickedest woman in Britain.

In the hallway downstairs Doug came straight to the point. 'What was that about prison, earlier?'

He didn't miss a trick.

'What?' Lola thought rapidly.

'Your friend Gabe mentioned prison. Then he looked embarrassed and apologised. Who's been to prison?'

'My father.'

'Really? God. *Alex?*' Doug frowned. 'What happened?'

Lola felt her throat tighten. 'Not Alex. My *real* father. His name's Nick James.' Her voice began to wobble. 'It's all been a bit strange really. I only met him for the first time yesterday. Well, that's not true, he's been coming into Kingsley's and chatting to me but it wasn't until last night that he actually told me he was my real d-dad. And there was me, dressed like a r-rabbit . . . oh God, sorry, I wasn't expecting this to h-h-happen.' Hastily she pulled a tissue out of her bra and wiped her eyes. 'To be honest I think it's all c-come as a bit of a sh-shock.'

'OK, don't cry.' There was a note of desperation in Doug's voice; this was rather more than he'd been expecting. Lola realised he'd never seen her crying before. It was something she hardly ever did in public, darkened cinemas excepted, largely because she always turned into a pink blotchy mess. In fact, the only way to hide her face from Doug now was to bury it in his chest.

If only he wouldn't keep trying to back away . . .

Finally she managed to corner him against the front door and conceal her blotchiness in his shirt. Oh, yes, this was where she belonged, back in Doug's arms at last.

Gingerly he patted her shoulder. 'Hey, sshh, everything'll be all right.'

Nuzzling against the warmth of his chest, Lola said in a muffled, hiccuppy voice, 'All these years my mum lied to me about my f-father.'

'And he's only just come out of prison?'

'No, that was years ago. Cigarette smuggling, nothing too terrible. He went to prison just before I was born. Pretty ironic really. My mother decided he wasn't good enough to be my dad, so she refused to let him see me. And then seventeen years later, *your* mother decided I wasn't good enough to be your girlfriend.'

'That *is* a coincidence.' Doug paused. 'Did she offer him twelve thousand pounds to stay away too?'

OK, still bitter.

'I haven't even told Mum yet. Heaven knows what she's going to say when she finds out he's been in touch. It's just so much to take in.' Lola raised her face and wondered if he ever watched romantic movies, because this would be the *perfect* moment for him to kiss her.

'You've got mascara on your nose.' Doug evidently hadn't read the romantic-hero rules.

Even less romantically, his phone burst into life in his jacket pocket, less than three inches from her ear.

The spell was broken. Doug disengaged himself and answered the phone. He listened for a few seconds then said, 'No, sorry, I was held up. I'm on my way now.' He ended the call and opened the front door. 'I have to go.'

'Mustn't be late. Or you'll get home and find your dinner in the dog.' She was longing—*longing*—to know who he was rushing off to meet, but all Doug did was give an infuriating little smile. Almost as if he knew she was fishing for clues.

'Why were you dressed as a rabbit when you met your father?'

Ha, he wasn't the only one who could smile infuriatingly. 'It's a long story.' Lola was apologetic. 'And you have to rush off.'

He had the grace to nod in amusement. 'Touché. So what's he like?'

'Nice, I think. Normal, as far as I can tell. We have the same eyebrows.'

'The same eyebrows? You mean you take it in turns to wear them when you go out?' Doug shook his head. 'You want to splash out, get yourselves a pair each.'

# Chapter 7

'LOOK, I'M SORRY about yesterday,' said Gabe.

Sally, just home from yet another pre-Christmas shopping trip, dumped her bags and took off her coat. 'Really? Yesterday you were like a grizzly bear with a sore head.'

Gabe shrugged and smiled. 'Yesterday wasn't the best day of my life. Now I've slept for thirteen hours I'm feeling a lot better and so I hope we can get along,' he continued, keen to make amends.

'Me too. Can I ask you something?'

'Fire away.'

Sally eyed him in his falling-to-pieces Levi's, bare feet and ancient T-shirt full of holes. 'Don't you think it's a bit weird to *be* so tidy and nit-picky and go around *looking* such a scruffy mess?'

It had been a genuine question—she was *interested*—but Gabe instantly got his hackles up.

'No. Don't you think it's weird that you go around looking like you've stepped out of *Vogue*, yet at home you live in a tip?'

She pointed a warning finger. 'Look, we're stuck with each other, for better or worse. *Please* don't start being annoying again.'

For several seconds their eyes locked. Sally could tell he was struggling to control his irritation. Lola had denied it, but she wouldn't be surprised if Gabe was a little bit gay. He was exceptionally good-looking for a start. Obsessive-compulsive when it came to tidiness. And what straight man would ever have eyelashes that long?

'Right. Sorry.' Evidently having reminded himself that he was supposed to be making amends, Gabe said, 'How about a cup of tea?'

Well, she could be conciliatory too. 'Great. White, please, one sugar.'

'And I'm making fettucine Alfredo if you're hungry.'

Ha, absolutely without a question gay. Bisexual anyway. But who cared, if he was a good cook? Sally slipped out of her shoes and removed her silver drop earrings. 'I love fettucine Alfredo. OK if I have a shower first?'

'Fine.' But the way the word came out, it didn't sound fine.

'What? Why are you looking at me like that?'

'You're going to take a shower *now*?'

Sally gazed at him. 'Am I supposed to make an *appointment*?'

A muscle was thudding away in Gabe's jaw. 'No, it's only that I don't want you doing what you've just done.'

Bewildered, Sally said, 'I don't know what you're talking about.'

'This!' He pointed to the dumped carriers, and to her coat and umbrella on the chair. 'This.' Her handbag on the coffee table. 'Those.' Her shoes on the carpet. 'And them.' Her silver earrings on the window ledge. 'You came into this flat one minute ago and look at the mess!'

'Oh. Sorry.' God, talk about neurotic. She rolled her eyes and retraced her steps around the living room, picking everything up.

'Good. Well done,' said Gabe when she'd finished.

You had to pity him really.

Sally said sarcastically, 'Thank you, Mr Anal.'

'My pleasure, Miss Slob.'

'**W**here's Sally? Have you strangled her yet?' Having followed the smell of cooking up the stairs, Lola gave Gabe a hug.

'Give me a couple more days.'

'Ooh, Alfredo. My favourite.' She inspected the pans on the hob. 'So apart from the tidiness thing, how d'you think the two of you'll get on?'

'God knows. If I met her in a bar I'd think she was fine,' said Gabe. 'But that's because I wouldn't know what she's really like.' He paused. 'She doesn't have a boyfriend, right?'

Lola pulled a face. 'No. Bit of a disastrous history with men. One of them jilted her practically at the altar.'

'And we don't have to wonder why.'

'That's mean. You've just been dumped yourself.'

Gabe shrugged and tipped fettucine into a pan of boiling water. 'I'm just saying, she could get a crush on me. I don't need that kind of hassle. Platonic flat-sharing only works as long as one person doesn't secretly fancy the pants off the other.'

Enthralled, Lola said, 'You think she fancies you?'

'I don't know. Maybe. And it's the last thing I need.'

Lola pinched a slice of Parmesan. 'Serves you right for being so gorgeous. What did Sally do to give herself away then?'

'Oh, you know those looks girls give you. She was doing it earlier.' Gabe added a carton of double cream to the garlic sizzling in the pan. 'That kind of moony, pouty thing. I can't be doing with— *shit!*'

The hairbrush whistled past his ear and ricocheted off the kitchen wall. 'What the . . .?' Gabe twisted round in disbelief.

'Sorry, but someone had to shut you up.' Sally was in the doorway, wrapped in a brown silk dressing gown, her hair wet from the shower and her face the picture of outrage. 'You can't go around saying stuff like that.' Her eyes glittered. 'Because it's not *true.*'

'OK, I'm sorry. I got it wrong. You could have done me an injury with that hairbrush,' said Gabe.

'I meant to. I'm just not a very good shot.' Turning to Lola, Sally said, 'And you believed everything he was telling you!'

Lola shook her head apologetically. 'He's usually right. Most girls do fancy him. Gabe's a bit of an expert when it comes to that sort of thing.'

'Well, he's got it wrong this time, because I *don't* fancy him, and I *definitely* wasn't giving him any kind of moony pouty look.' Brimming with derision, Sally said, 'If anything, I was thinking that any man who makes such a big fuss about keeping his flat perfect is probably gay.'

'I'm not gay,' said Gabe.

'And I don't fancy you. *At all.*'

'Fine. I believe you. And in return you have to stop thinking I'm gay.'

'Could we call a truce and stop talking about you two now?' Lola had been patient but enough was enough. Plaintively she said, 'If nobody minds, I'd quite like us to talk about me.'

Over dinner Lola brought them up to date with the New-found Father situation.

'I phoned Mum today to try to drop Nick's name casually into the conversation, and she said, "Oh, hello, darling, you've only just caught us, Malcolm and I are off to Cardiff." She told me they're spending the night with Malcolm's brother and his family. So I couldn't really say anything about Nick James, could I? To be honest, I hadn't realised she and Malcolm were getting so serious. Mum said he wants to introduce her to everyone.' Lola paused and tore into a chunk of focaccia. 'I don't know how I feel about that. I mean, it's not that I don't like Malcolm. He's just . . . well, he has this awful beard, and he wears weird baggy jumpers and sandals with the hairs on his toes poking through.'

'They're visiting his brother, not eloping to Gretna Green,' said Gabe.

Lola pulled a face. 'I really hope they're not sleeping together.'

Brightly Sally said, 'At least she's too old to get pregnant.'

Which was another mental image Lola could do without. Mopping up the last of the Alfredo sauce from her plate, she amused herself instead by watching Gabe pretend not to care that Sally had dripped Frascati from her glass onto the table.

'How would you have felt if you'd met your father for the first time,' Sally went on, 'and he looked like Malcolm? Would it put you off him?'

Oh crikey, it might. Especially the hairy toes. Lola went hot and cold at the thought. At least Nick James hadn't done that to her. She was almost sure he wasn't the type to get his toes out in public and—

'You've spilt a bit of wine,' Gabe blurted out.

Sally shrugged comfortably. 'Never mind, it's only white.'

Gabe sighed. Lola watched him pointedly not saying anything.

'Oh, look at yourself.' Sally grinned and reached behind her for a magazine she'd been allowed to leave—*neatly*—in the magazine rack. She opened it out, turned it upside-down and blotted up the wine. 'There, better now?'

'Yes. Although a normal person might have used kitchen roll.'

'This was closer.' Turning the magazine back over and studying the wet pages, Sally said, 'Anyway, it's only Jack Nicholson in his swimming shorts. He won't mind.'

Lola leaned across to peer at the shot. 'I had such a crush on that man when I first saw *One Flew Over the Cuckoo's Nest*.'

'She has pretty strange taste in crushes.' Gabe reached for the Frascati bottle. 'More wine?'

'Yes, please. Go on,' Sally said with a smile, 'who else does she like?'

'Ricky Gervais.'

'Euww.'

'That's supposed to be a secret.' Commandeering the magazine, Lola riffled through in search of inspiration. 'I have normal crushes too. Heath Ledger, he's one. And Johnny Depp, obviously.'

'Not to mention Alan Sugar,' said Gabe.

'And my brother,' Sally chimed in. She wrinkled her nose. 'To me, that's even weirder than fancying Alan Sugar.'

'They're both mean. But in a sexy way. Ooh, that reminds me, Tom Dutton.' Lola's eyes lit up and she puffed out her cheeks in appreciation. 'Now *he's* mean and sexy. And wasn't he fantastic in *Over You*? Gabe came with me to the cinema and . . . where are you going?' She swivelled round as Gabe jumped up and headed for his bedroom.

He returned with his camera and laptop. 'I forgot to tell you. I saw him.'

'Alan Sugar?' Lola's heart gave a little skip of excitement.

'Not him. Tom Dutton.'

'What? Where? At the airport?'

'On the way to it. Hang on, nearly there.'

'Let me see.' Lola jostled with Sally in front of the laptop in order to gaze at the photo Gabe had brought up on the screen. 'Wow, it *is* him. Who's he kissing?'

A second photo flashed up and Lola saw at once who it was. Next to her Sally let out a squeal of recognition and yelped, 'Jessica Lee!'

'I thought you'd like to see them.' Pleased with himself, Gabe clicked onto the third photo, the one showing Tom loping back to his car. 'They pulled up separately at this service station and disappeared together up a side alley. I just happened to have the camera in my hand. I knew you'd think I was making it up if I didn't have proof.' His fingers hovered over the laptop's touchpad. 'I could make this one your screen-saver if you like. Or shall I just delete them?'

'Excuse me! Are you *mad*?' To be on the safe side Sally grabbed his hand before he could press anything drastic and lose the photos for ever. 'It's Tom Dutton and Jessica Lee!'

'I *know*.' Gabe looked aggrieved.

Lola patted his shoulder. 'They're snogging.'

'So?'

'So, no one knows they're even seeing each other.'

'How do you know that?'

'Because if it *was* known, it would be in all the papers,' Sally patiently explained.

'Ri-ight.' Gabe was still looking baffled.

Sally tapped the photos on the screen. 'You can sell these, Gabe. For a lot of money.'

'Oh!' He frowned. 'What, to a newspaper?'

'To a picture agency,' Sally said promptly. 'They're the experts. This is what's known as a scoop.'

**T**he photographs appeared in the *Daily Mirror* two days later. They were also sold to newspapers and magazines all over the world. Colin Carter, from the picture agency Sally had suggested, had just phoned

Gabe and told him that he had a good eye for a picture; if he came up with any more photos he should be sure to give him a call.

It was Christmas Eve and Gabe now found himself with the possibility of a brand-new career as a member of the paparazzi.

He gazed at the newspapers spread out on the coffee table in front of him and frowned. 'I couldn't do it. Everyone hates the paparazzi.'

'It might be fun. All those celebs,' Lola said encouragingly.

Gabe hesitated. He really didn't want to go back to being a chartered surveyor. 'But you know what I'm like. I wouldn't recognise half the people I was supposed to be photographing.'

'God, listen to you.' Sally emerged from her room, her arms loaded with gift-wrapped presents. 'You old fogey! You don't say photographing, you say *papping*.' Never one to pass up the opportunity to have a dig, she said gleefully, 'You'll be playing *records* next, on your wind-up *gramophone*, while puffing away on a *Woodbine*.'

Gabe rolled his eyes. 'Are you off? Don't let us keep you.'

'Oh, are you leaving now?' Lola jumped up; it was seven in the evening and each of them was heading home to spend Christmas Day with their families. 'Are you getting a cab to Barnes?'

'No, I'm catching the tube to Doug's then we're going in his car.'

Doug lived in Kensington. 'You can't carry all those presents on the tube by yourself,' said Lola. 'Why don't I give you a hand? Kensington's practically on the way to Streatham.'

Sally frowned. 'But you've got loads of stuff to carry too.'

'Less than you have.'

'OK, better idea,' said Sally, 'how about if I call Doug and ask him to pick me up?' She paused, looked at the expression on Lola's face. 'What's wrong with that?'

'I don't know. It just doesn't seem fair on him . . .'

'I don't get this.' Sally shook her head, baffled. 'I thought you'd have liked the idea of Doug coming over. Don't say you've gone off him.'

Gabe grinned at her. 'The reason why Lola doesn't want your brother driving over is because . . . hmm, let me think, she'd far rather see where *he* lives and have a good look around *his* flat. Because she's nosy.'

'Is that why?' Sally turned to Lola, surprised.

Lola shrugged evasively; Gabe knew her too well. 'Might be.'

'For heaven's sake! Why didn't you just say so? What am I, a mind-reader?' Sally rolled her eyes. 'Get your coat on and let's go.'

**D**oug lived in the ground-floor flat of a huge Victorian pillar-fronted house in Onslow Gardens. If Lola thought she'd done pretty well for herself property-wise, his flat was several rungs further up the ladder.

Then again, he was a management consultant with a super-successful company he'd built up from scratch; it had to pay well.

'Phew, here we are,' panted Sally, climbing the white marble steps and ringing the bell with her shoulder.

Lola hugged the bags of presents and felt her stomach tighten with excitement. She'd watched *Love, Actually* enough times to know that magical things *could* happen on Christmas Eve.

The front door opened and there he was, barefoot and wearing a blue-and-white-striped shirt over jeans.

'About time too,' Sally complained, bustling past him. 'It's freezing out there.'

'OK, two things. I said to come over at nine.'

'I'm early!'

'And secondly,' Doug's dark eyes narrowed, 'what's Lola doing here? Because I'm fairly sure our mother hasn't invited her to spend Christmas Day with us.'

Lola's heart sank. So *he* hadn't ever watched *Love, Actually*.

'Don't be sarcastic. Lola's here because she's doing me a favour,' said Sally. 'I had too much stuff to carry so she offered to help me out.'

'See? I'm a nice person really.' Lola beamed hopefully. 'And don't panic, I'm on my way to my mum's. I just saw that Sal was struggling with all her parcels so I said I'd lend her a hand getting them here.'

'Fine. I'll take them off you.' Having seized the bags containing the presents, Doug stepped back. 'There. Thanks. Have a good Christmas.'

He was a man. He probably only watched testosterone-fuelled, action-packed films like *Mission: Impossible* and *The Great Escape*.

'Don't be so *rude*!' Sally exclaimed. 'Honestly, I'm *so* ashamed of you sometimes. I was going to ring earlier and ask you to come and pick me up, but Lola said I mustn't do that, you were far too busy to drive over to us, and that she really didn't mind struggling onto the tube and fighting through the crowds and *trudging* through the streets . . .'

Lola cleared her throat; Sally was getting carried away now.

'The least you can do is invite her in for a drink to say thank you.'

Doug gave her a long-suffering look, then turned and said, 'Lola, thank you for helping my sister. Won't you come in for a drink?'

'Doug, that's so kind of you.'

The living room was blissfully warm, L-shaped and comfortably furnished. Lola, greedily taking in every detail, noted that Doug was neither as chaotically untidy as his sister nor as obsessively neat as Gabe. Charcoal-grey curtains hung at the long sash windows, contrasting with the deep crimson walls. There were magazines beside the sofa, DVDs next to the TV, a dark blue sweater left hanging over the back of a chair, two discarded wineglasses on the coffee table . . .

Oh, and a blonde in the kitchen doorway. Now there was an accessory she could have happily done without.

'Hi,' said the blonde.

'Hi.' Lola felt as if she'd just stepped into a lift that wasn't there.

'Well, well, this is a surprise.' Sally, never backward in coming forward, said, 'Who are *you*?'

'This is Isabel. A friend of mine.' The way Doug moved towards her was oddly protective, almost as if he was preparing to defend an innocent gazelle from a couple of boisterous lion cubs. 'Isabel, this is my sister Sally.' In throwaway fashion he then added, 'And her friend Lola.'

Just to make crystal clear to everyone in the room how completely unimportant she was, how utterly irrelevant to his life.

To compound it, Isabel smiled widely and said, 'Sally. I've heard all about *you*. Doug's always talking about you!'

'Is he? He's kept *very* quiet about you.' Sally unwound her lime-green scarf, flung aside her handbag and plonked herself down on the sofa. 'So, how long have you two known each other?'

'Glass of red?' Evidently keen to be rid of her a.s.a.p., Doug appeared in front of Lola with the open bottle and a clean glass.

Talk about brisk. What could she ask for that would spin things out?

'Actually, I'd love a coffee.'

'We've known each other for ages.' Across the room, Isabel flipped back her ironed blonde hair and sat down cosily next to Sally. 'We work together,' she confided. 'I was seeing someone else but we broke up. After that, Doug and I just ended up getting together.'

Lola looked at Doug, sending him a telepathic message: *We could do that, you and me* . . .

'Coffee.' Doug's tone was brusque; he didn't appear to be telepathic. 'Why don't you sit down and I'll make it.'

'Actually I'll come with you.' Lola flashed him a sunny smile. 'Then I can make sure you don't palm me off with instant.'

As she followed Doug into the kitchen, Isabel was saying, '. . . and I'm going down to Brighton tonight, to stay with my parents. That's what Christmas is all about, isn't it? Mind you, I'm going to miss Doug! I can't wait to see what he's bought me. He wouldn't let me open it tonight.'

The kitchen was nice, black and white and boasting, among other items, a huge chrome Dualit toaster.

'Still keen on toast, then,' said Lola.

'What are you *doing*?'

'Inspecting the cupboards. What happened to the Pot Noodles? You used to love Pot Noodles.'

Exasperated, Doug said, 'When I was seventeen.'

'I bet you still secretly like them. Once a Pot Noodler, always a Pot Noodler.' Lola carried on opening and closing drawers and cupboards.

'Will you stop riffling through my cupboards?'

'Why, am I getting warm?'

'Here, just take your coffee.' Having sunk the plunger on the cafetière in record time, Doug shoved a small cup into her hands. 'Shall we head back through?'

'What did you buy Isabel for Christmas?'

Doug looked exasperated. 'I'm not telling you *that*.'

Sally, whose eavesdropping skills were second to none, said, 'You're not telling her what?' when they returned to the living room.

'I was wondering what he'd bought you for Christmas,' said Lola.

'Anything's fine by me.' Sally beamed at Doug. 'So long as he's kept the receipt.'

'I wouldn't *dream* of taking back anything Dougie bought me,' trilled Isabel.

'Remember when we bought each other the same CD? *Parklife*,' Lola fondly reminisced without thinking. 'God, we used to play that album nonstop. I can still remember the words to every song.'

'Hang on, you mean you and *Doug* bought each other the same CD?' Isabel looked confused. 'Oh, I'm sorry, I didn't realise . . .'

'Oh, yes,' Sally said helpfully. 'They were boyfriend and girlfriend.'

'That was a long time ago,' Doug cut in. 'How are things going with Gabe?' He swiftly changed the subject.

'Hideous.' Sally shuddered. 'Talk about pernickety. He's *so* gay, just won't admit it.'

'He's not gay.' Lola hadn't yet managed to convince Sally but she kept saying it anyway. 'You drive him insane, that's all it is. Some people leave tea bags in the kitchen sink,' she told Doug. 'Yesterday your sister left hers on the coffee table.'

Sally shrugged. 'Not on purpose. Only because I hadn't realised it was still in my mug.'

Lola had been making her coffee last as long as possible. Finally she was down to the lukewarm grounds.

'Finished? Good.' Doug whisked away her cup, clearly keen to see the back of her.

Which—and here was her optimism rushing to the fore again—could mean that her presence was disturbing him *in a good way*.

'Could I use your bathroom before I go?'

'Out in the hall. Second door on the left.'

It was actually a tricky exercise, walking the length of the living room in a natural manner, super-aware of Dougie's eyes upon her. What was he really thinking? Was he mentally comparing her with Isabel? Come to that, how *did* she compare with Isabel?

'I said second door on the left.' Out in the hall Doug's voice behind Lola made her jump. 'That's the second on the right.'

But he was a split second too late; she'd already opened the door and walked into his bedroom.

'Sorry. I'm always getting my left and right mixed up. Wow, this is nice!' Taking another step into the room, she drank in the burnt-orange walls, the duvet and pillowcases in bitter chocolate, the oak floorboards and mahogany furniture. This was where Doug slept, this was *his bed*. Lola did her best to picture him in it. 'Do you still sleep naked?'

Doug shook his head. 'You don't change, do you?'

Oh well. She shrugged. 'I like to know these things.'

'Even though "these things" aren't any of your business?'

But he wasn't sounding entirely pissed off. Encouraged, Lola said innocently, 'I just wondered if you'd turned into the kind of man who wears stripy cotton pyjamas, like Kenneth Williams in *Carry On Nurse*.'

His mouth twitched. 'Oh, yes, that's me. That's what I wear.'

'You don't.'

'I definitely do.'

'You still sleep naked.' Lola exhaled with relief; *now* she was able to picture him in his king-sized bed.

'OK, you've had your snoop around,' said Doug. 'Now I'll show you where the bathroom is.'

She couldn't help herself; the question was bubbling up. 'Do you really like her?'

'Do I really like who?'

'Isabel.'

As he steered her out of the bedroom and pointed her in the direction of the door opposite, Doug said, 'Again, not any of your business. But if it helps,' he paused, causing Lola's heart to expand with hope, 'then I suppose I'd have to say yes, I do.'

The pause had been deliberate. He knew exactly why she was asking and now he was getting his own back. Recklessly Lola said, 'Is sleeping with her as much fun as it was with me?'

There, *there* was that flicker behind his eyes again.

'Lola, you're talking about ten *years* ago. I don't even remember what sleeping with you was like.'

Which, if she'd believed him, might have counted as a put-down. Luckily Lola didn't for a minute.

'You know what I think? I think I must be having an effect on you if you're having to say stuff like that.' With a playful smile Lola said, 'Because I know you're lying now. I remember every detail of every minute of every time with you, Dougie. And I still will when I'm ninety. Because it was the most important thing in the world to me. It meant everything. And I know you remember it too.'

Another pause. He took a step closer and leaned forward, causing her to suck in her breath . . .

'It was *almost* the most important thing in the world to you.' Doug whispered the words. 'Remember? It came in second, behind money.'

Which put a bit of a dampener on a potentially promising moment. Doug turned and headed back to the living room and Lola paid her visit to the bathroom, which was white and modern and thankfully devoid of girlie toiletries.

OK. Time to say her goodbyes and leave. Gazing at her reflection in the bathroom mirror, Lola pinched her cheeks and jooshed up her hair. With a bit of luck, what with everyone being jolly and wishing each other Happy Christmas, she might get the chance to give Doug a festive hug and a fleeting kiss on the cheek.

Not much to pin your hopes on, maybe. But every little helped.

'**O**h, come here, don't you look gorgeous?' Blythe flung open the front door and enveloped her daughter in her arms. As the car pulled away and disappeared up the road she said, 'Did somebody give you a lift? Why didn't you invite them in for a drink?'

Lola closed her eyes and revelled in being in her mother's arms; at least it wasn't going to be a completely hug-free evening. And yes, she *was* looking gorgeous, not that it had had the desired effect.

'I would have,' she fibbed, 'but they were in a hurry. It was Doug.'

'Doug? You mean Dougie Tennant?' Blythe exclaimed. 'Oh, I'd love to have seen him again. You should have forced him to come in!'

Oh, yes, and wouldn't that have been relaxing? Earlier, as they'd all been preparing to leave Dougie's flat, Lola had briefly cornered him and murmured, 'By the way, my mum doesn't know about the money thing, OK? I really don't want her to find out.'

Doug had given her one of his withering looks. 'I bet you don't.'

It was horrible but there was nothing she could do. As far as Blythe was aware, the decision to finish with Dougie and move to Majorca had been Lola's alone, based on her decision that a long-term, long-distance relationship with Dougie could never work out.

'But if he gave you a lift over here, that's a good sign, isn't it?' Now, studying her daughter's face, Blythe said hopefully, 'Do you think he might be starting to forgive you yet?'

'Mum, stop it, don't get carried away. He was with his girlfriend. I went over to his flat with Sally. He only gave me a lift because she forced him to.' Maybe she was being extra-suspicious but Lola also wondered if Doug had done it in order to avoid the festive goodbye hug-and-a-kiss. When she'd clambered out of the back of the Mercedes with her bags of presents, he'd made reaching him a physical impossibility by remaining in the driver's seat with Isabel next to him.

'Oh, well, never mind. Men and their silly egos.' Blythe was nothing if not supportive. 'Come on inside, it's freezing out here. We're going to have such a lovely time,' she went on proudly. 'I've got smoked salmon and Madagascan king prawns from Marks and Spencer. Your favourites.'

It was the not knowing how her mother might react that was causing Lola to hesitate. On the one hand she wanted, more than anything, to talk about her father.

Not her stepfather, Alex. The biological one, Nick.

On the other hand, it was Christmas morning and the very last thing she wanted to do was upset Blythe. Their family Christmases had always been extra-special, but since Alex's death five years ago, she and her mother had made even more of an effort, drawing closer still, both of them treasuring this time together and cherishing all the shared happy memories that meant so much.

Which was why, despite longing to raise the subject of Nick James, every time she geared herself up to do it Lola felt the words stick in her throat. She had the number of his mobile keyed into her phone. Was he wondering why she hadn't contacted him yet? It was Christmas Day and the schmaltzy, happy-ever-after side of her—the kind that wept buckets over the festive films shown on Hallmark—had dared to fantasise about blurting everything out to her mother, followed by Blythe admitting that she'd made a terrible mistake all those years ago, and that she'd never stopped loving Nick. Cut to Nick, sitting alone in his flat on Christmas Day. A look of regret crosses his face; he made a mistake and has spent the last twenty-seven years paying for it. Blythe is still the only woman he's ever loved, but it's all too late now, she's—

The phone rings, *brrrrrr brrrrrr*. Nick hesitates then answers it. His eyes widen in wonder as he whispers, 'Blythe?'

'Okey dokey, that's the parsnips done.' Wiping her hands on her blue striped apron, Blythe counted the saucepans and consulted her list. 'Stuffing, check. Bread sauce, check. Chipolatas, bacon, baked onions, check check check. How are those carrots coming along?'

'Finished.' It was a ridiculous amount of work for one meal but that was tradition for you.

'Ready for a top-up?' Blythe took the bottle of sparkling Freixenet from the fridge and gaily refilled their glasses. 'Oh, sweetie pie, I love you so much, give me a hug.'

*Mum, guess whose number I've got stored on my phone . . .?*

*Mum, remember when I was born . . .?*

Lola decided to wait until lunch was over. Maybe this afternoon, when they were relaxing together in front of the fire eating Thorntons truffles, she could casually slide the conversation round to the opposite sex in general, then old boyfriends in particular and how they might have changed since they'd last seen them—

'I'll get that.' Blythe darted across the kitchen as the phone began to ring. 'It's probably Malcolm, calling from his brother's in Cardiff.'

It was Malcolm. Lola popped a chunk of carrot into her mouth, tipped the rest into a pan of sugared and salted water, and went upstairs to the bathroom. By the time she came back down, her mother was off the phone.

'What's wrong?' said Lola.

'Nothing's wrong.' Blythe's freckles always seemed to become more prominent when she was feeling guilty. 'That was Malcolm.'

'I know. He's staying with his brother's family in Cardiff.'

Blythe leaned against the dishwasher. 'He was. But now he's back. His brother's mother-in-law had a heart attack yesterday afternoon and they all had to rush up to the hospital in Glasgow. She's in intensive care, poor thing, and it's touch and go. But poor Malcolm too,' Blythe went on pleadingly. 'He had to drive back from Cardiff last night and now he's all on his own at home. On Christmas Day.'

It was so obvious what was coming next. Lola wanted to wail '*Noooo*' and hated herself for it. She wished she was less selfish, more generous, one of those kind people who wouldn't hesitate for a second to suggest what she knew perfectly well Blythe was about to suggest.

'Doesn't he have any other friends he could spend the day with?'

'I don't suppose he wants to be a burden.' Her mother tilted her head to one side. 'Everyone has their own families.'

So he has to pick on ours. God, she was horrible. How could she even think that? Awash with shame and self-loathing, Lola forced herself to say brightly, 'So he's coming over?'

'Is that all right, love? You don't mind?' Which meant the invitation had already been extended and accepted. 'Dear Malcolm, if it was the other way round he'd be inviting us to stay. He's an absolute sweetheart.'

'Of course I don't mind.' Disappointment hit Lola like a brick. Bang went the opportunity to raise the subject of her real father.

'Thanks, love. You're an angel. We'll have a lovely day together.'

'Ho ho ho! Happy Christmas one and all!' In celebration of the day, Malcolm was wearing a bright red, Santa-sized sweater over his plaid shirt and bottle-green corduroys. As he made his way into the house he grazed Blythe's cheek with a kiss and beamed at Lola. 'This is a treat! How kind of you both to invite me. I hope it's not too much trouble.'

'Of course it isn't.' Lola felt ashamed of herself; he was a sweet man, if not what you'd call a heart-throb. And at least he wasn't wearing sandals today, so the hairy toes weren't on show.

'The more the merrier,' Blythe gaily insisted.

'I didn't know if you had a Monopoly set, so I brought my own.' Triumphantly Malcolm produced it from his khaki haversack. 'Nothing like a few games of Monopoly to get Christmas going with a swing! Those people who just sit around like puddings watching rubbish on TV . . . what are they like, eh? They don't know what they're missing!'

Lola, who couldn't bear Monopoly and had been banking on sitting like a pudding watching TV, said brightly, 'What can I get you to drink, Malcolm?'

Evidently detecting the bat-squeak of panic in her voice, he looked anxious. 'Unless you don't like playing Monopoly?'

'Of course we do, Malcolm.' Blythe reassured him. 'We love it!'

The day was long. Verrrrrry lonnnnnng. Being relentlessly nice and having to pretend you were having *so much fun* had been exhausting. By ten o'clock, with Malcolm still showing no sign of leaving, Lola conceded defeat. Faking a few enormous yawns, she made her excuses and kissed Blythe good night.

'Sure I can't tempt you to one last game of Monopoly?' Malcolm's tone was jovial, his eyes bright with hope.

'Thanks, Malcolm, but I just can't stay awake.'

Upstairs in her old bedroom Lola sat up in bed with a book and tried hard to feel more like Mother Teresa, less like a selfish spoilt brat. Malcolm's last words to her had been, 'Thanks for being so welcoming, pet. I tell you, this has been one of the best Christmases of my life.'

Which had brought a bit of a lump to her throat. Because Malcolm was a sweet, genuinely good man who would never hurt Blythe.

Reaching for her mobile, Lola scrolled through the address book until she found Nick James's number.

As it began to ring at the other end she felt her chest fill with butterflies. Had he spent the last five days waiting for this moment, getting all jumpy every time his phone burst into life, then being disappointed each time it wasn't her? Or what if he'd given her a fake number?

Five rings. Six rings. Any moment now it was going to click onto answering machine and she'd have to decide whether to leave a—

'Hello?'

*Whoosh*, in a split second all Lola's nerves vanished. His voice was as warm and friendly as she remembered.

'Nick?' She couldn't call him Dad, that was too weird. 'Hi, it's . . . Lola.'

'Lola.' She heard him exhale. Then, sounding as if he was smiling, he said, 'Thank God. You don't know how glad I am to hear from you. I was beginning to think I wouldn't.'

She waggled her toes with relief. 'And I was just wondering if you'd given me a made-up number.'

'You seriously thought I'd do that?'

'Well, I was dressed as a rabbit. It could put some people off.'

'I'm made of sterner stuff than that. Hey, merry Christmas.'

Lola grinned, because her actual biological father was wishing her a merry Christmas. How cool was that? 'You too. Where are you?'

'Just got home. Spent the day with friends. How about you?'

'I'm at Mum's house.'

He sounded pleased. 'You mean you've told her?'

'Um, no. I wanted to, I was going to, then this friend of hers turned up and I couldn't. They're downstairs. I'm up here in bed. Too much Monopoly takes it out of you.'

'God, I can't stand Monopoly.' Nick spoke with feeling. 'Sorry. So how do you think she'll react when you do tell her?'

'That's the thing, I just don't know.' She hesitated. 'But I'm a bit worried that she might refuse to see you. And once Mum makes up her mind about something she can be a bit, well . . .'

'You don't have to tell me.' Nick's tone was dry. 'What are you doing tomorrow?'

'Working.' Lola shuddered, because tomorrow was going to be hell on wheels; when she was crowned Queen of the World, opening shops on Boxing Day wouldn't be allowed. 'But I'm off on Saturday.'

'How about Blythe? Would she be free then?'

'As far as I know.'

'OK, now listen,' Nick said slowly. 'How about this for an idea?'

**I**f there was anything more manic than working in the West End after Christmas when the sales were in full swing, it was shopping in the West End after Christmas when the sales were in full swing. Elbows were out, toes and small children were getting trampled on and everyone was carrying bags of stuff they'd either just bought or had been given for Christmas and were about to take back.

'Mum, we've been shopping for three hours. My feet hurt.'

'Lightweight!'

'And I'm thirsty,' Lola said whiningly.

'We'll buy you a bottle of water.' Her mother was in the grip of buying fever; her eyes were darting around, greedily taking in sequinny sparkly tops, dresses awash with flowers and frills . . . *all reduced in the sale* . . .

'And I'm hungry,' Lola pleaded. '*Sooo* hungry. Let's stop and have something to eat.'

Blythe heaved an impatient sigh. 'You were easier to take shopping when you were in a pram. OK, we'll eat. Where d'you want to go?'

'Marco's,' Lola said promptly.

The restaurant was busy, warm and welcoming. Lola slipped her shoes off under the table and took a big sip of Merlot. 'Oh, this is better. My feet thank you. My stomach thanks you. Are we both having the chicken?'

'Fine by me.'

She saw him twenty minutes later through the full-length front window, making his way across the street. Blythe, sitting with her back to the entrance, was chattering away about holidays. Lola took a deep breath; in an ideal world her mother's hair would be just brushed and she'd be wearing rather more make-up, but short of lunging across the table and forcibly applying a fresh coat of lipstick to her mouth, there wasn't a lot she could do about it. Yeek, and now the door was being pushed open, here he came, it was really going to happen.

'. . . so I said I'd think about it, although I'm not sure it's really my thing.' Blythe wrinkled her nose. 'I mean, hill walking in Snowdonia. In big clumpy hiking boots. Sleeping in a tent, for heaven's sake! It's all right for Malcolm, but where would I plug in my hair dryer? And what happens when I need to . . . to . . .' Her voice trailed away and the piece of chicken she'd been about to eat slid off her fork. All the colour drained abruptly from her face, leaving only freckles behind.

Nick, standing behind Lola's chair, said, 'Hello, Blythe.'

Blythe was in a state of shock. For a split second Lola thought she might bolt from the restaurant. Then, visibly gathering herself, she managed a fixed smile. 'Nick, what a surprise. How nice to see you. How are you?' Her shoulders were stiff, her jaw clenched with terror; mentally she was screaming *go away, go away, please go away.*

'I'm fine, thanks. And you haven't changed at all. It's incredible.'

Lola said, 'Mum—'

'Oh, sorry, love, this is Nick.' Blythe jumped in before Lola could ask any awkward questions. 'We knew each other years ago . . . well, nice to see you again, we mustn't keep you . . .'

'Mum, it's OK.' Desperate to explain, Lola blurted out, 'I know who Nick is. And this isn't a coincidence; he knew we'd be here today because I told him. We met before Christmas. He's my father. And we really like each other.' Hopefully, because her mother was staring at her as if she'd just sprouted an extra pair of ears, she said, 'So that's good, isn't it?'

Blythe's hand trembled as she took a gulp of wine. 'You planned this.' Her voice rose in disbelief. 'You met before *Christmas*?'

'I was going to tell you,' Lola said hurriedly, 'but I didn't know how you'd react. And then Malcolm turned up on Christmas morning . . .'

'OK if I sit down?' Nick indicated a spare chair.

'My God . . . how did it happen? Who found who?'

'Well, it wasn't me,' said Lola. 'It couldn't have been me, could it? Seeing as you told me my father was an American who never even told you his last name.'

Her mother rubbed her forehead with both hands and said nothing.

'I saw Lola being interviewed on the local news.' Nick pulled out the chair and sat down. 'Just for a few seconds, but it was enough. I had to find out if she was my daughter. And she is.' His eyes softening, he slid one hand across the table towards Blythe then withdrew it as she snatched hers out of reach. 'You've done a fantastic job, Blythe. She's an absolute credit to you.'

Lola felt ridiculously proud.

'And to Alex. Her stepfather,' Blythe said stiffly.

Nick nodded. 'Of course.'

'I've told him all about Alex,' said Lola.

'And did he tell you everything too?' Breathing rapidly, Blythe turned her attention to Nick. 'Hmm? Did you? *Everything*?'

'Yes, Blythe, she knows I went to prison. I made a mistake and I paid for it a hundred times over. I lost you and I lost my daughter. And before you ask, no, I *haven't* been in trouble with the police since then. I am a normal, decent, law-abiding citizen.'

'Congratulations. Some of us always have been,' Blythe said frostily.

'Hey, Blythe.' His smile crooked, Nick said, 'It really is fantastic to see you again. I never stopped thinking about you. About both of you.'

For a second her eyes flashed. 'And I never stopped thinking about the way you lied to me.'

'Mum, it's all in the past.'

'But it happened,' Blythe insisted. 'I was eight months pregnant when I got the phone call telling me my boyfriend was in prison. No warning, no hints, just . . . bam. I didn't know what to do, I was *desperate*. And now here you are, turning up again out of the blue, saying, hey, never mind all that, it's in the past, let's just put it behind us.'

'I'm Lola's father,' said Nick.

'Not as far as I'm concerned. Alex was the one who was there for her.' Heatedly Blythe said, 'And guess what? He didn't go to prison once!'

Lola closed her eyes; not quite the Hallmark reunion she'd been hoping for. 'Mum, you lied to me about Nick, remember? You didn't tell me the truth because you didn't want me to be hurt.'

Her mother said defensively, 'So? Was that wrong?'

'No! You did it because you loved me!' Spreading her arms wide, narrowly missing the groin of a startled passing waiter, Lola said, 'But that's exactly why Nick lied to you! He didn't tell you about being arrested and charged because he loved you and didn't want you to be upset!'

'And didn't *that* work well.' Bright spots of colour burned in Blythe's cheeks as she scraped back her chair and made a grab for her bag.

'Mum, where are you going?'

'I'm going to the ladies, then home.'

'Mum, don't!'

'It's OK.' Nick rose to his feet. 'I'll leave. I'm sorry.' He rested his hands on Lola's shoulders as Blythe, blindly ricocheting off chairs, hurried to the loo. 'We got that a bit wrong, didn't we? Give her a while to calm down. Maybe I'll see you later.'

## *Chapter 8*

ACROSS THE HALLWAY Lola's doorbell was ringing. Sally, engrossed in the ice skating on TV—and the bowl of Ben and Jerry's in her lap—wiggled her toes and imagined herself in a sparkly, hot-pink figure-hugging outfit twirling across the ice.

*Ddddrrrrrrinnnggggg*. Whoever was at the front door wasn't giving up. As the skating routine drew to an end, Sally put down her ice cream and clambered off the sofa.

She hauled up the sash window and leaned out. 'Hello? Lola's not at home.' Then she almost lost her balance and toppled out, because the man gazing up at her was just . . . *Wow*.

'Any idea when she'll be back? I've tried her mobile but it's switched off.' His dark hair gleamed in the light from the street lamp. Even at this distance his eyes were hypnotic. Effortlessly hypnotised, Sally said, 'She could be back any time now. Do you want to come in and wait?'

His teeth gleamed white. 'Are you sure?'

With a smile like that? Was he kidding? Praying Lola wouldn't be back too soon, Sally called out, 'Hang on, I'll buzz you up.'

'Thanks.' His smile broadened when she opened the door to her flat. 'I don't want to be a nuisance. But it's pretty icy out there.'

*No worries, come here, I'll soon warm you up!*

Thankfully she managed to keep these words inside her head. Oh, but he was to die for, with those expressive eyebrows and chiselled cheekbones. This was definitely lust at first sight. And wasn't there something familiar about those eyebrows?

'Come on in, I'll make us a cup of tea . . . I'm Sally, by the way.'

'I know. Lola's told me all about you.'

'*Has* she?' Ridiculously flattered, Sally turned to look at him as she filled the kettle at the sink. *Whooosh*, ice-cold water promptly ricocheted off the spout, drenching her from neck to navel. When you were in the grip of lust it was hard to concentrate.

'Why don't I make the tea?' Amused, he said, 'You'd better go and change out of those wet things.'

By the time she re-emerged in dry clothes she'd figured it out. 'I've heard all about you too,' Sally announced as he carried the tea through to the living room. 'You're Lola's dad.'

'Nick James.' His gorgeous dark grey eyes crinkled at the corners. And the way he dressed . . . a dark green shirt, black trousers and black shoes . . . his clothes were so plain and of such excellent quality.

Unlike grungy Gabe with his bleached T-shirts and disintegrating jeans, this was a man who knew how to dress. He even smelt fantastic. And he was Lola's father. Would this make things awkward?

Sally considered the facts then decided there was no reason why it should. If Lola was allowed to have a crush on her brother, it seemed only fair that she should be allowed a shot at Lola's dad. Crikey, if Lola married Doug and she married Nick, she'd be Lola's stepmother *and* her sister-in-law. OK, maybe getting a teeny bit carried away here . . .

'What are you thinking?' Nick was regarding her with interest.

Again, probably best not to tell him. 'Just wondering if I'm allowed to ask how it went today, meeting up with Lola and her mum.'

'Not brilliantly.' He paused, stirring his tea. 'Hardly surprising, I suppose. Bit of a shock for Blythe. That's why I came over to see Lola, to find out how things are now. Relationships are . . . complicated.'

'Ha, tell me about it.'

Nick grinned. 'Lola did happen to mention you'd had your share of bad luck with men.'

'That's a very polite way of putting it,' Sally said ruefully, 'but I think you mean my share of bastards.' On the TV a groan of disappointment went up from the audience and she pointed to the pair of skaters sprawled on the ice. 'It's like that, isn't it? One minute it's all going so well, you're twirling and flying through the air and actually starting to think you're in with a chance of gold. And the next minute, splat, you're flat on your face. That's why I love watching my old video of Torvill and Dean doing *Bolero*. Because I know nobody falls over and they carry on being perfect right to the end.' She paused, then said with a lopsided smile, 'Wouldn't it be great if our lives could be like that?'

Had that been too heartfelt? Was he going to make fun of her now?

But that didn't happen. Instead, he said, 'It's what everyone wants, if they're honest. We just can't help buggering things up.'

They carried on chatting for another hour. He was so wonderfully easy to talk to. She learned about his career in advertising and told him about her own job as a receptionist in a doctors' surgery in Wimbledon.

'I wouldn't have had you down as a doctors' receptionist.'

'Because I'm not tidy?' Hurt, Sally said, 'I'm *very* organised at work.'

'I actually meant you look too glamorous.'

She flushed at the compliment, smoothed back her hair. 'I love my job. OK, it's not high-powered and it isn't glamorous, but the doctors I work with are great. And I'm good at what I do,' she added with pride. 'Dr Willis says I'm the most efficient receptionist they've ever had.'

'So this surgery then, is it not a good place to meet men? What are these doctors like?'

'Old and married.' Hastily, because she knew Nick was forty-eight, Sally said, 'I mean, *ancient*. Sixties. Much older than you.'

His mouth curved at the corners. 'Glad to hear it. How about the patients, then? Must be a few promising ones there.'

'Well, yes, until you look through their medical notes.' Sally pulled a face. 'And read all about their erectile dysfunction and problems with wind and snoring . . . then somehow all the magic goes out of them.'

He looked appalled. 'I take your point. What's more,' said Nick, 'I'll never try to chat up my doctor's receptionist again.'

**Y**ou missed Nick. He left twenty minutes ago.' Sally beckoned Lola into the flat, eager to tell her everything. 'Isn't he great? He's been waiting here for you to get back. He's so—'

'Oh, no. Why didn't he ring me?' Distracted, Lola scrabbled for her phone. 'Damn, when did I switch that off?'

'It wasn't a problem. We've been chatting nonstop. In fact—'

'Hang on, let me just give him a quick call.'

Sally waited impatiently for Lola to get off the phone; she was long-ing to tell her how well they'd got along together and was going to jokily ask Lola's permission before making a proper play for him.

'Damn, now his phone's switched off.' Lola shook her head. 'What a day! So you met Nick. Did you like him?'

'He's great,' Sally said eagerly. 'I *really* liked him; in fact—'

'I'm so glad. He's a really nice person. That's why I know I can do it.'

'Do what?'

Lola looked smug. 'Get them back together.'

'But, but . . .'

'Wouldn't that be perfect?' Lola, her eyes shining, unwound her scarf and collapsed onto the sofa. 'OK, it didn't get off to the best of starts, but that was just the shock factor. I went home with Mum and we had a proper talk about everything. It was amazing, hearing all this stuff for the first time. And look what she gave me.' Lola took an envelope from her bag and carefully slid out a photograph. 'It's the two of them together, before I came along.'

Feeling numb, Sally gazed at the photograph. Lola's mother, her red-gold hair swinging round her shoulders, was wearing a purple sundress and white platform shoes. Nick was sitting on the wall next to her with a proprietorial arm round her narrow waist. He was twenty years old, good-looking in a denim shirt and jeans, with everything going for him.

'This is how I know I can do it,' said Lola, tapping the old photo. 'My mum kept it all these years. That means she still cares about him.'

Sally exhaled slowly. The disappointment was crushing. Why did stuff like this always have to happen to her? Struggling to sound normal, she said, 'Maybe she just forgot it was there. I've got photos at home of my seventh birthday party but it doesn't mean I care about the kids I was at infants' school with. I can't even remember their names.'

'That's completely different.' Lola shook her head. 'When it's boyfriend–girlfriend stuff, you don't hang on to photos of the ones you don't like any more. But if you *do* still care about the other person, you keep the photos. Like I've still got all mine of me and Dougie.'

'Maybe, but has he still kept his ones of you?'

Suddenly the door swung open behind them.

'They do it deliberately,' Gabe announced, tipping Lola's feet off the sofa and throwing himself down with a groan of despair. 'I swear to God, their mission in life is to officially do my head in. Celebrities.' He exhaled, pushing his hands through his floppy blond hair.

'Not a good night?' Lola was sympathetic.

'Complete waste of time. I waited three hours for this actress to come out of a hair place in Primrose Hill. I was getting thirsty, but I stuck it out because I knew she had to be finished soon. Finally, I couldn't stand it a minute longer and raced into the shop across the road. I was in there for fifteen *seconds*, no more than that. And when I came out, her limo was pulling away. I tell you, I felt like throwing rocks at it.'

'You'll get the hang of it.' Lola's tone was consoling. 'What about the other paps, are they friendly?'

'They're OK,' grumbled Gabe. 'But they're taking the mickey out of me because I keep getting things wrong. I thought I'd spotted Britney Spears coming out of Waterstones but it wasn't her. I'm a laughing stock. They keep pointing to old homeless guys in the street and saying, "Quick, Gabe, it's Pierce Brosnan!"'

'But your photos of Tom Dutton and Jessica Lee were in *Heat* this week,' said Lola. 'They're just jealous.'

'That was a fluke. I could work for the next five years and not get another chance like that.'

'Or it could happen again tomorrow,' Sally chimed in. 'That's the thing, you never know. It's like panning for gold.'

It was seven o'clock on New Year's Eve. 'You won't believe what's happened,' wailed Sally, bursting into Lola's flat. 'My bloody boss has only stood me up.'

Lola, hopping around with one shoe on and one shoe off, said, 'For your posh do? You can come along to the White Hart with us if you like. It won't be posh, but it'll be a good night.' It would actually be a sweaty, crowded, extremely rowdy night, but Tim from work had bullied everyone into buying tickets. Persuasively Lola added, 'A tenner a ticket and all the burgers you can eat.'

Sally looked horrified. 'My God, I can't imagine anything more horrible. My ticket for the Carrick cost a hundred and fifty pounds.'

'Blimey, I'd want gold-plated burgers for that price.'

But it was for charity, Lola learned. And they certainly didn't serve burgers at the five-star, decidedly glitzy Carrick Hotel overlooking Hyde Park. The event was dinner and a quiz, with tables of eight forming teams who were to compete against each other. Dr Willis, Sally's boss, had been due to partner her for the evening—in a platonic way, naturally, what with him being sixty-four years old, married and keen on astronomy.

'So the ticket's already been paid for,' Sally finished. 'Seems a shame to waste it. Wouldn't you rather come with me to the Carrick than squeeze into some scuzzy, sticky-carpeted pub?'

'Tim's expecting me to be there. I don't want to disappoint him.'

'Sure? It'll be fun.' Sally played her trump card. 'Doug's on our table.'

Oh well, everyone else from Kingsley's was going along to the White

Hart; it wasn't as if Tim would be all on his own. 'Go on, then.' Lola's heart began to beat faster, because this could be her chance to really impress Dougie. 'You've twisted my arm.'

**H**aving changed out of her beer-friendly black Lycra top and frayed jeans into an altogether more suitable peacock-blue dress with spaghetti straps and swishy sequinned hem, Lola entered the Carrick's ballroom feeling quite the bee's knees. Moments later those same knees quivered with excitement as, through the crowds, she spotted Dougie over by the bar, looking even more handsome than ever in formal black tie. He was gorgeous. Giving herself time to mentally get her act together, Lola hung back as Sally approached the group at the bar.

'Hey, you're here.' Doug turned when she tapped him on the shoulder. 'Everyone, this is my sister Sally, specialist subjects fashion and shopping. And rather more usefully she's brought along her boss who's a doctor, so any medical questions and he's our man. He's also excellent on astronomy, which . . . which is . . .' As he was speaking, Doug's gaze had veered past Sally, and when he spotted Lola his voice trailed off, his welcoming smile faded and he said, 'I don't believe it. You *again*?'

Which was, frankly, more than a little hurtful.

'Honestly.' Sally rolled her eyes at the rest of the group. 'Is this what he's like at work? Roger couldn't make it, so I asked Lola if she'd come along in his place. Otherwise we'd have been a team member short.'

Doug shook his head. 'So Lola's our medical expert for the evening. Perfect. Let's just hope no one needs an emergency tracheotomy.'

'Doug, calm down. I'll answer the medical questions,' said Sally.

The tall man next to Doug said intently, 'Are you a doctor too?'

'Not exactly, but I'm a GP's receptionist.' As the man's lip began to curl into a sneer Sally said, 'Do you know what papilloedema is?'

He looked startled. 'No.'

'See? I do. I know about systolic and diastolic blood pressure measurements. And I can tell you exactly what to do with a sphygmomanometer.'

The man took a gulp of his drink. Lola stifled a grin. Touché.

'Sally, *hiiii!*' Yeeurgh. Isabel joined the group, flicking back her silky, ice-blonde hair and clutching Sally's arms as if they were long-lost friends. Moments later, spotting Lola, she said with rather less enthusiasm, 'Oh, hello again.'

'I'm Tony, history and politics,' the tall man announced. Gesturing towards the others he said, 'Alice is biology and art. Jerry's Egyptology and maths. And this is Bob, whose speciality is classical music.'

'And cricket,' said Bob.

'Great,' said Lola.

'How about you?'

'Um . . . well, literature.'

'And?' Tony eyed her beadily; it appeared everyone was required to be an expert in two subjects.

'And . . . er, Sumo wrestling.' That would be safe surely?

'Excellent, excellent. So which should we be hoping for this evening, hmm? *Kachikoshi*? Or *makekoshi*?'

Bugger. And his lip was curling again. He *knew*.

'OK,' said Lola, 'I was lying. I don't know anything about Sumo. I only have one specialist subject, but I'm just here as a last-minute replacement. It's either me or an empty chair.'

The four-course meal, each course served between rounds of questions, was sublime. The glittering ballroom with its mirrored walls, opulent decor and hundreds of tethered gold-and-white helium balloons, was beautiful in every way. Lola began to enjoy the evening. It was, after all, a far cry from the White Hart.

Their team—the Sitting Tennants—were doing well and by the beginning of the fifth and final round they were joint leaders along with the Deadly Dunns, a team from another management consultancy. The rivalry was intense; reputations were at stake.

Sally got them off to a flying start by knowing the whereabouts in the body of the islets of Langerhans, which Lola privately felt should be found not in the pancreas but somewhere off the west coast of Scotland.

The questions continued and their table's points continued to mount up. Bob knew something ridiculously obscure about the composer Dmitri Shostakovich and earned himself a round of applause. Jerry the Egyptologist preened, having correctly answered a question about the identity of the tekenu. Alice dithered a bit but finally guessed correctly that David Hockney had attended Bradford Grammar.

Isabel let out a shriek of delight and smothered Doug in kisses when he correctly answered that David Campese was the player who'd scored the most tries in test rugby.

Lola helped herself to more wine. One question, that was all she asked, a question that nobody else knew the answer to. And when she answered it correctly, everyone would break into wild applause and Dougie would give her one of his heart-melting smiles.

From what she could tell, this thing with Isabel was hardly the romance of the century. Isabel might be beautiful but her personality wasn't exactly dazzling. Basically she was nothing but an airhead . . .

'The next question,' boomed the questionmaster, calling the room to attention, 'is in two parts. The first part is this. What is the speed of light?'

Lola's spirits sank: how was *anyone* supposed to know—

'Three hundred thousand kilometres per second,' Isabel whispered. *What?*

'Good girl.' Tony wrote down the answer without blinking.

'And now for the second part,' the questionmaster announced. 'In order for any object to escape the earth's gravitational pull, it must be flying at or above the earth's escape velocity. What is that velocity?'

Everyone at the table turned their gaze on Isabel. *No*, Lola wanted to yell, *no, you can't know the answer to that, you just can't . . .*

With a self-deprecating smile Isabel murmured, 'Eleven kilometres per second.'

Smirking, Tony scribbled down the answer on their table's card.

'OK, time's up, please raise your cards.'

All across the room, cards were lifted and checked. The question-master announced, 'The answers are three hundred thousand kilometres per second and eleven kilometres per second.'

A great cheer went up round their table. Isabel took a sip of iced water and continued to look modest. 'And Table Sixteen, the Sitting Tennants, were the only ones to get both parts of the question right.'

Lola's stomach clenched as she observed Isabel, with her dinky little nose and perfect smile. Geeky boffins were supposed to look like geeky boffins, not swan around like Grace Kelly in slinky sea-green silk with strappy Gucci sandals on their feet.

Finally it was the penultimate question of the quiz. Doug's table and the Deadly Dunns were still neck and neck. It's only a game, Lola told herself. But she felt sick anyway; it felt more important than that.

'Right, here we go,' said the questionmaster. 'James Loveless, George Loveless, John Standfield, Thomas Standfield, James Brine and James Hammett are the names of . . .?'

Lola, busy knocking back wine, froze in mid-glug. She knew who they were. Bloody hell, she actually knew an answer!

Everyone looked blank. Sally whispered, 'Is it the Arctic Monkeys?'

'Soldiers who won the VC?' guessed Bob.

History was Tony's specialist subject. He was shaking his head, gazing in turn at the others in search of enlightenment. Tony looked at Isabel, then at Doug, before glancing in Lola's direction. Hastily swallowing her mouthful of wine and keen not to let anyone at nearby tables overhear, she mouthed the answer at him. '*The Tolpuddle Martyrs.*'

Tony turned away as if he hadn't seen her. Reaching for the answer card he scrawled a few words and, leaning across to Isabel, whispered in her ear.

Lola watched open-mouthed as she cried, 'Oh, Tony, you're *brilliant.*'

'Everyone raise your cards,' called the questionmaster. 'And the correct answer . . . is . . . the Tolpuddle Martyrs!'

'Yayyyy!' Everyone else on the table let out a huge cheer. Bob and Jerry clapped Tony on the back and Lola waited for him to announce that, in fact, *she*, Lola, was the one who'd known the answer.

But he didn't. He just sat there lapping up the congratulations. Lola gazed around wildly; had none of them *seen* what had happened?

'Damn, the Deadly Dunns got it too,' said Doug. 'We're still level. It's right down to the wire.'

Bloody Tony, what a cheater! Lola was so busy being outraged and glaring at him that she barely listened to the final question.

'. . . famous writer died in 1880. Her nom de plume was George Eliot. But what was her real name?'

This was it. Lola sat up as if she'd been electrocuted. Ha, *and* it was a trick question! Everyone else was going to think the answer was Mary Ann Evans. More importantly, the Deadly Dunns were going to think that. But the clue was in the way the question had been phrased, and seven months before her death at the age of sixty-one, Mary Ann Evans had married a toy boy by the name of John Cross. So the question being asked was, in fact, what was her real name *when she died* . . .

'Well?' said Bob. 'Do you know it?'

'Of course.' Lola signalled for the answer card and a pen. With a flourish she wrote Mary Ann Cross. Was that a flicker of respect in Doug's eye? About time too! She was about to win his team the competition!

'Raise your cards, ladies and gentlemen.'

Trembling with excitement, Lola held it above her head.

'And the correct . . . answer . . . is . . .' the questionmaster strung it out *X Factor* style, '. . . Mary . . . Ann . . . Evans!'

'*No*,' Lola heard herself blurt the word out, shock prickling at the base of her skull. Shaking her head in disbelief, she said, 'That's wrong!'

Jerry's tone was bitter. '*You're* wrong.'

'YEEEAAAHHH!' Realising they'd won the competition, the Deadly Dunns were cheering their heads off.

'But I'm not wrong. Mary Ann Evans married a man called John Cross . . . she *did* . . .' The words died in Lola's throat as she realised it no longer mattered; the game was over and she'd lost it—irony of ironies—by trying to be too clever.

*Bam*, went the cork as it flew out of the Deadly Dunns' triumphantly shaken bottle of champagne. Everyone else in the room was applauding them. They rose to their feet and bowed, before breaking into a boisterous chorus of 'We Are the Champions'.

Tony said, 'They're never going to let us forget this.'

Lola was bursting for the loo. If she left the table now, they'd all talk about how rubbish she was. Oh well, who cared?

The ladies' loo was blessedly cool, a calm ivory-marble haven from the babbling crowds in the ballroom. Having touched up her make-up and enjoyed five minutes of peace and quiet, Lola was just putting away her lipstick when the door swung open and Doug said, 'There you are.' His miss-nothing gaze checked out her face. 'Are you OK?'

'Fine. You aren't allowed in here.'

'Come outside then.' He held the door open and ushered her past him. In the corridor he said, 'I thought you might have been upset.'

'You mean crying?' Lola was glad the whites of her eyes were still clear and white. 'I wouldn't give your friends the satisfaction. And I'm not upset, I'm just sorry I let you down.'

Doug shook his head. 'Hey, it doesn't matter. It was only meant to be a bit of fun. I had no idea Tony was going to take the whole thing so seriously. They're not my friends either,' he added. 'Tony works for me. Jerry and Bob are friends of his. Tony was the one who persuaded me that coming here tonight would be good PR. He can be a bit of an arse.'

'He's a cheating arse,' said Lola; it was no good, she couldn't not tell him. 'I gave him the Tolpuddle Martyrs answer. I *did*,' she insisted when Doug look amused. 'That was me! He just couldn't bear to admit it.'

'OK. Well, I'm glad you're all right. And I'm sorry about Tony.'

Touched by his concern—that had to be an encouraging sign, surely—Lola smiled and said, 'Thanks. Not your fault.'

Doug hesitated. 'How's it going with your father?'

Yay, another encouraging sign! 'Pretty good. I'm trying to fix him up with my mum but she's digging her heels in. I won't give up though. When you know two people would be perfect together, if one of them could just forgive the other for some silly mistake they made years ago, you have to persevere,' Lola said innocently. 'Don't you think?'

'Maybe your mother really isn't interested,' Dougie said.

'Ah, but that's the thing. Deep down, I think she still is.' Lola gazed at him, longing to touch his face. 'Remember that weekend we went to Brighton and you took loads of photos of me on the beach?'

Doug paused, clearly wondering if there was any point in trying to say no. He shrugged. 'Vaguely.'

Vaguely, right. He'd been eighteen, she'd been seventeen and they'd made love at midnight on a Lilo on the beach. How could any red-blooded male fail to remember a weekend like that?

'I'd love to see those photos again.'

His mouth twitched. 'You don't give up, do you?'

Lola smiled back, realising that he wasn't going to tell her whether or not he still had them. That was the trouble with trying to outsmart someone smarter than yourself. On the other hand, reminding him of the existence of the photos might prompt him to dig them out and the sight of her cavorting in the sea in her pink bikini might in turn remind him of how happy they'd been, and how happy they could be again.

'Well,' Dougie cleared his throat. 'I suppose we'd—'

'Yes, better get back.' She dived in, saying the words before he could say them himself. 'Don't want people wondering where we've got to. Just one thing first.' Her heart beating faster, Lola rested a hand on his arm. 'Seeing as it's New Year's Eve and I probably won't get the chance later, can I wish you a . . .' *move towards him* '. . . happy . . .' *slide your free arm round his neck* '. . . New . . .' *half close your eyes, half open your mouth . . .*

'Year,' said Doug, planting a kiss on her cheek before stepping back.

Damn, foiled again. This was a man with *way* too much self-control.

**I**'m not sure this is such a good idea,' said Lola. 'Remind me again why we're here?'

*Because I've got the most enormous crush on your father and I'm longing to knock him dead with my dazzling footwork and spinny twirls!*

Sally didn't actually say this out loud. Turning to Lola she explained, 'Because it's fun and it's something you've never done before. I mean, look at this place! Did you ever see anything so pretty?'

Lola followed the expansive sweep of her arm, dutifully taking in the flaming torches and architectural lighting illuminating the courtyard's classical façades. 'I'm going to fall over and break my ankles.'

'You won't. I'll show you how to do it properly. Besides, falling over's all part of the fun.' Personally Sally felt her choice of Somerset House ice rink, off the Strand, had been inspired. 'Ooh, look, there's Nick!'

Luckily the subzero temperatures meant that her cheeks were already pink. In her white fake-fur hat and matching gilet, Sally was ready to impress the hell out of Lola's dad. When Lola had idly wondered what father–daughter things she and Nick could do together on their road to getting to know each other, it had taken her . . . ooh, all of two seconds to think of something that could include her as well.

Oh God, look at Nick, he was *so* gorgeous, she could just—

'Over here,' Lola called out, windmilling both arms to attract his attention.

'Hey, you two.' Joining them, he gave Lola a hug and a kiss.

She beamed, delighted to see him again. 'Look at you, so *brown*.'

Nick, just back from ten days in St Kitts, in turn greeted Sally with a kiss on the cheek that made her quiver like a terrier on a leash.

Nick grinned. 'So you're going to be teaching us the moves tonight?'

Was that an unintentional double entendre or was he saying it like that on purpose?

'Absolutely. You're both going to love this.'

Lola was a revelation on the ice, more spectacularly useless than Sally would ever have guessed. Clinging to the barriers, she was edging her way round the outside of the rink at the speed of a lame tortoise.

Happily this meant Sally was free to coach Nick, who might not be any great shakes on the ice but who was fifty times better than Lola. At least he could manage circuits, so long as Sally was there to hold his hands. Which was heaven, almost as good as when, upon losing his balance and wobbling crazily in the centre of the rink, he had flung both arms round her waist.

Breathing into her ear, Nick protested, 'This can't be fun for you.'

Was he serious? This was the most fun she'd had in years. 'I'm fine.'

'No, it's not fair.' Nick shook his head. 'Why don't I have five minutes' rest, then you can do some proper skating without having to hold me up. I'll just watch and admire from the side.'

Oh dear, nobody liked a show-off. But she couldn't resist. Having guided him to the barriers then skated back to the less crowded centre of the rink, Sally struck a pose then pushed off into an impromptu routine. God, skating was so brilliant, she was *gliding* across the ice now, as accomplished and elegant as a swan. Was Nick watching? Would he be suitably impressed by her technique? Yes, there he was, Lola had managed to hobble-skate over to him and they were both hanging on to the barriers, watching her. Right, time for a double axel . . .

'*Ow!*' bellowed Sally, crashing to the ice like a felled tree. '*Ow, ow*, who did *that*?'

Because someone had come up behind her and delivered a vicious kick to the back of her calf. Letting out a shriek of pain she clutched her left leg as melted ice soaked into her jeans.

'Are you OK?' Nick and Lola slithered up to her, having somehow managed to weave their way through the crowds of skaters.

'Did you see who kicked me?'

'Nobody kicked you.'

'They did! I felt it!'

'There was no one near you.' Lola pulled an apologetic face. 'If it felt like being kicked, you've probably snapped an Achilles' tendon.'

'Nooo!' Sally sank down in despair and rested her face against the ice, because this was a nightmare.

Lola, valiantly attempting to help her into a sitting position, promptly lost her balance and gasped, 'Oof!' as she tumbled back like an upturned beetle onto the ice.

'**W**hat's going on?' Puzzled by the commotion on the stairs, Gabe emerged with wet hair and a dark blue towel draped round his hips.

'What does it look like?' Sitting on her bottom, inelegantly hauling herself up one stair at a time, Sally was looking fraught.

'Ice skating went well, then.' Gabe looked at Lola and her father, who were following her up the stairs carrying a pair of crutches.

'It's not funny,' Sally wailed. 'We've just spent three hours in casualty. When they told me I'd torn my calf muscle I was actually relieved because I thought it was better than snapping an Achilles' tendon, but it's not better at all, it's going to be a complete *nightmare*.' Finally, laboriously, she reached the top step. 'Don't just stand there. Help me up.'

Gabe's heart sank. Was his luck ever going to change? 'Sorry, *who's* going to be a complete nightmare?'

Nick, struggling to keep a straight face, said, 'She has to rest the muscle completely, keep the leg elevated at all times. She's going to need some serious looking after.'

Gabe winced as one of the aluminium crutches clunked against the door frame. 'Look, wouldn't it be easier to go and stay with your mother? Then she could look after you.'

*Crash* went the other crutch against the skirting board as Sally lurched inside. 'But if I went to my mother's house I'd be on my own because she and Philip are off on holiday tomorrow. So that wouldn't be very good, would it?' With a sigh of relief she lowered herself onto the sofa and stretched out across it, propping her leg up on a couple of cushions. 'There, that's better. All comfy now. Ooh, I'd love a cup of tea.'

## *Chapter 9*

SOMETIMES A NAME simply didn't register on your personal radar but it turned out that everyone else knew at once who it belonged to. Such was the case with EJ Mack, whom Lola had never heard of. But when his publisher had announced that he'd be available during the third week of January for signing sessions, everyone else at Kingsley's had got as overexcited as if Al Pacino had offered to turn up.

'But how can you know who he is?' Bemused, Lola had studied the publisher's press release. 'He's only a music producer.'

Cheryl, Tim and the new assistant, Darren, had exchanged despairing looks. 'He's *huge*,' said Darren. 'He's worked with everyone who's anyone.'

'Fine, we'll let him come here then.' Still unconvinced, Lola said, 'But it'll still be your fault if nobody turns up.'

It was always embarrassing when that happened. Watching the poor authors' faces fall as they sat there behind their teetering piles of books, gradually realising that not one single person was going to buy one.

Anyhow, it didn't seem as if this was a problem they were likely to encounter tonight with EJ Mack. Loads of customers had been thrilled to discover he was coming to Kingsley's. As Lola unloaded boxes of his books and arranged them in spiral towers round the signing table, people were already starting to gather in the shop.

'He's here!' squealed Cheryl.

Lola scanned the crowded shop, absolutely none the wiser. 'Where?'

'That's him, the one in the blue anorak.'

Oh, good grief, how could anyone be cutting-edge in an anorak? Then her eyes locked with those of EJ Mack.

'This is wicked,' gushed Darren, appearing out of nowhere.

Tim, next to him, breathed enviously, 'And he's slept with some of the most beautiful women on the planet.'

Lola opened her mouth but no sound came out. Flanked by his publisher's balding rep and blonde PR girl, EJ Mack approached them.

'This is a coincidence.' Smiling, he stuck out his hand. 'Who'd have thought we'd be bumping into each other again? How's your partner?'

Lola tried her best to come up with an answer. Tim, keen to bridge an awkward silence, leapt in with, 'Hi, I'm Tim! She doesn't have a partner.'

'You mean you broke up? What's going to happen with the baby?'

Funny how someone could look like a geeky speccy accountant-type one minute and not quite so geeky and accountanty the next, even if he was still wearing spectacles and that bizarre anorak.

'*Baby?*' Cheryl stared in disbelief at Lola's stomach. 'What baby?'

The signing session had been a great success. In the music world EJ was a thirty-one-year-old legend and devotees of his work were thrilled to have this chance to meet him. EJ in turn didn't disappoint them, he was charming, witty and interested in talking about music. He had worked with everyone who was anyone and plenty of tonight's book-buyers were keen for him to work with them too. By the time they'd finished, EJ had been saddled with a stack of CDs pressed upon him by starry-eyed wannabes.

'Occupational hazard,' he said good-naturedly.

'I'll get you a carrier bag,' Lola offered.

'I'd rather have a private word, if that's all right. In your office?'

Lola felt herself go pink, glanced awkwardly at her watch. 'Um . . .'

'Just for a couple of minutes.'

Once inside the office Lola said, 'OK, I'm sorry, I told a fib.'

'More than one, at a guess.' He counted off on his fingers. 'The pregnant woman isn't—never *was*—your partner. Was she even pregnant?'

Shamefaced, Lola said, 'No.'

'And the smell?'

'We boiled an awful lot of cabbage.'

'You really didn't want me moving into that flat, did you?'

'Oh, please don't take it personally. Whoever turned up, we were just going to do everything we could to put them off. Like playing that music . . .' Lola's voice trailed away, because they'd been playing Eminem. Damn, hadn't she overheard a fan earlier, gushing about the album EJ had worked on with Eminem?

'Hmm.' EJ raised an eyebrow. 'The music was fine, it was the dancing that worried me. So who lives there now?'

'Um, Sally. The one who wasn't pregnant. And the guy who was meant to be letting the flat unexpectedly came back from Australia so they're both in there now, driving each other nuts.' Eagerly Lola said, 'So in fact you had a bit of a lucky escape . . .'

'Look, it's not that big a deal.' He shrugged. 'I live in Hertfordshire and staying in hotels whenever I'm up in town gets tedious. I'm renting a place in Hampstead now.'

'Well, I'm sorry we messed you about.'

'Don't worry about it.' His gaze slid downwards to where, having eased off one shoe, Lola was surreptitiously flexing her aching toes. 'Been a long day?'

'Just a bit. I can't wait to get home and run a bath.' Relieved to have been forgiven, she confided, 'My feet are killing me and I'm shattered.'

'Shame, I was just about to ask if you fancied a drink.'

'Oh!' Lola's eyes widened. That was an invitation she hadn't expected. Following him, Lola said, 'Well, maybe a drink wouldn't be so—'

'No, no, you're too tired.' He turned back, his thin clever face pale beneath the overhead fluorescent strip lighting. 'Forget I asked. You get yourself home and jump into that hot bath.' With a glimmer of a smile he added, 'You do look exhausted.'

Ouch. Or maybe touché. Talk about getting your own back.

The advance proof copy of EJ Mack's book, given to her months ago by the publisher's sales rep, was lying under her bed unopened and covered in dust. Wiping it clean on the carpet, Lola raced barefoot across the landing to 73C. Oh, for heaven's sake, Gabe was bound to be out and he hadn't thought to leave the door on the latch; how long was she going to have to wait for Sally to hobble across and unlock it?

Impatiently she hammered on the door. 'Sal, quick, just roll off that sofa, crawl over here and let me in this minute because you are not going to *believe* who I met tonight!' Then, as the door began to open, 'And by the way, everyone at work was *agog* when they heard you were my pregnant lesbian lover—ooh!'

Of course it hadn't been Sally answering the door that quickly. Of course it had to be Doug, whom Lola hadn't seen for three weeks, not since New Year's Eve when she'd made such a dazzling impression.

'So now you're having a lesbian affair with my sister.' Doug shook his head in resignation. 'You really do want to give my mother a heart attack.'

'Sorry. Hi, Doug, I didn't know you were here.' Otherwise I'd have quickly redone my make-up and *definitely* not just made myself that cheese-and-pickled-onion toasted sandwich.

'You know, I wish I was gay,' complained Sally, lying in state across the sofa. 'We're far nicer people. It's got to be easier fancying women than fancying men.'

'Not when they reek of pickled onions,' said Doug.

Doing her best not to breathe, Lola said, 'No Isabel tonight?'

'Yes, I'm here too!' Emerging from the kitchen with a tray, Isabel said gaily, 'Hi, Lola, look at us, meals on wheels!'

'I ran out of milk.' Sally eased herself into more of a sitting position, wincing with pain as she shifted her leg a couple of inches on its pile of cushions. 'Gabe's been gone for hours and he gets cross with me when I keep phoning him, so I gave Doug a call instead.'

'Poor lamb, stuck here with no milk for a cup of tea,' Isabel trilled. 'Then when we said we'd pop over with a couple of pints she mentioned how hungry she was and asked us to bring her a takeaway.'

The poor starving lamb had the grace to look faintly ashamed at this point, as well she might. Lola said indignantly, 'What happened to the lasagne I brought over this morning? All you had to do was heat it up.'

'It's still in the fridge,' Sally admitted. 'Sorry, I was in the mood for a Chinese.' Hastily she changed the subject. 'So who did you meet tonight?'

'Remember the geeky speccy guy who wanted this flat? Him!'

'Yeek, you mean he came into the shop? Was it embarrassing?'

'Just a bit, seeing as he was doing a signing. By the way, he asked after you and the baby.'

Sally patted her stomach. 'We're doing great, thanks.'

Lola, still clutching the book in her hand, said, 'Have you ever heard of EJ Mack?'

'The music bloke? Worked with Madonna last year?' Popping a fork-ful of chicken Sichuan into her mouth, Sally shrugged. 'Kind of.'

'Well, it was him,' said Lola.

Sally almost choked on a mushroom. 'What? EJ Mack's the speccy geek? Oh my God, he's a mega-millionaire and we didn't even *know* . . .'

'Sounds like you missed your chance there, girls!' As she said it, Isabel slipped her arm round Doug's waist and gave it a proprietary squeeze, signalling, oh, you poor creatures, here I am with the perfect man and there's you two with not even a half-decent one to share between you . . .

Inwardly nettled—for heaven's sake, she was *still* clinging on to Doug—Lola said airily, 'Who says I missed my chance? EJ asked me out.'

'Seriously?' Isabel's eyebrows shot up.

Even Doug looked impressed.

Sally squealed, 'The geek asked you out?'

'Actually, he's not as geeky as we thought.' Lola rushed to EJ's defence. 'Behind those glasses his face is really quite interesting . . . and he has these amazing cheekbones . . .'

'So what you're saying is, the more money he has, the better looking he becomes,' Doug drawled with just a hint of eye-roll.

Reaching over to pinch a handful of Sally's prawn crackers, Lola said defiantly, 'No. Tonight I found out he has a really nice personality.'

Doug's mouth twitched. 'Of course you did.'

'So you're actually going out with him?' Sally was so excited she dropped her fork. 'On a *date*?'

'Let's hope he doesn't forget his platinum Amex,' said Doug.

'Could somebody pick my fork up, please?'

'He asked me out tonight,' said Lola. 'But I was worried about Sal being stuck here all on her own, so I turned him down.' *Now* who was the most selfless, thoughtful and downright saintly person in this room?

'Aah, isn't that nice?' Sally beamed. 'Then again, I bet your feet were killing you in those new shoes. And far nicer to have some notice to get yourself tarted up. So when are you seeing him instead?'

'I'm not. He asked me out and I said no, thanks. We left it at that.'

'Are you mad? You can't not see him again! He's EJ Mack!'

'Well, it's too late now.' Throwing up her hands, Lola said, 'At least I can say I turned him down.'

Doug's face was deadpan. 'Either that or he never asked her out in the first place.'

'*Doug*.' Isabel gave him a pretend slap. 'You can't call Lola a liar!'

'You'd be surprised what I can call Lola.' He scooped up his car keys from the coffee table and raised a hand in farewell. 'When it comes to scruples and honesty she's in a class of her own. Right, we're off . . .'

'You're not doing terribly well, are you?' said Colin Carter of the Carter Agency.

Gabe sighed and shook his head. Was he about to be told he should give up the day job? He hadn't had much luck during the past few weeks.

But Colin was a kindly soul. 'Don't be too downhearted. You're only ever one photo away from the next worldwide scoop. Look, we've had a tip-off that Savannah Hudson's holed up in a cottage in the wilds of Gloucestershire. She's been keeping a low profile lately. Here's the address.' He handed over a scrap of paper and said, 'No one else knows about it, so this could be your big chance. Don't bugger it up.'

The cottage was perched on the side of a hill, only slightly set back from the narrow lane winding its way down from the common towards the small country town of Nailsworth. There was a nondescript green Peugeot parked in the driveway and a couple of lights on in the cottage, indicating that Savannah Hudson was probably in there. Needless to say, there was nowhere to park outside the cottage; the lane was single-track with passing places dotted along its length. Which meant Gabe was going to have to leave his warm car further down the hill and spend the afternoon lurking in a wet hedge. It was probably one of the reasons Savannah had chosen to hide out in this cottage. Honestly, these camera-shy celebrities were so selfish.

Having parked in Nailsworth, Gabe stocked up in the bakery with a selection of pies and cakes to keep him going and stave off the tedium. He put a can of Coke and a bottle of water in the pockets of his Barbour. Back at the car he took out his camera, careful to keep it hidden from view, and slung it round his neck under the waxed jacket. Please God, make today the day he got a decent shot and could prove to Colin he wasn't a complete waste of space.

Two hours later Gabe was going out of his mind with boredom. He'd eaten all his food and it was obvious Savannah Hudson wasn't going to emerge from the cottage. The only good thing about the afternoon was that the pies from the bakery had been excellent.

Bugger, he wasn't going to be able to impress Colin after all and it was getting dark and starting to rain. He may as well get back to the car before the heavens opened. At least it was downhill.

As he set off down the lane, Gabe tried to work out what time he'd be home. His social life had taken a serious nose dive lately, what with work and having to look after Sally-the-whinge and getting over the whole soul-destroying business with Jaydena. Maybe a night off was what he needed, a few hours of mindless drinking and clubbing with old friends, chatting up girls, possibly even getting—

Bloody hell.

Having rounded a bend, Gabe saw a figure hurrying up the lane towards him with a bag of shopping in one hand and a dog on a lead in the other. His brain shot into overdrive as he took in the oversized jacket, the skinny legs in skinnier jeans, the blonde head almost hidden beneath the hood of the jacket . . . Bloody hell, it *was* her, Savannah Hudson was heading straight for him, this was his big chance.

Then her head tilted up and she saw him, her actress's antennae on instant alert. As her hood blew back she stopped in her tracks, like a deer hearing the click of the hunter's rifle. Gabe, already reaching for the camera slung round his neck, realised she was about to bolt and called out, 'Please, could I just take one picture of—'

But the wind whipped his words away. Savannah was backing off, dragging the black-and-tan Jack Russell with her. Then a ferocious blast knocked her off-balance and sent her staggering into the verge. She let out a shriek of alarm as the hawthorn hedge bordering the lane bent and swayed, grasping at her with branches like mad spiky fingers.

'Look, I'm sorry,' Gabe yelled above the noise of the wind, advancing towards her. 'I just wanted to . . .'

The words faded in his throat and he stopped dead, gazing in disbelief as the furiously waving branches clawed at her hair and, having yanked it free, waved it like an ecstatic contestant on *Supermarket Sweep*. Savannah Hudson let out a whimper of anguish and dropped her bag of shopping as she attempted to shield her exposed head—*click*—from Gabe. Letting go of the dog's lead, she used her other hand to grasp helplessly—*click, click*—at the blonde wig caught up on the spiky branches.

Good grief, she was as bald as an egg. This was a major scoop, bigger even than his petrol station exposé of Tom Dutton and Jessica Lee. Gabe hastily sidestepped as the dog raced up to him barking furiously.

'Sshh, it's OK, don't do that.' Reaching down, he grabbed the dog's lead. Together they made their way over to the verge where Savannah Hudson was still battling the needle-sharp spikes. Tears swam in her eyes and she ducked her face away at Gabe's approach.

'Here, let me. I'm so sorry. I'll do it,' said Gabe. 'You just hold the lead.'

'Please,' her voice broke, 'just leave me alone. Bunty, *shh*.'

Ignoring the scratches his hands were amassing, Gabe finally managed to liberate the blonde wig, although it did look as if it had just been dragged through a . . . no, no, not the moment to make a joke.

'Thank you.' Tears slid down Savannah Hudson's white face.

'Sorry,' Gabe said again as she crammed the wig onto her head, covering her naked scalp and pulling up the hood of her jacket for good measure. He retrieved the dropped carrier of shopping from a clump of dead stinging nettles in the ditch and handed that back too.

'Sorry? I doubt that.' Savannah's lip curled with derision. 'You've got just what you wanted, haven't you? I hope you're proud of yourself.'

She turned and hurried on up the lane with her shopping and her ridiculous yippy-yappy dog.

'*Wait*,' Gabe called out. He caught up within a few seconds and put a hand on her arm to slow her down.

'Please, just leave me alone,' Savannah said, snatching her arm away.

'OK, OK, just stop for a moment and watch me.' Closing his mind to what he was about to do, Gabe waited until he had her attention. His hands trembled as he showed her the photos on the camera screen. 'OK, see the delete button? You press it.'

If he'd expected Savannah Hudson's rosebud mouth to fall open, for her to turn to him in wonder and whisper, 'Seriously? Do you mean it?' he'd have been disappointed. In a nanosecond her index finger had shot out, pressing the button and deleting the images for ever.

*Dink, dink*, gone. Just like that. And if Gabe had been expecting her to fling herself at him in gratitude crying, 'Thank you, *thank you*,' well, he'd have been sorely disappointed there too. Instead she turned away, muttering, 'And don't tell anyone either.'

He watched her trudge up the hill with Bunty still yapping at her side. Then they rounded the bend and disappeared from view. A smattering of icy rain hit Gabe in the face and he shivered at the realisation of what he'd just done.

In retrospect, Lola was able to acknowledge that she'd made a big mistake in confiding to the others at work—OK, *boasting* to the others at work—about having been asked out by EJ Mack. Now, at least half a dozen times a day someone would clutch their chest and exclaim, 'Oh my God, here he is! Lola, EJ's here to beg you to go out with him . . . quick, look, he's crawling on his knees through the shop . . .'

Which might have been mildly amusing the first couple of times but was altogether less hilarious now.

Anyway, concentrate on the books that needed to be ordered. In the back office, Lola double-checked a list of ISBNs.

Across the desk, after hastily swallowing the last mouthful of her lunchtime prawn sandwich, Cheryl picked up the ringing phone.

Seconds later, windmilling her free arm in front of Lola, she squealed, 'It's for you! You'll never guess . . . it's *him*!'

'Who?' Lola couldn't help herself; her ever-hopeful heart leapt at the idea that it might be Doug.

'EJ Mack!'

God, weren't they sick to death of playing that game yet? Cross with herself for even thinking it could have been Dougie, Lola said, 'Well, tell him sorry, but I don't want to speak to someone who goes out in public wearing an anorak. Tell him to go pester Madonna instead.'

Hastily covering the receiver, Cheryl hissed, 'You berk, I'm serious. It really *is* him.'

'She's right,' EJ confirmed when Lola took the phone. 'It really is.'

'Oops. Hello.'

'And I'll have you know, the anorak is Jean Paul Gaultier.'

'OK,' said Lola. 'Sorry. I'm nothing but a fashion heathen.'

'The trouble is, you think I dress like a train spotter because I can't help myself. Whereas in fact I *choose* to dress like a train spotter because I am a leading proponent of cutting-edge, pseudo-supergeek fashion.'

Shit. 'Right. Sorry again.'

Gravely, EJ said, 'That's all right. You can't help being a heathen. How are your feet now?'

'*What's he saying?*' mouthed Cheryl frantically, her eyes like saucers.

'They're . . . much better.' Lola ignored her.

'And you're not feeling too shattered?'

'No, I'm fine, thanks.'

'So if I were to ask you if you'd like to meet me tonight, do you think you might say yes?'

'If *you* want to,' said Lola.

'You don't sound very enthusiastic. Do you want to see me?'

'Sorry, I'm playing it cool. Deep down I'd really like to see you.'

'Progress at last. Do you play snooker?'

'Er . . . crikey, not very well.'

'Great, more chance of me winning. Can I ask you something else?'

'Fire away.'

'If I looked like me and dressed like me but my job was collecting trolleys in a supermarket, would you still be agreeing to see me?'

Lola thought about it. Finally she said, 'No, I wouldn't.'

He laughed. 'Good for you. A bit of old-fashioned honesty does it for me every time. When shall I pick you up?'

'Um, eightish? I live at—'

'Don't worry,' EJ cut in, sounding amused. 'I know where you live.'

The Groucho Club, that was where they'd be playing snooker. Lola had now read EJ's book—not an autobiography as such, but the story of his experiences in the music industry—and there had been a couple of mentions of playing snooker at the Groucho, so she was pretty sure this was where he'd be taking her and—ooh, doorbell.

The car was, frankly, a bit of a disappointment.

'Is this yours?' Lola hesitated as EJ opened the door for her.

'Yes, that's why we're driving off in it. Otherwise it would be stealing.'

Oh well, maybe the car only looked like a grubby cherry-red Fiesta. Maybe it was actually a gleaming scarlet Ferrari Marinello in disguise.

'Where are we going?' Please say the Groucho, *please* don't say some grotty dive in the backstreets of Bermondsey.

EJ's mouth was twitching; had he read her mind? 'Wait and see.'

'**W**ell?' said EJ forty minutes later. 'What d'you think?'

'I think blimey.' The house was lit up like Buckingham Palace. They were in Hertfordshire, out in the depths of the countryside.

'I think blimey too,' EJ said cheerfully. 'Every time I see it. I grew up in a council flat in Chingford. Now I live here. Pretty cool, eh?'

'Better not let the Beckhams see it,' said Lola. 'They'll be jealous.'

'Come on, we've got a snooker match to play.'

Security lights zapped on as they crunched across the gravel. In the distance a couple of dogs began to bark.

As evenings went, it was an experience. The house was vast and Lola got the full guided tour. EJ beat her at snooker on the purple baize-covered table and she managed to shoot the yellow ball clear across the room, narrowly missing a mullioned window. There were nine bedrooms, each one with an en suite. He showed her his offices and recording studio, and the gold and platinum discs lining the bottle-green walls. There was also a home cinema complete with plush plum-velvet seats, a fully equipped gym, a stadium-sized living room and a kitchen bigger than Belgium.

'Are you hungry?' said EJ, reaching for his phone. 'I can give Myra a call and she'll make us something.'

Myra was the cook/housekeeper who lived with her husband Ted the handyman/gardener in a cottage in the grounds.

'I'm starving. No, don't drag her over here.' Having nosily inspected the fridge, so packed with food it resembled a Tesco Metro, Lola stopped him dialling the number. 'I'll do us both a frittata.'

'**A**t one o'clock in the morning EJ drove Lola back to Notting Hill and said, 'Thanks, I really enjoyed this evening.'

'Me too.'

'Want to do it again?'

'Maybe.' She paused. 'If you do.'

His cheekbones grew more pronounced. 'Hedging your bets.'

'I didn't know if it was a trick question. What if I said, yes please, and you said oh well then, good luck with finding someone to do it with.'

'Hey.' Taking her hand, EJ said, 'I like you. And I'd like to see you again. I'm off to New York tomorrow, but can I give you a ring next week when I get back?'

'Fine.' Lola liked him too; he had a dry sense of humour and was good company.

'At this point, as a general rule, I'd give you a good-night kiss.' EJ paused. 'But we're being watched.'

Gosh, he was observant. Peering up, Lola saw he was right; the lights were off but there was a face pressed avidly to the window.

'It's my pregnant lesbian lover.' Evidently Sally's bad leg wouldn't allow her to get up to make a cup of tea, but hobbling over to the window to spy on other people was another matter.

Waving up at Sally, EJ said, 'On the bright side, at least with her gammy leg she can't dance.'

Sally waved back. Seconds later, Lola's phone began to ring.

'Is he nice?' Sally demanded. 'Have you had a good time? Where did he take you? You can bring him up for a coffee, if you like. Are you going to have sex with him? Why's he driving such a godawful car?'

'I'm *very* nice.' EJ, who'd grabbed the phone, said, 'And yes, we had a great time, thanks. We played snooker at my place. I won. And my car isn't awful, it's reliable and doesn't get vandalised like the Lamborghini.'

'Sorry,' giggled Sally. 'Are you coming up for coffee?'

'Can't, I'm afraid. Early flight to catch.'

'How about sex?'

'Generous of you to offer, but aren't you supposed to be giving that leg of yours a rest?'

'OK, stop that.' Lola seized control of the phone.

'I like him,' Sally said. 'You should definitely sleep with him.'

'He can still hear you,' said Lola. 'I'm going to hang up now.'

'Tell her to move away from the window,' EJ added.

Into the phone Lola duly repeated, 'Move away from the window.'

'Why?'

'Because I want to kiss Lola and I can't do it if you're watching.'

At least at a film premiere you could safely assume that anyone turning up wouldn't object to being snapped. Gabe, who had high hopes for this evening, marvelled at the fact that the air temperature was minus several degrees and he was freezing in his leather jacket, yet the endless parade of starlets doing their beam-and-pose bit on the red carpet were wearing dresses the size of your average J-cloth.

Maybe the layers of fake tan kept them warm.

'Tania, over here!' bellowed a gaggle of paparazzi as a slinky brunette in a shimmering purple scrap of nothing emerged from the next limo in the queue. Gabe wasn't entirely sure who she was, but he clicked and snapped along with the rest of them.

As the next limo drew up, Gabe polished the lens of his Leica Digilux, ready for whoever might be about to—

'Hey, Savannah, this way!' The paparazzi lurched into a frenzy of action. With a jolt, Gabe saw her emerge from the car behind a huge security guy in a dark suit with the look of a debt collector about him.

This was the public face of Savannah Hudson. Tonight she was in full-on film-star mode. Her blonde hair was carefully styled, her make-up perfect. Round her narrow shoulders she wore a silvery velvet wrap; the rest of her body was draped in bias-cut white satin. Not a plastic carrier bag, not a pair of Wellington boots in sight.

No bald heads either, unless you counted the shaven one belonging to the security gorilla.

Savannah posed for the photographers. Having taken a few pictures, Gabe stopped and put his camera down in order to watch her. Maybe it was his stillness among the frenzied screaming horde that attracted her attention but moments later she spotted him. Their eyes met for a second. Gabe nodded, acknowledging her with a brief smile, but there was no flicker of acknowledgment in return. Savannah's gaze slid past him, and after a few more poses she was off up the red carpet to cheers of delight from the assembled fans.

Well, what had he expected?

Gabe got on with the business of snapping the next wave of celebs. Several minutes later, just as he'd bagged a telling shot of a husband and wife giving each other the kind of look that hinted their marriage might be on the rocks, he felt a firm hand grasp his shoulder. Looking round, Gabe saw that it belonged to the security guy.

'You've been pestering Miss Hudson.' The words were accompanied by a menacingly jabbed finger. 'My advice to you, *sonny*, is to leave her alone. Got that?'

For a split second Gabe thought he was being targeted by a pick-pocket. Then he realised his wallet wasn't being stolen, something was being pushed *into* his jacket pocket.

He murmured, 'Got it.'

'Bloody hell,' said one of the paps when the incredible hulk had stalked off. 'I thought he was going to hammer you into the ground.'

'Me too.' With a grimace Gabe raked his fingers through his hair. 'Close call. In fact I'm going to get myself a drink to celebrate still having a neck.'

**R**ound the corner, away from the crowds and the noise, Gabe pulled a folded cinema flier from his pocket. In the semidarkness he had to turn it over twice before spotting the mobile number scribbled diagonally across one corner. Mystified, he called the number. It was answered by the incredible hulk.

'It's me.' Feeling stupid, Gabe said, 'The photographer.'

'The boss wants to see you.'

'Who?' Why ever would his boss be asking to see him?

Evidently sensing his confusion, the hulk explained in a caring, gentle fashion, 'Savannah, you dozy pillock. Wait on the corner of Irving Street and Charing Cross Road. We'll be there in ten minutes.'

This was downright weird. Lost in thought, Gabe zipped the Leica inside his jacket and made for Irving Street. Was he out of his mind? If the hulk turned up with a couple of ready-for-trouble friends he could end up getting more than his camera broken.

Thirteen minutes later a limo with blacked-out windows slowed to a halt beside Gabe. The door slid open and the hulk said, 'Get in.'

'You must be joking,' Gabe retorted. 'Do I look stupid?'

The hulk grinned. 'Now you come to mention it . . .'

'Oh, *stop* that,' exclaimed a despairing female voice and Gabe's mouth fell open as Savannah Hudson's face came into view. Beckoning to Gabe she said, 'Ignore him. Just please get into the car.'

**I**t was something of a novelty, checking there were no paps lurking around the entrance to the Soho Hotel before diving out of the limo, through reception and into the lift.

The hulk waited downstairs in the bar. Up in her suite Savannah disappeared into the bedroom to change out of the liquid silk gown and into one of the hotel's oversized towelling robes. When she returned Gabe sat in a chair over by the window and she perched crosslegged on the vast bed.

'I wanted to say thanks properly,' she ventured at last, 'for doing what you did.'

'That's OK.' Gabe was nursing a bottle of tonic from the minibar.

'And for not doing what you could have done.' As she spoke, Savannah's hand fiddled nervously with a tendril of styled blonde hair. 'I should have thanked you when you deleted those pictures. I was just in such a panic at the time. Then when you'd gone I was convinced you'd only pretended to delete them. But it's been over a week. If you'd still had them they'd have been everywhere by now.'

'I deleted them. Actually,' Gabe pointed out, because it had been her index finger on the button, '*you* did.'

Savannah shrugged. 'You didn't tell anyone, either. My manager's been bracing himself for a barrage of phone calls about my health and there haven't been any. Not one.'

'When I make a promise I keep it.'

'I didn't trust you. I'm really sorry.'

'That's all right. To be honest, I don't think I'm cut out for this paparazzi business. Can I ask you two questions?'

Savannah took a deep breath then exhaled like a diver. 'Fire away.'

'Aren't you supposed to be sitting in that cinema watching the film?'

For a moment Savannah looked nonplussed. Then the corners of her mouth began to twitch. 'You're new, right? We might turn up at a premiere but it doesn't mean we watch the film. Most of us walk up the red carpet, disappear into the cinema and then head straight out again through the back door.'

'Oh. There's lots of things I don't know about this stupid job. Can I ask my other question now?'

She nodded, took a sip of water.

'Do you have cancer?' said Gabe.

Flushing, Savannah shook her head. 'No, I don't. And thank goodness I don't.' She put the bottle of water down on the bedside table and said, 'I have alopecia, which is something actresses like me aren't supposed to get because it's not attractive, and p-people would make f-fun of me . . . oh God, and my career would be over . . .' As she spoke, the tears rolled down her cheeks. She buried her face in her hands and began to sob.

'Oh, don't do that.' Appalled, Gabe jumped to his feet.

The next thing he knew, she was in his arms, as fragile as a baby bird, weeping helplessly and soaking the front of his grey sweatshirt.

'You're so k-kind,' Savannah hiccupped.

With a handful of tissues, Gabe wiped away the dregs of the professionally applied make-up. It was surreal, doing something as intimate as this to a face he'd seen so many times on cinema screens. She was beautiful, talented, fragile. And he was sitting with her on a king-sized bed, consoling her as she wept. To lighten the mood he said, 'I bet you never thought you'd be here doing this with someone like me.'

She managed a watery smile. 'Not in a million years.'

'Everyone hates us,' said Gabe. 'We're right up there with traffic wardens, tax inspectors and those people who club baby seals to death.'

'And bitchy journalists,' Savannah added, 'who always manage to find something horrible to say about you.' She tapped her wig. 'Can you imagine the field-day they'd have if they knew about *this*?'

'But it's not your fault.'

'They don't care about that.' Two more tears popped out. 'All they want is to sell a few more copies of their rotten magazines.'

'Listen to me,' Gabe said firmly, 'you're beautiful.'

Savannah shook her head. 'Not without hair I'm not. My agent told me I looked like a wing nut.'

'That's not true. I *saw* you,' Gabe insisted. 'And you didn't.'

In response, Savannah reached up and peeled off her wig. Minus the hair, her ears stuck out. She looked exactly like a wing nut. A weary, fearful, deeply ashamed wing nut.

'See?' whispered Savannah.

Gabe did the only thing he could possibly do. Reaching forwards, he cupped her damp, tear-stained face between his hands, drew her towards him and kissed her on the mouth.

He'd meant it to be a brief, reassuring kiss, but Savannah clung on, wrapping her arms round his neck. Time stood still for Gabe; bloody hell, this was Savannah Hudson he was kissing and now she was the one making sure it carried on . . .

**B**lythe had finally, reluctantly agreed to meet Nick again, so Lola was hosting a proper grown-up dinner party in her flat.

God, though, cooking proper grown-up food was hard work. She'd been slaving away for ages and there was still heaps to do, never mind getting herself ready and—

*Crash* went the kitchen door as Sally bashed it open with one of her crutches and came clunking through. 'So, how do I look?'

'Like someone who hasn't had anything else to do today except get herself dolled up.' Pausing with a saucepan of mangetout in one hand and a tray of roast potatoes in the other, Lola said, 'You look great. I can't believe you're wearing that dress. What if you spill something on it?'

'It'll dry-clean.' Sally patted her favourite, pale yellow dress. She had fastened her hair up with silver, crystal-studded combs and her make-up was flawless.

Lola was touched that she'd gone to so much trouble. 'And you're not even going to have anyone to flirt with. I should have invited some-one nice along for you. Here, at least help yourself to a drink—oh Lord, that can't be one of them already.'

Sally, already helping herself to wine from the fridge, said cheerfully, 'You never know, maybe it's someone gorgeous for me to flirt with.'

She was half right. It was Doug.

Lola's heart did its usual floppity skip-and-a-jump.

'Ma asked me to drop this off with you.' He dumped a light blue holdall on the table in front of Sally. 'What is it, more clothes?'

'Better than that.' Sally unzipped the holdall. 'Old photos!'

Lola, busy chopping courgettes, was entranced by the look on Doug's face. 'Only you could pick up a bag, wonder what's in it and not even think to take a sneaky look inside.' Thinking that this was why she loved him so much—OK, it was one of the many reasons.

Dougie shot her a look that suggested he didn't love her in return, before turning back to Sally. 'Why did you want them?'

'Lola's mum's bringing loads of photos over tonight to show Lola's dad. I thought it'd be nice to have some of mine here too, so I could join in. Don't worry, I won't pass round any embarrassing ones of you. Well, apart from that one of you naked in a paddling pool with a plastic bucket on your head.'

'I won't let her,' Lola hastily assured him, before Doug could seize the holdall and race off into the night. On an impulse she said, 'You could stay if you want.' Adrenaline sloshed through her body. 'I've made mountains of food. You can see Gabe and my mum again, and meet my dad . . . the more the merrier. It'd be great if you were here too.'

'Thanks,' Dougie cut into her happy fantasy, 'but I can't.'

Oh. Unable to hide her disappointment, Lola blurted out, 'But I've made chocolate pudding with real custard!'

He smiled, just slightly. 'Sorry. I'm seeing Isabel tonight.'

'Shall I get that for you?' Seeing that Lola's hands were wet, Sally picked up the ringing phone. 'Hi . . . no, this is Sally . . . oh hello, you! Yes, thanks, the baby's fine!' Beaming, she said, 'Where are you, still in New York? Oh, right. No, she's busy cooking, we're having a dinner party this evening . . . hey, why don't you come over? Don't be daft, of course you can—Lola's just invited my brother but he's busy.' Covering the receiver Sally whispered, 'That's all right, isn't it?'

What else could Lola say? 'Fine by me.'

Sally hung up a couple of minutes later. 'EJ's on his way.'

'Great.' Lola forced a smile because she'd have preferred Dougie.

'And I'm off.' Doug headed for the door. 'Have a good time.'

On the surface it seemed like a successful dinner party, buzzy and fun, but as far as Lola was concerned it wasn't going according to plan. Nor could she help wondering what EJ was making of it. Gabe, despite being as charming as ever, was definitely distracted. He'd been checking his watch all evening, as jumpy as a cat. Sally wasn't behaving normally either; she was laughing more loudly than usual and generally behaving like an overexcited teenager in the grip of a girlie crush.

Which was slightly weird, seeing as there wasn't anyone here for her to have a crush on. Unless Sally secretly fancied EJ . . . crikey, could that be it? Was that possible? When he was wearing *those* trousers?

Damn, why couldn't Doug be here now? That would help take her mind off the realisation that, across the table, her wonderful plan to get her parents back together wasn't going according to . . . er, plan.

They weren't even chatting to each other; her mother was talking to EJ and Gabe, while Nick and Sally were trading holiday stories. Honestly, it was as if neither of her parents was even *trying*.

'**D**o you know what might be helpful?' said Blythe when Lola tackled her in the kitchen. 'If you could just stop *watching* us all the time.'

'But I can't help it! I want to watch you!'

'Well, it makes us feel like two giant pandas in a zoo, with everyone waiting for us to mate.'

'Mum! Eeuuw!'

Blythe smiled faintly. 'See? That's how I feel too.'

'About Nick? But he's my father. You were in love with him.'

'Twenty-eight years ago,' Blythe reminded her.

'And now he's here again!' Lola couldn't understand how her mother could be this uninterested in Nick.

'Look, if your father and I had got married back then, we'd have been divorced by the time you were three. I know that now.' Blythe went on as Lola opened her mouth to protest. 'Look at your father and look at me.' She gestured at herself, at her wild red hair and pink glittery blouse, the crinkled leaf-green skirt that so strongly resembled a lettuce. Then, flipping a hand towards the living room, she said dismissively, 'And there's him in his trendy clothes, with his hair cut by some celebrity hairdresser chap off the telly. You see, that's the difference between us, love. Nick went in one direction, I went in the other. He's turned into the kind of person who thinks it's normal to spend a hundred pounds on a haircut. I mean, can you imagine?'

'Are you talking about me?' Nick appeared in the doorway.

'About your hair,' Blythe said cheerfully.

'Sorry,' said Lola. 'My mother's turning into a bit of a delinquent.'

Nick shrugged. 'That's OK, Blythe's entitled to her opinion about my hair, just as I'm allowed to have an opinion about her skirt. Would you like me to carry that coffee through?'

'Thanks.' Lola passed him the tray.

'Maybe I wore this skirt because I knew it would annoy you.' Blythe beamed.

Lola said, 'And maybe you're about to get a pot of coffee tipped over your head. Could you please be nice to each other or should I put you at opposite ends of the table?'

'Hey, we're fine.' Nick's tone was reassuring. 'Just having fun.'

'Of course we are.' Giving Lola a conciliatory hug, Blythe said, 'Don't take any notice of us. Dinner was gorgeous. And I like EJ, *very* much.'

'He's a good chap.' Nodding in agreement, Nick said, 'Is he wearing those trousers for a bet?'

Back in the living room, Lola poured out the coffee. Gabe drained his in one scalding gulp and jumped to his feet. 'Right, I'm off to work.'

'Now?' Lola said. 'But it's nearly midnight.'

'Colin wants me to get some shots outside Bouji's. It's somebody's birthday there tonight.'

Sally the Queen of *OK!* magazine said eagerly, 'Ooh, whose?'

'Um . . . can't remember.' Combing his hair with his fingers and shrugging on his battered suede jacket, Gabe said his goodbyes, gave Lola a thankyou kiss on the cheek and headed for the door.

'Um . . . Gabe? Aren't you forgetting something?'

He turned, eyebrows registering impatience. 'What?'

She pointed to the coffee table. 'Might help if you took your camera.'

## *Chapter 10*

'DO YOU TRUST ME?'

'I trust you.'

'Go on, then. Take it off,' said Gabe.

Savannah flushed and double-checked that the bedroom curtains were drawn shut. Not even the most persistent paparazzo could sneak a peek into the cottage. Reaching up, she removed the wig and put it on the dressing table in front of her.

'Maybe a bit of powder,' Gabe suggested. 'Just to take off the shine.'

She did as he said, then turned on the seat to face him.

'Round to the left a bit. I don't want you full on.' Keen to avoid the wing-nut effect, he wanted to minimise her ears. A three-quarter shot would be most flattering. 'And tilt your head slightly . . . relax your shoulders. Now give me a hint of a smile . . . perfect, that's *perfect* . . .'

Afterwards Savannah hugged him. Together they watched as the series of images emerged from the printer on high-gloss photographic paper. Gabe was pleased with the results; as their session had progressed, the tension in Savannah's muscles had dissolved. The final few had achieved what he'd been aiming for; a beautiful woman who happened to have no hair was gazing into the lens without fear.

'Thank you.' Savannah couldn't stop gazing at them. 'Thank you so much. Maybe if I keep looking at them, I'll get more used to them.'

'Let's hope so.' He watched her slide the glossy colour photographs into the wall safe, where no one else could get at them.

'You do the rest,' said Savannah, and Gabe set about deleting first the images from the memory card, then the files from the laptop itself.

'All done.' There was data recovery software on the market capable of retrieving deleted images but he didn't mention this to her.

'Thank you.' If she was aware of this she didn't mention it either. The point was that she had trusted him to take the photographs, which was good enough for Gabe. Slowly, Savannah was gaining in confidence.

She was also besotted with him, which was a pretty flattering thing to happen, even if it meant that for the last week or so he'd been getting less sleep than a new mother of twins with colic.

'You're doing it again,' Savannah chided.

'Doing what?'

'Looking at your watch. I hate it when you look at your watch.'

Gabe kissed the tip of her nose. 'I know, I'm sorry, it's called being a part of the real world. We can't all be A-list stars about to fly off to LA to make a movie. Some of us have to earn a living.'

Savannah gazed up at him, her eyes almost feverishly bright. 'Gabe, come with me to LA?'

Gabe's heart sank. 'Um . . .'

'Don't say um, say yes! It's the obvious answer. My agent's rented a house for me in Bel Air so that's all taken care of. And I know you'd feel funny about coming out just to keep me company, but that's the beauty of your job—you can work as easily over there as you can here!'

'Savannah, hang on a—'

'And it'll get you away from that messy flatmate of yours . . . I mean, I'm sure she's nice enough but I have to say she sounds a nightmare to live with. Plus, *she'll* be relieved to see the back of *you*.'

'Sav, listen—'

'So, talk about tough decisions, is it going to be picking used tea bags out of the sink in a disgusting bombsite of a flat in Notting Hill, or being waited on hand and foot by the live-in staff at an eight-bedroomed mansion in Bel Air?'

Gabe looked at her and said nothing. He didn't need to; Savannah read it in his eyes.

Finally, hesitantly, she said, 'So . . . is that a no?'

He nodded. 'I can't come to LA with you.'

'Can't? Or won't?'

'Can't, I suppose.' He rubbed the back of his neck. 'You're an amazing girl and I think the world of you, but there's . . . something missing.'

'Like, my hair?'

Shit. 'No. God, *no*.' Vehemently Gabe shook his head.

'It's all right, I believe you.' Savannah managed a ghost of a smile.

'Well, good, because your hair has nothing to do with it. If anything I'm thinking there must be something seriously wrong with me. I mean, you're Savannah Hudson,' said Gabe. 'And I'm a street pap.'

'And now you're turning me down. Does that mean you'll sell your story to the papers?'

'I'd never do that. You can still trust me.' Gabe's voice softened. He felt sorry for her. It couldn't be easy being Savannah Hudson.

Gabe collected together his few belongings. Having picked up his toothbrush and aftershave, he looked around the clinical white bathroom and Savannah's equally immaculate bedroom. He wouldn't miss this place; for all its traditional exterior, the inside of the cottage was modern and sparsely furnished, minimalist bordering on sterile . . .

Hang on a minute. That couldn't be right, surely? Taken aback, Gabe looked around again. He *liked* sterile, didn't he? Cool, clean lines and no clutter was his thing. And this was what he was seeing here; design-wise, he and Savannah couldn't be more perfectly matched. Yet somehow all these clean lines suddenly seemed a little bit . . . well, empty.

OK, this was too weird, like an alien invading his brain. An alien with shocking taste at that, and a predilection for gaudy knick-knacks.

Unable to face searching through pristine drawers for the sweater he knew was in here somewhere, Gabe left it and hurried downstairs.

Savannah, pale but composed, was waiting in the kitchen with her back to the Aga. 'So you're off then.'

'I should be getting back.' Thank God she wasn't crying.

'I just wasn't right for you, is that it?'

'Hey, you'll be perfect for someone else. You know that.' Gabe folded her into his arms and she clung to him.

Against his chest Savannah mumbled, 'I just have to find someone who likes bald girls. Mr Spock, maybe.'

'Don't think like that.' He dropped a kiss on her forehead. 'You're beautiful with hair or without it. Be proud.'

'**I** don't believe it,' cried Sally. 'Another living breathing human being! After months of being marooned up here all alone, I finally have the chance to speak to someone—that's if I can remember *how* to speak . . .'

Nick grinned up at her from the pavement. 'Want to buzz me in?'

Did she want to buzz him in? Was he kidding? Hastily clonking through to the bathroom and slapping on a bit of powder and lip gloss, Sally clonked her way back through the flat and pressed the buzzer.

When she opened the door to let him in, Nick, ever the gentleman, greeted her with a kiss on the cheek and said cheerfully, 'How are you?'

'Fed up. Gabe buggered off yesterday, God only knows where because *he* won't tell me, and Lola's gone out for the day with EJ.'

'So, not the best of days.'

'You could say that.' She broke into a smile to show she wasn't a complete grump. 'Not the best of weeks. See that?'

'See what?' Nick followed the direction of her gesturing hand.

'That empty mantelpiece.'

He frowned. 'It's not empty. There's loads of things on it. Fairy lights, photos, candles . . .'

'But no Valentine's cards,' said Sally.

'I didn't get any either.'

'Didn't you?' Hooray for that. 'Not even from Lola's mum?'

Nick laughed. 'Especially not from Blythe. It's OK, I think Lola's come round at last to the idea that she's not going to get us back together. Sweet of her to try, but let's face it, we're poles apart. That Disney happy ending was never going to happen.'

Better and better. Sally began joyfully concocting an alternative happy ending starring . . . *Ta-daaa!* . . . herself.

'Anyway, this is the reason I dropped by.' Nick took a couple of rolled-up leaflets from his pocket. 'Lola's got it into her head that we should be taking up badminton, so I've been to look at a couple of sports centres. I can leave these with you or slide them under her door.'

'Leave them with me. I'll give them to her when she gets home. Where are you off to this afternoon? Somewhere nice, I expect. Having fun, meeting friends . . .'

'The truth? There's an account I should be doing some work on, but to be honest I'm not in the mood. How about if I invited you out to lunch, would that cheer you up?'

'Really? Are you sure?' Sally was barely able to conceal her delight.

'Why not? Decent food, a few drinks and good company.' Nick's grey eyes crinkled with amusement. 'What could be nicer than that?'

**N**ick grew better and better looking as lunch progressed. By the time they had left the restaurant and got back into his car, Sally found him irresistible. And it no longer mattered that Nick was Lola's father because—thank God—he and Blythe had no intention whatsoever of getting back together. The hurdle had been removed and Sally felt her inhibitions disappearing too, possibly helped along by the bottle of wine she appeared to have played a large part in demolishing.

'Whoops, hang on, let me just . . .' Sally gave up the struggle to haul herself out of the passenger seat and allowed Nick to do the honours, providing a shoulder to lean on as she and her crutches navigated their way onto the pavement outside 73 Radley Road. Gathering herself, she handed the front-door key to Nick and said, 'Coming in?'

'I think someone has to ensure you don't fall downstairs, don't you?'

Sally took deep breaths; this was it, she knew it. Gabe was out, they had the place to themselves and the situation couldn't be more perfect. Well, OK, it would have been a teenier bit more perfect if she didn't have her gammy leg to contend with.

Finally they reached the flat. Somewhat unromantically, Sally discovered, all the wine she'd drunk had found its way to her bladder and she was forced to excuse herself in order to visit the bathroom. Returning, she found Nick gazing out of the living-room window. Lit from behind, he had a profile like a Greek god.

He turned, indicating the kitchen. 'I put the kettle on. Thought you might like a coffee.'

OK, it was time. He wanted her to be the one to make the first move. And he was smiling, waiting for her to make it. Approaching him— *clunk*—Sally smiled back then deliberately took her arms out of the crutches and propped them against the wall. Facing Nick, she said, 'I don't want a coffee.'

'No?' Amused, Nick said, 'Well, it's not compulsory.'

'Can you believe this is happening?' Without the support of the crutches, Sally felt herself beginning to sway.

'Steady.' He reached for her.

'It's the last thing I expected.' Sally gazed at him. 'Is it the last thing you expected?'

He looked bemused. 'Well, yes, but ice skaters do injure themselves.'

They appeared to be talking at cross-purposes, but Sally was beyond caring. 'It won't make any difference, I promise.' Curling her arms round his neck, she kissed him passionately, full on the mouth.

**M**aking his way along Radley Road, Gabe slowed and looked up at the window of the flat. Puzzled by the sight of what appeared to be two people locked in a passionate embrace, he reached instinctively for the camera round his neck and peered through the long lens, adjusting it until it slid into focus.

What the . . .?

Gabe's heart began to thud in his chest. Jesus. Sally and Lola's father.

For crying out loud, how long had this been going on? How long had they been carrying on behind his back? And not only his back, Lola's too, because she absolutely definitely didn't know about this.

Unable to watch any more, Gabe put down the camera and turned away. His hands were trembling and he felt as if he'd been punched hard in the stomach. Talk about sly, underhand, deceitful . . . How *dare* they? He swallowed and turned back; yes, they were still there, no longer kissing but only inches apart, holding each other and gazing into each other's eyes, murmuring sweet nothings . . . So this was the kind of man Nick James was, nothing but a sleazy Lothario. How dare he?

**S**omething truly horrible was happening. When Nick jerked away, Sally said, 'It's OK, you don't have to worry about Lola.'

Eyes wide with disbelief, Nick said, 'This isn't to do with Lola.'

'Wh-what do you mean? I d-don't understand.' It came out as a whisper. 'I thought you liked me.'

'I do like you.' Nick shook his head. 'You're Lola's *friend*.'

This was a nightmare. Sally felt sick and suddenly, hideously, sober.

'I'm so sorry.' Nick was clearly mortified. 'I had no idea.'

'No, *I'm* sorry. I thought you were flirting with me.'

Vehemently Nick shook his head. 'I was just being friendly. I want my daughter's friends to like me.'

Humiliation was washing over Sally in waves. How could she have got it so utterly, completely wrong? She'd never be able to forget the moment she launched herself at his mouth and felt him freeze in disbelief . . . oh, oh *God* . . .

'Come on, sit down.' Nick steered her away from the window and lowered her into a chair. 'I'm incredibly flattered. You're a beautiful girl. Any man would be proud to have you as his girlfriend.'

Any man except you, *obviously*.

'Look, I have to leave.' Nick checked his watch, obviously lying but desperate to escape. 'And don't worry, we'll just pretend this never happened. Lola doesn't need to know. I won't tell her,' Nick said gently. 'I won't breathe a word to anyone. That's a promise.'

**I**t took Gabe half a minute to reach his car. He zapped open the door and sank into the driver's seat, appalled by what he'd learned about himself in the last thirty seconds. Because he genuinely hadn't had any idea that the sight of Sally with another man could make him feel like this.

Yet . . . it had. Despite the fact that she drove him insane on a daily basis, that she lived her life surrounded by clutter and chaos and that domestically they were about as compatible as Tom and Jerry, in the space of just a few seconds Gabe discovered that he was capable of white-hot jealousy where Sally was concerned. Because he didn't *want* her to be seeing someone else.

Oh God, now he knew he was going stark staring mad. Sally, of all people. Gabe groaned aloud and rubbed his hands over his face. This couldn't be happening; he didn't *want* to want her. She was the last person on the planet he needed to get involved with.

Except . . . well, that wasn't going to happen anyway, was it? It wasn't as if it was even an option, because she was involved with Lola's dad.

'That's thirteen–three,' Nick called out. 'Ready? Or do you want to stop for a couple of minutes to catch your breath?'

Catch her breath? *What* breath? There was none left in her lungs, that was for sure. Lola shook her head, determined not to give in. This was *badminton*, for crying out loud. If it had been tennis or squash she could have understood being this exhausted, but badminton wasn't anywhere near in that league, everyone knew it was one of those namby-pamby games played by children and old people where you flicked a shuttlecock back and forth over a net.

'Oof,' Lola gasped, lunging after the shuttlecock as it whistled past her ear. Stupid, *stupid* racket . . .

'Fourteen–three.' Grinning, Nick prepared to serve again.

'*Oof.*'

'Game. Well done.' He came round to her side of the net.

'You can't say well done when it wasn't.' Clutching her sides where two stitches were competing to see which of them could hurt most, Lola panted, 'I'm your daughter. Aren't you supposed to let me win?'

He looked amused. 'Not when you're twenty-seven.'

To add insult to injury it had been her idea to come here tonight because Sally had told her that Merton's Sports and Fitness Club in Kensington was where Dougie was a member and that Thursday was his squash night. Lola had called up the club and asked if she and her father could try out the facilities before deciding whether or not to join.

And yes, Merton's did seem like a great place to socialise and expend a few calories, but there was one small drawback. No Doug. Anywhere.

'Ready for a drink?' said Nick as she wiped her face with a towel.

'Ready for loads of drinks.' How could she ever have thought that coming to this place tonight would be a good idea? As soon as they'd showered and dressed they were out of here.

'You've dropped your hairband,' said Nick as Lola just about managed to haul the strap of her sports bag onto her shoulder.

'I can't pick it up, it hurts too much.'

She waited as Nick went back to retrieve the pink hairband, then turned and pushed wearily through the glass swing doors.

Dougie was standing on the other side, watching her.

'Oh!' If there was a god, he really did have it in for her. A trickle of sweat slid down her forehead for that extra-glamorous finishing touch.

'Lola, what's going on?' Doug shook his head. 'Are you stalking me?'

Lola swallowed, realising that this was exactly what she was doing. Instantly on the defensive she said, 'Of course I'm not stalking you!'

Oh God, he was right, she was turning into one of those deranged females incapable of accepting rejection, madwomen who end up shouting in the street and getting arrested for harassment.

'Here's your hairband.' Catching up with them, Nick eyed Dougie coolly and said, 'What's this about stalking? I was the one who suggested we try this club. It wasn't Lola's idea to come here.'

And now she had her father covering for her, lying to protect his deranged-stalker daughter. Mortified, Lola gazed down at her feet and felt the trickle of sweat drip down to her chin.

'Sorry, I was just surprised to bump into her. Didn't have Lola down as the badminton-playing type.'

'Why wouldn't I be?' Defiantly Lola said, 'We had a fantastic game.'

'Really?' Dougie's mouth was twitching. 'When I looked through the window half an hour ago you didn't appear to be having much fun.' He turned to Nick. 'Hi, I'm Doug Tennant. You must be Lola's father.' Shaking Nick's hand, he said, 'You were wiping the floor with her.'

Nick relented. 'I was rather, wasn't I?'

*Oh terrific.*

'I'm going to get showered and changed,' said Lola.

'Me too. See you in the bar afterwards.' Nick nodded cheerfully at Doug. 'Nice to meet you.'

Ten minutes later Lola screeched to a halt at the entrance to the bar. Doug was standing with his back to her, talking to a couple of women with toned brown thighs. There was no sign of Nick. She retraced her steps and waited for him to emerge from the men's changing room.

He looked surprised when he did. 'What are you doing here? I thought we were meeting in the bar.'

'I don't want to stay for a drink. Doug's in the bar. He'll only think I'm stalking him again.'

'Hey, that's OK, it doesn't matter.'

'Yes, it *does* matter.' Lola wearily shook her head. 'Because he's right, I have been stalking him. And it's time to stop.'

They went to Café Rouge in Lancer Square. Over red wine Lola told Nick the whole story from beginning to end.

'So that's it, I've basically made the world's biggest fool of myself but it's all over now. Doug's not interested in me and I've finally accepted it. I gave it my best shot and I failed. Time to give up and move on. As everyone always loves to say, there are plenty more fish in the sea.' Lola curled her lip. 'Although whenever they say that, it really makes me want to get hold of a big fish and smack them round the face with it.'

'I won't say that then. Oh, sweetheart, I do feel for you.' Reaching across the table, Nick gave her hand a squeeze. 'I can't believe you haven't told me any of this before.'

'I didn't want you thinking you'd got yourself a scary daughter. You might have run for the hills.'

'I wouldn't.'

Lola shrugged. 'I wanted to impress you, make you think you had a daughter to be proud of.'

'Sweetheart, I *am* proud of you.'

Lola blinked back tears; he was being so nice to her and it felt lovely being called sweetheart. 'Yes, but I have behaved pretty stupidly. I mean, throwing myself at a man who kept telling me he didn't want me, it's hardly the brightest thing to do. *Anyway*,' hastily she drew a line with her free hand, 'I won't be doing that any more.'

'I wish there was something I could do to help.' Nick thought about it for a couple of seconds. 'Do you want me to have a word with him?'

Lola smiled bravely. 'Thanks, but it's over. He's with Isabel now.'

'And you've got EJ.' Nick's tone was encouraging. 'You like him, don't you?'

Lola sighed. Of course she liked EJ, but only as a friend. They kissed—which was fine—but hadn't slept together. He was a nice person and great company, but the magic wasn't there. It wasn't fair on EJ and she was going to have to finish that relationship—if you could call it a relationship when you weren't even having sex.

As they were leaving Café Rouge Nick said, 'So, what happened to the money Blythe mustn't know about? What did you spend it on?'

'I can't tell you.'

He laughed. 'Tell me!'

Lola spotted an approaching taxi. 'Really, I can't.' She stuck out her arm and flagged down the cab. 'Sorry, Dad, but I can't tell anyone. Ever.'

It was like being on a really strict diet and having someone present you with a year's supply of Thorntons truffles. Lola had never actually been on a really strict diet owing to her inability to give up . . . well, Thorntons truffles, but she just knew this was how it would feel. Toby Rowe was a multimillionaire music mogul and an old friend of EJ's. It had been thrilling enough being invited along to his fortieth birthday party, held at the kind of private members' club Lola had only ever dreamed of visiting, but now Toby was offering something more.

'Come on.' Toby's tone was cajoling. 'It's only a week. You can take a week off work, can't you? EJ, work your magic, make this girl say yes.'

Toby had a party of ten friends flying out in the first week of April to stay at his villa on St Kitts. Evidently it was large enough to accommodate two more. From the sound of things it could hold another twenty. And the people joining Toby and his girlfriend were all major players in the music business. Lola would be practically the only civilian.

'Go on,' EJ said with a persuasive wink, 'you know you want to.'

Oh God, this was torture. 'I'm not sure if I can take the time off.'

'Couldn't you just phone in at the last minute,' said Toby, 'and tell the boss you've got flu?'

'Except I am the boss.' Lola pulled a face. 'And I wouldn't believe me. I'm always suspicious when people phone in with a croaky voice and tell me they have flu.'

Toby said, 'Or when they ring in with a croaky voice to tell you they've sprained an ankle.'

'What I really hate,' said EJ, 'is when we're recording an album and they phone up with a croaky voice to tell me they've got a croaky voice.'

Lola's heart sank as he grinned his quirky, lopsided grin. He was the kind of person anyone would love to have as a friend. And he had buckets of money . . . why, *why* couldn't she feel a frisson of lust?

But there you go, she couldn't and that was that. It was time to do what she had to do. Checking her watch, Lola saw that it was midnight and she had to be at work by eight tomorrow morning. She touched EJ's arm and said, 'I need to get home. If you want to stay on, I can get a cab.'

But EJ put down his orange juice. 'It's OK. I'm pretty shattered too.'

They said their goodbyes to Toby and his friends. As EJ drove back to Notting Hill, he told her more about Toby's villa on St Kitts, about the view over Half Moon Bay, the scuba diving—

'I'm sorry,' Lola blurted out, 'I can't go.'

'Don't say that. You haven't checked with work yet.'

Her fingernails dug into her palms as she squeezed her fists tight. 'It's not work.'

'No?' EJ pulled up at traffic lights, glanced sideways at her. 'Is it the plane tickets? Because that's not a problem. I'll pay for those.'

'OK, here's the thing.' Gearing herself up, Lola wished he could be driving the battered old Fiesta tonight; she didn't want to be responsible for him pranging his beloved Lamborghini. 'EJ, I really like you but we're going to have to stop seeing each other.' The lights changed and they moved forward; praying he wouldn't go careering into the bus ahead of them, she said hastily, 'But you're a fantastic person.'

EJ remained in control of the Lamborghini. Drily he said, 'But not quite fantastic enough.'

'Oh, don't say that! It's not you, it's me, I just—'

'Lola, it's OK. It's not your fault.' He indicated left and pulled into a side street. 'Would it help if I said I'd guessed this might be coming?'

'I'm sorry,' she said again. 'You're so *nice* . . .'

'I know I am. I also know I'm not the world's best-looking guy, but I was kind of hoping to win you over with my brilliant personality.' He shot her a lopsided smile. 'That's why I never tried to get you into bed. Because I knew you hadn't reached the stage yet where you really wanted to. I thought if I was patient . . . well, that the right time would come along and everything would be perfect. But there was always the risk that you'd bale out before it had a chance to happen.'

'But you've slept with so many incredible girls,' Lola protested. 'Famous ones! Loads more glamorous than me!'

'Maybe I have.' He shrugged. 'Maybe they don't mean so much.'

'Oh God, don't say that.' Lola felt terrible now.

'Sorry, I don't want you to feel guilty. Hey, it's OK. Really. Can't make chemistry happen if it isn't there. It's a shame, but I'll survive.'

'You deserve someone fantastic.' Lola really meant it.

'Thanks.' EJ started the Lamborghini up again and drove her home.

Before she climbed out of the car, Lola hugged him hard and said, 'Have a great time in St Kitts.'

He smiled, sad for a moment, then gave her waist a squeeze. 'I have to say, all credit to you for telling me tonight. A lot of girls would have waited until after the five-star, all-expenses-paid holiday.'

'I know.' Lola wondered if she'd live to regret it. 'I'm probably mad.'

As he planted a goodbye kiss on her cheek, EJ said with affection, 'That's probably why I liked you so much in the first place.'

Today was her last day of being an invalid. At midnight, Cinderella-style, her sick note expired. Tomorrow she was going back to work at the surgery and to celebrate she'd been invited over to dinner by her lovely boss Dr Willis and his wife Emily.

'You're leaving the practice?' Sally couldn't believe it; she loved working for Dr Willis. Why was her life crumbling around her? For the past ten days, Gabe had been withdrawn and moody, working all hours and spending less and less time at home. At first she'd been thrilled that he'd stopped nagging her to clear up after herself, but after a while she'd kind of begun to miss it. And now this.

'Isn't it exciting? We can't wait.' Emily beamed across the dinner table at her. 'Skipton's such a wonderful place to live.'

'It was Emily's idea.' Roger refilled their wineglasses. 'She spotted the ad in *Pulse*, organised a trip up to Skipton, even dragged me round the estate agents before I knew I'd got the job. We'd always planned to retire up there,' he went on. 'But this way we've got a few years of me working in the area first, becoming a real part of the community.'

'That's why we asked you over here this evening. We wanted you to be the first to know. Here, take a look at the place we're buying.' Bursting with excitement, Emily produced a glossy brochure. 'All my life I've dreamed of living in a house like this.'

The place was spectacular, a sprawling converted farmhouse on a hillside with lovingly tended gardens and stunning views across the valley. There were five bedrooms, three of them en suite, and a kitchen the size of a tennis court. There was even a granny annexe, a snooker room and—crikey—an *actual* tennis court.

Sally said, 'It's fantastic. Can I come with you?'

Emily paused, a forkful of fish pie halfway to her mouth. 'Really?'

'I was joking,' said Sally.

'Oh.' Emily's face fell. 'Shame.'

'Sorry?'

'No, my fault, you got our hopes up there for a minute.' Emily waggled her free hand. 'It's just that the current receptionist is the wife of the chap Roger's replacing. They're moving down to Cornwall. So the practice needs a replacement.'

Sally gazed again at the glossy brochure. Was this a sign?

'When we wake up in the morning we'll look out of our bedroom window and see all that.' Roger Willis proudly tapped the photograph of rolling green hills dotted with sheep.

Sally drank it in. Sheep. Was this a sign that she was meant to live somewhere hilly and popular with sheep?

*Heartbeat.* Was that set in Yorkshire? Yes, it was.

*Where the Heart Is*? Tick, ditto.

*The Royal.* Ha, yes, so was that. And there was a *reason* why so many feel-good cosy Sunday-evening dramas were set in Yorkshire. It was because Yorkshire was a cosy, feel-good place to live.

And there was a Harvey Nichols in Leeds . . .

'Hello? Sally?' Roger was holding the dish of fish pie, waving the ladle to attract her attention. Having caught it, he said jovially, 'What are you thinking? You're miles away!'

'I'm not.' Sally moved her fork to one side, allowing him to spoon another helping of fish pie onto her plate. 'But I could be.'

# *Chapter 11*

WHAT A SHAME you couldn't fall in love with a man as easily as you could fall in love with a coat.

'This is it.' Lola hugged herself and did a happy twirl in front of the antique, rust-spotted mirror propped against the side of the stall.

'Fabulous.' Sally nodded in agreement.

Blythe, ever practical, said, 'How much?'

But Lola didn't care. It was love at first sight. The moment she'd clapped eyes on the coat, fuchsia-pink velvet, long and swirly, she'd known it was the one for her. And they'd be happy together; the coat would never let her down, stand her up or make her cry.

Oh, yes, when everything else around you was going pear-shaped, there was always Portobello Market, with its bustle and colour and endless treasure trove of shops and stalls, to cheer you up.

Just as there was always someone to nag you about money.

'Lola. Tag,' Blythe prompted, pointing to the sleeve.

This was the downside of having a mother who went for quantity rather than quality every time.

'Um . . . forty-five.' Lola attempted to hide the tag up the coat's sleeve as her mother approached.

Too late. Blythe peered at the tag then dropped it as if it had barked at her. 'Two hundred and forty-five!' She gazed at Lola and Sally in disbelief. '*Pounds!* For a secondhand coat.' Blythe was indignant.

'Vintage,' said the stallholder.

'If this was in a charity shop you'd be able to buy it for twenty pounds! Lola, offer her fifty pounds and not a penny more.'

'Mum, sshh, look at the label. If this coat was on sale in Harvey Nichols it would cost thousands.'

'But see how thin it is—it won't even keep you warm!'

Lola looked the stallholder in the eye and said, 'Two hundred.'

The stallholder, who knew a pushover when she saw one, shrugged and said, 'Sorry, I can't go below two thirty.' The subtext being: *because I know how badly you want this.*

Lola took out her purse and began counting out twenties.

'Lola, you can't buy it.'

'Mum, I love this coat. It'll make me happy. And it's my money.'

At last the transaction was complete and they moved on. Sally, after a week back at work, was relishing her day off and getting along quite niftily now with the help of her walking stick. Blythe stopped at a stall selling patchwork waistcoats and said, 'Now these are fun, and they're only fifteen pounds!'

'They're horrible,' said Sally.

'Oh. Are you sure?' Blythe looked to Lola for a second opinion.

'Really horrible,' Lola confirmed.

'At least they're new. Ooh, how about this?' Excitedly Blythe waved a peacock-blue scarf adorned with silver squiggles. 'Seven pounds!'

What harm could a scarf do? The sooner her mother bought something, the sooner she'd stop going on about the coat. 'Yes, buy it.'

'No, don't buy it!' Sally let out a snort of laughter and waggled her hands in a bid to draw Lola's attention to something on the scarf.

'Honestly, you two,' Blythe grumbled. 'What's wrong with—'

'My God! Lola!'

Everyone turned in unison at the sound of the girl's voice. Next moment Lola found herself having the breath hugged out of her lungs.

At last Jeannie put her down and Lola said, 'I don't believe it. Look at you! You're so *brown*.'

'That's because I'm living in Marbella now! We're just back for a few days visiting my mum.' Jeannie's hair was sunbleached and her skin was the colour of a hazelnut. 'And you aren't brown,' she said cheerfully, 'so that must mean you live in unsunny Britain.'

'I do. I live right here in Notting Hill. And this is my mum.' Lola indicated Blythe. 'And my friend Sally. Mum, this is Jeannie from school.'

'Oh, the Jeannie you went off with to Majorca! How lovely to meet you at last,' Blythe exclaimed.

As things had turned out, Lola hadn't ended up spending more than a few days with Jeannie. Shortly after her arrival in Alcudia, Jeannie had hooked up with a boy called Brad who was moving on to work in a restaurant on a surfer's beach in Lanzarote. Jeannie had gone with him the following week and that had been the last she and Lola had seen of each other. Lola, aware that her mother and Alex would have been worried sick if they'd known she was out there on her own, had discreetly glossed over that snippet in her postcards home.

'I was just looking at Sarah's jacket, admiring it from a distance, then I saw who she was talking to and I was just, like, ohmigod!' Jeannie ran her fingers over the sleeve of Sally's caramel leather jacket and said appreciatively, 'It's even better close up.'

'Sally,' said Sally.

'Huh? My name's Jeannie.'

'I know. You just called me Sarah. I'm Sally, Sally Tennant.'

'Oops, sorry!' Jeannie tapped the side of her head, then stopped and began wagging her index finger in a thoughtful way. 'Hang on a minute, wasn't Tennant the name of that boyfriend of yours?'

The index finger was now pointing questioningly at Lola.

'Doug Tennant.' Sally gave a yelp of excitement. 'That's right, he's my brother!'

Lola experienced a sensation of impending doom, like an express train roaring out of a tunnel towards—

'You're kidding!' Her eyes and mouth widening in delight, Jeannie looked from Sally to Lola. 'So you and Doug got back together? My God, I don't believe it! That's so romantic! What happened about the money? Did his witch of a mother make you pay it all back?'

Lola's first instinct was to clap her hands over her ears and sing loudly, 'Lalala.' Her second was to clap her hands over her mother's ears and go, 'Lalala.' But it was too late; Blythe was frowning, looking as bemused as if everyone had suddenly started babbling away in Dutch.

'Oops, sorry!' Jeannie smacked her forehead and turned back to Sally. 'I just called your mother a witch!'

'What money?' said Blythe.

'Dougie and I didn't get back together,' Lola blurted out. 'Sally's my next-door neighbour.'

'Oh crikey, I'm getting everything wrong here, aren't I?' Jeannie shook her head dizzily.

'Excuse me.' The bored stallholder nodded at the scarf being twisted in Blythe's hands. 'Are you going to be buying that or what?'

'So did Doug ever find out about the money?' Jeannie said avidly.

Lola closed her eyes. In Alcudia she'd made a point of explaining to Jeannie that her mother didn't know about the money thing. How could her friend have forgotten?

Blythe carried on twisting the scarf. 'What money?'

'Yes, Doug found out.' Sally, attempting to ride to the rescue, said hastily. 'But that's all in the past, everyone's moved on, it's—'

'Oh, Lola, I've always wanted to know what you spent all that money on. God, I wish someone had given me ten grand to dump any of the loser boyfriends I've hooked up with over the years.' Apologetically, Jeannie touched Sally's arm. 'Not that your brother was a loser.'

Desperate to get away—although it was too late now, the cat was out of the bag—Lola grabbed the blue and silver squiggly scarf from Blythe. 'Mum, are you going to buy this?'

'No, she isn't,' Sally repeated.

'Why not?' Lola gave the scarf a flap to try and get the creases out. 'It's pretty!' Useful too. She could strangle blabbermouth Jeannie with it.

'It's obscene.' Jeannie pointed to the squiggles. 'Rude Spanish word.'

God, it was too. Lola hurriedly put down the scarf.

'That's disgusting.' Rounding on the hapless stallholder, Blythe said, 'You should be ashamed of yourself, selling something like that.'

'I don't speak Spanish.' The man shook his head in protest.

Nobody was listening to him, nobody cared. Blythe had already swung round and pointed an accusing finger at Lola. Her voice scarily controlled, she said, 'But he shouldn't be as ashamed of himself as *you*.'

'I can't believe this.' Blythe's cup of coffee sat in front of her untouched. She shook her head and gazed across the tiny café table at Lola. 'I can't believe you did something like that. In God's name, *why*?'

Lola felt sick with shame. She'd never imagined her mother would find out about the money. She wished she still had Sally here to be on her side.

'Well?' Blythe demanded.

'I've told you. Because Dougie's mother hated me and Dougie was moving up to Scotland. We were so young, what were the chances of us staying together? I mean, realistically?' Lola's coffee cup rattled as she tried to lift it from the saucer. Her whole life, she'd loved earning praise from her mother, making her happy and proud of everything she did. Blythe's approval was all that mattered and until today she'd known she'd always had it, unconditionally.

Until an hour ago. What were the chances of bumping into Jeannie and the whole sorry story spilling out like that?

'And the money,' said Blythe. 'The ten thousand pounds. What happened to it?'

Lola shifted in her seat. She wasn't completely stupid, she did have a plausible lie put by in case of absolute emergencies.

'OK, it wasn't ten thousand pounds. It was twelve and a half.' May as well get as many of the facts correct as possible. 'And I used most of it to buy a Jeep so I could get around the island.'

'A *Jeep*? Dear God! But you hadn't even passed your test!'

'I know. That's why I didn't tell you. It's also why I couldn't get it taxed and insured.' Her palms growing damp, Lola forced herself to carry on with the lie she'd concocted years ago and hoarded for so long. 'Which is why, when it was stolen a week later, I couldn't do anything about it. I'd spent the money on a Jeep then, *boom*, it was all gone. I was back to square one.'

'No, you weren't.' Blythe was shaking her head again. 'At square one you had Dougie. Oh, Lola, what were you thinking of? I thought we'd brought you up better than that. Relationships are more important than money! Look at Alex and me, we were happy whether we had it or not. If you love someone, money's irrelevant. You sold your chance of happiness with Dougie for a . . . a Jeep! That's a terrible thing to do.'

'I know. I know that now.' Lola was perilously close to tears.

'And you know what? If you were capable of doing that to Dougie, you don't deserve him. How could you be so stupid? I feel like phoning that boy up and apologising to him myself, I really do.'

Oh God. Her mother's disappointment in her was too much to bear. Tears rolled down Lola's cheeks as she clenched her fingers and blurted out, 'I was seventeen, I was stupid and I did a terrible, *terrible* thing. I don't blame you for hating me,' she shook her head in despair, 'because I know it was wrong. And I'll regret it f-for the r-rest of my l-l-life.'

Blinded and sniffing helplessly, she fumbled in her pocket for a tissue. None there. The next moment she felt her mother's arms go round her and a paper napkin being pushed into her hand.

'Oh, sweetheart, of course I don't hate you. You're impetuous and you don't always think things through, but you're my daughter and I love you more than anything in the world. There, shh, don't cry.' Blythe rocked her, just as she'd always done as a child. 'You made a mistake and you've learned your lesson.' Pulling away, she smiled and tenderly wiped rivulets of mascara from Lola's wet face with her finger. 'My God, the antics you've got up to over the years. Just you wait, one of these days you'll have children of your own and then you'll know how it feels when they do things that shock you.'

'I've got some good news for you,' said Sally.

'Oh?' Gabe halted in the doorway, clearly surprised to see her up at one o'clock in the morning.

'You're going to be thrilled. It might even make you crack a smile.' Sally was drinking Pernod and water, which was unbelievably disgusting but she'd been in need of Dutch courage and there hadn't been anything else alcoholic in the flat. Talking things through with Lola would have helped, but Lola was staying with Blythe for the night.

'Go on, then,' said Gabe. 'Thrill me.' Gabe chucked his jacket over the back of a chair.

Having psyched herself up to tell him, Sally abruptly lost her temper. 'I'm trying to tell you something that you'll want to hear and you're being all distant and sarcastic.'

'I'm sorry. Right, I'm listening. See?' Gabe made his face deliberately blank. 'Not being sarcastic at all.'

And now he was treating her like a child. Her stomach in knots, Sally blurted out, 'Well, don't worry, soon you can be as sarky as you like because I won't be here to see it. I'm moving out.'

A muscle was going in Gabe's jaw. For a couple of seconds he just stood there looking at her. Then he turned away. 'Right. Good for you.'

'Is that it?' Adrenaline was sloshing through her body. 'Is that all you're going to say?'

'What else do you want me to say? OK, I've got something. Have you told Lola yet?'

'What? No, because she's not here. I'll tell her tomorrow.'

Gabe raised an eyebrow. 'And how do you think she'll react?'

'Oh, come on, it's not that big a deal.'

'But you haven't mentioned it before now, have you?'

'Because I only decided tonight! My God, why are you *being* like this? I'm leaving.' Pernod flew out of Sally's glass as she flung her arms wide. 'Isn't that enough? I thought you'd be delighted to have me out of here. And what's *this* about?' Agitatedly jabbing a finger at his discarded jacket, she cried, 'You spend your life nagging me but it's OK for you to act like a slob. Would it kill you to hang that up?'

Slowly and deliberately, Gabe picked up the jacket. As he made his way past her he murmured, 'Poor sod, does he know what he's letting himself in for?'

'Will you shut up? I've worked for him for the last two years, haven't I? So I can't be that unbearable!'

Gabe stopped dead. 'Worked for who?'

'Dr Willis!'

He gazed at her in disbelief. 'You're having an affair with Dr Willis?'

'What?' Sally let out a shriek. 'For crying out loud, what are you *on*? How could you *think* I'm having an affair with Dr Willis?'

'But . . . but . . .'

'He's *old*.' Sally wailed. 'And he's *married*.'

'So who are you moving in with?'

'Dr Willis. And his wife. But I won't be living *with* them, not in the same house. It's a self-contained annexe.' Sally mimed self-containment with her hands. 'When I wake up in the morning I'll see sheep.'

Gabe was gazing at the almost empty glass of Pernod. 'How many of those have you had?'

'One. It's vile. And can we please stop arguing now, because I'm not moving out tonight. I'm going to be here for another four weeks yet.'

He shook his head in confusion. 'I don't understand the bit about the sheep. At all.'

'There's loads of them, all over the hills.'

Gabe said evenly, 'Where are these sheep? Where is this house?'

'Near Skipton. In Yorkshire. That's where I'm going to be living.' As she said the words, Sally wondered if she really wanted to go. 'Living and working. It's a fresh start.'

'Why?'

'Why? Because I'm hoping it's going to be nicer than living in London. My boss is moving to Yorkshire and he offered me a job in his new practice. You don't want me here in this flat, you've made that obvious. Of course I'll miss Lola, but it's not going to stop me—'

'So what happened? You and Nick broke up? Or is he moving up there too?'

For a split second she couldn't work out who he meant. 'Nick who?'

Gabe gave her a look. 'Come on. I know.'

Sally didn't know what he knew, but she felt herself flushing anyway. If Gabe knew, that meant that Nick must have told him. Except . . . it was more likely that Nick would have told Lola, who in turn had told Gabe, so basically they'd *all* been laughing at her behind her back.

'I get it,' Gabe said dismissively. 'You're moving up there together.'

'What are you *talking* about?' Sally stared at him; how could he even think this? 'I'm not having an affair with Lola's dad!'

'You mean it's over?'

'I mean it never happened!'

'No? Take a look in the mirror.' Gabe's tone was triumphant. 'If it's not true, tell me why you've gone redder than a traffic light.'

'Oh, I'm sorry, are we in court?' That was it; Sally lost the last vestige of control. 'Are you the lawyer for the prosecution? Not that it's *any* business of yours, but just to shut you up, the reason I've gone red is because, OK, I *did* have a bit of a crush on Lola's dad and I did make a complete idiot of myself one afternoon telling him I liked him. But he turned me down, and I don't know what makes you think it ever went any further than that, but it definitely didn't.' Unable to meet his gaze, she said, 'Can we stop talking about this now? It's humiliating.'

No reply. Sally carried on staring at the floor. Finally she heard Gabe say, 'There's nothing going on between you?'

Her hands clenched in frustration. 'Isn't that what I just *said*?'

'Sorry. Just checking. The afternoon you made a bit of an idiot of yourself . . . was it a Sunday afternoon?'

Sally nodded and gritted her teeth, cringing at the memory. The ridiculous thing was she no longer even thought about Lola's dad. The crush had died as quickly as it had sprung up.

'And you and Nick were standing over there, by the window.' As he pointed, a glimmer of a smile appeared at the corners of Gabe's mouth.

'I suppose so. Yes.' Admittedly she'd been slightly the worse for drink at the time but she could still remember the way the sunlight had streamed through the window . . . *oh!* The penny dropped. 'You were outside the flat! You were watching me make a prat of myself!'

'I didn't know you were making a prat of yourself. He had his arms round you.'

'He was keeping me upright. And I don't know if I ever mentioned this, but I've had a bit of a bad leg.' Sally couldn't believe what she was witnessing; before her very eyes Gabe was metamorphosing from the tetchy grump of the past few weeks back into the old sparkly-eyed *human* Gabe she'd missed so desperately since the evil twin had taken his place.

'I thought you were shagging him.' Gabe's whole face had changed, cleared. He was smiling now with what appeared to be relief.

Glad the misunderstanding had been cleared up, but mystified by the relief, Sally said, 'Is that why you've been so stroppy and weird?'

He hesitated, then nodded. 'You could say that.'

'All because you thought I was having a thing with Nick? Would Lola really have hated it that much?'

'No idea.'

'But that's why you were so iffy?'

A longer pause this time. Much longer. Finally Gabe raked his hair back with his fingers and took a deep breath. 'OK, I can't quite believe I'm standing here saying this, but the reason I wasn't happy about it was because I was . . . . I was . . .'

Encouragingly Sally said, 'Spit it out.'

'Oh, for crying out loud, it was because I was jealous.' He threw both hands up in the air. 'There. Said it. Now you know.'

Sally stopped dead in her tracks. Surely not, *surely not* . . .

Gabe shrugged. 'Sorry.'

'Oh my God. Gabe! That explains so much,' Sally blurted out. 'I even guessed! I asked Lola and she said I was wrong, but I *knew*.'

'You did?' It was Gabe's turn to look stunned.

'The whole tidiness thing.' She was triumphant. 'It's so *obvious*.'

'You really think I'm gay?'

Flummoxed, Sally said, 'Isn't that what you're telling me?'

'*No.*' Gabe clutched his head, looking as if he was on the brink of tearing his hair out. His eyes, wide with disbelief, fixed on hers. The next moment he reached out and grabbed her. Before Sally knew what was happening, she was being kissed. His warm mouth covered hers, her whole body was pressed against Gabe's, her skin was zinging like sherbet and . . . *cut.*

Just as abruptly as it had begun, the kiss ended. Gabe let her go and she was left standing there like a cartoon character, dazed and panting and with giant question marks exploding out of her head.

'I can't believe you thought I was gay.'

'But . . .'

'Oh shit, this is all going wrong. I thought I could do it but I can't.'

Before she could react, he was gone. The door of the flat slammed shut behind him and Sally heard his footsteps clattering down the staircase. She sank down onto the sofa and clutched her hands tightly together to stop them trembling.

OK, concentrate. Gabe had jumped to the wrong conclusion. And so had she. He wasn't gay, she was convinced of that now. And if he wasn't jealous at the thought of Nick being involved with someone else, then he had to be jealous at the thought of *her* seeing another man . . .

Shaking now, Sally replayed the incredible thought in her mind. But how could this be happening, exploding like a bomb in front of her with no warning at all? And why was she feeling, among all the confusion and disbelief, as if it was something she'd been longing to happen for months? But so secretly that she'd barely even acknowledged it, because it was simply *the* most unlikely scenario on the planet.

Sally wrapped her arms round her waist, rocking back and forth in order to think more clearly. Had she, deep down, been seriously attracted to Gabe since the first time she'd clapped eyes on him?

Yes.

Had she ever considered doing anything about it?

No. Because although Gabe was gorgeous and funny and pretty damn fanciable—if a bit overzealous in the tidiness department—you knew categorically you weren't Gabe's type.

She had to find him before he had time to change his mind about her. How much of a start had he got on her?

Stumbling to her feet, Sally reached for her stick and hurried out of the flat. Where was Gabe? It was a cold night and all he was wearing was jeans and an old polo shirt. Clunk-step, clunk-step went the stick against the stairs, interspersed with the sound of her rapid breathing. Then halfway down the staircase she saw a scruffily dressed figure with messy hair leaning against the far wall of the darkened hallway.

Sally stopped abruptly. Now that she'd found him she didn't know what to say. 'I thought you'd left.'

'I was going to. Then I realised I didn't have my keys.'

'Or your jacket. You'd have been cold.'

'That too.' The whites of his eyes gleamed in the darkness.

'You could have stayed upstairs,' said Sally.

'I couldn't. Too scared. I told you, I never expected to feel like this.'

'Me neither.'

She saw him nod. 'Bit of a shock?'

'A lot of a shock.' Gathering her courage, Sally said, 'But a nice one.'

He was watching her carefully. 'Really?'

'Really. I thought I drove you mad.'

'You do. Are you really moving up to Yorkshire?'

How could everything change so drastically in a matter of minutes? 'I suppose I don't have to. Seeing as the main reason I was doing so was to get away from the miserable old git I was sharing a flat with.'

Gabe stepped out of the shadows, came to stand at the foot of the staircase. He touched his chest. 'Me?'

'Yes, you.' Feeling braver, Sally said, 'Come here.'

He climbed the stairs separating them. This time she knew he was going to kiss her. What she hadn't expected was for her knees to give way, mid-kiss. Smiling broadly, Gabe lowered her onto the stairs and carried on kissing her. God, he was so good at it and . . . *whoops* . . .

The walking stick she'd left propped against the banister toppled over and went clattering down the staircase. Sally squeaked, 'Oh no!' and attempted to muffle her laughter against Gabe's shoulder.

Gabe whispered, 'Don't worry, he's asleep.'

He wasn't. The door to the ground-floor flat was wrenched open and the tenant, Mr Kowalski, his white hair standing on end, bent down and picked up the walking stick. He eyed Sally and Gabe balefully.

'Vot arr you doing? Making sex on ze stairs in ze mittle of ze night?'

'Sorry, Mr Kowalski. Didn't mean to wake you.' Gabe grinned apologetically. 'We weren't . . . um, making sex on the stairs.'

'Ha. Pretty close, if you ask me.' Shaking his head, the old man skilfully threw the stick up to them, Gene Kelly style.

Equally skilfully, Gabe caught it. 'Thanks.'

'Off, off you go! You make sex in your own beds and leave me to sleep in mine.' Having gestured extravagantly at the ceiling he shuffled back into his flat muttering, 'Too much noise, too much sex, *tuh*.'

Sally buried her face in Gabe's chest.

'Sounds good to me,' Gabe murmured, standing and helping her to her feet.

By the time they reached the flat, Sally was light-headed with lust, dizzy with joy and minus her shoes. Gabe lifted her into his arms and carried her through to his bedroom. As he lowered her onto the crisp, spotless, geometrically aligned white duvet, Sally, her arms entwined round his neck, whispered, 'I'm warning you, I'm going to make your bed awfully untidy.'

Gabe's eyes softened as they sank down together. 'I'm counting on it.'

'**W**hat's going on?' She walked into Gabe's flat and saw the look on Sally's face. Total, *total* giveaway.

'What?' Sally half laughed in that way people do when they're trying so hard to appear innocent.

'Hey, you're back!' Gabe, emerging from the kitchen with a tea towel slung over one shoulder and a cold beer in his hand, said with delight, 'Come here,' and gave her a smacking kiss on the cheek.

Ha! Confirmation if any was needed. He'd been like a bear with a sore brain for weeks. And now he was kissing her. What's more, the atmosphere in the room was positively zingy.

'We've missed you,' Gabe went on cheerfully—and he definitely hadn't been cheerful for weeks. 'How's your mum?'

'We've talked it all through. I was just asking Sal what's going on.'

'Hmm? In what way?' Now it was Gabe's turn to look innocent, like a six-year-old being asked what had happened to the last Jaffa Cake.

'You and Sally,' said Lola. She narrowed her eyes. 'Shagging.'

'Oh my God!' Sally let out a shriek of disbelief. 'How can you *tell*?'

'OK, three reasons. One,' Lola counted on her fingers, 'Gabe's stopped being a miserable old git. Two, you look so sparkly there's only one thing that can have caused *that*.'

'Sparkly? Do I really?' Sally rushed over to the mirror.

'And three, I bumped into Mr Kowalski on his way out to the paper shop. He happened to mention you'd been making sex on ze stairs.'

'OK, but we weren't actually doing it, not out there on the stairs. I just accidentally dropped my stick.'

Lola was still struggling to take in the news, but in all honesty was not as stunned as she could have been. It was one of those scenarios that was so bizarre it made sense, so wrong it was almost right.

'I know what you're thinking,' said Gabe. 'But I'm crazy about her.'

'She'll drive you mad,' said Lola.

'Probably. OK, definitely.' He slid an arm round Sally's waist. 'But she's been doing that since the day she moved in. I'm used to it now.'

'She's never going to be tidy,' Lola warned.

'We're going to hire a cleaner.' Sally was glowing with happiness.

Lola knew she should be thrilled for them and on one level she was. But at the same time, and she was deeply ashamed to have to admit it even to herself, there was that niggling worry that the balance of the relationship between the three of them was about to tip. Before, the triangle had been more or less equal. Now it was changing shape, lengthening, drawing two of the points closer together and distancing the third. She was going to feel left out and unwanted and—oh God—*lonely* . . .

'Are you worried that we won't have time for you any more?'

Effortlessly reading her mind, Gabe let go of Sally and gave Lola a reassuring hug. 'There's no need, we won't abandon you.'

'Don't be daft, of course I wasn't worried. We're all grown-ups.' Lola submitted happily to the hug; how could she have thought everything wouldn't be fine? 'Ooh, that reminds me, I just saw a sign outside the King's Head—that comedian you love is doing a show there on Saturday night. Johnny thingummy? I thought we could all go.'

She felt Gabe hesitate. Sally exclaimed, 'Oh, what a shame, we'd have loved to, but . . .' She looked over at Gabe to help her out.

'The thing is, we kind of decided to fly over to Dublin,' said Gabe.

*Zooouuuup*, that was the sound of the triangle lengthening.

'You can at least stay for dinner.' Gabe was persuasive, eager to make amends. 'I'm doing a cannelloni.'

Lola smiled, because the last thing they really wanted was a gooseberry sitting at the table. 'It's OK, I've just eaten. And I'm shattered—all I really want is a shower and an early night.'

Which was probably top of their agenda too.

The following evening Nick came round to Lola's flat after work. She was just telling him about Gabe and Sally when there was a tap at the door.

'Hi, come in.' Nick, answering it because he was closest, grinned at Sally and said, 'Congratulations, I've just been hearing your news.'

'Th-thanks.' Sally tucked her hair behind her ears and looked flustered. 'Um, Lola, about this weekend.'

'Is something wrong?' Had their flights been cancelled?

'No, no, it's just that I thought you might be at a bit of a loose end and Doug just called. His company's taken a table at another of those charity dinners and he wanted to know if we'd like to go along. Of course we can't make it, but I wondered if you'd be interested.'

Lola shook her head, not even remotely tempted. 'No, thanks.'

'Oh, go on. It's at the Savoy! On Saturday night!' Sally's eyes were bright, her tone cajoling. 'And there isn't a quiz this time.'

Up until a few weeks ago, Lola knew, she would have leapt at the chance to spend an evening in the same room as Dougie. Just breathing the same air and being able to gaze adoringly at him across the dinner table would have been enough.

But that had been then, when she'd still had hope, and this was now. Besides, Dougie would be there with Isabel doing the adoring bit at his side, leaving her, Lola, stuck at the far end of the table.

'Well?' Sally was still doing her persuasive thing. 'Wouldn't it be fun?'

'I don't think it would be much fun at all. In fact I'd rather boil my own head.'

Nick stood by the mirrored doors at the entrance to the Savoy's Lancaster Ballroom. Everyone had enjoyed an excellent dinner and the babble of voices was deafening. Scanning the room, he spotted Doug Tennant at one of the circular tables close to the stage.

Nick weighed up the situation. Should he be doing what he was about to do? Sod it, why not?

Doug was leaning to one side, laughing at something the girl next to him had just said, when he saw Nick making his way towards the table. Recognising him at once, Doug straightened and said, 'Hello, there. On your own tonight?'

'Yes.'

Doug raised an eyebrow and smiled slightly. 'Don't tell me your daughter's got you following me now.'

'Not at all,' said Nick. 'She doesn't know I'm here.' The blonde girl at his side must be Isabel; oh well, couldn't be helped. Keeping his tone light, he went on, 'Anyway, she's given up on you. You had your chance and you blew it. It's your loss. I just hope you don't live to regret it.'

'Excuse me.' An older woman who'd only just begun paying attention demanded, 'What's going on? Who *is* this man?'

'My name's Nick James. My daughter knows Doug. I just came over to say hello, and to tell him that in my view he's made a big mistake. Sorry,' Nick added, addressing the girl at Doug's side, 'but it's something that needed to be said. I can't help myself; I think she's had a rum deal.'

'Doug?' The older woman was sitting there, stiff-backed like a judge, clearly dissatisfied with the answer. 'Who's this person talking about?'

Doug said flatly, 'Lola.'

'What? Oh, for heaven's sake!' The woman stared at Nick in disbelief. 'You're the father?'

'I am. And you're Doug's mother. How very nice to meet you at last.'

They both knew he didn't mean it. 'And you seriously think my son made a mistake?'

Nick flashed her his most charming smile. 'I do.'

'The only mistake he made was getting himself involved with your daughter in the first place,' Adele flashed back. 'Do you *know* what that girl did to him?'

'Yes, I know exactly what she did. And she made a mistake too, I'm not denying that. But she had her reasons. My point is, we all make mistakes,' said Nick, 'but there's such a thing as forgiveness. I made a huge mistake twenty-eight years ago, but Lola's forgiven me. So has her mother. And we're all here tonight for the same reason. To help people who've made mistakes.' Noting the look of incomprehension on Adele's carefully made-up face he picked up one of the glossy embossed programmes from the table. 'This is a charity dinner in aid of the Prince's Trust. Some of the money raised this evening will go to help former prisoners who are being rehabilitated into the community.'

Adele had clearly only come tonight because of the royal connection.

'Anyway, lecture over. It seems that some people are more easily forgiven than others.' Nick looked at Doug. 'As I've already said, Lola's accepted that you aren't interested and she's moving on. I may not have known her for long but she's an amazing girl, loyal and generous. And I'm proud to be her father.' He paused, then said evenly, 'One last thing. I wonder if you've ever asked yourself why she needed that money?'

Nobody spoke. Up on the stage the MC was preparing to introduce the band.

Nick nodded fractionally at Doug. 'I'll leave you to enjoy the rest of the evening.'

He was upstairs in the bar when Doug appeared beside him twenty minutes later.

'I thought you'd left,' said Doug.

'Just had to get away from that bloody awful music. Not my thing.' Nick signalled to the barman. 'Can I get you a drink?'

'Scotch and water. Thanks. I was rude earlier,' Doug dipped his head, 'and I apologise. I shouldn't have made that remark about Lola sending you here to follow me. That was below the belt.'

'Look,' said Nick, 'I love my daughter to bits, but I can admit that she's done her fair share of chasing after you. Up until a few weeks ago she might well have tried that trick. But it's over now.' He paused, paid for the drinks and said, 'I'm sorry too. It probably wasn't very sensitive of me to say all that stuff in front of everyone.'

Doug smiled slightly, shrugged it off. 'Never mind. It's this business with the money that I'm interested in.'

*Thought you might be.*

'Did you ever ask Lola why she took it?' said Nick.

'Of course I did. She said she couldn't tell me.' Doug waited, took a sip of his drink, then said with a trace of impatience, 'Well? I'm assuming she told you.'

'No. I asked her but she said she could never tell me.'

'Same here.' Doug looked disappointed; he'd clearly thought he'd been about to find out the truth.

'Sorry. But something interesting happened last week. You know Lola never *ever* wanted her mother to find out about the money thing?' Nick waited for Doug to nod before proceeding. 'Well, Blythe *did* find out about it. You can imagine how shocked she was. She called me to tell me about it. She couldn't believe Lola had done such a thing to you.'

'And?' Doug was gazing at him intently.

After a pause, Nick said, 'Blythe asked Lola what she'd spent the money on and Lola told her. A Jeep, apparently. Which was stolen a week later. She hadn't insured it, so that was it, the money was gone.'

'Really? A Jeep?' Doug frowned.

'That's the story.' Nick held his gaze for a long moment before knocking back his Scotch in one go. 'Think about it,' he added, ready to leave and wondering if Doug Tennant was smart enough—*surely*—and cared enough—*hopefully*—to work it out. 'Then ask yourself whether you think the story Lola told her mother was the truth.'

## *Chapter 12*

THE WOMAN PLACING the order rested threadbare elbows on the counter and said, 'It's the most marvellous book, you know. Called *When Miss Denby went to Devon*. By Fidelma Barlow. Have you heard of it?'

'Sorry, no.' Lola typed the details into the computer.

'Oh, it's unputdownable, an absolute joy! I can't understand why it isn't a *Sunday Times* best seller. It deserves to be made into a film!' The woman nodded enthusiastically. 'Miss Denby would be a wonderful role for Dame Judi Dench.'

Lola checked the screen. 'Okaaay, we can get that for you by Friday.'

'Lovely!' The woman's face lit up. 'Can I order fifty copies, please?'

'Fifty! Gosh.' Maybe it was for a book club. Hesitating for a moment, Lola said, 'You have to pay for them in advance, I'm afraid.'

'Oh, no.' The woman shook her head. 'I don't want to pay for them.'

'I know it's a lot of money. But somebody has to.'

'But not me! I just want you to put them on the shelves. Make a nice display like you do with the Richard and Judy books. Right at the front of the shop,' the woman said helpfully, 'so that people will buy them.'

By the time Lola had finished explaining the niceties of stock ordering to a disappointed Fidelma Barlow, it was almost eight o'clock, kicking-out time. Fidelma, shoulders drooping, left the shop. Lola, who knew just how she felt, dispiritedly straightened a pile of bookmarks and wondered if she could bear to go along to the party tonight that Tim and Darren had invited her to.

The next moment she looked up and almost fell over. There, standing six feet away like an honest-to-goodness mirage, was Doug.

Lola's heart, which never listened to her head and hadn't yet learned to stop hoping, went into instantaneous clattery overdrive.

'Hello.' She clutched the computer for support. 'Well, this is a nice surprise! What can I—'

'I'm here because of your dad.'

'You are?' She hadn't been expecting him to say *that*.

'We had a chat on Saturday night.'

'*You did?*'

'He obviously didn't mention it. Well, we were at the Savoy.'

Lola boggled. 'My dad was *there*?'

'Well, we didn't communicate by telepathy. He spoke to me about you. Quite forcefully, in fact.' Doug paused, then glanced over at a nervously hovering Darren who was waiting to empty the till. 'Sorry, could you just give us a couple of minutes?'

'Um, but I need to get the—'

'Darren?' Lola murmured the word out of the corner of her mouth. 'Go away.'

'OK.' Defeated, Darren slunk off.

'I was watching you with that woman just now. The one who wanted you to stock her book,' said Doug. 'You were really nice to her.'

'That's because I'm a really nice person. Believe it or not. And you were eavesdropping.'

'Not eavesdropping. Listening. Like I listened to your dad on Saturday night.' He waited, gazing directly into Lola's eyes. 'I know why you took that money when my mother offered it to you.'

'*What?*' Lola felt as if all the air had been vacuumed out of her lungs. How could he know that? It wasn't physically possible, it just wasn't.

Doug gave an infinitesimal shrug. 'OK, I don't know *exactly* why. But I do know it didn't have anything to do with a Jeep.'

'How? Why not?'

'Because you told me you could never tell me the reason you needed the money. And that's what you said to your father too.' Doug tilted an eyebrow at her. 'But if the Jeep story was true, there's no reason why you couldn't have told us that. Therefore it stands to reason that it wasn't.'

Lola felt dizzy. This was like being cross-examined on the witness stand by a barrister a zillion times cleverer than you. In fact this might be a good moment to faint.

'So basically,' Doug continued, 'you needed the money for something that meant far more to you than a Jeep. It was also something you were determined your mother was never to find out about. Well, there was only one other person on the planet who was that important to you back then.' Pause. 'And that was your stepfather Alex.'

Lola's eyes filled with tears. 'I can't tell you.' Helplessly she shook her head. 'I made a promise.'

'That's OK, I'm not asking you to. No digging.' Doug's voice softened. 'I know who you did it for. I don't need to know why. I didn't understand before, but I do now. That's enough. It's all in the past.'

Was this how Catholics felt when they were absolved of all sin and forgiven by God? Lola, who hated crying in front of people but seemed to have been doing a lot of it lately, could feel the tears rolling faster and faster down her face. She couldn't speak, only nod in a hopeless, all-over-the-place, nodding-doggy kind of way.

'You know, you've been pretty lucky as far as fathers go. First Alex, now Nick. He's so proud of you,' said Doug.

For heaven's sake, how was she supposed to stop crying if he was going to come out with stuff like this? Blindly Lola nodded again and wiped her sleeve across her wet cheeks.

'And he certainly made me think,' Doug went on, 'when he told me I'd missed my chance with you.'

'He said that?' Lola sniffed hard. This was the thing she'd forgotten about fathers; how much they loved to embarrass their daughters.

'And the rest. As if it hasn't been hard enough these past few months, reminding myself why I should be steering clear of you. Then along comes your father giving me all sorts of grief, *then* explaining to me why I should think again. That knocked me for six, I can tell you.'

*As if it hadn't been hard enough these past few months?* Desperate not to be getting this wrong, Lola said, 'So that night when you first saw me again at your mother's house . . . does that mean you didn't hate me after all?'

'Oh, yes, I did. With all my heart. Absolutely and totally.' Doug half smiled, causing her heart to lollop. 'But at the same time the old feelings were still there as well, refusing to go away. Like *you* were refusing to go away. It drove me insane having you back in my life, because I wasn't able to control the way I felt about you. I wanted to be indifferent, to see you and feel nothing. But it wouldn't happen.' He tapped his temple. 'You were in here, whether I liked it or not.'

Lola was trembling now, almost but not quite sure that his coming here tonight was a very good thing. 'Like a tapeworm.'

He looked amused. 'You always did have a way with words.'

'Oh, Dougie, all this time you've been hating me, I've been trying my best to change your mind.' The words came tumbling out in a rush. 'In the end I just had to give up, told myself to stop before I made a complete prat of myself . . . except I already *had*, over and over again . . .'

'I quite enjoyed those bits. I think watching you try to play badminton was my favourite.' He grinned, moved closer to the counter. 'I waited in the bar afterwards, but you didn't turn up.'

'In case you accused me of stalking you again.'

'I'm sorry. I haven't behaved very well either.' Ruefully Doug said, 'I've lied to you, for a start.'

'About what?'

'The photos of us when we were young. Of course I kept them. They're at home, hidden away in a cupboard,' his eyes glinted, 'along with my secret stash of Pot Noodles.'

'I knew it!' Triumphantly Lola said, 'Once a Pot Noodler, always a Pot Noodler. Did Isabel know about this?'

*Ach, Isabel . . .*

'What's wrong?' said Doug when she winced.

'Isabel. Your girlfriend.'

He relaxed. 'She isn't my girlfriend. I finished with her weeks ago. On the night of your dinner party, in fact.'

'What?'

'I smuggled away the photo album. By the time I'd finished looking through the old photos of us, I realised Isabel couldn't compete. I told her I couldn't see her any more and she handed in her notice.'

'Poor Isabel.' Lola did her best to sound as if she meant it.

'She's working in Hong Kong now.' Dougie moved towards Lola.

'Oh, Dougie . . .' It was no good; having a counter between them wasn't helping at all. She came out from behind it and threw herself into his arms.

Oh, yes, this was where she was meant to be. As he kissed her—*at last*—she knew everything was going to be all right.

Despite the odd potential drawback.

When he'd finished kissing her, Dougie smiled and said, 'What are you thinking?'

'That this is one of the happiest moments of my life.' Lola stroked his hair. 'And that your mother's going to be absolutely furious when she hears about this.'

'Don't worry about my mother. After Dad died, she became overprotective of us. When she made you that offer she thought she was doing the right thing. But it's OK, I've had a chat with her. All she wants is for me to be happy, and she accepts that now. She'll be fine.'

God, he was a heavenly kisser; no one else even came close. And there was so much more fantastic stuff to look forward to. Doublechecking that they were out of sight, Lola allowed her hands to start wandering in an adventurous fashion.

'What are you doing?'

'What I've been wanting to do for a long, long time.' She smiled playfully up at him. 'Ever got intimate in a bookshop before?'

Doug surveyed her with amusement. 'Is that a dare?'

Lola gazed into his dark eyes. Then, slowly and deliberately, she reached out and unfastened his belt.

'Shouldn't do that,' Dougie murmured, 'unless you're sure you've got the nerve to go through with it. From start to finish.' He trailed an index finger down her chest until he came to the top button of her shirt. It came undone, exposing the top of her lacy lilac bra.

'Are you calling me chicken?' Lola retaliated by pulling his shirt out of his trousers.

'I think you might lose your nerve.' Deftly he undid the next button on her shirt.

Trembling now, Lola struggled with the fastening on his trousers. 'I think you know me better than that. If I say I'm going to do something, I'll—*aaarrgh!*'

'Lola?' The door at the back of the shop opened and Tim poked his head round. 'Oh, sorry!' His eyes popped as he realised what he was interrupting.

'I thought you'd all left!' Flustered, Lola clapped both hands over her exposed bra.

'Everyone else has. I'm just off now. I wondered if you'd made up your mind yet about coming along to the party.'

Hmm, have sex with Dougie or go to a party with Tim and Darren. That was a tricky one.

'Um . . . I don't think so, Tim. But, thanks, anyway.'

'OK.' Hardly knowing where to look, Tim backed away. 'Well, have a . . . nice time.'

Lola nodded and somehow managed to keep a straight face. When the door had closed behind Tim, she looked at Dougie and said, 'OK, now I've lost my nerve.'

'Thank God for that.' Doug smiled his crooked smile and tucked his shirt back into his trousers.

'So, your flat or mine?'

He raised an eyebrow. 'I have Pot Noodles.'

Giddy with joy, Lola made herself decent. 'That settles it then. A nice time followed by Pot Noodles.'

Dougie put his arm round her. 'Who could ask for more?'

# Jill Mansell

**What is your routine when sitting down to write for the day?**

I write my books by hand, using a fabulous Harley Davidson fountain pen and Pukka Pads. I sit on the sofa in our living room and have the TV on while I work, although I could never listen to the radio or play music, that would be far too intrusive. I watch *This Morning* with Fern and Phil and pinch ideas for my books from their programme. I also get through rather a lot of crisps, fruit gums and cups of coffee. I work while my children are at school, and periodically take chunks of the completed manuscript to my typist, who deciphers my handwriting. My late mum used to type my novels for me, which is why there was never any explicit sex in them. Now my daughter's friends all read my books so there's still no explicit sex in them! And my daughter flatly refuses to read them at all because it's too embarrassing. Every time I ask her to look at a page, she sees one of my characters saying something I say or, worse, something she says.

**In *An Offer You Can't Refuse* Adele Tennant pays Lola to break up with her son. Where did this idea come from?**

Well, I never received an offer like that, unfortunately, though obviously this kind of thing has happened before in fiction and in films. But it always seemed to me that it was the unsuitable, baddie boyfriend who got paid off. And I thought, how about if it was somebody nice who was offered a pay-off? Someone who had a very good reason to take the money? That way, I could turn the original idea on its head.

**You have a son and a daughter. Would you ever contemplate paying off an unsuitable girlfriend/boyfriend of theirs?**

Do you know, it might be an idea in years to come. I'd better start saving.

**What would you buy if you visited the Cod Almighty fish-and-chip shop?**
Curry sauce and chips. I love curry sauce, especially the thick gloopy kind you get in fish-and-chip shops!

**Have you ever had any bad experiences at a book signing?**
When I first started writing I remember sitting there with people asking me the way to the toilets. Or they would come up and chat and not buy anything. But earlier this year I did some in Holland. My first thoughts were: Oh no, it's going to be a nightmare, it's going to be embarrassing, no one's going to turn up. But it was absolutely wonderful. Hundreds of people came. It was incredible. They brought me flowers, presents and I had my photo taken non-stop—I felt like Robbie Williams!

**Is it still a thrill to see your books in the shops?**
Yes, a massive thrill that never fades. I move them to the front too. If any writer tells you they don't do this, they are not telling the truth.

**To what extent have your own life experiences influenced your writing?**
I must use my life experiences while writing, but I'm not conscious of doing so. Knowing how something feels, and imagining how it might feel, all comes from the same place. Having said that, I will, of course, shamelessly recycle my own past experiences of growing up: dating disastrously, lusting after men and not getting them, getting them and then going off them, marriage, divorce, secretly giving birth to George Clooney's lovechild—oh sorry, that one hasn't happened yet—see what I mean about the lines between fantasy and reality becoming blurred?

**In the novel, Lola goes to her work's fancy-dress party dressed as a rabbit. What's the worst fancy-dress outfit you've ever had to wear?**
The last fancy-dress party I went to was when I worked at Burden Neurological Hospital. Everyone dressed up rather glam and sexy—waitress with a very short skirt, naughty schoolgirl—I went dressed as a convict with arrows all over my face and outfit. I looked ridiculous. The time before I went as a witch and nobody recognised me because my face was covered in green paint!

**Are you super-tidy like Gabe in the story or super-messy like Sally?**
Definitely super-messy like Sally. Though I'm much better than I was as a teenager. I guess by the time I'm ninety I might be almost decent.

**Picture the scene: you are having a 'duvet day' on the sofa and can choose three films to watch. What would you choose?**
A 'duvet day' sounds like my every day! Has to be *Four Weddings and a Funeral*, *When Harry Met Sally* and *The Great Escape*—I never get tired of that one. I always hope that Steve McQueen will get away at the end.

**What's the best thing about being a writer?**
In the old days, my general untidiness and aversion to housework meant I was a lazy slut. Now I'm allowed to be untidy because I'm a writer.

**Will you ever stop writing?**
What, and have to start doing housework all over again? No chance.

*Jane Eastgate*

# The Memory
# Keeper's Daughter

## KIM EDWARDS

On a freezing night in March 1964, with snow falling thickly on Lexington, Kentucky, Dr David Henry finds himself unexpectedly delivering his beautiful young wife of their first child. But joy turns to grief when a heart-rending discovery leads him to make a decision that will change the course of his life, and that of his family, for ever.

# March 1964

# I

THE SNOW STARTED TO FALL several hours before her labour began. A few flakes first, in the dull grey late-afternoon sky, and then wind-driven eddies around the edges of their wide front porch. He stood by her side at the window, watching sharp gusts of snow billow, then swirl and drift to the ground. All around the neighbourhood, lights came on, and the naked branches of the trees turned white.

After dinner he built a fire, venturing out into the weather for wood he had piled against the garage the previous autumn. The air was bright and cold against his face, and the snow in the driveway was already halfway to his knees. He gathered logs, shaking off their soft white caps and carrying them inside. The kindling in the iron grate caught fire immediately, and he sat for a time on the hearth, watching the flames leap, blue-edged and hypnotic. Outside, snow continued to fall quietly through the darkness, as bright and thick as static in the cones of light cast by the streetlights. By the time he rose and looked out of the window, their car had become a soft white hill on the edge of the street.

He brushed ashes from his hands and sat on the sofa beside his wife, her feet propped on pillows, her swollen ankles crossed, a copy of *Dr Spock* balanced on her belly. Watching her read, he felt a surge of love and wonder: that she was his wife, that their baby, due in just three weeks, would soon be born. Their first child, this would be. They had been married just a year.

She looked up, smiling, when he tucked the blanket round her legs.

'You know, I've been wondering what it's like,' she said. 'Before we're born, I mean. Do you suppose it's like being inside a great lantern? The book says light permeates my skin, that the baby can already see.'

'I don't know,' he said.

She laughed. 'Why not?' she asked. 'You're the doctor.'

'I'm just an orthopaedic surgeon,' he reminded her. 'I could tell you the ossification pattern for foetal bones, but that's about it.' He lifted her foot, both delicate and swollen inside the light blue sock, and began to massage it gently. Her breathing filled the quiet room, her foot warmed his hands, and he imagined the perfect, secret symmetry of bones. In pregnancy she seemed to him beautiful but fragile, fine blue veins faintly visible through her pale white skin.

She was eleven years younger than he was. He had first seen her not much more than a year ago, as she rode up an escalator in a department store downtown. He was thirty-three years old and new to Lexington, Kentucky, and she had risen out of the crowd like some kind of vision, her blonde hair swept back in an elegant chignon, pearls glimmering at her throat and on her ears. She was wearing a coat of dark green wool and her skin was clear and pale. He stepped onto the escalator, pushing his way upwards, struggling to keep her in sight. She went to the fourth floor, lingerie and hosiery. When he tried to follow her through aisles dense with racks of slips and brassieres and panties, a sales assistant in a navy-blue dress stopped him, smiling, to ask if she could help.

'A robe,' he said, scanning the aisles until he caught sight of her hair. 'A robe for my sister who lives in New Orleans.' He had no sister, of course, or any living family that he acknowledged.

The assistant disappeared and came back with three robes in sturdy towelling. He chose blindly, hardly glancing down, taking the one on top. Three sizes, the assistant was saying, but he was already in the aisle, a coral-coloured robe draped over his arm, moving impatiently to where she stood.

She was shuffling through the stacks of expensive stockings, sheer colours shining through slick cellophane windows. The sleeve of her green coat brushed his and he smelt her perfume, delicate and yet pervasive, like the dense pale petals of lilacs outside the grimy windows of the basement rooms he'd once occupied when a student in Pittsburgh.

He cleared his throat and held up the towelling robe, but the assistant behind the counter was laughing, telling a joke, and she did not notice him. When he cleared his throat again she glanced at him, annoyed, then nodded at her customer, now holding three packages of stockings like giant playing cards in her hand.

'I'm afraid Miss Asher was here first,' the assistant said.

Their eyes met then, and he was startled to see they were the same dark green as her coat. She was taking him in—the tweed overcoat, his face clean-shaven and flushed with cold. She smiled, amused and faintly dismissive, gesturing to the robe on his arm.

'For your wife?' she asked. She spoke with what he recognised as a genteel Kentucky accent, in this city of old money where such distinctions mattered. After just six months in town, he already knew this. 'It's all right, Jean,' she went on, turning back to the assistant. 'Take him first. This poor man must feel lost in here with all the lace.'

'It's for my sister,' he told her, desperate to reverse the bad impression he was making. The robe slipped to the floor and he bent to pick it up, his face flushing as he rose. His discomfort seemed to soften her, for when he met her eyes again, they were kind.

He tried again. 'I'm sorry. I don't seem to know what I'm doing. And I'm in a hurry. I'm a doctor. I'm late to the hospital.'

Her smile changed then, grew serious. 'I see.' She turned back to the assistant. 'Really, Jean, do take him first.'

She agreed to see him again, writing her name and phone number in the perfect script she'd been taught in third grade, her teacher an ex-nun who had engraved the rules of penmanship in her small charges. Eight years old, pale and skinny, the woman in the green coat who would become his wife had clenched her small fingers round the pen and practised cursive writing alone in her room, hour after hour, until she wrote with the exquisite fluidity of running water. Later, listening to that story, he would wonder at her tenacity. But on that day he did not know any of this. On that day he carried the slip of paper in the pocket of his white coat through one sickroom after another, remembering her letters flowing one into another to form the perfect shape of her name. He phoned her that same evening and took her to dinner the next night, and three months later they were married.

Now, in these last weeks of her pregnancy, the soft coral robe fitted her perfectly. She had found it packed away and had held it up to show him. 'But your sister died so long ago,' she exclaimed, puzzled.

He shrugged, sheepish. 'I had to say something,' he told her. 'I had to find a way to get your name.'

She smiled then, and crossed the room and embraced him.

The snow fell. For the next few hours, they read and talked. Then, at eleven, she rose and went to bed. He stayed downstairs, reading the latest issue of *The Journal of Bone and Joint Surgery*. He was known to be a very good doctor, with a talent for diagnosis and a reputation for skilful work. He had graduated first in his class. Still, he was young enough and—though he hid it very carefully—unsure enough about his skills that he studied in every spare moment. He felt himself to be an aberration, born with a love for learning in a family absorbed in simply scrambling to get by, day to day. When they went to the doctor at all it was to the clinic in Morgantown, fifty miles away. His memories of those rare trips were vivid, bouncing in the back of the borrowed pick-up truck. The dancing road, his sister had called it, from her place in the cab with their parents. In Morgantown the rooms were dim and the doctors had been hurried, distracted.

All these years later, he still had moments when he sensed the gaze of those doctors and felt himself to be an impostor, about to be unmasked by a single mistake. He knew his choice of specialities reflected this. Not for him the random excitement of general medicine or the delicate, risky plumbing of the heart. He dealt mostly with broken limbs, sculpting casts and viewing X-rays, watching breaks slowly yet miraculously knit themselves back together. Bones would last; it was easy for him to put his faith in something so solid and predictable.

He read well past midnight, until the words shimmered senselessly on the bright pages, then he tossed the journal on the coffee table and got up to tend to the fire. He tamped the charred logs into embers, opened the damper and closed the brass screen, then turned off the lights.

The stairs creaked with his weight. He paused by the nursery door, studying the shadowy shapes of the crib and the changing table, the stuffed animals arranged on shelves. His wife had made the Mother Goose quilt that hung on the far wall, sewing with tiny stitches, tearing out entire panels if she noted the slightest imperfection.

On an impulse he went into the room and stood before the window, pushing aside the sheer curtain to watch the snow, now nearly eight inches high on the lampposts, on the fences and the roofs. It was the sort of storm that rarely happened in Lexington, and the steady white flakes, the silence, filled him with a sense of excitement and peace. He stood there for a long time, until he heard her moving quietly. He found her sitting on their bed, her head bent, her hands gripping the mattress.

'I think this is labour,' she said, looking up. 'I don't know. I feel strange. This crampy feeling, it comes and goes.'

He helped her lie down on her side and then he lay down too, massaging her back. 'It's probably just false labour,' he assured her. 'It's three weeks early, after all, and first babies are usually late.'

This was true, he knew, he believed it as he spoke, and he was, in fact, so sure of it that after a time he drifted into sleep. He woke to find her standing over the bed, shaking his shoulder.

'I've been timing them. Five minutes apart. They're strong.'

He felt a surge, then, of excitement and fear. But he had been trained to be calm in emergencies, to keep his emotions in check. When the contractions came she squeezed his hand so hard he felt as if the bones in his fingers might fuse. He took the suitcase from the closet, feeling numb with the momentousness of these events. When he took her arm he felt strangely as if he himself were suspended in the room, watching them both from above, noting every nuance and detail.

He helped her into her green woollen coat, which hung unbuttoned, gaping around her belly. They stood together on the porch for a moment, stunned by the soft white world.

'Wait here,' he said, and went down the steps, breaking a path through the drifts. The doors of the old car were frozen and it took him several minutes to get one open. A white cloud flew up, glittering, when the door at last swung back, and he scrambled on the floor of the back seat for the ice scraper and brush. When he emerged his wife was leaning against a porch pillar, her forehead on her arms. He understood in that moment both how much pain she was in and that the baby was really coming, coming that very night. He resisted a powerful urge to go to her and, instead, put all his energy into freeing the car, brushing snow from the windshield and the windows.

'You didn't mention it would hurt this much,' she said when he reached the porch. He put his arm round her shoulders and helped her down the steps. 'I can walk,' she insisted.

'I know,' he said, but he did not let her go.

When they reached the car she touched his arm and gestured to the house, veiled with snow and glowing like a lantern in the darkness.

'When we come back we'll have our baby with us,' she said. 'Our world will never be the same.'

The windshield wipers were frozen, and snow spilled down the back window when he pulled into the street. He drove slowly, thinking how beautiful Lexington was, the trees and bushes so heavy with snow. Now and then he wiped at the windshield with the back of his hand, leaning to peer through the hole he'd made. 'I called Bentley before we left,' he said, naming his colleague, an obstetrician. 'I said to meet us at the office. We'll go there. It's closer.'

She was silent for a moment, her hand gripping the dashboard as she breathed through a contraction. 'As long as I don't have my baby in this old car,' she managed at last, trying to joke.

He smiled, but he knew her fear was real, and he shared it.

Methodical, purposeful: even in an emergency he could not change his nature. He came to a full stop at every light, signalled turns to the empty streets. Every few minutes she braced one hand against the dashboard again and focused her breathing, which made him swallow and glance sideways at her, more nervous on that night than he could ever remember being. More nervous than in his first anatomy class.

More nervous than on his wedding day, her family filling one side of the church, and on the other just a handful of his colleagues. His parents were dead, and so was his sister.

There was a single car in the clinic parking lot, the nurse's powder-blue Ford Fairlane. He'd called her, too. He pulled up in front of the entrance and helped his wife out. They were both exhilarated to have reached the office safely, laughing as they pushed into the waiting room.

The nurse met them. The moment he saw her, he knew something was wrong. She had large blue eyes in a pale face that might have been forty or twenty-five, and whenever something was not to her liking a thin vertical line formed across her forehead. It was there now as she gave them her news: Bentley's car had skidded off the road, into a ditch.

'You're saying Dr Bentley won't be coming?' his wife asked.

The nurse nodded. She was tall and angular, her large eyes solemn and intelligent. For months, there had been rumours, jokes, that she was in love with him. He had dismissed them as idle office gossip, annoying but natural when a man and a single woman worked in such close proximity, day after day. And then one evening he had fallen asleep at his desk. He'd been dreaming, back in his childhood home. His sister, aged five, sat holding a doll in one listless hand. A passing image that filled him with sadness and yearning. The house was his but empty now, deserted when his sister died and his parents moved away, the rooms filled only with the rustlings of squirrels and mice.

He'd had tears in his eyes when he opened them, raising his head from the desk. The nurse was standing in the doorway, her face gentled by emotion. Their eyes met, and it seemed to the doctor that he knew her—that they knew each other—in some profound and certain way. It was an intimacy of such magnitude that he was motionless, transfixed. Then she blushed severely and looked aside. For many days, her eyes would not meet his.

After that, when people teased him about her, he made them stop. 'She's a very fine nurse,' he would say, holding up one hand against the jokes, honouring that moment of communion they had shared. 'She's the best I've ever worked with.' This was true, and now he was very glad to have her with him.

'How about the hospital?' she asked. 'Could you make it?'

The doctor shook his head. 'This baby won't wait.'

'It's all right,' his wife said, stoic. 'This will be a better story to tell him, growing up—him or her.'

The nurse smiled. 'Let's get you inside, then,' she said. 'Let's get you some help with the pain.'

He went into his own office to find a coat, and when he entered

Bentley's examination room his wife was lying on the bed. He went to the sink and washed his hands.

'Everything's progressing,' the nurse said when he turned. 'I'd put her at ten centimetres; see what you think.'

He sat on the low stool and reached up into the soft warm cave of his wife's body. The amniotic sac was still intact, and through it he could feel the baby's head, smooth and hard like a baseball.

'Yes,' he said, 'ten centimetres.'

'Phoebe,' his wife said. He could not see her face, but her voice was clear. They had been discussing names for months and had reached no decisions. 'For a girl, Phoebe. And for a boy, Paul, after my great-uncle. I meant to tell you I'd decided.'

'Those are good names,' the nurse said, soothing.

'Phoebe and Paul,' the doctor repeated, but he was concentrating on the contraction now rising in his wife's flesh. He gestured to the nurse, who readied the gas. His wife tensed and cried out, and the baby moved in the birth canal, bursting the amniotic sac.

'Now,' the doctor said, and the nurse put the mask in place. His wife's hands relaxed, her fists unclenching as the gas took effect, and she lay still as another contraction moved through her.

'It's coming fast for a first baby,' the nurse observed.

'Yes,' the doctor said. 'So far so good.'

Half an hour passed in this way. His wife roused and moaned and pushed, and when he felt she had had enough—or when she cried out that the pain was overwhelming—he nodded to the nurse, who gave her the gas. Except for the quiet exchange of instructions, they did not speak. The doctor had delivered five babies during medical school, all live births and all successful, and he focused now on those, seeking in his memory the details of care. It was necessary, more necessary than usual, to keep his emotions in check. As time passed, the strange moment he had experienced in their bedroom came to him again. He began to feel as if he were somehow removed from the scene of this birth, observing from some safe distance. He watched himself make the careful, precise incision for the episiotomy. A good one, he thought.

The head crowned. In three more pushes it emerged, and then the body slid into his waiting hands and the baby cried out.

It was a boy, red-faced and dark-haired, his eyes alert, suspicious of the lights and the cold bright slap of air. The doctor tied the umbilical cord and cut it. My son, he allowed himself to think. *My son.*

'He's beautiful,' the nurse said. She waited while he examined the child, noting his steady heart, rapid and sure, the long-fingered hands and shock of dark hair. Then she took the infant to the other room to bathe him and to drop the silver nitrate into his eyes. The small cries drifted back to them, and his wife stirred.

'Where is the baby?' she asked. 'Is everything all right?'

'It's a boy,' the doctor replied, smiling down at her. 'We have a son. You'll see him as soon as he's clean. He's absolutely perfect.'

His wife's face, soft with relief and exhaustion, suddenly tightened with another contraction, and the doctor, expecting the afterbirth, pressed lightly against her abdomen. She cried out, and at the same moment he understood what was happening, as startled as if a window had appeared suddenly in a concrete wall.

'It's all right,' he said. 'Everything's fine. Nurse,' he called, as the next contraction tightened.

She came at once, carrying the baby, now swaddled in blankets.

'He's a nine on the Apgar,' she announced. 'That's very good.'

His wife lifted her arms for the baby and began to speak, but then the pain caught her and she lay back down.

'Nurse?' the doctor said. 'I need you here. Right now.'

After a moment's confusion the nurse put two pillows on the floor, placed the baby on them, and joined the doctor by the table.

'More gas,' he said. He saw her surprise and then her quick nod of comprehension as she complied.

'Twins?' the nurse asked.

The doctor, who had allowed himself to relax after the boy was born, felt shaky now, and he did not trust himself to do more than nod.

This baby was smaller and came easily, sliding quickly into his gloved hands. 'It's a girl,' he said, and cradled her, face down, tapping her back until she cried out. Then he turned her over to see her face.

The blue eyes were cloudy, the hair jet black, but he barely noticed. What he was looking at were the unmistakable features, the eyes turned up as if with laughter, the epicanthic fold across their lids, the flattened nose. 'A classic case,' he remembered his professor saying as they examined a similar child, years ago. 'A mongoloid. Do you know what that means?' And the doctor, dutiful, had recited the symptoms he'd memorised from the text: flaccid muscle tone, delayed growth and mental development, possible heart complications, early death. The professor had nodded. 'Poor kid. There's nothing they can do except try to keep him clean. They ought to spare themselves and send him to a home.'

The doctor had felt transported back in time. His sister had been born with a heart defect and had grown very slowly, her breath catching and coming in little gasps whenever she tried to run. For many years, until the first trip to the clinic in Morgantown, they had not known what was the matter. Then they knew, and there was nothing they could do. All his mother's attention had gone to her, and yet she had died when she was twelve years old. The doctor had been sixteen, already living in town to attend high school, already on his way to Pittsburgh and medical school and the life he was living now. Still, he remembered the depth and endurance of his mother's grief, the way she walked uphill to the grave every morning.

The nurse, beside him, studied the baby. 'I'm sorry, Doctor,' she said.

He held the infant, forgetting what he ought to do next. He imagined her heart, the size of a plum and very possibly defective, and he thought of his wife standing before their brightly veiled home, saying, 'Our world will never be the same.'

The baby's hand brushed his and he started. Without volition he began to move through the familiar patterns. He cut the cord and checked her heart, her lungs. Later, when he considered this night— the turning point of his life, the moments around which everything else would always gather—what he remembered was a silence so deep and encompassing that he felt himself floating to a new height, to some point above this room and then beyond, where this scene was something unfolding in a different life, as though glimpsed through a warmly lit window by someone walking on a darkened street.

'All right. Clean her up, please,' he said, releasing the slight weight of the infant into the nurse's arms. 'But keep her in the other room. I don't want my wife to know. Not right away.'

The nurse nodded. She disappeared and then came back to lift his son into the baby carrier they'd brought. The doctor was by then intent on delivering the placentas. Fraternal twins, male and female, one visibly perfect and the other marked by an extra chromosome in every cell of her body. What were the odds of that? He injected his wife with a sedative, then leaned down to repair the episiotomy. It was nearly dawn, light gathering faintly in the windows.

When the doctor finished, he found the nurse sitting in a rocker in the waiting room, cradling the baby girl in her arms. She met his gaze without speaking.

'There's a place,' he said, writing the name and address on the back of an envelope. 'I'd like you to take her there. When it's light, I mean. I'll issue the birth certificate and I'll call to say you're coming.'

'But your wife,' the nurse said, and he heard, from his distant place, the surprise and disapproval in her voice.

He thought of his sister, pale and thin, trying to catch her breath, and his mother turning to the window to hide her tears.

'Don't you see?' he asked. 'This poor child will most likely have a serious heart defect. I'm trying to spare us all a terrible grief.'

He spoke with conviction. He believed his own words. He did not imagine, as he would later that night, and in many nights to come, the ways in which he was jeopardising everything.

The nurse studied him with her blue, unreadable eyes. At last she nodded. 'The snow,' she murmured, looking down.

But by midmorning the storm had begun to abate, and the distant sounds of ploughs grated through the still air. He watched from the upstairs window as the nurse knocked snow from her powder-blue car and drove off into the soft white world. The baby was asleep in a box lined with blankets, on the seat beside her.

In the late morning, when the snow had stopped for good, the doctor's son cried out in hunger, and his wife woke up.

'Where's the baby?' she asked, rising up on her elbows, pushing her hair from her face.

He sat down beside her, settling the baby in her arms. 'Hello, my sweet,' he said. 'Look at our beautiful son. You were very brave.'

She kissed the baby's forehead, then undid her robe and put him to her breast. As he latched on, she looked up and smiled. He took her free hand, remembering how much he wanted to protect her.

'Is everything all right?' she asked. 'Darling? What is it?'

'We had twins,' he told her slowly, thinking of the shocks of dark hair, the slippery bodies moving in his hands. 'One of each.'

'Oh,' she said. 'A little girl too? Phoebe *and* Paul. But where is she?'

Her fingers were so slight, he thought, like the bones of a little bird.

'Oh, my love,' he said. His voice broke, and the words he had rehearsed were gone. When he could speak again, more words came, unplanned. 'I am so sorry. Our little daughter died as she was born.'

# II

CAROLINE GILL WADED carefully, awkwardly, across the parking lot. Snow reached her calves; in places, her knees. She carried the baby, swathed in blankets, in a cardboard box once used to deliver samples of infant formula to the office. It was stamped with red letters and cherubic faces, and the flaps lifted and fell with every step. Snow billowed, stinging her face, when she opened the car door. Instinctively, protectively, she curved herself round the box and wedged it into the back seat. The baby slept, a fierce, intent, newborn sleep, its face clenched.

The city streets were badly ploughed and difficult to navigate. Twice the car slid, and twice Caroline almost turned back. The interstate was clearer, however, and once Caroline got onto it she made steady time, travelling through the industrial outskirts of Lexington and into the rolling country of the horse farms.

Since the moment she had let her head dip in faint agreement to Dr Henry's astonishing request, Caroline had felt as if she were falling through the air in slow motion, waiting to hit land and discover where she was. What he had asked of her—that she take his infant daughter away without telling his wife of her birth—seemed unspeakable. But Caroline had been moved by the pain and confusion on his face as he examined his daughter, by the slow, numb way he seemed to move thereafter. Soon he'd come to his senses, she told herself.

She drove faster, images of the early morning running through her like a current. She crested the slight hill and began the long descent to the river far below. Behind her, in the cardboard box, the baby slept on. Caroline glanced over her shoulder now and then, both reassured and distressed to see it had not moved. Such sleep, she reminded herself, was normal after the labour of entering the world. She wondered about her own birth, but both her parents were long dead; there was no one who remembered those moments. Her mother had been past forty when Caroline was born, her father already fifty-two. They had long since given up waiting for a child. Their lives were orderly, content.

Until Caroline, startlingly, had arrived, a flower blooming up through snow.

They had loved her, certainly, but it had been a worried love, earnest and intent, layered with poultices and warm socks and castor oil. In the hot still summers, when polio was feared, Caroline had been made to stay inside, sweat beading on her temples as she stretched out on the day bed by the window on the landing, reading. Outside, the landscape shimmered in the light and heat, and children from the neighbourhood, whose parents were younger and thus less acquainted with the possibility of disaster, shouted to one another in the distance.

She was crossing the bridge now, the Kentucky River meandering far below. She glanced again at the baby. Surely Norah Henry would want to hold this child, even if she couldn't keep her?

Surely this was none of Caroline's affair.

She turned on the radio, found a station of classical music.

Twenty miles outside Louisville, Caroline consulted Dr Henry's directions, written in his sharp, close hand, and left the highway. Here, so near the Ohio River, the upper branches of hawthorns and hack-berry trees glittered with ice, though the roads were clear and dry. Soon, across a mile of pale hills, Caroline glimpsed the building, built of red brick at the turn of the century. It disappeared as she followed the curves and dips of the country road, then was suddenly before her.

She pulled into the circular driveway. Up close, the old house was in a state of mild disrepair. Paint was peeling on the wood trim and on the second floor a window had been boarded up. Caroline got out of the car. She slung the bag she had prepared—containing diapers, a Thermos bottle of warmed formula—over her shoulder, picked up the box with the baby and entered the building. A strip of threadbare carpet led across the foyer's wide-planked floor to a waiting room at the back of the house with tall windows and heavy draperies. She sat on the edge of a worn velvet sofa, the box close by her side, and waited.

The room was overheated. She unbuttoned her coat. She was still wearing her white nurse's uniform, and when she touched her hair she realised she was still wearing her sharp white cap, too. Above her, foot-steps moved and echoed. She closed her eyes.

'I need you here. Right now,' Dr Henry had called. And Caroline had hurried, fashioning that awkward bed out of pillows, holding the mask on Mrs Henry's face as the second twin, this little girl, slid into the world, setting something into motion.

Into motion. Yes, it could not be contained. Even sitting here in the stillness of this place, even waiting, Caroline was troubled by the feeling that the world was shimmering, that things would not be still. *This?* was the refrain in her mind. *This now, after all these years?*

For Caroline Gill was thirty-one, and she had been waiting a long time for her real life to begin. She had felt since childhood that her life would not be ordinary. A moment would come—she would know it when she saw it—and everything would change. In her twenties, as her friends from nursing school began to marry and have their families, Caroline too had found young men to admire. For a dreamy time she imagined that one of them would transform her life. When years passed she gradually turned her attention to her work.

She read, too, Pearl Buck's novels first and then everything she could find about life in China, Burma and Laos. She pictured herself moving through another life: an exotic, difficult, satisfying one. Her clinic would be simple, perhaps set in a lush jungle. People would line up outside and she would heal them all. She would transform their lives and hers.

Consumed by this vision, she had applied to become a medical mis-sionary. One brilliant late-summer weekend, she had taken the bus to St Louis to be interviewed. Her name was put on a waiting list for

Korea. But time passed; the mission was postponed, then cancelled altogether. Caroline was put on another list, this time for Burma.

And then, while she was still checking the mail, Dr Henry had arrived. It was late autumn by then, a season of colds, and the waiting room was crowded. Caroline herself could feel a dull scratching deep in her throat as she called the next patient, an elderly gentleman whose cold would worsen in the next weeks, turning into the pneumonia that would finally kill him. Rupert Dean. When he reached the desk he handed Caroline a photograph in a dark blue cardboard frame. The woman looking out wore a pale peach sweater. Rupert Dean's wife, Emelda, dead now for twenty years. 'She was the love of my life,' he announced to Caroline, his voice so loud that people looked up.

'She's lovely,' Caroline said. Her hands were trembling. Because she was almost thirty years old, and yet if she died the next day there would be no one to mourn her. Surely she, Caroline Gill, must be as deserving of love as the woman in the old man's photo?

She was still trying to compose herself when the door to the waiting room swung open. A man in a brown tweed overcoat hesitated in the doorway. He had brown hair with a reddish tinge and his face was lean, his expression attentive, assessing. Caroline's heart quickened. His eyes caught hers—and she knew. Before he crossed the room to shake her hand, before he opened his mouth to speak his name, 'David Henry,' in a neutral accent that placed him as an outsider. Before all this, Caroline was sure of a single simple fact: the person she'd been waiting for had come.

He had not been married then. Not married, not engaged and with no attachments that she could ascertain. Caroline listened carefully and heard what others, distracted by his unfamiliar accent, did not: that aside from mentioning his time in Pittsburgh now and then, he never made reference to the past. For Caroline, this reticence gave him an air of mystery, and the mystery increased her sense that she knew him in ways the others did not. When she overheard people joking about her crush on the new doctor, she was secretly pleased, for the rumours might reach him in a way that she, with her shyness, could not.

One late evening, she had found him, with his head resting on his hands, sleeping at his desk. In that moment the dreams Caroline had nurtured for years had all coalesced. They would go together, she and Dr Henry, to some remote place in the world, where they would work all day with sweat rising on their foreheads, and where of an evening she would play to him on the piano that would be sent across the sea and the lush land to where they lived. Caroline was so immersed in this dream that when Dr Henry opened his eyes she smiled at him openly.

His obvious surprise brought her to herself. She touched her hair, murmured some apology, blushed deep red. She disappeared, mortified but also faintly thrilled. For now he must know, now he would see her at last as she saw him.

Three weeks later, Caroline had opened the newspaper to find the wedding photo on the society page: Norah Asher, now Mrs David Henry, caught with her head turned, her neck elegant.

Caroline started, sweating in her coat. The waiting room was over-heated; she had almost drifted off. Beside her, the baby still slept. She stood and walked to the windows. Velvet drapes brushed the floor, remnants from the far-flung time when this place had been elegant. She touched the edge of the net curtains beneath; yellow, brittle, they billowed dust. Outside, half a dozen cows stood in the snowy field.

Caroline let the curtains fall and walked out of the room, moving towards the sound of human voices. She entered a hallway, fluorescent lights humming against the high ceiling. The air was thick with cleaning fluid, steamed vegetables, the faint odour of urine. Carts rattled; voices called and murmured. She passed several doors, glimpsing moments of people's lives: a man staring out of a window, his face cast in shadows; two nurses making a bed; a young woman wearing a white cotton slip sitting on the edge of a bed, her head bent. Another woman, a nurse, standing behind her, silver scissors flashing. Hair cascading darkly onto the white sheets. Caroline paused in the doorway.

'She's cold,' she heard herself saying, causing both women to look up. The woman on the bed had large eyes, darkly luminous in her face. Her hair, once quite long, now jutted raggedly at the level of her chin.

'Yes,' the nurse said, and reached to brush some hair off the woman's shoulder. 'But it had to be done.' Her eyes narrowed then as she studied Caroline's wrinkled uniform. 'Are you new here?' she asked.

Caroline nodded. 'New,' she said. 'That's right.'

The hair was scattered, irretrievable, and the cold light fell through the window. She felt tears in her eyes. Voices echoed in another hall, and Caroline remembered the baby, left sleeping in a box on the over-stuffed velvet sofa of the waiting room. She turned and hurried back.

Everything was just as she had left it. The box with its cheerful red cherubs was still on the sofa; the baby, her hands curled into small fists by her chin, was still sleeping. *Phoebe*, Norah Henry had said, just before she went under from the gas. *For a girl, Phoebe.*

Phoebe. Caroline unfolded the blankets gently and lifted her. She was so tiny, five and a half pounds, smaller than her brother, though with the same rich dark hair. Caroline changed her diaper and wrapped her back up, then she put the still-sleeping baby back into the box and tucked the blankets lightly around her.

There were footsteps, drawing nearer, and then a woman with grey hair and a white uniform very much like Caroline's stood in the doorway. She was solidly built, agile for her size, no-nonsense.

'Can I help you?' she asked. 'Have you been waiting long?'

'Yes,' Caroline said slowly. 'I've been waiting for a long time, yes.'

The woman, exasperated, shook her head. 'Yes, I'm sorry. It's the snow. We're short-staffed today because of it. What can I do for you?'

'Are you Sylvia?' Caroline asked, struggling to remember the name on the back of the envelope, below the directions. 'Sylvia Patterson?'

The woman's expression grew annoyed. 'No. I am not. I'm Janet Masters. Sylvia no longer works here.'

'Oh,' Caroline said, and then stopped. This woman didn't know who she was; clearly, she hadn't talked with Dr Henry.

Janet Masters planted her hands firmly on her hips and her eyes narrowed. 'Are you here from that formula company?' she asked, nodding across the room to the box on the sofa, the red cherubs smiling benignly. 'Sylvia had something going with that rep, we all knew that, and if you're from the same company you can just pack up your things and go.'

'I don't know what you mean,' Caroline said. 'But I'll just go,' she added. 'I won't bother you again.'

Janet Masters wasn't finished. 'Insidious, that's what you people are. Dropping off free samples and then sending a bill for them. This may be a home for the feeble-minded, but it isn't run by them, you know.'

'I know,' Caroline whispered. 'I'm truly sorry.'

'See that you're out of here in five minutes,' the woman said. 'Out of here and don't come back.' Then she was gone.

Caroline stared at the empty doorway, then she felt in her pocket for her keys. Quickly, before she could think about what she was doing, she picked up the box with Phoebe in it, went into the spartan hallway and out through the front door.

She settled Phoebe in the car again and pulled away. By the time she reached the interstate she was driving mechanically, shaking her head now and then to keep herself awake. It was late afternoon; Phoebe had been asleep for almost twelve hours. Soon she would need to be fed. Caroline hoped they would be in Lexington before this happened.

She had just passed the last Frankfort exit, thirty-two miles from home, when the brake lights of the car ahead of her flared. She slowed, then slowed some more. Dusk was already beginning to gather, the sun a dull glow in the overcast sky. As she crested the hill, the traffic came to a complete stop, a long ribbon of taillights that ended in a cluster flashing red and white. Caroline thought she might weep. The gas gauge hovered below a quarter of a tank, enough to get back to Lexington but nothing extra, and this line of cars—well, they could be here for hours.

She sat for several minutes, paralysed. The last exit ramp was a quarter of a mile back, separated from her by a chain of cars. Heat rose from the Fairlane's hood, shimmering in the dusk, melting the few flakes of snow that had started to fall. Caroline, following an impulse that would amaze her later, jerked the steering wheel and slid the Fairlane off the asphalt and onto the soft gravel shoulder. She put the car in reverse and then backed up, travelling slowly past the line of cars.

She reached the exit without incident. It took her to Route 60, where the trees were heavy with snow again. The fields were broken by houses, first a few and then many, their windows already glowing in the dusk. Soon Caroline was driving down the main street of Versailles.

A dark blue Kroger sign rose up a block away. That familiar sight, sale posters decorating its bright windows, comforted Caroline and made her realise suddenly how hungry she was. And it was what, now—Saturday, not quite evening? The stores would be closed all day tomorrow and she had very little food in her apartment. Despite her exhaustion, she pulled into the parking lot and turned off the engine.

Phoebe, warm and light, twelve hours old, was wrapped in sleep. Caroline shouldered the diaper bag and tucked the baby beneath her coat, so small, curled close and warm. She picked her way through the slush, afraid of falling and hurting the baby. A deep sense of responsibility flooded through her, making her light-headed.

The glass door swung open, releasing a rush of light and warmth. Caroline settled Phoebe in a metal cart and walked through the aisles. She pondered over formulas, a bottle warmer, over the rows of bottles, over bibs. She started for the check-out, then realised she had better get milk for herself, and some more diapers, and some kind of food.

While Caroline was picking out cans of soup, Phoebe stirred, and began to cry. Caroline vacillated for a moment, then picked up the baby and the bulky bag and went to the restroom at the back of the store. She sat on a plastic chair and poured formula from the Thermos into a bottle. It took several minutes for the baby to settle down, but eventually she caught on, and then Phoebe drank as she had slept: fiercely, intently. By the time she relaxed, sated, they were announcing that the store was about to close. Caroline hurried to the check-out, where a single cashier waited. When she left, they locked the doors behind her.

The parking lot was nearly empty, the last few cars idling or pulling slowly out into the street. Caroline rested her bag of groceries on the hood and settled Phoebe into her box on the back seat. Scattered flakes swirled in the cones from the streetlights. She reached into the bag and ripped open the covering round a loaf of bread, taking out a slice. She chewed as she shut the door, thinking with weary longing of her apartment. She was halfway round the back of the car before she realised that her taillights were glowing weakly red.

She stopped where she was, staring. While she had dithered in the grocery aisles, while she had sat in the unfamiliar restroom quietly feeding Phoebe, this light had been spilling out across the snow.

When she tried the ignition it merely clicked, the battery so dead the engine wouldn't even groan. She got out of the car and stood by the open door. 'I have a baby,' she said out loud, astonished. 'I have a baby in this car.' But the parking lot was empty now, the lights from the store windows making large rectangles in the slush. 'I have a baby here,' Caroline repeated. 'A baby!' she shouted then, into the stillness.

# III

NORAH OPENED HER EYES. Outside, the sky was fading into dawn, but the moon was still caught in the trees, shedding pale light into the room. She had been dreaming, searching in frozen ground for something she had lost. Beside her, in his cradle, her son was crying. In one smooth motion, she lifted him into the bed. The sheets beside her were cool. David was gone, then, called to the clinic while she slept. Norah pulled her son into the warm curve of her body, opened her nightgown. His small hands fluttered against her breast as he latched on. His cheeks moved rhythmically as he drank. Norah's heart surged with love, with vast unwieldy happiness and sorrow.

She had not cried about their daughter right away, though David had. 'A blue baby,' he had told her, tears catching in the stubble of his one-day beard. A little girl who never took a breath. Paul was in her lap and Norah had studied him: the tiny face, so serene and wrinkled. The infant fingers, so pink and delicate and curved. Tiny, tiny fingernails, still soft, translucent as the daylight moon. What David was saying— Norah could not take it in, not really. She remembered the second urge to push, and tension beneath David's voice like rocks in white water. But the infant in her arms was perfect, beautiful, more than enough. 'It's all right,' she had told David, stroking his arm, 'it's all right.'

It was not until they left the office, stepping tentatively into the chill, damp air of the next afternoon, that the loss had finally penetrated. It was nearly dusk, the air full of melting snow and raw earth. The sky was overcast, white and grainy behind the stark bare branches of the sycamores. She carried Paul, thinking how strange this was, to take an entirely new person to their home. Everything was in order, everything was prepared, her son was in her arms. Yet at the building entrance, she stopped, unable to take another step.

'David,' she said.

'What?' he asked, turning. 'What is it?'

'I want to see her,' she said, her voice a whisper. 'I have to see her.'

David shoved his hands in his pockets. 'Oh, Norah,' he said softly. 'Please, just come home. We have a beautiful son.'

'I know,' she said. Because it was 1964 and he was her husband and she had always deferred to him completely. Yet she could not seem to move, not feeling as she did, that she was leaving behind some essential part of herself. 'Oh! Just for a moment, David. Why not?'

Their eyes met, and the anguish in his made her own fill with tears.

'She isn't here.' David's voice was raw. 'That's why. There's a cemetery on Bentley's family farm. In Woodford County. I asked him to take her. We can go there, later in the spring. Oh, Norah, please. You are breaking my heart.'

Norah closed her eyes then, feeling something drain out of her at the thought of an infant, her daughter, being lowered into the cold March earth. Her arms, holding Paul, were stiff and steady, but the rest of her felt liquid, as if she too might flow away into the ditches and disappear with the snow. David was right, she thought; she didn't want to know this. When he climbed the steps and put his arm round her shoulders, she nodded, and they walked together across the empty parking lot, into the fading light. He secured the car seat; he drove them carefully home; they carried Paul across the porch and through the door; and they put him, sleeping, in his room. It had brought her comfort, the way David had taken care of everything, the way he'd taken care of her, and she had not spoken again about her wish to see their daughter.

But now she dreamt every night of lost things.

Paul had fallen asleep. Norah turned, shifted him to her other breast, closed her eyes again, drifting. She woke suddenly to dampness, crying, sunlight full in the room. It had been three hours.

On the changing table Paul cried louder, turning an angry mottled red. She stripped off his damp clothes, threw the diaper in the pail to soak, then dressed him again.

'Sweet baby,' she murmured, lifting him. 'Little love,' she said, and carried him downstairs.

In the living room the blinds were still closed, the curtains drawn. Norah made her way to the comfortable leather chair in the corner, opening her robe. Distantly, the bathroom door opened and shut and water ran faintly. Bree, her sister, came lightly down the stairs, wearing an old shirt. Her legs were white, her feet bare on the wooden floors.

'Don't turn on the light,' Norah said.

'OK.' Bree came over and touched her fingers gently to Paul's scalp. 'How's my little nephew?' she said. 'How's sweet Paul?'

Norah looked at her son's face, surprised, as always, by his name.

'Paul.' She said it out loud, solid and definite.

Silently, to herself, she added, *Phoebe.*

'He's hungry,' Norah added. 'He's always so hungry.'

'Ah. He takes after his aunt, then. I'm going to get some toast and coffee. You want anything?'

'Maybe some water,' she said, watching Bree, long-limbed and graceful, leave the room. How strange it was that her sister, who had always been her opposite, her nemesis, should be the one she wanted here.

Bree was only twenty, but headstrong and so sure of herself that she seemed to Norah, often, the elder. Three years ago, Bree had run away with the pharmacist who lived across the street, a bachelor twice her age. People blamed Bree's wildness on losing her father so suddenly when she was in her early teens. They predicted that the marriage would end soon and badly, and it had. But if they imagined that Bree's failed marriage would subdue her, they were wrong. She had not come home chastened and embarrassed. Instead, she'd enrolled at the university, changing her name from Brigitte to Bree because she liked the way it sounded: breezy, she said, and free.

Their mother, mortified by the scandalous marriage and more scandalous divorce, had married a TWA pilot and moved to St Louis, leaving her daughters to themselves. 'Well, at least one of my daughters knows how to behave,' she had said, looking up from the box of china she was packing. It was autumn, the air crisp, full of golden raining leaves. Her white-blonde hair was spun in an airy cloud, and her delicate features were softened with sudden emotion. 'Even if you never marry, darling, you'll always be a lady.'

Norah, sliding a framed portrait of her father into a carton, had flushed dark with annoyance and frustration. She too had been shocked by Bree's nerve, her daring, and she was angry that Bree had more or less got away with it—the marriage, the divorce, the scandal.

She hated what Bree had done to them all. She wished desperately that she'd done it first. But it would never have occurred to her. She'd always been good. She had been close to their father, a disorganised, affable man, an expert in sheep, who had spent his days in the closed-up room at the top of the stairs, reading journals. She'd loved him, and all her life she had felt a compulsion to make up, somehow, for his inattention to his family and for her mother's disappointment in having married a man so alien. When he died, this compulsion to make things right again, to fix the world, had only intensified. After graduation she had worked for six months at the telephone company, a job she'd not enjoyed and had given up quite happily when she married David. Their whirlwind courtship had been the closest she'd come to wild.

Norah's life, Bree was fond of saying, was just like a TV sitcom. 'It's fine for you,' she'd say, tossing back her long hair, wide silver bracelets halfway to her elbow. 'I couldn't take it. I'd go nuts in a day!'

Now Bree came back in carrying a tray with coffee, fresh bread, butter. Her long hair fell over her shoulder as she bent to put a tall glass of iced water on the table next to Norah. She slid the tray on the coffee table and settled onto the couch, tucking her long legs beneath her.

'David's gone?'

Norah nodded. 'I didn't even hear him getting up.'

'You think it's good for him to be working so much?'

'Yes,' Norah said firmly. 'I do.' Dr Bentley had talked to the other doctors in the practice, and they had offered David time off, but David had refused. 'I think it's good for him to be busy right now.'

'Really? And what about you?' Bree asked, biting into her bread.

'Me? Honestly, I'm fine.'

Bree waved her free hand. 'Don't you think—?' she began, but before she could criticise David again, Norah interrupted.

'It's so good you're here,' she said. 'No one else will talk to me, Bree. I had twins. I had a daughter, but no one else will say a word about her. They act like since I have Paul, I ought to be satisfied. But I had *twins*. I had a daughter too.'

'Everyone is sad,' Bree said softly. 'So happy and so sad, all at once. They don't know what to say, that's all.'

Norah lifted Paul, now asleep, to her shoulder, and rubbed his back. 'I know,' she said. 'I know. But still.'

'David shouldn't have gone back to work so soon,' Bree said. 'It's only been three days.'

'He finds work a comfort,' Norah said. 'If I had a job, I'd go.'

'No,' Bree said, shaking her head. 'No, you wouldn't, Norah. I hate to say this, but David's just locking up every feeling. And you're still trying to fill the emptiness. To fix things. And you can't.'

Even though Norah was inclined to agree with her sister, she felt obligated to defend David, who through his own sadness had taken care of everything: the quiet unattended burial, the explanations to friends, the swift tidying up of the ragged ends of grief.

'He has to do it his own way,' she said, reaching to open the blinds. 'I just wish I'd seen her, Bree. People think that's macabre, but I do wish it. I wish I had touched her, just once.'

'It's not macabre,' Bree said softly. 'It sounds completely reasonable.'

Paul's head was a warm weight, his fine thick hair soft against Norah's neck. Did he miss his twin? she wondered. Would he always feel a sense of loss? She stroked his head, looking out of the window at the fading sphere of the moon.

Later, while Paul slept, Norah took a shower. She tried on and discarded three different outfits, skirts that bound her waist, trousers that strained across the hips. She had always been petite, slender and well proportioned, and the ungainliness of her body amazed and depressed her. Finally, in despair, she ended up in her old denim maternity dress, gratifyingly loose. Dressed but barefoot, she wandered through the house. Like her body, the rooms were spilling over, wild, chaotic, out of control. There was a clean trail in the dust on the dresser, where David had placed a vase of daffodils, brown already at the edges; the windows were cloudy too. In another day Bree would leave and their mother would arrive. At the thought of this, Norah sat helplessly on the edge of the bed. The disorder of the house pressed on her like a weight. She didn't have the energy to fight it.

The doorbell rang. Bree's sharp footsteps moved through the rooms. Norah recognised the voices right away. For a moment longer she stayed where she was, feeling drained of energy, wondering how she could get Bree to send them away. But the voices came closer, near the stairwell, fading again as they entered the living room; it was members of the night circle from her church, eager for a glimpse of the baby.

Bree was calling. Norah went downstairs without bothering to put on lipstick or even brush her hair. Her feet were still bare.

'Paul's just gone to sleep,' she announced, entering the room. 'I won't wake him up.' There was anger in her voice, real aggression.

'It's all right, my dear,' Ruth Starling said, patting the sofa by her side. She was nearly seventy, with fine white hair. Her husband had passed away the year before. What had it cost her? Norah wondered. What did it cost her now, to maintain her appearance, her cheerful demeanour?

'How about some tea?' Bree asked, with cheery unease. Before anyone could answer, she disappeared into the kitchen.

Norah did her best to concentrate on the conversation: what people thought of the new pastor, whether or not they should donate blankets to the Salvation Army. Then Flora Marshall announced that her sister Kay's baby, a girl, had been delivered the night before.

'Seven pounds exactly,' she said. 'Kay looks wonderful. The baby's beautiful. They named her Elizabeth.'

There was a silence, then, as everyone realised what had happened, Flora flushed pink with regret. 'Oh, Norah,' she said. 'I'm so sorry.'

Norah wanted to speak and set things in motion again, but she could not seem to find her voice. Worse, she was crying.

'Now, now. You have a beautiful baby boy,' Ruth said, taking Norah's hand and pressing it hard.

'He had a sister,' Norah whispered, determined, looking around at all the faces. 'Her name was Phoebe. I want somebody to say her name. Do you hear me?' She stood up. 'I want someone to remember her name.'

There was a cool cloth on her forehead then, and hands helping her to lie down on the couch. They told her to close her eyes, and she did. Tears still slipped beneath her eyelids, a spring welling up; she couldn't seem to stop. Voices swirled around her like snow in the wind, but then Bree was there, calm and gracious, ushering them all to the door. When they had gone Norah opened her eyes to find Bree standing beside her.

'David said her hair was dark,' Norah said.

Bree looked at her. 'You said you were going to have a memorial service. Why wait? Why not do it now? Maybe it would bring you some peace.'

Norah shook her head. 'What David says, what everyone says, it makes sense. I should focus on the baby I have.'

Bree shrugged. 'Except you're not doing that. The more you try not to think about her, the more you do. David's only a doctor,' she added. 'He doesn't know everything. He's not God.'

'Of course he's not,' Norah said. 'I know that.'

'Sometimes I'm not sure you do.'

Norah didn't answer. She felt she should be angry, but she was not. The idea of a memorial service seemed to have stopped the draining of energy and will that had begun on the steps of the clinic.

'Maybe you're right,' she said. 'I don't know. Maybe. Something very small. Something quiet.'

Bree handed her the telephone. 'Here. Just start asking questions.'

Norah took a deep breath and began. She called the new pastor first and found herself explaining that she wanted to have a service, yes, and outside, in the courtyard. Yes, rain or shine. 'For Phoebe, my daughter, who died at birth.' Over the next two hours, she repeated the words again and again: to the florist, to the woman in classifieds at *The Leader*, to her sewing friends. Each time, Norah felt the calm within her swell and grow, something connecting her back to the world.

Bree left for class, and Norah walked through the silent house, taking in the chaos. In the bedroom, afternoon light slanted through the glass, showing every inattention. Now, for the first time since the birth, she felt energy rather than inertia. She pulled the sheets taut on the beds, opened the windows, dusted. Off came the denim maternity dress. She searched her closet until she found a skirt that would fit. She pulled on a sweater and took time to brush her hair before she went downstairs and found her flat beige shoes. Her feet, at least, were slim again.

She checked on Paul—still sleeping, his breath soft but real against her fingertips—put a frozen casserole into the oven, set the table and opened a bottle of wine. She was discarding the wilted flowers when the front door opened. Her heart quickened at David's footsteps, and then he stood in the doorway, his dark suit loose on his thin frame, his face flushed from his walk. She saw him register with relief her familiar clothes, the smells of cooking food. He held another bunch of daffodils, gathered from the garden. When she kissed him, his lips were cool.

'Hi,' he said. 'Looks like you had a good day here.'

'Yes. It was good.' She nearly told him what she'd done, but instead she made him a drink: whisky, neat, how he liked it. They went into the living room and sat together on the sofa. For a moment it was like before, just the two of them, and the world around them was an understandable place, full of promise. Norah had planned to tell David about her plans over dinner, but now, suddenly, she found herself explaining the simple service she had organised, the announcement she had placed. David's expression made her hesitate; it was as if he'd been unmasked, his eyes darker than she'd ever seen them.

'You don't like the idea,' she said.

'It's not that.'

Again she saw the grief in his eyes; she heard it in his voice. Out of a desire to assuage it, she nearly took everything back, but she felt her earlier inertia, pushed aside with such great effort, lurking in the room.

'It helped me to do this,' she said. 'That isn't wrong.'

'No,' he said. 'It isn't wrong. But damn it, Norah,' he added, his voice low and harsh, anger underlying his words, 'why, at least, didn't you tell me before you called the papers?'

'She died,' Norah said, angry now herself. 'There's no shame in it. No reason to keep it a secret.'

He stood up and walked to the window. Stiff-shouldered, he stared into the darkness.

'David,' she said, 'what is happening to us?'

He did not turn. Scents of meat and potatoes filled the room; she remembered the dinner, warming in the oven, and her stomach churned with hunger. Upstairs, Paul began to cry, but she stayed where she was, waiting for his answer.

'Nothing's happening to us,' he said at last. When he turned, the grief was still vivid in his eyes and something else—a kind of resolution—that she did not understand. 'You're making a mountain out of a mole-hill, Norah,' he said. 'Which, I suppose, is understandable.'

Cold. Dismissive. Patronising. Paul was crying harder. The force of Norah's anger pushed her to her feet and she stormed upstairs, where she lifted the baby and changed him, gently, gently, all the time trembling with rage. Then the rocking chair, buttons, the blissful release. She closed her eyes. Downstairs, David moved through the rooms. He, at least, had touched their daughter, seen her face.

She would have the service. She would do it for herself.

# IV

ONCE HER VOICE DWINDLED to nothing in the empty parking lot, Caroline slammed the car door and started picking her way through the slush. After a few steps, she stopped and went back for the baby. Phoebe's thin wails rose in the darkness, propelling Caroline across the asphalt, past the wide blank squares of light, to the automatic doors of the store. Locked. Caroline shouted and knocked, her voice weaving with Phoebe's cries. Inside, the brightly lit aisles were empty. For several minutes, Caroline stood still, listening to the crying baby and the rush of the wind. Then she pulled herself together and made her way to the back of the store. The rolling metal door off the loading platform was closed. She walked up to it and kicked it hard until she was breathless.

'If they're still in there, honey, which I kinda doubt, they aren't going to be opening up any time soon.'

A man's voice. Caroline turned and saw him standing below her, on the ramp that allowed tractor trailers to back into the loading area. He wore a bulky coat and a knitted hat.

'My baby's crying,' she said, unnecessarily. 'My car battery is dead. There's a phone right inside the front door, but I can't get to it.'

'How old's your baby?' the man asked.

'A newborn,' Caroline told him, hardly thinking.

'It's Saturday night,' the man observed, his voice travelling over the snowy space between them. 'Any garage in town is likely to be closed.'

Caroline didn't answer.

'Look here, ma'am,' he began slowly. 'I left my jumper cables with another trucker last week by mistake, so I can't help you that way. But I'm thinking, why don't you come sit with me in the rig? It's warm. I delivered a load of milk here a couple of hours ago and I was waiting to see about the weather. I'm saying that you're welcome, ma'am. To sit in the truck with me. Might give you some time to think this through.' When Caroline didn't respond, he added, 'I'm considering that baby.'

She looked across the parking lot then, to its very edge, where an articulated truck with a dark gleaming cab sat idling. In her arms Phoebe gasped, caught her breath and resumed her crying.

'All right,' Caroline decided. 'For the moment, anyway.'

When she reached the edge of the ramp he was there, holding up a hand to help her down. She took it, then looked up to see his face, thickly bearded, the knitted hat pulled down to his eyebrows and, beneath it, dark eyes, kind eyes. Stupid, she told herself, as they walked together across the parking lot. He could be an axe murderer. But the truth was, she was almost too tired to care.

He helped her collect some things from the car and get settled in the cab, holding Phoebe while Caroline climbed into the high seat, then handing her up. Caroline poured more formula from the Thermos into the bottle. Phoebe was so worked up that it took her a few moments to realise that food had come, and even then she struggled to suck. Caroline stroked her cheek gently, and at last she clamped down on the teat and started drinking.

'Kinda strange, isn't it?' the man said, once Phoebe had quietened. He had climbed into the driver's seat. The engine hummed in the darkness, comforting, like some great cat, and the world stretched away to the dark horizon. 'This kind of snow in Kentucky, I mean.'

'Every few years it happens,' she said. 'You're not from here?'

'Akron, Ohio,' he said. 'Originally, that is. But I've been on the road five years now.'

'Don't you get lonely?' Caroline asked, thinking of herself on a usual night, sitting alone in her apartment in the evening. She couldn't believe she was here, talking so intimately with a stranger.

'Oh, some,' he admitted. 'It's lonely work, sure. But just as often I get to meet someone unexpected. Like tonight.'

It was warm in the cab, and Caroline felt herself giving in to it, settling back on the high comfortable seat. Her car stood in the middle of the parking lot, a lone dark shape, brushed with snow.

'Where were you heading?' he asked her.

'Just to Lexington. There was a wreck on the interstate a few miles back. I thought I'd save myself some time and trouble.'

He smiled. 'If it's only Lexington we're talking about, I could give you a lift. I might as well park the rig there as here. Tomorrow—well, tomorrow's Sunday, isn't it? But on Monday, first thing, you can call a towing service about your car. It'll be safe here.'

Light from a streetlamp was falling across Phoebe's tiny face. He reached over and gently, gently, stroked her forehead with his large hand. Caroline liked his awkwardness, his calmness.

'All right,' she decided. 'If it doesn't put you out.'

'Oh, no,' he said. 'Lexington is on my way.'

He collected the rest of the things from her car, the grocery sacks and blankets. His name was Al, Albert Simpson. He groped on the floor and found an extra cup beneath the seat. This he wiped out carefully with a handkerchief before he poured her coffee from his Thermos. She drank, glad of the warmth and the company of someone who didn't know a thing about her. As he drove, Al talked, telling her stories of his life on the road. Lulled by the hum of the tyres, by the warmth and the snow rushing in the headlights, Caroline half drifted into sleep.

When they pulled into the parking lot of her apartment complex, Al got out to help her down. He left the truck idling while he carried her things up the exterior stairs. Caroline followed, Phoebe in her arms. Everything was just the same, but surely she was not the same woman who had left here in the middle of the previous night, wading through the snow to her car? Yet her familiar key slid into the lock, catching in the usual place. When the door swung open, she carried Phoebe into a room she knew by heart: the dark brown carpet, the plaid sofa and chair, the glass-topped coffee table.

Al hovered awkwardly, filling up the doorway.

'I have a sofa bed,' she said. 'You're welcome to use it tonight.'

After a moment's hesitation, he stepped inside. 'What about your husband?' he asked, looking around.

'I don't have a husband,' she said, then realised her mistake. 'Not any more.'

He studied her, standing with his hat in his hand, surprising dark curls sticking out of his head.

'I don't want to be any trouble to you,' he said.

'Trouble?' she said. 'I'd still be stranded in a parking lot except for you.'

He grinned then, went to his truck, and came back a few minutes later with a small duffle bag of dark green canvas.

Phoebe had been stirring, and Caroline took the bottle from its warmer, tested the formula on her arm, and sat down. Al, meanwhile, got straight to work. In no time at all he had pulled out the sofa bed and made it up, sharp military folds at each corner. When Phoebe had finished, Caroline nodded at him and whispered good night.

During the drive, Caroline had been making plans. Now she pulled a drawer from her dresser and dumped its neat contents in a pile on the floor. Then she folded two towels in the bottom and tucked a folded sheet around them, nestling Phoebe amid the blankets. When she climbed into her own bed, fatigue rolled over her like waves, and she slept at once, a hard and dreamless sleep.

Caroline woke to a flood of light and the smell of eggs and bacon. She stood, pulling her robe around her, and bent over to touch the baby's tranquil cheek. Then she went to the kitchen.

'Hey, there,' Al said, looking up. His hair was combed but still a little wild. He had a bald spot on the back of his scalp and he wore a gold medallion on a chain round his neck. 'Hope you don't mind my making myself at home. I missed dinner last night.'

'It smells good,' Caroline said. 'I'm hungry too.'

'Well, then,' he said, handing her a cup of coffee. 'Good thing I made plenty. It's a neat little place you've got here. Nice and tidy.'

'Do you like it?' she asked. The coffee was richer and darker than she usually made it. 'I'm thinking of moving.' Her own words surprised her, but once they were out, in the air, they seemed true. 'I'm thinking of going to Pittsburgh,' she said, surprising herself again.

Al stirred the eggs with a spatula, then lifted them onto plates. 'Pittsburgh? Great town. What would take you there?'

'Oh, my mother had family there,' Caroline said, as he put the plates on the table and sat down across from her. It seemed there was no end at all to the lies a person could tell, once she got started.

'You know, I've been meaning to say I'm sorry,' Al said. His dark eyes were kind. 'For whatever happened to your baby's father.'

Caroline had half forgotten that she'd made up a husband, so she was surprised to hear in his voice that Al didn't believe she'd ever had one. He thought she was an unwed mother, she marvelled. They ate without speaking much, passing remarks now and then about the weather and the traffic and Al's next destination, which was Nashville.

'I've never been to Nashville,' Caroline said.

'No? Well, hop aboard, you and your daughter too,' Al said. It was a joke, but within the joke was an offer.

'Maybe next time,' she said, reaching for the coffee. 'I've got some things to settle here. But thanks. I appreciate the thought.'

'My infinite pleasure,' he said seriously, and then he stood up to go.

Caroline watched from the window as he went to his truck, climbing up the steps into the cab and turning once to wave from the open doorway. She waved back, happy to see his smile, surprised by the tug in her heart. She had an impulse to run after him, but his engine caught and then he was pulling out of the parking lot and away.

For the next twenty-four hours, Caroline slept and woke on Phoebe's schedule, staying up just long enough to eat. It was as if she had entered some state halfway between sleep and waking, where she would not have to consider too fully the consequences of her decisions, or the fate of the baby sleeping in her dresser drawer, or her own.

On Monday morning she got up in time to call in sick to work. Ruby Centres, the receptionist, answered the phone.

'Are you all right, honey?' she asked. 'You sound awful.'

'It's the flu, I think,' Caroline said. 'Anything happening there?' She tried to make her voice casual. 'Dr Henry's wife have the baby?'

'Well, I sure don't know,' Ruby said. 'No one else is in yet, except about a hundred patients. Looks to be everyone else has got your flu, Miss Caroline.'

For the next two days, Caroline did not go out. The world came to her in the form of newspapers, grocery deliveries, milkmen. The weather changed and the snow was gone as suddenly as it had come. For Caroline, the broken days blurred together into a stream of random images: her Ford Fairlane, its battery recharged, being driven into the lot; the sunlight streaming through cloudy windows; a robin at the feeder. She had her spells of worry, but often, sitting with Phoebe, she was surprised to find herself completely at peace. She loved sitting in the sunlight and holding her. She warned herself not to fall in love with Phoebe; she was just a temporary stop. Caroline had watched David Henry often enough at the clinic to believe in his compassion. When he had raised his head from the desk that night and met her eyes, she had seen in them an infinite capacity for kindness. She had no doubt that he would do the right thing, once he got over the shock.

Every time the phone rang she started. But three days passed with no word from him.

On Thursday morning there was a knock on the door. Caroline hurried to answer it, adjusting the belt of her dress, touching her hair. But it was only a delivery man, holding a vase full of flowers: dark red and pale pink in a cloud of baby's breath. These were from Al. *My thanks for the hospitality,* he'd written on the card. *Maybe I'll see you on my next run.*

Caroline took them inside and arranged them on the coffee table.

Agitated, she picked up the local paper, which lay unread beside the vase. She skimmed through the articles, not really taking in any of them. Escalating tensions in Vietnam, social announcements, a page of local women modelling the new spring hats. She was about to throw the paper down when a black-bordered square caught her eye.

*Memorial Service*
*For Our Beloved Daughter*
*Phoebe Grace Henry*
*Born and Died March 7, 1964*
*Lexington Presbyterian Church*
*Friday, March 13, 1964, at 9 a.m.*

Caroline sat down slowly. She read the words once and then again. She even touched them, as if this would make them clearer somehow, explicable. With the paper still in her hands, she stood up and went to the bedroom. Phoebe slept in her drawer, one pale arm outflung against the blankets. *Born and died.* Caroline went back into the living room and called her office. Ruby picked up on the first ring.

'I don't suppose you're coming in?' she said. 'It's a madhouse here. Everyone in town seems to have the flu.' She lowered her voice then. 'Did you hear, Caroline? About Dr Henry and his babies? They had twins. The little boy is fine, but the girl, she died at birth. So sad.'

'I saw it in the paper.' Caroline's jaw, her tongue, felt stiff. 'I wonder if you'd ask Dr Henry to call me. Tell him it's important. I saw the paper,' she repeated. 'Tell him that, will you, Ruby?' Then she hung up.

An hour later he knocked at her door.

'Well,' she said, showing him in.

David Henry came in and sat on her sofa, his back hunched, turning his hat in his hand. She sat down in the chair across from him.

'Norah put the announcement in,' he said. When he looked up she felt a rush of sympathy despite herself, for his forehead was lined, his eyes bloodshot. 'She did it without telling me.'

'But you told her her daughter died?' Caroline said.

He nodded, slowly. 'I meant to tell her the truth. But when I opened my mouth, I couldn't say it. I thought I was saving her pain.'

Caroline thought of her own lies. 'I didn't leave her in Louisville,' she said softly. She nodded at the bedroom door. 'She's in there. Sleeping.'

David Henry looked up. His face was white.

'Why not?' he asked, on the edge of anger. 'Why in the world not?'

'Have you been there?' she asked, remembering the pale woman, her dark hair falling into the cold linoleum. 'Have you seen that place?'

'No.' He frowned. 'It came highly recommended, that was all.'

'It was awful,' she said, relieved. So he hadn't known what he was doing. She wanted to hate him still, but she remembered how many nights he had stayed at the clinic, treating patients from the country-side, from the mountains, who couldn't afford the care they needed. He wasn't an evil man, she knew that. He wasn't a monster. But this—a memorial service for a living child—that was monstrous.

'You have to tell her,' she said.

His face was pale, still, but determined. 'No,' he said. 'It's too late now. Do whatever you have to do, Caroline, but I can't tell her. I won't.'

It was strange; she disliked him so much for these words, but she felt with him also at that moment the greatest intimacy she had ever felt with any person. They were joined together now in something enor-mous, and no matter what happened they always would be. He took her hand, and raised it to his lips and kissed it. She felt the press of his lips on her knuckles and his breath, warm on her skin.

'I'll leave it in your hands, Caroline,' he said, releasing her. 'I believe the home in Louisville is the right place for this child. She will need medical care she can't get elsewhere. But whatever you have to do, I will respect that. And if you choose to call the authorities, I will take the blame. There will be no consequences for you, I promise.'

For the first time, Caroline thought beyond the immediate, beyond the baby in the next room. It had not occurred to her before that their careers were in jeopardy.

'I don't know,' she said slowly. 'I have to think.'

He pulled out his wallet, emptying it. Three hundred dollars—she was shocked that he carried this much with him.

'I don't want your money,' she said.

'It's not for you,' he told her. 'It's for the child.'

'Phoebe. Her name is Phoebe,' Caroline said, pushing away the bills. She thought of the birth certificate, left blank but for his signature in David Henry's haste that snowy morning. How easy it would be to type in Phoebe's name, and her own.

'Phoebe,' he said. He stood up to go, leaving the money on the table. 'Please, Caroline, don't do anything without telling me first. That's the only thing I ask. That you give me warning, whatever it is you decide.'

He left, then, and everything was the same as it had been. Yet the room seemed strangely impersonal now, as if she had never lived here at all. Twin threads ran through her: fear and excitement. She could start a new life somewhere else. She could leave this place today. She would have to do that, anyway. This was a small town; she couldn't go to the grocery store without running into an acquaintance.

*I'll leave it in your hands, Caroline.* His face aged, clenched like a walnut.

The next morning, Caroline woke early. It was a beautiful day and she opened the windows, letting in the fresh air and the scent of spring. Phoebe had woken twice in the night, and while she slept Caroline had packed and carried her things to the car in the darkness. She had very little, as it turned out—just a few suitcases.

By noon yesterday she had made all the arrangements: a charity would take the furniture; a cleaning service would handle the apartment. She had stopped the utilities and the newspaper, and she had written letters to close her bank accounts.

Caroline put Phoebe in her box on the back seat and drove into town. When she reached the church she parked in the street and left Phoebe asleep in the car. The group gathered in the courtyard was larger than she'd expected, and she paused at its outside edge, close enough to see the back of David Henry's neck, flushed pink from the cold, and Norah Henry's blonde hair swept up in a formal twist.

Words drifted on the still morning air. Mrs Henry wiped at her eyes with a lace handkerchief. What would happen if Caroline stepped forward now with the lost baby in her arms? If she interrupted this grief, only to introduce so many others?

'"Thou has set our misdeeds before thee, and our secret sins in the light of thy countenance."'

David Henry shifted his weight as the minister spoke. For the first time Caroline understood in her body what she was about to do. Her throat closed and her breath grew short.

'"For the things that are seen are transient, but the things that are unseen are eternal."'

Caroline watched the minister's hand and, when he spoke again, the words, though faint, seemed addressed not to Phoebe but to herself.

'"We have committed her body to the elements, earth to earth, ashes to ashes, dust to dust. The Lord bless her and keep her, the Lord make his face to shine upon her and give her peace."'

The voice paused, the wind moved in the trees, and Caroline pulled herself together, wiped her eyes with her handkerchief and gave her head a swift shake. She turned and went to her car, where Phoebe was still sleeping, a wand of sunlight falling across her face.

In every end, then, a beginning. Soon enough she was turning the corner, headed for the interstate. When she reached the split in the highway she chose to go north, to Cincinnati and then to Pittsburgh, following the Ohio River to the place where Dr Henry had lived a part of his mysterious past.

Caroline drove fast, feeling reckless, her heart filling with an excitement as bright as the day. The child who rode beside her was, in the eyes of the world, already dead. And she, Caroline Gill, was vanishing from the face of the earth. All that sunny afternoon, travelling north and east, Caroline believed absolutely in the future. And why not? For if the worst had already happened to them in the eyes of the world, then surely, surely, it was the worst that they left behind them now.

## February 1965

NORAH STOOD, BAREFOOT and precariously balanced, on a stool in the dining room, fastening pink streamers to the brass chandelier. Chains of paper hearts, pink and magenta, floated down over the table.

Paul, eleven months old, sat in the corner beside a basket full of wooden blocks. He had just learned to walk, and all afternoon he'd amused himself by stomping through this, their new house, in his first pair of shoes. Now, wide-eyed, he watched the streamers, as beautiful and elusive as butterflies, then pulled himself up on a chair and staggered in pursuit. He caught one pink strand and yanked. Then he lost his balance and sat down hard. Astonished, he began to cry.

'Oh, sweetie,' Norah said, climbing down to pick him up. 'There, there,' she murmured, running her hand over his soft hair.

Outside, headlights flashed and disappeared and a car door slammed. At the same time, the phone began to ring. Norah carried Paul into the kitchen, picking up the receiver just as someone knocked on the door.

'Hello?' She pressed her lips to Paul's soft forehead, straining to see whose car was in the driveway. Bree wasn't due for an hour. 'Sweet baby,' she whispered. And then into the phone she said again, 'Hello?'

'Mrs Henry?'

It was the nurse from David's new office—he'd joined the hospital staff a month ago—a woman Norah had never met. Her voice was warm and full: Norah pictured a hefty middle-aged woman, her hair in a careful beehive. Caroline Gill, who had held her hand through the rippling contractions, whose blue eyes and steady gaze were inextricably connected for Norah to that wild and snowy night, had simply disappeared—a mystery, that, and a scandal.

'Mrs Henry, it's Sharon Smith. Dr Henry was called into emergency surgery just as he was about to go home. There was a horrible accident out off Leestown Road. Teenagers, they're pretty badly hurt. Dr Henry asked me to call you. He'll be home as soon as he can. Between you and me, it may end up being hours.'

Norah nodded. The air was redolent with roast pork, sauerkraut and oven potatoes: David's favourite meal. Distantly, the front door opened, shut. There were footsteps, light and familiar: Bree, early, coming to pick up Paul, to give Norah and David this evening before Valentine's Day, their anniversary, to themselves.

Norah's plan, her surprise, her gift to him.

'Thanks for calling,' she told the nurse, before she hung up.

Bree walked into the kitchen, bringing with her the scent of rain. She'd come straight from work—she managed the office for a local radio station—and her bag was full of books and papers from the classes she was taking.

'Wow,' Bree said, sliding her bag on the counter and reaching for Paul. 'Everything looks great, Norah. I can't believe what you've done with the house in such a short time.'

'It's kept me busy,' Norah agreed, thinking of the weeks she'd spent steaming off wallpaper and applying new coats of paint. They had decided to move, she and David, thinking that, like his new job, it would help them leave the past behind. Yet it hadn't helped as much as Norah had hoped. Twice in this last month alone she'd hired a baby sitter for Paul and left the house, with its half-painted trim and rolls of wallpaper, behind. She had driven too fast down the narrow country roads to the private cemetery where her daughter was buried. Phoebe's stone was simple, made from pink granite, with the dates of her short life chiselled deeply beneath her name. In the bleak winter landscape, Norah had knelt on the brittle, frozen grass of her dream for a long time before she finally stood up and went home.

Now Paul was playing a game with Bree, trying to catch her hair.

'Your mom's amazing,' Bree told him. 'She's just a regular Suzy Homemaker these days, isn't she? No, not the earrings, honey,' she added, catching Paul's small hand in her own.

'Suzy Homemaker?' Norah repeated, anger lifting through her like a wave. 'What do you mean by that?'

'I didn't mean anything,' Bree said. She'd been making silly faces at Paul, and now she looked up, surprised. 'Oh, honestly, Norah. Lighten up. Why are you so angry?'

Norah waved her hand. 'Oh, darn it, David's in surgery. It's not his fault. There was an accident. But it stinks. It absolutely stinks, OK?'

'I'm sorry, sis,' Bree said, her voice surprisingly soft. Then she smiled. 'Look, I brought you and David a present. Maybe it will cheer you up.'

Bree shifted Paul to one arm and rummaged in her oversized quilted bag, pulling out books, a pile of leaflets, sunglasses in a worn leather case and, finally, a bottle of wine. The liquid glimmering like garnets as she poured a glass for each of them.

'To love,' she said, handing Norah one glass and raising the other. 'To eternal happiness and bliss.'

They laughed together and drank. The wine was dark with berries, faint oak. Rain dripped from the gutters. Years from now, Norah would remember this evening, the gloomy disappointment and Bree bearing shimmering tokens from another world, her energy like a kind of light.

'Hey—did your old house sell?' Bree asked, putting her glass on the counter. 'Did you decide to take the offer?'

'It's lower than we hoped,' Norah said. 'David wants to accept it, just to have it settled, but I don't know.'

She thought of their first house, standing dark and empty with a FOR SALE sign planted outside, and held on to the counter to steady herself.

'So how's your love life these days?' Norah asked, changing the subject. 'How are things with that guy you were seeing—Jeff?'

'Oh, him.' A dark expression crossed Bree's face. 'I didn't tell you? I came home two weeks ago and found him in bed—in *my* bed—with this sweet young thing who worked with us on the mayoral campaign.'

'Oh! I'm sorry.'

Bree shook her head. 'Don't be. It's not like I loved him or anything.'

'You didn't love him?' Norah repeated, hearing and hating her mother's disapproving voice coming from her own mouth.

'No,' Bree said. 'No, I didn't love him, though for a while I thought I might. But that's not even the point any more. The point is he turned our whole thing into a cliché. I hate that.' She put her empty glass on the counter and shifted Paul into her other arm. Her face, unadorned, was finely boned; her cheeks were flushed pale pink.

'I couldn't live like you do,' Norah said. Since Paul was born, since Phoebe had died, she'd felt the need to keep a constant vigil. 'I just couldn't do it—break all the rules. Blow everything up.'

'The world doesn't end,' Bree said quietly. 'Amazing, but it doesn't.'

Norah shook her head. 'It could. At any given moment, anything at all could happen.'

'I know,' Bree told her. 'You're right, Norah, anything can happen, any time. But what goes wrong is not your fault. You can't spend the rest of your life tiptoeing around to try and avert disaster. It won't work. You'll just end up missing the life you have.'

Norah did not know how to answer this, so she reached for Paul, who was squirming in Bree's arms, hungry, his long hair—too long, but

Norah couldn't bear to cut it—drifting slightly, as if underwater, whenever he moved.

Bree poured more wine for them and took an apple from the fruit bowl. Norah cut up chunks of cheese and banana, scattering them across the tray of Paul's high chair. She sipped from her wine as she worked. Gradually, the world around her became clearer, more vivid. She noticed Paul's hands, like small starfish, spreading banana in his hair.

'I bought David a camera for our anniversary,' Norah said, wishing she could capture these fleeting instants, hold them for ever. 'He's been working so hard since he took this new job. He needs a distraction. I can't believe he has to work tonight.'

'You know what?' Bree said. 'Why don't I take Paul anyway? I mean, so what if David gets home at midnight? You could just skip dinner and make love on the dining-room table.'

'Bree!'

Bree laughed. 'Please, Norah? I'd love to take him.'

She agreed, finally, and packed Paul's things. His dark eyes watched her seriously as Bree walked out of the door with him, and then he was gone. Norah watched from the window as Bree's taillights disappeared down the street, then she went into the kitchen, where she put foil over the roast and turned the oven off. Bree's bottle of wine was nearly empty. It was seven o'clock. In the kitchen, so silent she could hear the clock ticking, Norah opened another bottle, then, glass in hand, she walked through the house, her footsteps hollow on the polished floors.

Outside, the rain fell steadily, blurring the lights across the street. Norah remembered another night, the swirling snow. David had taken her by the elbow, helping her into her green coat. He was so concerned, so serious, so charged with nervous excitement; in that moment, Norah felt she knew him as she knew herself.

Yet everything had changed. David had changed. In the evenings, when he sat beside her on the couch, browsing through his journals, he was no longer really there. Sometimes, even after they had made love in the middle of the night and still lay together, heart beating against heart, she would look at him and feel her ears filling up with the dark, distant roar of the universe.

It was after eight o'clock. She went back to the kitchen and stood at the stove, picking at the dried pork. She ate one of the potatoes straight from the pan, smashing it into the drippings with her fork. The broccoli-cheese dish had curdled and was beginning to dry; Norah tasted that too. It burned her mouth, and she reached for her glass. Empty. She drank a glass of water, standing at the sink, and then another, holding on to the edge of the counter because the world was so unsteady. I'm drunk, she thought, surprised and mildly pleased with herself. She had never been drunk before.

The telephone seemed a long way away. Walking, she felt strange, as if she were somehow floating, just outside herself. She held on to the doorjamb with one hand and dialled with the other, the receiver pressed between her shoulder and her ear. Bree answered on the first ring.

'I know it's you,' she said. 'Paul's fine. We read a book and had a bath and now he's sound asleep.'

'Oh, good. Yes, wonderful,' Norah said. She'd intended to tell Bree about the shimmering world, but now it seemed too private somehow.

'How about you?' Bree was saying. 'Are you OK?'

'I'm fine,' Norah said. 'David's not here yet, but I'm fine.'

She hung up fast, poured herself another glass of wine and stepped onto the porch, where she lifted her face to the sky. The rain had stopped and a light mist hung in the air. Now the wine seemed to move through her like heat or light, spreading out through her limbs.

Where was David, she wondered, sudden tears in her eyes, and why had she married him anyway? Why had he wanted her so much? Those whirlwind weeks after they met he'd been at her apartment every day, offering roses and dinners and drives in the country. On Christmas Eve the doorbell rang and she went to answer it in her old robe, expecting Bree. Instead, she opened the door to find David, his face flushed with cold, brightly wrapped boxes in his arms. It was late, he said, he knew that, but would she come with him for a drive?

And she had laughed at the wildness of it, laughed and stepped back and let him in, pleased and amazed. There had been moments when Norah, so quiet and reserved, had believed she would be single all her life. Yet here was David, handsome, a doctor, standing in her apartment saying, 'Come on, please, there's something special I want you to see.'

It had been a clear night, stars vivid in the sky. Norah was wearing a red woollen dress and she felt beautiful, the air so crisp and David's hands on the wheel and the car travelling through the darkness. He pulled to a stop beside an old flour mill, and they stepped out of the car into the sound of rushing water, which caught the moonlight and poured over the rocks, turning the mill's great wheel.

'Are you cold?' David asked, shouting over the stream.

'I'm fine,' Norah shouted back, shivering, but he was already taking her hands in his, pressing them to his chest, warming them between his gloves and the dark, flecked wool of his coat.

'It's beautiful here!' she called to him, and he laughed. Then he leaned down and kissed her, releasing her hands and letting his own slide up her back, as water rushed, echoing off the rocks.

'Norah,' he shouted. 'Norah! Will you marry me?'

She laughed, letting her head fall back. 'Yes!' she shouted, pressing her palms against his coat. 'Yes, I will!'

He slid a ring on her finger then: a thin white-gold band, exactly her size, its marquise diamond flanked by two tiny emeralds. To match her eyes, he said later, and the coat she'd worn when they met.

She was inside now, standing in the doorway of the dining room, turning this ring on her finger. Streamers drifted. One brushed her face; another had dipped into her wineglass. Norah watched, fascinated, as the stain spread upwards. Wine had splashed from her glass and spattered across the tablecloth, staining the gold wrapping of her present to David. She picked this up and, on an impulse, tore the paper off.

The camera was compact, a pleasing weight. With complex dials and levers and numbers etched around the rings, to Norah it had resembled David's medical equipment. The salesman had plied her with information about apertures and f-stops and wide-angle lenses, all of which had washed over her like so much water, but she had liked the way the world was so precisely framed when she held the camera to her eye.

Tentatively, now, she pushed the silver lever. Click and then snap, loud in the room, as the shutter released. She turned the little dial, advancing the film—she remembered the salesman using that phrase—she looked through the viewfinder, framing the ruined table again, then turned two different dials to find the focus. This time, when she snapped the shutter, light exploded across the wall. Blinking, she turned the camera over and studied the blackened bulb. She replaced it, burning her fingers, but somehow distant from the pain.

She glanced at the clock: 9.45 p.m.

The rain was soft, steady. David had walked to work and she imagined him trudging wearily home. On an impulse she got her coat and the car keys—she would go to the hospital and surprise him.

The car was cold. She backed out of the driveway and by old habit turned in the wrong direction. Even after she realised her mistake, she kept driving on the same narrow rainy streets, back to their old house, where she'd decorated the nursery with such innocent hope. The truth was, she could not bear the idea of selling the place.

Except for being dark, the house looked much the same: the wide front porch with its four white columns. Norah could almost believe, walking up the steps, that she lived here still. But the door opened onto rooms that were bare, empty, shocking in their smallness.

Walking through the cold house, Norah struggled to clear her head. She held David's camera in one hand. There were fifteen pictures left in the camera and spare flashbulbs in her pocket. She took a picture of the chandelier, satisfied, when the bulb flashed, because now she would always have that image with her. She walked from room to room, still drunk but charged with purpose, framing windows, light fixtures, the swirling grain of the floor. It seemed vitally important that she record every detail. At one point, in the living room, a spent and blistered bulb slipped from her hand and shattered; when she stepped back, glass pierced her heel. She studied her stocking feet for a moment. She must have left her wet shoes by the front door, out of old habit. It was only on her way downstairs that she realised her foot was bleeding, leaving a splotchy trail: grim hearts, bloody little valentines.

Norah found her shoes and went outside. Her heel throbbed as she slid into the car, the camera still dangling from her wrist.

Later, she would not remember much about the drive, only the dark, narrow streets, the wind in the leaves, light flashing on the puddles and water spraying off her tyres. She would not remember the crash of metal against metal, but only the sudden startling sight of a trash can, glittering, flying up in front of the car. She remembered that it hit the hood and rolled up to shatter the windshield; she remembered the car, bouncing over the kerb and coming to a stop. She did not remember hitting the windshield, but it looked like a spiderweb, the intricate lines fanning out, delicate, beautiful and precise.

She did not get out of the car. The trash can was rolling in the street. Lights flashed on in the house to her right, and a man came out in his robe and slippers, hurrying down the sidewalk to her car.

'Are you all right?' he asked, leaning down to look in the window as she rolled it open. 'What happened out here? Your forehead's bleeding.'

'It's nothing,' Norah said. She pressed her palm gently to her forehead. The camera, still dangling from her wrist, tapped against the steering wheel. She slipped it off and put it beside her on the seat.

'Do you need a doctor?' the man asked.

'My husband's a doctor,' Norah said, noting the man's uncertain expression. 'He's a doctor,' she repeated firmly. 'I'll go find him.'

'I'm not sure you should be driving,' the man said. 'Why don't you leave the car here and let me call an ambulance?'

'No,' she said, becoming very careful of her words. 'I'm fine, really. A cat ran out and startled me. But truly, I'm fine. I'll just go home now.'

The man hesitated, then nodded and stepped back. Norah drove carefully, using her turn signals properly on the empty street. In the rearview mirror she saw him watching her until she turned the corner.

The world was quiet as she drove back through the familiar streets, the effects of the wine beginning to ebb. Her new house was ablaze with lights in every window. She parked in the driveway and got out, standing for a moment on the damp grass, rain falling softly and beading on her hair, her coat. Inside, she glimpsed David sitting on the sofa. Paul was in his arms, his head resting on his father's shoulder. She thought of how she'd left things, the spilt wine and trailing streamers, the ruined roast. She hurried up the steps.

'Norah!' David met her at the door, still carrying Paul. 'Norah, what happened to you? You're bleeding.'

'It's OK. I'm OK,' she said, refusing David's hand when he tried to help her. Her foot hurt, but she was glad of the sharp pain; a counterpoint to the throbbing in her head, it seemed to run straight through her and hold her steady. Paul was sound asleep and she rested the palm of her hand lightly on his small back.

'Where's Bree?' she asked.

'She's looking for you,' David said. 'When you weren't home, I panicked and called her. She brought Paul over, and then she went out looking for you.'

'I was at the old house,' Norah said. 'I hit a trash can.' She put her hand to her forehead and closed her eyes.

'You were drinking.' He made the statement calmly.

'Wine with dinner. You were late.'

'There are two empty bottles, Norah.'

'Bree was here. It was a long wait.'

The phone rang and she picked it up, heavy in her hand. It was Bree. 'I'm OK,' Norah said, trying to speak calmly and clearly. 'I'm fine.' David was watching her, studying the dark lines on her palm where the blood had settled and dried.

'Come here,' he said gently, once she hung up.

They went upstairs. While David settled Paul into his crib, Norah eased off her ruined stockings and sat on the edge of the bath. She blinked in the bright lights, trying to put the events of the evening in their proper order. When David came back, he brushed the hair from her forehead and started cleaning the cut.

'Hope you left the other guy in worse shape,' he said, and she imagined that he might say this same thing to the patients who came through his office: small talk, banter, empty words as a distraction.

'There was no one else,' she said, thinking of the silver-haired man leaning into her window. 'A cat startled me, and I swerved. But the windshield—Oh!' she said, as he put antiseptic on her cut. 'That hurts.'

'It won't last long,' he said, putting his hand on her shoulder for a moment. He knelt down by the tub and took her foot in his hand.

She watched him pick out the glass. He was careful and calm, absorbed in his thoughts.

'You are so good to me,' she whispered, longing to bridge the distance between them, the distance she had made.

He looked up. 'Good to you,' he repeated slowly. 'Why did you go to our old house, Norah? Why don't you want to let it go?'

'Because it's the final thing,' she said at once, surprised by the sureness and sorrow in her voice. 'The final way we leave her behind.'

In the brief instant before he looked away, there was, on David's face, a brief flash of tension, of anger quickly repressed.

'What would you have me do that I'm not doing? I thought this new house would make us happy. It would make most people happy, Norah.'

At his tone, fear rushed through her; she could lose him too. She closed her eyes briefly at the thought of the scene she had caused.

'All right,' she said. 'I'll call the realtor. We should take that offer.'

A film closed over the past as she spoke, a barrier as brittle and fragile as ice forming. It would become impenetrable, opaque. Yes, she would move on. This would be her gift, to David and to Paul.

Phoebe she would keep alive in her heart.

David wrapped her foot in a towel and sat back. 'You're so sad,' he said, gentler now that she'd conceded. 'Please don't be sad. I didn't forget, Norah. Not our anniversary. Not our daughter. Not anything.'

'Oh, David,' she said. 'I left your present in the car.' She thought of the camera, its precise dials and levers. *The Memory Keeper* it said on the box, in white italic letters; this, she realised, was why she'd bought it—so he'd capture every moment, so he'd never forget.

'That's all right,' he said, standing. 'Wait . . . wait right here.'

He ran down the stairs, while she stood and limped to Paul's room.

The carpet was dark blue and thick beneath her feet. She had painted clouds on the pale blue walls and hung a mobile of stars above the crib. Paul slept beneath the drifting stars, his small hands outflung. She kissed him gently, running her hand over his soft hair.

'Norah?' David came in and stood behind her. 'Close your eyes.'

A cool line shimmered on her skin. She looked down to see emeralds, a sequence of dark stones, caught in the gold stream of the chain against her skin. To match her ring, he was saying. To match her eyes.

'It's so beautiful,' she whispered. 'Oh, David.'

His hands were on her shoulders then, and for an instant she stood again amid the sound of rushing water from the mill, happiness as full around her as the night. Don't breathe, she thought. Don't move. But there was no stopping anything. Outside, rain fell softly and seeds stirred in the dark, wet earth. Paul sighed and shifted in his sleep. He would wake tomorrow, grow and change. They'd live their lives day by day, each one taking them another step away from their lost daughter.

# March 1965

THE SHOWER RUSHED and steam swirled, misting the mirror and the window. Caroline paced in the tiny purple bathroom, holding Phoebe close. Her breathing was light and rapid, her small heart beat so quickly. 'Be well, my baby,' Caroline murmured. 'Be better, sweet girl, be well.' She paused, tired. Phoebe's cough started again, deep in her chest. Her body grew rigid beneath Caroline's hands as she barked the air out of her constricted throat. This was croup, a textbook case.

Stairs creaked, then floorboards, nearer, and then the purple door swung open in a rush of cool air. Doro, wearing a black silk robe, her grey hair falling loose around her shoulders, came in.

'Is it bad?' she asked. 'It sounds just awful. Should I get the car?'

'I don't think so. But could you shut the door? The steam helps.'

Doro pushed the door shut and sat on the edge of the tub.

'We woke you,' Caroline said, Phoebe's breath against her neck. 'Sorry.'

Doro shrugged. 'You know me and sleep. I was up anyway, reading.'

'Anything interesting?' Caroline asked. She wiped at the window with the cuff of her robe; moonlight fell into the garden three floors below and shone like water on the grass.

'Science journals. Dull as dust, even for me. Sleep being the goal.'

Caroline smiled. Doro had a PhD in physics; she worked in the university department her father had once chaired. Leo March, brilliant and well known, was now in his eighties, physically strong but subject to lapses of memory and sense. Eleven months ago, Doro had hired Caroline as his companion.

A gift, this job: she knew that. She had emerged from the Fort Pitt tunnel onto the high bridge over the Monongahela River, emerald hills rising out of the river flats, the city of Pittsburgh gleaming before her, so startling in its vastness and vivid beauty that she had gasped and slowed, afraid of losing control of the car.

For one long month she had lived in a cheap motel on the edge of town, circling 'wanted' ads and watching her savings dwindle. By the time she'd come to this interview, her euphoria had turned into dull panic. She rang the bell and stood on the porch, waiting. Next door, a woman in a quilted housecoat swept soot from her steps. The people at this house had not bothered; Phoebe's car seat rested on dust like blackened snow; Caroline's footprints were stark and pale behind her.

When Dorothy March, tall and slender in a trim grey suit, finally opened the door, Caroline ignored her wary glance at Phoebe, lifted the car seat and stepped inside. She perched on the edge of an unsteady chair. Dorothy March sat across from her, on a couch of cracked leather supported at one end by a brick. She lit a cigarette. For several moments she studied Caroline, then she cleared her throat, exhaling smoke.

'Quite frankly, I wasn't counting on a baby,' she said.

Caroline pulled out her résumé. 'I've been a nurse for fifteen years. I'd bring a great deal of experience and compassion to this position.'

Dorothy March took the papers in her free hand and studied them. 'Yes, but it doesn't say here just *where* you've worked.'

Caroline hesitated. She had tried a dozen different answers to this question at a dozen different interviews in these last weeks.

'That's because I ran away from Phoebe's father,' she said. 'And so I can't tell you where I'm from, and I can't give you any references. That's the only reason I don't have a job. I'm an excellent nurse and you'd be lucky to get me, frankly, given what you're offering to pay.'

At this Dorothy March gave a sharp, startled laugh. 'What a bold statement! My dear, it's a live-in position. Why in the world would I take such a chance on a perfect stranger?'

'I'll start now for room and board,' Caroline persisted, thinking of the motel room with its peeling wallpaper, the room she could not afford to keep another night. 'For two weeks. Then you can decide.'

Dorothy March ground her cigarette in the overflowing ashtray.

'But how would you manage?' she mused. 'With a baby? My father is not a patient man. He will not be a patient patient, I assure you.'

'A week,' Caroline had replied. 'If you don't like me in a week, I'll go.'

Now nearly a year had passed. Doro stood up in the steam-softened bathroom. The sleeves of her robe slipped to her elbows.

'Let me take her,' she said. 'You look exhausted, Caroline.'

Phoebe's wheezing had abated and her colour had improved. Caroline handed her over, feeling the sudden coolness of her absence.

'How was Leo today?' Doro asked. 'Did he give you any grief?'

For a moment Caroline didn't answer. Somehow she had come to be here in this tiny purple bathroom, a mother to Phoebe, a companion to a brilliant man with a failing mind, an unlikely but certain friend to this woman Doro March: the two of them strangers a year ago, their lives now woven together by the demands of their days and a sure respect.

'He wouldn't eat. He accused me of putting scouring powder in the mashed potatoes. So—a fairly typical day, I'd say.'

'It's not personal, you know,' Doro said softly.

Caroline turned off the shower and sat on the edge of the purple tub.

Doro nodded at the steamy window. Phoebe's hands were pale, like stars, against her robe. 'That used to be our playground, over there on the hill. Herons used to nest in the trees, did you know that? Before they put the freeway in. My mother planted daffodils one spring, hundreds of bulbs. My father came home from work on the train every day at six o'clock, and he'd go straight over there and pick her a bunch of flowers. You wouldn't have known him,' she said. 'You don't.'

'I know,' Caroline said gently. 'I realise that.'

They were silent for a moment. The steam swirled.

'I think she's asleep,' Doro said. 'Will she be OK?'

'Yes. I think so.'

'What's wrong with her, Caroline?' Doro's voice was intent now, her words a determined rush. 'My dear, I know nothing about babies, but even I can sense that something's not right. She's nearly a year old and only now learning to sit up.'

Caroline closed her eyes. 'Phoebe has Down syndrome,' she forced herself to say. 'That's the term.'

'Oh, Caroline,' Doro said. 'I'm so sorry. This is why you left your husband, isn't it? Oh, my dear, I'm so sorry.'

'Don't be,' Caroline said, reaching for Phoebe. 'She's beautiful.'

'Oh, yes. Yes, she is. But, Caroline, what will become of her?'

Phoebe was warm and heavy in her arms, her soft dark hair falling against pale skin. Caroline touched her cheek.

'What will become of any of us? I mean, tell me honestly, Doro. Did you ever imagine that this would be your life?'

Doro looked away. Years ago, her fiancé had been killed while jumping from a bridge into the river on a dare. Doro had mourned him and never married, never had the children she longed for.

'No,' she said at last. 'But this is different.'

'Why? Why is it different?'

'Caroline,' Doro said. 'Let's not. You're tired. So am I.'

As Doro's footsteps sounded faintly down the stairs, Caroline settled Phoebe in her crib. Asleep in the dull glow of the streetlight, Phoebe looked like any child, her future as unmapped as the ocean floor, as rich with possibility. *What will become of her?* In truth, Caroline sometimes lay awake at night, struggling with this same question.

In her own room, the moonlight was strong enough to read by. On the desk there was an envelope with three photographs of Phoebe, next to a paper folded twice. Caroline opened it and read what she had written.

*Dear Dr Henry,*

*I am writing to say that we are well, Phoebe and I. We are safe and happy. I have a good job. Phoebe is generally a healthy baby, despite frequent respiratory concerns. I am sending photos. So far, touch wood, she does not have any problems with her heart.*

She should send this—she had written it weeks ago—but each time she went to mail it she thought of Phoebe, the soft touch of her hands or the cooing sounds she made when she was happy, and she could not do it. Now she put the letter away again and lay down, drifting quickly into sleep.

**W**hen Caroline woke, the room was full of sunlight and trumpet music. Phoebe, in her crib, was reaching, as if the notes were small winged things that she might catch. Caroline got them both dressed and took her downstairs, pausing on the first floor, where Leo March was ensconced in his sunny office, books tumbled all around the day bed where he lay, staring at the ceiling. Caroline watched him from the doorway—she was not allowed to enter this room except by invitation—but he did not acknowledge her. An old man, bald with a fringe of grey hair, listening intently to the music that blared from his speakers.

'Do you want breakfast?' she shouted.

He waved his hand, indicating that he'd get it himself. Well, fine.

Caroline descended another flight to the kitchen and put the coffee on. Even here the trumpets sounded. She put Phoebe in her high chair, feeding her apple purée and egg and cottage cheese. Three times she handed her the spoon; three times it clattered on the tray.

'Never mind,' Caroline said out loud, but her heart numbed. Doro's voice echoed: *What will become of her?* And what would? At eleven months, Phoebe should be able to grasp small objects.

She cleaned up the kitchen and went into the dining room to fold the laundry from the line. Phoebe lay on her back in the playpen, cooing, batting at the rings and toys Caroline had hung above her.

After about half an hour the music stopped and Leo's feet appeared on the stairs in precisely tied and polished leather shoes. Bit by bit he came into view—a tall man, flesh hanging loosely from his bony frame.

'Good,' he said, nodding at the laundry. 'We've been needing a maid.'

'Breakfast?' she asked.

'I'll get it myself.'

'Go right ahead, then.'

'I'll have you fired by lunchtime,' he called from the kitchen.

'You go right ahead,' she said again.

There was a cascade of falling pots, the old man swearing. Caroline imagined him stooped over to push the tangle of cookware back into the cupboard. She ought to go to help him—but no, let him cope by himself. In her first weeks she'd been afraid to talk back, afraid not to jump whenever Leo March called, until Doro had taken her aside. 'Look, you're not a servant. You answer to me; you don't have to be at his beck and call. You're doing fine, and you live here too,' she had said, and Caroline had understood that her period of probation was over.

Leo came in, carrying a plateful of eggs and a glass of orange juice.

'Don't worry,' he said. 'I'm taking my breakfast upstairs.'

He thumped up the stairs and she paused in her work, suddenly near tears. What was she doing here? And what would become of *her*?

After a few minutes, the trumpets started again upstairs and the doorbell rang twice. Caroline lifted Phoebe from the playpen.

'Here they are,' she said, drying her eyes with her wrist. 'Time to practise.'

Sandra was standing on the porch, and when Caroline opened the door she burst in, holding Tim by one hand and carrying a big cloth bag in the other. She was tall, large-boned, blonde and forceful; she sat down without ceremony in the middle of the rug.

'Sorry I'm so late,' she said. 'The traffic's awful out there. Anyway, check out what I found. Look at these stacking toys. Tim loves them.'

Caroline sat down on the floor, too. Like Doro, Sandra was an unlikely friend. They'd met in the library one bleak January day and had begun to talk. Sandra's son, Tim, was nearly four. He had Down syndrome too, but Sandra hadn't known it. That he was slower to develop than her three other children, this she had noticed, but Tim had been walking by the time he was two, toilet-trained by the age of three. The diagnosis had shocked her family; the doctor's suggestion—that Tim should be put into an institution—had angered her into action.

Caroline had listened intently, her heart lifting with every word.

They'd left the library and gone for coffee. Caroline would never forget those hours, the excitement she'd felt, as if she were waking from a long, slow dream. What would happen, they wondered, if they simply went on assuming their children would do *everything*? Perhaps not quickly. Perhaps not by the book. What if they kept their expectations but erased the time line? What harm could it do? Why not try?

They'd begun to meet, here or at Sandra's house with her older, rambunctious boys. They brought books and toys, research and stories, and their own experiences—Caroline's as a nurse, Sandra's as a schoolteacher and mother of four. A lot of it was simple common sense. If Phoebe needed to learn to roll over, put a bright ball just out of her reach;

if Tim needed to work on coordination, give him blunt scissors and paper and let him cut. For Caroline, these hours had become a lifeline.

'You look tired today,' Sandra said.

Caroline nodded. 'Phoebe had croup last night. I don't know how long she'll hold out, actually. Any news about Tim's ears?'

'I liked the new doctor,' Sandra said, sitting back. She smiled at Tim and handed him a yellow cup. 'But the news isn't great. Tim has some hearing loss, so that's probably why his speech has been so slow. Here, sweetie,' she added, tapping the cup he'd dropped. 'Show Miss Caroline and Phoebe what you can do.'

Tim was not interested; the nap of the carpet had his attention, and he ran his hands through it again and again. But Sandra was firm, calm and determined. Finally, he took the yellow cup, then put it on the floor and started stacking others in a tower.

For the next two hours, the two women played with their children and talked. Sandra had strong opinions about everything and was not afraid to speak her mind. Caroline loved sitting in the living room and talking with this smart, bold woman. They laughed together as Tim tried to stack the cups on their heads, as Phoebe reached and reached for a sparkly ball and finally, despite herself, rolled over. Several times that morning, Caroline dangled her car keys in front of Phoebe. They flashed, catching the morning light, and Phoebe's hands flew open, her fingers waving, splayed like starfish. But she could not catch them.

'Next time,' Sandra said. 'Wait and see. It will happen.'

At noon, Caroline helped them carry things to the car, then stood on the porch with Phoebe in her arms, tired already but happy too, waving as Sandra pulled her station wagon out into the street.

Caroline went back inside and cleaned up the kitchen, then carried out the garbage. She stood for a moment in the alley by the trash can, grateful for the cool air. Garages staggered, one after another, down the hill. Gradually, she became aware of a tall man, in dark jeans and a brown jacket, colours so muted he nearly became another part of the late-winter landscape, standing at the base of the alley. Something about him—something about the way he stood and stared in her direction—made Caroline uneasy. She put the metal lid back on the garbage can. He was walking towards her now, a big man, bearded, broad-shouldered. His jacket was not brown at all, but a muted plaid with streaks of red. He pulled a bright red hat from the pocket and put it on. Caroline felt oddly comforted by this gesture, though she didn't know why.

'Hey, there!' he called. 'That Fairlane running OK for you these days?'

She knew him, and she understood this in her relief before she could formulate it in thought. Then it was so bizarre she couldn't believe it.

The man had stopped a few feet away.

'How in the world—?' she began.

'It wasn't easy!' Al said, his teeth flashing white. His dark eyes were warm, pleased and amused. 'You are one tough lady to track down. But you said Pittsburgh. And I happen to have a layover here every couple of weeks. It kind of got to be a hobby, looking for you.' He smiled. 'Don't know what I'll do with myself now.'

Caroline couldn't answer. There was pleasure at the sight of him but a great confusion too. For nearly a year she had not let herself think too long or too hard about the life she had left, but now it rose up with great force and intensity. Her heart was pounding and she stared wildly down the alley, as if she might suddenly see David Henry too. This, she understood suddenly, was why she had never sent that letter. What if he wanted Phoebe back—or Norah did? The possibility filled her with an excruciating rush of fear.

'How did you find me?' Caroline demanded. 'And why?'

Taken aback, Al shrugged. 'I stopped in Lexington to stay hello. Your place was empty. Being painted. A neighbour of yours told me you'd been gone three weeks. Guess I don't like mysteries, because I kept thinking of you.' He paused, as if debating whether to go on. 'Plus— hell, I liked you, Caroline, and I figured you were in some kind of trouble, to cut out like you did. I figured maybe I could lend you a hand.'

'I'm doing just fine,' she said. 'So. What do you figure now?'

She hadn't meant the words to come out as they did, so tough and harsh. There was a long silence before Al spoke again.

'I guess I figure I was wrong about some things,' Al said. He shook his head. 'I thought we hit it off, you and me.'

'We did,' Caroline said. 'I'm just shocked, that's all. I thought I'd cut my ties.'

He looked at her then; his brown eyes met hers. 'It took me a full year,' he said. 'If you're worried about someone else tracking you down, remember that. And I knew where to start, and I had good luck. I started checking the motels I know, asking about a woman with a baby. Last week I hit pay dirt. The clerk at the place you stayed remembered you. She's retiring next week, by the way.' He held his thumb and fore-finger up, close together. 'I came this close to missing you for ever.'

Caroline nodded, remembering the woman behind the desk with her white hair in a careful beehive, pearl earrings glimmering.

Al nodded at the powder-blue hood of the Fairlane. 'I knew I'd found you when I saw that,' he said. 'How's your baby?'

She remembered the empty parking lot, the way his hand had rested, so gently, on Phoebe's tiny forehead.

'Do you want to come in?' she heard herself ask. 'I was just about to wake her. I'll make you some tea.'

Caroline took him down the narrow sidewalk and up the steps to the back porch. She left him in the living room and climbed the stairs, feeling unsteady. She changed Phoebe and splashed water on her own face, trying to calm herself down.

When she came downstairs, Al turned, his face breaking into a wide grin. He reached for Phoebe at once, exclaiming over how big she'd grown, how beautiful she was. Caroline felt a rush of pleasure, and Phoebe, delighted, laughed, her dark curls falling down around her cheeks. Al reached into his shirt and pulled out a medallion, clear plastic over gilded turquoise letters that said GRAND OLE OPRY.

Phoebe was making soft sounds, reaching. Her hands were brushing against Al's neck, his collarbone, his dark plaid shirt. At first, it didn't register with Caroline, what was happening; then, suddenly, it did.

Phoebe was reaching for the medallion. Not batting at air, as she had this morning, but using Al's chest for resistance, her small fingers scraping and scraping the medallion into her palm until she could close her fist around it. Rapt with success, she yanked the medallion hard on its string, making Al raise his hand to the chafing.

Caroline touched her own neck too, feeling the quick burn of joy. Oh, yes, she thought. Grab it, my darling. Grab the world.

# May 1965

NORAH WAS AHEAD OF HIM, moving like light, flashes of white and denim amid the trees: there, and then gone. David followed, leaning down now and then to pick up stones. Rough-skinned geodes, fossils etched in shale—he held each of them for a moment, pleased by their weight and shape, by their coolness against his palm, before he slipped them into his pockets. As a boy, the shelves of his room had always been littered with stones, and to this day he couldn't pass them up, their mysteries and possibilities, even though bending was awkward with Paul in a carrier against his chest and the camera scraping against his hip.

Far ahead, Norah paused to wave, then seemed to vanish into a wall of smooth grey stone. As David drew closer he realised that the stairway leading to the natural stone bridge rose up there, just out of sight.

'Better watch your step,' a woman, descending, warned him. 'It's steep. Slippery too.' Breathless, she paused.

David, noting her paleness, her shortness of breath, said, 'Ma'am? I'm a doctor. Are you all right?'

'Palpitations,' she said, waving her free hand. 'Had them all my life.'

He took her plump wrist and felt her pulse, swift but steady, slowing as he counted. He could tell at once that the woman was in no real distress. Not like his sister, who had grown breathless and dizzy and was forced to sit any time she so much as ran across the room.

'Heart trouble,' the doctor in Morgantown had said, shaking his head. There was nothing he could do. Years later, in medical school, David had remembered her symptoms and read late into the night to make his own diagnosis: a narrowing of the aorta, or maybe an abnormality of the heart valve. Either way, June had moved slowly and fought to breathe, her condition worsening as the years passed, her skin pale and faintly blue in the months before she died. She was always singing, made-up tunes she hummed softly to herself, and her hair was the colour of buttermilk. For months after she died he had woken in the night, thinking he heard her voice, singing like the wind in the pines.

'Well, I think you'll be fine,' he said now to the woman, releasing her hand. 'But don't push yourself too hard.'

She thanked him, touched Paul's head and said, 'You watch out for that little one.'

David nodded and moved off, protecting Paul's head with his free hand as he climbed between the damp stone walls. Paul patted softly at his chest, grabbing at the envelope he'd stuffed in his pocket: a letter from Caroline Gill, delivered that morning to his office. He had read it only once, swiftly, putting it away as Norah came in, trying to conceal his agitation. *We are well, Phoebe and I*, it had said. *So far, she does not have any problems with her heart.*

Now he caught Paul's small fingers in his own, gently. His son looked up, wide-eyed, curious, and he felt a deep swift rush of love.

'Hey,' David said, smiling. 'I love you, little guy. But don't eat that, OK?'

Paul studied him with large dark eyes, then turned his head and rested his cheek against David's chest, radiating warmth. He wore a white hat with yellow ducks that Norah had embroidered in the quiet, watchful days after her accident. With the emergence of each duck, David had breathed a little easier. He had seen her grief when he'd developed the spent roll of film in his new camera: room after empty room in their old house. And Norah's footprints, those erratic, bloody trails. But days had passed, now nearly three months, and Norah seemed to be herself again. She worked in the garden, or laughed on the telephone with friends, or lifted Paul from his playpen with her lean, graceful arms. David, watching, told himself she was happy.

Now he emerged from the narrow stairs onto the natural stone bridge spanning the gorge. Norah, wearing denim shorts and a sleeveless white blouse, stood in the centre of the bridge, the toes of her white sneakers flush with the rocky edge. Slowly, with a dancer's grace, she opened her arms and arched her back, eyes closed, as if offering herself to the sky.

'Norah!' he called out, appalled. 'That's dangerous!'

'It's spectacular!' Norah called back, letting her arms fall. She turned, causing pebbles to skid and slide over the edge. 'Come and see!'

Cautiously, he walked out onto the bridge and went to stand beside her at the edge. Tiny figures moved slowly on the path far below, where an ancient river had once rushed. He took a deep breath, fighting a wave of vertigo, afraid even to glance at Norah. He had wanted to protect her from loss and pain; he had not understood that loss would follow her regardless. Nor had he anticipated his own grief, woven with the dark threads of his past. When he imagined the daughter he'd given away, it was his sister's face he saw.

'Let me get a picture,' he said, taking one slow step back, then another. 'Come over to the middle of the bridge. The light's better.'

'In a minute,' she said, her hands on hips. 'It's just so beautiful.'

'Norah,' he said. 'You are really making me nervous.'

'Oh, David,' she said, tossing her head without looking at him. 'Why are you so worried all the time? I'm fine.'

He didn't answer, conscious of his lungs moving, the deep unsteadiness of his breathing. He'd had this same feeling when he opened Caroline's letter, addressed to his old office in her handwriting, half covered with a forwarding stamp. It was postmarked Toledo, Ohio. She had included three pictures of Phoebe, an infant in a pink dress. The return address was to a PO box, not in Toledo but in Cleveland. The place where Caroline Gill was apparently living with his daughter.

'Let's move away from here,' he said again. 'Let me take your picture.'

Norah nodded, but when he reached the safe centre of the bridge and turned, she was still near the edge, facing him, arms folded, smiling.

'Take it right here,' she said. 'Make it look like I'm walking on air.'

David squatted, fiddling with the camera dials, heat radiating up from the rocks. Paul squirmed against him and started to fuss. David would remember all this—which went unseen and unrecorded—when the image rose up later in the developing fluid, taking slow shape. He framed Norah in the viewfinder, wind moving in her hair, her skin tanned and healthy, wondering at all she kept from him.

They hiked back down, passing cave entrances and sprays of purple rhododendron. Norah led them off the main path and through the trees, following a creek, until they emerged in a sun-struck place she remembered for its wild strawberries.

They spread out their picnic: cheese and crackers and clusters of grapes. David sat down on the blanket, cradling Paul's head against his chest as he undid the baby carrier, thinking idly of his own father, stocky and strong, with skilled blunt fingers that covered David's hands as he taught him to heft an axe or milk the cow.

Free, Paul immediately pulled off one shoe. He studied it intently, then dropped it and crawled off toward the grassy world beyond the blanket. He yanked a fistful of weeds and put them in his mouth, a look of surprise flashing across his small features at the texture. David wished, suddenly, fiercely, that his parents were alive to meet his son.

'Awful stuff, isn't it?' he said, wiping grassy drool from Paul's chin.

Norah took out silverware and napkins. They ate lazily, then picked ripe strawberries, sun-warmed and tender. Paul ate them by fistfuls, juice running down his wrists. Two hawks circled lazily in the deep blue sky. 'Didi,' Paul said, lifting a chubby arm to point. Later, when he fell asleep, Norah settled him on a blanket in the grassy shade.

'This is nice,' Norah observed, settling with her back against a boulder. 'Just the three of us, sitting in the sun.'

Her feet were bare and he took them in his hands, massaging them. 'Oh,' she said, closing her eyes, 'that's good. You'll put me to sleep.'

'Stay awake,' he said. 'Tell me what you're thinking.'

'I was remembering this little field by the sheep farm. When Bree and I were little we used to gather huge bunches of black-eyed Susans and Queen Anne's lace. The sun felt just like this—like an embrace. Our mother put the flowers in vases all over the house.'

David released one foot and attended to the other. He ran his thumb over the thin white scar the broken flashbulb had left. 'I like thinking of you there.' He remembered sunny days from his own childhood, before June got so sick, when the family had gone hunting for ginseng, a fragile plant hidden amid the trees. His parents had met on such a search. He had their wedding photo, and on the day of their own marriage Norah had presented it to him in a handsome oak frame. 'My parents loved being outside,' he added. 'My mother planted flowers everywhere. There was a cluster of jack-in-the-pulpit by the stream up from our house.'

'I'm sorry I never met them. They must have been so proud of you.'

'Yes,' he said, nodding. 'I think they were proud and sorry both. They didn't like the city. They only visited me once in Pittsburgh.' He remembered them sitting awkwardly in his single student room, his mother starting every time a train whistle sounded. June was dead by then, and as they sat sipping weak coffee at his rickety student table, he remembered thinking, bitterly, that they did not know what to do with themselves without June to care for. 'After my father died, my mother went to live with her sister in Michigan. She wouldn't fly, and she never learned to drive. I only saw her once, after that.'

'That's too sad,' Norah said, rubbing away a smear of dirt on her calf.

'Yes,' David said. 'Too sad indeed.' He thought of June, the way her hair got so blonde in the sun each summer. And how he had hated coming home to find her lying on a pallet on the porch on sunny days, his mother's face drawn with concern as she sat beside her daughter's limp form. His love for June was so deeply woven with resentment that he could not untangle the two.

David looked at Paul, sleeping on the blanket with his head turned to the side. His son, at least, he had sheltered from grief. Paul would not grow up, as David had, suffering the loss of his sister. He would not be forced to fend for himself because his sister couldn't.

This thought, and the force of its bitterness, shocked David. He wanted to believe he'd done the right thing when he'd handed his daughter to Caroline Gill. Or at least that he'd had the right reasons. Perhaps it was not so much Paul he'd been protecting on that snowy night as some lost version of himself.

'You look so far away,' Norah observed.

He moved closer to her, leaning against the boulder too. 'My parents had great dreams for me,' he said. 'But they didn't match my own. What do you dream about, Norah?' he asked. 'What do you dream for Paul?'

Norah didn't answer right away. 'I suppose I want him to be happy,' she said at last. 'Whatever in life makes him happy, I want him to have that. I don't care what it is, as long as he grows up to be good and true to himself. And generous and strong, like his father.'

'No,' David said. 'You don't want him to take after me.'

She gave him an intent look, surprised. 'Why not?'

He didn't answer. After a long, hesitant moment, Norah spoke again. 'What's wrong?' she asked, not aggressively but thoughtfully. 'Between us, I mean, David.'

He didn't answer, struggling against a sudden surge of anger. Why did she have to stir things up again? Why couldn't she let the past rest?

'It hasn't been the same since Paul was born and Phoebe died. You still won't talk about her. It's like you want to erase the fact she existed.'

'What do you want me to say? Of course life hasn't been the same.'

'Don't get angry, David. That's just some kind of strategy, isn't it? So I won't talk about her any more. But I won't back down.'

He sighed. 'Don't ruin the beautiful day, Norah.'

'I'm not.' She lay down on the blanket and closed her eyes. 'I'm perfectly content with this day.'

'Norah,' he said. 'I don't know what you want.'

'No,' she said. 'You don't.'

'You could tell me.'

'I suppose I could. Maybe I will. I still think about her, David,' she said, turning on her side and meeting his gaze. 'Our daughter. What she would be like. Don't you ever miss her too?'

'Yes,' he said truthfully. 'I think about her all the time.'

Norah put her hand on his chest, and then her lips, berry-stained, were on his, a sweetness as piercing as desire against his tongue. He felt himself falling, the sun on his skin and her breasts lifting softly, like birds, against his hands. She sought the buttons on his shirt and her hand brushed against the letter he had hidden in his pocket.

He shrugged off his shirt, but even so, when he slid his arms round her again, he was thinking, I love you. I love you so much, and I lied to you. And the distance between them, the space of a breath, opened up and deepened, became a cavern at whose edge he stood. He pulled away, back into the light and shadow, the clouds over him and then not, and the sun-warmed rock hot against his back.

'What is it, David?' she asked, stroking his chest. 'What's wrong?'

He hesitated, on the edge of confessing everything, and then he could not. 'A patient. I can't get the case out of my mind.'

'Let it go,' she said. 'I'm sick and tired of your work.'

Hawks, lifting high on the updrafts, and the sun so warm. Everything circled, returning each time to the exact same point. He must tell her. *I love you. I love you so much, and I lied to you.*

'I want to have another baby, David,' Norah said, sitting up. 'Paul's old enough now, and I'm ready.'

David was so startled he didn't speak for a moment.

'Paul's only a year old,' he said at last. 'Things are fine right now. Why rock the boat?'

'How about for Paul?' She nodded to him, sleeping, still and peaceful, on his blanket. 'He misses her.'

'He can't possibly remember,' David replied sharply.

'Nine months,' Norah said. 'Growing heart to heart. How could he not, at some level?'

'We're not ready,' David said. 'I'm not.'

She sighed. 'I knew you'd say no.'

'I'm not saying no,' David replied carefully. 'But it wouldn't fix things, Norah, to have another baby. That's not the right reason.'

After a moment's silence she stood up, brushing her hands on her shorts, and waded off angrily through the field.

His shirt lay beside him, a corner of the white envelope visible. David did not reach for it; he did not need to. The note was brief, and though he had glanced at the photos only once, they were as clear to him as if he'd taken them himself. Phoebe's hair was dark and fine, like Paul's. Her brown eyes gazed at something behind the camera. Caroline, perhaps. He had glimpsed her at the memorial service, tall and lonely in her red coat, and he'd gone straight to her apartment afterwards, unsure of his intentions, knowing only that he had to see her. But by then she was gone. He had not tried to find her, and since her letter had no useful return address, he could not imagine where to start now.

Tired, David lay back. Insects hummed in the sunlight, and he felt faintly anxious about bees. As he drifted into sleep, he remembered the days when he went out with his father to catch rattlesnakes. Dusk to dawn, they'd walked through the woods, carrying forked sticks, cloth bags over their shoulders and a metal box swinging from David's hand. For the largest ones, coveted by zoos and scientists and sometimes snake handlers, they might receive five dollars apiece. There were weeks, in the summer and late fall, when they could make twenty-five dollars. The money paid for food; and it paid for the doctor in Morgantown.

'David!'

Norah's voice came to him faintly, urgently, through the distant past and the forest and into the day. He rose up on his elbows and saw her standing on the far edge of the field of ripening strawberries, transfixed by something on the ground. He felt a rush of adrenaline and fear. Rattlesnakes liked sunny logs like the one by which she'd stopped; they laid their eggs in the fertile rotting wood. He glanced at Paul, still sleeping quietly in the shade, and then he was up and running, already reaching into the pocket of his jeans and closing his fist round the largest stone. When he got close enough to glimpse the dark line of the snake, he threw the stone as hard as he could. It fell six inches short.

'What in the world is the matter?' Norah asked.

He'd reached her by then. Panting, he looked down. It was not a snake at all but a dark stick resting against the log. 'I thought you called me,' he said, confused.

'I did.' She pointed to a cluster of pale flowers. 'Jack-in-the-pulpits. Like your mother used to have. David, you're scaring me.'

'I thought it was a rattlesnake,' he said, gesturing to the stick. 'I was dreaming, I guess. I thought you needed help.'

She looked puzzled. 'Why were you dreaming of snakes?' she asked.

'I used to catch them,' he said. 'For money.'

'For money?' she repeated, puzzled. 'Money for what?'

The distance was back between them, a chasm of the past that he could not cross. Money for food, and for those trips into town. She came from a different world; she would never understand this.

'They helped to pay my way through school, those snakes,' he said.

She nodded and seemed about to ask more, but she did not. 'Let's go,' she said, rubbing her shoulder. 'Let's just get Paul and go home.'

They walked back across the field and packed up their things. Norah carried Paul; he, the picnic basket.

As they walked, he remembered one weekend when he came home from school to find the cabin empty, still. He sat on the porch, hungry and cold, waiting. Very much later, near dusk, he glimpsed his mother walking down the hill. She did not speak until she reached the steps, and then she looked up at him and said, 'David, your sister died. June died.' His mother's eyes were red-rimmed from crying. And when he stood and hugged her she broke down, weeping, and he could not think of anything to say. He put a blanket round his mother's shoulders and made her a cup of tea, but he could not cry. He went out to the hens and gathered the eggs she had not collected. He fed the chickens and milked the cow. He did these ordinary things, but when he went inside the house, June was still gone.

'Davey,' his mother said, a long time later, from the shadows where she sat, 'you go and learn something that could help in the world.'

He felt a resentment at that; he wanted his life to be his own, unencumbered by this loss. He felt guilty because June was lying in the earth and he was still standing here; he was alive. 'I'll be a doctor,' he said, and after a while his mother nodded.

When they finally reached the car, Norah paused to examine her shoulder, dark pink from the sun. She was wearing sunglasses, and when she looked up at him he could not read her expression.

'You don't have to be such a hero,' she said. Her words were flat and practised, and he could tell she had been thinking about them, rehearsing them, perhaps, during the walk back.

'I'm not trying to be a hero.'

'No?' She looked away. 'I think you are,' she said. 'It's my fault too. For a long time I wanted to be rescued, I realise that. But not any more. You don't have to protect me all the time now. I hate it.'

And then she took the car seat and turned away again. In the dappled sunlight, Paul's hand reached for her hair and David felt a sense of panic at all he didn't know; at all he knew and couldn't mend. And anger: he felt that too. At himself, but also at Caroline, who had made an impossible situation even worse.

# May 1970

## I

'HE'S ALLERGIC TO BEES,' Norah told the teacher, watching Paul run across the new grass of the playground. He climbed to the top of the slide and then sailed down, springing up with delight as he hit the ground. 'His father's allergic, too. It's very serious.'

'Don't worry,' Miss Throckmorton replied. 'We'll take care of him.'

'He picked up a bee,' Norah persisted, 'a *dead* bee. One that was lying on the windowsill. Seconds later, he was swelling up like a balloon.'

'Don't worry, Mrs Henry,' Miss Throckmorton repeated, a bit less patiently, and moved off to help a little girl with sand in her eyes.

Norah lingered in the new spring sun, watching Paul. He was play-ing tag, running with his arms straight down by his sides—he'd slept that way, too, as an infant. She saw herself in him, the same bone struc-ture and fair colouring, and David was there too, in the shape of Paul's jaw. But mostly Paul was simply himself. He loved music and hummed made-up songs all day long. Though he was only six, he'd sung solos at school, stepping forward with a confidence that astonished Norah.

Now he paused to squat beside another little boy who was skimming leaves from a puddle with a stick. Norah watched him, serious and utterly absorbed. Paul, her son. Here in the world.

'Norah Henry! Just the person I wanted to see.'

She turned to see Kay Marshall, pushing her baby daughter in an antique wicker carriage while Elizabeth, her oldest, walked by her side. Elizabeth, born just two days after Paul, in the sudden spring that had followed that strange and sudden snow. Impatiently, she pulled away from Kay and ran off across the playground to the swings.

'It's such a pretty day,' Kay said, watching her go. 'How are you, Norah?'

'I'm fine,' Norah said, looking at the baby, who gazed up at her with wide inquisitive eyes. 'Look how big Angela is getting!'

Impulsively, Norah leaned down and picked up the baby. She felt a rush of pleasure, remembering the way Paul had felt at this age, his scent of soap and milk, his soft skin.

'She's ten months today,' Kay said. 'Can you believe it?'

'No,' Norah said. 'Time goes so fast.'

'Have you heard?' Kay asked. 'What's happening at the campus?'

Norah nodded. 'Bree called last night.' She'd stood, the phone in one hand and the other on her heart, watching grainy news on TV: four students shot dead at Kent State. Even in Lexington, tension had been building for weeks, the newspapers full of war and protests and unrest.

'It's scary,' Kay said, but her tone was more disapproving than dismayed, the same voice she might have used to talk about someone's divorce. She took Angela, kissed her, and put her back into the pram.

'I know,' Norah agreed. She used the same tone, but to her the unrest seemed deeply personal, a reflection of what had been going on within her heart for years. Norah's world had changed when Phoebe died. All her joys were set into stark relief—by that loss and by the possibility of further loss. David was always telling her to relax. He grew irritated with her projects, her committees, her plans. But she could not sit still; it made her too uneasy. So she arranged meetings and filled up her days, always with the sense that if she let down her guard, even for a moment, disaster would follow. The feeling was worst in the late morning; she almost always had a quick drink then—gin, sometimes vodka—to ease her into the afternoon. She kept the bottles hidden from David.

'Anyway,' Kay was saying. 'I wanted to RSVP about your party. We'd love to come, but we'll be a little late. Is there anything I can bring?'

'Just yourselves,' Norah said. 'Everything's almost ready. Except I have to go home and take down a wasps' nest.'

Kay's eyes widened slightly. 'A wasps' nest? Poor you!'

'Yes,' Norah said. 'Paper wasps. The nest is hanging off the garage.'

She hoped the task would take all morning. Otherwise, she might find herself driving, as she had so often in these last weeks, fast and hard, a silver flask in her bag. She could make it to the Ohio River in less than two hours.

The school bell rang and Norah searched for Paul's dark head, watched him disappear.

'I just loved our two singing together,' Kay said, blowing kisses to Elizabeth. 'Paul has such a beautiful voice.'

'He loves music,' Norah replied.

'Actually, that's the other thing I wanted to ask you, Norah. This fund-raiser I'm doing next month. It's a Cinderella theme, and I've been sent out to round up as many little footmen as I can. I thought of Paul and of how he could sing a duet with Elizabeth.'

'I see,' Norah said, and she did. Elizabeth's voice was sweet but thin. It wouldn't be strong enough without Paul's. His voice was pure, winged.

'It would mean such a lot to everyone if he would.'

Norah nodded slowly. Paul would love to be a footman.

'Wonderful!' Kay said. 'Oh, marvellous. I hope you won't mind,' she added, 'I took the liberty of reserving a little tuxedo for him. I just knew you'd say yes!' She glanced at her watch, efficient now, ready to go. 'Good to see you,' she added, waving as she walked away.

Norah walked past the bright swings and slides to her car. The river, its calming swirl, called to her. Two hours and she could be there. The lure of the fast drive, the rushing wind, the water, was nearly irresistible. On the last school holiday she had been shocked to find herself in Louisville, Paul frightened and quiet in the back seat and the gin wearing thin. 'There's the river,' she had said, standing with Paul's small hand in hers, looking at the muddy, swirling water. 'Now we'll go to the zoo,' she announced, as if that had been her intention all along.

She left the school and drove into town, slowing as she passed World Travel. Yesterday, she had been interviewed for a job there. She'd seen the ad in the paper and she'd been drawn into the low brick building by the glamorous signs in the windows: glittering beaches and buildings, vivid skies. The agency was owned by a man named Pete Warren, fifty years old and balding. He had liked her, she could tell, even though her degree was in English and she had no experience.

Behind her, someone honked a horn. Norah speeded up. But as she neared the university the streets filled with people, and she slowed to a crawl, then had to pull over. She got out of the car and left it.

There was a crowd gathering by the Reserve Officers Training Corps building, where two young men stood on the steps. One of them was holding an American flag aloft. As she watched, the other young man held his fist near the edge. The flames were invisible at first, an intensity of shimmering heat; then they caught in the fabric.

Through the wavering air, Norah saw Bree moving along the perimeter of the crowd near the building, passing out leaflets. Her long hair was caught in a ponytail that swung against her white peasant top. She was so beautiful, Norah thought, glimpsing the determination and excitement on Bree's face in the instant before she disappeared.

Norah pushed her way through the crowd. When she finally reached her sister, Bree was standing on the kerb, talking to a young man with reddish hair. Their conversation so intent that when Norah touched her arm Bree turned, puzzled and unseeing, her expression blank.

'Norah?' she said, recognising her sister at last. She placed her hand on the red-haired man's chest, a gesture so intimate that Norah's heart caught. 'This is my sister,' Bree explained. 'Norah, this is Mark.'

He nodded without smiling and shook Norah's hand, assessing her. 'They set the flag on fire,' Norah said.

Mark's brown eyes narrowed slightly and he shrugged. 'They fought in Vietnam,' he said. 'So I guess they had their reasons.'

'Mark lost half his foot in Vietnam.'

Norah found herself glancing down at Mark's boots.

'The front half,' he said, tapping his right foot.

'I see,' Norah said, deeply embarrassed.

'Look, Mark, can you give us a minute?' Bree asked.

He glanced at the stirring crowd. 'Not really. I'm the next speaker.'

'It's OK. I'll be right back,' she said, then took Norah's hand and pulled her a few yards away. 'What are you doing here?' she asked.

'I'm not sure,' Norah said. 'I had to stop because of the crowd.'

Bree nodded. 'It's amazing, isn't it? There must be five thousand people here. It's because of Kent State. It's the end.'

The end of what? Norah wondered, leaves fluttering around her. Wasps swam lazily in the sunny air by her garage. Could the world end on such a day?

'Is that your boyfriend?' she asked.

Bree nodded, smiling a private smile.

'Oh, look at you! You're in love.'

'I suppose so,' Bree said softly, glancing at Mark. 'I suppose I am. Hey, can I bring him this weekend? To your party?'

'Sure,' Norah said, though she wasn't sure at all.

'Great. Oh, Norah, did you get that job you wanted?'

'I don't know yet,' Norah replied. Suddenly her aspirations seemed so trivial. 'I'm not sure I want it any more. It was just a little box of an office. You wouldn't be caught dead in it.'

'I'm not you,' Bree pointed out, impatient. 'You wanted this job, Norah. For the glamour. For the independence.'

'I'd be typing, not travelling. It would be years and years before I earned any trips. It's not exactly what I imagined for my life, Bree.'

'You make me so crazy, Norah. Why can't you just *be* and let the world unfold? You're sticking your head in the sand. That's what I see.'

'You don't see anything but the next available man.'

'All right. We're done.' Bree took a single step and was immediately swallowed by the crowd: a flash of colour, then gone.

At home, in her sunny kitchen, Norah made herself a gin and tonic, then paused before the photograph of herself standing on the stone bridge. *Let me take your picture,* David had called, insistent, and she'd turned to find him, kneeling, focusing, intent on preserving the moment. She'd been right about that camera, to her own regret. David, fascinated to the point of obsession, had built a darkroom above the garage.

Norah took her drink outside. She stood below the papery nest, watching the wasps circle it and disappear inside. Now and then one flew close to her, drawn to the sweet smell of gin. She finished the drink, put the glass down on the driveway, then went to find her gardening gloves and a long-handled hoe. She stepped round Paul's tricycle. He was already too big for it; she should pack it away with his baby clothes, his outgrown toys. David did not want more children, and now that Paul was at school she had given up arguing with him about it.

Norah pulled on her gloves and stepped back into the sun. The hoe was heavy in her hands. She lifted it slowly and took a bold swipe at the nest, the blade slicing easily through the papery skin. But as she pulled the hoe back, wasps, furious and determined, poured out of the torn nest and flew after her. One stung her wrist, another her cheek. She dropped the hoe and ran inside, slamming the door.

Outside, the swarm circled, buzzing angrily around the ruined nest. She went into the kitchen and made another drink, dabbing some gin on her cheek and her wrist, where the stings were beginning to swell.

'All right, you damned wasps,' she said out loud. 'You've had it now.'

There was insect repellent in the closet, above the coats and shoes and the vacuum cleaner—a steel-blue Electrolux, brand new.

The wasps were busy, already reassembling the nest, and they seemed not to notice Norah when she came outside again, carrying the Electrolux. She'd put her gloves back on, her hat and a jacket, and wrapped a scarf round her face. Boldly, she stuck the nozzle into what remained of the nest. The wasps buzzed and rushed, but were quickly sucked in with a rattling sound. She waved the nozzle in the air, a magic wand, collecting the angry insects. When she had them all, she looked for some way to cover the nozzle and noticed the tailpipe of the car. The nozzle fitted on it perfectly. Deeply satisfied, Norah turned the machine off and went inside.

At the bathroom basin, she undid the scarf and took off her hat, checking the mirror. An angry red welt rose on her cheek.

She glanced at her watch. It was time to get Paul. On the back steps Norah paused, groping in her bag for the house keys. A strange noise from the driveway made her look up. It was a kind of buzzing, and at first she thought the wasps had escaped. But the blue air was empty. The buzzing became a sizzling, and then there was the scent of burning wires. It was coming, Norah realised, from the Electrolux. She hurried down the steps. Her feet hit the driveway when suddenly the vacuum cleaner exploded and sprang out of reach, falling amid the rhododendrons, smoke billowing out in oily clouds.

Norah stood with her hand outstretched, trying to take in what had happened. A piece of the tailpipe had been pulled from the car. Seeing this, she understood: the gasoline fumes must have gathered in the vacuum cleaner's still-hot engine, causing it to explode. Norah thought of Paul, allergic to bees, who might have been in its path if he'd been home.

As she watched, a wasp drifted out of the tailpipe and flew off.

This was too much for Norah. Her hard work, her ingenuity, and now, despite everything, the wasps were going to escape. She crossed the lawn. With one swift motion, she opened the vacuum cleaner, reached in through the bloom of smoke to pull out the paper bag full of dust and insects, threw it on the ground and began to stamp on it.

Even after it was clear that all the wasps inside the bag must be dead, Norah kept dancing on the pulpy mess, wild and intent. Something was happening, in the world and in her heart. The next day she would replace the vacuum cleaner without mentioning the incident to David. She would cancel the tuxedo for Kay's fund-raiser; she would accept that job. Glamour, yes, and adventure, and a life of her own.

Norah stepped off the soggy paper bag. Dazed, cold sober, she walked across the lawn, fingering her keys. She got in the car, as if it were any other day, and drove off to get her son.

## II

'DAD? DADDY?'

At the sound of Paul's voice, his quick light steps on the garage stairs, David looked up from the exposed sheet of paper he had just slipped into the developer.

'Hang on!' he called out. 'Just a second, Paul.' But even as he spoke the door burst open, spilling light into the room.

'Damn it!' David watched the paper darken rapidly, the image lost in the sudden burst of light. 'Damn it, Paul, haven't I told you a million zillion *trillion* times not to come in when the red light is on?'

'Sorry. I'm sorry, Dad.'

David took a deep breath, chastened. Paul was only six, and he looked very small in the doorway. 'It's OK, Paul. Come on in. I'm sorry I yelled at you.' He squatted down and held out his arms.

Paul plunged into them, resting his head briefly on David's shoulder. Slight and wiry, Paul was a boy who moved through the world like quicksilver, quiet and watchful and eager to please.

'OK. What was so important?' David asked, sitting back on his heels.

'Dad, look!' Paul said. 'Look what I found!'

He unclenched his small fist. Several flat stones, thin disks with a hole in the centre, rested on his palm, the size of buttons.

'These are great,' David said. 'Where did you find them?'

'When I went with Jason to his grandfather's farm. There's a creek and we were wading and I found these by the edge of the water.'

'Wow.' David fingered the fossils; light and delicate, millennia old. 'These fossils were part of a sea lily, Paul. You know, a long time ago, a lot of Kentucky used to be under an ocean.'

'Really? Neat. Is there a picture in the rock book?'

'Maybe. We'll check as soon as I clean up. How are we doing on time?' he added, stepping to the darkroom door and glancing outside. It was a beautiful spring day, the air soft and warm, dogwoods in bloom all around the perimeter of the garden. Norah had set up tables and covered them with bright cloths. She'd arranged plates and punch, chairs and napkins, vases of flowers. A maypole, fashioned round a lean poplar tree in the centre of the back yard, streamed bright ribbons.

He stepped back into the darkroom, cool and hidden.

'Mom's getting dressed,' Paul said. 'I'm not supposed to get dirty.'

'A tough order,' David observed, sliding the bottles of fixer and developer onto a high shelf beyond Paul's reach. 'Go on inside, OK? I'll be right there. We'll look up those sea lilies.'

David washed out the trays and set them to dry, then removed the film from the developer and put it away. He stood in the quiet darkroom for a few seconds longer before he followed Paul across the lawn.

Norah was in the kitchen, wearing an apron over a suit of coral-coloured silk, arranging parsley and cherry tomatoes on a meat platter.

'It looks great out there,' he said. 'Anything I can do?'

'Get dressed?' she suggested, glancing at the clock. She dried her hands on a towel. 'But first put this platter in the fridge downstairs.'

David took the platter, the glass cool against his hands. 'Such a lot of work,' he observed. 'Why don't you have these parties catered?'

He had meant to be helpful, but Norah paused, frowning, on her way out of the door.

'Because I enjoy this,' she said. 'The planning and the cooking—all of it. Because it gives me a lot of pleasure. I have a lot of talents,' she added, coolly, 'whether you realise it or not.'

'That's not what I meant.' David sighed. These days they were like two planets in orbit round the same sun, not drawing any closer. 'I just meant, why not have some help? We can afford it.'

'It's not about the money,' she said, stepping outside.

He put the platter away and went upstairs to shave. Paul followed him in and sat on the edge of the tub, talking a mile a minute. He loved Jason's grandfather's farm; he had helped milk a cow there yesterday, and Jason's grandfather had let him drink some milk, still warm.

David lathered on the soap with a soft brush, taking pleasure in listening. The razor blade slid in smooth clean strokes against his skin.

'I used to milk cows,' David said. He reached for his shirt. 'I used to be able to squirt a stream of milk straight into the cat's mouth.'

'That's what Jason's grandpa did! I wish Jason was my brother.'

David, putting on his tie, watched Paul's reflection in the mirror and his thoughts travelled to his daughter. Every few months, shuffling through the office mail, he came across Caroline's loopy handwriting. Each envelope bore a different postmark. Sometimes she enclosed a new post-office box number—always in vast cities—and whenever she did this, David sent money. They had never known each other well, yet her letters to him had grown increasingly intimate over the years. He kept them locked in a filing cabinet in the darkroom so he would always know where they were. So Norah would never find them.

'Dad, you forgot to look up the fossils,' Paul said. 'You promised.'

'That's right,' David said, pulling himself back to the present, adjusting the knot in his tie. 'That's right, son. I did.'

They went downstairs together to the den and spread the familiar books on the desk. The fossil was a crinoid, from a small sea animal with a flowerlike body.

'I'm going to show Mom,' Paul said. He grabbed the fossil and ran off through the house and out of the back door. David got a drink and stood by the window. A few guests had arrived and were scattered across the lawn, the men in dark blue jackets, the women like bright spring flowers in pink and vibrant yellow and pastel blue. Norah moved among them, hugging the women, shaking hands, managing the introductions. She had been so quiet when David first met her: calm and self-contained and watchful. He could never have imagined her so gregarious and at ease, launching a party she had orchestrated. Yet David knew this success would not be enough, not even for a day. By evening she would have moved on to the next thing, and if he woke in the night and ran his hand along the curve of her back, hoping to stir her, she would murmur and catch his hand in hers and turn away.

Paul was on the swing now, flying high into the blue sky. He wore the crinoids on a long piece of string round his neck; they lifted and fell, bouncing against his small chest.

'Paul,' Norah called, her voice drifting in clearly through the open screen. 'Paul, take that thing off your neck. It's dangerous.'

David took his drink and went outside. He met Norah on the lawn. 'Don't,' he said softly, touching her arm. 'He made it himself.'

'I know. I gave him the string. But he can wear it later. If he slips while he's playing and it gets caught, he could choke.'

'That's not likely,' he said. 'Nothing bad will happen to him, Norah.'

'You don't know that.'

'Even so, David's right, Norah.'

The voice came from behind. He turned to see Bree. She was wearing a spring dress of filmy material, which seemed to float around her as she moved, and holding hands with a young man with reddish hair.

'Bree, honestly, it could choke him,' Norah insisted, turning too.

'He's swinging,' Bree told her lightly, as Paul flew high against the sky, his head tipped back, sun on his face. 'Look at him, he's so happy. Don't make him get down and get all worried. Nothing's going to happen.'

Norah forced a smile. 'No? The world could end. You said so yourself just yesterday.'

'But that was yesterday,' Bree said. She touched Norah's arm and they exchanged a long look, connected in a way that excluded everyone else.

'What happened yesterday?' David asked. 'Were you at the fire, Bree?' He and Norah had woken in the night to sirens, to the acrid smell of smoke and a strange glow in the sky. They had come outside to stand with their neighbours on the dark, quiet lawns, their ankles growing wet with dew, while on campus the ROTC building burned. For days the protests had been growing, while in towns along the Mekong River bombs fell and people ran, cradling their dying children in their arms. Across the river in Ohio now, four students lay dead. But no one had imagined this in Lexington, Kentucky.

Bree turned to him, her long hair swinging, and shook her head. 'No. I wasn't there, but Mark was.' She smiled at the young man beside her and slipped her slender arm through his. 'This is Mark Bell.'

'Mark fought in Vietnam,' Norah added. 'He's here protesting the war.'

'Ah,' David said. 'An agitator.'

'A protester, I believe,' Norah corrected, waving across the lawn. 'There's Kay Marshall,' she said. 'Will you excuse me?'

'A protester, then,' David repeated, watching Norah walk away.

'That's right,' Mark said. He spoke with self-mocking intentness. 'The relentless pursuit of equity and justice.'

'You were on the news,' David said, remembering. 'Last night. You were giving some kind of speech. So. You must be glad about the fire.'

Mark shrugged. 'Not glad. It happened, that's all. We go on.'

'Well,' Bree said, after a long moment of silence, 'I'm getting thirstier by the second. Mark? David? Want a drink?'

'I'll come with you,' Mark said, extending his hand to David.

David watched them merge into the bright milling crowd, then he went into the coolness of the garage and up the stairs, where he took his camera from the cupboard and loaded a new roll of film. Norah's voice lifted above the crowd and he remembered the feel of her skin when he'd reached for her that morning, the smooth curve of her back. He remembered the moment she'd shared with Bree, how connected they were, beyond any bond he'd ever share with her again.

He took his camera and moved around the edges of the party, smiling and saying hello, shaking hands, drifting away from conversations to catch moments of the party on film. He paused before a vase of tulips, focusing in close, the sounds of the party falling away as he concentrated. He was startled to feel Norah's hand on his arm.

'Put the camera away,' she said. 'Please. It's a party, David. You should get a drink and join in.'

'I have a drink,' he pointed out. 'No one cares that I'm taking a few pictures, Norah.'

'I care. It's rude.'

They were speaking softly, and during the whole exchange Norah had not stopped smiling. Her expression was calm; she nodded and waved across the lawn. And yet David could feel the pressed-back anger.

'I've worked so hard,' she said. 'Why can't you just enjoy it?'

'Hey, Dad!' Paul called, and David looked around, trying to locate his son. 'Mom and Dad, look at me. Look at me!'

'He's in the hackberry tree,' Norah said, shading her eyes and pointing. 'Look, up there, about halfway up. How did he do that?'

'I bet he climbed up from the swing. Hey!' David called, waving.

'Get down right now!' Norah called. And then, to David, 'He's making me nervous.'

'He's a kid,' David said. 'Kids climb trees. He'll be fine.'

'Hey, Mom! Dad! Help!' Paul called, but when they looked up at him, he was laughing.

'Remember when he used to do that in the grocery store?' Norah asked. 'Remember, when he was learning to talk, how he used to shout out "help" in the middle of the store?'

They laughed together and David felt a wave of gladness.

'Put the camera away,' she said, her hand on his arm.

'Yes,' he said. 'I will.'

Bree had wandered over to the maypole and picked up a purple ribbon. A few others, intrigued, had joined her. David started back to the garage, watching the fluttering ends of the ribbons. He heard a sudden rush and stirring of the leaves, a branch cracking loudly. He saw Bree lift her hands, the ribbon slipping from her fingers. David turned round in time to see Paul hit the ground with a thud. He ran, pushing through the guests, and knelt beside his son. Paul grabbed David's hand, trying hard to breathe.

'It's OK,' David said, smoothing Paul's forehead. 'You fell out of the tree and lost your wind, that's all. Just relax. Take another breath.'

'Is he all right?' Norah asked, kneeling down beside him in her coral suit. 'Paul, sweetie, are you OK?'

Paul gasped and coughed, tears standing in his eyes. 'My arm hurts,' he said, when he could speak again. 'My arm really hurts.'

'Which arm?' David asked, using his calmest voice.

It was his left arm, and when David lifted it carefully, supporting the elbow and the wrist, Paul cried out in pain.

'David!' Norah said. 'Is it broken?'

'Well, I'm not sure,' he said calmly, though he was nearly certain that it was. He rested Paul's arm gently on his chest. 'Paul, I'm going to carry you to the car. Then we're going to go to my office, OK?'

Slowly, gently, he lifted Paul. His son was so light in his arms. Their guests parted to let him pass. He put Paul in the back seat of the car, got a blanket from the trunk and tucked it around him.

'I'm coming too,' Norah said, sliding in the front seat beside him.

'What about the party?'

'There's lots of food and wine,' she said. 'They'll have to figure it out.'

They drove through the bright spring air towards the hospital. David glanced at Paul in the rearview mirror. He was quiet, uncomplaining, but tears streaked his pale cheeks.

In the Emergency Room, David used his influence to hurry the process of admission and X-ray. He helped Paul get settled in a bed, left Norah reading him stories from a book she'd grabbed in the waiting room, and went to pick up the X-rays. When he took them from the technician, he saw his hands were trembling, so he walked down the hall to his office.

The door swung shut behind him, and he groped for the light switch. A panel on the wall pulsed and then filled with a steady white light. He slipped Paul's X-rays beneath the clips. The damage was simple enough: clear, straightforward fractures of the ulna and the radius. He walked back down the hall, and found Norah holding Paul in her lap.

'Is it broken?' she asked right away.

'Yes, I'm afraid so,' David said.

'I was so careful about the wasps,' Norah said, helping him move Paul back to the examination table. 'I got rid of the wasps, and now this.'

'It was an accident,' David said.

'I know,' she said, near tears. 'That's the whole problem.'

David didn't answer. He had taken out the materials for the cast and now he concentrated on applying the plaster. Paul's arm was small and the cast grew steadily, as bright and seductive as a sheet of paper. In a few days it would be a dull grey, and covered with childhood graffiti.

'Three months,' David said. 'And you'll have the cast off.'

'That's almost the whole summer,' Norah said. 'You said nothing would happen and now he has a broken arm. Just like that. It could have been his neck. His back.'

David felt tired all of a sudden, torn up about Paul, exasperated with Norah too. 'It could have been, yes, but it wasn't. So just stop it, Norah.'

Away from the bright motion of the party, she carried her sadness like a dark stone clenched in her palm. He longed to comfort her.

'I wish you were happier,' he said softly. 'I wish there were something I could do.'

'You don't have to worry,' she said. 'I got a job yesterday.'

'A job?'

'Yes. A good job.' She told him all about it then: a travel agency, mornings. She'd be home in time to pick Paul up from school. As she spoke, David felt as if she were flying away from him. 'I've been going crazy,' Norah added. 'This will be a good thing.'

'OK,' he said. 'That's fine. If you want a job so much, take it.' He tickled Paul and reached for his otoscope. 'Here,' he said. 'Look in my ears. See if I left any birds in there.'

Paul laughed, and the cool metal slid against David's ear lobe.

'I knew you wouldn't like this,' Norah said.

'Well, what do you expect?' he said, trying to keep his voice even, for Paul's sake. 'It's hard not to see this as criticism.'

'It would only be criticism if it were about you,' she said. 'That's what you don't understand. It's not about you, David. It's about freedom.'

'Freedom?' he said. She'd been talking to her sister again, he'd bet his life on it. 'You think anyone is free, Norah? You think I am?'

There was a long silence and he was grateful when Paul broke it. 'No birds, Dad. Just giraffes.'

'Really? How many?'

'Six.'

'Six! Good grief! Better check the other ear.'

'Maybe I'll hate the job,' Norah said. 'But at least I'll know.'

'No birds,' Paul said. 'No giraffes. Just elephants.'

'Elephants in the ear canal,' David said, taking the otoscope. 'We'd better get home right away.' He forced himself to smile, squatting down to pick Paul up, cast and all. As he felt his son's weight, the warmth of his good bare arm round his neck, David let himself wonder how their lives would have been if he'd made a different decision six years ago. *David,* Caroline Gill had written in her most recent letter, *I've got a boyfriend now. He's very nice, and Phoebe is fine; she loves to catch butterflies and sing.*

Outside it was still a beautiful day, late afternoon, clear and sunny. By the time they got home, the guests had dispersed. David paused, surveying the lawn, scattered with chairs, then he carried Paul inside and up the stairs. He gave him a drink of water, and the orange chewable aspirin he liked, and sat with him on the bed, holding his hand.

'Read me a story, Dad,' Paul said, so David settled himself on the bed, holding Paul in his arms, turning the pages of *Curious George*, who was in the hospital with a broken leg. Downstairs, Norah moved through the rooms, cleaning up. The screen door swung open and shut, open and shut again. He imagined her walking through it, dressed in a suit, heading for her new job and a life that excluded him.

# June 1970

'WELL, PHOEBE CERTAINLY HAS your hair,' Doro observed.

Caroline touched the nape of her neck, considering. They were on the east side of Pittsburgh, in an old factory building that had been converted into a progressive preschool. At six, Phoebe was chubby, with dimpled knees and a winning smile. Her eyes were a delicate almond shape, upslanted, dark brown. This morning she wore a pink and white striped dress, which she had chosen and put on by herself—backwards.

'Do you think so?' she asked Doro, running her fingers through the hair behind her ear, knowing that no genetic connection existed. 'Do you think her hair's like mine?'

'Oh, yes. Sure it is.'

To the other children in this preschool Phoebe was simply herself, a friend who liked the colour blue and Popsicles and twirling in circles; her differences went unnoticed. In the first weeks, Caroline had watched warily, braced against the sorts of comments she'd heard too often. 'What a terrible shame!' 'You're living my worst nightmare.' And once, 'At least she won't live very long—that's a blessing.' But here the teachers were young and enthusiastic, and the parents had followed their example: Phoebe might struggle more, go slower, but like any child she'd learn.

'This place has been so good for Phoebe,' Doro said.

Caroline nodded. 'I wish the Board of Education could see her here.'

'You have a strong argument and a good lawyer. You'll be fine.'

Caroline glanced at her watch. Her friendship with Sandra had grown into a political force, and today the Upside Down Society, over 500 members strong, would ask the school board to include their children in public schools. Their chances were good, but Caroline was still very nervous. So much rested on this decision.

A speeding boy careened past Doro, who caught him gently by the shoulders. Doro's hair was pure white now, in striking contrast to her dark eyes. She swam every morning and she'd taken up golf, and lately Caroline often caught her smiling to herself, as if she had a secret.

'It's so good of you to come today to cover for me,' Caroline said, pulling on her coat.

Doro waved her hand. 'Don't mention it. I'd much rather be here, actually, than fighting with the department over my father's papers.' Her voice was weary, but a smile flickered across her face.

'Doro, if I didn't know better, I'd guess you were in love.'

Doro only laughed. 'What a bold conjecture,' she said. 'And speaking of love, can I expect Al this afternoon? It's Friday, after all.'

It was Friday, yes, but Caroline hadn't heard from Al all week. Usually he called from the road, from Columbus or Atlanta or even Chicago. He'd asked her to marry him twice this year and each time she'd said no. They had argued on his last visit—'You hold me at arm's length,' he'd complained—and he'd left angry, without saying goodbye.

'We're just close friends, Al and I. It's not that easy.'

'Don't be ridiculous,' Doro said. 'Nothing's simpler.'

So it *was* love, Caroline thought. She kissed Phoebe's soft cheek and went away in Leo's old Buick. Leo had been dead for almost a year. In the last months of his life he had grown frail, spending most of his days in an armchair near the window with a book in his lap, gazing out at the street. One day Caroline had found him slumped there, his skin so pale that she knew he was dead before she touched him.

After his funeral, a quiet affair crowded with physics professors and gardenias, Caroline offered to leave, but Doro wouldn't hear of it. 'I'm used to you. I'm used to the company. No, you stay.'

Caroline drove across the city she had come to love, found a parking spot on the narrow street and entered the building.

Sandra was already sitting in the shabby meeting room with half a dozen other parents from the Upside Down board. Their lawyer, Ron Stone, sat next to Sandra, whose blonde hair was pulled severely back, her face serious and pale. Caroline took the remaining seat beside her.

The door swung open almost immediately, and men from the Board of Education began to file in, relaxed, joking with one another, shaking hands. When everyone was settled and the meeting had been called to order, Ron Stone stood and cleared his throat.

'All children deserve an education,' he began, his words familiar. The evidence he presented was clear, specific: steady growth, tasks accomplished. Still, Caroline watched the faces in front of her turn impassive, masked. When Ron paused, a young man with dark wavy hair spoke.

'Your passion is admirable, Mr Stone. We on the board appreciate everything you say, and we appreciate the commitment and devotion of these parents. But these children are mentally retarded; that's the bottom line. Their accomplishments, significant though they may be, have taken place within a protected environment, with teachers capable of giving extra, perhaps undivided, attention.'

Caroline met Sandra's eye. These words were familiar too.

'Mentally retarded is a pejorative term,' Ron Stone replied evenly. 'These children are delayed, yes, no one's questioning that. But they are *not* stupid. The best hope for their growth and development, as for all children, is an educational environment without predetermined limits. We ask only for equity today.'

'Ah. Equity, yes. But we haven't got the resources,' said another man. 'To be equitable, we would have to accept them all, a flood of retarded individuals that would overwhelm the system. Take a look.'

He passed around copies of a report and began doing a cost–benefit analysis. Caroline took a deep breath.

'It's not about numbers,' she said. 'It's about children. I have a daughter who is six years old. It takes her more time, it's true, to master new things. But what I see is a little girl who wants to learn and who loves everyone she sees. And I see a roomful of men who appear to have forgotten that in this country we promise an education to every child—regardless of ability.'

The voice of the dark-haired man was gentle. 'I have—we all have—great sympathy for your situation. But how likely is it that your daughter, or any of these children, will master any academic skills? If it were me, I'd rather have her settled in a productive and useful trade.'

'She's six years old,' Caroline said. 'She's not ready to learn a trade.'

Ron Stone had been watching the exchange, and now he spoke. 'Actually,' he said, 'this entire discussion is beside the point.' He opened his briefcase and took out a thick cluster of papers. 'This is not just a moral or logistical issue. It's the law. This is a petition, signed by these parents and by five hundred others. It's appended to a class-action lawsuit filed on behalf of these families to allow the acceptance of their children into Pittsburgh's public schools.' He shut his briefcase. 'We'll be in touch.'

Outside on the old stone steps, they burst into talk; Ron was pleased, cautiously optimistic, but the others were ebullient.

Agitated, still, from her speech, Caroline drove back to the preschool. Phoebe jumped up from the circle group and ran to Caroline, hugging her knees. Briefly, Caroline told Doro what had happened. Doro, late for work, touched her arm. 'We'll talk more tonight.'

The drive home was beautiful, leaves on the trees and lilacs blooming like drifts of foam and fire against the hills. Caroline parked in the alley, disappointed to see that Al hadn't arrived. Together, she and Phoebe walked beneath the shade of the sycamores. Caroline sat on the porch steps and turned on the radio. Phoebe started spinning on the soft grass, her arms held out and her head flung back, face to the sun.

Caroline watched her, still trying to shed the tension of the morning. There was reason to hope, but after all these years of struggling to change the world's perceptions, Caroline made herself stay cautious.

The sunlight touched amber glints in Phoebe's dark hair, and Caroline remembered Norah Henry beneath the bright clinic lights. For an instant she was stung with weariness and doubt.

Phoebe stopped in her twirling, arms held out to keep her balance. Then she gave a shout and ran across the lawn and up the steps to where Al stood, looking down, a brightly wrapped package in one hand for Phoebe and bunch of lilacs that Caroline knew were for her.

Her heart lifted and she stood, feeling a rush of pleasure. How afraid she'd been that this time he would stay away.

'Pretty day,' he said, squatting to hug Phoebe, who flung her arms round his neck in welcome. The package contained a filmy butterfly net with a carved wooden handle, which she took at once, running off toward a bank of dark blue hydrangeas. 'How did the meeting go?'

She told him the story and he listened, shaking his head.

'Well, school's not for everyone,' he said. 'I sure didn't like it much. But Phoebe's a sweet kid and they shouldn't keep her out.'

'That was a nice gift,' she said, nodding across the grassy space where Phoebe was running, the net making bright arcs in the air.

'Fellow in Georgia made it,' Al said. 'Nicest guy. Had a whole bunch of them he'd carved for his grandkids. Spent the whole night talking, me and him. Now, that's the plus of the wandering life. Oh, yeah,' he went on, reaching into his pocket and pulling out a white envelope. 'Here's your mail from Atlanta.'

Caroline took the envelope without comment. Inside there would be several twenty-dollar bills folded neatly into a plain white paper. Al brought them back from Cleveland, Memphis, Atlanta, Akron: cities he frequented on his runs. She told him simply that the money was for Phoebe, from her father. When it came, she put it in the bank and didn't think about it until the next envelope arrived. She had done this for five years now, and she had saved almost $7,000.

Phoebe was still running, chasing after butterflies, birds, motes of light. Al was fiddling with the radio dial.

'The nice thing about this city is that you can really find some music. Some of the podunk little towns I stay in, all you get is the Top Forty.' He began to hum along with 'Begin the Beguine'.

'My parents used to dance to this song,' Caroline said.

'We ought to go dancing,' Al said. 'You like to dance, Caroline?'

Caroline felt something shift in her then, some excitement. She couldn't place its source: something to do with her anger from the morning passing, and the vibrant day.

'Why wait?' she asked, and extended her hand.

He was puzzled, bemused, but then he was standing with his hand resting on her shoulder and they were moving on the lawn to the thin strains of the music. Sunlight mingled in her hair and they moved together so easily, dipping and turning. They swayed in the grass, turning with the music, connected by it. The traffic rushing by was as present and soothing as the ocean. Other sounds, thin, lifted through the strands of music, through the bright day. Caroline didn't register them at first. Then Al turned her and she stopped dancing. Phoebe was kneeling in the soft warm grass by the hydrangeas, crying too hard to speak, holding up her hand. Caroline ran and knelt beside her, studying the angry swollen circle on Phoebe's palm.

'It's a bee sting,' she said. 'Oh, sweetie, it's all right,' she said, smoothing Phoebe's hair.

But Phoebe's sobs were giving way to a wheezing like the croup she'd suffered as a child. Her palm was swelling; the back of her hand and her fingers too. Caroline rose swiftly and called to Al.

'Hurry!' she cried, her voice loud. 'Oh, Al, she's allergic.'

She was lifting Phoebe, heavy in her arms, and then Al was there, taking Phoebe and running to the car, and Caroline got the keys and her bag from the kitchen counter. She drove as fast as she dared through the city streets. By the time they reached the hospital, Phoebe's breath was coming in short, desperate gasps. They left the car at the entrance and Caroline grabbed the first nurse she saw.

'It's an allergic reaction. We need to see a doctor *now*.'

The nurse led them through a set of steel doors, and Al put Phoebe gently, gently, on a gurney. The nurse swept Phoebe's hair back, touching her fingers to the pulse in her neck. And then Caroline watched her see Phoebe as Dr Henry had seen her on that snowy night so long ago. She saw the nurse taking in the beautifully sloped eyes, the small hands that had gripped the net so hard as she ran after butterflies, saw her eyes narrow slightly. Still, she was not prepared.

'Are you sure?' the nurse asked, looking up and meeting her eyes. 'Are you really sure you want me to call a doctor?'

Caroline stood fixed in place and then her fear transformed itself into anger, fierce and piercing. She raised her hand to slap the bland, impassive face of the nurse, but Al caught her wrist.

'Call the doctor,' he said to the nurse. 'Do it now.'

He put his arm round Caroline and didn't let go, not when the nurse turned away or when the doctor appeared, not until Phoebe's breathing began to ease and some of the colour returned to her cheeks. Then they went together to the waiting room and sat on the orange plastic chairs.

'She could have died,' Caroline said, beginning to tremble.

'But she didn't,' Al said firmly, taking her hand.

Al had been so patient all these years, he had come back again and again, saying he'd wait. But he'd been away two weeks this time, not one. He could drive away in his truck and never come back, never give her another chance to say yes.

She raised his hand and kissed his palm, so rough, so marked with lines. He turned, startled from his thoughts.

'Caroline.' His tone was formal. 'There's something I want to say.'

'I know.' She placed his hand on her heart, held it there. 'Oh, Al, I've been such a fool. Of course I'll marry you,' she said.

## July 1977

'LIKE THIS?' NORAH ASKED.

She was lying on the beach, and beneath her hip the gritty sand slid and shifted. The sun was so hot, like a shimmering metal plate against her skin. She had been here for over an hour, posing and re-posing, the word 'repose' like a taunt, for it was what she longed to do and could not. It was her vacation, after all—she had won two weeks in Aruba for selling the highest number of cruise packages in the state of Kentucky last year—and yet here she was, pressed between sun and beach.

To distract herself, she kept her gaze on Paul, who was running along the shore, a speck on the horizon. He was thirteen and he'd shot up like a sapling in this last year.

Waves crashed slowly against the beach. The tide was turning, coming in, and the harsh noon light would soon change, making the picture David wanted impossible until tomorrow. A strand of hair was stuck against Norah's lip, tickling, but she willed herself to stillness.

'Good,' David said, bent over his camera and clicking off a rapid series of shots. 'Just a few more minutes. We're almost done.' He was on his knees now, his thighs winter pale against the sand. 'Think about the sea. Waves in the water, waves in the sand. You're part of that, Norah.'

She lay still beneath the sun, watching him work, remembering days early in their marriage when they'd gone out for long walks in the spring evenings, holding hands. What had she imagined, that younger version of herself, walking in the soft still light of dusk, dreaming her dreams? Not this life, certainly. Norah had learned the travel business inside out over the past five years. She'd organised the office, built a stable client list and learned to sell, pushing glossy brochures across her desk. Last year, when Pete Warren decided to retire, she'd taken a deep breath and bought the business. Her days were hectic, busy, satisfying—and every night she came home to a house full of silence.

'I still don't see it,' she said, when David finally finished, when she was standing up and shaking sand from her hair. 'Why take the photo of me at all, if you're hoping I'll just disappear into the landscape?'

'It's about expectations,' David said, looking up from his equipment. 'People will look at this picture and see a beach, rolling dunes. And then they'll glimpse something a little odd, something familiar in your curves, or they'll read the title and look again, searching for the woman they didn't see the first time, and they'll find you.'

There was intensity in his voice; the wind coming off the ocean moved through his dark hair. It made her sad, because he spoke of photography as he had spoken once of medicine, of their marriage. Norah had hoped this dream vacation would be a path back to the closeness they'd once shared. This was what had compelled her to spend so many hours lying in the hot sun, holding herself still while David took roll after roll of photos, but they had been here three days now, and nothing but the setting was significantly different from home.

Norah shaded her eyes and looked down the golden curve of the beach. A runner's shape had emerged, but it wasn't Paul. The man was tall, lean, maybe thirty-five or forty. As he drew close to them, he slowed and then stopped, hands on his hips, breathing heavily.

'Nice camera,' he said. Then, looking straight at Norah, he added,

'Interesting shot.' He was beginning to go bald; his eyes were dark brown, intense. She turned away, feeling their heat, as David began to talk: waves and dunes, sand and flesh, two conflicting images at once.

The man had introduced himself as Howard; she wondered where he was from. She gazed down the beach. There, barely visible, was another running figure, her son.

'So you're the inspiration for this study,' Howard said, turning to include Norah.

'I suppose,' she said, brushing sand off her wrist. 'It's a bit hard on the skin,' she added.

'You have beautiful skin,' Howard said. David's eyes widened—he looked at her as if he'd never seen her before—and Norah felt a surge of triumph. *See?* she wanted to say. *I have beautiful skin.*

'You should see David's other work,' Norah said. She gestured to the cottage, tucked low beneath the palms, bougainvillea cascading off the porch trellises. 'He brought his portfolio.'

'I would like that,' Howard said, turning back to David. 'I'm interested in your study.'

'Why not?' David said. 'Join us for lunch.'

But Howard had a meeting in town at one o'clock.

'Here comes Paul,' Norah said. He was running fast along the edge of the water, pushing through the last hundred yards, his arms and legs flashing in the light. 'Our son,' she said to Howard. 'He's a runner too.'

'He has good form,' Howard observed.

Once he reached them, Paul bent down with his hands on his knees, dragging deep breaths into his lungs.

'And good time,' David said, glancing at his watch. 'I hate to see him miss his vocation. Look at that height. Think what he could do on a court. But he doesn't give a damn about basketball.'

Paul looked up, grimacing, and Norah felt a flare of irritation. Why couldn't David understand that the more he pushed basketball, the more Paul would resist?

'I like running,' Paul said, standing up.

'Who can blame you,' Howard said, reaching to shake hands, 'when you run like that?'

Paul shook his hand, flushing with pleasure.

'Come to dinner,' Norah suggested impulsively, inspired by Howard's kindness to Paul. 'Bring your wife, of course,' she added. 'Bring your family. We'll build a fire and cook out on the beach.'

Howard frowned, looking out over the shining water. He clasped his hands and put them behind his head, stretching. 'Unfortunately,' he said, 'I am here alone. A retreat of sorts. I am about to be divorced.'

'I'm sorry,' Norah said, though she was not.

'Come anyway,' David said. 'Norah throws wonderful dinner parties. I'll show you the rest of the series I'm working on—it's all about perception. Transformation.'

'Ah, transformation,' Howard said. 'I'm all for that. I'd love to come to dinner.'

**A**fter lunch, David dozed in the hammock and Norah lay down on the bed beneath the window, feeling abundantly alive. Howard was just an ordinary person, almost scrawny, beginning to go bald, yet he was mysteriously compelling too, conjured perhaps from her own deep loneliness and wishing. She imagined Bree, delighted with her, laughing.

'Well, why not?' she would say. 'Really, Norah, why not?'

Norah stood and fixed herself a gin and tonic with lime. She sat on the porch swing, lazy in the breeze, watching David dozing. Notes from Paul's guitar floated through the soft air. She imagined him, sitting cross-legged on the narrow bed, head bent in concentration over the new Almansa guitar that he loved, a gift from David on his last birthday.

At four o'clock she roused herself, dreamily. She chose a sundress splashed with flowers, gathered at the waist, thin straps over her shoulders. She put on an apron and began to cook, simple but luxurious foods: oyster stew with crisp crackers on the side, corn yellowing on the cob, a fresh green salad, small lobsters she'd bought that morning at the market, still in buckets of sea water. As she moved in the tiny kitchen, the air, warm as breath, glanced across her arms. Outside, Paul and David worked to light a fire in the half-rusted grill, its holes patched with aluminium foil. There were paper plates on the weathered table and wine poured into red plastic glasses. They would eat the lobster with their fingers, butter running down their palms.

She heard his voice before she saw him, another tone, slightly lower than David's and slightly more nasal, with a neutral northern accent. Norah dried her hands on a kitchen towel and went to the doorway.

The three men—it shocked her that she thought of Paul this way, but he stood shoulder to shoulder with David now—were clustered on the sand beyond the porch. Paul, shirtless, stood with his hands thrust into the pockets of his cutoffs, answering with awkward brevity the questions that came his way. They did not see her, her husband and her son; their eyes were on the fire and on the ocean, smooth as glass at this hour. It was Howard, facing them, who lifted his chin to her and smiled.

For an instant, before the others turned, their eyes met. It was a moment real to only the two of them, his face and hers opening in pleasure and promise, the world crashing around them like the surf.

They ate on the porch. Darkness fell swiftly, and David lit the candles set at intervals along the railing. Beyond, the tide came in, waves rushing invisibly against the sand. In the flickering light, Howard's voice rose and fell. He talked about a camera obscura he had built. The camera obscura was a mahogany box that sealed out all light, except for a single pinpoint. This pinprick cast a tiny image of the world onto a mirror. The instrument was the precursor to the camera; some painters—Vermeer was one—had used it as a tool to achieve an extraordinary level of detail in their work. Howard was exploring this, too.

Norah listened, struck by his imagery: the world projected on a darkened interior wall, tiny figures caught in light but moving.

After dinner, Paul went to his room. A few minutes later, notes from his guitar cascaded amid the sounds of the waves. He had a concert to play a few days after they got home. David had insisted that he come on this vacation; he did not take Paul's musical ambitions seriously. But Paul was passionate about the guitar, determined to go to Juilliard.

The conversation moved from optics to the rarefied light of the Hudson River Valley, where Howard lived, and southern France, where he liked to visit. David poured more wine and then they were standing, stepping into the brightly lit living room. David pulled his series of black and white photos from his portfolio, and he and Howard launched into a discussion about the qualities of light.

Norah turned and walked into the kitchen. All around her were dirty pots and the fiery red husks of lobsters. Such a lot of work for such brief pleasure. Usually David did the dishes, but tonight Norah tied an apron round her waist and filled the sink. In the living room the voices went on and on. What had she been thinking, putting on this dress? She was Norah Henry, the wife of David, the mother of Paul. Howard had come to discuss photography with David, and that was that.

She stepped outside, carrying the garbage to the Dumpster, then she walked to the edge of the ocean and stood gazing at the vivid white sweep of stars. Behind her the screen door opened and swung shut. David and Howard came out, walking through the sand and darkness.

'Thanks for cleaning up,' David said. He touched his hand briefly to her back. 'I guess we got talking. Howard has some good ideas.'

'Actually, I was mesmerised by your arms,' Howard noted, referring to the hundreds of shots David had taken. He picked up a piece of driftwood and flung it out to sea.

Behind them the house was like a lantern, casting a bright circle, but the three of them stood in darkness. The conversation meandered, circling back to technique and process. Norah thought she might scream. She put one bare foot behind the other, meaning to turn and leave, when suddenly Howard's fingers ran lightly up the seam of her dress, and then his hand was slipping inside her pocket, a sudden secret warmth against her flesh.

Norah held her breath. David talked on about his pictures. After a moment she made a slight turn, and Howard's hand flowered open against the flatness of her stomach.

'Well, that's true,' Howard said, his voice low and easy. 'You'd sacrifice something in clarity if you were to use that filter. But the effect would certainly be worth it.'

Norah let her breath out, slowly, slowly. Warmth radiated from Howard's fingers and she was filled with such yearning that she ached.

'Now, with the camera obscura you're one step closer to the process,' Howard said. 'It's really quite remarkable, the way it frames the world. I wish you'd come by and see it. Will you?' he asked.

'I'm taking Paul deep-sea fishing tomorrow,' David said. 'Maybe the next day.'

'I think I'll go inside,' Norah said faintly.

'Norah gets bored,' David said.

'Who can blame her?' Howard said. Then he slid his hand from her pocket. 'Come tomorrow morning if you want,' he said. 'I'm making some drawings with the camera obscura.'

He left a few minutes later, disappearing into the darkness.

'I like that guy,' David said later, when they were inside.

Norah was standing at the window looking out at the dark beach.

'Yes,' she agreed. 'So do I.'

The next morning, David and Paul rose before sunrise to drive up the coast and catch the fishing boat. Norah lay there in the dark, listening to them bump around awkwardly in the living room, trying not to make any noise. Footsteps, then, and the roar of the car starting, then fading into silence. She showered and got dressed and made herself a cup of coffee. She ate half a grapefruit, washed her dishes, then walked out of the door. She was wearing shorts and a turquoise blouse patterned with flamingos.

Howard's cottage, a mile down the beach, was nearly identical to her own. He was sitting on the porch, bent over a darkly finished wooden box. He was wearing white shorts and an orange shirt, unbuttoned.

He stood up as she drew near. 'Want some coffee?' he called. 'I've been watching you walk down the beach.'

'Maybe in a minute.' She climbed the steps and ran her hand over the polished mahogany box. 'Is this the camera obscura?'

'It is,' he said. 'Come. Take a look.'

She sat down on the chair and looked through the aperture. The world was there, the long stretch of beach and the cluster of rocks, and a sail moving slowly in the horizon, everything tiny and rendered in such sharp detail, framed and contained, yet alive, not static.

'Oh,' she said. 'It's astonishing. The world is so precise, so rich.'

Howard laughed. 'It's wonderful, isn't it? I knew you'd like it. Go. Be in it. Let me draw you.'

She rose and walked out onto the hot sand. She turned and stood before Howard, his head bent over the aperture, watching his hand move across the sketch pad. How many times had she stood just this way, the subject and an object too, posed to evoke or to preserve what really did not exist, her true thoughts locked away?

So she stood now, a woman reduced to a perfect miniature of herself, every fact of her cast by light onto a mirror. The ocean wind, warm and damp, moved in his hair, and Howard's hands moved quickly as he sketched her, fixing her image on the page. Then she remembered that hand, warming her pocket and her flesh.

She reached down to her waist and caught the hem of her blouse. Slowly, she pulled it over her head and let it fall on the sand. Howard stopped drawing, though he did not lift his head. Norah unzipped her shorts. They slid down over her hips and she stepped out of them. Now she reached behind and unhooked the straps of the bikini top. She pushed the bottoms over her hips and down her legs, kicking them away.

Howard raised his head from the camera obscura and stared. 'You are so beautiful,' he whispered. He rose then, carefully, as if she were a bird he might startle into flight, and crossed the few feet of beach. He pushed a strand of hair from her lip, tucking it gently behind her ear. 'I could never capture what you are in this moment,' he said.

Norah smiled and splayed her hand flat on his chest, feeling the thin madras cotton and the warm flesh. He cupped his hands lightly round her face and she let her own hand fall. Together, without speaking, they walked to the little cottage. She left her clothes on the sand; she did not care that anyone might see them.

The room seemed dim after the light of the beach, and the world was framed in the window as it had been in the lens of the camera obscura, bright and vivid. She sat on the edge of the bed. 'Lie down,' he said, pulling his shirt over his head. 'I just want to look at you for a moment.' She did, and he stood over her, his eyes moving across her skin. 'Stay with me,' he said, and he shocked her by kneeling and resting his head on her belly. She reached down, weaving her hands through his thinning hair, and pulled him up to kiss her.

Later, she would be astonished, not that she had done these things or any of those that followed, but that she had done them on Howard's bed beneath the open, unscreened window. Yet she did not stop, then or later. She went back to Howard again and again, even after David remarked about how many walks she was taking. Even when, lingering in bed while Howard fixed them both a drink, she fished his shorts off the floor and found a photo of his smiling wife and three small children inside a letter that said: *My mother is better, we all miss and love you and will see you next week.*

The ceiling fan clicked in the dim room and she held the photo, gazed outside into the landscape of the imagination, the brilliant light. In real life this photo would have cut, swift and sure, but here she felt nothing. Norah slid the photo back and let his shorts slip back to the floor. Here, this did not matter. Only the dream mattered, and the fevered light. For the next ten days, she met him.

# August 1977

## I

DAVID RAN UP THE STEPS and stepped into the quiet foyer of the school. He was late for Paul's concert, very late. A burst of applause drew him down the hall to the big double wooden doors of the auditorium. He pulled one door open and stepped inside, letting his eyes adjust. A young woman handed him a programme, and as a boy in low-slung jeans walked out onto the stage and sat down with his saxophone, she pointed to the fifth name down. David took a deep, grateful breath. Paul was number seven; he had made it just in time.

The saxophonist began, playing with passion and intensity. David scanned the audience and found Norah in the centre near the front, with an empty seat beside her. He hadn't been sure she would save him a place; he wasn't sure, any more, of anything. Well, he was sure of his anger, and of the guilt that kept him silent about what he'd seen in Aruba; those things certainly stood between them. But he did not have the smallest glimpse into Norah's heart, her desires or motivations.

The sax player finished with a flourish and stood up to bow. During the applause, David made his way down the dimly lit aisle, climbing awkwardly past those already seated to take his place by Norah.

'David,' she said, moving her coat. 'So. You made it after all.'

He could feel her anger, radiating in waves. Her short blonde hair was perfectly styled, and she was all shades of cream and gold, wearing a natural silk suit she'd bought on her first trip to Singapore. As the business had grown, she'd travelled more and more, taking tour groups to places both mundane and exotic.

'You have no right to be angry with me, Norah,' he whispered.

She smelt very faintly of oranges, and her jaw was tense. Onstage, a young man in a blue suit sat down at the piano, flexing his fingers. After a moment he plunged in, the notes rippling.

'I'm not angry. I'm just nervous about Paul. You're the one who's angry.'

'No, it's you,' he said. 'You've been like this ever since Aruba.'

A hand fell on his shoulder, then. He turned to see a heavy woman.

'Excuse me,' she said. 'You're Paul Henry's father, aren't you? Well, that's my son Duke playing the piano, and if you don't mind, we'd really like to hear him.'

David met Norah's eyes then. She was even more embarrassed than he was. He settled back and listened. Duke, a friend of Paul's, played the piano with an intent self-consciousness, but he was technically proficient and passionate too. David watched his hands move over the keys, wondering what Duke and Paul talked about when they rode their bikes through the quiet neighbourhood streets. What did Paul tell his friends that he would never tell his father?

Norah's clothes, discarded in a bright pile against the white sand, the wind lifting the edge of her wildly coloured blouse: that was one thing they would never discuss, though David suspected that Paul had seen them too. They'd risen very early that morning for their fishing trip and had driven up the coast at dawn. But the trip had been cancelled. Disappointed, they'd driven back to the cottage.

The light was good that morning, and David, though disappointed, was also eager to get back to his camera. He'd had another idea, in the middle of the night, about his photos. Howard had pointed out a place where one more image would tie the whole series together. Their conversation had been on David's mind all night, generating a quiet excitement. He'd hardly slept, and now he wanted to get home and shoot another roll of Norah on the sand. But they found the cottage still and cool and empty. Norah had left a bowl of oranges centred on the table. Her washed coffee cup was draining in the sink. 'I think I'll take a run,' Paul said, a shadow in the bright doorway.

Alone in the cottage, David moved the bowl of oranges to the counter and spread his photos on the table. Norah complained that he was becoming obsessed with photography, but he didn't use the camera to escape the world. Sometimes, watching images of her emerge in the bath of developer, he was stilled by a deep sense of his love for her. He was still arranging and rearranging the photos when Paul returned, the door slamming hard behind him.

'That was fast,' David said, looking up.

'Tired,' Paul said. 'I'm tired.' He disappeared into his room.

'Paul?' David said. He went to the door and tried the handle. Locked.

'I'm just tired,' Paul said. 'Everything's fine.'

David waited a few more minutes. Paul was so moody lately. Nothing David did seemed to be the right thing, and the worst were talks with Paul about his future. Paul was gifted in music and sports, with every possibility open to him. David often thought that the difficult choices he had made in his own life would be justified if Paul would only realise his potential. He lived with the nagging fear that his son would throw his gifts away. He knocked again, lightly, but Paul didn't answer.

Finally, David sighed and went back into the kitchen. Then, following an impulse, he went outside and started walking down the beach. He'd gone at least a mile before he glimpsed the bright flutter of Norah's shirt from a distance. When he got closer, he realised that they *were* her clothes, left lying on the beach in front of what must be Howard's cottage. Had they gone for a swim, then? He stopped and scanned the water but didn't see them. Then Norah's familiar laughter, low and musical, drifted out of the cottage windows. He heard Howard's laugh too, an echo of Norah's. He knew then, and he was gripped by a pain as gritty and searing as the hot sand beneath his feet.

Howard, with his thinning hair, giving advice about photography the night before. With Howard. How could she?

And yet, all the same, he had expected this moment for years.

He was filled with the old, sure sense that the snowy night when he had handed their daughter to Caroline Gill would not pass without consequence. He had given their daughter away. This secret stood in the middle of their family. He knew it, he saw it as a rock wall grown up between them. And he saw Norah and Paul reaching out and striking rock and not understanding what was happening, only that something stood between them that could not be seen or broken.

Duke Madison finished playing with a flourish, stood and bowed. The stage was empty then, and the applause faded. One moment passed, and another. People began to murmur.

'Where is Paul?' David asked, glancing down at his programme.

'Don't worry, he's here,' Norah said. To David's surprise, she took his hand and he was washed with an inexplicable relief, believing, for a moment, that nothing had changed; that nothing stood between them after all. 'He'll be out soon.'

Even as she spoke there was a stirring, and then Paul was walking onto the stage: tall and lanky, wearing a clean white shirt with the sleeves rolled up and flashing a wry, crooked smile at the audience. David was aware of Norah's hand in his own as Paul leaned over the guitar, testing a few notes, and then began to play.

It was Segovia, the programme noted: two short pieces, 'Estudio' and 'Estudio Sin Luz'. The notes of these songs, delicate and precise, were intimately familiar. All during the vacation in Aruba this music had spilled out of Paul's room, faster or slower, measures and bars repeated again and again. And yet now David felt he was hearing it for the first time. His heart filled, tears rose in his eyes and his throat ached.

He thought of his sister, singing in her clear, sweet voice; music was a silvery language it seemed she'd been born speaking, just as Paul had. A deep sense of loss rose up in him, woven of so many memories. Too much. He opened his eyes and pushed it all back: June, the music, the powerful rushing love he felt for his son. Paul's fingers came to rest on the guitar. David pulled his hand from Norah's. Fiercely, he applauded.

'Are you all right, David?' Norah asked, glancing at him.

'He's good,' he said at last, barking the words out. 'He's good.'

'Yes.' She nodded. 'That's why he wants to go to Juilliard.' She was still clapping, and when Paul looked in their direction she blew him a kiss. 'Wouldn't that be wonderful? He has a few years left to practise still, and if he gives it everything he has—who knows?'

Paul bowed, left the stage with his guitar. The applause swelled high.

'Everything he has?' David repeated. 'What if it doesn't work out? He's only thirteen. He's too young to shut doors.'

'He's so talented, David. What if this is a door opening?'

'But—it's such an unpredictable life. Can he make a living?'

Norah's face was very serious. She shook her head. 'I don't know. But don't shut the door on his dream.'

'I won't,' David said. 'But I want him to be secure in life.'

Norah opened her mouth to speak, but the auditorium grew quiet as a young woman in a dark red dress came on with her violin, and they turned their attention to the stage.

David watched the young woman and all those who followed, but it was Paul's music that was with him still. When the performances were over, he and Norah made their way to the lobby, stopping to shake hands every few feet, hearing praise for their son. When they finally reached Paul, Norah pushed through the crowd and hugged him, and Paul, embarrassed, patted her on the back. David caught his eye and grinned, and Paul, to his surprise, grinned back. An ordinary moment: again David let himself believe that things would be all right. But seconds later Paul seemed to catch himself. He pulled away from Norah.

'You were great, son,' David said. He hugged Paul, noting the tension in his shoulders, the way he was holding himself: stiff, aloof.

'Thanks. I was kind of nervous.'

'You didn't seem nervous.'

'Not at all,' Norah said. 'You had wonderful stage presence.'

Paul shook his hands at his sides, loosely. 'Mark Miller invited me to play with him at the arts festival. Isn't that the best?'

Mark Miller was David's guitar instructor, with a growing reputation. David felt another surge of pleasure.

'Yes, it is the best,' Norah said, laughing. 'That's absolutely the best.'

She looked up and caught Paul's pained expression.

'What?' she asked. 'What is it?'

Paul shifted, shoving his hands in his pockets, and glanced around the crowded lobby. 'It's just—I don't know—you sound kind of ridiculous, Mom. I mean, you're not exactly a teenager, OK?'

Norah flushed. David watched her grow still with hurt, and his own heart ached. She didn't know the source of Paul's anger, or his own. She did not know that her discarded clothes fluttered in a wind that he himself had set in motion so many years ago.

'That's no way to talk to your mother,' he said, taking on Paul's anger. 'I want you to apologise right now.'

Paul shrugged. 'Right. Sure. OK. Sorry.'

'Like you mean it.'

'David'—Norah's hand was on his arm now—'let's not make a federal case out of this. Please. Let's go home and celebrate. I was thinking I'd invite some people over. What do you think, Paul? I don't know Duke's parents very well, but maybe they'd like to come over?'

'No,' Paul said. 'I don't want to invite anyone. I just want to go home.'

For a moment they stood, an island of silence in the midst of the buzzing room.

'All right, then,' David said at last, 'let's go home.'

The house was dark when they got there, and Paul went straight upstairs. They heard his footsteps moving to the bathroom and back again; they heard his door shutting, the turn of the lock.

'I don't understand,' Norah said. She had slipped off her shoes and she looked very small, very vulnerable, standing in the kitchen in her stocking feet. 'He was so good onstage. He seemed so happy—and then what happened?' She sighed. 'Teenagers. I'd better go and talk to him.'

'No,' David said. 'Let me.'

He climbed the stairs without turning on the light, and when he reached Paul's door he paused in the darkness, remembering how his son's hands had moved with such delicate precision over the strings. He had done the wrong thing all those years ago, when he handed his daughter to Caroline Gill. He'd made a choice, and so he stood here, on this night, in the darkness outside Paul's room. He knocked on the door, but Paul didn't answer. He knocked again, and when there was still no answer David went to the bookcase and found the thin nail he kept there and slid it into the hole in the doorknob. There was a soft click and the door swung open. It did not surprise him to see that the room was empty. When he turned on the light, a breeze lifted the curtain.

'He's gone,' he told Norah. She was still in the kitchen, standing with her arms folded, waiting for the kettle to boil.

'Gone?'

'Out of the window. Down the tree, most likely.'

She pressed her hands to her face.

'Any idea where he went?'

She shook her head. 'I don't know. With Duke, maybe.'

The kettle started to whistle and then a persistent wailing filled the room. David crossed the room and pulled the kettle from the burner.

'I'm sure he's OK,' he said.

Norah shook her head. 'No,' she said. 'That's the thing. I really don't think he is.'

She picked up the phone. Duke's mother gave Norah the address of a post-show party and Norah reached for her keys.

'I'll go,' David said. 'I don't think he wants to talk to you right now.'

'Or to you,' she snapped.

But he saw her understand, even as she spoke. In that moment something was stripped away. It all stood between them then, her long hours away from their cottage, the lies and the clothes on the beach. His lies too. She nodded once, slowly, and he was afraid of what she might say or do, of how the world might be for ever changed.

'I blame myself,' he said. 'For everything.'

He took the keys and went out into the soft summer night. The moon was full, the colour of rich cream. David kept glancing at it as he drove through the silent neighbourhood, along streets solid and prosperous, the sort of place he'd never even imagined as a child. This is what he knew that Paul didn't: the world was precarious and sometimes cruel. He'd had to fight hard to achieve what Paul simply took for granted.

He saw Paul a block before the party, his hands shoved into his pockets, his shoulders hunched. David slowed and tapped the horn. Paul looked up, and for a moment David was afraid he might run.

'Get in,' David said. And Paul did.

David started driving. He was aware of Paul sitting beside him, aware of his soft breathing, aware that he was staring out of the window at the silent lawns they passed.

'You were really good tonight. I was impressed.'

'Thanks.'

They drove two blocks in silence.

'So. Your mother says you want to go to Juilliard.'

'Maybe.'

'You're good,' David said. 'You're good at so much, Paul. You'll have a lot of choices in your life. You could be anything.'

'I like music,' Paul said. 'It makes me feel alive.'

'I understand that,' David said. 'But there's being alive and there's making a living.'

'Right. Exactly.'

'You can talk like this because you've never wanted for a thing,' David said. 'That's a luxury you don't understand.'

They were close to home now, but David turned in the opposite direction. He wanted to stay with Paul in the car, driving through the moonlit world where this conversation was possible.

'You and Mom,' Paul said, his words bursting out, as if he'd been holding them back. 'What's wrong with you? You live like you don't care about anything. You don't have any joy. You just get through the days. You don't even give a damn about that Howard guy.'

So he did know.

'I give a damn,' David said. 'But things are complicated, Paul. I'm not going to talk about this with you. There's a lot you don't understand.'

Paul didn't speak. David stopped at a traffic signal. They sat in silence, waiting for the light to change. He'd made a choice, on the beach; he'd left Norah's clothes lying on the sand, her laughter spilling into the light. He'd gone back to the cottage and worked with the photos, and when she'd returned, he hadn't said a thing about Howard. He'd kept this silence because his own secrets were darker, more hidden, and because he believed that his secrets had created hers.

'Let's stay focused here,' David said at last. 'You don't need to worry about your mother and me. That's not your job. Your job is to find your way in the world. To use all your many gifts. And it can't all be for yourself. You have to give something back. That's why I do that clinic work.'

'I love music,' Paul said softly. 'When I play, I feel like I'm doing that—giving something back.'

'And you are. You are. But, Paul, what if you have it in you to discover, say, another element in the universe? What if you could discover the cure for some rare and awful disease?'

'Your dreams,' Paul said. 'Yours, not mine.'

David was silent, realising that once, indeed, those had been exactly his dreams. He'd set out to fix the world, to change it and shape it, and instead every aspect of his life seemed beyond his grasp.

'Yes,' he said. 'Those were my dreams.'

'What if I could be the next Segovia?' Paul asked. 'Think of it, Dad. What if I have it in me to do that, and I don't try?'

David didn't answer. He'd reached their street again and this time he turned towards home. They pulled into the driveway and stopped in front of the detached garage. David turned off the car.

'It's not true that I don't care,' David said. 'Come on. I want to show you something.'

He led Paul out into the moonlight and up the exterior stairs to the darkroom above the garage. Paul stood by the closed door, his arms folded, radiating impatience, while David set up the developing process, pouring out the chemicals and sliding a negative into the enlarger. Then he called Paul over.

'Look at this,' he said. 'What do you think it is?'

After a moment's hesitation, Paul crossed the room and looked. 'A tree?' he said. 'It looks like a silhouette of a tree.'

'Good,' David said. 'Now look again. I took this during surgery, Paul. I stood up on the balcony of the operating theatre with a telephoto lens. Can you see what else it is?'

'I don't know . . . Is it a heart?'

'A heart, yes. Isn't that amazing? I'm doing a perception series, images of the body that look like something else. That mystery of perception—I care about that. So I understand what you mean about music.'

David sent concentrated light through the enlarger, then slid the paper into the developer. 'Photography is all about secrets,' he said, after a few minutes, lifting the photo with a pair of tongs and slipping it into the fixer. 'The secrets we all have and will never tell.'

'That's not what music is like,' Paul said, and David heard the rejection in his son's voice. He looked up, but it was impossible to read Paul's expression in the soft red light. 'Music is like you touch the pulse of the world. Music is always happening, and sometimes you get to touch it for a while, and when you do you know that everything's connected to everything else.' He opened the darkroom door and stepped out.

After a moment, David pulled open a drawer and removed something from a folder. Then he went to where Paul stood in the gallery room, and showed his son the photograph in his hand. It was black and white, with a scalloped white border.

Paul took the photograph. There was a low, ramshackle house fastened to the side of a hill. In front of it stood four people: a woman in a dress to her calves, wearing an apron, her hands clasped in front of her. A man, gaunt, bent like a comma, stood next to her, holding a hat to his chest. The woman was turned slightly towards the man, and they both had suppressed smiles on their faces, as if in another instant they would burst out in laughter. The mother's hand rested on a girl's blonde head, and between them was a boy, not far from his own age, staring seriously straight into the camera.

'Do you know who these people are?' David asked.

'No,' Paul said, then seemed to change his mind. 'Oh,' he said, pointing to the boy on the steps. 'Oh. That's you.'

'Yes. I was your age. That's my father right behind me. And beside me is my sister. Her name was June. She was good at music, like you. This is the last photo that was ever taken of us all. You can keep it, if you like. I've got another copy. My sister had a heart condition, and she died the next fall. It just about killed my mother, losing her.'

Paul studied the woman in the picture. 'Did she die?' he asked.

'My mother? Yes. Years later. Your grandfather too. They weren't very old, either of them. My parents had hard lives, Paul. Sometimes they didn't know if we were going to have food to eat. It pained my father, who was a hard-working man. And it pained my mother, because they couldn't get much help for June. When I was about your age, I got a job so I could go to high school in town. And then June died, and I made a promise to myself. I was going to go out and fix the world.' He shook his head. 'Well, of course I didn't really do that. But here we are, Paul. We have plenty of everything. We never worry about having enough to eat. You'll go to any college you want. Read any subject you want.'

'But I love music,' Paul said. 'Playing is my life. I'll never give it up.' He turned angrily from his father and ran from the room, clattering down the exterior steps.

David crossed to the window, watching the boy run through the moonlight and up the back stairs and disappear inside, then he turned back to the darkroom and went to the mini-refrigerator where he kept his chemicals and film. He'd wanted to connect with Paul, to have a moment when they understood each other, but his good intentions had come to nothing. He opened the door of the fridge. The envelope was tucked behind several bottles. It was full of twenty-dollar bills. He counted out ten, then twenty, and put the envelope back.

Usually he mailed the money wrapped in a sheet of blank paper, but tonight, Paul's anger lingering in the room, David sat down at the table in the gallery space and wrote a letter. He wrote swiftly, letting the words pour out, all his regrets about the past, all his hopes for Phoebe. Who was she, this child of his flesh, the girl he had given away? He had not expected that she would live this long, or that she would have the sort of life Caroline had told him about. He thought of the loneliness Paul carried with him everywhere. Was it the same for Phoebe? What would it have meant to them to grow up together? *I would like very much to meet Phoebe,* he wrote. *I would like her to know her brother, and for him to know her.* Then he folded the letter round the money, put it all in an envelope, and addressed it. He would mail it tomorrow.

Now he went back into the darkroom and searched through his most recent roll of film. He'd taken some photos during the dinner party in Aruba: Norah, carrying a tray of glasses, various shots of them all relaxing on the porch. It was the final image he wanted; once he found it, he cast it with light onto the paper. In the developing bath, he watched as the image took shape: Norah and Howard on the porch, lifting their glasses of wine in a toast, laughing. A moment both innocent and charged; a moment when a choice was being made.

David took the photograph from the developer, went into the gallery room and stood in the moonlight with the wet photo in his hands, looking at his house, darkened now, Paul and Norah inside, moving in their own orbits, their lives constantly shaped by the gravity of the choice he'd made so many years ago.

In the darkroom again, he hung the photograph of that moment to dry. Unfinished, unfixed, the image wouldn't last. Over the next hours, the picture of Norah laughing with Howard would slowly darken until—within a day or two—it would be completely black.

# II

THEY WERE WALKING towards Duke Madison's place, a little shotgun house right by the railway. Dean with his hands shoved in his jacket pockets, Paul kicking at stones. Paul had been born over here, a few streets down, but even though his mother sometimes drove him over to see the house where he'd first lived, she didn't like him coming over here or to Duke's. But what the hell, she was never around, and as long as his homework was done, which it was, and as long as he'd mowed the lawn and practised the piano for an hour, which he had, he was free.

What she didn't see wouldn't hurt her. What she didn't know . . .

His mind went back once more to that morning in Aruba, when he had gone running on the beach with a carefree heart, pleased because the fishing trip with his father had fallen through. As a child he had loved to fish, but as he'd grown older the fishing trips had come to seem more like something his father planned because they might bond; Paul imagined him reading it in some manual for parents. He'd got the facts of life on one vacation, sitting trapped in a boat on a lake in Minnesota as his father talked about the realities of reproduction. These days, Paul's future was his father's favourite topic, his ideas about as interesting to Paul as a glassy, flat expanse of water.

So he'd been happy to run on the beach, he'd been relieved, and he'd thought nothing of the pile of clothes at first, discarded in front of one of the little cottages. He had run right past them, making for the rocky point. Then he stopped and ran back, more slowly. The clothes had shifted: the sleeve of the blouse was flapping in the ocean wind, and the flamingos, bright pink, danced against the dark turquoise background. He slowed. It could have been anybody's shirt, but his mother had one like it. They had laughed about it in the tourist shop in town and she had bought it as a joke.

So, OK, maybe there were a hundred, a thousand shirts like this around. Still, he leaned down and picked it up. His mother's bikini, nubbly, the colour of flesh and unmistakable, fell out of the sleeve. Paul stood still, unable to move. Finally, he dropped the shirt and started walking, and then he was running back to their own cottage as if seeking sanctuary. He stood in the doorway, trying to pull himself together. His father was arranging photos on the big wooden table. 'What's wrong?' he asked, looking up, but Paul couldn't say. He went to his room and slammed the door and didn't open up, not even when his father came and knocked on it.

His mother was back two hours later, humming, the flamingo shirt tucked neatly into her shorts. 'I thought I'd take a swim before lunch,' she said, as if everything might still be normal. 'Want to come?' He shook his head and that was that, the secret, his secret, hers and now his, between them like a veil.

His father had secrets too, a life that happened at work or in the darkroom, and Paul had figured it was all normal, just the way families were, until he started hanging out with Duke, an awesome piano player he'd met in the band room one afternoon. Paul knew he ought to feel sorry for Mrs Madison, his parents would; she had five kids and a husband who worked at the General Electric plant and wouldn't ever make much money. But Duke's dad liked to play ball with his boys and he came home every night at six when the shift was over.

'So whaddya want to do?' Duke asked him.

'Dunno,' Paul said. 'How about you?'

'We could shoot some hoops.'

'Nah.'

They had crossed Rosemont Garden and were surrounded by tall grass. Duke stopped, fishing in the pockets of his leather jacket.

'Look here,' he said. 'I got this from my cousin Danny.'

It was a small plastic bag full of dried green clippings.

'What is it,' Paul asked, 'a bunch of dead grass?' As he spoke he understood, and he flushed, embarrassed at what a geeky dork he was.

Duke laughed. 'That's right, man, "grass". You ever get high?'

Paul shook his head, shocked despite himself.

'You don't get hooked, if that's what's scaring you. I've done it twice. It's totally amazing. You wanna try it?'

'Sure.' Paul looked around. 'But let's go to my place. No one's home.'

So they walked back to Duke's house, where they'd left their bicycles after school, then cycled slowly through the neighbourhoods to Paul's.

The house was locked, the key hidden under the loose flagstone by the rhododendron. Inside, the air was faintly stale. While Duke called home to say he'd be late, Paul opened a window and the breeze lifted the curtains his mother had made. They had a creamy background with country scenes in dark blue that matched the dark-striped wallpaper.

Duke looked around. 'Man,' he said. 'You're rich.' He sat at the dining-room table and spread out a thin rectangular paper. Paul watched, fascinated, as Duke arranged a line of ragged weed, then rolled a thin white tube.

'Not in here,' Paul said, uneasy at the last minute. They went outside and sat on the back steps; the joint flared orange on the tip and moved back and forth between them.

They went inside at some point, though not before the rain had started, leaving them soaked and suddenly chilled. His mother had left a casserole on the stove but Paul ignored it. Instead Duke ordered a pizza and Paul got out his guitar and they went into the living room, where the piano was, to jam. Paul sat on the edge of the raised hearth and strummed a few chords, then his fingers started moving in the familiar patterns of the Segovia pieces he'd played at the concert. He felt himself being lifted up, the waves riding in and he was on them, and they were carrying him up and up, rising to a crest.

When he finished there was silence for a minute, before Duke said, 'Damn, that was good!' He ran a scale on the piano and launched into his piece from the recital, Grieg's 'March of the Trolls', with its energy and dark joy. Duke played and then Paul did and they didn't hear the doorbell or the knocking; suddenly the pizza delivery boy was standing in the open door. It was dusk by then; a darkening wind surged into the house. They ripped open the boxes and ate furiously, quickly and without tasting, burning their tongues. Paul felt the food settling in him, holding him down like a stone.

'Damn,' Paul said. He put his hands flat on the oak floor, glad to find it there and himself on it and the room around him totally intact.

'No joke,' agreed Duke. 'Some stuff. What time is it?'

Paul stood up and walked to the grandfather clock in the hall. Minutes or hours earlier they had stood here, convulsing with laughter as the seconds ticked off, a gaping stretch of time between each one. Now he looked back on the afternoon and saw it had gone, condensed into a memory no larger than a drop of rain, and the sky was already dark.

The phone rang. Duke was lying flat out on the living-room rug, and it seemed like hours passed before Paul picked up the receiver.

'Sweetie,' his mother said, over noise and silverware in the background. He pictured her in her suit, maybe the dark blue one. 'I've got to take these IBM clients out to dinner. It's important. Is your father home?'

'I did my homework,' he said, studying the grandfather clock, so recently hilarious. 'I practised the piano. Dad's not home.'

There was a pause. 'He promised he'd be home,' she said, sighing. 'Well, that's good about your homework, anyway. Look, Paul, I'll call your father, and I'll be no later than another two hours myself.'

'I'm OK,' he said, remembering last night, how he'd sat on the edge of the windowsill and thought about jumping, and then he was in the air, falling, landing with a soft thud on the ground. 'I'm not going anywhere tonight,' he said.

'I don't know, Paul. I'm worried about you.'

*So come home*, he wanted to say, but in the background laughter rose and fell. 'I'm OK,' he said again. 'You don't need to call Dad.'

'He told me he'd be home,' she said, her tone cool, clipped.

'These people,' he asked, 'from IBM. Do they like flamingos?'

There was a pause, the roar of laughter and clinking glasses.

'Paul,' she said at last. 'Are you all right?'

'I'm fine,' he said. 'It was just a joke. Never mind.'

When she'd hung up, Paul stood listening to the dial tone. In the living room, Duke was still lying on the rug. Paul picked up the empty pizza box and carried it out to the garbage can. He was thirsty like a desert, and he carried a half-gallon of milk back with him to the living room, drinking straight from the jug and then passing it to Duke. He sat down and played again, more quietly. The guitar notes fell through the air, slowly, gracefully, like winged things.

Eventually, Duke got up, muttered goodbye and went outside. Paul stopped playing and went to the window. He watched Duke coast down the driveway on his bike, his right leg swinging over the bar before he disappeared into the street. The house rose around him, silent. It wasn't like the silence in the auditorium, expectant and charged, but rather an emptiness. He wondered about his sister. If she hadn't died, would she like to run? Would she sing?

When he was nine or ten, his mother had taken him to the country cemetery where his sister was buried. Paul had stood, reading the name—PHOEBE GRACE HENRY—and his own birth date, feeling an uneasiness, a weight he could not explain.

'Why did she die?' he asked.

'No one knows,' his mother said and then, seeing his expression, she put her arm round him. 'But it wasn't your fault,' she said fiercely.

But he hadn't believed her then, and he didn't now. If his father secluded himself in his darkroom every evening and his mother worked long past dinner most days and, on their vacations, shed her clothes and slipped into the cottage of a strange man, whose fault could it be? Not his sister's, who had died at birth and left this silence. He was alive, after all. He was here. So surely it was his job to protect them.

## September 1977

CAROLINE CAUGHT THE CORNER of the Polaroid between her thumb and first finger as it slipped from the camera, the image already emerging. On a sea of dark grass, Phoebe was a pale blur in her confirmation dress. Caroline waved the photo dry in the fragrant air.

'One more,' she said.

'Oh, Mom,' Phoebe protested, but she stood still.

The minute the camera clicked she was off, running across the lawn to where their neighbour Avery, aged eight, was holding a tiny kitten with hair the same dark orange as her own. Phoebe, at thirteen, was short for her age, chubby, still impulsive and impassioned.

'I'm confirmed!' she shouted now. Skirt swirling, she ran to Sandra's son Tim, now a teenager too. She wrapped her arms round him, kissing him exuberantly on the cheek.

Then she glanced back anxiously at Caroline. Hugging had been a problem earlier this year, at school. 'I like you,' Phoebe would announce, enveloping a smaller child. Caroline had told her again and again, 'Hugs are special. Hugs are for family.' Slowly Phoebe had learned.

'It's OK, honey,' Caroline called. 'It's OK to hug your friends today.'

Phoebe relaxed. She and Tim went off to pet the kitten. All across the lawn people moved, talking and laughing. A cake, three tiers and frosted white, stood on the table, decorated with dark red roses from the garden. Three layers, for three celebrations: Phoebe's confirmation, her own wedding anniversary and Doro's retirement, a *bon voyage*.

'It's my cake.' Phoebe's voice floated over the rise and fall of conversations, the physics professors and neighbours and choir members and school friends, families from the Upside Down Society. Caroline's new friends from the hospital, where she'd started working part-time once Phoebe was at school, were here too. 'It's my cake.' Phoebe's voice came again, high and floating. 'I'm confirmed.'

Caroline sipped her wine, the air warm as breath on her skin. She didn't see Al arrive but he was suddenly there, sliding a hand round her waist and kissing her cheek, his presence, his scent, sweeping through her. Five years ago they had married at a garden party much like this one, strawberries floating in champagne and the air full of fireflies, the scent of roses. Five years, and the novelty had not worn off.

'Happy anniversary,' he said now, pressing his hands on her waist.

Caroline smiled, filled with pleasure. She took Al's hand, solid and sure, and almost laughed because he'd just arrived and didn't yet know the news. Doro was leaving on a year-long world cruise with her lover, a man named Trace. Al knew that already; plans had been evolving for months. But he didn't know that Doro, in what she called a joyful liberation from the past, had given Caroline the deed to this old house.

Doro was arriving even now, coming down the stairs from the alley in a silky dress. Trace was just behind her, carrying a bag of ice. He was a year younger than she, sixty-five, with short grey hair, a pale, narrow face. He was kind and good to Doro, who clearly adored him.

A gust of wind swept a pile of napkins off the table and Caroline stooped to catch them.

'You're bringing the wind,' Al said, as Doro drew near.

'It's so exciting,' she said, lifting her hands. She had come to resemble Leo more and more, her features sharper, her hair pure white. 'It's such a beautiful party, a wonderful farewell.'

Phoebe ran up, holding the tiny kitten, a ball of pale orange, in her arms. 'Can we keep him?' she asked.

'No,' Caroline replied as she always did. 'Aunt Doro's allergic.'

'Mom,' Phoebe complained, but she was distracted at once by the beautiful table. She tugged on Doro's sleeve. 'Aunt Doro. It's my cake.'

'Mine too,' Doro said, putting one arm round Phoebe's shoulders. 'I'm going on a trip, don't forget, so it's my cake too. And your mother's and Al's because they've been married five years.'

The party lasted until eleven. Doro and Trace lingered after the last guests had left, carrying trays of glasses and left-over cake. Phoebe was asleep by then; Al had carried her inside after she dissolved into tears, overcome by Doro's leaving, weeping with great heaving sobs.

'Don't do any more,' Caroline said, stopping Doro at the top of the steps, brushing past the dense, supple leaves of the lilacs. 'I'll clean up tomorrow, Doro. You have an early flight. You must be eager to be off.'

'I am,' Doro said, her voice so soft Caroline had to strain to hear her. She nodded to the house where Al and Trace were working in the kitchen. 'But, Caroline, it's so bittersweet. I've spent my life here.'

'You can always come back,' Caroline said, fighting a swell of emotion.

'I hope I won't want to,' Doro said. 'Not for more than a visit.' She took Caroline's elbow. 'Let's go and sit on the porch.'

They walked along the side of the house, under arching wisteria, and sat in the swing seat, a river of cars moving by on the parkway.

'You won't miss the traffic,' Caroline said.

'No, that's true. It used to be so quiet. They used to close the street off in the winter. We rode our sleds straight down the middle.'

Caroline pushed the swing, remembering that long-ago night when moonlight flooded the lawns and fell through the bathroom windows, Phoebe coughing in her arms.

The screen door swung open and Trace stepped out.

'Well?' he asked. 'Are you about ready, Doro?'

'Just about,' she said.

'I'll go and get the car, then, and bring it round to the front.' He went back inside.

'I'll miss you, Doro,' Caroline said. 'Phoebe will too.'

Her friend nodded. 'I know. But I'll send postcards from everywhere.'

Headlights poured down the hill, and then the rental car was slowing and Trace's long arm was lifting in a wave.

'It's the call of the road!' he shouted.

'Be well,' Caroline said. She hugged Doro, feeling her soft cheek. 'You saved my life all those years ago, you know.'

'Honey, you saved mine too.' Doro pulled away. Her dark eyes were wet. 'It's your house now. Enjoy it.'

And then Doro was down the steps, her white sweater catching in the wind. She was in the car and waving goodbye; she was gone.

A storm was circling in the hills now, flashing the sky white, dull thunder echoing far away. Al came out with drinks, pushing the door open with his foot, and they sat together in the swing.

'So,' Al said. 'Nice party.'

'It was,' Caroline said. 'It was fun. I'm exhausted.'

'Have you got enough energy to open this?' Al asked.

Caroline took the package and undid the clumsy wrapping. A carved wooden heart fell out, smooth as a water-worn stone in her palm.

'It's beautiful,' she said, pressing the heart against her cheek. 'So warm. It fits right here exactly, in the palm of my hand.'

'I carved it myself,' Al said. 'Nights, on the road. This waitress I know in Cleveland said you'd like it. I hope you do.'

'I do,' Caroline said, linking her arm in his. 'I got something for you too.' She handed him a small box. 'I didn't have time to wrap it.'

He opened the box and took out a new brass key.

'What's this, the key to your heart?'

She laughed. 'No. It's a key to this house.'

'Why? Did you change the locks?'

'No.' Caroline pushed at the swing. 'Doro gave it to me, Al. Isn't that amazing? I have the deed inside the house. She wanted a fresh start.'

One heartbeat. Two, three, and the creak of the swing, back and forth.

'That's pretty extreme,' Al said. 'What if she wants to come back?'

'I asked her that same thing. She said Leo had left a lot of money.'

'Generous,' Al said.

'Yes.'

Al was silent. Caroline listened to the porch swing creaking.

'We could sell it,' he mused. 'Take off ourselves. Go anywhere.'

'It's not worth much,' Caroline said slowly. The idea of selling this house had never crossed her mind. 'Anyway, where would we go?'

'Oh, I don't know. You know me. I've spent my life wandering.'

The comfort of the darkness gave way to a deeper unease. 'So you'd rather not have a house?' Caroline pressed. 'Because it ties you down?'

'I like coming home to you, Caroline. I like coming down that last stretch of highway and knowing you and Phoebe are here, in the kitchen cooking, or planting flowers, or whatever. But, sure, it's appealing, what Doro's doing. Taking off. Wandering the world.'

'I don't have those urges any more,' Caroline said, looking out into the dark garden. 'And Phoebe doesn't handle change well.'

'Well, there's that too,' Al said. He turned to her. 'You know, Caroline, Phoebe's starting to grow up. She's not a little girl any more.'

'She's only thirteen,' Caroline said, thinking of Phoebe and how easily she slipped back into the carefree joys of childhood.

'That's right. She's thirteen. She's—well, you know—starting to develop. I feel uncomfortable picking her up.'

'So don't,' Caroline said sharply.

'You don't have to get mad, Caroline. It's just that we've never once talked about what's going to become of Phoebe. What it'll be like for us when we retire.' He paused. 'I'd like to think we might consider travelling. It makes me a little claustrophobic, that's all, to imagine staying in this house for ever. And what of Phoebe? Will she live with us for ever?'

'I don't know,' Caroline said wearily. She had fought so many fights already to make a life for Phoebe in this indifferent world. For the time being she had all the problems solved, and for the last year she'd been able to relax. But how Phoebe might live when she grew up—this remained unknown. 'Oh, Al, I can't think about all this tonight. Please.'

The porch swing glided back and forth.

'We'll need to think about it sometime, Caroline. You know I love Phoebe. But we're not always going to be around to take care of her. And there may come a time when she doesn't want us to. I'm just asking if you've thought about this. I'm just raising the topic for discussion. I mean, wouldn't it be nice if you could come on the road with me now and again? Just for a weekend?'

'Yes,' she said softly. 'That would be nice.'

Al nodded, drained his glass, and started to stand up.

'Don't go just yet,' she said, putting her hand lightly on his arm. 'I have to talk to you about something.'

'Sounds serious,' he said, settling back into the swing. He gave a nervous laugh. 'You're not leaving me, are you? Now that you've come into this inheritance and all?'

'Of course not; it's nothing like that.' She sighed. 'I got a letter this week,' she said. 'From Phoebe's father.'

Al nodded and folded his arms, but he didn't speak. He knew about the letters, of course. They'd been arriving for years, bearing cash in varying amounts and a note with a scrawled sentence: *Please let me know where you are living.* She had not done this, but in the early years she'd told David Henry everything else. Heartfelt confessional letters, as if he were a friend close to her heart. As time passed she'd become more efficient, sending photos and a line or two, at best. What a shock it had been, then, to find a fat letter from David Henry. A passionate letter that started with Paul, his talent and his dreams, and his anger.

*I know it was a mistake. What I did, handing you my daughter, I know it was a terrible thing and I know I can't undo it. But I would like to meet her, Caroline. I would like to make amends, somehow.*

She was unnerved by the images he'd given her—Paul, a teenager, playing the guitar and dreaming of Juilliard, Norah with her own business, and David, fixed in her mind all these years, bent over this piece of paper, filled with regret and yearning. She'd slipped the letter into a drawer, but the words had hovered in her mind.

'He wants to meet her,' Caroline said. 'To be a part of her life again.'

'Nice of him,' Al said. 'After all this time.'

Caroline nodded. 'He *is* her father, though.'

'Which makes me what, I wonder?'

'Please,' Caroline said. 'You're the father Phoebe knows and loves. But I didn't tell you everything, Al, about how I came to have Phoebe.'

He took her hand in his. 'Caroline, I hung around in Lexington after you left, and I heard lots of stories. Now, I didn't get much schooling, but I'm not a stupid man, and I know that Dr David Henry lost a baby girl about the time you moved away. What I'm saying is that whatever happened between the two of you doesn't matter. Not to me. Not to us. So I don't need the details.'

'He didn't want her,' she said. 'He was going to put her in a home— an institution. He asked me to take her there and I did. But I couldn't leave her. It was an awful place.'

Al didn't speak for a while. 'I've heard of things like that,' he said at last. 'You were brave, Caroline. You did the right thing. It's hard to think of Phoebe growing up in a place like that.'

Caroline nodded. 'I'm sorry, Al. I should have told you years ago.'

'Caroline,' he said. 'It's OK. It's water under the bridge.'

'What do you think I should do?' she asked. 'I mean, about this letter. Should I answer it? Let him meet her?'

'I don't know what to say,' he said, slowly. 'It's not for me to decide.'

She nodded. That was fair.

'But I'll support you,' Al added, pressing her hand. 'Whatever you feel is best, I'll support you and Phoebe one hundred per cent.'

'Thank you. It doesn't touch us, then?' she asked. 'The fact that I didn't tell you this before—it doesn't touch you and me?'

'Not with a hundred-foot pole,' he said. He stood up, stretching. 'Long day. You coming up?'

'In a minute, yes.'

The screen door squeaked open, fell shut. The wind stirred and it began to rain, softly against the roof at first, and then a drumming. Caroline locked the house—her house now. Upstairs, she stood for a minute in Phoebe's room, moved by her daughter's smallness, and by all the ways she would not be able to protect her in the world. Then she went to her own room, slipping between the cool sheets next to Al. A good husband to her, a good father to Phoebe, a man who would get up on Monday morning and disappear in his truck for the week, trusting her to do whatever she felt was best about David Henry and his letter.

She woke at dawn, Al thundering down the stairs to take the rig in early for an oil change. Rain cascaded from the gutters and the drains, teemed in puddles and poured downhill in a stream.

Caroline went downstairs and made coffee, so absorbed in her own thoughts that she didn't hear Phoebe until she was standing behind her.

'Rain,' Phoebe said. Her bathrobe hung loose. 'Cats and dogs.'

'Yes,' Caroline said. They'd spent hours once, learning this idiom, working with a poster Caroline made of angry clouds, cats and dogs teeming from the sky. 'Do you want some toast?'

'Want a cat,' Phoebe said.

'What do you want?' Caroline asked. 'Use your sentences.'

'I want a cat, please,' Phoebe said.

'We can't have a cat.'

'Aunt Doro went away,' Phoebe said. 'I can have a cat.'

'Look, Phoebe, here's your toast. We'll talk about the cat later, OK?'

'I want a cat,' Phoebe insisted.

'Later.'

'A cat,' Phoebe said.

'Damn it.' The palm of Caroline's hand came down on the counter, startling them both. 'Don't talk to me any more about a cat.'

'Sit on the porch,' Phoebe said, sullen now. 'Watch the rain.'

'What do you want? Use your sentences.'

'I want to sit on the porch and watch the rain.'

'You'll get cold.'

'I want—'

'Oh, fine,' Caroline interrupted, waving one hand. 'Fine. Go out, sit on the porch. Watch the rain. Whatever.'

The door opened and swung shut. Caroline looked out to see Phoebe sitting on the porch swing with her umbrella open and her toast on her lap. She was angry with herself for losing her patience. She took out a piece of paper, then went to sit on the sofa, where she could still keep an eye on Phoebe, and wrote to David.

*Phoebe was confirmed yesterday. She was so sweet in her white dress. She sang a solo at the church. I'm sending a picture of the garden party we had later. I'm starting to feel worried about what the future holds. I suppose this was what was on your mind the night you handed her to me. I've fought so hard all these years and sometimes I'm terrified of what will happen next, and yet*

Here she paused, wondering at her impulse to reply. It wasn't for the money. Over the years Caroline had saved nearly $15,000, all of it held in trust for Phoebe. Perhaps Caroline had simply wanted him to understand what he was missing. 'Here,' she wanted to say, grabbing David Henry by the collar, 'here is your daughter: Phoebe, thirteen years old, a smile like the sun on her face.'

She pushed the letter aside. Instead, she paid some bills, then stepped outside to slip them in the mailbox. Phoebe was now sitting on the front steps, holding her umbrella high against the rain. Caroline let the door fall shut and went to the kitchen to get another cup of coffee. She stood for a long time at the back door, gazing out at the dripping leaves, the wet lawn, the little stream running down the sidewalk.

The rain came harder suddenly, hitting the roof, and some powerful instinct made Caroline turn and walk into the living room. She knew before she stepped out on the porch that she'd find it empty.

Phoebe gone.

Gone where? Caroline went to the edge of the porch and searched up and down the street, through the teeming rain. A train sounded in the distance; the road to the left climbed the hill to the tracks. To the right, it ended in the freeway entrance ramp. *All right, think. Think! Where would she go?*

Down the street the Swan children were playing barefoot in the puddles. Caroline remembered Phoebe saying that she wanted a cat, and thought of Avery standing at the party with the furry bundle in her arms. And sure enough, when she asked the Swan children about Phoebe, they gestured across the road to the copse of trees. The kitten had run away. Phoebe and Avery had gone to rescue it.

At the first break in traffic, Caroline darted across the road. She pushed through the copse and broke into the clearing. Avery was there, kneeling by the pipe that drained water from the hills into the concrete ditch. Phoebe's yellow umbrella was discarded, like a flag, beside her.

'Avery!' She squatted down beside the girl. 'Where's Phoebe?'

'She went to get the cat,' Avery said, pointing into the pipe. 'In there.'

Caroline swore softly and knelt in the edge of the pipe. Cold water rushed against her knees, her hands. She inched her way inside. The water was so cold. 'Phoebe!' she shouted. 'Phoebe!' A sound then, faint. Caroline crawled further in, through the water, and then her hand brushed fabric, cold flesh, and Phoebe, trembling, was in her arms.

'We have to get out of here, honey. We have to get out.'

But Phoebe wouldn't move. 'My cat,' she said, her voice high, determined, and Caroline felt the squirming beneath Phoebe's shirt, heard the small mewing. 'It's my cat.'

'OK,' Caroline said, water rushing higher now. 'OK, OK, it's your cat.'

Phoebe began to move, inching towards the circle of light, until finally they emerged, water streaming around them in the concrete ditch.

'It's all right.' Caroline put her arm round Phoebe. The kitten twisted, thin claws scratching the backs of her hands.

'There's the mailman,' Phoebe said.

'Yes,' Caroline said, watching him climb the porch.

Her letter to David Henry sat unfinished on the table. She had stood at the back door thinking only of Phoebe's father, while Phoebe wandered into danger. It suddenly seemed like an omen, and the fear she'd felt at Phoebe's disappearance turned to anger. She wouldn't write to David again; he wanted too much from her, and he wanted it too late.

# April 1982

# I

CAROLINE STOOD AT THE BUS-STOP near the corner of Forbes and Braddock, watching the kinetic energy of the children on the playground, their happy shouts lifting up over the steady roar of the traffic. Beyond them, on the baseball field, figures in blue and red from competing local taverns moved with silent grace against new grass. She and Al watched the games there when they made it out for an evening. Tonight he was gone, however, speeding through the gathering night, south from Cleveland to Toledo, then Columbus. Years ago, in those strange days after Doro left, Caroline had hired someone to watch Phoebe while she travelled with Al. Hours slid away, the road spinning out beneath them, a dark ribbon bisected by mesmerising flashes of white. Finally, Al would pull into a truck stop and take her to a restaurant that didn't differ appreciably from the one they had left behind in whatever city they'd stayed in the day before. Only the names were different, the faces. She'd gone with Al twice, then never again.

The bus rounded the corner and roared to a stop. The doors folded open and Caroline climbed in and took a window seat. Trees flashed as they roared over the bridge, then they lumbered on to Oakland, where Caroline got off. She stood before the Carnegie Museum, collecting herself. A banner strung along the top of the portico fluttered in the wind—MIRROR IMAGES: PHOTOGRAPHS BY DAVID HENRY.

Tonight was the opening: he would be here to speak. Caroline had carried the newspaper clipping in her pocket for two weeks. A dozen times she had changed her mind. What good could come of it? And then, in the next breath, what harm? If Al had been here, she would have stayed home. She would have let the opportunity slip away unremarked, glancing at the clock until the opening was over and David Henry had disappeared back into whatever life he now led.

But Al had called to say he'd be away tonight, and Mrs O'Neill was home to keep an eye on Phoebe. Caroline stood still, taking deep breaths, while streams of people, dressed in silk and heels and dark expensive suits, flowed up the museum's stone steps. She took one step and then another, merging with the crowd.

The museum had high white ceilings and gleaming oak floors. Caroline was given a programme of thick creamy paper with David Henry's name across the top. She walked into the gallery and found his most famous photo, the undulating beach that was more than a beach: the curve of a woman's hip, then the smooth length of her leg, hidden among the dunes.

Caroline sat down in a seat, watching everything intently. The lights dimmed once and went on again, and then there was applause and David Henry was walking in, smiling at the audience. Tall and familiar, but fleshier now and greying, he walked to the podium and gazed out at the audience. Caroline caught her breath, sure he must have seen her.

He spoke with melodious assurance, though Caroline paid almost no attention to what he was saying. Instead, she studied the familiar gestures of his hands, the new lines at the corners of his eyes. His hair was longer, thick and luxurious despite the grey.

When his talk was over, the applause rose, strong, and then he was stepping from behind the podium, taking a long drink from his glass of water, answering questions. Tension mounted in Caroline's body and her heart pounded until she could barely breathe. The questions ended and the silence grew, and David Henry cleared his throat, a smile forming as he thanked the audience and turned away. Caroline felt herself rising then, almost beyond her own volition. She crossed the room and joined the group collecting around him. He glanced at her and smiled politely, without recognition. She waited through more questions, growing calmer as the moments passed, then, when a break came in the questions, she stepped forward and put her hand on David's arm.

'David,' she said. 'Don't you know me?'

He searched her face.

'Have I changed so much?' she whispered.

She saw him understand, then. His face altered, the shape of it even, and a flush crept up his neck. They stared at each other without speaking, as if the room and all the people in it had fallen away.

'Caroline,' he said at last, recovering. 'Caroline Gill. An old friend,' he added, speaking to the people still clustering around them. A smile broke across his face, though it did not touch his eyes. 'Thank you.' He nodded to the others. 'Thank you all for coming. Now, if you'll excuse us.'

And then they were crossing the room. David walked beside her, one hand lightly but firmly against her back.

'Come in here,' he said, stepping behind a display panel, where an unframed door was barely visible in the wall. He guided her inside and shut the door behind them. It was a storage closet, small, one bare bulb lighting shelves full of paint and tools. They stood just inches apart.

'Caroline,' he said. 'Do you live here? In Pittsburgh? Why wouldn't you tell me where you were?'

'I wasn't hard to find. Other people found me,' she said slowly, remembering Al walking up the alley, understanding for the first time the depth of his persistence. For if it was true that David Henry had not looked very hard, it was also true that she had wanted to be lost.

When he spoke again his tone had softened. 'I went to your apartment, Caroline. That day, after the memorial service. I went there, but you were already gone. All this time—' he began, and then he fell silent.

There was a light tap on the door, a muffled questioning voice.

'Give me a minute,' David called back.

'I was in love with you,' Caroline said in a rush, astonished at her confession, for it was the first time she had ever voiced this, even to herself. The admission made her feel reckless, and she went on. 'I spent all sorts of time imagining a life with you. And it was in that moment by the church when I realised I hadn't crossed your mind at all.'

He'd bent his head as she spoke and now he looked up. 'I knew,' he said. 'I knew you were in love with me. How could I have asked you to help me, otherwise? I'm sorry, Caroline. So sorry.'

She nodded, tears in her eyes, that younger version of herself still alive, still standing by the edge of the memorial service, unacknowledged, invisible. It made her angry, even now, that not knowing her at all he hadn't hesitated to ask her to take away his daughter.

'Are you happy, Caroline?' he asked. 'Has Phoebe been happy?'

His questions, and the gentleness in his voice, disarmed her. She thought of Phoebe, struggling to learn to shape letters, to tie her shoes. Phoebe, putting her soft arms round Caroline's neck for no reason at all and saying, 'I love you, Mom.' She thought of Al, gone too much but walking through the door at the end of a long week, carrying flowers or a small gift for her, always, and something for Phoebe.

'Do you really want to know?' she asked at last, looking him straight in the eye. 'Because you never wrote back, David. Except for that one time, you never asked a single thing about our lives.'

As Caroline spoke, she realised that this was why she had come. Not out of love, or any allegiance to the past, or even out of guilt. She had come out of anger and a desire to set the record straight.

'For years you never wanted to know how I was. How Phoebe was. You just didn't give a damn, did you? And then that last letter, the one I never answered. All of a sudden, you wanted her back.'

David gave a short, startled laugh. 'Caroline, I asked you for your address. Again and again—every time I sent money. And in that final letter I simply asked you to invite me back into your life. What more could I do? I kept every letter you ever sent. When you stopped writing, I felt like you'd slammed a door in my face.'

Caroline thought of all her heartfelt confessions flowing into ink on paper. 'Where are they?' she asked. 'Where do you keep my letters?'

He looked surprised. 'In my darkroom filing cabinet, bottom drawer. It's always locked. Why?'

'I didn't think you even read them,' Caroline said. 'I felt I was writing into a void. Maybe that's why I thought I could say anything at all.'

David rubbed his hand on his cheek, a gesture she remembered him using when he was tired or discouraged. 'I read them. At first I had to force myself, to be honest. Later, I wanted to know what was happening, even though it was painful. You gave me little glimpses of Phoebe. Little scraps from the fabric of your lives. I looked forward to that.'

She didn't answer, remembering the satisfaction she'd felt on that rainy day, when she'd sent Phoebe upstairs with her kitten, Rain, to change out of her wet clothes while she stood in the living room, tearing his letter in four pieces, then eight, and dropping it in the trash.

'I couldn't lose her,' she said. 'I was angry with you for a long, long time, but by then I was mostly afraid that if you met her you'd take her away. That's why I stopped writing.'

'That was never my intention.'

'You didn't intend any of this,' Caroline answered. 'But it happened.'

David Henry sighed, and she imagined him in her deserted apartment, walking from room to room and realising she was gone for good.

'If I hadn't taken her,' she added, 'you might have chosen differently.'

'I didn't stop you,' he said, meeting her gaze again. His voice was rough. 'I could have. You wore a red coat that day at the memorial service. I saw you and I watched you drive away.'

Caroline felt suddenly faint. 'You saw me?' she said.

'I went straight to your apartment afterwards. I thought you'd be there.'

Caroline closed her eyes. She had been driving towards the highway then. She'd probably missed David Henry's visit by minutes.

'You didn't answer me,' David said, clearing his throat. 'Have you been happy, Caroline? Has Phoebe? Is her health OK? Her heart?'

'Her heart's fine,' Caroline said, thinking of the early years of constant worry over Phoebe's health. 'She was lucky, I guess. She loves to sing. She has a cat named Rain. She's learning to weave. That's where she is right now. At home. Weaving.' Caroline shook her head. 'She goes to school with all the other kids. I had to fight like hell for them to take her. And now she's nearly grown I don't know what will happen. I have a good job. I work part-time in a clinic at the hospital. My husband— he travels a lot. Phoebe goes to a group home each day. She has a lot of friends there. She's learning how to do office work. What else can I say? You missed a lot of heartache, sure. But, David, you missed a lot of joy.'

'I know that,' he said. 'Better than you think.'

'And you?' she asked. 'Have you been happy? Has Norah? And Paul?'

'I don't know,' he said slowly. 'Paul's so smart. He wants to go to Juilliard and play the guitar. I think he's making a mistake, but Norah doesn't agree. It's caused a lot of tension.'

Caroline thought of Phoebe, how she loved to clean and organise, how she sang to herself while washing the dishes, how she loved music with her whole heart and would never have a chance to play the guitar.

'And Norah?' she asked.

'She owns a travel agency,' David said. 'She's away a lot.'

'A travel agency?' Caroline repeated. 'Norah?'

'I know. It surprised me, too. She's very good at it.'

The doorknob turned and the door swung open a few inches. The curator of the show stuck his head inside, his eyes bright with curiosity and concern. 'Dr Henry?' he said. 'You know, there are a lot of people out here. There's a kind of expectation that'll you'll—ah—mingle.'

David looked at Caroline. 'No problem,' he said. 'I'm coming. You'll stay, won't you?' he said, turning to Caroline, taking her elbow.

'I need to get home,' she said. 'Phoebe's waiting.'

'Please.' He paused outside the door. 'There so much to say. Please say you'll wait.' She felt an uneasiness she couldn't place, but she nodded slightly and David Henry smiled. 'Good. We'll have dinner.'

His hand was on her arm and they were moving back into the crowd. People were glancing in their direction, curious and whispering. She reached into her bag and handed David the envelope she'd prepared, with the latest photographs of Phoebe. David took it, met her eyes and nodded, and then a woman in a black dress was taking him by the arm.

Caroline stood where she was for a few minutes, watching him gesture to a photo that resembled the dark branches of a tree. 'Wait,' he'd said. And he'd expected that she would. But she didn't want to wait. Nothing good had ever come to her from waiting.

David was standing with his head bent, nodding, listening to the woman in the black dress, the envelope clasped in his hands, behind his back. As she watched, he reached up and put the envelope casually into his pocket, as if it contained something trivial and mildly unpleasant—a utility bill, a traffic ticket.

In moments she was outside, hurrying down the steps into the night.

# II

SHE WAS A PROFESSOR of art history at Carnegie Mellon and she was asking him about form. 'What is beauty?' she wanted to know. 'Is beauty to be found in form?'

He stared down at her smooth, pale face. 'Intersections,' he said, glancing back to where Caroline lingered, relieved to see her still there. With an effort, he turned back to the professor. 'Convergence. That's what I'm after. I don't take a theoretical approach. I photograph what moves me.'

'No one lives outside of theory!' she exclaimed.

The room swirled around him, voices rose and fell. He realised that he still held the envelope Caroline had given him. He glanced across the room again—yes, she was still there—and tucked it carefully into his pocket.

Her name was Lee, the dark-haired woman was saying now. She was the visiting critic-in-residence. David nodded, only half listening. Did Caroline live in Pittsburgh, or had she come from somewhere else?

He scanned the room again and did not see her, and the first threads of panic began. She had said she would stay. Surely she would not leave?

'Excuse me,' he murmured, then walked across to the entrance foyer, where he paused to survey the gallery room, searching the crowd. Surely, after all this time, he couldn't possibly lose her again?

But she was gone. Loss and grief rushed through him like a wave, so powerful that he leaned against a wall and bent his head, fighting a deep nausea. They were excessive, his emotions, disproportionate. He reached into his pocket with a trembling hand and took out the envelope

Caroline had given him; maybe she'd left an address or a phone number. Inside were two Polaroids. The first showed Caroline, smiling, her arm round the girl beside her, who wore a stiff blue dress with a sash. The girl was sturdy; the dress fitted her well but did not make her graceful. Her hair fell around her face in soft waves and she smiled a bright smile. It might have been only the angle of the camera that made her eyes slant upwards. *Phoebe on her birthday*, Caroline had written on the back. *Sweet sixteen.* He slid the first photo behind the second, more recent one. Here was Phoebe again, playing basketball, the sport Paul refused to play. David looked on the back, but there was no address.

He walked to the doorway, then turned and watched with curious detachment, as if this scene were something he'd stumbled on by accident, nothing to do with him. Then he turned away again and stepped out into the soft, cool, rain-dampened air. He slipped the envelope with its photos into his breast pocket and began to walk.

Oakland, his old college neighbourhood, was changed. Forbes Field, where he had spent so many afternoons cheering when bats cracked and the balls rose over the bright green fields, was gone. A new university building, square and blunt, rose into the air where the cheers of thousands had once roared.

He walked on, down the dark city streets. He did not really think about where he was going, though he knew. He saw he'd been caught, frozen for all these years in that moment when he handed Caroline his daughter. What had been held still in his heart had been set in motion again by his meeting with Caroline. He thought of Norah, who had become a self-sufficient and powerful woman. She'd had more than one affair over the years, he knew that, and her secrets, like his own, had grown up into a wall between them. They lived together now like strangers in their vast house. And Paul suffered for it.

The streets converged, coming together at odd angles, as the city narrowed to the point where the great rivers met, the Monongahela and the Allegheny, their confluence forming the Ohio. He walked to the very tip of the point. As a young man he had stood here often, with his toes suspended above the dark skin of the river, wondering how cold this black water might be, whether he would be strong enough to swim to shore if he fell in.

Far below the water swirled, foamed white against the cement piling, surged away. If he fell or jumped and couldn't swim to safety, they would find these things: a watch with his father's name inscribed on the back, his wallet, his driver's licence and the photos in the envelope.

His funeral would be crowded. The cortege would stretch for blocks. But it would stop there, the news. Caroline might never know. Nor would word travel back to where he'd been born. Even if it did, no one there would recognise his name.

The letter had been waiting for him one day after school. The University of Pittsburgh logo was clear. He'd carried the envelope upstairs and placed it on the table by his bed, too nervous to open it.

For two hours he had not allowed himself to look. And then he did, and the news was good: he had been accepted with a full scholarship. *It is my pleasure to inform you . . .*

But then he noticed the error: the name on the letter was not his. Every other detail from his date of birth to his social security number—all these were correct. And his first two names, David for his father and Henry for his grandfather, those were fine as well, typed precisely by a secretary who had perhaps been interrupted by a phone call.

His last name, McCallister, had been lost.

He had never told anyone. He had gone off to college and registered, and no one ever knew. David Henry was a different person from David Henry McCallister, that much he knew, and it seemed clear it was as David Henry he was meant to go to college, a person with no history, unburdened by the past. And he had done just that. In the early days, surrounded by people wealthier and better connected than he would ever be, he would sometimes allude to a distant but important lineage, invoking false ancestors to stand behind him and lend support.

This was the gift he'd tried to give Paul: a place in the world that no one could question.

The water between his feet was brown, edged with a sickly white foam. The wind rose and the swirling water flashed, drew closer, and then there was acid in his throat and he was on his hands and knees, vomiting into the wild grey river. He lay there for a long time, in the darkness. Finally, slowly, he stood and walked back into the city.

**H**e sat in the Greyhound bus terminal all night, and in the morning he caught the first bus to his childhood home in West Virginia. After seven hours, the bus stopped where it always had, on the corner of Main and Vine, then roared away, leaving David Henry in front of the grocery store. The street was quiet, a newspaper plastered against a telephone pole and weeds growing up through cracks in the sidewalk. He'd worked in this store to earn his room and keep above it, the smart kid come down from the hills to study. Now red and black graffiti covered the plywood-boarded windows, bleeding into the grain, unreadable.

In the narrow room above the store, books spread out on his bed, he had been so homesick he couldn't concentrate, and yet when he went back to the mountains his yearning did not diminish. In his parents' small clapboard house, set into the hill, the hours stretched, measured out by the tamping of his father's pipe and his mother's sighs. There was life below the creek and life above it, and loneliness everywhere.

A light rain, delicate as mist, began to fall. He walked, though his legs ached. He thought of his bright office, a lifetime or a dream away. It was late afternoon. Norah would still be at work and Paul would be up in his room, pouring his loneliness and anger into music. They expected him home tonight, but he would not be there. He slid his hands under his arms to warm them. It was a season earlier here, and crusts of snow broke under his feet.

It took him nearly an hour to reach the old house, now weather-beaten a soft grey, the roof sagging at the centre of the ridgepole and some of the shingles missing. David stopped, taken so powerfully into the past that he expected to see them again: his mother coming down the steps, his sister sitting on the porch, and the sound of the axe striking logs from where his father chopped firewood, just out of sight. He had left for school and June had died, and his parents had stayed on here as long as they could, reluctant to leave the land. But then his father died, too young, and his mother went north, travelling to her sister and the promise of work in the auto factories. David had come home from Pittsburgh rarely and never again since his mother died.

He walked up the steps. The door hung crookedly on its hinges and would not close. The air inside was chilly, musty. It was a single room, the sleeping loft compromised now by the sagging ridgepole. As far as David knew, no one had been here for years. Yet a frying pan sat on the old stove, cold, the grease congealed but not, when he leaned to smell it, rancid. In the corner there was an old iron bed, its frame covered with a layer of blankets and a worn quilt like his grandmother and his mother had made. The plank floor was swept clean and there were three crocuses in a jar in the window.

Someone was living here. A breeze moved through the room, stirring the paper cut-outs that hung everywhere. David examined them with a sense of wonder. They were like the snowflakes he'd cut out in school, but infinitely more intricate and detailed, showing entire scenes to the last detail. Who had made these with such delicate skill and patience?

He lay down on the hard bed and pulled the damp quilt around him. It was so quiet here. There was only the sound of the wind fluttering the old leaves and, distantly, the murmuring of water in the stream beneath the ice. He thought of the two rivers converging, and the dark water swirling. Not to fall but to jump: that was what had hung there in the balance. His head throbbed and he shivered, then he closed his eyes, just for a few minutes, to rest.

'**D**on't suppose you're anyways useful,' the voice was saying, and David, not sure if he was dreaming or hearing voices in the wind, shifted at the tugging at his wrists, at the muttering voice, and ran his dry tongue against the roof of his mouth. He turned and his wrists hurt. Startled, he woke fully, his eyes opening and drifting over the room.

She was standing at the stove, just a few feet away, olive fatigues tight round her slim hips, flaring fuller round her thighs. She wore a sweater the colour of rust shot through with luminous strands of orange, and over this a man's green and black plaid flannel shirt. She had cut the fingertips from her gloves, and she moved around the stove with deft efficiency, poking at some eggs in the frying pan.

Grease spattered and the girl's hand flew up. He tried to sit up then, but was stopped again by his wrists. Puzzled, he turned his head: a filmy red chiffon scarf tied him to one bedpost; the strings from a mop to the other. She noticed his movement and turned.

'My boyfriend's coming back any minute now,' she announced.

She was slight, perhaps even younger than Paul, out here in this abandoned house. Shacking up, he thought, wondering about the boyfriend, realising for the first time that maybe he ought to be afraid.

'What's your name?' he asked.

'Rosemary,' she said, then looked worried. 'You can believe that or not,' she added.

'Rosemary,' he said, thinking of the piney bush Norah had planted in a sunny spot, 'I wonder if you would untie me.'

'No.' Her voice was swift and bright. 'No way.'

'I'm thirsty,' he said.

She looked at him for a moment, then she went outside, releasing a wedge of cold air into the room. She came back with a metal cup of water from the stream.

'Thanks,' he said, 'but I can't drink this lying down.'

She attended to the stove for a minute, then rummaged through a drawer, coming up with a plastic straw, which she thrust into the cup.

'I suppose you'll use it,' she said, 'if you're thirsty enough.'

He turned his head and sipped the water, while she slid the eggs onto a metal plate and sat down at the wooden table. She ate quickly, pushing the eggs onto a plastic fork. In that moment he understood somehow that the boyfriend was fiction. She was living here alone.

He drank until the straw sputtered dry, then he said, 'My parents used to own this place. In fact, I still do own it. I have the deed in a safe. Technically, you're trespassing.'

She smiled at this and put her fork down carefully in the centre of the plate. 'You come here to claim it, then? Technically?'

She was so young, yet there was something fierce and strong about her too, something lonely but determined.

'No,' he said. 'My name is David Henry McCallister.' His real name, so long unspoken. 'How old are you?' he asked. 'Fifteen?'

'Sixteen,' she corrected.

'Sixteen,' he repeated. 'I have a son older than you. Paul.'

A son, he thought, and a daughter.

'Is that so?' she said, indifferent.

'Why don't you untie me?' he suggested. 'I'm a doctor. Harmless.'

'Right.' She stood and carried her plate to the sink.

She was pregnant, he realised with shock, catching her profile as she turned. Just four or five months, he guessed.

'Look, I really am a doctor. There's a card in my wallet. Take a look.'

She didn't answer, just washed her plate and fork and dried her hands on a towel. David thought how strange it was that his own family should have disappeared so completely and that this girl, so young and tough and so clearly lost, should have tied him to the bed.

She crossed the room and pulled his wallet from his pocket. One by one she placed his things on the table: cash, credit cards, the miscellaneous notes and bits of paper.

'This says photographer,' she said, reading his card.

'That's right,' he said. 'I'm that, too. Keep going.'

'OK,' she said a moment later, holding up his ID. 'So you're a doctor. So what? What difference does that make?'

Her hair was pulled back in a ponytail and stray wisps fell around her face; she pushed them back over her ear.

'It means I'm not going to hurt you, Rosemary. "First, do no harm."'

'You'd say that no matter what. Even if you meant me harm.'

He studied her, the untidy hair, the clear sherry-brown eyes.

'There are some pictures,' he said. 'Somewhere here . . .' He shifted and felt the sharp edge of the envelope through his shirt. 'Take a look. These are pictures of my daughter. She's about your age.'

Rosemary slipped her hand into his pocket.

'What's her name?' she asked, studying the photographs.

'Phoebe.'

'Phoebe. That's pretty. She's pretty. Is she named for her mother?'

'No,' David said, remembering the night of her birth, Norah telling him the names she wanted. Caroline had heard this and had honoured it. 'She was named for a great-aunt. On her mother's side.'

'I was named after both my grandmothers,' Rosemary said softly. 'Rose on my father's side, Mary on my mother's.'

'Does your family know where you are?' he asked.

She shook her head. 'I can't go back,' she said, both anguish and anger woven in her voice. 'I can't ever go back. I won't.'

She looked so young, sitting at the table, her hands closed in loose fists and her expression dark, worried. He wanted to put his arm round her, take her home, protect her. 'Why not?' he asked.

She tapped the photo of Phoebe. 'You say she's my age?'

'Close, I'm guessing. She was born on March the 6th, 1964.'

'I was born in February 1966.' Her hands trembled a little as she put the photos down. 'My mom was planning a party for me: sweet sixteen.'

David watched her swallow, brush her hair behind her ear again, gaze out of the dark window. He wanted to comfort her, just as he had so often wanted to comfort others—June, his mother, Norah—but now, as then, he couldn't. He had only wept once for June, standing with his mother on the hillside in the raw evening wind, holding the Bible in one hand as he recited the Lord's Prayer over the newly turned earth. He wept with his mother, and then they hid their grief away.

'Phoebe is my daughter,' he said, astonished to hear himself speaking, yet compelled to tell this secret he'd kept for so many years. 'But I haven't seen her since she was born.' He hesitated, then forced himself to say it. 'I gave her away. She has Down syndrome, which means she's retarded. So I gave her away. I never told anyone.'

Rosemary's glance was shocked. 'I see that as harm,' she said.

'Yes,' he said. 'So do I.'

They were silent for a long time. Everywhere David looked he was reminded of his sister, his mother, his father. Gone, all of them gone, and his daughter too. He struggled against grief from old habit, but tears slipped down his cheeks; he could not stop them. He wept for June, and he wept for the moment in the clinic when he handed Phoebe to Caroline Gill and watched her turn away. Rosemary sat at the table, grave and still. Once their eyes met and he held her gaze, a strangely intimate moment. He remembered Caroline watching him from the doorway as he slept, her face softened with love for him. He might have walked with her down the museum steps and back into her life, but he'd lost that moment too.

'I'm sorry,' he said, trying to pull himself together. 'I haven't been here for a long time.'

She didn't answer and he wondered if he sounded crazy to her.

He took a deep breath. 'When is your baby due?'

Her dark eyes widened in surprise. 'Five months, I guess.'

'You left him behind, didn't you?' David said softly. 'Your boyfriend.'

She turned her head, but not before he saw her eyes fill.

'I'm sorry,' he said at once. 'I don't mean to pry.'

She shook her head a little. 'It's OK. No big deal.'

'Where is he?' he asked, keeping his voice soft. 'Where's home?'

'Pennsylvania,' she said. She took a deep breath, and David understood that his story, his grief, had made it possible for her to reveal her own. 'Near Harrisburg. I used to have an aunt here in town,' she went on. 'She's dead now. But when I was a little girl we came here. We used to wander all over these hills. This house was always empty. We used to come here and play, when we were kids. Those were the best times.'

He nodded, remembering the rustling silence of the woods.

'Untie me,' he said, softly.

She laughed bitterly, wiping her eyes. 'Why?' she asked. 'Why would I do that, with us alone up here? I'm not a total idiot.'

It had grown dark outside and she rose and lit some candles, then gathered her scissors and a small stack of paper from the shelf above the stove. Shards of white flew as she cut and the candle flames flickered.

'Those paper things you make,' he said. 'They're beautiful.'

'My grandma Rose taught me. It's called *Scherenschnitte*. She grew up in Switzerland, where I guess they make these all the time.'

'She must be worried about you.'

'She's dead. She died last year.' She paused, concentrating on her cutting. 'I like making these. It helps me remember her.'

David nodded. 'Do you start with an idea?' he asked.

'It's in the paper,' she said. 'I don't invent them so much as find them.'

'You find them. Yes.' He nodded. 'I understand that. When I take pictures, that's how it is. They're already there and I just discover them.'

'That's right,' Rosemary said, turning the paper. 'That's exactly right.'

'Look,' he said. 'Rosemary. Please. Untie me.'

'How could you give her away?' she asked.

'Is that what worries you?' he asked. 'That you'll give your baby away?'

'Never. I'll never do that,' she said fiercely, her face set. So someone had done that to her, one way or another, and tossed her out to sink or swim. To be sixteen and pregnant and alone, to sit at this table.

'I realised it was wrong,' David said. 'But by then it was too late.'

'It's never too late.'

'You're sixteen,' he said. 'Sometimes, trust me, it's too late.'

Her expression tightened for an instant and she didn't answer, just kept cutting, and in the silence David started talking again, trying to explain at first about the snow and the shock. How he had stood outside himself and watched himself moving in the world. How he had woken up every morning of his life for eighteen years thinking maybe today, maybe this was the day he would put things right. But Phoebe was gone and he couldn't find her, so how could he possibly tell

Norah? The secret had worked its way through their marriage, an insidious vine, twisting; she drank too much and then she began to have affairs; he'd tried not to notice, to forgive her, for he knew that in some real sense the fault was his. Photo after photo, as if he could stop time or make an image powerful enough to obscure the moment when he turned and handed his daughter to Caroline Gill.

She cut and listened. Her silence made him free. He talked like a river, words rushing through the old house with a force and life he could not stop. At some point he began to weep again, and he could not stop that either. He talked until the words slowed, ebbed, finally ceased.

Silence welled and he closed his eyes.

Her footsteps and then the metal, cold and bright, against his skin.

The tension in his wrists released. He opened his eyes to see her stepping back, her eyes, bright and wary, fixed on his, her scissors glinting.

'All right,' she said. 'You're free.'

# III

'PAUL,' SHE CALLED. Her heels were a sharp staccato on the polished stairs and then she was standing in the doorway, slender and stylish in a navy suit. Through barely opened eyes, Paul saw her shake her head. 'Get up, Paul,' she said. 'Do it now.'

'Sick,' he mumbled, pulling the covers over his head, making his voice hoarse. Through the loose weave of the summer blanket he could still see her hair, highlighted yesterday, glinting with red and gold. He'd heard her on the phone with Bree, describing the strands of hair wrapped up in foil and baked.

She'd been sautéing ground beef as she talked, her voice calm, her eyes red from crying earlier. His father had disappeared, and for three days no one knew if he was dead or alive. Then last night his father had come home, walking through the door as if he'd never been gone, and their tense voices had travelled up the stairs for hours.

'Look,' she said now, glancing at her watch. 'I know you're not sick. So get yourself out of bed and get dressed. I'll drop you at school.'

'My throat's on fire,' he insisted.

She hesitated, then sighed, and he knew he'd won.

'If you stay home, you stay home,' she warned. 'I'm serious, Paul. I have all I can deal with on my plate right now.'

'Right,' he croaked. 'Yep. I will.'

She stood a moment longer without speaking. 'I'd stay with you, Paul,' she said at last. 'But I promised to take Bree to the doctor.'

He pushed up on his elbows then, alerted by her tone. 'Is she OK?'

His mother nodded, but she wouldn't meet his eyes. 'I think so. But she's having some tests and she's a little worried. Which is natural. I promised her I'd go. Before all this with your father.'

'It's OK,' Paul said, remembering to make his voice sound hoarse. 'You should go with her. I'll be OK.'

'It shouldn't take long. I'll come straight back.'

'Where's Dad?'

She shook her head. 'I have no idea. But how unusual is that?'

Paul didn't answer. Not very, he thought. Not unusual at all.

His mother put her hand on his cheek and then she was gone. Downstairs, Bree's voice rose from the hall. Over these last years they'd become very close, his mother and Bree. They'd even started to look alike. Bree was still a cool and together person, she was still the one who'd take a risk, the one who told him to follow his heart and apply to Juilliard like he wanted. Everyone liked Bree: her sense of adventure, her exuberance. She brought in a lot of business. She and his mother were complimentary forces, he'd heard her say. Now their voices mingled, and then the door slammed and the house was quiet.

Paul got up, stretching, and went downstairs. He stood in the cool light of the refrigerator, eating macaroni and cheese from a dish with his fingers, studying the shelves. Not much. He took a handful of mint chocolate cookies and then, with the milk jug swinging from his hand, he walked through the living room to the den.

The girl was still there, sleeping. He slipped a cookie in his mouth, studying her. Last night the familiar angry voices of his parents had risen up to his room, and although they were arguing, the stone he had felt in his throat at the thought of his father lying dead somewhere— immediately, that had dissolved. Paul had got out of bed and started down the stairs, but on the landing he stopped, taking in the scene: his father, limp and bedraggled, a full beard on his face; his mother in her peach satin robe; this stranger, standing in the doorway in a black coat. She had looked up, past the swirling anger, and her eyes had met his.

'Three days,' his mother was saying, 'and then you come home like—my God, look at you, David—like *this* and with this girl you've just met. Pregnant, you say? And I'm supposed to take her in?'

The girl flinched then and looked away. Paul stood very still. The argument went on; it seemed to last a long time. Finally, his mother, silent and tight-lipped, had pulled sheets, blankets, pillows from the linen closet and thrown them at his father, who had taken the girl very formally by the elbow and led her to the den.

Now she slept on her back on the fold-out couch, her head turned to the side, one hand resting near her face, her belly rising up like a low wave. Paul studied this girl, her paleness and long dark hair, her scattered freckles. Who was she? He reached out, touched her hair lightly, then let his hand fall. Her eyes blinked open and for a moment she stared at him, unseeing. Then she sat up quickly, pushing her hands through her hair. She was wearing one of his T-shirts.

'What are you looking at?' She swung her feet to the floor.

He shook his head, unable to speak.

'You're Paul,' she said. 'Your father told me about you.'

'He did?' he asked. 'What'd he say?'

She shrugged, pushing her hair behind her ears, and stood up. 'Let's see. You're headstrong. You hate him. You're a genius on the guitar.'

Paul felt the heat rising to his face. 'I don't hate him,' he said. 'It's the other way round.'

She leaned down to gather up the blankets, then sat with them in her arms, looking around. 'This is nice,' she said. 'Someday I'm going to have a place like this.'

Paul gave a startled laugh. 'You're pregnant,' he said.

'Right. So what? I'm pregnant. Not dead.' She spoke defiantly.

'You might as well be,' he said.

She looked up sharply, tears in her eyes, as if he'd slapped her.

'I'm sorry,' he said. 'But what are you doing here anyway?' he demanded, angry at her tears, at her very presence. 'I mean, who do you think you are to latch on to my father and show up here?'

'I don't think I'm anyone,' she said, but his tone had startled her and she dried her tears. 'And I didn't ask to come. It was your father's idea.'

'That doesn't make sense,' Paul said. 'Why would he do that?'

She shrugged. 'How should I know? I was living in that old house where he grew up, and he said I couldn't stay there any more. And it's his place, right? What could I say? In the morning we walked into town and he bought bus tickets and here we are.'

She pulled her long hair back and Paul watched her, thinking how pretty her ears were, wondering if his father thought she was pretty too.

'What old house?' Paul asked, feeling something sharp in his chest.

'Like I said. The one where he grew up. I was living there. I didn't have anywhere else to go,' she added, glancing at the floor.

Paul felt something fill him then, some emotion he couldn't name.

Envy, maybe, that this girl, this thin, pale stranger, had been to a place that mattered to his father, a place he himself had never seen.

'My father's a doctor,' Paul said. 'He just likes to help people.'

She nodded, then looked at him straight on, her expression full of something—pity for him, that's what he read there.

'What?' he asked.

She shook her head. 'Nothing. You're right. I needed help. That's all.'

'My father had a sister,' Paul said, remembering the story and his father's voice, pushing to see if it was true, that she'd been there.

'I know. June. She's buried on a hillside above the house. We went there, too.'

His breathing was low and shallow. Why should it matter that she knew this? What difference did it make?

'So what?' he said. 'So what that you've been there?'

She seemed about to speak for a moment, but then she turned away. He watched her go into the kitchen, heard the refrigerator door open and shut. Then he went upstairs and got the photograph his father had given him that night they'd talked in the darkroom.

He took the picture and his guitar and went out onto the porch, shirtless, barefoot. He sat in the swing seat and played, keeping an eye on this girl as she moved through the rooms. He kept on playing. It soothed him, the music, in a way that nothing else did. He reached the end and stopped, closing his eyes and letting the notes die away.

When he opened his eyes, she was leaning against the doorjamb. She pushed open the screen door and came out onto the porch. 'Wow. Your father was right,' she said. 'That was amazing.'

'Thanks,' he said, ducking his head to hide his pleasure. The music had released him; he was not so angry any more. 'You play?'

'No. I used to take piano lessons.' She frowned. 'Are you an only child?' she asked.

He was startled. 'Yes and no. I mean, I had a sister. A twin. She died.'

Rosemary nodded. 'Do you ever think about her?'

'Sure.' He felt uncomfortable and looked away. 'Not *about* her, exactly. I never knew her. But about what she might have been like.' He flushed then, shocked to have revealed so much to this stranger. 'Hey,' he said. 'I want to show you something.' He laid the guitar flat on the swing seat and picked up the grainy black and white photo. 'Was it this place?' he asked, handing it to her, 'where you met my father?'

She took the print and studied it, then nodded. 'Yes. It looks different now. I can see from this picture—those sweet curtains in the window, and the flowers growing—that it was a nice house once. It's empty now. The wind comes through because the windows are broken.

When I was a kid we used to play there. We used to run wild in those hills, and it was like my secret place.'

He nodded, taking the photo back and studying the figures as he had so many times before.

'OK. It's your turn again,' she said after a minute. 'Tell me something your father doesn't know.'

'I'm going to Juilliard,' he said, the words coming in a rush. He'd told no one but his mother yet. 'I was first on the waiting list and I got accepted last week. While he was gone.'

'Wow.' She smiled a little sadly. 'That's great, Paul. I always thought college would be great.'

'You were going to go,' he said, realising suddenly what she'd lost.

'I will go. I will definitely go.'

'I'll probably have to pay my own way,' Paul offered, recognising her fierce determination, the way it covered fear. 'My father's set on me having some kind of secure career plan. He hates the idea of music.'

'You don't know that,' she said, looking up sharply. 'You don't really know the whole story about your father at all.'

Paul did not know how to answer this, and they sat silently for several minutes. They were screened from the street by a trellis, clematis vines climbing all over it and the purple and white flowers blooming, so when two cars pulled into the driveway, one after the other, his mother and his father home so oddly in the middle of the day, Paul glimpsed them in flashes of colour, bright chrome. He and Rosemary exchanged looks. The cars doors slammed shut, echoing against the neighbouring house. Then there were footsteps, and the quiet, determined voices of his parents, just beyond the edge of the porch. Rosemary opened her mouth as if to call out, but Paul held up one hand and shook his head, and they sat together in silence, listening.

'This day,' his mother said. 'This week. If you only knew, David, how much pain you caused us.'

On the day after his father disappeared, his mother had called the police, who had remained noncommittal and jocular, until his father's briefcase was found in the cloakroom of the museum in Pittsburgh, his suitcase and camera in his hotel.

'I'm sorry. You're right. I should have called. I meant to.'

'That's supposed to be enough? Maybe *I'll* just go away,' she said. 'Just like that. Maybe I'll just take off and come back with a good-looking young man and no explanation. What would you think of that?'

There was a silence, and Paul remembered the discarded pile of bright clothes on the beach. He thought of the many evenings since when his mother had not made it home before midnight. 'Business,' she always sighed, slipping off her shoes in the hall, going straight to bed.

'She's sixteen and pregnant,' his father said. 'She was living in an abandoned house, all alone. I couldn't leave her there.'

His mother sighed. 'Is this a midlife crisis?' she asked quietly.

'A midlife crisis?' His father's voice was even, thoughtful. 'I suppose it might be. I know I hit some kind of wall, Norah. In Pittsburgh. I went back to try to figure out some things. And there was Rosemary, in my old house. But trust me. I'm not in love with her. It's not like that.'

Paul looked at Rosemary. Her head was bent so he couldn't see her expression, but her cheeks were flushed pink.

'I don't know what to believe,' his mother said slowly. 'This week, David, of all weeks. Do you know where I was just now? I was with Bree, at the oncologist's. She had a biopsy done last week: her left breast. It's a very small lump, her prognosis is good, but it's malignant.'

'I didn't know, Norah. I'm sorry.'

'No, don't touch me, David.'

Paul, listening, felt the world slow down a little bit. He thought of Bree, with her quick laugh, who would sit for an hour listening to him play. He couldn't imagine the world without her.

'What do you want?' his father was asking. 'I'll stay, if you want, or I'll move out. But I can't turn Rosemary away.'

There was a silence and he waited, hardly daring to breathe, wanting his mother never to answer.

'What about me?' he asked, startling himself. 'What about what *I* want?'

'Paul?' His mother's voice.

'Here,' he said, picking up his guitar. 'On the porch. Me and Rosemary.'

'Oh, good grief,' his father said. Seconds later, he came round to the steps. Since last night he'd showered and shaved. He looked tired. So did his mother, coming to stand beside him.

Paul stood and faced him. 'I'm going to Juilliard, Dad. They called last week: I got in. And I'm going.'

He waited for his father to be resistant, but to his surprise he only nodded. 'Good for you,' he said. 'Go and work hard and be happy.'

Paul stood uneasily on the porch. All these years, each time he and his father talked, he'd felt he was running into a wall. And now the wall was mysteriously gone but he was still running, giddy and uncertain.

'Paul?' his father said. 'I'm proud of you, son.'

Everyone was looking at him now, and he had tears in his eyes. He didn't know what to say, so he started walking, at first just to get out of sight, and then he was truly running, the guitar still in his hand.

'Paul!' his mother called after him, and when he turned, running backwards for a few steps, he saw her newly streaked hair lifting in the breeze. He thought of Bree, what his mother had said, how much they'd come to be like each other, his mother and his aunt, and he was afraid. His father had turned into someone else. Behind, half screened by the clematis, Rosemary stood listening, and he imagined her in that house set into the hill, talking with his father, riding the bus with him for hours, somehow a part of this change in his father, and again he was afraid.

So he ran.

He was three blocks away from home, five, ten. Across the street, in front of one low bungalow, an empty car stood running. It was a tan Gremlin, the ugliest car in the universe, edged with rust. He crossed the street, opened the driver's door and slipped inside. No one shouted; no one came running from the house. He yanked the door shut and adjusted the seat, putting the guitar on the seat beside him. The car was an automatic, scattered with empty cigarette packs. A total loser owned this car, he thought, as he put it into gear and backed up.

Still nothing: no shouts, no sirens. He hadn't driven much, but geared into DRIVE and pulled away. The guitar slipped. He pulled over and strapped it in with the seat belt. Then he drove through town, stopping carefully at every light, the day vibrant and blue. He reached the interstate where the road split and went west, to Louisville. California glimmered in his mind: music there, and an endless beach. Soon he'd be on that beach, playing in a band and living cheap and easy all summer long. In the fall, he'd find a way to get to Juilliard.

He pressed the pedal to the floor, climbing between the limestone walls where the highway had been cut into the hill, and then he descended towards the curve of the Kentucky River, flying.

# IV

BEYOND NORAH'S GLASS-PANELLED DOOR, the office hummed. Neil Simms, the personnel manager from IBM, walked through the outer doors, a flash of dark suit, polished shoes. Bree, standing in reception, turned to greet him. She was wearing a yellow linen suit and dark yellow shoes; a fine gold bracelet slipped down her wrist as she reached to shake his hand. She'd become thin and sharp-boned beneath her elegance. Still, her laugh was light, travelling through the glass to where Norah sat with the phone in one hand, the glossy folder she'd spent weeks preparing on her desk, IBM in bold black letters across the front.

'Look, Sam,' Norah said. 'I told you not to call me and I meant it.'

A cool, deep current of silence welled up against her ear. Sam was an investment analyst. Norah had met him in the parking garage six months ago. Her keys had slipped and he had caught them in midair. His fingers brushed her skin; the keys fell coldly against her palm.

That night he left a message on her machine. Norah's heart had quickened, stirred at his voice. Still, when the tape ended, she had forced herself to sit down and count up her affairs. Four. She had walked into each of them with a sense of hope and new beginnings, swept up in the rush of secret meetings, of novelty and surprise. Each had begun at moments when she thought the roar of silence in her house would drive her mad.

'Norah, please, just listen,' Sam was saying now: a forceful man, a person she didn't even particularly like.

In the reception room, Bree turned to glance at her, enquiring, impatient. Yes, Norah gestured through the glass, she would hurry.

'I just want to ask about Paul,' Sam was insisting. 'If you've heard anything. Because I'm here for you, OK? Do you hear what I'm saying, Norah? I'm totally, absolutely, here for you.'

'I hear you,' she said, angry with herself—she didn't want Sam talking about her son. Paul had been gone for twenty-four hours now. She'd watched him run off, carrying his guitar, and she'd nearly gone after him. But she'd let herself think that maybe he needed some time to work this out on his own.

'Norah?' Sam said. 'Norah, are you OK?'

She closed her eyes briefly. 'I'm focusing on Paul right now,' she said, and then, sharply, she added, 'Look, Sam, I've had it, actually. I was serious the other day. Don't call me again.'

She hung up. Her hand was trembling. She felt Paul's disappearance like a punishment: for David's long anger, for her own. The car he'd stolen had been found deserted on a side street in Louisville last night, but there had been no trace of Paul. And so she and David were waiting. The girl from West Virginia was still sleeping in the den. David hardly spoke to her, except to ask if she needed anything. And yet Norah sensed an emotional connection, which pierced her as much, perhaps more, than any physical affair would have done.

Bree knocked on the glass, then opened the door a few inches. 'Everything OK? Because Neil's here, from IBM.'

'I'm fine,' Norah said. 'How are you doing? Are you OK?'

'It's good for me to be here,' Bree said brightly, firmly.

Norah nodded. All night and into this morning she had paced the house in her bathrobe, imagining every possible disaster. The chance to come to work had felt like sanctuary. 'I'll be right there,' she said.

She hurried through the lobby, but Sally stopped her at the reception desk, holding out the phone. 'You'd better take this, honey,' she said.

'They found him.' David's voice was quiet. 'The police just called. They found him in Louisville. Our son was caught stealing cheese.'

'He's OK, then,' she said, releasing a breath she hadn't realised she'd been holding all this time.

'Yes, he's fine. Hungry, apparently. I'm on my way to get him.'

'Maybe I should go. You might say the wrong thing, David.'

'Norah, he's eighteen. He stole a car. He has to take responsibility.'

'You're fifty-one,' she snapped. 'So do you.'

She imagined him standing in his office, so reassuring in his white coat. No one seeing him would imagine the way he'd come back home: unshaven, his clothes filthy, a pregnant girl in a shabby coat by his side.

'Look, just give me the address,' she said. 'I'll meet you there.'

'He's at the police station, Norah. I'll give you the address.'

As Norah was writing it down, she looked up to see Bree.

'Paul's OK?' Bree asked.

Norah nodded, too moved, too relieved, to speak. The office staff, hovering in the reception room, began to clap, and Bree crossed the room to hug her. So thin, Norah thought, tears in her eyes.

'I'll drive,' Bree said, taking her arm. 'Come on. Tell me as we go.'

Norah let herself be led down the hall and into the elevator, to the car in the garage. Bree drove through the crowded downtown streets while Norah talked, relief rushing through her like a wind.

'I was awake all night,' she said. 'I know Paul's an adult now and in a few months he'll be off to college, but I couldn't stop worrying.'

'He's still your baby.'

'Always. It's hard, letting him go. Harder than I thought.'

They were passing the low, dull buildings of IBM, and Bree waved at them. 'Hey, Neil,' she said. 'Be seeing you soon.'

'All that work.' Norah sighed.

'Oh, don't worry,' Bree said. 'I was very charming. And Neil's a family man. We'll get the account, don't worry.'

Norah didn't reply. White fences flashed and blurred against the lush grass. Horses stood calmly in their fields. Early spring, Derby time soon, the redbuds bursting into bloom. They crossed the Kentucky River, muddy and glinting.

'I can't lose you, Bree,' she said. 'I don't know how you're being so calm about everything.'

'I'm calm,' Bree said, 'because you're not going to lose me. But I was awake last night too. I have the feeling something's changing. It's funny how things seem different, suddenly. This morning I found myself staring at the light coming in the kitchen window. It made a long rectangle on the floor, and the shadows of new leaves were moving in it, making all their patterns. Such a simple thing, but it was beautiful.'

Norah studied Bree's profile, remembering her as she had been. Where had that young girl gone? 'Oh, Bree,' she managed, at last.

'It's not a death sentence, Norah.' Bree was speaking crisply now. 'More like a wake-up call. I did some reading, and my chances really are very good. And I was thinking this morning that if there's not a support group for women like me, I'm going to start one.'

Norah smiled. 'That sounds just like you. That's the most reassuring thing you've said yet.'

They drove on in silence. The world flashed by: grass, trees, sky. Then, increasingly, buildings. They had entered Louisville now and Bree was merging into the heavy traffic. The parking lot of the police station was nearly full, shimmering in the noon sun. They got out of the car, their slammed doors echoing, and walked in through the revolving doors.

Paul was on a bench on the far side of the room, hunched over, his elbows on his knees and his hands dangling between them. Norah's heart caught. She walked past the desk and the officers to her son.

'I'm glad to see you,' she said quietly. 'I was so worried, Paul.'

He looked at her, his eyes darkly angry and suspicious, and turned away suddenly, blinking back tears. 'I stink,' he said.

'Yeah,' Norah agreed. 'You really do.'

He scanned the lobby, his gaze lingering on Bree, who stood at the desk. 'So. I guess I'm lucky he didn't bother to come.'

David, he meant. Such pain in his voice. Such anger.

'He is coming,' Norah said, keeping her voice even. 'He'll be here any minute. Bree drove me over. Flew, really.'

She had meant to make him smile, but he only nodded. 'Is she OK?'

'Yes,' Norah said, thinking of their conversation in the car. 'She's OK.'

He nodded again. 'Am I going to jail?' Paul's voice was very soft.

She took a breath. 'I don't know. I hope not.'

They sat in silence. Bree was talking to an officer, nodding, gesturing. Beyond, the revolving door turned and turned, spilling strangers inside or out, one by one, and then it was David striding across the terrazzo floor. Norah felt Paul tense beside her, but to her astonishment, David walked straight to Paul and grabbed him in a powerful hug.

'You're safe,' he said. 'Thank God.'

She drew a deep breath, grateful for this moment. An officer with a white crew cut crossed the room, a clipboard under one arm. He shook Norah's hand, David's. Then he turned to Paul.

'What I'd like to do is put you in the slammer,' he said conversationally. 'But it seems your neighbours think they're doing you a favour and won't press charges about the car. So since I can't lock you up, I'm releasing you in the custody of your parents.'

Paul nodded. His hands were trembling; he shoved them in his pockets. They all watched as the officer tore a paper off his clipboard, handed it to David and walked slowly back to the desk.

'I called the Bolands,' David explained, folding the paperwork and tucking it into his breast pocket. 'They were reasonable. But don't think you won't be paying back every red cent of what it will cost to get that car repaired, Paul. And don't think your life is going to be very happy for a while. No social life.'

Paul nodded, swallowing. 'I have to rehearse,' he said. 'I can't just drop the quartet.'

'No,' David said. 'What you can't do is steal a car from our neighbours and expect life to go on as usual.'

'Fine,' Paul said. 'Then I'm not coming home. I'd rather go to jail.'

'Well, I can certainly arrange that,' David answered.

'Go ahead,' Paul said. 'Arrange it. Because I'm a musician. And I'd rather sleep in the streets than give it up. Hell, I'd rather be dead.' His eyes narrowed. 'My sister doesn't know how good she's got it.'

Norah, who had been holding herself very still, felt the words like shards of ice. Before she knew what she'd done, she'd slapped Paul across the face. The stubble of his new beard was rough against her palm—he was a man, no longer a boy, and she'd hit him hard. He turned, shocked, a red mark already rising on his cheek.

'Paul,' David said, 'don't make things worse than they are. Don't say things you'll regret for the rest of your life.'

Norah's hand was still stinging; her blood rushed. 'We'll go home,' she said. 'We'll settle this at home.'

'I don't know. A night in jail might do him good.'

'I lost one child,' she said, turning to him. 'I will not lose another.'

Now David looked stunned, as if she'd slapped him too.

'OK,' he said. 'Maybe you're right to pay no attention to me. God knows I'm sorry for the things I've done to fail you both.'

'David?' Norah said, as he turned away, but he didn't respond. She watched him walk across the room and enter the revolving doors. Outside, he was visible for an instant, a middle-aged man in a dark jacket, part of the crowd, then gone.

'I didn't mean—' Paul began.

Norah held up her hand. 'Don't. Please. Don't say another word.'

It was Bree, calm and efficient, who got them to the car. They opened the windows against Paul's stench, and Bree drove, her thin fingers steady on the wheel. Norah glanced at Paul in the rearview mirror. He sat, pale and sullen, arms folded, slouching, clearly furious, clearly in pain. She had done the wrong thing back there, lashing out at David like that, slapping Paul; she had only made things worse. His angry eyes met hers in the mirror, and she remembered his soft, plump infant hand pressed against her cheek, his laughter trilling through the rooms. Another boy altogether, that child. Where had he gone?

## July 1988

# I

DAVID HENRY SAT UPSTAIRS in his home office. Through the window, he watched a squirrel retrieve a nut and run up the sycamore tree. Rosemary was on her knees by the porch, her long hair swinging as she leaned to plant bulbs and annuals in the flowerbeds she had made. Jack sat near her, playing with a truck. He was a sturdy boy, five years old now, cheerful and good-natured, with dark brown eyes and traces of red in his blond hair.

On the evenings when David watched the boy, while Rosemary went to work, he loved to read him stories, feeling his weight and warmth, his head against his shoulder. It pained David that his memories of Paul at this age were so sparse, so fleeting. He had been establishing his career then, of course, busy with his clinic, and his photography, but really it was his guilty secret that had kept him distant.

He had never been able to tell Norah the truth about Phoebe, knowing he would lose her entirely—and perhaps Paul too—if he did. So he had devoted himself to his work and, in those areas of his life he could control, had been very successful. But, sadly, from those years of Paul's childhood he remembered only a few moments.

David tapped on the window and waved to Jack and Rosemary. He'd bought this old, two-storey house six years ago, in great haste, looking at it only once and then going home to pack while Norah was at work. It was split almost exactly in half, with thin partitions dividing what had been expansive rooms. David had taken the larger apartment and given Rosemary the keys to the other; for the last six years they had lived side by side, separated, but seeing each other every day.

Rosemary had tried to pay rent from time to time, but David had refused, telling her to go back to college and get a degree; she could pay him back later. He knew that his motives weren't entirely altruistic, yet he couldn't explain even to himself why she mattered so much to him.

'I fill up that place left by the daughter you gave away,' she had said once. He'd nodded, thinking it over, but that wasn't it either, not exactly. It was more, he suspected, that Rosemary knew his secret. He'd poured his story out to her in such a rush, the first and last time he'd told it, and she'd listened without judging him. There was freedom in that; David could be completely himself with Rosemary, who had listened to what he'd done without rejecting him and without telling anyone, either. Strangely, over the years Rosemary and Paul had established a friendship, a kind of earnest ongoing argument about issues that mattered to them both—politics and music and social justice—arguments that started over dinner during Paul's rare visits and lasted into the night.

Sometimes, David suspected that this was Paul's way of keeping a distance from him. A way of being in the house without having to talk about anything deeply personal.

Now Rosemary looked up, brushing a wisp of hair from her cheek with her wrist, and waved back. David saved his files and walked along the narrow landing and down the stairs. His running shoes were on the back porch. He put them on, tying the laces tightly, and walked round to the front. Jack was standing by the trellis, pulling blossoms off the roses. David squatted down and pulled him close, feeling his soft weight, his steady breathing. Jack had been born in September, early in the evening. David had driven Rosemary to the hospital and had sat with her during the first six hours of labour. He'd been the first one after her to hold Jack and he'd come to love the boy like his own.

'You smell funny,' Jack said now, pushing at David's chest.

'It's my old stinky shirt,' David said.

'Going running?' Rosemary asked. She sat back on her heels, brushing dirt from her hands. She was lean these days, almost bony, and he worried about the pace she kept, how hard she pushed herself.

'I am. I can't look at those insurance files another minute.'

'I thought you hired someone.'

'I did. She'll be good, I think, but she can't start until next week.'

Rosemary nodded, pensive. Her dark eyelashes caught the light. She was young, just twenty-two, but she was tough and focused.

'Class tonight?' he asked, and she nodded.

'My last one ever. July the 12th.'

'That's *right*. I'd forgotten.'

'You've been busy.'

He nodded, feeling vaguely guilty, troubled by the date. July 12; it was hard to understand how time passed so quickly. Rosemary had gone back to college after Jack was born, the same dusky January in which he had left his former practice because a man who'd been his patient for twenty years had been turned away at the door for lack of health insurance. He'd started his own practice, and he took anyone who showed up, insurance or no. He wasn't in it for the money any more. Paul was through college and his own debts were long since paid off; he could do as he liked.

'I have a chemistry final today,' Rosemary said, pulling off her gloves, 'and then, hooray, I'm done.' Bees hummed in the honeysuckle. 'There's something else I need to tell you,' she said, tugging at her shorts and sitting next to him on the warm concrete steps.

'Sounds serious.'

She nodded. 'It is. I was offered a job yesterday. A good one.'

'Here?'

She shook her head, smiling and waving to Jack as he tried to do a cartwheel. 'That's the thing. It's in Harrisburg.'

'Near your mother,' he said, his heart sinking. Two years ago, after her father died quite suddenly, Rosemary had been reconciled with her mother and her elder sister, and they were anxious for her to come home and raise Jack nearby.

'That's right. It's the perfect job for me: four ten-hour days a week. They'll pay for me to study too. I could work on getting my physical therapy degree. But mostly I'd have more time with Jack.'

'And help,' he said. 'Your mother would help. And your sister.'

'Yes. That would be really nice. And as much as I love Kentucky, it's never been home to me, not really.'

He nodded, glad for her, not trusting himself to speak.

'We'll visit,' she said. 'You'll visit us.'

'That's right,' he said. There were tears in his eyes. 'I'm sure we'll see a lot of each other.'

'We will.' She put her hand on his knee. 'Look, I know we never talk about it. But what it meant to me—how you helped me—I'm so grateful. In many ways, you saved my life.'

'Well, if that's true, I'm glad. God knows I've done enough damage elsewhere. I never could seem to do Norah much good.'

'You ought to tell her,' Rosemary said softly. 'Paul too. You really must.' Jack was squatting on the walkway now, making little piles of gravel. 'It's not my place to say anything, I know that. But Norah ought to know about Phoebe. It isn't right that she doesn't. It isn't right, what she's had to believe about us all this time, either.'

David shrugged. 'I told her the truth. That we're friends.'

'Not the whole truth. David, in some weird way we're connected, you and I, because of Phoebe. Because I know that secret. The thing is, I used to like that: feeling special because I knew something no one else did. But lately I don't like it so much. It's not really mine to know, is it?'

'No,' David said. He thought of Caroline's letters, which he'd burned when he moved into this house. 'I suppose it's not.'

'So. You see? You will? Tell her, I mean.'

'I don't know, Rosemary. I can't promise that.'

They sat quietly in the sun for a few minutes, watching Jack try again to turn cartwheels on the grass. David had come back from Pittsburgh set free from the grief and loss he'd locked away all those years. When June died he'd had no way to give voice to what had been lost, no real way to move on. Somehow, going back had allowed him to settle it. He had come home to Lexington drained, yes, but also calm and sure. After all these years, he'd finally had the strength to give Norah the freedom to remake her life.

**W**hen Jack was born, David set up an account for him in Rosemary's name, and one for Phoebe, in Caroline's name. It was easy enough; he'd always had Caroline's social security number, and he had her address too. It had taken a private investigator less than a week to find Caroline and Phoebe, living in Pittsburgh, in a tall, narrow house near the freeway. David had driven there and parked, meaning to go up the steps and knock on the door. What he wanted was to tell Norah what had happened, and he couldn't do that without telling her where Phoebe was. Norah would want to see their daughter, he was sure, so he had come here to tell Caroline what he was hoping to do.

David got out of the car and stood at the bus-stop, trying to look inconspicuous even as he gazed across the darkening lawn at Caroline's house. As he watched, a light went on in a ground-floor room. Inside, moving in the square of light, Caroline picked up newspapers and folded up a blanket. She stood up and stretched, looked over her shoulder, and spoke.

And then David saw her: Phoebe, his daughter. She was in the dining room, setting the table. She had Paul's dark hair and his profile, and for an instant David felt as if he were watching his son. He took a step forward, and Phoebe walked out of his line of vision and then came back with three plates. She was short and stocky, and her hair was thin, held back with clips. She wore glasses. Even so, there was Paul's smile, his nose. Caroline came into the room and stood beside her, then put her arm round Phoebe in a quick affectionate hug.

By then it was fully dark. David stood, transfixed, glad there was little foot traffic. Now he understood that he was not in control of this situation; he was excluded from it as completely as if he didn't exist. Phoebe had been invisible to him all these years: an abstraction, not a girl. Yet here she was, putting water glasses on the table. She looked up, and a man with curly dark hair came in and said something that made Phoebe smile. Then the three of them sat down at the table to eat.

David went back to his car. He imagined Norah, standing next to him in the darkness, watching their daughter move through her life, unaware of them. He had caused Norah pain; his deception had made her suffer in ways he had never imagined or intended. But he could spare her this. He would drive away and leave the past undisturbed.

'I don't understand.' Rosemary was looking at him. 'Why can't you promise? It's the right thing to do.'

'It would cause too much grief.'

'You don't know what will happen. Promise me you'll think about it?'

'I think about it every single day.'

She shook her head, troubled, then smiled a small, sad smile. 'All right, then. There's one more thing.'

'Yes?'

'Stuart and I are getting married.'

'You're far too young,' he said at once, and they both laughed.

'I'm as old as the hills,' she said. 'That's how I feel half the time.'

'Well,' he said. 'Congratulations. It's no surprise, but it's good news all the same.' He thought of Stuart Wells, a respiratory therapist, tall and athletic. 'I'm glad for you, Rosemary. Stuart's a good young man, and he loves Jack. Does he have a job in Harrisburg, too?'

'Not yet. He's looking. His contract here finishes this month.'

'How's the job market in Harrisburg?'

'So-so. But I'm not worried. Stuart's very good.'

'I'm sure he must be.'

'You're angry.'

'No. No, not at all. But your news makes me feel old. Sad and old.'

She laughed. 'Old as the hills?'

Now he laughed too. 'Oh, much, much older.'

They were silent for a moment. 'It all just happened,' Rosemary said. 'Everything came together in this last week. I didn't want to mention anything about the job until I was sure. And then, once I got the job, Stuart and I decided to get married. I know it must seem sudden.'

'I like Stuart,' David said. 'I'll look forward to congratulating him.'

She smiled. 'Actually, I wondered if you'd give me away.'

He looked at her then, her pale skin, the happiness she could no longer contain shining through her smile.

'I'd be honoured,' he said gravely.

'It's going to be here. Very simple and private. In two weeks.'

'You're not wasting any time.'

'I don't need to think about it,' she said. 'Everything feels completely right.' She glanced at her watch and sighed. 'I'd better get going.' She stood up, brushing off her hands. 'Come on, Jack.'

'I'll keep an eye on him, if you want, while you get dressed.'

'That would be a lifesaver. Thanks.'

He sat on the steps, lazy in the sun, while Jack played with his truck. *You should tell her.* He shook his head. After he'd sat watching Caroline's house, he'd called a lawyer and set up those beneficiary accounts. When he died, they would skip probate; Jack and Phoebe would be taken care of and Norah would never need to know.

Rosemary came back, smelling of Ivory soap, dressed in a skirt and flat shoes. She took Jack's hand and hefted a turquoise backpack onto her shoulder. She looked so young, strong and slender. She would drop Jack at the sitter's house on the way.

'Oh,' she said, 'with everything else, I almost forgot: Paul called.'

David's heart quickened. 'Did he?'

'Yes, this morning. It was the middle of the night for him; he'd just come from a concert. He was in Seville, he said. He's been there for three weeks, studying flamenco guitar with someone.'

'Was he having a good time?'

'Yes. It sounded like he was. He said he'd call again.'

David nodded, glad Paul was safe. Glad he'd called.

'Good luck in your exam,' he said, standing.

'Thanks. As long as I pass, that's all that matters.'

She smiled, then waved and walked with Jack down the stone path to the sidewalk. David watched her go, trying to fix this moment—the vivid backpack, her hair swinging against her back, Jack's free hand reaching out to grab leaves and sticks—for ever in his mind. It was futile, of course; he was forgetting things with every step she took. But he hadn't picked up a camera since he went to stand by the confluence of those two rivers in Pittsburgh. He had simply ceased caring. Sometimes his photographs amazed him, pictures he came across stored in old boxes or folders, moments he could not remember even when he saw them. And what would he have of this moment in another year, in five? The sun in Rosemary's hair and the faint clean scent of soap.

And somehow, that would be enough.

He stood, stretched, and loped off to the park. About a mile into his run, he remembered the other thing that had been nagging him all morning, the importance of this day beyond Rosemary's test: July 12. Norah's birthday. She was forty-six. Hard to believe.

He ran, falling into an easy stride, veering away from the park, heading instead for his old neighbourhood. Rosemary was right. Norah should know. He would tell her today. He would go to their old house, where Norah still lived, and wait until she returned, and he would tell her.

David turned down his old street. He had not been over here in months and he was surprised to find the porch roof supported by pairs of two-by-fours. Rot in the porch floor, it looked like, but no workmen were in sight. The driveway was empty; Norah wasn't home. He paced across the lawn to catch his breath, then walked to where the key was still hidden beneath a brick beside the rhododendron. He let himself inside and got a drink of water. The tile floor was new, as was the refrigerator. Then he walked through the house, curious to see what else had changed. Small things, everywhere: a new mirror in the dining room, the living-room furniture reupholstered.

Upstairs, the bedrooms were the same, Paul's room a shrine to adolescent angst, the walls painted a hideous dark blue, like a cave. He'd gone to Juilliard, and although David had given his blessing and paid half his bills, what Paul still remembered was when David didn't believe his talent would be enough to sustain him in the world. He was always sending programme reviews, along with postcards from every city where he'd performed, as if to say, 'Here, look, I'm a success.'

The master bedroom was unused. Norah had moved to the smaller front bedroom; here the bedspread was wrinkled. David reached to straighten it, but pulled his hand back and went downstairs.

He didn't understand; it was late in the afternoon and Norah should be home. He picked up a yellow legal pad from the desk by the phone, carried it back to the breakfast nook and sat down. He began to write.

*Our little girl did not die. Caroline Gill took her and raised her in another city.* He crossed this out. *I gave away our daughter.*

He sighed and put the pen down. He couldn't do this; he could hardly imagine what his life would be without the weight of his hidden knowledge. He'd come to think of it as a penance. It was self-destructive, he could see that, but that was the way things were.

Distantly, the taps in the downstairs bathroom dripped, something he had always meant to fix. He tore the page off the legal pad into small pieces and put them in his pocket to discard later. Then he went out into the garage and rummaged around in the tools he had left until he found a wrench and a spare set of washers. Probably he had bought them one Saturday for just this reason.

It took him more than an hour to fix the taps in the bathroom. He took them apart and washed sediment from the screens, replaced the washers, tightened the fixtures. The brass was tarnished. He polished it, using an old toothbrush he found in a coffee can beneath the basin. When he'd finished, he stood in the bathroom for a moment, feeling deeply satisfied by the way the brass was shining, by the silence. Then the phone rang in the kitchen and an unfamiliar voice came on, speaking urgently about tickets for Montreal, interrupting itself to say, 'Oh, damn, that's right, I forgot you were off to Europe with Frederic.' And he remembered too—she'd told him, but he'd let it slip from his mind; no, he'd pushed it from his mind—that she'd gone to Paris on a holiday. That she'd met someone, a Canadian from Quebec, someone who worked at IBM and spoke French. Her voice had changed when she spoke of him, somehow softened, a voice he'd never heard her use before.

Well, at least she would be happy about the taps. And he was too— he'd done a careful, meticulous job. He stood in the kitchen and picked the yellow legal pad up again.

*I fixed the bathroom taps,* he wrote. *Happy Birthday.*

Then he left, locking the door behind him, and ran.

# II

NORAH SAT ON A STONE BENCH in the gardens at the Louvre, a book open in her lap, watching the silvery poplar leaves flutter against the sky.

'He's late,' she said to Bree, who sat beside her, long legs crossed at the ankle, leafing through a magazine. Bree, now forty-four, was very beautiful, tall and willowy, turquoise earrings brushing against her olive skin, her hair a pure silvery white. During the radiation she'd cut it very short. She was lucky and knew it; they'd caught the tumour early and she'd been cancer-free now for five years.

'Paul will come,' Bree said now. 'It was his idea, after all.'

'That's true,' Norah said. 'But he's in love. I just hope he remembers.'

The air was hot and dry. Norah closed her eyes, thinking back to the late-April day when Paul had surprised her at the office. Tall and still lanky, he sat on the edge of her desk, describing his plans for a summer tour of Europe, with a full six weeks in Spain to study with guitarists there. She and Frederic had scheduled a trip to France, and when Paul discovered that they'd be in Paris on the same day, he grabbed a pen from her desk and scrawled *Louvre* on the wall calendar in Norah's office: *Five o'clock, July 21. Meet me in the garden and I'll take you out to dinner.*

He'd left for Europe a few weeks later, calling her now and then from rustic pensions or tiny hotels by the sea. He was in love with a flautist, the weather was great, the beer in Germany spectacular. Norah listened; she tried not to worry or ask too many questions.

She was so discreet she'd never even asked him for an itinerary, so when Bree called from the hospital in Lexington she had not known how to reach him with the shocking news: David, running through the arboretum, had suffered a massive heart attack and died. She had flown home alone, waking on the plane from uneasy dreams of searching for Paul. Bree had helped her through the funeral and wouldn't let her return to Paris alone.

'Don't worry,' Bree said. 'He'll come.'

'He missed the funeral,' Norah said. 'I'll always feel awful about that. They never really resolved things, David and Paul. I don't think Paul ever got over David's leaving.'

'And you did?'

'I don't know,' Norah replied slowly. They had been divorced for six years and married for eighteen before that. When Bree had called with news of his death, she simply could not believe it. It was only later, after the funeral, that grief had caught up with her. 'There are so many things I wish I'd said to him. But at least we did talk. Sometimes he just stopped by: to fix something, to say hello.'

'Did he know about Frederic?' Bree asked.

'I tried to tell him once, but he didn't seem to take it in.'

'Where is Frederic, anyway? Didn't you say he was coming?'

'He wanted to, but he got called to Orléans to work. I told him to go. He and Paul are great friends, but it's better that I give him this news alone.'

'Yes. I'm planning to slip away too, once he comes.'

'Thank you,' Norah said, taking her hand. 'Thank you for everything. I couldn't have got through the last week without you.'

'You owe me big-time,' Bree said, smiling. Then she grew pensive. 'I thought it was a beautiful funeral. There were so many people. It surprised me to know how many lives David touched.'

Norah nodded. 'It was the clinic,' she said. 'Most of the people had been his patients.'

'I know. It was amazing. People seemed to think he was a saint.'

'They weren't married to him,' Norah said.

Leaves fluttered against the hot blue sky. She scanned the park again, looking for Paul, but he was nowhere in sight.

'Oh,' she said, 'I can't believe David's really dead.'

Bree took her hand and they sat quietly for several minutes. Tonight Norah would meet Frederic at their pension by the river. They would drink wine and she would wake in the night, moonlight flooding in, his steady breath soft in the room. He wanted to marry her.

Norah's book slipped from her hand and she leaned over to pick it up. When she sat up again, Paul was crossing the park.

'Oh,' she said, with the sudden rush of pleasure she always felt on seeing him. She stood up. 'There he is, Bree. Paul's here!'

'He's so handsome,' Bree observed, standing up too. 'He must get that from me.'

Paul raised one hand to wave, grinning, and Norah started walking towards him, leaving her book on the bench. Her heart was beating with excitement and gladness, as well as grief and trepidation. He wore a white shirt with the sleeves rolled up, khaki shorts. How it changed the world, his being there. She reached him at last and hugged him.

'Hey, Mom,' Paul said, pulling back to look at her. He'd grown a dark beard. 'Fancy meeting you here,' he said, laughing.

'Yes, fancy that.'

Bree was beside her then. She stepped forward and hugged Paul too.

'I have to go,' she said. 'I was just hanging around to say hello. You're looking good, Paul. The wandering life agrees with you.'

He smiled. 'Can't you stay?'

Bree glanced at Norah. 'No,' she said. 'But I'll see you soon, OK?'

'OK,' Paul said, leaning to kiss her on the cheek. 'I guess.'

Norah wiped the back of her wrist against her eye as Bree turned and walked away.

'What is it?' Paul asked; then, suddenly serious, 'What's wrong?'

'Come and sit,' she said, taking his arm.

Together, they crossed back to her bench. She picked up her book.

'Paul, I have bad news,' she said. 'Your father died nine days ago. A heart attack.'

His eyes widened in shock and grief and he looked away, staring without speaking at the path he'd walked to reach her.

'When was the funeral?' he asked at last.

'Last week. I'm so sorry, Paul. I thought about contacting the embassy to help me track you down, but I didn't know where to start. So I came here today, hoping you'd show up.'

He nodded and leaned forward with his elbows on his knees, his hands clasped between them. He clenched his fists, then released them.

She took her son's hand in hers. 'It's OK to be upset,' she said.

Paul nodded, but his face was still closed. When he finally spoke, his voice was on the edge of breaking. 'I never thought he'd die. I never thought I'd care. It's not like we ever really talked.'

'I know.' And she did. 'But he loved you,' she said. 'Don't ever think he didn't.'

Paul gave a short, bitter laugh. 'No. That sounds pretty, but it's just not true. I'd hang out and talk with Dad about this and that, but we never went any further. I could never get anything right for him.' His voice was still calm, but tears were slipping down his cheeks.

Norah felt her own grief and sadness gather in her throat. 'Your father,' she said at last, 'had a hard time revealing himself to anyone. I don't know why. He grew up poor and he was always ashamed of that. I wish he could have seen how many people came to the funeral, Paul. Hundreds. It was all the clinic work he did. A lot of people loved him.'

'Did Rosemary come?' he asked, turning to face her.

'Rosemary? Yes.' She'd glimpsed Rosemary when the service ended, sitting in the last pew in a simple grey dress. She looked older, more settled. David had always insisted there had never been anything between them; in her heart, Norah knew this was true. 'They weren't in love,' Norah said. 'Your father and Rosemary. It wasn't what you think.'

'I know.' He sat up straighter. 'Rosemary told me. I believed her.'

'She did? When?'

'When Dad brought her home. That first day.' He looked uncomfortable. 'I'd see her at his place sometimes. When I stopped in to visit Dad. We'd all have dinner together. I could tell there wasn't anything between them. She was OK, Rosemary. She wasn't the reason I couldn't ever really talk to him.'

Norah nodded. 'But, Paul, you mattered to him. Look, I know what you're saying, because I felt it too. That distance. That sense of a wall too high to get over. But behind that wall, he loved us both. I don't know how I know that, but I do.'

Paul didn't speak. Every now and then he brushed tears from his eyes. Finally, he sat back and looked straight at her. 'Has your visit been good?' he asked. 'Do you like France?'

'I've been happy here,' Norah said, and it was true. Frederic felt congestion had ruined Paris, but for Norah the charm was infinite, the boulangeries and the patisseries, the crepes sold from street stands, the spires of ancient buildings, the bells. The sounds, too, of the language flowing like a stream. She wondered if it was Frederic's voice she had loved first. They had so much in common—grown children, divorces, demanding jobs—but because Frederic's life had happened in another country, it felt exotic to Norah, familiar and unknown all at once. 'How about you? How's the tour? Are you still in love?'

'Oh, yes,' he said, his face easing a little. He looked straight at her. 'Are you going to marry Frederic?'

She ran her finger round the corner of her book. This was the question, of course. Should she change her life?

'I don't know,' she said slowly. 'Bree's willing to buy the business. Frederic has two more years on his contract, so we don't have to make any decisions for a while. But I can imagine myself in a life with him.'

Paul nodded. 'Is that how it was last time? You know, with Dad?'

Norah looked at him, wondering how to answer this.

'Yes and no,' she said at last. 'I'm much more pragmatic now. Then, I just wanted to be taken care of. I didn't know myself very well.'

'Dad liked to take care of things.'

'Yes. Yes, he did.'

They sat for a time in silence, air moving lightly around them. Then Paul was standing up, waving across the park, the sadness on his face giving way to a joyous smile. Norah followed his gaze across the dry grass to a slender young woman with a long, delicate face and skin the colour of ripe acorns, her dark hair in dreadlocks to her waist. She wore a soft print dress and carried herself with a dancer's grace.

'It's Michelle,' Paul said. 'I'll be right back. It's Michelle.'

Norah watched him move towards her as if pulled by gravity. He cupped her face lightly in his hands as they kissed, a gesture so intimate that Norah looked away. They crossed the park then, heads bent, talking. At one point they paused and Michelle rested her hand on Paul's arm, and Norah knew he had told her.

'Mrs Henry,' she said, shaking hands when they reached the bench. Her fingers were long and cool. 'I am so sorry about Paul's father.'

For a few minutes they all stood in the garden, talking. Paul suggested that they go for dinner, and Norah was tempted to say yes, but she hesitated, aware that between Paul and Michelle there was a warmth, a radiance, a restlessness to be alone. She thought of Frederic again, perhaps already back in their pension.

'How about tomorrow?' she said. 'What if we meet for breakfast?'

On the way to the metro, Paul walked just ahead, and Michelle took Norah's arm.

'You raised a wonderful son,' she said. 'I'm so sorry I won't get to know his father.'

'That would have been hard in any case—to get to know him. But yes, I'm sorry too,' Norah said. 'Have you enjoyed your tour?'

'Oh, it's a wonderful feeling, travelling,' Michelle observed.

It was a soft evening, the bright lights of the metro station a shock as they descended. A train clattered in the distance.

'Come by around nine tomorrow,' Norah told Paul. And then, as the train came nearer, she leaned forward, close to his ear, shouting. 'He loved you! He was your father, and he loved you!'

Paul's face opened for an instant: grief and loss. He nodded. There was no time for more. The train stopped, squealing, and the hydraulic doors burst open with a sigh. Norah got on and sat by the window, watching a flash, a final glimpse of Paul. There, then gone.

# November 1988

HIS NAME WAS ROBERT and he was handsome, with a shock of dark hair that fell across his forehead. He went up and down the aisle of the bus, introducing himself to everyone and commenting on the route, the driver, the day. 'I'm having a great time here,' he announced, shaking Caroline's hand on his way. She smiled, patient; his grip was firm and confident. Other people would not meet his eye. Yet Robert went on, undaunted, as if within his persistence, Caroline thought, was some deep desire to find a person who would really see him.

That person, it appeared, was Phoebe, who seemed to brighten, awash in some internal light, when Robert was around. When he finally settled down in the seat next to her, still talking, Phoebe simply smiled up at him. It was a radiant smile; she held nothing back. Caroline closed her eyes at her daughter's naked expression of emotion—the wild innocence, the risk! But when she opened them again, Robert was smiling back, as pleased by Phoebe, as wonderstruck.

Well, yes, Caroline thought, and why not? Wasn't such love rare enough in the world? She glanced at Al, who sat next to her, nodding off, his greying hair lifting as the bus sped across the ravine, up the incline to Squirrel Hill. Headlights were already on in the early winter dusk. Phoebe and Robert sat quietly, facing the aisle, dressed for the Upside Down Society's annual dance. Robert's shoes were polished to a high shine; he wore his best suit. Beneath her winter coat, Phoebe wore a flowery white and red dress, a delicate white cross from her confirmation on a slender chain round her neck. She stared out of the window, smiling faintly, lost in her thoughts. Robert studied the ads above Caroline's head. He was a good man, prepared in every moment to be delighted by the world, though he forgot conversations almost as soon as they were finished and asked Caroline for her phone number every time they met.

Still, he always remembered Phoebe. He always remembered love.

'We're almost there,' Phoebe said, tugging on Robert's arm as they neared the top of the hill.

'Al,' Caroline said, shaking his shoulder. 'Al, honey, it's our stop.'

They stepped off the bus into the damp chill of the November evening and walked in pairs through the dusky light.

'You're tired,' Caroline said, sliding her hand round Al's arm. 'You've had a long couple of weeks.'

'I'm OK,' he said.

'I wish you didn't have to be away so much.' She regretted her words the moment she'd said them. The argument was old by now, a tender knot in the flesh of their marriage.

Al sighed heavily, his breath a faint cloud in the cold. 'Look, I'm doing the best I can, Caroline. The money's good just now and I'm pushing sixty. I have to milk it while I can.'

Caroline nodded. His arm beneath her hand was firm and steady. She was so glad to have him here, so tired of the strange rhythms of their lives that kept him away for days at a time. What she wanted was to have breakfast with him every morning and dinner every night.

'It's just that I miss you,' Caroline said softly. 'That's all I meant. That's all I'm saying.'

Phoebe and Robert walked ahead of them, holding hands. Phoebe wanted to marry Robert, to have a life with him; lately this was all she talked about. Linda, the day-centre director, had warned, 'Phoebe's in love. She's twenty-four, a bit of a late bloomer, and she's starting to discover her own sexuality. We need to discuss this, Caroline.' But Caroline had put the discussion off.

Then last week, while Al was still away, a letter had arrived from a law firm downtown. Caroline, puzzled, had ripped it open and read it on the porch, in the chill November air.

*Please contact this office regarding an account in your name.*

She called at once, and stood at the window as the lawyer gave her the news: David Henry was dead. He'd been dead, in fact, for three months. They were contacting her to tell her about a bank account he'd left in her name. Caroline had pressed the phone to her ear, something sinking through her at this news. It was a beneficiary account. David had established it in their joint names and therefore it stood outside the will and probate. They wouldn't tell her how much was in the account over the phone. Caroline would have to come in to the office.

After she had hung up, she went back out onto the porch and sat in the swing, trying to take in the news. It shocked her that David had remembered her this way. It shocked her more that he'd actually died. What had she imagined? That she and David would both somehow go on for ever, living their separate lives yet still connected to that moment when he put Phoebe in her arms? She couldn't figure out what to do, and in the end she'd simply gone back inside and got ready for work, sliding the letter into the top desk drawer.

Light spilled onto the sidewalk from the day centre and they pushed through the double glass doors into the hall. A dance floor had been set up at one end and a disco ball turned, scattering bright shards of light over the ceiling, the walls and the upturned faces. The music played, but no one was dancing. Phoebe and Robert stood on the edge of the crowd, watching the light shifting on the empty floor.

Al hung up their coats and then, to Caroline's surprise, he took her hand. 'You remember that day in the garden, the day we decided to get hitched? Let's teach them how to rock'n'roll, what do you say?'

He slid his hand round her waist and they stepped onto the floor. Caroline had forgotten—it had been a long time—how easily their bodies moved together, how free it made her feel to dance. Slowly, other people drifted onto the dance floor, smiling in their direction. Caroline knew almost everyone in the room, the staff of the day centre, the other parents from Upside Down, the residents from the facility next door. Phoebe was on a waiting list for a room there, a place where she could live with several other adults and a house parent. It seemed ideal in some ways—more independence and autonomy for Phoebe, at least a partial answer to her future—but the truth was that Caroline could not imagine Phoebe living apart from her. The waiting list for the residence had seemed very long when they applied, but in the last year Phoebe's name had moved up steadily. Soon Caroline would have to make a decision. She glimpsed Phoebe now, smiling such a happy smile, stepping shyly onto the dance floor with Robert.

She danced with Al for three more numbers, letting herself drift, following his steps. He was a good dancer, smooth and sure, and the music seemed to run straight through her. 'Nice,' Al murmured, pulling her closer, pressing his cheek to hers. When the music shifted to a fast rock number, he kept his arm round her as they left the floor.

Caroline, a little giddy, scanned the room for Phoebe by long habit.

'I sent her down for more punch,' Linda called from behind the table. She gestured to the dwindling refreshments on the table. 'Can you believe this turnout, Caroline? We're running out of cookies too.'

'I'll get some,' Caroline offered, glad for an excuse to go after Phoebe.

'She'll be OK,' Al said, catching her hand and gesturing to the chair beside him.

'I'll just check,' Caroline said. 'I won't be a minute.'

She walked through the empty halls, so bright and quiet, Al's touch still present on her skin. She went downstairs and into the kitchen, pushing open the swinging metal doors with one hand and reaching for the light switch with the other. The sudden fluorescence caught them like a photograph: Phoebe in her flowered dress, her back against the counter; Robert standing close, his arms round her. In the instant before they turned, Caroline saw that he was going to kiss her and Phoebe wanted to be kissed and was ready to kiss him back. Her eyes were closed, her face awash with pleasure.

'Phoebe,' Caroline said, sharply. 'Phoebe and Robert, that's enough.'

They pulled away from each other, startled but not contrite. 'It's OK,' Robert said. 'Phoebe is my girlfriend.'

'We're getting married,' Phoebe added.

Caroline tried to stay calm. Phoebe was, after all, a grown woman. 'Robert,' she said, 'I need to talk to Phoebe for a minute. Alone, please.'

Robert hesitated, then walked past Caroline, all his gregarious enthusiasm evaporated. The doors swung shut behind him.

Caroline turned to Phoebe. 'You can't get married, sweetie.'

Phoebe looked up, her face set in a stubborn expression Caroline knew well. 'Why not?'

'Sweetheart, marriage . . .' Caroline paused. 'Look, it's complicated, honey. You can love Robert without getting married.'

'No. Me and Robert, we're getting married.'

Caroline sighed. 'All right. Say you do. Where are you going to live?'

'We'll buy a house,' Phoebe said, her expression intent. 'We'll live there, Mom. We'll have some babies.'

'Babies are an awful lot of work,' Caroline said. 'I wonder if you and Robert know how much work babies are? And they're expensive. How are you going to pay for this house? For food?'

'Robert has a job. So do I. We have a *lot* of money.'

'But you won't be able to work if you're watching the babies.'

Phoebe considered this, frowning, and Caroline's heart filled. Such profound and simple dreams, and they couldn't come true.

'I love Robert,' Phoebe insisted. 'He loves me. Plus Avery had a baby.'

'Oh, honey,' Caroline said. 'Remember when you and Avery rescued Rain? We love Rain, but he's a lot of work. Having a baby is like having twenty Rains.'

Phoebe's face was falling, tears slipping down her cheeks. 'It's not fair,' she whispered.

'It's not fair,' Caroline agreed.

They stood for a moment, quiet in the bright harsh lights.

'Look, Phoebe, can you help me?' she asked finally. 'Linda needs some cookies, too.'

Phoebe nodded, wiping her eyes. They walked back upstairs and through the hallway, carrying boxes and bottles, not speaking.

Later that night, Caroline told Al what had happened. He was sitting beside her on the couch, arms folded, already half asleep. In the morning he would rise at dawn and drive away.

'She wants to have her own life, Al. And it should be so simple.'

'Mmm,' he said, rousing. 'Well, maybe it is simple, Caroline. Other people live in the facility and they seem to manage OK.'

Caroline shook her head. 'She certainly can't get married, Al. What if she did get pregnant? I'm not ready to raise another child and that's what it would mean.'

'I don't want to raise another baby either,' Al said.

'Maybe we should keep her from seeing Robert for a while.'

Al turned to look at her, surprised. 'You think that would be a good thing? From the minute I met you, Caroline, you've been demanding that the world should not slam any doors on Phoebe. "Do not underestimate her"—How many times have I heard you say that? So why won't you let her move out? Why not let her try? She might like the place. You might like the freedom.'

'I can't imagine my life without her,' she said softly, struggling with the difficult truth.

'No one's asking you to do that. But she's grown up, Caroline. That's the thing. Why have you worked all your life, if not for some kind of independent life for Phoebe?'

'I suppose you'd like to be free,' Caroline said. 'You'd like to travel.'

'And you wouldn't?'

'Of course I would,' she cried, surprised at the intensity of her response. 'But, Al, even if Phoebe moves out, she'll never be completely independent. And I'm afraid you're unhappy because of it. I'm afraid you're going to leave us.'

Al didn't speak for a long time. 'Why are you so mad?' he asked at last. 'What have I ever done to make you feel like I'm going to leave?'

'I'm not mad,' she said quickly, knowing she'd hurt him. 'Al, wait here a second.' She walked across the room and took the letter from the drawer. 'This is why I'm upset. I don't know what to do.'

He took the letter and studied it.

'How much is in this account?' he asked, looking up.

She shook her head. 'I don't know. I have to go in person to find out.'

Al nodded, studying the letter again. 'It's strange: a secret account.'

'I know. Maybe he was afraid I'd tell Norah. Maybe he wanted to make sure she had time to get used to his death. That's all I can imagine.' She thought of Norah, never suspecting that her daughter was still alive. And Paul—what had become of him?

'What do you think we should do?' she asked.

'Well, find out the details first. We'll go down to see this lawyer fellow together when I get back. I can take off a day or two. After that, I don't know, Caroline. We sleep on it, I guess.'

'All right,' she said. Al made it sound so easy. 'I'm so glad you're here.'

'Honestly, Caroline.' He took her hand in his. 'I'm not going anywhere. Except to Toledo, at six o'clock tomorrow morning. So I think I'll go up and hit the sack.'

He kissed her then, and pulled her close. Caroline pressed her cheek against his, taking in his scent and warmth, thinking of meeting him that day in the parking lot outside Louisville, the day that defined her life.

Al got up, his hand still in hers. 'Come upstairs?' he invited.

She nodded and stood, her hand in his.

In the morning, she rose early and made breakfast, decorating the plates of eggs, bacon and hash browns with sprigs of parsley.

'That sure smells good,' Al said, as he came in, tossing the paper on the table, along with yesterday's mail. There were two bills, plus a bright postcard of the Aegean Sea with a note from Doro on the back.

Caroline ran her fingers over the picture and read the brief message. 'Trace sprained his ankle in Paris.'

'That's too bad.' Al snapped open the paper and shook his head at the election news. 'Hey, Caroline,' he said after a moment, putting the paper down. 'I was thinking last night. Why don't you come with me? Linda would take Phoebe for the weekend, I bet. You and I could get away. You'd get a chance to see how Phoebe might do on her own.'

'Right now? Just leave, you mean?'

'Yeah. Seize the day. Why not?'

'Oh,' she said, flustered. 'I don't know. There's so much to do this week. Maybe next time.' She didn't want to turn him away. 'It's a really good idea,' she added, thinking with surprise that it was.

He smiled, disappointed, and leaned to kiss her, his lips cool on hers.

After Al drove off, Caroline hung Doro's postcard on the refrigerator. It was a bleak November, and she liked looking at that bright, alluring sea, the edge of warm sand. All that week, helping patients or making dinner or folding laundry, Caroline remembered Al's invitation. She thought about the passionate kiss she'd interrupted between Robert and her daughter, and about the residence where Phoebe wanted to live. Al was right. Phoebe had a right to a life of her own.

On Friday, Caroline arranged to pick Phoebe up from work on her way back from her hospital shift. That evening, she sat in her car, waiting, watching Phoebe through the window as she moved behind the counter, binding documents or joking with Max, her co-worker. Phoebe had worked here for three years now. She loved her job and she was good at it. Caroline thought back to all the fights and presentations it had taken to make this moment possible. Yet Phoebe didn't earn enough to live on and she simply would not be able to stay by herself, not even for a weekend. If a fire broke out, or the electricity failed, she would be frightened and would not know what to do.

And then there was Robert. On the drive home, Phoebe chatted about work, about Max, and about Robert, Robert, Robert. He was coming over the next day to make a pie with Phoebe. Caroline listened, glad that it was almost Saturday and Al would be back.

When they walked in the door, the phone was ringing. Caroline sighed. It would be a salesman or a wrong number. Rain mewed in welcome, weaving round her ankles. 'Scat,' she said, picking up the phone.

It was the police, the officer on the other end asking for her.

'Yes,' she said, watching Phoebe pick up Rain and hug him. 'This is Caroline Simpson.'

He cleared his throat and began. Al's truck had left the road on a bend, breaking through a guardrail and flying into a low hill. He was in hospital with a broken leg.

Caroline told Phoebe what had happened as she drove. In the tiled hospital corridors, the same trauma centre where Caroline had long ago agreed to marry Al, she found herself swimming in memories of that earlier day: Phoebe's lips swelling, her breathing laboured. Now Phoebe was a grown woman; she and Al had been married for sixteen years.

He was awake, his dark and silver hair standing out against the pillow. He tried to sit up but then grimaced in pain.

'Oh, Al.' She crossed the room and took his hand.

'I'm OK,' he said, and he closed his eyes and took a deep breath. She felt herself going very still inside, for she had never seen Al like this.

'Hey, you're starting to scare me,' she said, keeping her tone light.

He opened his eyes then, and for an instant they were looking straight at each other, everything between them falling away. He reached up and touched one large hand lightly against her cheek.

'What happened?' she whispered.

He sighed. 'I don't know. It was such a sunny afternoon. I was moving right along, singing with the radio. The next thing I knew, the truck was sailing through the guardrails. And after that I don't remember. Not until I woke up in here. I totalled the truck.'

Caroline leaned forward and put her arms round him. She heard his heart beating steadily in his chest. 'Oh, Al.'

'I know,' he said. 'I know, Caroline.'

Beside them, Phoebe started to cry, pressing the sobs back into her mouth with her hand. Caroline sat up and put an arm round her.

'Phoebe,' Al said. 'Look at you here, just getting off work. Did you have a good day, honey? I didn't get to Cleveland, so I didn't get those rolls you like so much, sorry to say. Next time, OK?'

Phoebe nodded, wiping her hands across her cheeks. 'Where's your truck?' she asked, and Caroline remembered the times Al had taken them both for a ride, Phoebe sitting high up in the cab.

'Honey, it's broken,' Al said. 'I'm sorry, but it's really smashed up.'

Al was in the hospital for two days, then he came home. Caroline's time passed in a blur of work, tending to Al, making meals, trying to do the laundry. Al was an awful patient, short-tempered and demanding.

A week passed. On Saturday, Caroline, exhausted, put a load in the washer and went into the kitchen to get something made for dinner. She pulled a pound of carrots out of the refrigerator for a salad and rummaged in the freezer, hoping for inspiration. Nothing. Upstairs, the bell she'd left with Al rang insistently. Caroline sighed and hurried up the stairs. How much was one woman supposed to do?

'You're supposed to be patient,' she said, walking into their room, where Al was sitting with his leg propped on an ottoman, a book in his lap. 'I know it's exasperating, but healing takes time.'

'You're the one who wanted me home more,' Al retorted. 'Be careful what you wish for.'

Caroline sat down on the edge of the bed. 'I didn't wish for this.'

'You're right. I'm sorry.' He looked out of the window. 'I'm not going to drive a truck any more,' he said, blurting the words out.

'All right,' she said, trying to imagine what this might mean for their lives. She was suddenly a little apprehensive. Not once since they were married had they spent more than a week together.

'I'll be getting in your hair all the time,' Al said, as if reading her mind.

'Will you?' She looked at him intently, taking in his pallor, his serious eyes. 'Are you planning to retire completely, then?'

He shook his head. 'Too young for that. I was thinking I could transfer into the office, maybe. Drive a city bus.'

Caroline nodded. She'd driven out to the accident site, seen the hole torn in the guardrail. The truth was, another few yards and Al would have died, and she could be a widow, facing the rest of her life alone.

'Maybe you should retire,' she said slowly. 'I went down to the lawyer, Al. I'd already made the appointment and I kept it. It's a lot of money that David Henry left for Phoebe.'

'Well, even if it's a million dollars, it's not mine,' Al said.

She remembered, then, how he'd responded when Doro had given them the house: this same reluctance to accept anything he hadn't earned with his own hands.

'That's true,' she said. 'The money is for Phoebe. But you and I, we raised her. If she's taken care of financially, we can worry less. We can have more freedom. Al, maybe it's time for us to retire.'

'What do you mean?' he asked. 'You want Phoebe to move?'

'No. I don't want that at all. But Phoebe wants it. She and Robert . . . Who am I to say? Maybe they *will* be OK, more or less, together.'

He nodded, thinking, and she was struck by how tired he looked, how fragile all their lives were. All these years she had tried to imagine every possibility, and yet here was Al, grown a little older, with a broken leg—an outcome that had never crossed her mind.

'I'll make a pot roast tomorrow,' she said, naming his favourite meal. 'Will pizza be OK tonight?'

'Pizza's fine,' Al said. 'Get it from that place on Braddock, though.'

She touched his shoulder and started downstairs to make the call.

# July 1, 1989

THE STUDIO OVER THE GARAGE, with its hidden darkroom, had not been opened since David moved out seven years ago, but, now that the house was going up for sale, Norah had no choice but to face it. Curators were coming tomorrow to view the collection of David's work. So Norah had been sitting on the floor since early morning, slicing through boxes, lifting out folders full of photographs and negatives and notes, determined to be ruthless in this process of selection. It should not have taken long; David had been so meticulous and everything was neatly labelled. A single day, she'd thought, no more.

She hadn't counted on memory, the slow lure of the past. It was early afternoon already, growing hot, and she had only made it through one box. A fan whirred in the window and a fine sweat gathered on her skin; the glossy photos stuck to her fingertips. They seemed at once so near and so impossible, those years of her youth. There she was with a scarf tied gaily in her carefully styled hair, Bree beside her in sweeping earrings, a flowing patchwork skirt. And here was a rare photo of David, so serious, with a crew cut, Paul just an infant in his arms. Memories rushed up, filling the room.

A wasp roamed the ceiling. Each year the wasps returned and built a nest somewhere in the eaves. Now that Paul was grown, Norah had given up worrying about them. She stood and stretched and got a Coke from the refrigerator where David had once stored chemicals and packages of film. She drank it, gazing out of the window at the wild irises and honeysuckle in the back yard. Norah had always meant to make something of it, but now she never would. In two months she would marry Frederic and leave this place for ever.

He had been transferred to France for two years. They had already rented a little riverside cottage. Frederic was there at this very moment, putting in a greenhouse for his orchids. Even now it filled Norah's imagination: the smooth red tiles of the patio, the slight river breeze in the birch tree by the door. She could walk to the station and be in Paris in two hours, or she could walk to the village and buy fresh cheese and bread, and dark, gleaming bottles of wine. On the patio, in the evenings she'd spent there, the moonflowers had opened with their lemony fragrance and she and Frederic had sat drinking wine and talking. Such simple things, really. Such happiness.

Norah drained her Coke and went back to work, bypassing the box in which she'd got so mired and opening another. Inside this one there were file folders neatly arranged, organised by year. The first held shots of anonymous infants, sleeping in their carriages, held in the arms of their mothers. The second folder was very similar, and the third and the fourth. Photos of girls, not babies any more but two- and three- and four-year-olds. Girls in their Easter dresses at church, girls running in the park, dancing, throwing balls, laughing, crying. Norah frowned, flipping more quickly through the images. There wasn't one child she recognised. The photos were arranged carefully by age. When she skipped to the end, she found not girls but young women, walking, shopping, talking to each other. The last was a young woman in the library, her chin resting in her hand as she gazed out of the window.

Norah let the folder fall into her lap, spilling photos. What was this? All these girls, young women: it could have been a sexual fixation, yet

Norah knew that it was not. Loss lingered in the play of lights and shadows; these were photos full of yearning. Of longing, not lust.

She flipped back the box lid to read the label. SURVEY was all it said.

Quickly, careless of the disorder she was creating, Norah went through all the other boxes. In the middle of the room she found another with that bold black word SURVEY. She opened it and pulled the folders out. Not girls this time, not strangers, but Paul. Folder after folder of Paul in all his ages, his transformations and his growth. His anger, his intentness and his stunning gift of music, fingers flying over his guitar.

For a long time Norah sat very still, agitated, on the edge of knowing. And then suddenly the knowledge was hers. She longed to talk to David, for now she realised he'd missed his daughter too.

All these years, she had felt her daughter's presence, a shadow, standing just beyond every photograph. Norah had kept this feeling to herself, fearing that anyone who heard her would think her crazy. It brought tears to her eyes to realise how deeply David, too, had felt their daughter's absence. He had looked for her everywhere, it seemed.

Finally, into the expanding rings of silence in which she sat, gravel popped faintly: a car in the driveway. Distantly she heard a slammed door, footsteps, the doorbell ringing in the house. She shook her head and swallowed, but she did not get up. She was wiping tears from her eyes; whoever wanted her could wait.

But no. The furniture appraiser had promised to stop by this afternoon. So Norah pressed her hands across her cheeks and entered the house from the back, pausing to splash water on her face and run a comb through her hair. 'I'm coming,' she called, when the doorbell rang again. She walked through the rooms, the furniture clustered into the centre and covered with tarps: the painters were coming tomorrow.

She opened the door, still drying her hands.

The woman on the porch was vaguely familiar. She was dressed practically, in crisp, dark blue trousers. She wore a white cotton sweater and her thick hair was grey and cut very short. Even at first glance she gave the impression of being organised, efficient, the sort of person who wouldn't stand for any sort of nonsense. She didn't speak, however. She seemed startled to see Norah, taking her in so intently that Norah folded her arms defensively. She caught the woman's gaze and focused on her wide-set eyes, so blue, and then she knew.

Her breath snagged. 'Caroline? Caroline Gill?'

The woman nodded, her blue eyes falling shut for a moment as if something had been settled between them. But Norah did not know what. The presence of this woman from the long-lost past had set up a fluttering deep in her heart, taking her back to that dreamlike night when she and David had ridden to the clinic through the silent, snow-filled streets; when Caroline Gill had administered gas and held her hand during the contractions.

'What are you doing here?' Norah asked. 'David died a year ago.'

'I know,' Caroline said, nodding. 'I know, I'm so sorry. Look, Norah—Mrs Henry—I have something I need to talk to you about, something rather difficult. I wonder if you could spare me a few minutes. When it's convenient. I can come back if this isn't a good time.'

There was both an urgency and a firmness in her voice, and Norah found herself stepping back and letting Caroline Gill step into the hall. Boxes, neatly filled and taped, were stacked against the walls.

'You'll have to excuse the house,' she said, gesturing at the furniture all pushed to the centre of the living room. 'I have painters coming. And a furniture appraiser. I'm getting married again,' she added. 'I'm moving.'

'I'm glad I caught you, then,' Caroline said. 'I'm glad I didn't wait.'

Caught me? Norah wondered, but from force of habit she invited Caroline into the kitchen, the only place they could comfortably sit. She filled two glasses with ice and water, while Caroline took a seat in the breakfast nook. David's final note—*I fixed the bathroom taps. Happy Birthday*—was tacked onto the bulletin board just behind Caroline's shoulder. Norah thought impatiently of the photos waiting in the garage, of all she had to do that couldn't wait.

'You've got bluebirds,' Caroline observed, nodding at the garden.

'Yes. I hope the next people will feed them.'

'It must be strange to be moving.'

'It's time,' Norah said, putting the glasses on the table. She sat down. 'But you didn't come to ask about that.'

'No.' She took a drink of water. When she spoke she seemed calm, resolved. 'Norah—may I call you Norah? That's how I've thought of you, all these years.'

Norah nodded, perplexed. When was the last time Caroline Gill had crossed her mind? Not in ages.

'Norah,' Caroline said. 'What do you remember about the night your son was born?'

'Why do you ask?' Norah's voice was firm, but she was leaning back, pulling away from the intensity in Caroline's eyes. 'Why are you here, and why are you asking me that?'

Caroline Gill didn't answer right away. The lilting voices of the blue-birds flashed through the room like motes of light.

'Look, I'm sorry,' Caroline said. 'There isn't an easy way to say this, so I'll just come out with it. Norah, that night when your twins were born, Phoebe and Paul, there was a problem.'

'Yes,' Norah said sharply, thinking of the bleakness she had felt after the birth. 'My daughter died,' she said. 'That was the problem.'

'Phoebe did not die,' Caroline said evenly, looking straight at her. 'Phoebe was born with Down syndrome. David believed the prognosis was not good. He asked me to take her to a place in Louisville where such children were routinely sent. Most doctors, in 1964, would have advised the same. But I couldn't leave her there. I took her and moved to Pittsburgh. I've raised her all these years. Norah,' she added gently, 'Phoebe is alive. She's well.'

Norah sat very still. Then she felt a rush, a loss of control. Shaking, she held on to the edge of the table. 'What did you say?'

Caroline said it again: Phoebe, not dead but taken away. All these years. Phoebe, growing up in another city. 'Safe,' Caroline kept saying. Safe, well cared for, loved. Phoebe, her daughter, Paul's twin. Born with Down syndrome, sent away.

David had sent her away.

'You must be crazy,' Norah said, though even as she spoke so many jagged pieces of her life were falling into place.

Caroline reached into her bag and slid two Polaroids across the table. Norah couldn't pick them up, she was trembling too hard, but she leaned close to take them in: a little girl in a white dress, chubby, with a smile that lit her face, her almond-shaped eyes closed in pleasure. And then another, this same girl years later, about to shoot a basketball, caught in the instant before she jumped. She looked a little like Paul in one, a little like Norah in the other.

'But why?' The anguish in her voice was audible. 'Why would he do this? Why would you?'

Caroline shook her head and looked out into the garden again. 'For years I believed in my own innocence,' she said. 'I believed I'd done the right thing. The institution was a terrible place. David hadn't seen it; he didn't know how bad it was. So I took Phoebe and I raised her, and I fought many, many fights to get her an education and access to medical care. To make sure she would have a good life. It was easy to see myself as the hero. But I think I always knew, underneath, that my motives weren't entirely pure. I wanted a child and I didn't have one.' She shook her head again. 'I can't speak for David. He was always a mystery to me. I know he loved you, and I believe that, as monstrous as this all seems, his initial intentions were good ones. He told me once about his sister. She had a heart defect and died young, and his mother never got over her grief. For what it's worth, I think he was trying to protect you.'

'She is my child,' Norah said, the words torn out of some deep place in her body. 'Protect me? By telling me she'd died?'

Caroline didn't answer, and they sat for a long time, the silence gathering. Norah thought of David. She had planned the memorial service without telling him. What must it have been like for him, that service, carrying this secret with him. She hadn't known, she hadn't guessed. But now that she'd been told, it made a terrible kind of sense.

At last Caroline opened her bag again and took out a piece of paper with her address and telephone number on it. 'This is where we live,' she said. 'My husband, Al, and I, and Phoebe. This is where Phoebe grew up. She has had a happy life and she's a lovely young woman. Next month, she's going to move into a group home. It's what she wants. She has a good job in a photocopy shop. She loves it there.'

'A photocopy shop?'

'Yes. She's done very well, Norah.'

'Does she know about me?' Norah asked. 'About Paul?'

Caroline glanced down at the table, fingering the edge of the photo. 'No. I didn't want to tell her until I'd talked to you. I didn't know what you'd want to do, if you'd want to meet her. But if you want to come, we're there. Just call. Next week or next year.'

'I don't know,' Norah said slowly. 'I think I'm in shock.'

'Of course you are.' Caroline stood up.

'May I keep the photos?' Norah asked.

'They're yours. They've always been yours.'

On the porch, Caroline paused. 'David always loved you, Norah.'

Norah nodded, remembering that she'd said much the same thing to Paul in Paris. She watched as Caroline walked to the car. Phoebe was alive, in the world. Loved, Caroline had said. Well cared for. But not by Norah. The dreams she'd had came back to her, pierced her. She went back into the house, crying now, walking past the shrouded furniture. The appraiser would come. Paul was coming too, today or tomorrow. She washed the water glasses, then stood in the silent kitchen, thinking.

David had sent their daughter away and told her she was dead.

Norah slammed her fist on the counter, making the glasses jump. She made herself a gin and tonic and wandered upstairs. She called Frederic, and hung up when the machine answered. After a time she went back out to David's studio. Everything was the same, the air so warm, so still, the photographs and boxes scattered all over the floor, just as she'd left them. At least $50,000, the curators had estimated.

Norah picked up the first box and lugged it across the room. She heaved it up onto the counter, then balanced it on the windowsill overlooking the back yard. She paused to catch her breath before she opened the screen and pushed the box out, using both hands, hearing it land with a satisfying *thunk* on the ground below. She went back for the next one and the next. In less than an hour, the studio was cleared. She walked back into the house, passing the photographs spilling out and scuttling across the lawn in the late-afternoon light.

Inside, she took a shower, standing beneath the rushing water until it ran cold. She put on a loose dress, made another drink and sat on the sofa. When it got dark, hours later, she was still there. The phone rang, and she heard herself, recorded, and then Frederic, calling from France. She yearned to be there, to be in that place where her life had made sense, but she didn't pick up the phone or call him back.

She dozed, off and on, but didn't sleep. Now and then she got up to make another drink, walking through the empty rooms, shadowy with moonlight, filling her glass by touch. Not bothering, after a time, with tonic or lime or ice. Once she dreamt that Phoebe was in the room, emerging somehow from the wall where she had been all these years, Norah woke then, weeping. She poured the rest of the gin down the sink and drank a glass of water.

Finally, she fell asleep at dawn. At noon, when she woke, the front door was standing wide open and in the back yard there were photos everywhere: caught in the rhododendrons, plastered up against the foundation. Glimpses of their lives, as David had seen them, as David had tried to shape them. Negatives, dark celluloid, scattered on the grass. Norah imagined the shocked and outraged voices of the curators, friends, of her son, even of a part of herself.

She drank two more glasses of water and took some aspirin, then started hauling boxes to the far side of the overgrown yard. One box, the one full of images of Paul throughout his life, she pushed into the garage again to save.

There were stones piled behind the garage. She dragged these out, one by one, and arranged them in a wide circle. She dumped the first box, the glossy black and white images, all the unfamiliar faces of young women gazing up at her from the grass. Squatting in the harsh noon sun, she held a lighter to the edge of an eight-by-ten. When a flame licked and rose, she slid the burning photo into the shallow pile inside the ring of stones. Wisps of blackened paper wafted on the shimmering waves of heat, like butterflies. As the fire in the circle of stones took hold and began to roar, Norah fed it more photos, these memories of David's, so carefully preserved.

'You bastard,' she whispered, watching the photographs flame high before they blackened and curled and disappeared.

Light to light, she thought, moving back from the heat.

Ashes to ashes.

Dust, at last, to dust.

# July 2–4, 1989

PAUL DROVE to the neighbourhood where he had grown up, past the stately houses and deep front yards, the sidewalks and eternal quiet. The front door of his mother's house was closed. He turned off the engine and sat listening to the birds and the sound of lawn mowers.

His father had been dead for a year and his mother was marrying Frederic and moving to France. He was here not as a child or as a visitor but as caretaker of the past. His to choose, what to keep and what to discard. He leaned back, searching in his pocket for the house key.

When Paul got out of the car, he stood for a moment on the kerb, looking around the neighbourhood. It was hot; a high faint breeze moved through the tops of the trees. Strangely, too, the air seemed to be full of snow, a feathery grey-white substance drifting down through the blue sky. Paul reached out and caught a flake in one palm. When he closed his hand into a fist and opened it again, his flesh was smeared with black. Ashes were drifting down like snow in the dense July heat.

He left footprints on the sidewalk as he walked up the steps. The front door was unlocked, but the house was empty. 'Hello?' Paul called, walking through the rooms, the furniture pushed into the middle of the floor and covered with tarps. He hadn't lived here for years but he found himself pausing in the living room, stripped of everything that had made it meaningful. Upstairs, he stood in the doorway of his own room. Boxes were piled here, too, full of old things he had to sort. She hadn't thrown anything away; even his posters were neatly rolled.

'Mom?' he called. He went downstairs to the back porch.

She was there, sitting on the steps, wearing old blue shorts and a limp white T-shirt. He stopped, wordless, taking in the strange scene. A fire still smouldered in a circle of stones, and the ashes and wisps of burnt paper that had fallen around him in the front yard were here too, caught in the bushes and in his mother's hair.

She looked up, her face streaked with ashes and with tears. 'It's all right,' she said. 'I've been burning your father's photographs but I've stopped burning them now. I was so angry with him, Paul, but then it struck me: this is your inheritance too. I only burned one box. It was the box with all the girls, so I don't imagine it was very valuable.'

'What are you talking about?' he asked, sitting down beside her.

She handed him a photo of himself, one he'd never seen. He was about fourteen, sitting on the porch swing, bent over his guitar, playing intently, oblivious to everything around him, caught up in the music.

'OK. But I don't understand. Why are you so mad?'

His mother pressed her hands to her face and sighed. 'Do you remember the story of the night you were born, Paul? The blizzard?'

'Sure.' He waited for her to go on, not knowing what to say.

'Did we tell you about the nurse, Caroline Gill?'

'Yes. Not her name. You said she had blue eyes.'

'She does. Very blue. She came here yesterday, Caroline Gill. I haven't seen her since that night. She brought news, shocking news. I'm just going to tell you, since I don't know what else to do.'

She took his hand. His sister, she told him calmly, had not died at birth after all. She'd been born with Down syndrome, and his father had asked Caroline Gill to take her to a home in Louisville.

'To spare us,' his mother said, and her voice caught. 'That's what she said. But she couldn't go through with it, Caroline Gill. She took your sister, Paul. She took Phoebe. All these years your twin has been alive and well, growing up in Pittsburgh.'

'My sister?' Paul said. 'In Pittsburgh?'

'Caroline went to Pittsburgh and started a new life,' his mother said. 'She raised your sister. I keep trying to be thankful that she was good to Phoebe, but there's a part of me that's just raging.'

Paul closed his eyes, trying to hold all these ideas together. All these years he'd tried to imagine what his sister would be like, but now he couldn't bring a single idea of her to mind.

'How could he?' he asked finally. 'How could he keep this a secret?'

'I don't know,' his mother said. 'I've been asking myself the same thing. And how dare he die and leave us to discover this alone?'

She got up, went inside and came back with two Polaroids. 'Here she is,' she said. 'This is your sister: Phoebe.'

Paul took them and stared from one to the other: a posed picture of a girl, smiling, and then a candid shot of her shooting a basket. This stranger with the almond eyes and sturdy legs was his twin.

'You have the same hair,' Norah said softly, sitting down next to him again. She laughed. 'And guess what—she's a basketball fan.'

Paul's laugh was sharp and full of pain. 'Well,' he said, 'I guess Dad chose the wrong kid.'

His mother took the photos in her ash-stained fingers. 'Don't be bitter, Paul. Phoebe has Down syndrome.'

They sat in silence, looking at the scattered photos and damp boxes.

'What does it mean?' he asked at last. 'That she's retarded? I mean, day to day.'

'I don't know. Caroline said she has a job. A boyfriend. She went through school. But apparently she can't really live on her own.'

'This nurse—Caroline Gill—why did she come here now, after all these years? What did she want?'

'She just wanted to tell me,' his mother said softly. 'That's all. She was opening a door, Paul. Whatever happens next is up to us.'

'And what is that?' he asked. 'What happens now?'

'I'll go to Pittsburgh. I know I have to see her. But after that, I don't know anything. We'll be strangers to her. And I have to talk with Frederic; he has to know.' She put her face in her hands. 'Oh, Paul—how can I go to France for two years and leave her behind? I don't know what to do. It's too much for me, all at once.'

Paul sat quietly, struggling with many confused emotions: anger at his father, and surprise, and sadness for what he'd lost. Worry, too; it was terrible to be concerned about this, but what if he had to take care of this sister who couldn't live on her own?

'I don't know either,' he said. 'Maybe the first thing to do is clean up this mess.'

'Your inheritance,' his mother said.

'Not just mine,' he said, testing the words. 'It's my sister's too.'

They worked through that day and the next, sorting the photos and repacking the boxes, dragging them into the cool depths of the garage. While his mother met the curators, Paul called Michelle to explain, and to tell her he wouldn't be able to get back to Cincinnati for her concert.

On Tuesday morning, full of apprehension, he and his mother got into her car and drove over the river and through the lush late-summer green of Ohio. It was hot, the leaves of the corn shimmering against the expansive blue sky. They arrived in Pittsburgh amid returning Fourth of July traffic, travelling through the tunnel that opened onto the bridge in a breathtaking view of the two rivers merging. They crawled through downtown traffic and finally pulled up on a busy tree-lined street.

Caroline Gill had told them to park in the alley and they did, getting out of the car and stretching. Paul took the house in, so different from his own quiet childhood, its suburban ease and comfort. Traffic rushed by on the street, past the little postage-stamp yards, into the city.

The gardens all along the alley were thick with flowers. In this garden a woman was working, tending a row of tomato plants. She was wearing blue shorts and a white T-shirt and bright, flowered cotton gloves. She sat up where she was kneeling and ran the back of her hand across her forehead. The traffic rushed; she hadn't heard them coming.

'Is that her?' Paul asked. 'Is that the nurse?'

His mother nodded. Her sunglasses masked her eyes, but even so he could see how nervous she was.

'Yes. That's Caroline Gill. Paul, maybe we should just go home.'

'We've driven all this way. And they're expecting us.'

She smiled weakly. 'They can't possibly be expecting us. Not really.'

Paul nodded. The back door swung open and Caroline stood, brushing her hands on her shorts.

'Phoebe!' she called. 'There you are.'

Paul felt his mother grow tense beside him, but the figure on the porch was hidden in the shadows. The moment stretched out, until at last a young woman emerged, carrying two glasses of water.

He stared hard. She was short, much shorter than he was, and her hair was cut in a simple bowl shape around her face. From this distance her features seemed delicate in a broad face, a face that seemed somewhat flattened. Her eyes were slightly upslanted, her limbs short. She wore flowered shorts and she was stocky, a little plump, her knees brushing together when she walked.

'Oh,' his mother said. She had placed one hand on her heart. Her eyes were still hidden by the sunglasses, and he was glad.

'It's OK,' he said. 'Let's just stand here for a while.'

Caroline and Phoebe sat on the porch steps, drinking their water.

'I'm ready,' his mother said at last, and they went down the steps.

Caroline Gill saw them first; she shaded her eyes, squinting against the sun, then stood up, taking Phoebe's hand, bringing her to her feet. They met by the tomato plants, the heavy fruit already starting to ripen. No one spoke. Phoebe was gazing at Paul, and after a long moment she reached across the space between them and touched his cheek, lightly, gently. Paul nodded without speaking, looking at her gravely; her gesture seemed right to him, somehow. Phoebe wanted to know him, that was all. He wanted to know her too, but he had no idea what to say to her, this sudden sister, so intimately connected to him yet such a stranger.

It was Phoebe who recovered first.

'Hello,' she said, extending her hand to him formally. 'I'm Phoebe. Pleased to meet you.' Her speech was thick, hard to understand. Then she turned to his mother and did this again.

'Hello,' his mother said, taking her hand. Her voice was charged with emotion. 'Hello, Phoebe. I'm very glad to meet you too.'

'It's so hot,' Caroline said. 'Why don't we go inside? I have the fans on. And Phoebe made iced tea this morning.'

Phoebe smiled, suddenly shy. They followed her into the coolness of the house. The rooms were small but immaculate, with French doors opening between the living room and dining room. A massive loom sat in the far corner of the living room.

'I'm making a scarf,' Phoebe said.

'It's beautiful,' his mother said, crossing the room to finger the yarns, dark pink and cream and yellow and pale green. She'd taken off her sunglasses and she looked up, her eyes watery, her voice still charged with emotion. 'Did you choose these colours yourself, Phoebe?'

'My favourite colours,' Phoebe said, sitting down at the loom.

'Mine too,' his mother said. 'When I was your age, those were my favourite colours too.'

'You can have this scarf,' Phoebe said. 'I'll make it for you.'

'Oh,' his mother said. 'Phoebe, that's lovely.'

Caroline brought iced tea, and the four of them sat uneasily in the living room, talking awkwardly about the weather. Phoebe sat quietly at the loom, moving the shuttle back and forth, looking up now and then. At last his mother drained her tea and spoke.

'Well,' she said. 'Here we are. And I don't know what happens now.'

'Phoebe,' Caroline said. 'Why don't you join us?'

Quietly, Phoebe came over and sat next to Caroline on the couch.

Caroline began, speaking too quickly, nervous. 'There are no maps for this place we're in, are there? But I want to offer my home to Phoebe. She can come and live with us, if she wants to do that. I've thought about it so much, these last days.' She turned to Phoebe, who was looking at her with wide, wary eyes. 'You're my daughter, Phoebe, do you understand that? This is Paul, your brother.'

Phoebe took hold of Caroline's hand. 'This is my mother,' she said.

'Yes.' Norah glanced at Caroline and tried again. 'That's your mother,' she said. 'But I'm your mother too. You grew in my body, Phoebe.' She patted her stomach. 'You grew right here. But then you were born, and your mother Caroline raised you.'

'I'm going to marry Robert,' Phoebe said. 'I don't want to live with you.'

Paul, who had watched his mother struggle, felt Phoebe's words physically, as if she'd kicked him. He saw his mother feel them too.

'It's OK, Phoebe,' Caroline said. 'No one's going to make you go away.'

'I didn't mean—' His mother stopped and took a deep breath. She tried again. 'Phoebe, Paul and I, we'd like to get to know you. That's all. Please don't be scared of us, OK? What I want to say—what I mean—is that my house is open to you. Always. I hope you'll come and visit me some day, that's all. Would that be OK with you?'

'Maybe,' Phoebe conceded.

'Phoebe,' Caroline said, 'why don't you show Paul around for a while? Give Mrs Henry and me a chance to talk a little bit. And don't worry, sweetheart,' she added. 'No one's going anywhere.'

Phoebe nodded and stood up. 'Want to see my room?' she asked Paul. 'I got a new record player.'

Paul glanced at his mother and she nodded, watching them as they crossed the room together. Paul followed Phoebe up the stairs.

'Come on,' she said, leading him along the landing. 'I got some new records, too.'

They sat on the floor of her room. The walls were pink, with pink and white checked curtains at the windows. Phoebe put an album on and turned the volume up loud on her record player, blasting 'Love, Love Me Do', singing along to the music with her eyes half shut. She had a nice voice, Paul realised, turning the volume down a bit.

'I like trombones,' she said, pretending to pull a long slide, and when Paul laughed, she laughed too. 'I really love trombones.' She sighed.

'I play the guitar,' he said. 'Did you know that?'

She nodded. 'My mom said. Like John Lennon.'

He smiled. 'A little,' he said, surprised to find himself in the middle of a conversation. 'You ever hear of Andrés Segovia?'

'Uh-uh.'

'He's really good. Someday I'll play his music for you, OK?'

'I like you, Paul. You're nice.'

He found himself smiling. 'Thanks,' he said. 'I like you too.'

'But I don't want to live with you.'

'That's OK. I don't live with my mother either. I live in Cincinnati.'

'Lucky.'

'I suppose,' he said gravely. The things he took for granted in life were the stuff of Phoebe's dreams. 'I'm lucky, yes. It's true.'

'I'm lucky too,' she said, surprising him. 'Robert has a good job, and so do I.'

'What's your job?' Paul asked.

'I make copies.' She said this with pride. 'Lots of copies. Max works there. She's my friend. We have twenty-three different colours of paper.'

She hummed a little as she put the first record away and chose another. Her movements were not fast, but they were efficient, focused. Paul imagined her at the copy shop, doing her work, joking with her friend. He realised, with a deep sense of shame, that his pity for Phoebe, like his mother's assumption of her dependence, had been foolish and unnecessary. Phoebe liked herself and she liked her life; she was happy.

'Where's your father?' he asked.

'At work. He drives a bus. Do you like *Yellow Submarine*?'

'Yes. Yes, I do.'

Phoebe smiled a wide smile and put the album on.

# September 1, 1989

NOTES SPILLED from the church, into the sunlit air.

To Paul, standing just outside the red doors, the music seemed almost visible, scattering on the lawn like motes of light. The organist was a friend of his, a woman from Peru named Alejandra, who wore her burgundy hair pulled back in a long ponytail.

Now his mother appeared in the doorway, laughing, one hand resting lightly on Frederic's arm. They stepped together into the sunlight, into a bright rain of bird seed and petals.

'Pretty,' Phoebe observed, beside him.

She was wearing a dress of silvery green, holding the daffodils she'd carried in the wedding loosely in her right hand. She was smiling, her eyes narrowed with pleasure, deep dimples in both plump cheeks. The petals and the seeds arched against the bright sky; Phoebe laughed, delighted, as they fell. Paul looked at her hard: this stranger, his twin. They had walked together down the aisle of the tiny church to where their mother waited with Frederic by the altar. There were swallows winging in the rafters during the exchange of vows, but his mother had been sure of this church right from the beginning, just as she'd insisted, during all the strange and tearful discussions of Phoebe and her future, that both of her children would stand with her at her wedding.

Another burst, confetti this time, and a wave of laughter, rippling. His mother and Frederic bent their heads, and Bree brushed bright specks of paper from their shoulders, their hair.

'You're right,' he said to Phoebe. 'It's pretty.'

She nodded, thoughtful now, and smoothed her skirt with both hands. 'Your mother is going to France.'

'Yes,' Paul said, though he tensed at her choice of words: *your mother.* A phrase you'd use for strangers, and of course they all were. This, finally, was what had pained his mother most, the lost years standing between them, their words so tentative and formal where ease and love should have been. 'You and me too, in a couple of months,' he said, reminding Phoebe of the plans they'd finally agreed on.

An expression of worry, fleeting as a cloud, crossed Phoebe's face.

'We'll come back,' he added gently, remembering how scared she'd been by his mother's suggestion that she come with her to France.

Phoebe nodded, but she still looked worried.

'What is it?' he asked. 'What's wrong?'

'Eating snails.'

Paul looked at her, surprised. He'd been joking with his mother and Bree in the vestibule before the wedding, kidding about the feast they'd have in France. He hadn't thought Phoebe was listening.

'Snails aren't so bad,' he said. 'They're chewy. Kind of like garlic gum.'

Phoebe made a face and then she laughed. 'That's gross, Paul,' she said. The breeze moved lightly in her hair, and her gaze was still fixed on the scene before them: the moving guests, the sunlight, the leaves. Far across the lawn, his mother and Frederic lifted a silver cake knife.

'Me and Robert, we're getting married too.'

Paul smiled. He'd met Robert on that first trip to Pittsburgh; they'd gone to the grocery store to see him, tall and attentive, dressed in a brown uniform, wearing a name tag. When Phoebe introduced them, Robert had immediately taken Paul's hand and clapped him on the shoulder, as if they were seeing each other after a long absence.

'It's too bad Robert couldn't come,' he said.

Phoebe nodded. 'Robert likes parties.'

Paul watched his mother slip a bit of wedding cake into Frederic's mouth, touching the corner of his lip with her thumb. She was wearing a dress the colour of cream and her hair was short, blonde turning silver, making her green eyes look larger. He thought of his father, wondering what their wedding had been like.

'I like pink flowers,' Phoebe said. 'I want lots and lots of pink flowers at my wedding.' She grew serious then, frowned and shrugged. 'But me and Robert, we have to save the money first.'

The breeze lifted and Paul thought of Caroline Gill, tall and fierce, standing in the hotel lobby in downtown Lexington with her husband, Al, and Phoebe. They'd all met there yesterday, on neutral ground. His mother's house was empty, a FOR SALE sign in the yard. Tonight, she and Frederic would leave for France. Caroline and Al had driven in from Pittsburgh, and after a somewhat uneasy brunch together they had left Phoebe here for the wedding while they went on a trip to Nashville.

'Do you like Pittsburgh?' Paul asked. He'd been offered a good job there, with an orchestra.

'I like Pittsburgh,' Phoebe said. 'My mother says it has a lot of stairs, but I like it.'

'I might move there,' Paul said. 'What do you think?'

'That would be nice,' Phoebe said. 'You could come to my wedding.' Then she sighed. 'A wedding costs a lot of money. It's not fair.'

Paul nodded. It wasn't fair, no. None of it was fair. Not the challenges Phoebe faced in a world that didn't welcome her, not the relative ease of his own life, not what their father had done—none of it.

'You could elope,' he suggested.

Phoebe considered this, turning a green plastic bracelet on her wrist. 'No,' she said. 'We wouldn't have a cake.'

'Oh, I don't know. Couldn't you? I mean, why not?'

Phoebe, frowning hard, glancing at him to see if he was making fun of her. 'No,' she said firmly. 'That's not how you have a wedding, Paul.'

He smiled, touched by her sureness of how the world worked. 'You know what, Phoebe? You're right.'

Laughter and applause drifted across the sunny lawn as Frederic and his mother finished with the cake. Bree, smiling, raised her camera. Paul nodded to the table where the small plates were being filled. 'The wedding cake has six layers, Phoebe. You want some?'

Phoebe smiled and nodded in reply. 'My cake is going to have *eight* layers,' she said, as they walked across the lawn through the voices and the laughter and the music.

Paul laughed. 'Only eight? Why not ten?'

'Silly. You're a silly guy, Paul,' Phoebe said.

They reached the table. His mother was smiling, and she touched Phoebe's hair, smoothed it back, as if she were still a little girl. Phoebe pulled away and Paul's heart caught; for this story, there were no simple endings. There would never be the ordinary ease of daily life.

'You did a good job,' his mother said. 'I'm so glad you were in the wedding, Phoebe, you and Paul. It meant a lot to me. I can't tell you.'

'I like weddings,' Phoebe said, reaching for a plate of cake.

His mother smiled a little sadly. 'I'm glad you're coming to visit us in France, Phoebe,' she went on. 'Frederic and I, we're both so glad.'

Phoebe looked up, uneasy again.

'It's the snails,' Paul explained. 'She doesn't like snails.'

His mother laughed. 'Don't worry. I don't like them either.'

'And I'm coming back home,' Phoebe added.

'That's right,' his mother said gently. 'Yes. That's what we agreed.'

Paul watched, feeling helpless against the pain that had settled in his body like a stone. He wondered, as he had wondered so often in these past weeks, how his father could have betrayed her, betrayed them all.

'How?' he asked softly. 'How could he never tell us?'

She turned to him, serious. 'I don't know. But think how his life must have been, Paul. Carrying this secret with him all those years.'

He looked across the table. Phoebe was scraping whipped cream off her cake with her fork.

'Our lives could have been so different.'

'Yes. But they weren't different, Paul. They happened just like this.'

'You're defending him,' he said slowly.

'No. I'm forgiving him. I'm trying to, anyway. There's a difference.'

'He doesn't deserve forgiveness,' Paul said.

'Maybe not,' his mother said. 'But you and I and Phoebe, we have a choice. To be bitter and angry, or to try to move on.'

He considered this. 'I was offered a job in Pittsburgh,' he said.

'Really?' His mother's eyes were intent. 'Are you going to take it?'

'I think so,' he said, realising he'd made up his mind. 'It's a good offer.'

'You can't fix the past, Paul,' she said softly. 'Your life is your life. You're not responsible for what happened. Phoebe's OK, financially.'

Paul nodded. 'I know. I don't feel responsible for her. I truly don't. It's just—I thought I'd like to get to know her. Pittsburgh's a beautiful city and it's a good job. So, I guess—why not?'

'It would be nice,' his mother admitted slowly, 'to have the two of you in the same place. But you're so young, and you're just beginning to find your way. Please know it's OK for you to do that.'

Before he could answer, Frederic was there, tapping on his watch, saying they had to leave soon to catch their flight. After a moment's conversation Frederic went to get the car, and his mother turned back to Paul, put one hand on his arm.

'We're just about to go, I think. You'll be taking Phoebe home?'

'Yes. Caroline and Al said I could stay at their place.'

She nodded. 'Thank you,' she said, 'for being here. It can't have been easy for you, for all sorts of reasons. But it has meant so much to me.'

'I like Frederic,' he said. 'I hope you'll be happy.'

She smiled and squeezed his arm. 'I'm so proud of you, Paul. Do you have any idea how proud I am of you? How much I love you?' She turned to gaze across at Phoebe. 'I'm proud of both of you.'

'Frederic is waving,' Paul said, speaking quickly to cover his emotion. 'I think it's time. I think he's ready. Go and be happy, Mom.'

She looked at him, tears in her eyes, then kissed him on the cheek.

Frederic crossed the lawn and shook Paul's hand. Paul watched his mother embrace his sister and give Phoebe her bouquet; he watched Phoebe's tentative hug in return. Their mother and Frederic climbed into the car, smiling and waving amid another shower of confetti.

The car disappeared, and Paul made his way back to the table, keeping Phoebe's figure in sight. When he drew near he heard her talking happily to another guest about Robert and her own wedding. Her voice was loud, her speech a little thick and awkward, her excitement uncontained. He saw the guest's reaction—a strained, patient smile—and winced. Because he himself had reacted to such conversations in the same way, just weeks earlier.

'How about it, Phoebe,' he said, interrupting. 'You want to go?'

'OK,' she said, and put her plate down.

They drove through the lush countryside. It was a warm day. Paul turned off the air conditioner and rolled down the windows, remembering the way his mother had driven so wildly through these same landscapes to escape her loneliness and grief. He had never understood her sadness, though he had carried it with him later, wherever he went.

Now it was all gone, that sadness; that life was gone, as well.

He drove fast, edges of autumn everywhere. The dogwoods were already turning, clouds of brilliant red against the hills. Pollen tickled Paul's eyes and he sneezed several times. Phoebe, sitting in the seat beside him, took a Kleenex from a small pack in her large black plastic bag and offered it to him.

His sister. His twin. What if she'd been born without Down syndrome? Or what if she'd been born as she was, simply herself, and their father had not raised his eyes to Caroline Gill? The sunny playroom adjoining his would have belonged to Phoebe. She'd have chased him down the stairs, through the kitchen and into the wild garden, her face always with him, his laughter an echo of her own.

They were close to town now. Paul waited for a break in traffic, then turned into the Lexington cemetery. He parked beneath an elm tree and got out of the car. He walked round to Phoebe's door and opened it, offering his hand. She looked at it, surprised, then pushed herself out of the seat. They followed the path for a while, until he guided her across the grass to the stone that marked their father's grave.

Phoebe traced her fingers over the names and dates engraved in the dark granite. He wondered what she was thinking. Al Simpson was the man she called her father. It couldn't mean anything to her, this slab of granite, this name.

David Henry. Phoebe read the words out loud, slowly. They filled her mouth and fell heavily into the world.

'Our father,' he said.

'Our father,' she said, 'who art in heaven hallowed be thy name.'

'No,' he said, surprised. '*Our* father. My father. Yours.'

'Our father,' she repeated, and he felt a surge of frustration, for her words were agreeable, mechanical, of no significance in her life. 'You're sad,' she observed then. 'If my father died, I'd be sad too.'

Paul was startled. Yes, that was it—he was sad. His anger had cleared and suddenly he could see his father differently. His very presence must have reminded his father, in every glance, of the choice he'd made and could not undo. Those Polaroids of Phoebe that Caroline had sent over the years, found hidden in the back of a darkroom drawer after the curators had gone; the photograph of his father's family too, the one Paul still had, standing on the porch of their lost home. And the thousands of others, his father layering image on image, trying to obscure the moment he could never change.

Phoebe, his sister, a secret kept for a quarter of a century.

Paul walked a few feet back to the gravel path. He paused, his hands in his pockets, leaves swirling up in the eddies of wind.

At first the notes were thin, almost an undercurrent to the breeze, so subtle that he had to strain to hear them. He turned. Phoebe, still standing by the headstone, her hand resting on its dark granite edge, had begun to sing. It was a hymn, vaguely familiar. Her words were indistinct, but her voice was pure and sweet, and other visitors to the cemetery were glancing in her direction, at Phoebe with her greying hair and bridesmaid's dress, her awkward stance, her unclear words, her carefree, fluted voice. Paul stared at his shoes. For the rest of his life, he realised, he would be torn like this, aware of Phoebe's awkwardness, the difficulties she encountered simply by being different in the world, and yet propelled beyond all this by her guileless love.

By her love, yes. And, he realised, awash in the notes, by his own new and strangely uncomplicated love for her.

The words of the old hymn came back to him and Paul picked up the harmony. Their singing merged, her voice a twin to his own. When the song ended, they stayed as they were in the clear, pale light of the afternoon. The wind shifted, pressing Phoebe's hair against her neck.

Everything slowed, until the whole world was caught in this single hovering moment. Paul stood very still, waiting to see what would happen next.

For a few seconds, nothing at all.

Then Phoebe turned, slowly, and smoothed her wrinkled skirt. A simple gesture, yet it set the world back in motion.

Paul noted how short and clipped her fingernails were, how delicate her wrist had looked against the granite headstone. His sister's hands were small, just like their mother's. He walked across the grass and touched her shoulder, to take her home.

# Kim Edwards

**What was your main inspiration for starting to write a novel?**
I have always enjoyed the demands and pleasures of the story form and my first
book was a collection of short stories called *The Secrets of a Fire King*, but I
knew from the beginning that the idea for *The Memory Keeper's Daughter* was
too big to be a story. It came from one of the pastors of a church I'd recently
joined. It was just a few sentences about a man who'd discovered, late in life,
that his brother had been born with Down syndrome, placed in an institution at
birth and kept a secret from his family—even from his mother—all his life. I
remember thinking right away that it would make a good novel. It was the idea
of the secret at the centre of this family.

**Did you settle to writing the story straight away?**
No, but when I started I wrote the first chapter very quickly, having thought
about the idea for several years. I was simply intrigued by the characters and
wanted to find out where the events of that night in 1964 would take them in
their lives. Writing is always a process of discovery—I never know the end, or
even the events on the next page, until they happen.

**How long did it take you to write the book?**
I wrote it in about three years, from start to finish, of pretty steady work. I write
every day, in the mornings, for several hours. I spent another year in the
process of editing and production.

**What was the most surprising thing you discovered while researching *The
Memory Keeper's Daughter*?**
I discovered so many things: exploring photography, the ancient geography of

Kentucky, and of course Down syndrome. I discovered any number of quiet heroes, people who made a difference in individual lives and also inspired social change. I learned about the difficult landscape parents of children with Down syndrome faced when they started questioning conventional thinking, which recommended institutionalising children, and opted to raise their young at home instead. I remain very grateful to all the people who shared their own experiences and perceptions wth me while I was writing the book, helping me to gain a deep appreciation for their struggles and their joys.

**The novel begins in 1964. Did you meet any couples who had brought up a child with Down syndrome in the Sixties? Are we more enlighted now?**

The first couple I spoke with has a daugher whom they'd raised during the time period of this book. When I showed them the opening chapter, their immediate response was that I'd got the doctor exactly right: the attitudes David has about Down syndrome may seem outrageous to us now, but there was a time, not all that long ago, when these ideas were widely held. Certainly, writing this novel was a process of enlightenment for me. When I began, I didn't know how to imagine Phoebe. I was compelled by the secret and its impact on the family, but I wasn't very knowledgable about Down syndrome. To create a convincing character, one who was herself and not a stereotype, seemed a daunting task.

**Do you think our attitudes towards people with disabilities have changed?**

Yes, things have changed for the better over the past decades, but I'd say also that it's an ongoing process, with more progress yet to be made. The reason attitudes have improved, quite simply, is because the parents of children with Down syndrome refused, as Caroline does in this novel, to accept imposed limitations for their children. Changes do not happen easily, or without personal costs for those who struggle—and struggle still—to make their children visible to the world.

**As David's creator, were you able to sympathise in any way with his motives?**

Oh, yes, definitely. Even though none of us may ever experience a moment this dramatic, nonetheless we all have times when we react powerfully to an event in ways we may not completely understand. He makes absolutely the wrong decision, but he acts out of a desire to protect Norah from grief, and to do what the medical community in that time and place had deemed best for a child with Down syndrome. In addition, his own grief at the loss of his sister, and the greater loss of his family that resulted, is something he's never confronted or resolved. When Phoebe was born with Down syndrome, an event he could not anticipate or control, his old grief welled up.

**What are you working on now?**

I'm working on a new novel, *The Dream Master*. It's set in upstate New York and, like *The Memory Keeper's Daughter*, it turns on the idea of a secret.

*Taken from:* www.memorykeepersdaughter.com
and 'A Conversation with Kim Edwards'

# Death at Dawn

## Caro Peacock

*Miss Lane,*

*You do not know me, but I take the liberty of addressing you with distressing news. Your father, Thomas Jacques Lane, was killed this Saturday, 17th June, in a duel at Calais . . .*

When Liberty Lane receives this anonymous note, her first thought is to find her father's body. But, as her initial grief and the shock settle, Liberty knows that she must to do more than just bury her beloved father—she has a murderer to unmask . . .

# Chapter One

'WOULD YOU BE KIND ENOUGH to tell me where they keep people's bodies,' I said.

The porter blinked. The edges of his eyelids were pink in a brown face, lashes sparse and painful-looking like the bristles on a gooseberry. Odd the things you notice when your mind's trying to shy away from a large thing. When he saw me coming towards him over the cobbles among the crowds leaving the evening steam packet, he must have expected another kind of question altogether. Something along the lines of 'How much do you charge to bring a trunk up from the hold?' or 'Where can I find a clean, respectable hotel?' Those kinds of questions were filling the air all round us, mostly in the loud but uneasy tones of the English newly landed at Calais. I'd asked in French, but he obviously thought he'd misheard.

'You mean where people stay, at the hotels?'

'Not hotels, no. People who've been killed. A gentleman who was killed on Saturday.'

Another blink and a frown. He looked over my shoulder at his colleagues carrying bags and boxes down the gangplank, regretting his own bad luck in encountering me. 'Would he not be in his own house, mademoiselle?'

'He has no house here.'

Nor anywhere else, come to that. He would have had one soon, the tall thin house he was going to rent for us, near the unfashionable end of Oxford Street when we . . . Don't think about that.

'If an English gentleman were killed in . . . in an accident and had no family here, where might he be taken?'

'The morgue is over there, mam'selle.' The porter nodded towards a group of buildings a little back from the seafront then turned, with obvious relief, to a plump man who was pulling at his sleeve and burbling about cases of books.

I walked in the direction he'd pointed out but had to ask again before I found my way to a low building, built of bricks covered over with tarry, black paint. A man who looked as thin and faded as driftwood was sitting on a chair at the door, smoking a clay pipe. The smell of his tobacco couldn't quite mask another smell coming from inside the building. When he heard me approaching he gave me a considering look.

'It's possible that you have my father here,' I said.

He took a long draw on his pipe and spoke with it still in his mouth. 'Would he be the gentleman who got shot?'

'Possibly, yes.'

'English?'

'Yes.'

'She said his clothes had an English cut.'

'Who said?'

Without answering, he got up and walked over to a narrow house with a front door opening onto the cobbles only a few steps away from the morgue. He thumped on the door a couple of times and a fat woman came out in a black dress and off-white apron, straggly grey hair hanging down under her cap. They whispered, heads together, then he gave her a nudge towards me.

'Your father, oh, you poor little thing. Poor little thing.'

Her deep voice was a grieving purr in my ear, her hand moist and warm on my shoulder. Her breath smelt of brandy.

'May I see him, please?'

She led the way inside, still purring, '*Pauvre petite, oh, pauvre petite.*' Her husband in his could of pipe smoke fell in behind us. There were flies buzzing around the low ceiling and a smell of vinegar. Three rough, pinewood tables took up most of the space in the room but only one of them was occupied by a shape covered in a yellowish sheet. The woman signed to the man to pull the sheet back. I knew almost before I saw his face. I suppose I made some noise or movement because the man started pulling the sheet back again. I signed to him to leave it where it was.

'Your father?'

'Yes. Please . . .'

He hesitated, then, when I nodded, reluctantly pulled the sheet further down. They'd put my father in a white cotton shroud with his hands crossed on his chest. I took a step forward and untied the strings at the neck of the shroud. The woman pulled at my arm and tried to stop me. *Trust your own eyes and ears*, he'd said. *Never let anybody persuade you against them*. I tried to keep the sound of his voice in my head as I lifted up his right hand, cold and heavy in mine. I pulled the shroud aside with my other hand and looked at the round hole the pistol ball had made in his chest, right over the heart, and the livid scorch-marks on his skin surrounding it. No blood. They'd have sponged his body before they put it in the shroud. That probably accounted for the vinegar smell. The thought made me feel sick. I pulled the shroud up and watched while they covered him up again.

'His clothes?' I asked.

She looked annoyed and left us, wooden clogs clacking. The flies buzzed and circled. After a minute or two she was back with an armful of white linen, streaked with rusty stains. Breeches, stockings, a shirt. On the left breast of the shirt was a small round hole. I bent over it and smelt, through the iron tang of blood, a whiff of scorched linen and black powder. The man was repeating some question insistently.

'You will need an English priest?'

'I don't think . . . Oh, I see. For the burial. Yes.'

He produced a dogeared calling card from his pocket. I took the card. The woman had tried to be kind to me so as I left I slid some coins from my bag into the pocket of her apron. It came to me that she hadn't shown me his outer clothes, shoes, hat or jacket. One of the perquisites of her job, probably. Some lumpish son or cousin of hers might be wearing them even now. There should have been rings as well. I made myself picture the crossed hands against the shroud. They'd let him keep the narrow, silver ring on his left hand that he wore in memory of my mother. He usually wore a gold one with a curious design on his right hand, but I was certain that the hand I'd held had been bare. The thought of somebody else wearing his ring made me so angry that I almost turned back. But that was not sensible, and I must at all costs be sensible. I walked by the sea for a long time, watching the sun go down. Then I found a pile of fishing nets heaped in a shed, curled myself up in them and alternately slept and shivered through the few hours of a June night. In the shivering intervals, every word of the note that had jolted my world out of its orbit came back to me:

*Miss Lane,*

*You do not know me, but I take the liberty of addressing you with distressing news. Your father, Thomas Jacques Lane, was killed this Saturday, 17th June, in a duel at Calais . . .*

Everybody knows the place in Calais where gentlemen go to fight duels, the long stretch of beach with the sandhills behind. People point it out to each other from the deck of the steam packet. By the time the first grey light came in through the doorway of the fisherman's hut I knew that the one thing I wanted to do was follow the route my father would have taken three days before, at much this time of the morning. I unwrapped myself from the nets, brushed dry fish scales from my dress and walked along the harbour front, past shuttered houses and rows of tied-up fishing boats. Eventually the cobbled road runs out in a litter of nets and crab pots, just above the fringe of bladderwrack and driftwood that marks the high-tide line. They would have left their carriage there.

No carriage this morning, nothing but a fisherman's cart made of old planks. The owner of the cart probably lived in one of the little row of tilted and ramshackle hovels built of rocks and ships' timbers. The windows were closed with warped wooden shutters. There was nobody looking out of them so early in the morning, not even a fisherman's wife watching for her husband.

Later, I'd come back and try to talk to the fishermen's wives.

*I am sorry for disturbing you, madame, but can you recall a carriage drawing up there where the road runs out, three mornings ago? Just as it was getting light, it would have been, or even while it was still dark.*

I'm sure if he had met a fisherman's wife that morning, he'd have raised his hat and wished her good day. But almost certainly he did not meet her, the morning being so early. And even if she had met him or seen the carriage standing there, I don't suppose for one moment she'd tell me. The men and women who live in that ruckle of cottages must be used to seeing carriages drive up in the early morning, dark silhouettes of gentlemen against the pale dawn sky walking across the sands, but I'm sure they don't talk about them to strangers. These gentlemen and their purposes have nothing to do with the fishermen's world.

Now that I considered, there should have been two carriages, not one. But then, he might not have come by carriage. It was only a short way out here from the town and he might have walked here and seen the other carriage drawn up already.

Alone? He shouldn't have been alone. There should have been a friend with him—or at least somebody he called a friend. They would have stayed the night together in an inn. If I asked around the town somebody surely would have seen them together and be able to describe the other man. I'd do that later, when I come back from my walk.

The sand was firm underfoot, only I wished I'd brought stouter footwear. But then my escape from Chalke Bissett had been so hurried I'd had no time to go to the bootroom and find the pair I keep for country walking. Besides, when I escaped I had no notion in my head of walking over French beaches. A day or two on English pavements was the very worst I'd thought to expect. Still, the shoes were carrying me well enough. The ramshackle cottages were already a mile behind me, the sand dunes and the point at the far end of the beach in sight. Nearer the tideline, there was a gloss of salt water over the sand, splashing up to the hem of my skirts, making them drag damply round my ankles. From here, if there were figures on the point you'd be sure to see them. He would have seen them—three of them—waiting there, and my father and the man he called his friend would have walked over to them. They'd have shaken hands and serious words would have been spoken.

*Since your principal refuses to offer an apology, then things must proceed to their conclusion. Would you care to choose, sir?*

And the black, velvet-lined case would have been snapped open. As the man challenged, my father would have had first choice. So he'd have taken a pistol, weighed it in his hand and nodded, and the other man would have taken the other. How do I know? The way that anybody who reads novels knows. I confess with shame that ten years or so ago, around the age of twelve when much silliness is imagined, the etiquette of the duel had a morbid fascination for me. I revelled in wronged, dark-haired heroes, their fine features admitting not the faintest trace of anxiety as they removed their jackets to expose faultless, white linen shirt-fronts over their noble and so-vulnerable breasts, shook hands with their seconds (who—not being heroes—were permitted a slight tremor of the fingers), then strode unconcernedly to the fatal line, as if . . . Oh, and any other nonsense you care to add. That's why I knew enough to imagine how it would have happened. The two pistol shots, almost simultaneous. Then the frightened sea birds wheeling and crying. A figure flat on the sand, the two seconds bending over him, the doctor opening his bag.

*It really is the most appalling nonsense*, my father had said. *I wish you would not read these things.*

Back to being twelve, and my father—who was so rarely angry with anything or anybody—much annoyed with me. I had just twirled into the room in my new satin shoes, enjoying a fantasy of being a princess carelessly mislaid at birth—trilling that I hoped one day men might fight a duel for love of me. He'd caught me in mid-twirl, plumped me down in a chair and talked to me seriously.

*Some day another man besides myself and your brother will love you. But hear this, daughter, if he proves to be the kind of fool who thinks he can demonstrate that love by violently stealing the life of another human being, then he's not the man for my Liberty.*

*But if he were defending my honour, Papa . . .*

*Honour's important, yes. But there's wise honour and foolish honour. I wish to say something serious to you now, and I know if your mother were alive she'd be in utter agreement with me. Are you listening?*

I had nodded, looking down through gathering tears at my new satin shoes and knowing the gloss had gone from them for ever. He seldom mentioned our mother, who'd died when I was six years old and Tom four, but when he did, it was always in connection with something that mattered very much.

*If you ever—may the gods forbid—get yourself into the kind of scrape where your honour can be defended only by a man being killed for you, then you must live without honour. Do you understand?*

I had said *yes*, as firmly as I could, hoping the tears would not fall. He had crouched beside the chair so that my eyes were on a level with his.

*Don't cry, my darling. Only, duelling is wasteful, irrational nonsense. Lecture over. Now, shall we go out and feed the goldfish in the fountain?*

So that's how I knew, you see—knew for sure that I'd been told a black lie. The duel never happened. My father was dead, that was true enough, even though not a fibre of my mind or body believed it yet. But it was impossible that he died that way, no matter what the note said or what the couple at the morgue believed. I was as sure of that as the sun rising behind the point, turning the rim of sea to bright copper. I followed my own footsteps back over the sand, making a slow curve to the line of fishermen's cottages. It looked as if the people in them must have started their day's work, because there was a figure in front of the cottages looking out to sea. It would be a fine day for him, I thought. The sky was clear blue, with only a little breeze ruffling my bonnet ribbons. When I got to the town I'd drink some coffee and plan what questions to ask and where to ask them. Who saw him? Who were his friends in Calais? Who brought his body to the morgue? Above all, who wrote that lying and anonymous note to me at Dover? Insolent as well as lying, because the unknown writer had added a command:

*Remain where you are for the present and talk about it to nobody. People concerned on your behalf will come to you within two or three days.*

As if I could read that and wait tamely like a dog told to stay.

The man I'd noticed was still standing by the cottages. Closer to, he didn't look like a fisherman. His clothes were black, like a lawyer's or doctor's, and he was wearing a high-crowned hat. He was thin and standing very upright, not looking out to sea now but back along the sands towards the point. Almost, you might think, looking at me. But of course he had no reason to look at me. He was simply a gentleman admiring the sunrise. Something about the stiff way he was standing made me think he might be an invalid who slept badly and walked in the sea air for the sake of his health. Perhaps he came there every morning, in which case he might have been standing just there three days ago, watching whatever happened or did not happen. I raised my hand to him. Of course, that was overfamiliar behaviour to a man I'd never met, but the rules of normal life didn't apply any more. Either he didn't see my gesture, or he did and was shocked by it, because he turned and walked away in the direction of the town, quite quickly for a supposed invalid. Strange that he should be in such a hurry after standing there so long, but then everything was strange now.

Two mornings before, I'd woken up on a fine Sunday in the inn at Dover, with nothing in the world to cause me a moment's anxiety. Nothing, that is, beyond whether my aunt might have sent one of her servants to recapture me. It was a small room, the cheapest they had, looking out over the stableyard of the larger hotel next door. My escape from the dim, sour-faced house at Chalke Bissett had gone entirely to plan. Even before the servants were up I was on my way across the field footpath to the village, knowing the area well enough by then to guess that there'd be a farm cart taking fruit and vegetables into Salisbury.

From Salisbury, I took a succession of stage and mail coaches to Winchester. At Winchester I managed to secure the last outside place on another coach that took me all the way across Hampshire.

It was a glorious evening to be flying along on the top of the coach behind four fast horses with the scent of hay and honeysuckle in the air, seeing haymakers out late with their scythes and rakes and the sun sinking in the west behind us. We arrived at the changing point of Hartfordbridge in the early hours of the morning, when it was already getting light, so that spared me the expense of a room in the inn. I simply sat on the edge of a horse trough, wrapped my mantle round me and ate the last slice of bread and butter I'd taken from my aunt's kitchen.

From Hartfordbridge it was a long and expensive day's journey into Kent and Tunbridge Wells. In this fashionable place, spending the night on the edge of a horse trough was out of the question, but luckily I'd made friends with a lady on the journey, travelling to meet her husband at Chatham. We shared a room and a large but lumpy double bed at a modest inn. Over a supper of cold beef pie and two pots of tea, she glowed with happiness at the idea of seeing her husband again.

'And I'll soon be seeing my father,' I said.

Now I'd put two good days' travelling between myself and my aunt, it seemed safe to talk about myself.

'Has he been away long?'

'Only since September.'

It seemed longer. I remember that my companion asked the waiter if he had any news of the King. He shook his head gravely. King William was elderly and ill, probably dying, but that was not causing any great outbreak of grief among his subjects. I thought he was probably one of the dullest men ever to sit on the throne of England and in any case our family's sympathies were far from Royalist. But I said nothing for fear of offending my companion, who was a kind woman.

Next morning we breakfasted together on good bread and bad coffee, then she took the coach for Chatham while I waited for the coach that would take me on the last stage of my journey to Dover.

I reached the port in the evening. I knew it quite well, from the occasions when I'd crossed to the Continent with my father and Tom, but I'd never been there on my own before. I stood at the inn where the coach had put me down, feeling for the first time scared at what I'd done. Then, determined that my father should not come back to find a feeble young woman, I adjusted my bonnet and picked up my bag. I was wearing my second-best dress in plain lavender colour, with tight-fitting sleeves and a little lace at the neck. My bonnet had suffered from travelling outside and my hair felt plastered with dust, but I hoped I looked respectable, though travel-worn. The inns and hotels along the seafront were too expensive and conspicuous. If my aunt sent somebody after me, those were the first places he'd try. I walked along a side street and hit on an old inn called the Heart of Oak that looked as if it catered for the better class of tradesperson rather than the gentry. The dark, panelled hall smelt of beer and saddle leather. A bell stood on a counter. I rang and after some time a plump bald-headed man arrived, wearing a brown apron stained with metal polish.

'I should like to engage a room,' I told him, as confidently as I could. 'Not one of your most expensive ones.'

'Just for yourself, ma'am?' His voice was polite enough, but his boot-button eyes were weighing me up.

'Just for myself.' Then, losing my nerve a little, I added, 'I'm here to meet my father. He's coming across from Calais.' Which was the perfect truth, even though the look in those eyes made it feel like a lie.

'How many nights, ma'am?'

'He may be arriving as early as tomorrow . . .'

'Tomorrow's Sunday.'

'. . . or I might have to wait a day or two. I am not sure of his plans.'

That was true as well, although one thing I was entirely sure of was that my father's plans did not include having his daughter there to meet him at Dover. His latest letter—in my bag and marking my place in a volume of Shelley, which was the only book I'd brought with me—made it quite clear that I was to wait at Chalke Bissett until called for. The innkeeper grudgingly admitted there was a room on the second floor he could let me have.

'I'll take supper in my room,' I told him. 'Mutton chop, some bread and cheese and a jug of barley water.'

He nodded gloomily and called the bootboy to carry my bag upstairs to a small but reasonably clean room, furnished with bed, chair and washstand. I tipped the boy and, as the door closed behind him, spread out my arms and opened my mouth in a silent but most unladylike yell of triumph. When supper arrived I ate it to the last crumb, then slept in the deep feather bed as comfortably as any dormouse.

I idled Sunday away pleasurably enough, tipping the little maid a shilling to bring warm water upstairs so that I could wash my hair. When it was dry I strolled along the front in the sunshine, watching families driving in their carriages and sailors walking arm in arm with women friends. In such a busy place, nobody was in the least disturbed by a young woman walking unescorted. I revelled in being alone and the mistress of my own time for once.

But on Monday morning I woke at first light with a little demon of anxiety in my mind. Now that I might be meeting my father within hours, it occurred to me that he would perhaps be annoyed because I had disobeyed instructions. I took his letter out of my bag and read it by the window as the horses stamped and the ostlers swore down in the stableyard of the larger hotel next door. It had been written from a hotel in Paris, posted express, and had arrived at Chalke Bissett just the evening before I left, too late to change my plan of escape:

*My dearest Daughter,*

*I am glad to report that I have just said farewell to my two noble but tedious charges and am now at my liberty and soon to be on the way home to my Liberty. I have faithfully conducted His Lordship and cousin around Paris, Bordeaux, Madrid, Venice, Rome, Naples. All wasted, of course, like feeding peaches to donkeys. They pined for their playing fields, their hunters, their rowing boats at home. The stones Virgil and Cicero trod were no more than ill-kept pavement in their eyes, the music of Vivaldi in his own city inferior to a bawled catch in a London tavern.*

*But enough. I have justly earned my fee and we may now set about spending it as we planned. If I had travelled home with my charges I should have rescued you from Aunt Basilisk sooner, but I'm afraid my princess must fret in her Wiltshire captivity a week longer. I had business here in Paris, also friends to meet. To be candid, I valued the chance of some intelligent conversation with like-minded fellows after these months of listening to asses braying. Already I have heard one most capital story which I promise will set you roaring with laughter and even perhaps a little indignation. You know 'the dregs of their dull race . . .' But more of that when we meet. Also, I have just met an unfortunate woman who may need our help and charity when we return to London. I know I may depend on your kind heart.*

*I plan to be at Chalke Bissett about a week from now. Since even five minutes of my company is precisely three hundred seconds too many for dear Beatrice/Basilisk I'm sure she will not detain us. So have your bags packed and we shall whisk away. Until then, believe me your loving father.*

Then, after his signature, a scrawled postscript:

*If you'd care to write to me before then, address your letter to poste restante at Dover. I shall infallibly check there on my arrival, in the hope of finding pleasant reading for the last stage of my journey.*

As I reread it, I was seized with a panic that he might at that very moment be stepping off a boat and posting to Chalke Bissett, not knowing I was waiting for him less than a mile away. I ran downstairs and secured paper, pen and ink from the landlord:

*Dearest Father,*

*I am here in Dover at an inn called the Heart of Oak. Anybody will direct you to it. I could not tolerate the company of La Basilisk one hour longer. So you need not brave her petrifying eye and we may travel straight to London. Please forgive your disobedient but loving daughter.*

I didn't tell him in the note, and never intended to tell him, that the real reason I'd fled the house of my mother's elder sister was that I couldn't tolerate her criticisms of him. She'd never forgiven his elopement with my mother and used every opportunity to spray poisonous slime, like a camel spitting.

*Your father the fortune hunter . . .*

He is not. He had not a penny from my mother.

*Your father the Republican . . .*

He said it was wrong to cut off the head of Marie Antoinette.

*Your father the gambler . . .*

Do not all gentlemen play games of hazard occasionally?

She had called me argumentative and said I should never get a husband with my sharp tongue.

I sealed my scrawled note and was waiting on the steps of the poste restante office as it opened. When I handed it over the counter I asked if there were any more letters waiting for Mr Thomas Lane. Three, the clerk told me, so I knew I hadn't missed him. I strolled by the harbour for a while, watching the steam packet coming in. The novelty of my escape was wearing off now and I was beginning to feel lonely. But that was no great matter because soon my father would be with me and a whole new part of my life would be starting. My father had talked about it back in September, nine months before, as he was packing.

*I'm quite resolved that if I have to leave you again it will be in the care of a husband.*

I was folding his shirts at the time. Indeed. *And have you any one in mind?*

*As yet, no. Have you, Libby?*

*Indeed I have not.*

*Then we can look at the question like two rational beings. You agree it is time you were married? People should be old enough to know their own minds before they marry. Thirty for a man, say, and around twenty-two for a woman.*

I was twenty-one and six months at the time.

*So I have six months to find a husband?* I said.

He had smiled. *Hardly that. In fact, I am proposing that we should leave the whole question on the shelf . . .*

*And me on the shelf too?*

*Exactly that, until I return next summer and we can set about the business in a sensible fashion.* He must have seen the hurt in my face. *I'm not talking about the marriage market. I'm not proposing you trade your youth and beauty for some fat heir to a discredited peerage.*

*I don't think they'd rate higher than the second son of a baronet,* I said, still defensive.

He came and took my hand. *You know me better than that. I'm not a young man any more.* (He was forty-six years old.) *I must think of providing for you in the future. I shan't die a rich man and Tom has his own way to make.*

*I'd never be a burden on Tom, you know that.*

*I've not been as much of a father to you as I should. But I have tried to give you the important things in life. Your education has been better than most young women's. You speak French and German adequately and your musical taste is excellent.*

*That reminds me, I've broken another guitar string.* I was uneasy at hearing myself praised.

*And we've travelled together. You've seen the glaciers of Mont Blanc at sunrise and the Roman Forum by moonlight.*

I was wonderfully fortunate, I knew that. When I was back with my father it was easy to forget the other times, lonely and homesick in a cold French convent, or boarded out with a series of more or less resentful aunts or cousins. It was almost possible, though nowhere near as easy, to forget the glint of my brother's handkerchief waving from the rail of the ship as it left Gravesend to carry him away to India.

*Couldn't we just go on as we are?* I had asked. *Tom will come back one day and I can keep house for him and you. Do I really need a husband?*

He had become serious again. *The wish of my heart is to see you married to a man you can love and respect and who values and cares for you.*

I watched the steam packet go out again, arching sparks from its funnel. In three hours or so it would be in Calais, then perhaps bringing my father back with it. Around noon I felt weary from my early start and went back to my room. I must have dozed because I woke with a start, hearing the landlord's voice at the bottom of the stairs, saying my name.

'Miss Liberty Lane? Don't know about the Liberty, but she called herself Miss Lane, at any rate. Give it me and I'll take it in to her.'

As his heavy footsteps came upstairs my heart thumped because either this was a message from my father or my aunt had tracked me after all. But as soon as the landlord handed me the note I knew it had nothing to do with Chalke Bissett. The handwriting was strong and sprawling, a man's hand. The folded paper was sealed with a plain blob of red wax, entirely anonymous. I broke the seal and read: . . . *take the liberty of addressing you with distressing . . .*

'Bad news, miss?' The landlord was still in the room, his eyes hot and greedy. I gripped the edge of the washstand, shaking my head. I think I was acting on instinct only, the way a hurt deer runs.

'I must go to Calais. When's the next boat?'

'**W**as your father a confirmed and communicant member of the Church of England?'

The clergyman was plump and scowling. I'd traced the address on the card I'd been given at the morgue to a terraced house in a side street, with a tarnished brass plate by the door: *Rev. Adolphus Bateman, MA (Oxon).* This representative of the Anglican Church in the port of Calais smelt of wet woollen clothes and old mouse droppings, familiar to me from enforced evensongs in country churches with various aunts. It was a late-autumn, English smell and quite how he'd contrived to keep it with him on a fine June morning in Calais was a mystery.

'Yes, he was.' I supposed that, back in his schooldays, my father would have gone through the usual rituals. There was no need to tell this clergyman about his frequently expressed view that the poets talked more sense about heaven and hell than the preachers ever did.

'I shall arrange the interment for half past three. The Protestant chapel is at the far side of the burial ground. The total cost will be five pounds, sixteen shillings and fourpence. I assume you would wish me to make all the arrangements?'

'Yes, please.'

I took my purse out of my reticule and counted the money onto the faded crochet mat in the middle of the table. It left the little purse as floppy as the udder of a newly milked goat. I'd had to sell a gold locket belonging to my mother and my grandmother's silver watch to pay for my journey. In normal times I'd have cried bitterly at parting with them but, turned hard by grief and need, I'd bargained like an old dame at market. As I stowed the purse away the clergyman asked, with just a touch of sympathy in his voice, 'Have you no male relatives?'

'A younger brother. He is in Bombay with the East India Company.' I had a suspicion he intended to pray over me, so I hastily thanked him and left the house, filling my lungs with the better smells outside—fish, fresh baked bread and coffee. This reminded me that I had eaten and drunk nothing since the message had arrived, back in Dover. I was almost scared of doing either. That message had divided my life into before and after, like a guillotine blade coming down. Everything I did now—eating, drinking, sleeping—was taking me further away from the time when my father had been living. I still couldn't think of eating, but the smell of coffee was seductive. I followed it round the corner and on-to a small quay. The coffee shop was no more than a booth with a counter and a woman with a coffeepot. She poured, watched me drink, poured again, making no attempt to hide her curiosity.

'Madame is thirsty?'

'Very thirsty,' I told her. It was a pleasure to be speaking French again.

'Is madame staying in Calais for long?'

'Not long, I think. But my plans are uncertain. Tell me, where do the English mostly stay these days?'

She named a few hotels: Quillac's, Dessin's, the Lion d'Argent, the London. I thanked her and walked around the town for a while, trying to get my courage up, past the open-fronted shops with their gleaming piles of mackerel, sole and whiting, the stalls piled high with plump white asparagus, bunches of bright red radishes. At last I adjusted my bonnet, took a deep breath and tried the first hotel.

'Excuse me for troubling you, monsieur, but I am looking for my father. He may have arrived in Calais some time ago, but I am not sure where he intended to stay.' After the first few attempts I was able to give a description of my father without any trembling in my voice. 'His name is Thomas Jacques Lane. In France he probably uses Jacques. Forty-six years old, speaks excellent French. Tall, with dark curling hair, a profile of some distinction and good teeth.'

But the answers from the hotels were all the same. *No, madame, no English gentleman of that description.*

It was midday before I came to the last of the big hotels. It was the largest one, newly built, close to the pier and the landing stage for the steam packet, with a busy stableyard. I went up the steps into a foyer that was all false marble columns and velvet curtains, like a theatrical set, crowded with fashionably dressed people arriving or leaving.

I queued at the desk behind an English gentleman disputing his account. Clearly he was the kind of person who, if he arrived at Heaven's gateway, would expect to find St Peter speaking English and minding his manners. He was working his way through a bill several pages long, bullying the poor clerk and treating matters of a few francs as if there were thousands at stake. I had plenty of time to study him from the back. He was tall and strongly made, his shoulders broad, the neck above his white linen cravat red and wide as a farm labourer's. His hair was so black that I suspected it might owe something to the bottles of potions kept by Parisian barbers.

After a while my attention wandered to a young man and woman standing by a pillar and arguing. She was about my age, and beautiful. Her red-gold hair was piled up and she wore a rose-pink satin mantle that could only have come from Paris. The man with her was several years older, elegantly, but not foppishly, dressed in grey and black. He was tall and dark-haired with a handsome face and a confident, rather cynical air. They might have been taken for husband and wife, except for the strong family resemblance in their fine dark eyes and broad brows. Except, too, for the way they were carrying on their argument. When a husband and wife disagree in public they do it in a stiff and secretive way. Brothers and sisters are different. They have been arguing from the nursery onwards and are not embarrassed about it. Although I loved Tom more than anybody in the world except my father, it was the arguments I missed almost as much as all the more gentle things. So it went to my heart to see the way the young woman frowned at her brother, and how he laughed and said something that was no doubt patronising and elder-brotherly.

'Stephen, come here.' The man disputing his bill turned and called across the foyer. I'd been wrong to think his black hair might be dyed because his eyebrows, which joined in a single bar over dark and angry eyes, were just as black. He was looking at the brother and sister. As he turned back to the desk I saw them give each other that rueful grimace children exchange when in trouble with parents, their argument instantly forgotten in the face of a shared opponent. It had been a father's command, although there was no obvious likeness between the two men. I watched as Stephen crossed the foyer, obediently but none too quickly.

'Did you really order two bottles of claret on Sunday?'

I heard the older man's impatient question, saw the younger one bending over the bill, but nothing after that because, shamingly, my eyes had blurred with tears. That look between brother and sister had caused it. I felt suddenly and desperately how I needed Tom and how far away he was. I ran behind one of the pillars to hide myself and bent over gasping as if somebody had punched me in the stomach, hands to my face, rocking backwards and forwards to try to ease the pain.

'Is . . . is there anything wrong?' A soft English voice. Through my fingers I saw pink satin, smelt perfume of roses. A gentle hand came down on my shoulder. 'Are you ill? Perhaps if you sat down . . .'

I stammered that I was all right really. Just a . . . a sudden headache. She was so soft and kind that I had to fight the temptation to lean on her and cry all over her rose mantle.

'Oh, you poor darling. I suffer such headaches too. I have some powders in my room, if you'd let me . . .'

I straightened up, found my handkerchief and mopped my face. 'No, it's quite all right, thank you. I have . . . I have friends waiting outside. I am grateful for . . .'

And I simply fled, through the foyer, down the steps and out to the street. I couldn't risk her kindness. It would break me down entirely.

I walked around until I'd composed myself, then began enquiring at the lodging houses and smaller, less expensive hostelries in the side streets. There was a different spirit to this part of the town, away from where the rich foreigners stayed. The narrow streets were shadowed, shutters closed, eyes looking out at me through doors that opened just a slit. People here did not care for questions because Calais had so many secrets. Forty years ago those streets would have sheltered cloaked and hooded aristocrats, trying to escape from the guillotine. Not much more than twenty years ago, in the late wars with Napoleon, spies from both sides would have come and gone there. Whatever had happened to my father was only the latest in a long line of things that were never to be mentioned. Always the answer was the same. They regretted, madame, that they had knowledge of no such man.

And yet my father must have stayed somewhere, or at the very least drunk wine or coffee somewhere. In his last letter, written from Paris, he'd said he expected to be collecting me from Chalke Bissett in a week. Allow two days for travelling from Paris to Calais, one day for crossing the Channel, the next to travel on to Chalke Bissett, that meant three days spare. Had he spent the time in Paris with his friends, or at Calais? Was it even true that he'd died on the Saturday? How long had his body been lying in that terrible room? I was angry with myself for all the questions I had not asked and resolved to do better in future.

A clock struck two. There were roads straggling out of town with more lodging places along them, but they'd have to wait until later. I tried one more hostelry with the sign of a bottle over the door, was given the usual answer, and added another question: could they kindly give me directions to the burial ground? It was on the far side of the town. My lavender dress and bonnet were hardly funeral wear but my other clothes were on the far side of the Channel. My father wouldn't mind. Too little care for one's appearance is an incivility to others: too much is an offence to one's intelligence. Reverend Bateman's expression as he waited for me by the grey chapel in its grove of wind-bent tamarisks showed that my appearance was an offence to him.

'Are there no other mourners?'

'None,' I said.

An ancient carriage stopped at the gates, rectangular and tar-painted like a box for carrying fish, drawn by two rawboned bays. Two men in black slid off the box and another two unfolded from inside. The coffin came towards us on their shoulders. The black cloth covering it was so thin and worn that even the slight breeze threatened to blow it away.

I refuse even to remember the next half-hour. It had nothing to do with my living father. We had our five pounds sixteen and fourpence-worth of English funeral rites and afterwards the four bearers and two men in gardener's clothes, whom I took to be gravediggers, stood around fidgeting. It seemed that I was required to tip them. As I handed over some coins, I realised that the thinnest of the bearers was the man from the mortuary. I'd been trying to work up the resolution to go back there with some of the questions I'd been too shocked to ask on the first visit. At least this spared me the journey.

'Were you there when my father's body was brought in?'

He gave a reluctant nod.

'I was as well,' said one of the others, a fat man in a black tricorn hat, with a nose like a fistful of crushed mulberries.

'Who brought him in?'

They looked at each other. 'Friends,' said the thin one.

'Did they leave their names?'

A double headshake.

'How many?'

'Two,' said the fat one.

'Or three,' said the thin one.

'What did they look like?'

An exchange of glances over my head. 'English gentlemen,' said the fat one.

'Young, old, fair, dark?'

'Not so very young,' said the fat one.

'Not old,' said the thin one. 'Not particularly dark or fair. They said they'd be back soon to make the funeral arrangements.'

'And did they come back?'

Another double headshake.

'What day was it that they brought him in?'

'Three days ago. Saturday,' the fat one said. 'Early in the morning.'

Behind the two men, the gravediggers were shovelling the earth over my father's coffin. Reverend Bateman was looking at his watch, annoyed. 'I have an appointment back in town. I don't wish to hurry you, but we should be going.'

He clearly expected to escort me back. It was a courtesy of a kind, I suppose, but an unwanted one.

'Thank you, but I shall stay here for a while. I am grateful to you.'

I offered him my hand. He shook it coldly and walked off. The four bearers nodded to me and followed him. Reverend Bateman assumed, of course, that I wanted to be alone at my father's grave. I did indeed want to be on my own, but that was because I needed to think about what the bearers had said. Most of it supported the black lie. Two or three nameless gentlemen arriving with a shot corpse—that might be how things were done after a duel. But wasn't it odd—even by the standards of duellists—that the supposed friends who brought his body to the morgue didn't return to make his funeral arrangements?

I began walking to the graveyard gates as I thought about it. I suppose I had my eyes on the ground because when I looked up the figure was quite close, walking towards me. He was dressed entirely in black, elderly and a gentleman, although not a wealthy one. His jacket was frayed at the cuffs, his muffler clean and neat but old and threadbare. A mourner, I thought; probably come to visit his wife's grave. Indeed, his thin and clean-shaven face was severe, his complexion greyish and ill-looking. He might have been sixty or more. When he saw me looking at him he hesitated, then raised his hat. 'Bonjour, madam.'

The accent was so obviously English that I answered, 'Good afternoon, sir.'

He blinked, came forward and glanced towards the gravediggers. 'Do you happen to know whom they are burying over there?' he said.

It was not a bad voice in itself, low and educated. But there was something about the way he said it that made me sure I'd seen him before, and I went cold.

'Thomas Jacques Lane.' I tried to say it calmly, just as a piece of information, but saw a change in his eyes. So I added, 'My father.'

'Do I then have the honour of addressing Miss Liberty Lane?'

'You were watching me,' I said. 'This morning on the sands.'

He didn't deny it, just asked, 'What are you doing here?'

'As you see, arranging my father's burial.'

He said nothing. I sensed I'd caught him off-balance.

'You knew him, didn't you?' I said. 'It was you who sent me that note.' I'd guessed right about his watching me, so this was only a step further.

'What note?' He sounded genuinely puzzled.

'That lying note, telling me he'd been killed in a duel, ordering me to wait at Dover.'

'I sent you no such note. But if you were at Dover, you should never have left there. Go back. I tell you that as your father's friend.'

All my misery and shock centred on this black stick of a man.

'There was only one person in the world who had the right to give orders to me, and he's lying over there. And you, sir, are lying too—only far less honourably.' I was glad to see a twitch of the tight skin over his cheekbones that might have been anger, but he mastered it.

'How have I lied to you?'

'Did you not write me that note? My father would never in his life have fought a duel, and anybody who knew him must know that.'

He looked at me, frowning as if I were some problem in arithmetic proving more difficult than expected. 'There has clearly been some misunderstanding. I wrote you no note.'

'Who are you? What do you know about my father's death?'

He stared at me, still frowning. I was aware of somebody shouting a little way off, but did not give it much attention.

'I think it would be best,' he said at last, 'if you permitted me to escort you back to Dover. You surely have relatives who—'

'Why don't you answer my questions?'

'They will be answered. Only I must appeal to you to have patience. In times of danger, patience and steadfastness are the best counsel.'

'How dare you sermonise me. I have a right to know—'

Two men were coming towards us along the path from the cemetery gates, where a four-horse coach was waiting. One was dressed in what looked like a military uniform—buff breeches and highly polished boots, jacket in royal-blue, frogged with gold braid. The other appeared to be a coachman and had brought his driving whip with him. The man in black seemed too absorbed in the problem I presented to hear their heavy footsteps on the gravel path.

'Is this man bothering you, missy?' The hail from the man in the blue jacket was loud and cheerful, with tones of hunting in the shires. The man in black spun round. 'You!'

'Introduce me to the lady.'

'I'll see you in hell first!'

Both the words and the cold fury were so unexpected from the man in black that I just stood there, blinking and staring.

'Such language before a lady. Don't worry, missy, you come with us and we'll see you safe.' He stepped forward and put a hand on my sleeve.

'On no account go with him,' the man in black shouted.

I shook off the hand. It came back instantly, more heavily. 'Oh, but we really must insist.' The fingers tightened painfully.

'Let her go at once,' said the man in black.

He advanced towards us, but the hearty man didn't slacken his hold on my arm. He jerked his chin towards the coachman, who immediately grabbed the man in black, left arm round his windpipe like a fairground wrestler, and lifted his feet off the ground. The man fought back more effectively than I'd expected, driving the heel of his shoe hard into the coachman's knee. The coachman howled and dropped him and the whip. The man in black got up and took a step towards us, but the coachman grabbed him by his jacket and twirled him round. As he spun, the coachman landed a punch like a kick from a carthorse on the side of his bony temple. The man fell straight as a plank. He must have been unconscious before he hit the gravel path.

'I hope you haven't gone and killed him,' the hearty man said to the coachman, still keeping a tight hold on my arm.

'Let me go at once,' I said.

I'm sure there were many more appropriate emotions I should have been feeling, but the main one was annoyance that my man should have been silenced before I extracted any answers from him. At this point, I still regarded the hearty man as a rough but well-intentioned meddler and simply wanted him to go away.

'Oh, we can't leave a young English lady at the mercy of ruffians in a foreign country. We'll see you safely back to your friends.'

He assumed, I supposed, that I had a party waiting for me back in town. More to make him release his grip on my arm than anything, I accepted. 'You may take me back to the centre of town if you insist. My friends are at Quillac's.' I named the first hotel that came into my head.

'Are they now? Well, let's escort you back to them.'

He let go of my arm and bowed politely for me to go first.

'What about him?' I said, looking down at the man in black. His eyes were still closed but the white shirt over his narrow chest was stirred by shallow breaths.

'He'll live. Or if he doesn't, at least he's in the right place.'

We walked along the path to the carriage at the gates. It was an expensive travelling coach, newly lacquered, the kind of thing that a gentleman might order for a long journey on the Continent. Perhaps they'd left in a hurry because there was an oval frame with gold leaves round it painted on the door, ready for a coat of arms to go inside, but it had been left blank. The hearty man gave an overelaborate bow, suggesting I should climb in first.

'You might at least introduce yourself,' I said.

'I apologise. Harry Trumper, at your service.'

I didn't quite believe him. It was said like a man in a play.

'My name is Liberty Lane.'

'We knew that, didn't we?'

He was talking to somebody inside the coach.

'How?'

'We knew your father.'

It seemed unlikely that my clever, unconventional father would have wasted time with this young squire. As for the man inside, I could only make him out in profile. It was curiosity that took me up the three steps to the inside of the coach. The man who called himself Harry Trumper followed. The harness clinked, the coachman said, 'Hoy hoy' to the horses, and we were away.

There was a smell about the man inside the carriage. An elderly smell of stale port wine, snuff and candlewax. My nose took exception to it even as my eyes were still trying to adapt themselves to the half-darkness. Harry Trumper and I were sitting side by side with our backs to the horses, the other man facing us with a whole seat to himself. As my sight cleared, I could see that he needed it. His corpulent, unwieldy body spread out like a great toad's, with not enough in the way of bone or sinew to control its bulk. His face was like a suet pudding, pale and shiny, with two mean raisins for eyes, staring at me over a tight little mouth. He seemed not to like what he saw.

'Miss Lane, may I introduce . . .'

Before Trumper could finish, the fat man held up a hand to stop him. The hand bulged in its white silk glove like a small pudding in a cloth.

'Were you not told to stay at Dover?' He rumbled the words at me as if they'd been hauled from the depths of his stomach.

'The note,' I said. 'Did you write it, then?'

'I wrote you no note.'

'I don't believe you.'

By my side, Trumper burbled something about not accusing a gentleman of lying. I turned on him.

'You said you knew my father. What happened to him?'

'He took something that didn't belong to him,' Trumper said.

I think I'd have hit him, only another rumble from the fat man distracted me.

'I said I wrote you no note. That is true, but if it matters to you, the note was written on my instructions. As soon as I knew of your father's misfortune, I sent a man back to England with the sole purpose of finding you and saving you unnecessary distress.'

But there was no concern for anybody's distress in the eyes that watched my face unblinkingly.

'He hated duels,' I said. 'He'd never in his life have fought a duel.'

'Sometimes a man has no choice,' Trumper said.

The fat man paid no attention to him, his eyes still on me. 'That is beside the point. Tell me, did your father communicate with you at all when he was in Paris or Dover?'

Why I answered his question instead of asking my own, I don't know, unless those eyes and that voice had a kind of mesmeric force.

'He wrote me a letter from Paris to say he was coming home.'

There was no reason not to tell him. Even talking about my father seemed a way of fighting them. The fat man leaned forward.

'What did your father say in this letter?'

I was more cautious now. 'He said he'd enjoyed meeting some friends in Paris, but was looking forward to being back in England.'

'Gentlemen friends or women friends?' said Trumper, eager as a terrier at a rat hole. The fat man let him take over the questioning.

'Gentlemen friends,' I said.

'Did he mention any women?'

The eagerness of Trumper's question, practically panting with his tongue hanging out, made me feel that my father's memory was being dirtied. In defence of him, I told the truth. 'He mentioned that he'd met an unfortunate woman who needed his charity.' And realised, from the look on Trumper's face, that I'd made a mistake.

'Did he mention a name?' Trumper said.

'No.'

'Or any more about her?'

'Nothing.'

'What did he propose to do about her?'

His letter had implied that he was bringing her back to London with him. 'I really don't know,' I said. 'It was only a casual mention of her.'

'She's lying.' The fat man growled it without particular enmity, as if he expected people to lie. 'He was bringing her back to England with him, wasn't he, miss?'

'It seems you know more than I do, so why do you ask me?'

'He abducted her from Paris. We know that, so you need not trouble yourself to lie about it.'

'My father would not take away any woman against her will.'

'Did he write to you from Calais?'

'No. That letter from Paris was his last.'

'Are you carrying it with you?'

'No!'

From the fat man's stare, I expected him to order Trumper to search me there and then, and shrank back in the corner of the seat.

'Did he tell you to meet the woman at Dover?'

'No, of course not. I was waiting to meet him, although he didn't even know it.'

'Do you know where he lodged in Calais?'

It heartened me that their enquiries round Calais must have been as fruitless as mine. 'No. Not at any of the big hotels, I know that much.'

'So do we,' Trumper said, rather wearily.

The horses were moving at a fast trot now. There was something I hadn't noticed until then, with the shock and the questioning. 'This isn't the way back to Calais.'

'It's a better road,' Trumper said.

I didn't know enough about the area to contradict him, but I edged forward in my seat, trying to see out of the window. We were stirring up such clouds of dust that I couldn't make out much more than the outlines of bushes. Trumper pulled down the window and shouted something to the coachman that I couldn't hear. The whip cracked and the four powerful horses stretched out in a canter. I'd never travelled so fast before. Trumper hastily shut the window as a cloud of white dust blew up round us. I reached for the door handle. I don't know whether I'd have been capable of flinging myself out at such a speed, but there was no chance to tell, because Trumper's heavy hand clamped mine and forced it down on my lap. 'Sit still. We're not doing you any harm.'

'Please take me back to Calais at once.'

'You must understand . . .' Trumper said. He had both of my hands now. When I struggled it made things worse. Sweat ran down his forehead. 'We are only trying to protect you,' he pleaded. 'You wouldn't stay in Dover as you were told, so all we intend is to take you somewhere safe until the trouble your father's stirred up settles down again.'

'Take me where?'

'There's a nice little house by a lake, very friendly and ladylike.'

'The truth is, you're kidnapping me.'

'No. Concern for your safety, that's all.'

'My family will miss me. My brother will come after you.'

'Your brother's in India. You have no close family.'

This growl from the fat man froze me, both from the bleak truth of it and the fact that this creature knew so much about me. For a while I could do nothing but try to keep back the tears. I suppose Trumper must have felt me relax because he let go of my hands. The horses flew on, sixteen hoofs thudding like war drums on the dry road. Dust stung my eyes, at least giving me an excuse for tears. Then—'What the hell . . .?'

We'd stopped so abruptly that Trumper and I were propelled off our seats and onto the fat man. It was like being flung into a loathsome bolster. Above the unclean smell of it, and Trumper's curses from floor level, I was aware of things going on outside—whinnying and the coachman's voice, high with alarm, yelling at the horses. The carriage started bouncing and jerked forward several times. My face was level with the fat man's belly, a vast bulge of pale breeches, like a sail with the wind behind it.

*There are better uses for your head than employing it as a bludgeon.*

My father's voice from fifteen years back, on the occasion of a schoolroom quarrel when I'd butted my brother and caused his nose to bleed. I thought, Well, I'm sorry, Father, but even you are not always right, closed my eyes, drew my head back, and used all my strength to propel it like a cannonball towards the bulging belly.

There is no arrangement of letters that will reproduce the sound that resulted, as if an elephant had trodden on an ill-tuned set of bagpipes. The smell of foul air expelled was worse. The combination must have disconcerted Trumper because he made no attempt to stop me as I stood up and grasped the door handle. As the door began to open I let my weight fall on it and tumbled out into the road, dust in clouds round me. I rolled sideways. Something in the dust cloud. Legs. A whole mobile forest of short pink legs. A herd of pigs. By some dispensation of Providence, the flying carriage had met with the one obstacle that couldn't be whipped or bullied aside. Many horses fear pigs and, judging by the way the lead horse was rearing and whinnying, he was of that persuasion.

I pushed a snout aside and stood up. The coachman was standing on the ground, trying to pull the horse down with one hand, threshing the butt of his whip at a milling mass of pigs and French peasantry. I turned and ran into the bushes beside the road, following animal tracks, with no sense of direction except getting as far away as I could. After some time I stopped, heart beating.

'Miss Lane. Come back, Miss Lane.' Trumper's voice, but sounding breathless and mercifully coming from a long way off. I judged he must still be on the road, so I struck off as far as the tracks would let me at right angles to it. It was hard going in my heeled shoes so I took them off and went stocking-footed. After a while I came onto a wider track, with a ditch and bank on either side. I scrambled up the bank and saw, not far away, the sun glinting on blue sea. From there, it was a matter of two or three miles to the shore, with Calais a little way in the distance.

**I** thought a lot as I walked along the shore towards the town, chiefly about how strange it was when pieces of time refused to join together to make a past or future. I realise that is not expressed with philosophic elegance, in the way of my father's friends, but then I'm no philosopher. A few days ago I had a future that flowed in quite an orderly way from my life up to then. I also possessed twenty-two years of a past that accounted for how I had come to be at a particular place and time. But since that message had arrived at the inn at Dover, I'd been as far removed from my past as if it existed in a half-forgotten dream. As for my future, I simply did not possess one. I didn't know where or when I would sleep or eat or what I would do, not then or for the rest of my life.

It was only when I came to the first of the houses that I remembered I was supposed to be a rational being and that, if a future was necessary, I had better set about stringing one together. Small things first. I sat down on the grass at the edge of the shingle and examined the state of my feet. Stocking soles were worn away, several toes sticking through. I put my shoes back on, twisting what was left of the stocking feet round so that the holes were more or less hidden. The bottom of my skirt was draggled with bits of straw and dried seaweed, but a good brushing with my hand dealt with that. My hair, from the feel of it, had reverted to its primitive state of tangled curls, so all I could do was push as much of it as possible under my bonnet.

All the time I was tidying myself up, my mind was running over the events in the carriage and coming back to one question. Who was this woman they wanted so much? In my father's letter, she'd been not much more than a passing reference. If she was so important, why hadn't he given me some notion of it? But I had to tear my mind away from her and decide what I was going to do with myself. I reasoned it out this way. My father, without meaning to, had bequeathed me two sets of enemies, one represented by the thin man in black, the other by so-called Trumper and the fat man. The second set hated the first set so much that they were prepared to commit murder—since for all I knew the man in black might have died from the blow to his head. Both sides had wanted me to stay at Dover. Now the man in black wanted me to go back there, while Trumper and the fat man were planning to carry me off to some unknown destination by a lake. I feared the fat man and Trumper more than the man in black. If I stayed in France, they might capture me again. Quite probably they were looking for me already. So Dover seemed the safer option, and as quickly and inconspicuously as possible. Footsore and hungry, I started towards the centre of town, queued at a kiosk and milked my small purse almost to its limits to buy a ticket to Dover on the steam packet.

The quay was already reassuringly crowded with fellow passengers, most of them English. There was no sign of Trumper or the fat man. I bought a tartine and a cup of strong coffee and found a refuge on the edge of the harbour wall, behind some packing cases.

I sat with my back to a bollard until puffs of steam came out of the funnel of the packet and a shrill whistle blew. That was the signal for the carriages with the richer passengers to set out from the hotels. I watched from the shelter of the packing cases as three of them arrived in a line. Still no sign of Trumper's coach. The gentry from the carriages went on board, fashionably dressed and obviously proud of themselves for surviving their tours of Europe. Their servants followed, arms full of blankets, sunshades, shawls, umbrellas and large china bowls in case the sea turned impolite in mid-Channel.

I was on the point of leaving my hiding place when another carriage came rattling up in a hurry. A tall, dark-haired young man was first out. I recognised him as the brother of the girl who'd been kind to me at the hotel. She followed him out, in a travelling cloak of sky-blue merino, and they crossed the wharf towards the gangplank. I dodged back out of sight, not wanting her to notice me again after my weakness in the hotel. The man I took to be their father followed them over the cobbles. I waited until the three of them had disappeared on board, then, as the steam whistle blew a last long blast, pushed into the middle of a final rush of people.

Most of the fashionable passengers had gone below. I made my way to the stern and stood by the rail. The little crowd that had watched the steam packet depart was drifting away. A man in a royal-blue jacket was walking slowly towards the town, head bent and hands in his pockets. My heart pounded like a steam engine. There was no mistaking the man who called himself Harry Trumper. I got myself as quickly as I could to the far rail. When the first shock had passed, I marvelled at my luck. Trumper had got there in time after all and only my embarrassed wish not to be seen by the girl had saved me. Without meaning to, she'd done me another kindness.

I stayed on a bench at the stern for most of the crossing. The smoke from the funnel blew back over it, dropping a rain of ash and smuts. Towards the end of the passage, as the lamplit windows round Dover harbour came closer, a woman in a sky-blue travelling cloak walked slowly in my direction, though not seeing me. Her head was bent and she seemed thoughtful or dejected. Then a shower of red sparks came out of the funnel and a man called from behind her. 'Be careful, Celia.'

'I'm quite all right, Stephen. Why can't you leave me alone?'

I whispered into the darkness, 'Thank you, Celia.'

# Chapter Two

WE'D SLOWED DOWN for some reason towards the end of the journey, so the packet didn't tie up at Dover until the dark hours of the morning. Tired passengers filed down the gangplank into a circle of light cast by oil lamps round the landing stage. A two-horse carriage was waiting for Celia and her family. It whirled away as soon as they were inside, so they must have left servants to bring on the luggage.

With no reason to hurry, I disembarked with the last group of passengers. I felt as wary as a cat in a strange yard, not quite believing I'd managed to leave Trumper and the fat man on the far side of the Channel. I walked along the dark seafront, listening for footsteps behind me but hearing nothing. There were very few people about. When I turned into a side street, a few sailors were lying senseless on the doorsteps. An old woman, so bent that her chin almost touched the pavement, scavenged for rags in the gutter, disturbing a great rat that ran across the pavement in front of me. It was holding a piece of black crepe in its teeth, a mourning band from a hat or sleeve. Lamplight fell on the arm of one of the horizontal sailors and I saw that he too was wearing a mourning band.

'Has somebody died?' I asked the rag woman.

I had to stoop down to hear her reply. 'The King.'

She was adding something else, hard to make out. Itty icky? I made sense of it at the third try. 'Oh yes, so it's Little Vicky.'

William's niece, Victoria Alexandrina, a girl of eighteen, now Queen of Great Britain, Ireland and a large part of the globe besides. So a reign had ended and another begun while I'd been in Calais. It seemed less important than the coldness of my toes through the stocking holes.

I walked until it was around six in the morning and I could show myself at the Heart of Oak. It had a new black bow on the door knocker.

'You again,' the landlord said, bleary-eyed.

I collected my bag that I'd left in his keeping, secured my cheap room again and slept for a couple of hours. Then I put my head out of the room as a maid was hurrying past and asked for tea, also writing materials. The pen she brought me was the same crossed-nibbed one that I'd used to write that foolish, light-hearted note to my father. It now served to write a very different letter to my brother Tom.

*Dear Tom,*

*I am sorrier than anything in the world to be sending such grief to you. I have to tell you that our beloved father is no more. He was killed in an accident in Calais, on his way home from escorting his charges on their Grand Tour of Europe. I was present at his burial. I know that when you read this, the first impulse of your kind heart will be to come home to me, whatever the cost to your career. I am certain that I speak with the authority of our father in saying that you must do no such thing. I am as well as may be expected in the face of such news, and as you know we have relatives who—while they may not be over-brimming with the milk of human kindness towards our father's children—are much aware of the demands of Family Duty.*

*May God bless you, my dear, dear brother and help you to bear your grief. I am at present at Dover, and shall write again as soon as I am more settled, with an address.*

*Your loving sister Libby*

Accident? Well, murder is an accident to the victim, is it not? Suppose I had written *Dear Tom, Our father has been murdered . . .* would he have waited tamely in Bombay? No, and all our sacrifice in parting with him for the sake of his future would have been wasted. Surely there had been enough waste already. And the relatives? That was no lie either. Three or four aunts would have indeed taken me in from cold Duty. I was not bound to write in my letter what I felt—that I should sooner ride horses in a circus than accept the wintry charity of any of them. I should have had to pay dearly for it in endless days of criticism of my father. Over the years, I'd dwindle to the grey and dusty poor relative in the corner of the room furthest from the fire. I'd have no freedom, hardly allowed to walk in the garden without asking permission. They would certainly not permit me to do the only thing in my life that made sense—discover who killed my father and why.

I addressed my letter by his full name, Thomas Fraternity Lane, care of the Company's offices in London. They would send it on by the first available boat, but it would still be weeks or months before it came into Tom's hands. I drew the curtains across the window and started to dress myself to take it to the post. The stockings I'd walked in were beyond mending and had to be thrown away. This reminded me that most of my clothes and possessions were in a trunk at Chalke Bissett. I was making a list of the few clothes I had with me when the maid came in for the tray. She looked so tired and was so shy that I couldn't refrain from tipping her sixpence, which reminded me of the thinness of my purse. I shook the coins out on the bed and counted: 1 sovereign, 7 shillings, 3 pennies, 2 halfpennies, Total: £1 7s 4d.

This was not inspiring. I'd have to make my rounds of the jewellers again, this time selling the last thing I had, a gold-mounted cameo ring my father had bought for me in Naples. I put on my lavender dress and went out to take my letter to the post. The streets were crowded, full of carts and carriages coming and going from the harbour. I kept glancing round, wary of anybody who seemed interested in me.

It was worse when I reached the office and had to stand in a queue behind several others. The fat man's agent had come looking for me in this place. The only way he could have known to deliver the note to the Heart of Oak was by intercepting the letter I'd left there for my father. When it came to my turn, I said, 'Is there anything poste restante for Mr Thomas Jacques Lane?' trying to make my voice sound casual. There had been three letters when I first inquired. The clerk went over to a bank of pigeonholes. My heart thumped when he took out just one sheet of folded paper. Who'd taken the others?

'You have his authority to collect this?'

'Yes. I am his daughter.'

He gave me a doubtful look, asked me to sign the ledger, then handed it over. I hurried out with my prize, looking for a quiet place to read. It was thick, coarse paper with a smell about it, oddly familiar and comforting: hoof oil; memories of stables and warm, well-tended horses. I took refuge in a doorway and unfolded it.

> With Ruspect Sir, We be here safly awayting yr convenunce if you will kindly let know where you be staying.

This in big, disorderly writing and a signature like duck tracks in mud: *Amos Legge*. I couldn't help laughing because it was so far from what I'd been expecting. Neither the man in black nor the one who called himself Trumper would write like that. I went back to the office and left a note for Mr Amos Legge, saying that I was Mr Lane's daughter and I'd be grateful if he would call on me at the Heart of Oak. Then I strolled back to the inn by way of the seafront. As I passed a baker's shop, the smell of fresh bread reminded me that I was hungry. I paid a penny for a small white loaf and fourpence for two almond tartlets, then carried them back to the Heart of Oak.

The landlord was in the hall. 'How long are you planning to stay here—madam?' The moment's pause before 'madam' just stopped short of being insulting.

'Tonight at least, possibly longer.'

'It's payment on account for ladies and gentlemen without luggage.'

In other words, I was not respectable and he expected me to bilk him. Biting back my anger, I parted with my sovereign, salving my pride by demanding a receipt. As he went away, grumbling, to write it, the door from the street opened. "Scuse me for troubling you, ma'am, but be there a Miss Lane staying 'ere?'

I stared. He filled the door frame, six and a half feet tall at least with shoulders in proportion. His hair was a shiny, light brown colour, topped with a felt hat, his eyes blue as speedwells. The clean tarry smell of hoof oil wafted off him.

'You must be Amos Legge,' I said. 'I am Mr Lane's daughter.'

He grinned, good white teeth against the brown of his face.

'I thought you was when I see'd you back there, only I didn't like to make myself familiar, look. You do resemble 'im. 'E be 'ere then?'

For an instant, seeing and feeling the cheerfulness of him, I was in a safer world again and I think I smiled back at him. Then it hit me that the world had changed and he didn't know it.

'I think we had better go in here,' I said, indicating the snug.

His grin faded but he followed me. I left the door open to the hall, otherwise the landlord would have put the worst interpretation on it.

'Had you known my father long?' I asked him.

His speech might be slow but his mind wasn't. He'd already caught a whiff of something wrong. 'Nobbut ten days or so, miss, when he helped me out of a bit of a ruckus in Paris. We was to go on to Dover and wait for 'im 'ere. Yesterday morning we got in.'

'We?'

'Rancie and me.'

'Rancie?'

'That's right. Is 'e not 'ere yet, then?'

'He's dead,' I said.

His eyes went blank with shock, as if somebody had hit him. He shook his head from side to side, like an ox troubled by flies. 'When 'e said goodbye to me and Rancie, 'e was as healthy as any man you'd ever see. Was it the fever, miss?'

'He was shot,' I said.

He blinked. Amazingly, his blue eyes were awash with tears. 'Oh, the poor gentleman. Those damned thieving frogs . . . He should've come back with Rancie and me. I'd 'ave seen 'im safe.'

'I don't know that he was shot by a Frenchman.' I'd decided to trust him. I had to trust somebody, and he was as unlike Trumper or the man in black as any person could be. 'The fact is, there's some mystery about it, and I need to find out everything I can.'

I told him about the black lie and what had happened in Calais.

'How did you and my father meet?' I said. 'You mentioned something about a . . . a ruckus.'

'I got in a bit of disaccord with a frog on account 'e was driving an 'orse that was as lame as a three-legged dog. The frog took a polt at me, only I fetched 'im one first, and 'arder. 'Is friends were creating about it and I reckon they'd've 'ad me in prison except Mr Lane saw what 'appened and made them see sense.'

Of course my father would side with the defender of a lame horse.

'So you see, when Mr Lane mentioned 'e was puzzled 'ow to get Rancie back to England, I was glad to be of use.'

It amazed me that while the fat man and his agents were scouring Paris and Calais for this mysterious and fatal woman, this well-meaning giant should have escorted her across the Channel, apparently without fuss. 'Is she here in Dover?'

He nodded. 'I've got 'er here safe, yes.'

'Then I suppose I'd better come and see her.'

The landlord was lurking in the hall. 'Your receipt—madam.'

I tore it out of his hand. He looked up at Amos Legge then down at me with a greasy gleam in his eyes that made me want to kick him. I wanted to kick the entire world. I stalked out of the door, Legge behind me. I more than half resented him for bringing this female.

Who was this Rancie person? Badly treated servant girl? Wronged wife? Betrayed sweetheart? Any of those could have appealed to my father's chivalrous and romantic instincts. He'd eloped with my mother and they lived ten years blissfully together until fever took her. He grieved all his life, but there is no denying that his nature inclined to women. He loved their company, their beauty, their wit. In our wandering life together there'd been Susannas, Rosinas, Conchitas, Helenas . . . I do not mean that my father was a Don Juan, a ruthless seducer. If anything, quite the reverse: he'd do almost anything to help a woman in distress. Undeniable, too, that some of the Susannas, Conchitas, Helenas and Rosinas took advantage of his chivalrous nature.

'There's no 'urry, miss. She won't run away,' Amos Legge protested.

I suppose I was walking fast. We were clear of the town now, only a farm on one side of the road, a broken-down livery stable on the other.

Well, if it had happened like that, it wouldn't have been the first time. But it had been the last. Violent husband or bullying father had resented it, caught up with him. For the first time, my unbelief in the black lie wavered. Suppose he had been forced into a duel after all?

'Nearly there, miss,' Amos Legge said.

We were level with the farm. I expected him to turn in at the gateway, but we walked past and turned in under the archway of the livery stable. Amos Legge walked over to a loose-box in the corner, letting out a piercing whistle. A horse's head came over the door, nostrils flared in curiosity, eyes bold and questioning.

'What . . .?' I was caught off-balance.

'Well, miss, 'ere's Rancie for you.' Then to me, alarmed, 'My poor little maid, what be you crying for?'

**I** had the story of Rancie from Amos Legge, sitting in a broken-down chair in the tack room, saddles and harness all round us.

'You see, miss, it all starts with a Hereford bull, look. Red Sultan of Shortwood 'is name was in the 'erd book, only we called 'im Reddy.'

He was clearly one of those storytellers who liked to take his time. I'll abandon my attempt to record his accent because in truth the broad Hereford he talked is the hardest thing in the world to pin down.

'Reddy belonged to this farmer I used to work for, name of Priest. Well, there was this Frenchman at a place called St Cloud, just outside Paris, decided he was going to build up a herd of Herefords. They do well anywhere, only you can't get the same shine on their coats away from the red soil at home, no matter how—'

'But Rancie and my father?'

'I'm getting to them, miss. Anyways, this Frenchman got to hear about Reddy and nothing would content him except he should have him. He offered old Priest a thousand guineas and all the expenses of the journey met, so we made Reddy a covered travelling cart fit for the sultan he was, and off to St Cloud we went, old Priest and Reddy and me. It took us ten days. Old Priest pocketed his thousand guineas, and what do you think happened then?'

'You met my father?'

'Not yet, I'm coming to that. What happened was the old dev—, excuse me . . . He just took off for home and left me. He said all that travelling had brought on his arthritics and as a result he was going home the quickest way by coach. I was to follow him with the travelling cart. So there I was in a foreign country, not knowing a blessed soul. I took myself into Paris, thinking I'd have a look at it after coming all this way, and that's when I met your father. He mentioned he had a mare he wanted to bring back, and it came to me that if the cart had been good enough for Reddy, it would do for the mare, as long as I washed it down.'

354 | Caro Peacock

'Did he tell you how he came by the horse?'

Amos swatted a fly away from his face. 'Won her at cards, from some French fellow.'

'Did he say if the French fellow was angry about it?'

'No. From the way he told it, the mare had already changed hands three times on a turn of the cards. Your father was thinking of selling her in Paris, only he looked at her papers and decided to keep her.'

'Papers?'

'Oh yes, she's got her papers. And he wanted you to see her. He said he'd got a daughter at home with an eye for a horse as good as any man's, and it would be a surprise for her.'

I had to blink hard to stop myself crying again. My father loved a good horse as much as he loved music or wine or poetry, and I suppose I caught it from him. 'Was my father to travel with you?'

'No. He had things to do before he left Paris. I was to wait for him at Dover and leave a message.'

'How was he, when you saw him? Harassed or anxious at all?'

'Blithe as a blackbird, miss.'

'Did you meet any of his friends?'

'Yes, I did. When he'd finished sorting out my bit of business it was late so I had to stay the night in the same hotel where he was. He had friends there and they were up all hours talking and playing music. I looked into the room at midnight to say did he want me any more or could I go to bed? He said to sit down and take a glass of punch to help me sleep, which I did.'

'These friends, how many would you say?'

He thought, rubbing his head. 'Half a dozen at least, maybe more.'

'English or French?'

'Mostly English, but a couple of Frenchmen.'

'Did they seem angry?'

'Not in the world. They were as comfortable a crew as you'd see any-where; bowl of punch, pipes going, some books open on the tables—and fiddles and flutes and so on all over the place.'

It rang true. My father had a knack of finding friends wherever he happened to be. 'Were there any women there?'

'Not one. All gentlemen.'

'Do you remember what any of the men looked like? Was one of them a thin, elderly man with a greyish face, dressed all in black?'

'I don't recall any elderly men there.'

'Or a very fat man?'

'A couple of them stoutish, I wouldn't say very fat.'

'Or a young, fair-haired Englishman in a blue jacket?'

'I don't recall a blue jacket, no.'

A blank. If my father's convivial party had included a snake in the grass, I was no nearer to him. 'Can you describe anybody there at all?'

Amos thought hard. 'There was this little black-haired gentleman, played the fiddle like he was possessed by Old Nick.'

'Not much taller than I am?'

He nodded.

'In his mid-thirties, and very thin?'

'Thin as a peeled withy.'

'With his hair coming to a point like this?'

I sketched a widow's peak on my forehead with my finger.

'Yes, that's the gentleman. You know him, miss?'

'Daniel Suter.'

I felt myself smiling as I said the name, it brought back so many good memories. Daniel Suter was one of my father's dearest friends, although around ten years younger than he was. He had ambitions as a composer but had to earn his living as a musician, playing everything from a piccolo to a cello. It was not surprising that he should be in Paris or that, being there, he and my father should have found their way to each other. It was my first step forward, that at least I knew the name of someone who'd shared part of my father's last week on earth. Daniel was witty, observant. If anything had happened in Paris, he'd know about it. The only drawback was that he was presumably still in Paris.

'Did you see any of them again?'

'No. Next morning your father met me downstairs at the hotel and took me round the corner to where the horse was kept in the stables, then I took her off to the waiting cart.'

'And that was the last you saw of him?'

'Waving us on our way, yes. Happy as a lad on a day's holiday.'

He asked if I wanted a proper look at the mare. My tearful reaction had clearly disappointed him, and indeed it was poor recompense for having brought her so far. We crossed the yard to the loosebox and he put a head collar on her and walked her into the sun.

'Well, miss?'

No tears this time, but precious little breath to answer him. You know sometimes when you see a special picture or hear a few bars of music you feel a shock to the heart, as if you'd just breathed in frosty air, a delight so intense that it feels like fear? Well, that was the way I felt seeing the mare. She was a bright bay, not tall, no more than fifteen and a half hands at most, clean legs and a long build suggesting speed. Her eye was remarkably large and intelligent, ears well-shaped and forward-pricked, small white blaze shaped like a comma. She moved a step towards me, took the fabric of my sleeve very gently between flexible lips as if testing it, seemed to approve. I took off my glove and ran a hand down her neck, over her firmly muscled shoulder.

'The papers are here, if you want to see.'

When Amos had gone for the head collar he'd also fetched an old leather saddlebag. There were two papers inside. One, dated the day before my father's last letter to me and written on a leaf torn from a pocketbook, made over the mare, Espérance, to T. J. Lane Esq., in quittance of all debts incurred. The other was her pedigree. Now, as far as human lineage was concerned, my father was the least respectful person in the world. Horses were a different matter. His friends joked that he could recite the breeding of any racehorse that ever ran, right back to the two that Noah took into the Ark. I unfolded the paper and . . . 'Oh Lord.'

'Something the matter, miss?'

'She's a great-great-granddaughter of Eclipse. And there's the Regulus Mare in there, and she's half-sister to Touchstone that won the Ascot Gold Cup last year and . . .' The more I read, the more my head reeled.

'He reckoned she was a good horse,' Amos said.

The flies were gathering and he said he'd better take her back inside. I followed slowly, trying to get back some composure. We were standing in the shadowy box, watching her nosing at the hay in the manger, when a dark shape came hurtling out of nowhere and landed on her back. I shouted, but Amos laughed.

'Don't worry, miss. It's nowt but her cat.'

A cat like a miniature panther, sleek black fur, golden eyes, stretched full-length along the horse's back. Rancie simply turned her head as if to make sure that the cat was comfortable and went back to her hay.

'Won't go anywhere without that cat,' Amos said. 'We tried chasing her out of the cart when we left Paris, but they made such a caterwauling, the two of them, we had to bring her into the bargain. Lucy, I calls her.'

We watched horse and cat for a while, then went out into the sunshine. A man with white hair and a red face was standing outside the tack room, looking our way.

'The owner,' Amos said, with a jerk of the head and a grimace.

I'd been thinking hard. 'The money my father gave you to bring her over—I suppose it's spent by now?'

He looked comfortable. 'I can account for every farthing of it, if it hadn't been most of it foreign, that is. It was all spent on her.'

'And the owner's watching us in case we flit with the mare?'

An unhappy nod.

'So we owe him for her keep. How much?'

'Two pounds three shillings, he says. He reckons it would have been more, only I've been helping him out a bit.'

I slid the cameo ring from my finger and put it into Amos's large palm. 'Would you please sell that in the town for me and pay him what's owed. If there's any over, keep it for your trouble.'

His reluctant fingers closed over it. 'What do you want me to do with Rancie, then?'

I said I'd let him know as soon as I'd decided. He insisted on seeing me back to the door of the Heart of Oak, where I went straight up to my room, took off shoes, dress and stays, and lay down on the bed. *Well*, I said to myself, *so what are you going to do with her?*

Instead of answering that very reasonable question I fell into a daydream, thinking of the way she'd soft-lipped my sleeve. I thought of what Amos had said about my father wanting me to see her. He hadn't mentioned her in his letter, so as not to spoil the surprise. Then she'd turned out to be the last of his many presents to me. Espérance, meaning Hope. And then a hard little bit of my mind, not daydreaming at all, said, 'At least a thousand guineas at Tattersalls.' I could solve some of my problems at a stroke by instructing Amos to take the mare for sale at Tattersalls, along with her papers and the note transferring ownership. Once sold, I could give Amos something handsome for his trouble. Most of the money would go into the bank, but some of it—fifty pounds, say—I'd keep to find out the truth about my father.

Having decided that, my mind felt clearer. The thing to do was talk to Daniel Suter, the last friend I knew of to see him alive. I'd return to Paris and, if necessary, enquire at every opera house or theatre until I found him. I took my father's letter out of my bag to reread:

*My dearest Daughter,*
   *I am glad to report that I have just said farewell to my two noble but tedious charges . . . I had business here in Paris . . .*

One of the ways in which my father earned money was by acting as a go-between for objects of art. His excellent taste, wide travels and many friends meant that he was often in a position to know who needed to sell and who was aching to buy. Some classical statue or portrait of a Versailles beauty was probably his additional business in Paris.

He'd been there long enough to pick up some gossip:

*. . . I have heard one most capital story . . . You know 'the dregs of their dull race . . .'*

It had puzzled me when I first read it, and still did. I knew the quotation from Shelley. It came from the poet's tirade against His Majesty

George III and his unpopular brood of royal duke sons: *An old, mad, blind, despis'd, and dying king, Princes, the dregs of their dull race . . . mud from a muddy spring.* A fine insult, but King George was seventeen years dead. I might never hear the story, unless Daniel knew it. Still, I was making some progress. The mare to Tattersalls and I to Paris.

Soon after that, I fell asleep and, for the first time since hearing that my father was dead, I slept deeply and dreamlessly. When I opened my eyes, the wall had turned copper-coloured in the light from the setting sun. The buzz and clinking of people at dinner and drinking came up from below. The strange thing was that—although I woke unhappy—there was a little island of warmth in my mind, where before there had only been cold greyness. I saw, as vividly as if they had been in the room with me, the generous eye of Espérance, Amos Legge's kind look, even the golden stare of Lucy the cat. I had family of a kind after all, three beings who in some fashion depended on me.

And I was going to sell them. I'd decided that before going to sleep. Now, quite as clearly, the thing was impossible. Sell my father's last gift to me, for a hatful of greasy guineas? Use as my agent in this betrayal the good giant who'd brought her to me so faithfully? Even the cat had shown more loyalty than that. I jumped out of bed and opened my purse. My small store was now seven shillings and fourpence, not even enough to pay the rest of my score at the Heart of Oak. And yet here was I, proposing to make a trip to Paris and pay board and lodging indefinitely for an equine aristocrat. I heard myself laughing out loud.

Somebody else heard too. I froze, aware of a board creaking just outside. There was a knock at the door. The landlord, I thought. 'You'll have to wait,' I said.

I put back the money in my purse and dressed. Then I went to the door and opened it, expecting to be looking into a podgy face above a stained apron. Instead there was the gentleman in black, as straight and severe as when I'd last seen him at the Calais burial ground, although this time he was vertical, not horizontal. His high white cravat was the brightest thing in the shadowy passageway, the face above it grey as moonlight on slate.

'I thought you might be dead,' I said.

Admittedly it was hardly a cordial greeting, but when I'd last seen him he was barely breathing.

'It might be best if you would permit me to come in Miss Lane. I have a proposition to put to you,' he said.

I came close to slamming the door in his face. My reputation was low enough with the landlord, without entertaining gentlemen in my room. But something told me that my virtue was in no immediate danger, though everything else might be. I opened the door wider. He walked in.

'Our last conversation was interrupted,' I said. 'I was asking you what you knew about my father's death.'

'And I believe I counselled you to have patience.'

As before, his voice was low and level.

'An overrated virtue. Were you present when he died?'

'No.'

'But you know what happened?'

He raised a narrow black-gloved hand in protest. 'Miss Lane, that is not what I have come to speak to you about.'

'Do you know what happened?'

He sighed and walked towards the window, sliding a hand into his coat pocket. 'Miss Lane, do you recognise this?'

He was holding something small in his palm. I walked over to him and picked it up. When I saw it close, I felt as if somebody had caught me a blow.

'It's his ring.' A signet with a curious design of an eye and a pyramid. The one that should have been on his hand in the morgue.

'Yes,' he said. 'It was taken from his body. Not by me.'

'Who, then?'

'By persons at the morgue in Calais.'

'The fat drunken woman and her husband?'

The slightest of nods from him.

'I thought so,' I said. 'But what concern was it of yours?'

'I bought it from them,' he said. 'It should have stayed on his hand and been buried with him, but they'd only have stolen it again.'

'So you've come to return it to me?'

'No. I show it to you only to convince you that I knew your father.'

He pulled off his right glove and stretched out his hand to me. On his middle finger was a ring identical to my father's. Then he turned the hand over, palm up. 'If you please.'

He expected me to give him my father's ring back. Instead I dropped it down the front of my stays. It was cold against my hot, angry skin. The shock in his eyes was the first human reaction I'd had from him.

'I had heard that you possess an excellent understanding, Miss Lane. I fear you are not using it rationally.'

'The only understanding I care about is how my father died. Who is this woman he was trying to bring back to England?'

He couldn't hide his surprise. 'Who told you about a woman?'

'The man who kidnapped me in the graveyard and a fat man in the carriage. The fat man said my father had abducted a woman from Paris. They thought I knew where she was. I don't. I know nothing about her.'

'That's good. You must continue to know nothing.'

'No! She's the reason my father was killed, isn't she? Don't I at least have the right to know who she is?'

'I'm not sure myself who she is.'

'But there is a woman, you admit that?'

'I have reason to believe that your father left Paris in company with a woman, yes.'

'He wouldn't have taken her away against her will. So, whoever she is, she went with him of her own accord. But Trumper and the fat man found out about that and wanted her back.'

A reluctant nod from him.

'So they chased him from Paris to Calais?'

'Not chased, exactly. I understand that it took them some days to connect your father with the woman's disappearance.'

'How do you know about this?'

'I have no obligation to tell you how I know about anything. You must accept that I have been doing my best to observe these people for several months.' There was a hint of weariness in his voice.

'Who are these people? Why are they looking for this woman?'

He didn't answer for some time. There were chalky rings round his grey pupils, a sign of bad health. He sighed. 'Miss Lane, your father became involved in something that was nothing to do with him. You are probably right in thinking that it cost him his life. Since I met you in Calais, I have discovered two things about you. One is that you are, unfortunately, not on good terms with those whose natural duty it should be to shelter you. The other is that you are a young lady of some resource. Those two men in the carriage did not wish you well. I have heard some of the story of how you contrived to escape from them . . .'

How? From the toadlike man, the peasant with the pigs . . .?

'. . . and it suggests resolution and quick-wittedness. If it were not for these two discoveries, I should have had no hesitation in restoring you to some relative and counselling you to mourn your father and ask no more questions.'

'You have no rights over me. All I want from you is to know what happened to him.'

'In due course, you shall know everything. Only you must have—'

'Patience? What's to stop me opening this window and shouting to people to fetch a magistrate, that my father's murderer is in this room?'

He didn't move a muscle.

'I did not kill your father. If I could have prevented his death, I should have done so. As for the magistrates, I should be able within a few minutes to convince them that your accusation was untrue. And you, Miss Lane, would appear a young lady driven out of her senses by grief. Is that a desirable outcome?'

What he said was true. I could imagine the cold, official looks and what would follow: my aunt sent for and my return to Chalke Bissett as a captive. Or, worse than that, straitjacketed to a common asylum. He must have seen from my face that he'd won the round, because his voice became just a shade more soft.

'Miss Lane, I give you my promise that, when it is possible, I shall tell you more about what happened to your father. But the time is not yet right, and there are more things bound up in this than the fate of any single man or woman. Your father was a good man on the whole . . .'

'On the whole!'

'. . . but of an impulsive temperament, as you clearly are. That, above all, was what led to his death.'

We stared at each other. 'You said you had a proposition.'

He made it, standing there with his hand on the edge of the wash-stand. I let him talk without a word of interruption and tried not to show what I thought.

'There is a small part which you may play in a great cause of which I believe your father would approve. It may even in some measure help to put right the harm which your father unintentionally has done.'

How can I defend him, when I don't even understand what you're accusing him of? I hate you, as much as I've hated anybody in my life.

'So here is the proposal. It has the merit that it would meet, for a short time, your need for sustenance, a roof over your head, while permitting you to be of some service to a greater cause.'

Am I intended to assassinate somebody, like Charlotte Corday? Or does he wish me to put on a man's uniform and go for a soldier?

'I am proposing that you apply for the post of governess.'

'What?' That ended my silence, all this secrecy and drama leading to the most commonplace of conclusions. 'You invade my lodgings, insult my father—to tell me that? I could have come to that conclusion myself.'

The fact was, for a woman like myself with some education but no means of support, becoming a governess was the only respectable alternative to the workhouse, and only slightly less miserable: an underpaid drudge, ignored by gentry and servants alike, neither the one nor the other, condemned to a lifelong diet of chalk dust and humble pie.

'Not just any governess,' he said. 'There is a particular family . . .'

'Friends of yours, I suppose.'

'No, anything but friends of mine. Opponents.'

'So am I expected to put ground glass in their stew and saw through the brakes on their carriage?'

'Nothing so deleterious. You have merely to observe certain things and inform me, by means which shall be arranged for you.'

'In other words, to spy?'

'Yes.'

Honest, at least. My father's ring was now warm against my chest and I kept my hand on it through my stays to help me think.

'Are this family something to do with why my father was killed?'

'We think so, yes.'

'How long should I have to stay there?'

'A few weeks, probably. Months at most.'

'And what are you in all this—a government spy?'

'Far from it. No government has any reason to love me.'

I waited for him to enlarge on that, but he just stood there looking at me in that arithmetical way I'd noticed in the churchyard.

'You must tell me more about this family,' I said.

'Their name is Mandeville. They hold a baronetcy, conferred on them by Charles II. The present holder, the ninth baronet, Sir Herbert, is a very wealthy man and until recently was a Conservative MP.'

'Until recently? Do you mean he was one of those who lost their seats through the Great Reform?'

They'd been a huge joke to my father's circle, those lost Members of Parliament. They were mostly country squires and their friends who thought they had something like hereditary rights to seats in the House of Commons. For centuries they'd owned pocket boroughs, consisting of a mere half-dozen easily bribed or bullied electors. The Reform Act of five years before had swept them away, and not before time.

'Great Reform, you call it. I should have thought it a singularly small reform. Did it give a vote to every working man? Did it do anything to help the tens of thousands toiling in the workshops and factories of our great cities? Did it take away a single shilling from the rich to give to children hungry for bread?'

'Sadly, no.'

His eyes were glittering, his thin body swaying to the rhythm of his words. So, I thought, the man is an orator. That explained his sparing way with words, like an opera singer guarding his voice. Perhaps he realised the effect he was having, because he smiled a thin smile.

'I am sorry to become warm, Miss Lane. You suppose, correctly, that Sir Herbert lost his seat because of the Reform Act. But you would be mistaken to see him as simply a buffoon from the shires. He is a man of ability and ambition. In fact, he has held ministerial office under both Whig and Tory governments.'

'A turncoat, then.'

'Certainly a man of hasty and arrogant temperament.'

'Since he's rich, couldn't he simply buy himself another constituency?'

'For the present he prefers sulking in his tent, so to speak. Sir Herbert has become something of a focus for other men who think the country is going to the dogs.'

'But what does that have to do with how my father died?'

'Quite probably nothing personally. Your father, unfortunately, blundered into something mortally serious that touches many people.'

'You keep criticising him and not telling me why.'

He said nothing. I could feel him willing me into doing what he wanted and tried to play for time.

'They are very rich, then, these Mandevilles?'

'They own substantial estates in the West Indies. The seventh baronet had profitable dealings in slaves.'

'I shall hate them.'

'Governesses can't afford hate.'

'Nor spies?'

'No.'

'Do they live in London?'

'They have a house there, but their main estate is at Ascot in Berkshire, not far from Windsor. If successful in your application, you would probably spend most of your time there.'

Ascot. A picture came to my mind of heathland, horses galloping across it. An idea began to form. 'I may not be successful. If they are opponents, you can hardly recommend me.'

'That will be attended to. They are advertising for a governess, so an application would not be unexpected.'

The sun was down, the room almost dark. I went over to light the candle on the washstand. The idea was growing. 'Very well,' I said. 'I shall apply for the post, but on two conditions. One, you must tell me what I am looking for. I can't be expected to guess. Is it this woman again?'

'No. Put the woman out of your mind. The main thing required of you will be to communicate to me news of any guests or new arrivals at Mandeville Hall. In particular, I have reason to believe that they will be holding a reception or ball in the next few weeks, and it would be very useful to us to know the guest list in advance. You will also inform me of the comings and goings of Sir Herbert himself and his family.'

'How am I to inform you?'

'Wait here for two days. Either I shall come and see you again, or instructions will be sent to you.'

As the candle flame steadied, I saw satisfaction on his face—and was pleased to be able to erase it instantly. 'I said there were two conditions.'

'What else?'

'I have inherited a mare from my father. If you can arrange and pay for her stabling at some place convenient to Ascot, I shall do as you suggest. If not, then I refuse your proposition.'

He almost lost his self-possession. 'A governess with a horse?'

'A *spy* with a horse,' I said. 'That's different.'

He thought about it for half a minute or so. 'Very well, I accept your condition. If you will let me know where the mare is, I shall arrange—'

'No. Find a stables and I'll make the arrangements.'

We glared at each other. Then he said, 'Three days, in that case. Do not move from here. For necessary expenses . . .' He clinked something down on the washstand, and went. As the door closed behind him I saw a handful of coins glinting in the candlelight. Ten sovereigns. I sorely needed them, but it was some time before I could bring myself to pick them up.

Three days passed. I slept, ate, walked by the sea, slept and ate again. The landlord had become polite now that I'd paid my reckoning to date and let him see the flash of sovereigns in my purse. In my wandering round the town I kept an eye open for Trumper but saw no sign of him. Several times I was tempted to take the road out of town and visit Rancie and Amos Legge, but made myself defer that pleasure until I had news for them. It came on Saturday evening. A knock at my door and the landlord's voice. 'Letter for you, miss, just come.'

> Miss Lane,
>
>   The mare may be sent to the Silver Horseshoe livery stables on the western side of Ascot Heath. The manager of the stables, Coleman, has agreed to pass on your letters to me, which should be addressed to Mr Blackstone, care of 3 Paper Buildings, Inner Temple. You will present yourself at 16 Store Street, near the new British Museum, on Monday. Ask for Miss Bodenham and act according to her instructions.

Early on Sunday morning I walked to the stables, with choirs of skylarks carolling overhead. Amos Legge was looking in at Rancie, leaning over the half-door. He turned when he heard my step and gave a great open smile that did my heart good because it was so different from the man in black. 'Just given Rancie her breakfast, I have.'

She was munching from a bucket of oats and soaked bran.

'I've found a place for her,' I said. 'The Silver Horseshoe, on the west side of Ascot Heath. You can take her there in the bull's cart, then you're on the right side of London for getting home to Herefordshire.'

I'd expected him to be pleased, but his face fell. I supposed he was calculating how little profit his long journey would have brought him.

'You won't go home quite empty-handed,' I said. 'This is for the expenses of the journey, and what's left over you are to keep.' I put five sovereigns into his hand. He deserved them. 'I'm sorry it isn't more. I am very grateful to you.'

The sovereigns went slowly into his pocket, but his hand came out holding something else.

'My cameo ring? But you were to sell it.'

'We managed after all, miss. She do resemble you, the lady on it.'

Tears came to my eyes. That was what my father had said when he bought it for me. I drew out the ribbon I wore round my neck with my father's ring and knotted the cameo beside it. 'Thank you, Mr Legge. That was a great kindness.'

He murmured something, then went away across the yard. I spent some time with Rancie, stroking her soft muzzle.

'I shall come and see you at Ascot when I can,' I told her. It occurred to me that, by sending her ahead, I'd committed myself to winning the governess's post. I was thoroughly enmeshed. 'And I suppose you'd better go too,' I said to the cat Lucy.

She gave a little mewing sound in answer. I left them there. In the yard, Amos was filling buckets at the pump. I held out my hand and wished him goodbye, but he insisted on escorting me back to town.

The London Flyer drew out on Monday, prompt to the minute. I'd arrived early and secured a seat by the window and when I looked out there was Amos Legge. I waved to him as we clattered away, but if he waved back I didn't see it for the cloud of dust we were raising.

# Chapter Three

STORE STREET IS NOT in a fashionable part of London. It lies, as Blackstone had said, near the British Museum. They'd been building the new museum for almost my entire life and were still nowhere near to finishing it, so the streets around it were dusty in summer and muddy in winter from the coming and going of builders' wagons. It was an area I knew quite well because, being cheap, it provided rooms for exactly the kind of musicians, writers, actors and wandering scholars who tended to be my father's friends. So when I got down from the Flyer on Monday afternoon, I had no need to ask directions.

In other circumstances it would have delighted me to be back among the London crowds, on this sunny day with the season at its height, the barouches whirling their bright cargoes of ladies, the shouts of the hawkers and snatches of songs from ballad sellers, the smell compounded of soot and hothouse bouquets, sewage from the river and grass from the parks, baked potatoes and horse dung. Even now, my heart kept giving little flutters of delight, like a caged bird that wanted to be let out, only the bars of the cage were the memory that this was not how I was meant to come back to London. I should have been walking at my father's side.

It was evening by the time I got to Store Street. The sound of a man singing drifted from an open window. From another window, a woman's laughter rang out over a green-painted balcony with pots of geraniums and a parrot in a cage. I couldn't help smiling to myself. According to one of my aunts, the combination of green balcony, geraniums and parrot were unmistakable signs of what she called a 'fie-fie'—a fallen woman. Well, that woman sounded happy enough. Number 16 was drab by comparison. I knocked and the door was opened by a frizzy-haired maid. I gave her my name and said Miss Bodenham was expecting me.

'Second floor left.'

The bag and I had to bump and stumble up the two flights, so it was hardly surprising that Miss Bodenham heard us coming.

'Miss Lane? Come in.'

An educated voice, but weary and rasping. She held the door open for me. It was hard to tell her age. No more than thirty-five or so, I'd have guessed from her face, but her dark hair already had wide streaks of grey, and her complexion was yellowish. She was thin and dressed entirely in grey. The room was almost as colourless, dominated by a large wooden table piled with sheets of paper covered in small, regular script, with stones for paperweights. The furniture consisted of two upright chairs and a shelf of well-used books. The floor was of bare boards and even the rag rug was in shades of brown and grey. The place smelt of ink and cheap pie.

'Please sit down, Miss Lane. Have you eaten?'

I hadn't. The smell came from half a mutton pie. It was as cold as poverty and mostly gristle.

'There is tea, if you like.'

The tea suited the rest of the room, being cold and grey.

'I have your letter of application,' she said. 'You will need to copy it out in your own hand.'

She went to her bookcase, moved some volumes aside and brought out more written sheets of paper. She cleared a space for me among the papers. I looked at the letter I was to copy and recognised the severe hand from the note he'd sent me. 'Is this by Mr Blackstone?' I said.

She had already sat down on the other side of the table and started writing something herself. She looked up, annoyed. 'Who?'

'The gentleman who sent me to you.'

'It is not necessary for you to know that.' She bent back to her writing. She was copying something too, although the hand was different.

'Is Mr Blackstone his real name?'

Only the scratching of her pen for an answer.

'What did he tell you about me?' I said.

'That I was to lodge you, assist you in applying for this post, and instruct you in your duties.'

'As a governess?'

I meant '. . . or spy?', wondering how much she knew.

'As a governess, what else? I understand you have no experience of the work.'

'No.'

'Then we should not waste time. Copy it carefully.'

The address was given as 16 Store Street, the date the present: June 26.

> Dear Lady Mandeville,
>
> I am writing to make application for the post of governess in your household. I have recently returned to London after being employed for three years with an English family resident in Geneva and am now seeking a position in this country.
>
> The reason for leaving my former position, in which I believe I gave perfect satisfaction, is that the gentleman who is head of the family has recently been posted to Constantinople and it was considered best that the three children who were my charges should be sent back to school in England. I enclose with this a character reference which my previous employer was kind enough to furnish.
>
> As well as the normal accomplishments of reading, writing, arithmetic, history, geography, use of globes and Biblical knowledge, I am competent to teach music, both keyboard and vocal . . .

'Should I mention that I could also teach them guitar and flute?' I said.

She didn't look up from her writing. 'The flute is not considered a ladylike instrument. Keep strictly to what is written there.'

368 | Caro Peacock

*. . . plain sewing and embroidery. If I were to be fortunate enough to be offered*
*the position, I should be able to commence my duties as soon as required.*
  *Yours respectfully,*
  *Elizabeth Lock*

'Must I use a false name?' I said.

'Apparently.'

So even my poor father's name was denied to me. With so much else gone, I should have liked to keep one scrap of identity.

'Could I not still be Liberty at least?'

'Who in the world would employ a governess named Liberty?' Miss Bodenham stood up, flexing her fingers, and lit candles on the table and mantelpiece. 'Have you finished? Put it in the envelope with the character reference. You'll find the address on the back of the letter. Seal it up and I'll deliver it first thing tomorrow.'

The address was St James's Square, so presumably Lady Mandeville was at her town house. I lodged the application on the mantelpiece and, with nothing else to do, sat and watched Miss Bodenham copying. She was amazingly sure and quick, like a weaver at his loom. I noticed the pages she was copying from were a horrid mess of scratching out and overwriting. When, around midnight, she paused to mix some more ink, I risked a question. 'Is it a novel?'

'Political economy. I am copying it for money. Printers are very clever on the whole at deciphering an author's intentions, but there are some writers whose hands are so vile the printers won't take them. The publishers send them to me to make sense of them.'

The fingers of her right hand seemed permanently bent, as if fixed for ever in the act of holding a pen. Once she'd mixed the ink she yawned and said the rest would wait for tomorrow after all. She bent down and pulled out from under the table two straw-stuffed pallets with rough ticking covers and a bundle of thin blankets.

'You can put yours by the fireplace. I'll go nearer the door because I'll be up earlier in the morning.'

Quite true. Around four o'clock in the morning she was up and out, taking with her my letter from the mantelpiece and the cold teapot from the grate. I rose soon afterwards, tidied our pallets and blankets back under the table, and found a kind of cubbyhole on the first landing with a privy and a jug of water for washing. With nothing else to do, I looked round her room. Her bookshelves were interesting—old and well-used books, mostly from reformers and radicals of previous generations: Tom Paine, William Godwin, Mary Wollstonecraft, even Rousseau himself in the original French. If they were her choice, then Miss Bodenham and I had views in common.

Before six o'clock she was back with the teapot, a small loaf and a slice of ham.

'Your books . . .' I said.

'Are my own business. I've delivered your application. She will probably want to see you tomorrow, Wednesday. We have a lot of work to do.'

All that long summer day, with the scent of lime trees and coos of courting pigeons drifting in through the window, Miss Bodenham coached me in my part.

'The family lived in Geneva, down by the lake. Your charges were two girls and a boy: Sylvia who is now twelve, Fitzgeorge, nine and Margaret, five. Repeat.'

'Sylvia, twelve, Fitzgeorge, nine, Margaret, five. Was I fond of them?'

'It is unwise for a governess to express fondness. The mother may be jealous. You found them charming and well behaved.'

'Were you ever a governess?'

'Yes. But you must cure yourself of asking questions. Governesses don't, except in the schoolroom.'

'Is it very miserable?'

'How old is Fitzgeorge?'

She seemed pleased, in her gruff way, with my speed in getting this fictional family into my head. Less pleased, though, when it came to my accomplishments.

'She will probably ask you for a sample of your needlework.'

'I don't possess one.'

'Not even a handkerchief?'

I eventually found in my reticule a ten-year-old handkerchief which the nuns had made me hem. She looked at it critically.

'The stitches are too large.'

'That's what Sister Immaculata said. She made me unpick it nine times.'

'It will have to do, but you must wash and iron it.'

I washed the handkerchief in the basin on the landing, hung it from the windowsill to dry, and went downstairs to beg the loan of a flatiron from the frizzy-haired maid and the favour of heating it on the kitchen range. I was ironing it in the scullery when somebody knocked at the door. The maid had gone upstairs, so I went to answer it and found a footman outside in black and gold livery, powdered wig and hurt pride from having to stand on a doorstep in Store Street.

'I have a letter for a Miss Lock.'

Scented paper, address written in violet ink, seal a coat of arms with three perched birds. Inside, a short note hoping that Miss Lock would find it convenient to call at eleven o'clock on Wednesday, the following day, signed Lucasta Mandeville. I told the footman that Miss Lock would keep the appointment, then fled to the scullery from which a smell of burnt linen was rising. Handkerchief ruined. Miss Bodenham sighed and found me one of her own. It was more neatly stitched, but I had to go through the whole laundering and ironing process again.

In the evening, Miss Bodenham put on her bonnet, bundled together a sheaf of papers, and said she must go and deliver it to the printers in Clerkenwell. 'You stay here. I'll bring back something for a supper.'

I watched from the window as her straw bonnet turned the corner, then caught up my own bonnet and hurried down the stairs. I was tired of being obedient. Blackstone and Miss Bodenham might think they'd taken control of my life, but I had my own trail to follow. It took me southwards down Tottenham Court Road towards St Giles. It was the busiest time of the evening with the streets full of traffic; at the point where Tottenham Court Road met Oxford Street there was such a jam of carriages that I could hardly find a way through. It seemed worse than the usual evening crush so I asked a crossing sweeper the cause of the commotion. He spat into the gutter.

'Layabouts from the country making trouble as usual.'

From further along Oxford Street, above the grinding wheels and the swearing, came the funereal beat of a drum and voices chanting, 'Bread. Give us bread. Bread. Give us bread.'

I went towards the sound and saw a procession of working men in brown and black jackets and caps, mufflers round their necks in spite of the warmth of the day. They were walking and chanting in perfect unison, keeping time to the beat of the drum. Some of them carried placards: *No Corn Laws*, *Work Not Workhouse*. Their faces were pinched, their boots falling apart, as if they'd come a long way. Then, above the chanting, a shrill cry: 'The peelers are coming!' A line of about a dozen policemen came pushing past me at a run. They carried stout sticks and their treatment of political demonstrators over recent years had shown they weren't slow to use them. Ordinarily, I'd have stayed to see what happened, but now I couldn't afford to be caught up in a riot, so I pushed my way back through the crowd and got safely into St Giles High Street. From there it was an easy journey to Covent Garden.

I reached the theatre, as I'd hoped, just before the interval. I went round to the stage door, confident that it would only be a matter of minutes before I met somebody I knew. There was not a theatre orchestra in London without a friend of my father in it, and on such a warm night some of them would surely come out to take the air. The first were three men I didn't recognise, brass players, by their hot, red faces. Long minutes passed. I worried that the interval would soon be over.

Then a group of men came out slowly, talking together. I recognised one of them and stepped in front of him, trying to drag a name up from my mind. 'Good evening, Mr . . . Kennedy.'

He stopped, obviously racking his brains, then said, in a soft Irish accent, 'Well, it's Jacques Lane's daughter. How are you and how is he?'

Foolishly, it hadn't occurred to me that I should have to break the news. Because it filled my heart, I was sure the whole world knew it.

'I'm afraid he's dead,' I said.

His face went blank with shock. He asked how and I told him that my father was supposed to have been shot in a duel, only I didn't believe it. There were a lot more questions he wanted to ask, but already sounds of instruments retuning were coming from inside.

'I'm hoping to send a message to Daniel Suter,' I said. 'He was in Paris, and I think he's still there.'

'I knew he was going to Paris,' Kennedy said. 'He disagreed with the conductor here about the tempo of the overture to *The Barber* and took himself off in a huff. He should be back soon though. Will you ever come in and wait, if I find you a seat? We can talk afterwards.'

'I'm sorry, I must go. When you see Daniel, or anybody who knows him, could you please ask him to write to me urgently at . . . at Mandeville Hall, near Ascot, Berkshire.' The other men were going inside. 'You must go too,' I said.

Kennedy's hand went to his pocket. 'Are you all right for . . .?'

'Yes, thank you.'

'Friends of yours, these people at Ascot?'

I nodded. The truth was too complicated, and somebody was calling from inside for the damned fiddles to hurry up. He squeezed my hand and departed, still looking shocked. I headed back to Store Street at a fast walk. I just had time to take off my bonnet before I heard Miss Bodenham's footsteps coming wearily up the stairs.

**A**lthough my interview with Lady Mandeville was not until eleven o'clock on Wednesday morning, we were up at dawn for more coaching. 'Where did you learn French?'

'In Geneva, with the family who employed me. Some German, too. Should I mention Spanish?'

'Only if asked, and I don't suppose you will be. And don't speak so loudly. You're a governess, not an actress. Also, you should look down more, at your hands or at the floor. If you try to stare out Lady Mandeville like that, you'll seem impudent and opinionated.'

'These Mandevilles—have you ever met them?'

'No, of course not.'

'But you know something about them?'

'A little, yes.' She hesitated, then seemed to come to a decision. 'I am acquainted with a young woman who was a governess with them. She was dismissed last year. I believe there has been another since then.'

'Two in a year. Are they ogres who eat governesses?'

She risked a fleeting twist of her lips. 'Sir Herbert Mandeville has a black temper, and his mother-in-law, Mrs Beedle, has strict standards.'

Just as well, I thought, that Mr Blackstone only expected me to stay for a few weeks. 'How many children shall I be teaching?'

'He has three from this marriage, two boys and a girl. The elder boy, the heir, is twelve.'

'So there were other marriages?'

'One. Sir Herbert's first wife had several miscarriages and died in childbirth. He married his present wife, Lucasta, thirteen years ago. She was then a young widow with two children of her own, a boy and a girl. They are now both of age, live in the Mandeville household, and have taken his name.'

'And this Lucasta, Lady Mandeville, was she rich when Sir Herbert married her?'

'No, but she was regarded as a great beauty in her time. He needed to father a son to inherit the property and title.'

'And she'd proved she could bear a son. How like an aristocrat, to choose a wife by the same principles as a brood mare.'

'That is a most inappropriate sentiment for a governess.'

Later, we turned our attention to my appearance, which caused her more anxiety. She discovered my particular curse, that my hair is naturally crinkly and no amount of water or brushing will make it lie smoothly or stop it popping out of pins. In the end, we managed to trap it under my bonnet with the strings tied so tightly under my chin that I could hardly speak.

'Good,' Miss Bodenham said. 'It will keep you quiet.'

We had decided that my lavender dress, worn with a white muslin tucker at the neck, was suitable. My shoes were scratched from scrambling around at Calais, so I would tuck them away under my skirt.

'You can't wear those stockings.'

'Why not?' They were my only good pair.

'Governesses don't wear silk stockings.'

'Very well. I'll wear my blue thread ones.'

'Blue stockings are even worse. They suggest unorthodox opinions. You'll have to borrow a pair of mine.'

White cotton gone yellowish from much washing, darned nubbly around toes and heels. I had to garter them tightly to take out the wrinkles and what with that and the bonnet strings felt as thoroughly trussed as a Christmas goose. Miss Bodenham looked at me critically.

'It will have to do. Make sure you arrive ten minutes early.' Then she added, unexpectedly, 'Good luck.'

As instructed, I arrived precisely ten minutes early at the house in St James's Square. A footman opened the door to me and led me to a small drawing room, where I was to wait until summoned.

The drawing room told me nothing that I didn't know already—that the Mandevilles were rich and proud of their ancestry. The room bulged and writhed with marquetry, carving, and gilding as if the sight of a plain piece of wood were an offence against society. The chairs, gilt-framed and needlepoint-embroidered, looked as comfortable as thorn hedges for sitting on, so I stood and stared back at the Mandeville family portraits that adorned the silk-covered walls. Hatchet-like noses and smug pursed mouths seemed to be the distinguishing features of the men. There was the first baronet, with his full wig and little soft hands, and his lady who, from her expanse of white bosom and complaisant expression, was probably the reason King Charles gave the family their title. An eighteenth-century baronet stared at the world from between white marble pillars with palm trees to the side, presumably the Mandeville West Indian plantations. One portrait near the door clearly belonged to the present century and seemed more amiable than the rest. It showed the head and shoulders of a beautiful, golden-haired woman in a blue muslin dress. Puzzlingly, she seemed familiar, but I couldn't think why. I was still staring at her when the door opened and the footman told me to follow him.

Two women sat facing me, side by side in gilt-framed armchairs. The older woman, in her late sixties, wore a ruffled black silk dress and a black-and white widow's cap framing a sharp little face. The other was the girl from the portrait, twenty years older. The realisation of that fact, and the feeling that I'd seen her before, made me forget Miss Bodenham's tuition and stare at her. She was handsome still, but the twenty years had not been good to her. Even with her back to the light, her complexion was sallow. Her eyes met mine and looked away.

'Please sit down, Miss Lock,' the older woman said.

The younger woman—Lady Mandeville, presumably—had my letter of application and character reference. 'I see you have worked abroad.' Her voice sounded tired. The character reference trembled in her hand. 'It all seems . . . satisfactory, I should say.'

The older woman, whom I assumed to be Mrs Beedle, fired a question at me. 'What's nine times thirteen?'

'One hundred and seventeen, ma'am.'

She nodded. It was Lady Mandeville's turn, but she seemed to find it difficult to gather her thoughts. 'You are accustomed to teaching boys?'

'Yes, ma'am. I had charge of Master Fitzgeorge from six to nine years old.'

'What is the Fifth Commandment?' Mrs Beedle again.

'Honour thy father and thy mother, ma'am.'

We went on like that for some time; Lady Mandeville, with that same distracted air, asking questions about my past that I found it easy enough to deal with after Miss Bodenham's coaching. Her mother was another matter. It wasn't the questions themselves, although they covered everything from the Old Testament prophets to the rivers of America. Her eyes were what made me uneasy. They were dark and shrewd and took in every detail of my appearance from bonnet ribbon to scuffed shoes, as if she saw me for the impostor I was.

'Did your previous employer expect you to darn the children's stockings?'

I faltered for the first time in the interview. Miss Bodenham hadn't foreseen this and I didn't know what the answer should be.

'I . . . I always tried to do whatever . . .'

'Did Mrs McAlison expect you to darn their stockings?'

She'd even remembered the name of my fictitious employer. I felt my face turning red. 'No, ma'am.'

Mrs Beedle nodded, though whether in approval or because her suspicions had been confirmed, I had no notion. Lady Mandeville murmured something about Betty always seeing to that sort of thing. The two women looked at each other. 'Well?' said Lady Mandeville, fingers pressed to either side of her forehead, as if for an aching head.

'Wait outside, please,' Mrs Beedle said to me.

I went into the corridor leading to the front door. A door opened at the far end of the corridor. It must have led to the servants' quarters because the footman appeared and held it open for a maid with an armful of dust covers. I caught what the maid was saying.

'Just wish they'd make up their minds, that's all. Get it all uncovered, then have to cover it up again. When are they off back down there?'

'First thing tomorrow she is, and the old lady. Supposed to be the day after, only a letter came from over the water this morning and her ladyship was running around like a hen with its head cut off. New curtains, complete set of new silverware, six dozen of champagne, all to go down in the old coach after them.'

They noticed me in the corridor and went quiet, casting curious looks at me as they passed by on their way to the front drawing room.

Soon after that a bell tinkled from Lady Mandeville's room, which I took as my signal to go back in. This time they didn't invite me to sit down. Lady Mandeville was making a visible effort to be businesslike.

'I understand from your letter that you are free to take up your duties immediately. We are living in the country at present.'

'Yes, ma'am.'

'Your wages will be forty pounds a year. You will please make your own way to Windsor. You will be met at the White Hart, near the castle, at two o'clock tomorrow.'

So I found myself going down the steps, engaged as a governess, within half an hour of entering the house. I'd known women take longer to choose a pair of gloves. And what, if anything, had I discovered in that half-hour? One, that Lady Mandeville was unhappy. Two, that her mother, Mrs Beedle, was a woman to be treated warily. Three, the household was confused and on edge because of changes of plan. Four, and probably most important, her footman attributed the latest change of plan to a letter from over the water. When people said 'over the water' they usually meant the Channel. Therefore it was possible at least that the letter had come from France and . . . Yes, hundreds of letters did come to England from France every day and there was no logical connection at all with the fact that my father died there. But Blackstone had said that my post as spy in the household was somehow connected with his death. Logic is a plodding horse and now and then you need one which will take a leap.

As I turned the corner into Store Street I added a fifth fact to my list: judging by the silverware and the champagne, the Mandevilles were preparing their country home for entertainment on a grand scale. Presumably this was the reception or ball that interested the black one.

I spent the afternoon booking a seat on the first stagecoach I could find leaving for Windsor next morning and shopping for clothes and other necessities. My farewells to Miss Bodenham early on Thursday morning did not take long. I shook her hand and thanked her and she said, 'You have nothing to thank me for.'

I hired a loitering boy to carry my bag and arrived in plenty of time to take up the seat I'd reserved on the Windsor coach, only to find the vehicle surrounded by a crowd of people trampling on each other's toes. For some reason, half London seemed possessed of a desire to travel the twenty miles or so to Windsor. It was only when I'd claimed my place, after some unladylike elbowing and shoving, and we were going past Hyde Park Corner that I recalled the reason for this migration of people. They all hoped for a chance to see the new queen. She was expected any day to travel to her castle at Windsor. I was wedged in between a lawyerlike man with an umbrella and an Italian confectioner with—of all things—a large cake on his lap.

'For Her Majesty,' he explained.

'Has Her Majesty asked for it?' the lawyerlike man said.

'Poor little Vicky,' said a man in the corner, who seemed at least three parts drunk. 'Such a weight on such young shoulders.'

From the murmur of approval round the carriage, he did not mean the cake. Their voices mingled like pigeons in a loyal cooing: so young, so beautiful, so dignified. I said nothing. Even if my own world had not fallen apart, I could have raised no great enthusiasm about a granddaughter of mad King George succeeding to a thoroughly discredited throne. Of course, that was the kind of thing said by my father's friends, but even to hint at it in this patriotic coachload would bring down on my head accusations of republicanism, atheism, treason and revolution.

Well, that explains the six dozen of champagne, at any rate, I thought. Any person of consequence living within an easy drive of Windsor Castle would be expected to entertain housefuls of guests drawn by the mere chance of seeing Her Majesty riding in Windsor Great Park. The advantage was that, in the middle of such a stir, nobody was likely to pay attention to a new governess. The disadvantage, from a spy's point of view, was that one of the puzzles had such a simple explanation.

We reached Windsor half an hour late because of the amount of traffic. I stood outside the inn where the coach had put us down, wondering how I was to recognise the vehicle from Mandeville Hall in the confusion of broughams, barouches, fourgons, calashes, landaus and every other type of conveyance that clogged the centre of town.

'You Miss Lock, the governess?' A phaeton drew up beside me, drawn by a bay cob with a grey-haired coachman in the driving seat. It was crowded with packages, a large fish kettle, crates of bottles. 'Where you got to?' the driver grumbled. 'I been looking for you an hour or more. Now we'll be back late and they'll say it's my fault as usual.'

It was no use pointing out that it wasn't my fault either. I managed, without his help, to find a gap for myself and my bag between a box of wax candles and a large ham, and settled back for a ride through the Berkshire countryside. For much of the journey we went through Windsor Great Park, with cattle grazing under oak trees old enough to have seen Queen Elizabeth out hunting. Every time I looked back, there was the castle, silver in the sun, dwindling gradually into a child's toy castle as we trotted in a cloud of our own white dust between hedges twined with honeysuckle and banks of frothy white cow parsley.

We came out of the parkland alongside an area of common land that

I guessed must be Ascot Heath. The horse races had been run earlier in the month, while the old king was still alive, but a string was at exercise in the distance, stretching out at an easy canter. I thought of Espérance and longed to see her. We trotted on past various walls and gatehouses until we came alongside a park railing, newly painted, topped with gilt spearheads. Three men were at work with pots and brushes, regilding the spearheads. Behind the railing an expanse of parkland sloped upwards, with oaks like Windsor Castle's but much younger. At the top of the slope was . . . 'Good heavens, another castle.'

I said it aloud, to the ham and the fish kettle. At second glance it wasn't quite a castle, only a very grand notion of an Englishman's country house. It had enough towers and turrets for a whole chorus of fairy-tale princesses. Three storeys of windows dazzled in the sun. The whole thing was a perfection of the modern Gothic style. We slowed to a walk, approaching two open gates. They were wrought iron, twenty feet high, freshly painted and gilded like the railings. Cast-iron shields, as tall as a man, with the device of three perched birds, were attached to each gate. A small lodge stood beside the right-hand gate, built like a miniature Gothic chapel to match the house.

'Is this Mandeville Hall?' I asked the driver, appalled at such magnificence. He nodded, without turning round.

I knew the Mandevilles lived in some style, but had expected nothing as extravagant as this. The memory of my father's body in the morgue came into my mind and I felt a black depression. I was wasting my time. How could his life or death be connected with all this pomp?

A man in a brown coat and leggings came out of the lodge. The driver jerked his head towards the house and asked him, 'They back, then?'

'She is. He isn't.'

'When's he expected?'

'No telling. I haven't slept these two nights past, listening for him. You know what he's like if he has to wait while the gates are opened.'

The driver nodded. 'Seeing as they're open, might as well go up the straight way.'

'Better not. What if her ladyship sees you?'

'See two of me, if she does.'

The driver made a tilting motion with his elbow and they both laughed. He jerked the reins and the cob went trotting slowly up the steep drive towards the castle. We hadn't gone more than a few hundred yards when a shout came from the gate lodge behind us. I turned round and there was the gatekeeper, waving his arms and pointing back the way we'd come. The driver turned too and his face went slack.

A great cloud of white dust was coming along the road from

Windsor. At the centre of it was a travelling carriage drawn by four horses, coming at a fast canter. My driver swore and jerked at the cob's head, as if intending to go back down to the gate lodge. But it was too late. The carriage was thundering between the gates, at a trot now but still fast. The gatekeeper had to jump aside. My driver tried to pull our phaeton off the drive and onto the grass. The wheel must have stuck in a rut because it lurched and wouldn't go. By now the carriage was so close the air was full of the sweat of the four labouring horses.

'Oh God.'

It was the gentleman who'd disputed his bill in the hotel at Calais. He must have seen that the phaeton was stuck in his path, but he was still whipping up the horses. I believed that the driver of the carriage must swerve at the last minute. But he didn't. The phaeton lurched and juddered as the cob, writhing under the driver's lash, tried to drag us clear. Then the world came apart in a confusion of whinnying, swearing and splintering wood, and I was in the air with a great downpour of wax candles falling alongside as I landed with my face on the gravel of the drive and my knee on the fish kettle.

When I managed to get to my feet I found that the cob had saved us at the last second by managing to drag the phaeton out of its rut and far enough onto the grass for the carriage to give us no more than a glancing blow. But the blow had been enough to tear the nearside wheel from its axle and throw the phaeton sideways. The cob, trapped in the shafts, had gone with it and was threshing on his side.

'Sit on his head, for Gawd's sake,' he yelled at me.

As instructed, I sat on the cob's head. That kept him still enough for the driver to release him. When he told me I could get up, the cob scrambled to his feet. His face and neck were grazed, his eyes terrified.

'He'll live,' said the driver, having run his hands down the cob's legs.

'He could have killed him. He could have killed all of us.' I was boiling with the anger that follows terror.

'Shouldn't have been coming up that way, should we?'

'But he must have seen us,' I said. 'Is he a guest here? Surely Sir Herbert will be angry that—'

'What are you talking about, girl? That *was* Sir Herbert.'

**M**y hot anger turned to something colder and harder. Until then, I'd had misgivings about entering any man's house as a spy. Now I knew that if there was any way I could find to repay Sir Herbert for treating my life (and the horse's and coachman's lives) so lightly, I would find it. I looked for my bag and found it in the wreckage.

'Where are you going, then?' the driver said.

'To the house. I'm allowed to walk on their sacred drive, I suppose.'

'In that case, you can go through to the stableyard and tell them to send a man down.'

The bag was heavy and my knee hurt. I walked slowly up the drive, my eyes taking in the place like any sightseer. A broad terrace dotted with marble statues—Apollo, Aphrodite, Hercules, Minerva—stretched from the row of windows on the ground floor, which looked out onto the grazing cattle in the park. Gleaming white steps ran down from it to a formal garden with box hedges in clipped geometric shapes. A ha-ha divided the formal garden from the pasture, and a bridge carried the drive across it, decorated with more marble mythology.

I felt very conspicuous, as if the hundreds of windowpanes were eyes watching me. They're not the spies though, I said to myself. I am. I gloried in the word now because I thought that I'd found my enemy at the very start. A man who could deliberately run down his own groom driving one of his own vehicles was surely capable of anything, murder included. I'd seen for myself that he'd been in Calais three days after my father died and might well have been there for some time. What my father had done to earn the hatred of this money-swollen bully I didn't know, but I'd find it out and tell the world.

On the far side of the bridge the drive divided itself into two unequal parts. The broader, left-hand one passed through a triumphal stone arch to the inner courtyard of the house. I glanced inside and there was the carriage Sir Herbert had driven. Evidently this was the entrance for the Mandevilles and guests, not limping governesses. I stopped at the point where the drive divided and put my bag down to change arms. Before I could pick it up again, the carriage wheeled round and came towards me, this time at a slow walk.

I let it go past, then picked up my bag and followed. The side of the house was on my left, with fewer windows than the front. To the right, a high brick wall probably enclosed the vegetable garden. There was a wall on the other side as well and a warm smell of baking bread. We had come out of grandeur, into the domestic regions. I followed the carriage through a high archway with a clock over the top of it, into the stableyard. A dozen or so horses looked out over loose-box doors as their tired colleagues were unharnessed from the carriage, flanks and necks gleaming with sweat. The coachman was having a dejected conversation with a sharp-faced man in gaiters who looked like the head stableman. I picked my way towards them over the slippery cobbles.

'The driver of the phaeton asks will somebody please go to help him.'

'And who may you be?'

'I'm the new governess. The phaeton is smashed and the cob . . .'

He clicked his fingers. Two grooms immediately appeared beside him. 'Bring in the cob and phaeton,' he told them. Then, to me: 'Beggs—can he walk?'

'The driver? Yes, he's not badly hurt, he—'

Cutting me short, he turned back to the men. 'So you needn't waste time bringing Beggs back. Tell him from me he's dismissed. If there's any wages owing, they'll go towards repairing the phaeton.'

'But it wasn't his fault,' I said. 'Sir Herbert . . .'

He walked away. I went and sat on the mounting block with my bag at my feet. After a while an older groom with a kindly face came over to me. 'Anything wrong, miss?'

'I'm . . . I'm the new governess and I don't know where to go.'

He pointed to the archway. 'Through there, miss, and get somebody to take you to Mrs Quivering.' He even carried my bag as far as the archway, though he didn't set foot into the inner courtyard.

'The driver,' I said, 'it isn't at all just . . .'

'There's a lot that's not just, miss.'

The courtyard I walked into was sandwiched between the stableyard and the back of the house. A low building on the left was the dairy; the smell of bread was coming from a matching building on the right. The back of the house itself towered over it all, with a line of doors opening onto the courtyard. A footman was going inside and I followed him into a dark corridor. 'Excuse me,' I said to his back. 'Can you please tell me who Mrs Quivering is and where I can find her?'

He turned. 'Housekeeper. Straight on and last on the left.'

The passage was a long one; at the end was a door marked *Housekeeper*. I knocked, and a voice told me to come in.

Mrs Quivering reminded me of the nuns. She looked to be in her thirties, young for somebody holding such a responsible position, and handsome, in a plain black dress with a bundle of keys at her belt and smooth dark hair tucked under her white linen cap. But her eyes were shrewd. She looked carefully at me as I explained my business.

'Yes, you are expected, Miss Lock. I understand there was an accident on the drive.'

'I'd hardly call it an accident. What happened—'

'You are unhurt?'

'Yes, but—'

'I'm sorry that I can't allocate you the room used by your predecessor. We are expecting a large number of house guests shortly and I am having to set rooms aside for their servants. You might share with Mrs Sims, or there is a small room two floors from the schoolroom that you might have to yourself.'

I had no notion who Mrs Sims might be. I said I'd take the small room two floors up, please, and she made a note.

'I'm sure Lady Mandeville will want to talk to you about your duties, but she's occupied at the moment. I shall let her know you've arrived.'

She rang a bell on her desk and a different footman appeared.

'Patrick, this is Miss Lock, the children's new governess. Please show her to the schoolroom.'

He bent silently to pick up my bag. We'd gone no more than halfway along the corridor before he dropped it like a terrier discarding a dead rat and gave a low but carrying whistle. A boy appeared from nowhere. Patrick nudged the bag with his foot and the boy picked it up. It was clearly beneath the dignity of a footman to carry servants' bags. The boy followed us through a doorway and up two flights of uncarpeted stairs. I tried to keep note of where we were going, aware that much might depend on knowing my way round.

'How many servants are there?' I asked the footman.

'Fifty-seven.' He said it over his shoulder, adding, 'That's inside, not counting stables or gardens, of course.'

We went from the landing into a carpeted corridor with sunlight streaming through a window at the end. The footman knocked on a door halfway along it. 'It's the governess, Mrs Sims.'

The door was opened from the inside, into one of the most pleasant rooms I'd seen in a long time. A square of well-worn Persian carpet softened the polished wood floor. A doll with a smiling porcelain face lolled on the window seat, alongside an old telescope. A dappled rocking horse stood on one side of the window and a battered globe on the other. Three small desks were lined up along the wall, blotters, pens and inkwells all neatly ranged. Three children, two dark-haired boys and a yellow-haired girl, were sitting at a table with bowls of bread and milk in front of them. Overseeing them was a grey-haired woman in a navy-blue dress and white cap and apron. She turned to me, smiling.

'You'll be Miss Lock. I'm right glad to see you. I'm Betty Sims, the children's nursemaid.' Her accent was Lancashire, her welcome seemed genuine. 'And these are Master Charles, Master James and Miss Henrietta. Now, stand up and say good afternoon to Miss Lock.'

The children did as she told them, obediently but with no great enthusiasm. The older boy, Charles, at twelve years old, already had his father's black bar of eyebrows and something of his arrogant look. His brother James was three or four years younger and more frail, glancing at me sidelong as if weighing me up. The girl, Henrietta, was between them in age, masses of fair ringlets framing a round face.

'Did anyone offer you a cup of tea?' Betty asked.

I shook my head. She told me to take the weight off my feet and keep an eye on the children, then went out. I sank into a chair by the window. It was upholstered in worn blue corduroy

'That's my chair,' Henrietta said. 'But you can sit in it for now if you want to.'

'Thank you.'

'Do you know Latin?' Charles said.

'Yes.'

'I don't suppose you know as much of it as I do. Do you know about Julius Caesar? He was the greatest general who ever lived, apart from Wellington. Did you ever meet the Duke of Wellington?'

'No.'

'Papa met the Duke of Wellington.'

James dropped his spoon and wailed, 'Where's Betty? I feel sick.'

'He doesn't really,' Henrietta said. 'He's a terrible liar. Did you know you've got dust all over your shoes? I have fifteen pairs of shoes.'

'You're a lucky girl.'

'A red leather pair, a green leather pair, pink satin, white brocade . . .' She was still reciting her wardrobe when Betty came back carrying a tray with tea things and half a seed cake.

'I feel sick,' James said. 'I want some cake.'

Unperturbed, Betty cut thick slices for herself and me, thin ones for the children. When they'd finished them, she said they should go to their bedrooms and be quiet. She'd come along in five minutes and help them change.

'Change for bed?' I asked her, when they'd filed out of the room. It wasn't yet six o'clock.

'No, changed in case their mother and father want them downstairs before dinner. They usually do, but they might not this evening because of Sir Herbert only just getting back.'

'Getting back from where?' It felt mean, commencing my career as a spy on a person who'd been kind to me, but I had to begin somewhere.

'London, I expect. He's always up and down from London. Sir Herbert's an important man in the government.'

Said with simple confidence, but if Blackstone and Miss Bodenham were right, any importance he might have had was in the past.

'So he has a lot of business to attend to?' I said.

'Yes.' But her attention was on something else. She was staring at the draggled and dusty hem of my dress. 'If the children are sent for, their governess and I usually take them down together—when there is a governess, that is.'

She was hinting gently that I wasn't fit for company. My heart lurched at the thought that I might soon be standing in the same room as Sir Herbert Mandeville.

'But you do look tired out, Miss Lock. If you like, I could make your excuses for you . . .' She sounded worried about that.

'Thank you, but of course I must come down with you. I'll go and change at once, only . . .'

'Did Mrs Quivering say you were to share with me?'

She was obviously relieved when I said I'd opted for the little room.

'It's through the door at the end and up past the maids' dormitory. Shall I ring for a boy to take your bag?'

I refused out of pity for the overworked boys, so my bag and I made the final stage of our journey together, up two steep and narrow staircases. The room was small, no more than eight steps in either direction, with a tiny square of window at shoulder height. It was clean and simply furnished. I had to go down to the maids' floor to find a cubicle with a privy and water to wash myself. Water pails stood in a line, and I found one quarter-full, carried that upstairs, and sponged myself as well as I could. A green cotton dress I'd bought in London would have to do, along with my lace-trimmed fichu pelerine for a modest touch of style, white thread stockings and black shoes, also bought in London.

I went down to find the children changed into their best clothes— boys in breeches, waistcoats and short blue jackets with brass buttons, Henrietta in white-and-pink-striped silk with frills and a ribbon in her ringlets. Betty Sims was on the window seat, eyes on the little bell on its spring over the door. She seemed nervous.

'They usually ring about now if we're wanted.'

'Do the children always have to dress up, even if they're not wanted downstairs?'

'Oh, yes. But they're wanted more often than not.'

'When did the last governess leave?'

'Three weeks ago. I've been trying to teach them a bit on my own since then, but I can't keep all the tables in my head, and if I make a mistake Master James goes running to Mrs Beedle.'

'Mrs Beedle seems a holy terror,' I said.

I'd overstepped the mark, I could see that in her face.

'Mrs Beedle might have her funny ways, but she takes more notice of the children than anybody else does. Several times a week, she'll be up here hearing them recite their lessons.'

'They have regular times for their lessons, I suppose?'

'Yes. I get them up in the morning and washed at half past six, and they have a glass of milk, then an hour with their governess for prayers and reading. Then, if it's fine, we usually take them out for a walk in the flower garden or the orchard. Breakfast is sent up for all of us at nine o'clock, then it's studying from ten o'clock till two. Their lunch is at half past two, then Master Charles usually has his pony brought round. Master James hasn't cared for riding since his pony bit him, so he and Miss Henrietta play or work in their gardens. They're supposed to be in bed by half past eight, but it's not easy these light evenings.'

'And then we have the rest of the day to ourselves?' I was secretly appalled at the amount of work demanded.

'I mend their stockings and things of an evening— There you are.'

The bell over the door had started ringing, bouncing up and down on its spring. The children stood up obediently at the sound of the bell; the five of us went quickly along the corridor, down a flight of stairs and paused on the first-floor landing outside another grander door, painted white with gilt mouldings, while Betty checked the boys' neckcloths and retied Henrietta's ribbon. When she was satisfied, she tapped nervously on the door and it opened inwards, apparently of its own accord.

It seemed at first like magic, but there was a footman on the other side of it. Betty gave Charles a nudge on the shoulder and he walked through it, with his brother and sister following him, then Betty, then me. I was reciting in my mind, *A man's a man for a' that*, to remind myself that I was my father's daughter. In spite of that, I was dazzled and breathless. We were standing at the top of a double staircase, which curved down in a horseshoe, left and right, to a circular hallway. The floor was white and blue mosaic. A carved stone fountain played in the centre of the floor, surrounded by real hart's-tongue ferns. Orange and lemon trees alternated in bays round the walls, their scent rising round us as we went down the left staircase, treading an aisle of soft carpet between expanses of white marble. We crossed the hall; on the far side was another white and gilt door, with yet another footman waiting to open it to us. It led into what they called the small drawing room, as I found out later, the one the family used when there were few or no guests in residence. Still, it was at least twice as large as any room I was accustomed to.

Lady Mandeville was sitting on a sofa by the window, with her mother, Mrs Beedle. She smiled when she saw the children. James went running to her and buried his face in her chest. Charles followed at a slow march over the blue and red Turkey carpet. Henrietta stood just inside the doorway, very much aware of her own reflection in the many mirrors round the walls.

'Good evening, Papa.'

She dropped a grand curtsy. Sir Herbert Mandeville had been standing by the fireplace, talking to a grey-haired man I hadn't seen before. He broke off what he was saying, smiled and kissed his fingers at her.

'Say good evening to your father, James,' Lady Mandeville said.

He glanced towards his father and mumbled, 'Good evening, sir.' Sir Herbert nodded but hardly looked at him.

'What about you, Charles?' he said. 'Cat got your tongue?'

'Good evening, sir.'

Charles stood stiff and straight, as if for inspection. His father looked him over and gave a more approving nod, and turned back to his conversation. I saw Lady Mandeville blow out her cheeks in a look of relief. There was only one other person in the room. She was standing close to Mrs Beedle's chair but with her back to the company, looking out over the terrace. Her red-gold hair was swept up and held with a pearl-studded comb. Would Celia recognise me from the hotel at Calais? Possibly not. Servants are invisible. Lady Mandeville was looking in my direction, signalling with a lift of the chin that I should come over and speak to her.

'Good evening, ma'am,' I said. 'Good evening, Mrs Beedle.'

I could see Lady Mandeville struggling to remember my name.

'Good evening, Miss . . . Lock. I hope you had a pleasant journey.'

'Yes, thank you.' Celia spun round and our eyes met. There wasn't a shade of doubt about it. She'd recognised me. Mrs Beedle turned.

'Celia, this is Miss Lock, the new governess. Miss Lock, my granddaughter, Celia.'

Celia murmured something, gracious enough, I think, and I suppose I replied in kind. She opened her mouth to say something else, closed it again. If she had thought of saying, in front of the family, But I met you at Calais, the thought died in that second.

For the next few minutes the children clustered round their mother's sofa, more relaxed now that their father's attention was not on them. Betty and I stood out of the way near the door. Sir Herbert finished his conversation and announced that it was high time to go in to dinner. Lady Mandeville gently put the children aside and stood up.

'You must go, darlings. Sleep well. See you tomorrow.'

The family began filing through a door on the opposite side, presumably to the dining room, while we went towards the hall. I was almost through the doorway when I felt a hand gripping my arm.

'Miss Lock?' Celia's voice. I turned.

'I need very much to speak to you,' she whispered.

'Now?'

'No. Tomorrow. Will you meet me at six o'clock in the flower garden. And not tell anybody?'

'Celia?' Mrs Beedle's voice, sharply, from the drawing room.

'You will, won't you? Please.'

I nodded. She put a finger to her lips and moved away.

Later, when the children were in bed and Betty Sims and I were sharing supper in the schoolroom, I asked her where the flower garden was.

'Right-hand side of the house looking out, behind the big beech hedge.'

She showed no curiosity about why I wanted to know, because by then I'd asked her a lot of questions about the house and the Mandevilles—all perfectly reasonable for a new governess. She'd been there thirteen years, from a few months before the birth of Master Charles, but her time of service with Lady Mandeville went back longer than that. 'She wasn't Lady Mandeville then, of course, she was Mrs Pencombe. I came to her as nursemaid when her son Stephen was six years old and she was confined with what turned out to be her daughter, Celia.'

'So you've known Celia from a baby?' I wanted to know everything I could about Celia. It might help me decide how far to trust her.

'From the first breath that she drew.'

'What was she like as a child?'

'Pretty as a picture and sweet winning ways. But headstrong. She was always a child who liked her own way.'

'What happened to Mr Pencombe?'

'He died of congestion to the lungs when Celia was six years old. We thought we'd lose Mrs Pencombe too, from sheer grief. It was a love match, you see. With her looks, she could have married anybody.'

'And yet she must have married Sir Herbert quite soon afterwards.'

Betty put down her slice of buttered bread and gave me a warning look. 'Two years and three months, and I hope you're not taking it on yourself to criticise her for that.'

'Indeed not.'

'What would anyone have done in her place? Mr Pencombe hadn't been well advised in the investments he made and he left her with nothing but debts and two children to bring up. She was still a fine-looking woman, but looks don't last for ever.'

'Did she love Sir Herbert?'

'A woman's lucky if she marries for love once over. I don't suppose there's many manage it twice. May I trouble you to pass the mustard?'

That was her way of telling me I was on the edge of trespassing. It might also have been a gentle hint that she'd made a comfortable little camp for herself and the children in this great house and it was kind of her to let me into it.

The tea and candlelight were so soothing I could scarcely keep my eyes open.

'You're for your bed,' Betty said. 'Take that candle up with you. You can sleep in tomorrow, if you like. I'll see to the children.'

# Chapter Four

IN SPITE OF MY TIREDNESS I slept lightly. By four o'clock it was growing light. An hour after that the floorboards below creaked as the earliest maids dragged themselves downstairs. I got up too. There was still nearly an hour to go before my meeting with Celia but I was too restless to stay inside. I crept down the dark backstairs, with only the faintest notion of where I was going. But it was mostly a matter of travelling on downwards down zigzagging staircases and across narrow landings towards the sounds coming from the kitchen.

The last turn of the staircase brought me into the light, a smell of piss and a glare of white porcelain. Chamber pots, dozens of them. They must have been gathered from bedrooms and brought down for empty-ing. I picked my way carefully through them and out into the court-yard. There was an archway on the far side. I walked through it and the parkland stretched out in front of me, glittering with dew.

On the other side of the ha-ha, cows were already up and grazing. Nearer to hand, a narrow flight of steps led up to the back of the ter-race. At right angles, a freshly mown grass path stretched to an archway cut into a high beech hedge. I followed it and found myself in an old-fashioned kind of garden. Four gnarled mulberry trees stood at the cor-ners of the lawn, with an old sundial at the centre. Hollyhocks grew at the back of the borders, love-in-a-mist and mignonette at the front, with stocks, bellflowers and pentstemons in between. The whole area, no more than half an acre or so, was enclosed by the beech hedges, with a semicircular paved area on the south side, a rustic bench and a summerhouse dripping with white roses.

I sat down on the bench and made myself think how to manage the conversation with Celia Mandeville when she arrived. She wanted some-thing from me but—although she didn't know it—I badly wanted several things from her. The most important by far was confirmation that Sir Herbert had been in Calais the day my father died.

She was late. Ten minutes or so after the stable clock had struck six she came running through the archway in the beech hedge, face anx-ious and hair flying. 'Oh, here you are. Thank you, thank you.'

She was wearing a rose-pink muslin morning dress, thrown on

hastily. Perhaps I should have stood up, since she was my employer's daughter, but it never occurred to me. She sat down beside me and took my hand, panting from her run.

'Last night . . . I couldn't believe it. What are you doing here?'

'Your mother was kind enough to engage me as governess.'

'But when we met in Calais, I thought . . .'

I think she might have been on the point of saying that she'd taken me for a social equal. She glanced at me, then away.

'I suppose you've had some misfortune in life?'

'Yes,' I said.

Another glance at my face. She seemed nervous, poised to run away. 'I liked you,' she said. 'Liked you at once. Your poor head. Is it better now?'

'Head? Yes, oh yes. Thank you.'

We stared at each other. Her eyes were a deep brown.

'Can I trust you?' she said. The question should have been offensive, but somehow it wasn't. She seemed to be asking herself rather than me. 'You see, I do very much need to trust somebody.'

I watched her face as she came to a decision.

'I must trust you, I think. Goodness knows, there's nobody else.'

'You have a mother and a brother,' I said.

'Stephen doesn't always do what I want, and my poor mother is . . . has other things to worry her. Then if he found out that I'd confided in her and she hadn't told him, he'd be so angry with her . . .'

'"He" being your stepfather?'

She looked away from me and nodded. 'Miss Lock, would you do something for me and keep it secret?'

'What?'

'Promise me to keep it secret, even if you won't do it?'

'I promise. What is it that you want me to do?'

'Take a letter to the post for me.'

'Only that?' I felt both relieved and disappointed.

'Only that, but nobody must know. I can't trust any of the servants, you see. They're nearly all his spies. Or they're so terrified of him, they'd tell him at the first black look. But he'd never guess it of you, being so newly come here.'

'This letter is to a friend?'

'Yes. A gentleman friend. Not a love letter, in case that's what you're thinking.' She glanced sideways at me and must have caught my sceptical look. 'It's more important than that. It's . . .' She hesitated. 'If . . . if a certain thing happens, my life may be in danger.'

There was a flatness about the way she said it, more convincing than any dramatics might have been.

'What certain thing?'

'I mustn't tell you, and you mustn't ask any more questions. But you'll take the letter for me?'

'I've already said so. But how am I to get it to the post?' With the amount of work demanded from a governess, I couldn't see how I was to find the time to get to the Silver Horseshoe, let alone make regular reports to Mr Blackstone.

'There surely must be a way,' she said.

I let her see that I was thinking hard. 'There must be some livery stables near here, with carriages that meet the mail coaches,' I said. 'If I could take your letter to one of those . . .'

'Yes. Oh, Miss Lock, how very clever of you. Could you do that?'

'I think so, yes. I've heard somebody talking about a place called the Silver Horseshoe, on the west side of the heath.'

'Yes. We pass it in the carriage sometimes. They keep racehorses there as well as livery. It's about two miles away, I think.'

'If I were to walk there, in the very early morning, say, do you suppose anybody would notice me?'

'You must not be noticed. You simply must not be noticed.'

Which was hardly an answer to my question.

She turned her head suddenly. 'What was that?'

A chesty cough came from the far side of the beech hedge. A bent old gardener in a smock limped through the arch into the garden, trug over his arm. He didn't glance in our direction and moved on slowly to a bed of delphiniums.

'I must go,' she said. 'We must not be seen alone together.'

I kept a firm hold of her hand. 'It was strange, wasn't it, meeting in Calais like that?' I said.

She nodded, but her hand was tense and her eyes were on the old man. 'Yes.'

'What were you and your stepfather doing in Calais?'

'He had business in Paris. He wanted me to go with him.'

'I suppose you stayed several days in Calais?'

'Not even a day. He'd worked himself into such a fume about getting home, we hardly had time to sleep. It was nearly two o'clock on Tuesday morning before we got to Calais and we were on the packet out on Tuesday afternoon.'

She said it so naturally, with half her mind still on the old gardener, that it sounded like the truth. If she was right, by the time the Mandevilles had arrived in Calais, my father was nearly three days dead. And yet a memory came to me of the foyer of the Calais hotel, and her stepfather disputing a bill several pages long.

'You'd built up a very long hotel bill in a few hours,' I said.

She blinked, as if she didn't understand what I meant at first.

'Oh, that was mostly Stephen's. He was there waiting for us. My step-father frets if he thinks Stephen's being extravagant.'

She let go of my hand and stood up. The stable clock was striking seven. 'My maid Fanny will wonder what's become of me. I shall say I couldn't sleep. I'll make some excuse to come to the schoolroom and give you the letter.' She took a step or two, then turned round. 'I *can* trust you, can't I?'

'Yes.'

Then she was gone through the gap in the beech hedge. I went back to my room in the attic. From there, I hurried down to the schoolroom as if I'd just got up. Betty had the three children round the table, choosing pictures to paste into their scrapbooks.

'Say good morning to Miss Lock.'

They chorused it obediently.

'It's such a lovely morning, I thought we might all have a walk on the terrace before breakfast,' Betty said.

So we went downstairs and out onto the terrace through a side door, and the children played hide-and-seek among the marble statues.

After breakfast it was time to start my governess duties. I realised that, with all my other concerns, I'd given no thought to the question of teaching. Still, we managed. I devoted most of the morning to finding out how much they knew already, and the results were patchy. They were very well drilled in their tables and the Bible, adequate in grammar and handwriting and able to speak a little French. Their geography and history seemed sketchy. Charles's Latin was nowhere near as good as he believed. That possibly explained why he had not been sent away to school yet, although he was clearly old enough.

Around midday, we moved on to poetry. To my astonishment they'd never even heard of Shelley, so I fetched the treasured volume from my bag and read to them:

> *I met a traveller from an antique land,*
> *Who said: Two vast and trunkless legs of stone*
> *Stand in the desert. Near them, on—*

The door opened suddenly and Mrs Beedle walked in. She was wearing her usual black silk and widow's cap and carrying an ebony walking cane. I stopped reading. She came over and looked at my book.

'I don't approve of Mr Shelley. If they must have poetry, Mr Pope is best. Mr Pope is sensible.'

'I'm sorry, ma'am.'

It was no part of my plan to be dismissed on my first morning. She turned to the children. At least they did not seem scared of her. She fired questions at them for several minutes and, from the nod she gave me, seemed reasonably satisfied. Yet, now and again, I caught her looking at me in a thoughtful way. Perhaps it was only to do with my suspect taste in poetry, because at the end of it she simply wished me good morning and went with as little fuss as when she'd arrived.

Our dinner at half past two was shepherd's pie and blancmange with bottled plums. In the afternoon I helped Henrietta and James cultivate their plots on the south side of the walled vegetable garden. Every time Henrietta saw a worm she screamed and one of the gardeners' boys had to come running over to take it away.

When the stable clock struck five it was time to take the children back to the schoolroom for their bread and milk and have them washed and changed for their summons downstairs. This time there was no sign of Sir Herbert. Lady Mandeville was on her sofa, Mrs Beedle and Celia sitting by the window sewing. A tall, dark-haired young man was standing looking out of the window: Celia's brother. Lady Mandeville nodded at me to come over to her. 'Miss Lock, may I introduce my son Stephen. Stephen, Miss Lock, our new governess.'

It was graceful in her, to introduce us properly. Her son's response was equally graceful, a touch of the hand, a slight movement of the upper body that was an indication of a bow, though not as pronounced as it would have been to a lady. The dark eyes that met mine gave no indication that he remembered seeing me before. Celia glanced up.

'Miss Lock, do you sketch? Should you mind if I consulted you sometimes about my attempts?'

'I should be delighted,' I said. Soon after that they went in to dinner and we were free to escape to the nursery quarters.

The next day, Saturday, followed much the same pattern in the schoolroom. On Sunday we all went to church, the children travelling with their parents in the family carriage a mile across the park to the little Gothic church by the back gates, the rest of us walking in the sunshine.

After church, once the family had driven away in the carriage, there was a chance for the servants to linger in the sun and gossip. I strolled among the gravestones, catching the occasional scrap of conversation.

'. . . all the bedrooms opened, even ones they haven't used for years . . .'

'. . . bringing waiters in from London, just for the weekend. Where they're going to put them all . . .'

'So I said I didn't think it was very respectful having a ball, with the poor old King not even buried yet.'

'Well, he will be by then, won't he?'

'I think they're going to announce an engagement for Miss Celia.'

'They'd never go to all that trouble, would they?'

I tried to hear more, but the women who were talking saw me and lowered their voices. I wandered away to look more closely at some of the gravestones. Nearest the church were the big table tombs of the Mandeville family themselves. I was reading the florid description of the virtues of the fifth baronet, *as distinguished in his Piety and Familial Duty as in the high service of his Country*, when I heard footsteps.

'He really was the worst villain of the lot of them,' a man's voice said over my shoulder. 'Made a fortune selling bad meat to the army.'

I turned round and saw Stephen Mandeville standing there smiling. I dare say my mouth dropped open. I'd assumed he'd gone back in the carriage with the rest of the family. He came and stood beside me.

'I'm sorry. Did I startle you?'

I tried to compose myself and answer him in the same light tone. 'Not in the least. I suppose he had some good qualities.'

'Not that I've heard of.'

The irreverence for the family surprised me, until I remembered that they weren't his ancestors. He strolled on to the next tomb and in politeness I had to follow him. 'The carving on this one is thought to be quite fine, if you have a taste for cherubim.'

To anyone watching—and I was quite sure that some of the servants would be watching—the son of the house was simply being polite. I knew there was more to it than that.

'I am glad that you're here, Miss Lock. My sister needs a friend.' He said it simply in a quiet voice.

I glanced up at him. 'I'm sure Miss Mandeville has many friends.'

'Not as many as you might think. She leads a very quiet life here. You seem to be around the same age as she is, if you'll permit me to be personal, and I think she's taken a liking to you already.'

'Has she said so?'

From the lift of his eyebrow I could see he hadn't expected a direct question, but I wanted very much to know if they'd talked about me.

'She doesn't have to say it. I can read my sister like a book. So, you'll be a friend to her?'

'If I can, of course I will.'

'Thank you. Now, if you'll excuse me, I must go and join my family.'

**I** walked back across the park with Betty and her friend Sally, the bread and pastry cook, a plump woman. For some time the three of us strolled in silence. I broke it by going back to the talk I'd overheard.

'There's to be a ball, then?'

'Two weeks on,' Sally said. 'A hundred people invited and a dinner the day before.'

*I have reason to believe that they will be holding a reception or ball in the next few weeks . . .* So Blackstone had been right. But how did he know and what in the world did it matter to him?

'Don't worry, Miss Lock,' Betty said. 'We shan't have much to do with it, except keeping the children looking nice when they're wanted.'

'Her ladyship looks worn out with worry about it already,' Sally said.

Betty gave her a look that said some things should not be discussed in front of new arrivals and turned the conversation to a bodice she was trimming for Sally, leaving me with plenty of time to wonder why Miss Mandeville should be so much in need of a friend.

**O**n Monday afternoon, Mrs Quivering intercepted me and led me into her office. 'A letter has arrived for you, Miss Lock.'

My heart leapt. The only person to whom I'd given my address was Daniel Suter. 'Oh, excellent.' I held out my hand, expecting to be given the letter, and received a frown instead.

'Miss Lock, you should understand that if anybody has occasion to correspond with you, letters should be addressed care of the house-keeper and they will be passed on when the servants' post is distributed. Is that quite clear?'

Since childhood, I'd never felt so humiliated. When she brought an envelope from under the ledger, I took it without looking at the writing on the envelope, thanked her and marched out.

At least dear Daniel had not failed me. I carried it back upstairs to my attic room and turned the envelope over, expecting to see Daniel's fine italic hand. It was like running into a thorn hedge where you'd expected lilacs—not Daniel's hand after all but the upright, spiky characters of Mr Blackstone.

*Miss Lock,*
*    Livery bills will be paid for the mare Espérance at the Silver Horseshoe until further notice. Please let me know of your safe arrival as soon as is convenient.*

That was all; no greeting, no signature. When I read it a second time I saw that it contained a small threat. I had not told him the mare's name. He'd discovered that for himself and used it, I guessed, quite deliberately to show I could hide nothing from him. Well, I was being a good, obedient spy. In my first few days I'd found out something he wanted to know and had even seized a chance of getting it to him with the help of the daughter of the house.

Celia paid a visit to the schoolroom just before the end of our morning session. 'Miss Lock, may I steal you, please?'

As it was so close to their dinner time I told the children they could put their books away and joined her in the corridor.

'It was so obliging of you to offer to help with my sketching. It's driving me quite distracted.' I realised that she'd said it loudly for the benefit of Betty, who'd come hurrying out of her room to see who the intruder was. 'Would you come and give me your opinion?'

'Now?'

'Why not? Betty can see to the children, can't you, Betty?'

I followed her along the corridor and down the stairs to the first floor, where the family had their rooms. Celia opened a door into a sunny room with a blue canopied bed, blue velvet window curtains, two chairs and a sofa upholstered to match. A half-open doorway showed a dressing room with a screen and a full-length mirror.

'Where's your sketch?' I said, humouring her.

'Don't worry, it's quite safe to talk. I've sent Fanny down to the laundry. My letter's ready.' She brought it over to me. It was plump and scented, addressed to Philip Medlar Esq. at an address in Surrey. She dropped a smaller packet into my hands. 'There's some money in there to give whoever takes it to the post. I've tried to think of everything.'

She was anxious to please me. Perhaps she'd caught the look on my face when she gave me the letter. The smell and feel of it had convinced me that it was nothing more than a love letter after all and she'd not been truthful with me. Still, it suited my plans.

'How soon can you take it? Tomorrow?'

'Yes. If I leave at first light, I can be back by the time the children have to be got up.'

She knelt on the carpet and clasped my hands between both of hers.

'Oh, I am so very grateful. I do believe you've saved my life.'

I said gently, 'Are you so very scared of your stepfather?'

'I am scared of him, yes, but that isn't the worst of it. Miss Lock . . . Oh, I can't go on "miss"-ing you. What's your name?'

'Lib—, Elizabeth.'

'Elizabeth, there are things I mustn't tell you. But do believe that I might be in the most terrible danger of being put in prison or . . . or killed even, for something that isn't my fault at all.'

I wanted to say that there was no need for this drama because I'd carry her letter in any case, but I bit my tongue and slipped my hand from hers.

'I'd better go back to the children.'

'How shall I know you've sent it?' she said.

'That bench we sat on, in the flower garden—if I'm back safely, I'll pick a flower and leave it there.'

'Yes. I mustn't be seen talking with you too much, specially now Stephen's back. He notices more than Mama.'

'Where has your brother been?'

'He stays in London, mostly. He's studying to be a lawyer.'

I wondered whether to tell her about my conversation with Stephen. It would have reassured her, but I was still annoyed by her dramatics.

Or perhaps I was falling into the spy's habit of secrecy.

I got back to the schoolroom just in time for my share of minced mutton and green peas. In the afternoon, as a treat for the children, we were allowed the use of the pony phaeton to take them over to the keeper's cottage to see a litter of month-old puppies. Mrs Beedle had half promised Charles he might have one for his own, if my reports on his progress in Latin and arithmetic were satisfactory. It was good to see them playing and laughing with the puppies, so much at ease.

'I shall tell her he's doing well, whether he does or not,' I whispered to Betty.

'Yes. Goodness knows, they don't have an easy life, poor mites.'

It seemed an odd thing to say about three children who lived lives of such privilege, but that evening I had an illustration of what she meant. The bell rang as usual, and we escorted them downstairs. Only the immediate family were present, including Stephen. He was sitting on a chair beside his mother's sofa, showing her something in a book. Lady Mandeville was smiling. When James went running to her, she hugged the boy, but still with half her attention on Stephen. Celia was sitting by the piano, Mrs Beedle was at the window, sewing, and Sir Herbert was standing by the fireplace, reading a letter. Henrietta, who hated to be ignored, went over and stood beside him.

'Papa, may I have a puppy too?'

He ignored her and went on reading.

'Papa, may I . . .?'

He gestured to her to be quiet. Lady Mandeville called across from the couch, 'Henrietta, come here and stop bothering your father.'

Anybody could tell the letter was annoying him. His face was going red, his shoulders rigid. But the child wouldn't budge.

'Cowards. Miserable, temporising pack of damned cowards!' He shouted it at the top of his voice, crumpled the letter and threw it into the empty fireplace. As he turned, his elbow caught Henrietta on the side of the face. He might not have intended it, but when she cried out and went sprawling on the carpet, he made no move to pick her up.

'Herbert, the children . . .' Lady Mandeville protested.

James had started to cry and was clinging to her, so she couldn't get up and go to her daughter.

'Damn you and damn the children.'

Betty and I ran to Henrietta. Sir Herbert cannoned into Betty and almost knocked her off her feet as he made for the door to the hall. By now Henrietta was howling and even Charles was biting his lip and looking scared. Mrs Beedle was the first to recover.

'Henrietta, please stop that noise. Celia, see to James. Betty, have you arnica ointment in your room?' She wanted the children out of the drawing room, back to the safety of the schoolroom and, in spite of James's reluctance to leave his mother, we managed it.

We calmed the children, fed them bread and milk and put them to bed. Henrietta had a bruise developing on her jaw where her father's elbow had struck. Betty and I didn't discuss what had happened until we were sitting at the schoolroom table over a pot of tea.

'Is he often as bad as that?' I said.

'He's always had a black temper, but it's been worse in the last few months. A lot worse.'

'How does Lady Mandeville stand for it?'

'What can she do?'

'She could leave, couldn't she? She must have family or friends.'

'And lose the children? Children are a father's property, remember. If she walks out of here, she'll never see them again.'

'Can't anybody do anything? What about the son?'

'Mr Stephen's part of the trouble. If it weren't for him, she might stand up for herself more than she does.'

'Why?'

Betty took her time deciding whether to answer. 'After university, he took up with some bad company and got himself into debt. He doesn't have any money of his own, of course, not a shilling. So . . .' She hesitated, looking into her cup. 'He got put into debtors' prison.'

She whispered it, her eyes scared. I was perhaps not quite as shocked as she expected me to be. The fact was, some of my father's friends had been put into debtors' prison from time to time and seemed to regard it as no worse an inconvenience than an attack of fever or rheumatics.

'Not even the gentlemen's part of the prison,' Betty insisted. 'In there with the common criminals with rats running over him. And Sir Herbert let him stay there for three whole weeks.'

I thought of Stephen's elegant manners and quizzical eyebrows failing to impress the rats and did feel rather sorry for him.

'Lady Mandeville was on her knees to Sir Herbert, begging him to have her son out,' Betty said. 'But he wouldn't do it, not until Stephen had learned his lesson, he said. Ever since then, she's been terrified. That was what started . . . you know.' She tipped a hand towards her mouth, as if holding a glass. She might have said more, but Henrietta was crying out and we had to go to her. What with that and James wetting his bed, we had a hard night with them.

I didn't sleep because I was too scared about the journey I must make in the morning. At first light, I crept down the backstairs to the drawing room and retrieved from the fireplace the crumpled letter that Sir Herbert had flung there. It was the kind of thing that spies did, after all. I took it back to my room to read. It had the address of a gentleman's club at the top and was in small, cramped writing.

> Dear Mandeville,
>
> Yours of the 23rd ult. has only just come to my hand. I am writing in haste to urge you to desist from this most dangerous folly. You are aware of the extent to which I share all the concerns of yourself and others about the deplorable weakness of the present administration and the threat to our dignity, profits and rights of property which must inevitably result if they continue cravenly to appease the masses. But there are remedies which are more perilous than the disease and, if I understand your hints aright, your proposed cure is one such.
>
> If in the past my too-great warmth on such subjects has led you to the erroneous conclusion that I might in any way support what you propose, I can only apologise for unwittingly misleading you. Bluntly, I want no part in this. If indeed a wrong was done, then it was done twenty years ago. To attempt to right it in these changed times would be no service to our country or to him you wish to serve. Let him not cross the Channel. If a pension must be discussed, then—provided that stretch of water remains forever between him and England—I might be prepared to say a word in certain ears. Otherwise I must ask you not to correspond with me on the subject again.
>
> Believe me, your most alarmed well-wisher,
> Tobias

I added a postscript to the note I'd written to Blackstone and sealed up the letter. Then I put the note and Celia's letter into my reticule and went stocking-footed down the backstairs so as not to wake the maids.

Even so early in the morning it was unthinkable to walk down the main drive, with all those windows watching me. The back road was reassuring by comparison. After passing a lightning-scarred oak, it dipped between high banks crowded with cow parsley and wild geraniums.

Once clear of being seen from the house, my mind was free to think about other things, like the letter I'd taken from the fireplace. *Let him not cross the Channel.* The man who had written that was scared, and the reason for his fear—as the reason surely for my father's death—came from France. So did the unknown, unfortunate woman that the fat man was hunting. And yet my last letter from my father, hinting at a secret, had not mentioned danger, rather the reverse: . . . *one most capital story which I promise will set you roaring with laughter* . . .

The back road joined the main road that I'd travelled on from Windsor. Half a mile in that direction were the great gates of Mandeville Hall. I turned in the opposite direction, making for what I hoped was the heath.

After a while a lane went off to the right, marked with hoofprints, and a signboard with a horseshoe pointed to the stables. The heath opened out, with skylarks singing overhead and from far away a vibration of drumming hoofs. I envied what must surely be the uncomplicated happiness of the people riding those horses. Then the line of them came towards me, but the lads riding them didn't give me a glance. They had their hands full, bringing the excited horses back to a walk before they came to the harder ground of the path. The air was full of the smell of horse-sweat and leather. There were five horses, three of them bunched together, then a calmer, cobby type with a big man aboard. Then a gap and a bright bay mare a little smaller and more finely made than the others. The lad riding her was having trouble slowing her to a walk, but that was because he was so heavy-handed. He was trying to hold her by sheer force so that she was dancing on the spot, fighting the bit. His face was white and terrified. He looked no more than twelve or so and I supposed they'd put him on the mare because he was the lightest. A sideways jerk of her head tugged the reins out of his hands. She reared up and, as her head came round towards me, I recognised the comma-shaped blaze and intelligent eye, now terrified.

The boy rocketed out of the saddle. Rancie galloped past the other horses. One of them wheeled round to get out of her way and barged into his neighbour, who kicked him. I ran after her, scared that she'd catch a leg in the trailing reins. Some way along the path I caught up with her. She'd stopped and was snatching at grass. She rolled her eye at me and flinched as if expecting punishment.

'Rancie, girl, it's all right, Rancie . . .' I put a hand on her sweat-soaked shoulder. 'It's not your fault. Poor Rancie.'

With my other hand, I gathered up the trailing reins. By then, the other horses were coming past us. The man on the cob called out to me as he passed. 'Well done, miss. I'll take her.'

If an oak tree could have spoken, it would have been in that deep Hereford voice. Amos Legge, my light-brown giant. He sprang off the cob's back, landing neatly beside Rancie and me.

'Thought it was you, miss. You be come to see Rancie, then?'

He didn't even sound surprised. As he ran his hand down Rancie's legs, checking for injuries, she bent her head and nuzzled his back with that deep sigh horses give when anxiety goes out of them.

'No great mishtiff done. Will you lead her in then, miss?'

We followed Amos and the cob along the lane and into the yard, Rancie as quiet as a pet dog. The yard was busy. Amos seemed to sense that I didn't want to attract attention and led us to a box in the corner.

'You two wait in there, while I go and see to this fellow.'

The straw in the box was deep, and there was good clean hay in the manger. I stayed in a dark corner, talking to Rancie, until Amos came back. He untacked her, plaited a hay wisp and used it in long, sweeping strokes to dry off the sweat. As soon as her rug was on, the gold-eyed cat jumped down from the manger and settled in her usual place on Rancie's back.

'I thought you'd have gone home to Herefordshire by now,' I said.

'No hurry, miss. There's work for me here if I want it, so I thought I might stay for a bit, see her settled. And it was in my mind I might be seeing you again.'

'I have letters for the post,' I said. 'Could you see they go on the next mail coach?'

Blackstone had instructed me to send letters through the owner of the stables, but this was the chance of a little independence. Amos nodded, took both letters from me but gave back Celia's coins.

'I'm doing well enough, miss, but what about you?'

'I'm employed at Mandeville Hall, only they mustn't know about this.'

A voice from the yard called, 'Amos. Where's Amos?'

The call was impatient. Amos picked up the saddle and bridle.

'You wait here till I come. You'll be safe enough.'

'I can't wait.' Betty would surely be getting the children up soon and I'd be missed. Still, one thing was urgent. 'Rancie must be exercised properly. Isn't there anybody who can ride her?'

'I'm too heavy and the lads are feared of her, miss. That's the third she's had off.'

'It's because she's light-mouthed. They'll kill her spirit if they go on like this. Can you tell them you've had word from her owner that nobody should ride her until further instructions?'

He nodded, but looked worried. 'Needs a lady's hand, she does.'

I don't know if he was deliberately putting an idea into my mind.

'I'll think of something,' I said. 'I'll be back on . . .'—I did a quick calculation. In four days there might be an answer to one or both of the letters—'. . . on Saturday.'

'You look feverish,' Betty said. 'Did you sleep badly?'

She'd been kinder than I deserved, getting the children up and dressed, taking them for their walk before breakfast. I'd almost bumped into them on my way back from the flower garden where I'd put a clove carnation on the rustic seat for Celia to find. I'd had to hide behind the beech hedge then rush up the backstairs to wash and tidy myself.

'She's wearing rosewater,' Henrietta said, sniffing.

Observant little beast. The maids had taken most of the water as usual, and there had only been enough left for a superficial wash, not enough to abolish the lingering smell of stables.

'It smells just like my rosewater.'

It was. Desperate, I'd gone into her room and sprayed myself from the bottle on her white and gilt dressing table. What do nine-year-old girls need with rosewater in any case? It marked the start of a difficult day in the schoolroom. The children were short of sleep and sullen, still shaken by their father's anger the evening before; I could hardly keep my eyes open. Towards the end of the morning, when we'd moved on to French conversation, Mrs Beedle paid us a visit of inspection. She sat listening for a while, very stern and upright, but from the thoughtful way she looked at her grandchildren I guessed she was trying to tell if they were affected by what had happened. What was more alarming was that I caught her looking at me with a puzzled frown, nostrils flaring. She'd certainly noticed the rosewater and probably guessed where it came from, but had she caught a whiff of horse as well?

'Miss Lock, I am concerned . . .' she said, and paused, '. . . that you are teaching Henrietta the wrong kind of French.'

I tried not to show my relief. 'I hope not, ma'am. Her accent has improved quite remarkably in a few days.'

'Please do not contradict me. I couldn't understand a word she was gabbling. I shall examine her again next week and expect her to be speaking French like an English gentlewoman.'

The children slept in the afternoon and so did I. I woke thinking I was back at my aunt's house, until the clash of saucepans from the kitchens below reminded me. I cried for a while, then dressed and went down. Betty was laying out Henrietta's white muslin frock with the blue sash.

'We're surely not taking them down tonight?' I said.

'If they're sent for, they'll have to go.'

At first, James flatly refused to change into his best clothes. He wanted to see his mother but his fear of his father was greater.

'Your papa is a very important man,' Betty told him. 'He's angry sometimes because he works hard, that's all.'

But her eyes, meeting mine over his bowed head, told a different story. Henrietta was impatient with her brother.

'Don't be silly. Papa didn't mean to hurt me.'

I looked at the blue bruise on her jaw and thought there was a kind of courage in her. James let himself be dressed at last, but began crying when the bell rang for us and clung tightly to my hand as we went down the staircase to the grand hall. There were servants at work, dusting and polishing. The reason seemed to be a rearrangement of the pictures. There were dozens of them round the hall, some of bewigged Mandeville ancestors, others of great moments from British history. Julius Caesar confronting the Druids had been one of the most prominent. Now it had been taken down and propped against the wall and a portrait was being put up in its place. Sir Herbert himself was supervising, with Mrs Beedle, the butler, Mrs Quivering and two footmen in attendance. Since all this was barring the way to the drawing room, we could only stand there with the children and wait. The portrait was a comparatively modern one of a pleasant-looking though somewhat popeyed young woman, hair piled in curls on top of her head, surrounded with a wreath of roses, all in the easy Empire style of our parents' time. To my surprise, I recognised her from other portraits I'd seen, and when James whispered, 'Who is she?' I was able to whisper back, 'That's poor Princess Charlotte.'

Even a Republican's daughter may be interested in princesses, especially young ones who ended sadly. So although I was no more than a baby when Princess Charlotte died, I knew a little about her. She was a granddaughter of mad King George III, the only legitimate child of his son George IV and his unruly and hated queen, Caroline. Charlotte showed signs of being one of the best of the Hanoverian bunch, which to be sure is not saying a great deal. They married her before she was twenty to one of those German princelings who are in such constant supply, and she became pregnant with a child who would have succeeded her and become King of England—only she died in childbirth and her baby boy died too. Which was why we were about to celebrate the coronation of a different granddaughter of mad King George, Charlotte's cousin, little Vicky. In the circumstances, going to such trouble to commemorate Charlotte seemed eccentric.

'Is she the new queen?' James whispered to me.

'No. I'm afraid she died.'

Sir Herbert stood staring at the picture. None of us could move before he did. James gripped my hand even more tightly. 'What did she die of?'

An awkward question. I could hardly explain death in childbirth to the boy, especially in such public circumstances. I began, in a whisper, that she had caught a fever, but a higher voice came from my other side.

'She was poisoned.'

Henrietta, in that terribly carrying tone of hers, determined to be the centre of attention. There was a moment of shocked silence, then her father's head swung round, slow and heavy like a bull's, from the picture to where we were standing. After his violence the night before, I was terrified of what he might say or do to the child. I was scared for myself too, certain that I should be blamed for Henrietta's lapse both in manners and historical knowledge. I forced myself to look Sir Herbert in the eye, determined on dignity at least, and the expression under his black brow so disconcerted me that I fear my mouth gaped open. The man was smiling. He took a few heavy steps towards us, then, amazingly, bent down until his eyes were level with Henrietta's, and put a finger to his lips. 'Shhh,' he said to her.

I think everybody there was as amazed as I was, not believing him capable of such a kindly and humorous rebuke. He tweaked one of her ringlets and said, 'It is a pity you are not ten years older.'

The words were said in an undertone, and I think I was the only one apart from Henrietta who caught them. Then he walked into the drawing room and we followed him.

That evening, Betty went to her room soon after the children were in bed. I stayed on my own in the schoolroom, preparing notes on the geography of India for next day's lesson. I was dozing over the tributaries of the Ganges when the door opened and somebody came in.

'Is one of the children awake?' I said, thinking it must be Betty.

'I hope not,' Celia said, coming over to the table. She was in evening dress. Her face was pale in the candlelight, eyes scared. 'You were seen.'

'By whom?'

'One of the laundry maids has a sweetheart who works at the stables.'

'Why didn't you warn me?'

'Am I supposed to know every servant's sweetheart? I only heard about it from Fanny when she was doing my hair for dinner.'

'What did she tell you?'

'The stableboy was sent up here on some message. He told his laundry maid a tale of a woman catching a horse that was bolting.'

'She wasn't . . . I mean, how did he know it was me?'

'He didn't. Only he described you and what you were wearing and the laundry maid said it sounded a bit like the new governess.'

'They don't know for certain, then?'

'Not yet, no. I was shaking. Fanny must have felt it. Then I had to sit through dinner wondering if Sir Herbert had heard about it yet.'

'Did he give any sign?'

'No, but then he may just be waiting for his time to pounce.'

I put down my pencil and found my hand was shaking too.

'What are we to do?' Celia said. 'I must have the reply to my letter.'

'Oh, there's certain to be a reply, is there?' I was nettled at her refusal to consider any problem but her own.

'I'm sure Philip will reply by return of post. I told him to write care of the stables. It should be there by Friday or Saturday at the latest.'

'Is a love letter so important that I must risk dismissal for it?'

She sat down heavily on Henrietta's blue chair. 'It's more than that. I wish . . . oh, I must trust you.' She looked down at the map of India. 'I've asked him to elope with me.'

'Doesn't the suggestion usually come from the gentleman?'

'I'm certain Philip would suggest it if he knew. But he can't know until he reads my letter. You see, somebody's coming soon and I want Philip to take me away and marry me before he arrives.'

'This other person, is he the one your stepfather wants you to marry?'

She nodded.

'When is he arriving?'

'I don't know. He's expected any day and it would be so much safer in every way if I weren't here.'

I supposed she was referring to Sir Herbert's violent temper. I felt sorry for her, but wished she hadn't planted her burden on me. 'So what are we to do about your letter?' I said. Whatever happened, I must keep open a way of communicating with Blackstone.

'If I can think of something, will you do it, Elizabeth?'

'If I can, yes.'

'Don't fail me. You're my only hope.'

# *Chapter Five*

THE NEXT FEW DAYS were almost calm, probably because Sir Herbert was away in London. I gathered that from Betty, who picked up most of the gossip from the other servants. I say 'almost calm' because even I was aware that the staff were having to work harder than ever, cleaning rooms, washing the paintwork, trimming lawn edges and clipping box hedges. Relays of boys trotted from the vegetable garden to the back door of the kitchen with baskets of carrots, white turnips, new pota- toes, radishes, spring onions, salsify, artichokes, sage, thyme. The appetite of the house seemed endless, but Betty said this was all just practising. They were making sure they had the new recipes right.

'But what are they celebrating?' I asked Betty.

She shrugged. Sir Herbert was a law unto himself. When we took the children down on Friday evening, he was still away. Stephen was there, talking to his sister. Soon afterwards Celia came across to me.

'Miss Lock, my trees simply will not come right. Do look.'

Stephen gave me a glance and a nod of approval. We bent over the sketch, heads together.

'Will you be in the schoolroom around midnight?' she said, under her breath. 'Will Betty have gone to bed by then?'

'Yes, usually.'

'I've thought of a way, only . . . You see, they look like cabbages and I promise you I've tried so hard.'

This for the benefit of Mrs Beedle, who was coming over to look. The three of us pored over Celia's mediocre landscape until it was time for the family to go in to dinner. Betty was tired and went to bed early. I waited in the schoolroom with *Gallic Wars* and a single candle, listening to the stable clock striking the hours. Celia arrived soon after midnight, dragging a blanket-wrapped bundle.

'What's that?' I said.

'Some things to make you invisible.'

When I undid the blanket a tangle of clothes flopped out: plain brown jacket, tweed cap, coarse cotton shirt, red neckcloth, corduroy breeches, gaiters and a pair of that hybrid form of footwear known as high-lows, too high for a shoe and too low for a boot.

'Boys' clothes. It's the next best thing to being invisible. Boys go everywhere and nobody gives them a second glance.'

'I can't wear these. It's not decent.'

'Why not? Women in Shakespeare are always dressing up as boys.'

I picked up the breeches carefully.

'They're clean,' she said. 'I saw to that.'

'Where did you get them?'

'My grandmother collects old clothes from the household for the vicar to give to the poor. She was pleased when I offered to help her. Do the high-lows fit?'

I slipped my feet into them. They did, more or less. Somehow the touch of the leather against my stockings made the idea more thinkable, as if the clothes brought a different identity. 'Very well,' I said. 'I'll try it.'

She put her arms round me and kissed me on the forehead. 'Oh, you brave darling. You're saving my life, you know that?'

I turned away, not wanting to encourage her dramatics.

'You'll go tomorrow morning, early? There'll be a reply for me, I know. Leave a flower on the bench again when you get back, and I'll find an occasion for you to give the letter to me.'

**I** got up at four in the morning and puzzled my way into the boys' clothes by the first grey light of the day, not daring to light a candle in case the light or smell of it penetrated to the maids' rooms downstairs. It took time because my fingers were shaking, but I managed at last to work out the buttons and to pin my hair up under the cap so tightly that it dragged at my scalp. I slid my arms into the sleeves of the brown jacket and put my latest report to Blackstone into a pocket.

When I took my first steps across the courtyard, the feeling was so exposed and indecent that I felt as if the eyes of a whole outraged world were staring at me. I missed the gentle movement of skirt hems against my ankles, the soft folds of petticoats. The roughness of breeches against my thighs seemed an assault on my softest and most secret parts. The high-lows were a little too large, so, once through the archway and at the point where the drive divided, I sat down on the bank, plucked handfuls of grass and used it to pad them out so that my feet didn't slip round so much. After that, walking became easier. I learned to bend my knees and swing my legs less stiffly.

It was full light when I arrived at the Silver Horseshoe. I waited by the gate until I saw Amos Legge coming out of one of the loose boxes.

'Good morning, sir. Any horses to hold?' I'd been practising my boy's voice as I walked along. A hoarse mumble seemed to work better than a boyish treble. He turned round.

'You'd best ask . . . Well, I'll be dankered. It issun May Day, is it?'

'May Day?'

'When the maids dress up for a lark,' he said. 'None of them made as good a lad as you, though. I thought it was in your mind, only I didn't know you'd do it. I'll go and get the tack on her.'

'Tack?'

All I'd intended was to give him my letter for Blackstone, collect Celia's reply and go. Before I could explain that a big, red-faced man came up to us.

'Who's that, Legge?'

'Lad come to ride the new mare, Mr Coleman. Recommended especial by the owner.'

The man gave me a quick glance, then nodded and walked away.

'Ride Rancie?' I said.

'That's what you came here to do, isn't it?'

In a daze, I followed him to her loose box and helped him tack up. When he led Rancie out to the yard with me following, some of the lads were already mounting. I watched as they faced inwards to the horse and crooked a knee so that a groom could take them by the lower leg and throw them up into the saddle. When it was my turn, my legs were trembling so much that Amos must have felt it, but he gave no sign. Amos helped my toes into the stirrups and my hands to gather up the reins, and stood watching as the string of six of us walked out of the yard, Rancie and I at the rear. It felt oddly unsafe at first to be riding astride instead of sidesaddle, but the mare's pace was so smooth that after a half-mile or so I wondered why anybody should ever ride any other way.

Oh gods, we're cantering. Cantering, then galloping. Rancie stretched out, mane flying. I bent forward as the other boys were doing, the whole world a blur of green and blue and a pounding of hoofs. It was the memorial to my father that the wretched ceremony by the grave in Calais had not been, this flying into the morning light, this certainty that in spite of everything it was worth going on living and breathing.

For a few minutes fear, confusion and even grief itself were swept away in the sunlight and the rush of cool morning air against my face. I hardly needed to touch the rein because Rancie seemed responsive to my very thoughts. When the others drew up panting at the end of the gallop, her breath was coming as lightly as at the beginning. We turned back to the stables in a line, some of the horses jogging and fidgeting from excitement, but Rancie walking calmly like the lady she was.

Amos was waiting outside the gate, looking down the lane for us. He walked alongside as we came back into the yard and caught me as I slid down from the saddle. 'Best get her inside her box quickly, with all this bother going on.'

The stableyard was in confusion. A large travelling carriage had arrived. The nearside front wheel was off and leaning against the drinking trough, its iron rim half torn away and several spokes broken.

'What happened?' I asked Amos as we went across the yard.

'Hit a tree a mile up the road. Driving too fast, he was, and . . .'

He went on telling me, but I wasn't listening because I'd noticed something on the door of the coach. An empty oval shape, framed with a wreath of gold leaves, waiting for a coat of arms to go inside it.

'What's the trouble, lad?'

I suppose I must have stopped dead. Amos pushed me gently by the shoulder. Once the half-door of the loose box had closed on us, he was all concern. 'You look right dazed, miss. Are you not feeling well?'

'Mr Legge, whom does the carriage belong to?'

'Two gentlemen from London, wanting to get to the hall. The fat one's in a right miff because there's nobody to get the wheel fettled. The guvnor's sent a boy galloping for the wheelwright.'

'Is he a very fat man, like a toad?'

'If a toad could wear breeches and swear the air blue, yes, he is. You know him, miss?'

'I think I might.' I was sure of it, cold and trembling at the thought of being so near him again. 'I don't want him to see me. Where is he?'

'In the guvnor's office, last I saw. He was trying to convince the guvnor to take a wheel off one of his own carriages to put on the travelling coach. The guvnor offered him the use of his best barouche and horses instead and said he'd send the coach up to the hall later, but that wouldn't answer. It's the travelling coach or nothing.'

'So he could be here for hours.'

And me trapped in the loose box in my boys' clothes, with Betty and the rest wondering what had become of me, probably being found out and dismissed. All the time, Amos Legge was untacking Rancie.

'I'll have a look for you, while I take this over. If he's still going on at the guvnor, you can slip out like an eel in mud and he won't notice.'

He left with the saddle and bridle and I cowered back into the dark corner by the manger. He'd mentioned two gentlemen and I assumed the other one was the man who called himself Trumper. I feared him too, but not nearly as much as the fat man.

There was still a lot of noise and activity going on in the yard. Amos seemed to have been gone for a long time. I'd almost decided to make a run for it, when the square of sunlight above the half-door was obscured by a figure in silhouette. 'Mr Legge, thank good—' Then I shut my mouth because the person looking over the door wasn't Amos.

'Well, well, well,' he said. 'Why are you hiding in there, boy?' Then he slid open the bolt on the half-door and walked inside the box.

The voice was a high drawl. As he turned and the sunlight came on him I knew that I'd never seen him before. There was no doubt, though, that he was one of the two gentlemen just arrived from London. He walked delicately into the rustling straw, looking as if he'd just stepped off the pavement of Regent Street. He wore a plum-coloured coat, a waistcoat in plum and silver stripes, breeches of finest buckskin and beautiful boots of chestnut leather. He was about my age, soft and plump. His eyes were pale blue and protruding, his expression vacant, but amiable enough. As he waited for an answer from me, he reached into a pocket and brought out a round gold box. He opened it, drew off a glove, ran his little finger round the contents of the box and applied it delicately to his rather full lips. Lip salve.

'What's the trouble, boy? Lost your voice, have you?'

Rancie turned her head to see if he had a titbit for her. He stroked her nose cautiously, but his eyes never left me.

'What are you hiding from? Have you been naughty? Threatened you with a birching on the seat of your little pants, have they?'

His affected lisp made it 'thweatened'. There was such a gloating in his voice that I was sure he'd discovered my secret and knew I was no boy. In my shame and confusion, I thought he was taunting me. There was a strange greed in the pale eyes. I turned away, trying to cram myself into the dark corner, but he stepped towards me. His hand slid over my haunches, then round towards my belly. I opened my mouth to scream and closed it again, unwillingly gulping in the smell of him: bay-leaf pomade, starched linen, peppermint breath. Then a warmer, earthier smell as Rancie caught my fear, lifted her tail and splatted steaming turds onto the straw. I wriggled away from him and dodged under Rancie's neck, putting her body between him and me. He came round behind her.

'Don't be shy, boy. Don't stand on ceremony.'

He was between me and the door. I took hold of Rancie's mane, wondering if somehow I could manage to clamber up on her back, when a larger shape appeared at the half-door.

'You all right in there, boy?'

Amos Legge, a pitchfork in hand. The word 'boy' that had sounded a slithery thing in the fashion plate's voice was different and reassuring in his. I said 'no', trying to make it sound masculine and gruff, but the fashion plate's high drawl cut across me, speaking to Amos.

'He's been a naughty boy and I'm dealing with him. Go away.'

Amos took no notice. He slid back the bolt and walked in, giving the fashion plate a considered look. He said or did nothing threatening, but the size and assurance of him was enough. Fashion plate took a step away from me and his voice was less confident.

'Go away. You can come in and clear up later.'

'Best do it now, sir.'

Amos picked up Rancie's droppings with the pitchfork. In the process he let some fall on the toe of fashion plate's polished boot.

The man let out a howl. 'You clumsy oaf!'

'I'm sorry, sir. Mucky places, stables.'

Fashion plate opened his mouth, then looked up at Amos and decided not to say anything. He pushed past us to the door and went.

'You all right, miss?' Amos said.

I nodded, not trusting my voice.

'You'd best be off, miss. You just walk along with me as far as the midden and no one will take any notice.'

We went side by side across the yard, Amos carrying the bundle of soiled straw on his pitchfork. Most of the people in the yard were fussing round the travelling coach and took no notice of us. There was no sign of the fat man. The muck heap was right alongside the gate.

'Off you go then,' Amos said. 'If you're in any trouble, you get word to me, look. And here's your letters—'

He took a slim bundle out of his pocket and slid it into mine. Until then, I'd forgotten, in my fear and distress, the reason for being there.

'Here's another one for the post,' I said, almost dropping it in my haste to hand it over and be gone.

I covered the first half-mile or so at a pace between a stumbling run and a walk, fearful all the time of hearing shouts or horses' hoofs behind me. Fashion plate would surely tell the fat man about the woman in disguise, and if the fat man guessed who she was . . .

I know the fear wasn't reasonable. Perhaps it should have occurred to me that fashion plate had hardly cut a noble picture in the loose box so might not be eager to talk about it. The fact was, I credited the fat man with almost demonic powers and wanted to get as far away from him as I could. A stitch stabbed at my ribs, but I would not slow to an ordinary walk until I was on the main road again, within sight of Mandeville Hall. I went up the back road as usual, into the kitchen courtyard and up to my room. The stable clock was striking seven and I was already late for the children's prayers. I put the letters in my bag, changed, did my hair and ran downstairs.

The two boys were already dressed and sitting at the schoolroom table. Betty was brushing Henrietta's hair.

'There's straw on your dress,' Henrietta said.

The child was worse than a whole army of spies. I brushed it off. Betty looked a little disapproving, probably convinced I was a lazy lie-abed. Once prayers had been said, I made amends by volunteering to take the children for their before-breakfast walk on my own. The fact was, I wanted to go to the flower garden to leave my signal for Celia. As they ran around among the flowerbeds, I chose a spray of white sweet peas and wove it into the curlicues of the rustic bench.

After that, I yawned my way through breakfast and the morning session in the schoolroom. Luckily, Saturdays were less formal than the rest of the week and the children were put into pinafores and allowed to do things involving paint or paste. Seeing them happily occupied, I was wondering whether I might sneak upstairs and read my letter when there was a knock on the door. Patrick the footman stood outside.

'Mrs Quivering's compliments, and would Miss Lock kindly go down to the housekeeper's room.'

Betty gave me a look that said, Oh dear, what have you done? and I followed Patrick's black-liveried back down the stairs, almost certain that in the next few minutes I faced dismissal.

Mrs Quivering was sitting at her desk with a pile of papers in front of her. She looked tired and worried, but not especially hostile.

'Miss Lock, it's good of you to come down. I'm sorry to take you away from your pupils.'

Was it sarcasm? If so, there was no sign of it on her face.

'As you may have heard, Miss Lock, we are planning to entertain a large number of people next weekend, a dinner for forty people on Friday and a ball for more than a hundred on Saturday.'

I nodded, not sure if I was supposed to know even as much as that.

'Among other things, there is a deal of writing to be done: place cards, table plan, menus and the like. Mrs Beedle has suggested that you might take on the duty.' She must have mistaken my look of amazement for reluctance and went on, rather impatiently, 'I am sure you could accommodate it with your other duties. Mrs Sims could supervise some of the children's lessons, if necessary.'

Almost overcome by relief and my good luck, I assured her, truthfully, that nothing would give me more pleasure.

'Thank you, Miss Lock. I suggest you start this afternoon. The first thing I want you to do is make a complete and accurate copy of the guest lists here.' She picked up from her desk several pages pinned together. 'Then you may use it to work from when you do the place cards. You understand?'

'Perfectly, Mrs Quivering. I'm delighted to be of use.'

By midafternoon I was sitting by the window in the housekeeper's room, the precious lists on the table in front of me. There were three of them, the longest, some 120 names, consisted of those invited to the ball on the Saturday night. A shorter one listed the 40 guests who would also be at dinner the night before. An even more select group of 20 would be staying at Mandeville Hall for the weekend.

I read through the lists, looking for names I recognised. The house guests included one duke, two lords, four baronets and their ladies, and six Members of Parliament. The duke was eighty years old or so, and I remembered from accounts of Reform Bill debates in the Lords that he had been a bitter opponent of it. The same applied to two of the Members of Parliament, both to my knowledge die-hard Tories of the old school. I'd heard my father talk about them. It was a reasonable guess that the other four, of whom I'd never heard, shared their opinions.

'Have you everything you need, Miss Lock?'

Mrs Quivering came sweeping into the room, followed by her assistant, who was burdened with a bad cold and an armful of bedsheets.

'Yes, thank you, Mrs Quivering.'

I started mixing ink. Mrs Quivering took a bedsheet from the pile in her assistant's arms and spread it out on her table. They were on the far side of the room from me, so I couldn't hear all of their conversation but gathered that some wretch in the laundry room had ironed them with the creases in the wrong places. Then they started talking about other things. I caught 'wheel off' and 'didn't get here till nearly midday' and stopped stirring ink powder so that I could listen more carefully.

'. . . blue room all ready for him, then we have to change it because his man must sleep in the room next to him. So Mr Brighton offers to take the blue room, his valet goes upstairs with the others, and Lord Kilkeel has the oak room, which was . . .' She unfolded another sheet, muffling the end of what she was saying. I looked at the papers I was to copy. A Mr H. Brighton was at the top of the list of guests who would be staying at Mandeville Hall, with Lord Kilkeel just below him. Which was the fat man and which was fashion plate?

'Take them back,' Mrs Quivering said, sighing. 'Tell her she's to do them again in her own time, and I don't care how long she has to stay.' She heaped the sheets back into her assistant's arms. 'Miss Lock, Mrs Beedle says when you do the place cards you must make your s's the English way, not the French way.'

Soon afterwards she went out, leaving me alone with the lists. It was clear to me that I must make not one but two copies, one to stay in Mrs Quivering's office, the other for Mr Blackstone. I was never a tidy worker, not even in my convent days, and got blots on my cuffs, smears on my face, and the top two joints of my pen finger so soaked with ink I thought it must be black to the very bone. I had no time now to register the names I was copying: they were just words to be harvested. Mrs Quivering came back towards evening and seemed to approve of my industry, even showed some concern.

'You'll miss your supper, Miss Lock.'

'I think I should like to finish the lists today, Mrs Quivering.'

The true reason was that I wanted to have a reason not to be there if the children were sent for. The fat man and fashion plate were under Mandeville's roof now and would surely be in the drawing room before dinner. Fashion plate might not recognise the boy from the loose box, but the fat man would surely remember the woman who'd butted him in the stomach. How I'd avoid him for a whole week, I didn't know.

Mrs Quivering was so pleased by my zeal that she had beef sandwiches and a pot of tea sent in. I tried not to get ink on the sandwiches as I ate, then went back to copying. I was near the end of the ball guest list when the door opened. It was Celia, in a flurry of pink silk.

'Betty said you were here. Have you got my letter?'

I'd brought it down with me and had it under the blotter. She went over to the window and read, her hand shaking.

'Oh, thank God.' Her body sagged in a swish of silk and muslin and I think she'd have fallen to the floor if I had not jumped up and caught her. I put her down in my chair.

'What's wrong?' I said.

'Nothing's wrong. Everything's right. Philip will come for me. He'll come to Ascot and be ready for a word from me. Oh, I can't think. You must help me think.'

I had no wish to be an accomplice in an elopement—my life was too tangled already—but I could hardly desert her.

'When will he get to Ascot?'

'Tuesday, he says. Wednesday at the latest. But how shall I get away? If I as much as walk in the garden, somebody notices. And now Mr Brighton's here . . .' She said the name as if she'd bitten into something bad-tasting.

'Mr Brighton?'

'Didn't you see him? Oh, you didn't come down with the children.' She made a face, pushed out her lips and pretended to smear something on them with her little finger. Fashion plate with his lip balm.

'So the fat one is Lord Kilkeel,' I said.

'Yes. Isn't he the most hideous person you've ever seen? He's a great friend of my stepfather's. But tell me, Elizabeth, you're clever, how do I get away without them noticing?'

'If there are a hundred and twenty people coming here for a ball, will anybody notice an elopement?' I said.

'But that means waiting until next weekend—a whole week.'

'Is that so bad?'

'A lot of things may happen in a week. But I'll think about it.' She stood up. 'Philip says I must write to him at Ascot poste restante. I'll decide tomorrow, so you must take the letter on Monday morning.'

I thought, Must I? but didn't argue because I knew I'd go to the stables in any case to send my copies of the lists to Mr Blackstone. Celia was on her way to the door.

'If anybody sees me and asks what I was doing here, say I brought you a message from my grandmother. I think she approves of you. She keeps asking me questions about you.'

'What sort of questions?'

She went without answering.

I finished copying the list and, in the last of the daylight, took the note from Mr Blackstone out from under the blotter and read it.

*My dear Miss Lock,*

*You have done well. Please do your best to communicate with me every day. In particular, be alert for the arrival of a person calling himself Mr Brighton and let me know at once.*

On Sunday afternoon I wrote my reply.

*Dear Mr Blackstone,*

*Mr Brighton arrived Saturday, in the company of Lord Kilkeel. He will be staying until the dinner and ball next weekend. I enclose lists of the guests at the dinner and ball, and also of the house guests. I hope you will consider that I have earned the right to ask why you wish to know about Mr Brighton and how it concerns my father's death. What is Lord Kilkeel's part in it?*

I wrapped it up with the lists and addressed it.

That same afternoon Celia came into the flower garden when Betty and I were there with the children. She'd brought scissors and a trug with her, to cut some sweet peas for her dressing table. When Betty wasn't looking, she slid a letter out of the trug and into my hands.

'I've taken your advice. I'm telling him to come for me on Saturday.'

When she'd gone, I watched the children and worried. It was wrong that Celia should depend on me for advice in something so important. I wondered whether she really knew her own mind. I supposed I should have to speak seriously to her but did not look forward to it with any pleasure. Betty said she was happy to look after the children while I went back to my other work. Now that the lists were done, I turned to a stack of place cards that Mrs Quivering had set out for me. They gave me the excuse for missing the children's visit to the drawing room again and a close-quarters encounter with Kilkeel and Brighton.

On Monday morning I woke with my eyes still tired from all that penmanship, body stiff and weary after an uneasy night. I fumbled in the half-dark with the buttons and buckles of my boys' clothes, hating them for the memory of Mr Brighton's hands. No ride on Rancie this morning. The delight of that had been lost in what followed it and I had more serious things to do. I hurried down the backstairs and across the courtyard, where I came to the drive and took the turning for the back road. Rain threatened. About a hundred yards down, to the right of the road, was the big lightning-scarred oak tree. I passed the tree and had my back to it when a voice came from the other side of the trunk.

'Good morning, Miss Lock'.

A woman's voice. An elderly voice. Even before I turned round I knew whom I'd see. She'd come out from behind the tree and was standing there dressed exactly as she always was, in her black dress and black-and-white widow's cap, ebony walking cane in her hand. She stood where she was, clearly expecting me to walk towards her. I did.

'Well, aren't you going to take off your cap to me?'

Confused, I snatched off my boys' cap. My face, my whole body felt as red as hot lava while her cool, old eyes took in everything about me.

'I wondered where those clothes had got to,' she said. 'Where are you going so early, if I might ask?'

I didn't answer, conscious of the two letters padding out my pockets and sure she was aware of them too.

'It's going to rain,' she said. 'You are likely to get wet before you reach the Silver Horseshoe, so I hope you have those papers well wrapped up. It would be a pity if they were spoilt, after all your careful copying.'

'Oh.' I was numb, expecting instant dismissal or even arrest.

'So you had better hurry, hadn't you?' she said.

'Umm?'

She gave a sliver of a smile at my astonishment. 'May I ask for whom you are spying? Is it the Prime Minister? I wrote to him and to the Home Secretary. I was afraid that they'd taken no notice of me, but it seems one of them has after all.' Then, when I didn't answer, 'Well, it's no matter and I'm sure it is your duty not to tell me. I did not know that they used women. Very sensible of them.'

'You mean . . . ?'

'Only I must impress on you, and you must pass this on to whoever is employing you, action must be taken at once. This nonsense has gone quite far enough, and it must stop before somebody dies.'

'Somebody has already died,' I said.

'All the more reason to stop it then. What are you waiting for? Hurry!'

There was a letter for Celia at the stables that Monday morning, but nothing from Mr Blackstone. On Tuesday, when Mrs Beedle came up to see the children at their lessons, she gave not the slightest sign that she regarded me as anything but the governess.

'I notice that you haven't been coming down with the children, Miss Lock.'

'I'm sorry, ma'am, but there is a great deal to do for Mrs Quivering.'

In fact, the place cards were all written and she probably knew that, but she gave me a nod and corrected a spelling mistake on James's slate.

On Wednesday morning I made my usual journey to the livery stables, but there was no sign of her. There were two letters that day, one for Celia and a thinner one for me. I opened it on the journey back:

*You have done well, Miss Lock. Your duties are at an end. You need not communicate with me any further. I shall see you again when this affair is over, or provide for you as best I can.*

I crumpled it in my hand, furious. So Blackstone thought I could be dismissed with a pat on the head, like an unwanted hound.

Just one phrase of his note interested me: *when this affair is over . . .* It added to the sense I had of things moving towards a crisis. It increased all through the day as house guests began arriving in advance of the weekend. Every hour brought another grand carriage trotting up the drive and the children wouldn't settle and kept jumping up to look at them. It was a relief when Mrs Quivering summoned me downstairs again.

'Miss Lock, do you understand music?'

She had a new pile of papers on her desk and a more than usually worried expression.

'Understand?'

'There are musicians arriving tomorrow who, it seems, must have parts copied for them.'

'Will they not bring their own music?'

'It is something newly written. Sir Herbert ordered it from some great composer in London and is in a terrible passion . . . I mean, is seriously inconvenienced because the person delivered it late and with the individual parts not written out.'

'I'll do it gladly,' I said, meaning it.

It was just the excuse I needed for keeping behind the scenes on the servants' side of the house for the next two evenings. I'd often done the same service for my father's friends, so it was a link too with my old life.

She dumped the score on my desk and left me to look at it. A few minutes were enough to show that Sir Herbert's 'great' composer was a competent hack at best. The piece was headed *Welcome Home* and came in three parts: a long instrumental introduction, scored for woodwind, two trumpets and a side drum; then a vocal section for woodwind, strings, baritone and high tenor, with pinchbeck words about past glories and future triumphs, followed by an instrumental coda with so much work for the trumpets that I hoped they'd demand an extra fee. I wondered if Mrs Beedle had proposed me for the copying work and, if so, what I was expected to gain from it. As the afternoon went on, I guessed that it had nothing to do with the music, but very much to do with keeping me in a convenient place for spying. Everything in a household, from kitchen maids with hysterics to guests mislaying their toothbrushes, came to the housekeeper's room.

There was one particular incident that afternoon. The assistant housekeeper came into the room and whispered something to Mrs Quivering, who followed her out to the corridor. She left the door half-open and I saw one of the under footmen leaning against the wall, pale-faced, with tears running down his cheeks. His name was Simon and he was fourteen years old, tall for his age but childish in his ways. Mrs Quivering gave him a handkerchief to mop his eyes and listened with bent head to what he was saying. I couldn't hear him, but her voice carried better.

'It is not your fault, Simon, but you must not talk about it. While he is here, you will work in the kitchen, then we'll see.'

Her assistant led the boy away and she came back into the room, heaving a sigh. Soon after that, the butler came in. They carried on a conversation in low voices with Mrs Quivering doing most of the talking. 'I will not tolerate it, Mr Hall. The servants are under our protection. A word must be said.'

'He won't take it well.'

'I am almost past caring how he takes it. I had Abigail in tears this morning too. She said Lord Kilkeel swore at her most vilely when he found her in his room. She'd gone in there to clean and make the bed, and he told her nobody was to set foot in there, for any reason, without his express permission. The poor girl was so terrified she's been quite useless since. And now the other one and Simon. If you won't speak to him about the two of them, then I shall.'

Towards the end of the afternoon, I grew tired of having to draw musical staves with Mrs Quivering's knobble-edged ruler and went up to the schoolroom for a better one. I found Charles and James arguing, Henrietta sulking and Betty so worn out with having to cope with them on her own that it was the least I could do to give her an hour's relief by taking them for a walk in the flower garden.

'Celia? Celia, where are you?'

Stephen's voice came from the other side of the hedge. Henrietta stopped. I whispered to her to go on, but she put her eye to the hedge.

'He's with Mr Brighton,' she said in a loud whisper.

I caught Henrietta by the arm and fairly dragged her to the safety of a little ornamental orchard behind the flower garden, with the boys following. It was a pleasant acre of old apple and pear trees with a thatched wooden summerhouse in the middle. Once we were safely there, I encouraged the children to play hide-and-seek. Soon they were absorbed in their game and I sat on the bench in the summerhouse, still uneasy at having come so close to Mr Brighton, even more so in case Kilkeel came to join him.

'Elizabeth.' Celia's whisper, from behind me. I spun round. One alarmed eye and a swath of red-gold hair showed in a gap between the planks that made up the back wall of the summerhouse.

'Miss Mandeville, what are you doing there? Your brother's looking for you.'

'I know. Would you please keep the children here long enough for them to get tired of looking for me.'

'Why?'

'Because my stepfather wants me to be pleasant to Mr Brighton.' She said the name with such scorn and anger that I half expected it to scorch the planks between us.

'But why should you be . . .?' I was puzzled. She had no reason, as far as I knew, to share my abhorrence of the man.

'He's the reason why Philip must take me away.'

'You mean your stepfather wants you to marry that . . .'

'Shh. Yes.'

My voice must have risen in surprise. Luckily, it was masked by Henrietta's shriek of triumph as she discovered James hiding behind a pear tree. 'My turn to hide! My turn to hide!'

'I've been trying to keep away from him all afternoon,' Celia whispered. 'He must surely get tired soon.'

Henrietta plunged round among the trees, looking for a hiding place. Then she came running towards the summerhouse.

'No, don't let her,' Celia hissed through the planks.

I stood up, but too late.

Henrietta ran behind the summerhouse. 'I've found Celia. I've found Celia.'

'Go away, you little pest.'

But Henrietta's voice must have carried over the hedges. Stephen called, 'Celia?' Two pairs of footsteps sounded on the gravel path, one quick, one slow and heavy.

'Go to them,' Celia said. 'Tell them she's lying and I'm not here.'

By then I was in a fair panic myself. 'I can't. Mr Brighton saw me at the stables dressed as a boy. Supposing he guesses?'

A gasp from behind the planks, then Stephen appeared at the gap in the hedge. I sat down again, curling into the darkest corner of the summerhouse.

'Celia, are you there?' he called.

Celia came out from behind the summerhouse looking far cooler than I'd expected.

'Celia, where have you been? We've been looking for you.'

'Here, with the children,' Celia said. 'But Henrietta's made herself overexcited running about. I'm taking her back to the house.' She took a firm grip of her half-sister's hand and began walking towards the hedge. She was almost there when Mr Brighton arrived, flushed of face but gorgeously dressed in a pale green cutaway coat with a green-and-pink-striped waistcoat. He stood staring at Celia like an actor unsure of his cue. Anything less like an ardent suitor I'd never seen.

'Charles, James, come here,' Celia said, ignoring him entirely.

She collected the boys and shepherded the three children straight past Mr Brighton as if he were no more than another apple tree. When they'd disappeared, he prodded his walking cane into the grass a few times with a vacant look, then his hand went to the pocket in his coat-tail, the gold box came out and his little finger carefully applied pink balm to his full lower lip. He seemed lost. Stephen had to escort him away in the end, much as Celia had done with the children.

I stayed in the summerhouse, surprised by her resourcefulness and weak with relief at not having come face to face with Mr Brighton. Something about him was nagging at my mind—when I saw the vacant expression on his face, a kind of half-recognition had come to me, as if I'd seen that look before. I remained there for some time. It was cool and restful. I think I must have fallen into a half doze, because I didn't hear the footsteps coming back on the gravel path until they were almost at the hedge. I hoped it was simply a guest taking a stroll and started to stand up, intending to say a polite good afternoon and leave. But it wasn't a guest. Stephen Mandeville was standing in front of me.

'Miss Lock, I was hoping you'd still be here. No, please, sit down.'

So he'd seen me after all. He seemed weary, dark hair disordered. I waited, heart thumping. It was in my mind that Mr Brighton might have told him about seeing me at the stables.

'I'm very glad to find you on good terms with my sister,' he said. His voice was low and gentle, no hint of accusation in it.

'Miss Mandeville is very kind. I fear I'm not as much help as I should like to be with her sketching.' I looked down at our feet—his polished brown boots, my serviceable black—just as a governess should. In fact, I was feeling too guilty to meet his eyes. Here he was, showing concern for a sister, and I was helping her deceive him.

'My sister knows no more about sketching than my spaniel does, and cares even less.'

'Oh.'

'I'm not blaming you, Miss Lock. I suggested you should make a friend of Celia, after all. But we've always been close and I sense sometimes when things are not well with her. I hope I'm wrong, but I think Celia may be contemplating a step that might be very harmful for her.'

'Harmful?'

'A young woman's reputation is easily harmed. My sister is the most warm-hearted girl in the world but without much forethought.'

'Then I'll be frank as well,' I said. I looked him in the eyes now, not even trying to talk like a governess but doing my best for both of them. 'The most important decision a woman makes is whom she'll marry. Shouldn't she follow her own wishes?'

'It's not always as simple as that, is it, Miss Lock?' He paused. 'I'm not asking you to betray a confidence. I can only hope if you knew that Celia were on the point of doing something really unwise, you'd give a hint to me. In that case, I might be able to convince her to draw back before things went too far and came to other ears.'

The meaning was plain—Sir Herbert's ears. 'I understand.'

He gave me a brief nod, as if something important had been agreed, and walked away through the gap in the hedge.

I waited in the summerhouse until I thought family and guests would be dressing for dinner, then slipped in at the side entrance and returned to my copying. Near midnight, Mrs Quivering found me there and insisted I must go to bed. Crotchets and quavers danced behind my eyes all night and by six o'clock in the morning I was back at work. Mrs Quivering rewarded me with a cup of chocolate and warm sweet rolls for breakfast. 'Just like Lady Mandeville has. Shall we be ready in time? The musicians are supposed to be arriving by midday.'

Soon after midday, she put her head round the door. 'They've arrived and they're eating. Then they want to start rehearsing in the damask drawing room.'

'I'm just finishing. I'll take them in.'

I finished the page and carried the whole pile of parts to the damask drawing room. It was one of the largest and most pleasant rooms in the house, with blue damask curtains and upholstery and a plaster ceiling with a design of musical instruments. When I arrived the musicians were trickling in. I asked a flautist where I might find their director.

'Just coming in, ma'am.' A dapper little figure came through the doorway, dark hair shining in the sun. 'Mr Suter,' the flautist started saying, 'there's a lady—'

But he got no further because Daniel Suter and I were embracing like long-lost sister and brother and my carefully copied parts had gone flying all over the carpet. Indecorous, certainly, but he had been part of my life for as long as I could remember and was dearer to me than almost all of my relatives by blood.

'What a miracle,' I said, when at last I got my breath back. 'What a coincidence.'

'Miraculous I may be, child, but I disdain coincidence. Kennedy gave me your message two days ago. I'd been in France until then.'

'But how did you manage to be here with the orchestra?'

'An acquaintance of mine had accepted, but was more than happy to pass on the honour when I helped him to three days of more congenial work.' Then his smile faded. 'Forgive me, child, running on like this. Your father . . .'

'I want so much to talk to you.'

'And I to you, child. But what are you doing here?'

I knelt down and began gathering the scattered parts. 'I'm the governess. I can't tell you now. May we meet later?'

'Later, when I've come all this way to find you? Not at all.'

'But your rehearsal . . .' I handed him the score.

He looked through the first few pages, eyebrows raised. They came together as his forehead pinched in artistic pain, rose again in amusement as he flipped to the last few pages. 'Ah, child, the sacrifice I have made for you.' He tossed the score across the room to one of the other musicians, who caught it neatly. 'Take them through it,' he said. 'Sir Herbert informs me that he has no liking for pianissimo—or indeed any other fancy foreign issimo—so kindly keep that in mind.'

Daniel took the rest of the parts from me and dumped them on the pianoforte. 'Now, my dear lady, let us wander in the garden.'

'People might see us.'

'Am I such a disgrace?'

'Please be serious. I should be dismissed if I were seen walking with you.'

'Very well, we shall hide ourselves among the vegetables.'

Half a dozen gardeners were at work behind the warm brick walls when we got to the vegetable garden, but they hardly looked up from their hoeing. Daniel Suter offered me his arm.

'My dear, why did you run away? All of your father's friends will help you. There was no need for this servitude.'

'I want to know who killed my father.'

'What have they told you?'

'They? Nobody's told me anything, except one man, and I don't know how far to believe him.'

'Who?'

'A man who calls himself Mr Blackstone.'

I felt his arm go tense under mine. We'd come to the end of our path, facing the wall, and had to choose right or left. There were beans growing on strings up the wall, their red and white flowers just opening, and fat furry bees blundering round them. Daniel stood, apparently staring at the bees, but I guessed he was not seeing them.

'So what do you know?' I asked him.

'Child, please leave it be. I'd give my own life, if I could, to bring your father back to you. But since I can't . . .'

'Since you can't, at least do this for him. You know very well he wasn't killed in a duel, don't you?'

He gave the faintest of nods.

'What else do you know?' I said.

'Very little. He'd been dead two weeks before I even heard about it. A few days after he left Paris, I went to Lyons. Somebody wrote to me there . . .'

'Who?'

'A friend.' He mentioned a name that meant nothing to me. 'He said he'd been shot, no more.'

We started walking again, turning left between beds of lettuces. I told him everything that had happened to me. When I came to how I was almost carried off by Lord Kilkeel and Mr Trumper, he said, 'Damn them!'

'You know them?'

'The man Trumper, I think, yes. But go on.'

It took us three complete tours of the garden. I stopped before I came to Mr Brighton's arrival and the incident in the loose box. I couldn't quite bring myself to talk about that.

'So Blackstone sent you here?' he said at the end.

'Yes.'

'He had no right.'

'He had my father's ring.' I brought it out, untied the ribbon and put it into his hand. He held it for a while, then gave it back to me. 'He wears a ring like it. Who is he? Did he have some kind of power over my father?'

'No.' He sounded angry; then, more gently, 'But Blackstone is a man involved in many wild schemes, always has been. I think your father may unwittingly have been caught up in one of them.'

'What?'

'Child, if I had the slightest idea, I'd have dragged your father back to England. But how could any of us tell? It seemed no more than a joke.'

'He talked about a joke in his letter, then the quote from Shelley about princes. I couldn't understand it, for a long time. Only I think I do now. There was somebody in Paris, wasn't there? Somebody you were laughing at?'

'Yes.' He said it reluctantly, head bowed.

'That person, I think he's here now, in this house.'

'What?' His head came up.

'He's the reason Mr Blackstone wants me to spy. I think I know now why my father was killed. I knew yesterday.' When I'd seen Mr Brighton in the orchard, the look on his face, his whole posture, had gathered so many threads together. Daniel's large dark eyes were fixed on mine. He took my right hand between both of his.

'Child, you are coming with me now, back to London. We shall go to the stables and steal a horse if necessary.'

'I don't believe I'm in danger. Another person may be.'

'Why did you want to find me, if you won't let me care for you?'

'I wanted to know what happened when you were with my father in Paris. But I believe I've guessed most of it now. There are two other things I need you to do for me: look at a picture and look at a person.'

'What?' His eyebrows went up to his hairline.

'The picture is to the left of the big drawing-room door,' I said. 'The person is an honoured guest and will probably be sitting close to Sir Herbert at dinner. If I am right, you'll have seen him before.'

'We are to play quartets to them after dinner. If I do this, will you come back to London with me?'

'After the weekend, yes.' Whatever happened, I could not desert Celia until either I'd talked her out of elopement or she was safely in the arms of her Philip. I gave his hand a squeeze. 'I'll leave first. Will you meet me here tonight, after you've played your quartets?'

For reply, he hummed a few bars from *Figaro* about meeting in the garden, but his dark eyes were miserable.

Back in the schoolroom, Betty was mending a pinafore. 'Where did you get to? Miss Mandeville came looking for you. She said to tell you she'd be on the terrace.'

I found her sitting alone on a bench by a statue of Diana.

'Where's Mr Brighton?' I said.

'Playing billiards with Stephen.' She stuck out her lower lip, moistened her finger on it and dabbed at an imaginary billiard cue. 'How could anybody think I'd marry such a rag doll of a man?'

'Your brother spoke to me about you,' I said. 'He thinks you might be on the point of doing something unwise.'

'You didn't tell him? Surely you didn't.' She gripped my arm.

'No, I didn't. He said you were close.'

'We were. Until this.'

It was no more than a murmur. I thought of Tom and how he'd feel if I were to elope without telling him. 'I do believe he cares about you,' I said. 'Perhaps if you were to make him understand how totally opposed you are to Mr Brighton . . .'

'No. Stephen does care for me, but he doesn't understand. And I think he's scared of my stepfather.'

'He did not strike me as a person easily scared.'

'Sir Herbert bought off his IOUs to get him out of prison. He could use them to put him back, if he wanted. You *mustn't* tell him, Elizabeth.'

'Why did you want to see me?' I asked.

'Philip is coming for me on Saturday night, at nine o'clock. He'll have a carriage waiting on the back road. I want you to come with me as far as the carriage. I don't know my way down the back road and I'll have things to carry. And we must be so much more careful now, if Stephen suspects.' Her fingers picked nervously at her dress.

'It's a serious decision to make, leaving your family,' I said.

'Do you think I don't know that? I'll probably never see my mother again, or Stephen, or Betty.' Tears ran down her cheeks.

'Perhaps if you were to speak to your mother . . .'

'What good would that do? She's terrified of my stepfather too, surely you've seen that. I dread to think what he'll do to her after I've gone.'

'He could hardly blame her.'

'He will. But she chose to marry him and she'll always be unhappy now, whatever happens. Does that mean I must waste my life too?'

'So you won't speak to either of them?'

'No. If I spoke to anybody it might be my grandmother, but . . .'

'Perhaps you should.'

'No, I've made my choice and I choose Philip.'

'Do you know Philip well?' I cared enough for her to hope she wasn't throwing herself away on some worthless man, just to escape.

'Of course I do. A year ago, we were practically engaged.'

'But your stepfather disapproved?'

'No, that's the cruel part of it. Philip and I met at Weymouth last summer. Sir Herbert was prescribed sea bathing for pain in his joints, and Philip's father was there for the bathing too. I think my stepfather approved, as far as he cared at all. It would get me off his hands without having to pay a settlement because Philip's family are very comfortably situated. They have an estate in Buckinghamshire and Philip will inherit a baronetcy, so . . .' She paused for breath.

'So altogether a most suitable match,' I said.

She looked sharply at me. 'The fact is, I love Philip, he adores me and I'd marry him even if he were a pauper.'

'I'm sorry.'

'Only I'm glad he isn't, of course.'

I believed her, both about that and loving him, which was a relief in its way.

'When did your stepfather change his mind?'

'Only in the last month or so.'

'When Mr Brighton came on the scene?'

She nodded. 'It would be treason, wouldn't it?' She asked the question very softly.

'I think so, yes.'

'And my stepfather's trying to drag me into it, for his own ambition. So I've no choice, you see, no choice at all. There are just two days and seven hours to live through and it will be all over. Only there's that terrible dinner to get through first. I know they'll make me sit next to him. I'm glad you'll be there, at least.'

'I? At the dinner?'

'Didn't Mrs Quivering tell you? You're to fill a gap in the table. My grandmother said you were perfectly ladylike and they could put you down at the far end. Why are you looking so scared?'

'He'll recognise me! He can't fail to if we're sitting at the same dinner table!' My panic was about Lord Kilkeel, but she naturally thought it applied to Mr Brighton.

'How can he? There are forty people, remember, and you'll be at the very far end of the table, and in candlelight.'

I hoped she was right. Mrs Beedle had been clever, seizing the chance to provide her spy with a seat at the dinner. I might have tried again to persuade Celia to confide in her, but two of the house guests were approaching from the far side of the terrace.

'Botheration,' Celia said. 'I suppose they're coming to talk to me.'

She rose from the bench to face them while I slipped away.

Mrs Quivering's assistant was in the housekeeper's room, drinking sage tea for her sore throat. 'There's a letter come for you, Miss Lock.' She handed over a coarse grey envelope.

I went into the corridor and opened it.

*Miss Lane,*

*Ther is a thing I heard about the two gentlemen in the travling coach. I will come when I can and ask for you at the back door.*

*Yours ruspectfully,*

*A. Legge*

If I could, I'd have gone straight to the livery stables to find him, but I was needed back in the schoolroom to superintend the children. At least we were spared taking them down before dinner.

'Lady Mandeville has one of her headaches,' Betty said.

That saved me from having to invent a headache of my own as an excuse. We got the children into their beds by half past eight. When we'd set the schoolroom straight, it was time to keep the appointment with Daniel. The light was fading, the walls of the vegetable garden radiating back the heat of the day. I sat on the edge of the water trough and waited.

'Liberty.' Daniel Suter's voice, from the door in the wall. He came over to me, practically running, tripping on the gravel path.

'Well?' I said.

'You were right, child. Ye gods, what a situation.' He sat down beside me, breathing hard. I'd never seen him discomposed before.

'You recognised somebody here who was in Paris?'

'As you thought, the man they call Mr Brighton.'

My heart jolted. 'And you saw the portrait?' I said.

'Yes. You're right. There is a very strong resemblance.'

'My father saw it. *The dregs of their dull race*—I should have guessed.'

'It wasn't only your father who saw. They were flaunting it. They were a laughing stock among the Parisians. The very waiters would bow to him in jest, only he took it in deadly earnest.'

'Tell me, please, everything that happened in Paris.'

He took a deep breath. 'It was pure good luck meeting your father in Paris. And, as chance would have it, half a dozen of our mutual friends were there, musicians mostly and . . .'

'And?'

'Lodge brothers. We spent the afternoon in each other's company. Your father was in excellent spirits, money in his pocket, looking forward to reaching home and being with you. We talked a lot about you. We all had dinner together and your father asked if there was anywhere we might have a hand or two of cards, simply for amusement.'

'I know. Money never stayed in his pockets for very long.'

'This time he was determined it should. We went to a place I knew, off the Champs Elysées. He did not intend to play for high stakes, but . . .'

'He won a horse.'

'Indeed he did, from some old marquis. But how did you know that?'

'From the same person who told me you were together in Paris. So how does Mr Brighton come into the story?'

'The table next to ours was playing high. There were about half a dozen of them, all English. They'd been drinking heavily. Mr Brighton was totally drunk and kept yelling out remarks in that terrible high bray of his. At one point, Mr Brighton pushed his chair back suddenly and sent your father's tokens scattering all over the floor.'

'Did my father resent it?'

'No. He had too much good sense to quarrel with a man in drink. We went on playing. It happened a second time and we did the same thing. By the third time, it was obvious that the fool was doing it deliberately.

I said something about taking more care. Mr Brighton went as red as a turkey cock's wattles and said, "Do you know to whom you're speaking, sir?" "A clumsy buffoon, it would appear, sir," I said. Not the most politic speech, but I was annoyed. A man they called Trumper . . .'

'A fair-haired, country-squire kind of man?'

'Yes, the very same oaf who tried to carry you off. Anyway, he seemed to realise that his friend was making an ass of himself and took him into a side room. We finished our hand and left.'

'And nothing was said about a duel?'

'Good heavens, no. It had been an unpleasant few minutes, that's all. We went to supper and stayed up late over our pipes. And there it might have ended if we hadn't been joined by some Frenchmen your father knew. Something they said seemed to amuse your father mightily so we asked him to translate . . .'

He hesitated. A barn owl flew overhead; further off, a fox barked.

'Your father turned to me, pulling a long face. "Daniel," he said, "you are in very serious trouble. In fact, you will be lucky to escape with your head. Have you any notion of the identity of our young friend whom you so grossly insulted?" Well, by then we were near the bottom of the punch bowl and we all began imitating the young ass's bray. "Do you know to whom you're speaking, sir?" Your father sat watching us, grinning over his pipe, until we became tired of it. "Well, Daniel," he said, "my Parisian friends here tell me he goes by the *nom de guerre* of Mr Brighton, but his identity is well known. Young Mr Brighton is none other than . . ." Then he couldn't go on for laughing. I played the farce out, "Don't keep me in suspense," I said. "Who is this gentleman to whom my humble head is forfeit?" And your father, still laughing, replied, "Only the rightful heir to the throne of England, that's all."'

# Chapter Six

'YOU'D GUESSED, hadn't you?' Daniel said. 'Only I've no notion how you did.' His voice was sad at all that laughter gone sour.

'Sir Herbert's desperate to marry him into the family,' I said. 'His daughter's too young, so his stepdaughter has to do, poor thing. She came very near to telling me. Then there was the portrait. As soon as I saw Brighton, he reminded me of somebody. But why should it be poor Princess Charlotte?'

'I've been thinking about that. Do you remember when the princess died?'

'Of course not. I was only two years old.'

He sighed. 'I'd forgotten how young you are, or perhaps how old I am. I do remember. I was in my last year at school. She'd been popular and people mourned her. Then later there were some ugly rumours going round. You're cold?'

I must have shivered. 'The child Henrietta said she was poisoned.'

'Yes, that was part of it. Charlotte was healthy, you see, with the very best of medical attention. She and the baby should not have died.'

'But women do die in childbirth, even healthy ones,' I said.

'So they do. But some years later rumours started that she and her baby had both been poisoned just after the birth.'

'Why would anybody do such a terrible thing?'

'She was Queen Caroline's daughter. In some people's opinion, Caroline was well-nigh a lunatic, certainly an adulteress. Some distinguished persons at court were said to be determined that neither her daughter nor her grandson should ever come to the throne.'

'Did many people believe it?'

'It was a persistent rumour, helped by another unfortunate fact. A few months after Charlotte and her baby son died, the gentleman who'd had charge of the birth, her *accoucheur*, shot himself. He was an honourable man and, so it's said, blamed himself for not foreseeing the plot and preventing their deaths.'

'Daniel, do you believe this?'

'No. I believe their deaths were sheer misfortune. But it seems some people, including Sir Herbert Mandeville, are determined to revive the rumour—with one essential difference. Can you not see it?'

'The baby didn't die after all. Charlotte died, but her baby didn't.'

'And was spirited away by Charlotte's friends and brought up safely on the Continent, until the time came to claim what was rightfully his. It's a fairy tale, a horrible, warped fairy tale. And yet it's what Sir Herbert and Trumper and all the other greedy fools think they can get the country to believe. I'm sorry, Liberty. I'm ranting. But their idiocy has killed your father and could do so much other damage.'

'But why are they doing it?' I said.

'Why do men do most things? Money and power. Sir Herbert and his like have been running the country since the Conqueror. Now they're beginning to see their power stripped away. When they knew the buffoon William was dying and there'd be a mere child on the throne—a girl at that—they decided to take their chance. Put in another king, one beholden to them, and no more nonsense about reform.'

'But even if he were Princess Charlotte's son, why should they suppose people would support him rather than little Vicky? He is hardly Bonnie Prince Charlie, is he?'

Daniel laughed bitterly. 'So-called Bonnie Prince Charlie was a fat, red-faced, drink-sodden wreck, yet men died for him.'

'And my father died because of Mr Brighton?'

'Yes. He must have threatened their plans in some way.'

'But he thought it was all a joke. He said so in his letter. And my father wasn't important. He couldn't have made any difference.'

'It puzzles me, I admit. But he must have known something, otherwise why should they have tried to kidnap you?'

'It was a woman they wanted to know about. Daniel, do please think. There must have been a woman somewhere, those last days in Paris.'

He hesitated.

'There's still something you're not telling me, isn't there?' I said.

'Very well. There was a wine shop on the corner of the street near our hotel. I happened to be walking past and I'm nearly sure he was sitting with a woman. The wine shop was used quite a lot by the local *femmes de la nuit*. Now, don't rush to conclusions. As you know, your father would talk to anybody and . . .' His voice trailed away.

'It might explain something,' I said. 'Supposing there'd been an English girl there, fallen on hard times. He might have promised to bring her home to her family.'

'Yes, he might.' Daniel sounded embarrassed and unhappy. 'But your father was the most open man in the world. If he had decided to help some poor dove out of the gutter, I'm sure he'd have discussed it with us that evening when we were all together.'

'The evening that Amos Legge came to make arrangements for Espérance?'

'Who? Oh, the amiable horse-transporter. Yes. Your father said goodbye next morning in the best of health and spirits. That was the last I saw of him.'

I was crying and sensed he might be near tears too. I felt for his hand. 'Do you think it was Mr Brighton or Trumper who shot him?'

'I simply don't know. You said your father died on Saturday?'

'Yes.'

I could see he was thinking back. 'That's the morning I left for Lyons. I saw both Brighton and Trumper in the street the evening before. In fact, Trumper came striding up to me like a man wanting a quarrel and said, "Where's your friend gone?" I guessed he meant your father and said my friend would be back home in England by now. That didn't seem to please him.'

'They must have known that he'd gone away with the woman.'

'Yes, but Trumper couldn't possibly have got to Calais in time to kill him, however fast he rode.'

'What about the fat man—Lord Kilkeel?' I said.

'To the best of my knowledge, I never saw him in Paris.'

'So he might have been in Calais on the Saturday. He was certainly there three days later.' We lapsed into silence. My brain was tired. 'If you think Charlotte's baby died twenty years ago . . .' I said.

'I do, yes.'

'Then who is Mr Brighton?'

'Take your pick from twenty or more. You understand what I mean?'

'There is certainly no shortage of Hanoverian bastards,' I said. That was common knowledge.

'From his looks, I've no doubt he's one of that stock,' Daniel said.

'And tomorrow, Sir Herbert intends to introduce him to all his friends and supporters as their rightful king. Why else all the preparations? Why else that ridiculous *Welcome Home* piece you're rehearsing?'

'It is indeed an offence in itself. I think you're mostly right, Libby, only it probably won't happen in quite so blatant a way. They'll have their dinner party and ball. Mr Brighton is affable, the likeness unmistakable. Gossip gets back to London, the newspapers pick it up . . .'

'But why should anybody just take their word that he's Princess Charlotte's son?'

'A good question. Do you suppose that's what this whole occasion is about—that they intend to produce something that might be regarded as proof by people who want to believe?'

'Then what should we do?' I said. 'Tell somebody in authority?'

'If I were to go straight up to London and bang on the door of the Home Secretary, would he believe me?' he said. 'Besides . . . There is the question of what Blackstone is doing.'

There was a change in his voice, more guarded.

'You know him well?' I said.

'Quite well, yes.'

'Is Blackstone another *nom de guerre*?'

'I believe not. We've always known him as Alexander Blackstone.'

'We?'

'Your father and the rest of us.' He hesitated, then, 'Liberty, that ring of your father's—did you understand anything by it?'

'Only that it was a favourite of his. He often wore it.'

'He was a Freemason, Liberty, that's what it signifies. So am I; so is

Blackstone. I should not be telling you this, but I think you are owed it.'

'But where's the harm in that? Weren't Haydn and Mozart Masons?'

'Yes, and you're right, there's no harm in it at all. Mostly we're no more than people with a liking for intelligent company who wish to do good rather than harm. But some people will tell you otherwise.'

'That you wish to do harm?'

'That we are revolutionaries. They may not be entirely wrong. Some of the leaders of the Revolution in France and the War of Independence in America were Masons. We believe in equality among men and have no exaggerated respect for kings or princes.'

'A man's a man for a' that.'

'Who taught you that?'

'My father, of course. I am not in the least shocked that you and my father should believe in equality, but I'm at a loss to see what it has to do with Mr Blackstone and Mr Brighton.'

'Because Alexander Blackstone is a revolutionary. As a young man he was put in prison for writing a pamphlet supporting the French Revolution. He came from a good family and had a considerable income, but he's given all his life and fortune to the cause, and I believe now there's precious little of either left. What did you make of him?'

'He's like a black rock with ice on it.'

'You didn't know him in his prime. Neither did I, come to that, but people who did tell me he could have marched ten thousand men on Whitehall by the power of his oratory alone. He was a dangerous man.'

'I think he still is.'

'Perhaps. But he's a sick man now. He's never wavered in his belief that there'll be no end to poverty or injustice here until England has a revolution and we become a republic like the Americans. I think whatever he's doing now is his final desperate attempt, before he runs out of money and strength.'

'But why is he so concerned with Mr Brighton? Why did he make me spy for him?'

'I'm angry with him for that, and I don't know why he is interested. But, believe me, it certainly isn't for any devotion to the House of Hanover.' He sighed. 'Liberty, I'll ask you again. Please leave this and let me take you away.'

'No. Not before Saturday night.'

'Why?'

I wanted to tell him about Celia's elopement. I knew I could trust him, but I'd implied a promise to her. 'There's the question of the horse.'

'What is this about a horse?'

'The one my father won: Espérance. She's in a livery stables near here with Amos Legge. There's a cat as well. I can't just go and leave them.'

He laughed and his arm came round me. 'Then I suppose the horse must come too. Are you able to communicate with this man Legge?'

'Yes.'

'Well, tell him to bring the horse here on Saturday night. I'll stay for the ball and we'll go straight back to London the moment it's over, even if I have to steal somebody's carriage.'

What I'd do in London with a horse, a cat and Amos Legge's expenses to pay, nowhere to live and not a shilling in my purse, was something so far distant that it hardly seemed worth worrying about.

'Very well, I'll tell him,' I said.

Daniel insisted on escorting me all the way back to the kitchen door, although I was afraid one of the other servants might see us together. At the door, he put a hand on my shoulder and said softly, 'Child, do as little as possible tomorrow and Saturday. Stay safe in the schoolroom, if you can. Leave the fools to their folly.'

Something touched my forehead, light as a leaf. It was only after he'd walked away that I realised he'd kissed me.

Friday, July 14. *Le Quatorze Juillet.* I woke up thinking about that, of all things. Forty-eight years ago the people of Paris had stormed the Bastille and the world had changed for ever. It had always been a day of celebration in our household, with Tom and I allowed a glass of watered wine to drink to the Revolution and, as it happened, our own names: Liberty, Fraternity. But today Revolution had a colder feel to it. I got up at about six o'clock. I'd hoped to go early to the stables to see Amos Legge, but Betty had unknowingly ended that plan when I'd got back to the schoolroom the evening before.

'I'm sorry, Miss Lock, but you'll have to get the children up on your own tomorrow. Two of the lady visitors have come without their maids so Mrs Quivering said would I oblige.'

With the house full of guests and the kitchen preparing for the grand dinner in the evening, all the servants were doing two or three times their normal work. This was in spite of the fact that thirty extra maids, waiters and footmen had been brought in from London and Windsor for the occasion. The maids in the room below me were having to sleep two to a bed to make space for them. I roused the children at half past six as usual, but getting them washed and dressed took much longer than when Betty was there. There was only time for a truncated prayer session before breakfast was brought up. Betty arrived as we were finishing it, full of the gossip she'd gathered downstairs.

'You didn't tell me that you're to be at the dinner, Miss Lock.' She was not envious, simply pleased at what she saw as my good fortune. 'What shall you wear?'

'My lavender with the silk fichu, I suppose.'

She looked doubtful. 'Will that do?'

'It will have to. Besides, I'll be right at the end of the table and nobody will notice me,' I said, sincerely hoping that would be the case.

When the children's dinner time came, at half past two, I said I wasn't hungry and would go for a walk outside to clear my head. I was desperate to find a way of communicating with Amos Legge. My idea was to find a boy and give him sixpence to deliver a note asking if Amos could meet me at the bottom of the back road at six o'clock the following morning. Since the stableyard was usually the best place to find a spare boy, I walked across the courtyard and through the archway. The cobbled yard was almost deserted. Not a boy in sight, just a man sitting peacefully on the mounting block, smoking a clay pipe.

'Amos Legge!'

'Good afternoon, miss.' He stood up. 'I asked one of the maids to let you know I was here, but I couldn't tell if she'd heard me right.'

'Just the man I wanted to see. Mr Legge, could you please have Rancie here in the stableyard tomorrow night, after dark?'

'On the move again, are we?'

'I think so. Only there's so much I don't know, where we're going . . .'

'Don't you worry, miss, I'll have her here. Did you get that message I sent you?'

'About the two men in the travelling coach? Yes.'

'That's why I came. I've been turning it over in my mind. I didn't hear about it until after they'd gone, and with the others saying the lad was a bit simple, I didn't quite know what to make of it.'

It was no use trying to hurry him. I suggested we should sit down.

'When I left, they were still waiting for the wheelwright,' I said. 'What happened after that?'

'They got the wheelwright in the end. The two gentlemen were waiting in the guvnor's office. He kept offering them one of his own vehicles to go on up to the Hall, but it was go in the travelling coach or nothing. Anyways, there's this lad helps out in the yard sometimes. They make out he's a gawby, but I reckon he's clever enough when he wants to be. He says they had a woman in there.'

'Where?'

'In the travelling coach. You know how gentlemen's travelling coaches usually have a place under the floorboards, nice and convenient for anything that they might need on a day's journey without having to have the trunks unstrapped? Quite a tidy space in some of them, big enough to take a woman, if she didn't mind curling up a bit.'

'The boy says he saw a woman under the floorboards?'

'Not saw, heard. He reckons he heard a moithering voice calling for help and for somebody to bring her a glass of water.'

'Do you believe him?'

'Can't say whether I believe him or not. But it seemed to me somebody here ought to know about it.'

A groom came into the yard and gave us a curious look.

'I must go,' I said. 'I expect you must, too. Thank you for telling me.'

How seriously should I take his information? Very seriously, I thought. Gawby or not, the lad had impressed Amos. And if Lord Kilkeel and Brighton had a woman imprisoned in the well of the travelling coach, that explained why they'd refused to leave it at the stables. Could this be the woman from my father's letter?

I looked up from the courtyard at the back of Mandeville Hall, a great brick cliff with hundreds of windows. She might well be in there somewhere, among dozens of guests, plus nearly a hundred servants counting the extra ones brought in, so many rooms that a person might spend months there without seeing them all. I might as well try to search an entire town.

As soon as I stepped inside the house, one of the footmen said Mrs Quivering wanted me. I found her in her room.

'There's a note for you from Miss Mandeville.'

She handed me a folded lilac sheet.

*Dear Miss Lock,*

*If you would care to come to my room when you are free, we may plan what you are to wear this evening. There may be some things which I should be happy to lend you.*

I went back to the schoolroom to tell Betty where I was going. She was wide-eyed at my luck. 'You might even be sitting next to a lord who will fall in love with you. Stranger things have happened.'

'In fairy tales. But no, I'm not. I've looked at the table plan. I have a cathedral canon on my left hand and a Mr Disraeli on my right.'

'Who's he?'

'A writer, I believe. I'm nearly sure I read one of his novels once.'

Betty was clearly disappointed for me. I went as confidently as I could manage downstairs and through the door into the family's bedroom corridor. Compared to the last time I'd been there, it was as busy as a beehive on a sunny afternoon. Bells tinkled, maids I'd never seen before ran in and out with armfuls of lace or cans of hot water, voices called from half-open doorways and the sharp smell of frizzled hair mingled with rosewater and lavender. I knocked on Celia's door.

'Come in.' Celia held out her hands to me. 'Oh, Elizabeth, I'm so glad you've come. I'm so scared. Feel—I'm trembling like an aspen.'

I took her hands. Indeed, they were cold and trembling. 'I wish you'd told me more,' I said. The conversation with Daniel had hardened me. I was still sorry for her, but angry at what was going on round her. 'Queen to His Majesty King George the Fifth, was that the idea?'

'The creature's name is Harold, so it would be Harold the Third, wouldn't it? It wasn't my idea, you know that.' She stared back at me.

'How long have you known?'

'About the Harold creature being the rightful king? A month or two. My stepfather told me when we knew King William was going to die.'

'Miss Mandeville, he is not the rightful king at all. It's utter nonsense about Princess Charlotte being poisoned and the baby saved. And even if he were, what is your stepfather doing? If he tries to put this Harold on the throne, it may mean another civil war.'

'But there'll be one anyway. It's happening already. People have been stirred up by agitators so that they aren't content any more. They march and burn things down until they're given votes, then when they've got votes they're not satisfied with that and demand other things . . .'

'Like food for their families. Miss Mandeville, your stepfather's talking nonsense. There won't be a revolution here.'

'That's what they said in France. And little Vicky won't be able to stand up to them because she's a girl and even younger than we are.'

'What about Queen Elizabeth and Queen Anne? In any case, can you see your Bonnie Prince Harold standing up against a revolution?'

'You know very well he's not my Bonnie Prince anything. I find him entirely loathsome. Two days from now I'll be married to Philip, and nobody will be able to do anything about it.'

I realised it was useless to be angry about her political naiveté.

'And that's really the wish of your heart?'

'More than anything in the world. Sit down and I'll show you his letter about meeting me tomorrow.'

'I don't think . . .'

But she was already up and rummaging in a drawer. I settled in a blue armchair and she watched, smiling, as I read. It was brave and loving, with a bedrock of common sense to it as well. As I handed it back, I was annoyed to hear myself giving a sigh of envy. 'Yes, I think your Philip really loves you.'

'Of course he does. Now, where are you and I to meet tomorrow night? Philip will have the coach on the back road from nine o'clock.'

'Let's meet at nine then, in the stableyard. You slip out through the kitchens, into the back courtyard and through the archway.'

'Through the kitchens in *that*?' She laughed and whipped the sheet off a tailor's dummy. Underneath was a shining cloud of white silk and silver embroidery. 'My stepfather chose it in Paris. He insists I wear it.'

'Like a bride.'

'Or a sacrifice,' she said. 'And altogether the worst garment in the world for eloping. I must come up and change first, I suppose. We'll meet here instead. Now, what can I find that's drab-coloured?'

She walked over to a white-and-gilt-painted wardrobe and opened the door on a rainbow of dresses, skirts and bodices. With some trouble we discovered a plain grey dress, a dark gaberdine travelling cloak and the stoutest pair of shoes she owned.

'Now, let's choose a dress for you to wear tonight.' She pulled dress after dress out of the wardrobe, trying each colour against my face. After a while she narrowed the choice to a deep rose damask with silver-grey silk trim, or a moss-green ribbed silk with enough lace on the bodice to have kept Nottingham employed for weeks.

'Which do you prefer, Elizabeth?'

'Either.'

'You must have an opinion.'

She was as shocked by my unconcern as I'd been at her politics. To please her, I opted for the rose damask, as the skirt was less full.

'You must try it on. You're taller than I am.'

I went behind a leather screen in the corner. When I came out feeling awkward in the grandest dress I'd ever worn, she clapped her hands.

'It suits you so much better than me. It's a great thing I'm not jealous.' She looked critically. 'You're too thin for it, though. It hangs awkwardly at the waist. Come here and let me pin it.' She was as deft as a seamstress. 'It's just a bit short and your ankles will show when you walk. Still, you have good ankles and the shoes might have been made for you.'

She laughed, delighting in it like a child dressing a doll. She made me sit down at her dressing table and did my crinkly hair with her own hands, pinning it up to one side with a mother-of-pearl comb of her own. Then she rummaged in her jewel case, brought out a necklace of opals and garnets on a silver chain and clasped it round my neck.

'There, look at you. You're quite a beauty.'

I'd hardly dared glance in the mirror. When I did, I couldn't help gasping. The woman who stared back at me had a Spanish look with her dark hair and eyes and pale skin, set off by the rich rose of the bodice.

'You're crying,' Celia said. 'Why?'

And indeed there was a tear trickling down the cheek of the dark beauty. I wiped it away. 'Because my father will never see me and I'll probably be old before my brother comes home.'

She put a hand on my shoulder. 'Oh, my dear.'

We stayed silent for a while, looking at our faces in the mirror. I said I must go and reached up to unclasp the necklace.

'Keep it as your bridesmaid's present,' she said.

'Bridesmaid?'

'The nearest I'll have to one.'

She took the pins out of the dress and said I'd have to get Betty to help me alter it. While I was changing I remembered something:

'Miss Mandeville . . .'

'Please, call me Celia. After all, I call you Elizabeth.'

'But my name's . . . Celia, do you know if Mr Brighton and Lord Kilkeel brought a maid with them?'

'Maid? Why would they do that? I know there's a French valet. Here, I've found the rose-tinted silk stockings. You must have them.'

She kissed me on the cheek when I left.

Back in the schoolroom, Betty made me try the rose damask on again so that she could pin and tack the alterations, then left me stitching while she took the children downstairs to make their public appearance. When they came back, I ran up the rickety stairs to my own room and changed into the damask dress and the pumps. I had to go down to the mirror in the schoolroom to put the mother-of-pearl comb in my hair and fasten the necklace. Betty gasped when she saw me.

'Oh, Miss Lock, you look quite the lady.'

She bent suddenly and kissed me on the cheek. I kissed her back then ran along the corridor and down the main stairs. I paused at the door to the first-floor landing and put a hand to my chest to steady my breathing. 'I'm still who I am,' I told myself. 'I'm still Liberty.'

But I didn't feel it as I pushed open the door and stepped through.

The chandelier blazed with dozens of candles. More lights flashed up to meet them from the grand hall below: the jewels in the hair of the women, the decorations on the chests of the men, the champagne glasses. From here, the noise their talk made was something between a purr and a low roar. On a dais by the bottom of the staircase a small group of musicians were playing Mozart, with Daniel directing from the violin. A fire blazed in the enormous Gothic fireplace. Alongside, Mr Brighton outblazed the fire, gorgeous in a purple coat and a whole jeweller's window of gold chains and rings. Beside him, Sir Herbert Mandeville looked stiff and statesmanlike in black and white. Lady Mandeville stood next to her husband, her smile as fixed as if it had been cast in plaster of Paris. Celia was talking to an elderly lady in black velvet, her back firmly turned to her stepfather and Mr Brighton. Then I saw Kilkeel, standing in a corner. My nerve almost failed me and I thought I couldn't go down after all.

The scene below me began to change. The noise faded to a quiet buzz. Sir Herbert held out his arm to a woman in purple-and-pink stripes. One of the Garter knights offered his arm to Lady Mandeville. This left Mr Brighton by the fireplace, a vacant grin on his face. Sir Herbert went up to him and said something. Mr Brighton nodded and moved towards Celia without enthusiasm. She kept her back turned.

'Celia.' Sir Herbert's sharp command was loud enough to be heard at the top of the staircase. Celia turned reluctantly, but would not take the smallest step towards Mr Brighton. He had to come across the room to her; her stepfather's brows were a black bar. When, finally, she let her white-gloved fingers rest very lightly on his arm, the whole room seemed to relax in a sigh of relief and Sir Herbert and the striped woman led the way into the dining room. Celia's eyes were everywhere but on her partner, looking desperately all round the room. I realised with guilt that she was looking for me and must have willed her to look up, because just before they went through the door to the dining room, she did and caught my eye. She smiled, then mouthed 'Hurry,' and motioned me, with a flick of a fingertip, to come down.

I came as quickly as I could, still unused to the sway of rich fabric and stiff petticoats round my ankles, and tripped on the bottom stair. A hand came on my arm to steady me. I looked up and there was Mrs Beedle, in black silk as usual. Her only concession to the occasion had been to replace her customary widow's cap with a black velvet turban trimmed with white lace and jet beads. She was frowning. I assumed she was angry with me for being so nearly late and began apologising, but she took no notice and kept her grip on my arm, guiding me to the side of an orange tree in a pot at the bottom of the staircase.

'Miss Lock, something has occurred.' She said it in a low voice. 'You had better go in to dinner as arranged, but as soon as the first couple of courses are over, please make an excuse and meet me in the school-room. You must say you're indisposed, or anything you like.'

'But what . . .?'

She shook her head, forbidding questions, and started to move away. 'I hope you won't let me down.' Then she disappeared through a door behind the orange tree that I hadn't even noticed before.

By now almost everybody had gone through to the dining room. Just one man was waiting, his back to me and his foot tapping impatiently. I hurried towards him, knowing he must be the one obliged to take me in to dinner. When he turned I regret to say I stopped and gawped at him. He was beautiful. The dandyism that was an offence to the eye in Mr Brighton had reached a higher level entirely in him. He wore a claret-coloured cutaway coat and black velvet trousers with broad claret stripes down the outside legs. The fingers of his white kid gloves sparkled with gold rings. Black ringlets cascaded almost to his collar, his face was pale, his lips full and as well shaped as a woman's. He stood poised and conscious of his effect on others, like an actor.

'Miss Lock? I understand I am to have the privilege of taking you in to dinner.' His voice was languid, with a tinge of annoyance. I thought of my guest list. He certainly was not a cathedral canon.

'Mr Disraeli?' I said.

He was justifiably annoyed at my lateness. I was prepared for that. What took me by surprise was the look in his eyes when he straightened up from the most perfunctory of bows. There was approval there, the kind a man bestows on a pretty woman. I realised he was seeing the dark-haired beauty who'd looked back at me from Celia's mirror. It was a strange feeling, as if that made both of us into actors who could stroll across the stage, arm in arm, knowing our lines and our business.

We'd only just reached our seats at the far end of the table when the bishop was on his feet saying grace. I've sat through sermons shorter than that grace, but at least it gave me a chance to look around, as far as I could with head bowed. The white-clothed table seemed to extend far into the distance. Footmen in black and gold jackets with powdered wigs stood along the walls. Silver candelabra blazed all down the middle of the table. Posies of gardenias and tuberoses alternated with the candles, giving off a scent so sweet that it was almost oppressive.

The air quivered from the candle flames so that the group at the top of the table were little more than a blur. Kilkeel must be up there somewhere, but if I couldn't see him, he probably couldn't see me. Trying to keep the seating plan in mind, I managed to put names to some of the faces around the middle of the table. There were ladies whose political salons were famous, gentlemen whose speeches in the Lords and Commons were respectfully noted by *The Times*.

'. . . keeping our minds humbly obedient to Thy will . . .'

The cathedral canon on my left was echoing every word *sotto voce*. On my right, Mr Disraeli was also looking around. I sensed an increasing tension in him, at odds with his languid dandy air.

'. . . humble gratitude for Thy bountiful gifts. Amen.'

The footmen pushed forward chairs for the ladies to sit down, mine included. A buzz of talk started.

'Have you any notion why we are all here?' said Mr Disraeli.

I stared. I'd expected small talk; caught off-balance by his directness, I was tempted for a moment to be honest with him. I had the strangest feeling of fellowship, but then I reminded myself that he was presumably a friend of Sir Herbert, and that honesty to strangers was a luxury I could no longer afford. I smiled at him, trying to look quizzical. 'Have you?'

'A lady of my acquaintance was most insistent that I should attend.' He glanced towards one of the political salon hostesses. 'She said it would be useful to my career to meet our new monarch as soon as possible.'

'You were expecting to find the Queen here?'

'I believed that was being hinted. I've stolen time from my election campaign. I confess I am wondering why.'

'You do not know Sir Herbert well?'

'Only by reputation.' He did not sound as if he admired him. 'Are you a friend of the family, may I ask?'

I nodded. Any other way of explaining my presence would have been too complicated. I could see he was trying to judge my importance. My place at the far end of the table argued against it; on the other hand a man with an eye for jewellery could hardly have missed the value of Celia's opals.

'What did the old lady want with you so urgently?'

So he was sharp-eyed, as well as impudent.

'That was Mrs Beedle,' I said. 'Our hostess's mother.'

A waiter was ladling turtle soup into our plates.

'What did she mean about your not letting her down? Are you accustomed to letting people down?'

'I hope not.' I must have put more feeling into that than I intended, because he gave a sharp sideways glance. 'So you write novels,' I said, trying to take refuge in the small talk I'd prepared.

'Yes.'

It did not seem to please him. He was looking intently towards the top of the table.

'And you're in the midst of an election campaign?'

His eyes came back to me. 'In a few weeks' time I shall be the Member of Parliament for Maidstone. You haven't forgotten there must be a general election when a new monarch comes to the throne?'

I had forgotten. Too much had happened in the past few weeks for me to care about elections.

The waiters cleared the soup plates away and served turbot. By rights, with the change of courses, I should have turned to converse with my neighbour on the other side, but the canon seemed happily occupied with his fish. I noticed there was an empty place opposite him, and that the woman next to it looked put out at not being provided with a second gentleman. After all the trouble taken with the table plan, this struck me as odd, but I had little time to think about it.

'Are you in Sir Herbert Mandeville's confidence?' This time there was undisguised urgency in Mr Disraeli's question. Neither of us was eating.

'No.' At least I could answer that truthfully.

'Do you know if he's on particularly friendly terms with Kilkeel?'

A shiver ran up my spine. 'Why do you ask?'

'I know of the man, also by reputation.'

'So what is Lord Kilkeel's reputation?'

'As one of the greatest rogues who ever graced the Bar.'

'Oh.'

'That offends you? Are you connected in some way with him?'

'No!' I couldn't help saying it so loudly that the canon glanced up.

'He's a constitutional lawyer, probably the best of his generation. He's also the greatest political turncoat of our times. Whatever party is in or out, Kilkeel always has the ear of the men who matter. It's a question of knowing where all the bodies are buried.'

'Bodies?'

'You look alarmed. I speak metaphorically, of course. Any government ever formed has work to do which it can never admit to and, as often as not, Kilkeel is the man called upon to do it.'

'What sort of work?'

He glanced at me over the rim of his wineglass. 'For one thing, he helped fabricate some of the evidence against the late Queen Caroline.'

I held his gaze. Charlotte again. Caroline was her mother. He put down his glass and looked me in the eye.

'When Kilkeel is present on any occasion, the prudent man asks himself why. And for some reason, Miss Lock, I think you know a lot more about all this than you're telling me.'

By any normal standards, this was intolerably bad manners. After all, I'd claimed to be a friend of the family. When I got to my feet and asked him to excuse me, he must have thought that was the reason. He was, I think, drawling an unflustered apology as I went, but I didn't stop to hear because it was time to keep my appointment with Mrs Beedle upstairs.

The hall was deserted. I ducked behind the orange tree and went through the door that Mrs Beedle had used. It led into a servants' corridor that connected with a back staircase. I went up another flight of stairs and into the schoolroom corridor. It felt like home. The schoolroom had come to represent the nearest thing to familiarity and safety I'd known at Mandeville Hall.

The door to the schoolroom was shut. I tapped on it. When nothing happened I opened the door. The curtains were drawn across the window. I went towards the table and started feeling around for the lamp, intending to light it ready for when Mrs Beedle arrived. I couldn't find the lamp so I moved round the table. My foot caught on something and I fell to one knee, petticoats tangling round the heel of my shoe. A ruck in the carpet, I thought. But even as I thought it, I knew it wasn't that. It was the smell that warned me. There was a harsh metallic reek that didn't belong there.

My knee was nudging against something like a cushion or a bolster, but heavier. Scared now, I leaned forward and let my hand rest on it. An upholstered silk curve, slithery under my fingers. My hand moved along and it wasn't silky any more. Trying to get away from it, I backed into the rocking horse. Eventually I managed to pull myself upright and stumble to the door. Without knowing it, I'd picked something off the schoolroom floor and had it clenched in my hand. It was quite small: a turban of black velvet trimmed with white lace and jet beads.

# Chapter Seven

'SHE WAS AN OLD LADY,' Mrs Quivering said. 'Her heart failed, that's all.'

We were in the housekeeper's room, just the two of us. Mrs Quivering was sitting behind her desk, I—at her invitation—in a chintz armchair. It was just after one o'clock in the morning.

'Yes.'

'She must have gone upstairs to make sure the children were asleep. She knew Betty couldn't be with them.'

'Yes.' I had not told her, and had no intention of telling her, that Mrs Beedle had gone to the schoolroom to meet me.

'It's possible that she felt herself becoming faint and went to the schoolroom to sit down. Then she must have fallen and hit her head on something—the rocking horse, perhaps.'

The story was improving all the time. We both knew very well that she was talking nonsense. Mrs Quivering had organised the removal of the body from the schoolroom to Mrs Beedle's bedroom by two footmen. The grey hair above Mrs Beedle's left ear was clotted with blood, the side of her dress soaked with it. Mrs Quivering had had to run for towels from the nursery bathroom because blood was seeping onto the carpet. She told the footmen to carry the body down the backstairs, so as not to alarm any guests who might be going to their rooms, and left me to hold the lamp for them. Then she disappeared for a while.

I was sure she'd gone to report to Sir Herbert. By the time we reached Mrs Beedle's bedroom, Mrs Quivering was there to meet us. She told the footmen to lay the body on the bed, then sent them outside and dispatched me to the kitchen for hot water. I came back with it to find that she'd stripped Mrs Beedle of her black silk and replaced it with a long nightdress. Mrs Beedle looked older and smaller in death. I thought of the immense effort of will it must have cost her to protect her family, and was close to tears, knowing that I'd failed her after all.

Mrs Quivering told me sharply to come and hold the bowl while she sponged the worst of the blood off. We used a scarf to bind up the sagging jaw, then put on a nightcap over the injured head. When we left, she ordered one of the footmen to stay on guard by the closed door. By that time, the gentlemen guests had joined the ladies in the drawing room and were listening to music. I heard a snatch of a Vivaldi oboe and violin concerto, and imagined Daniel with his fiddle to his chin. I knew I should never hear that concerto again without smelling blood.

'It must have been most unpleasant for you, finding her,' Mrs Quivering said.

I didn't reply. How could I explain to her that it was doubly bad because it had catapulted me back to the room in Calais, and my father's body?

'It might be best if you didn't talk about this to any of the servants, Miss Lock. These things are very unsettling for them.'

I promised. It would have been easy to assume, because Mrs Quivering was weaving such a hard-wearing lie, that she was responsible in some way for Mrs Beedle's death. I didn't believe that. Mrs Quivering was a very efficient housekeeper, and the centre of a housekeeper's work is to deal with any unpleasantness before it troubles the life of the family. The death was nothing to do with Mrs Quivering and everything to do with me, and that first great lie about my father.

'Does Lady Mandeville know?' I said.

'She went to her room as soon as the ladies left the table. I'm sure she'll be sleeping now. It will wait until she wakes up.'

It was clear from the way she said it that Lady Mandeville had retired to bed the worse for drink.

'And Miss Mandeville?' I asked. 'She was fond of her grandmother.'

I could see from Mrs Quivering's face that Sir Herbert had given no instructions about that.

'Yes, it would be wrong for her to hear it from one of the servants. I should go to her, I suppose.' Mrs Quivering began to stand up, so weary that she could hardly force her body out of the chair.

'I'll go and tell Miss Mandeville, if you'd like me to,' I said.

She sank back in the chair. 'Thank you, Miss Lock. You will do it as kindly as you can, won't you?'

I promised to do it kindly. I went up the backstairs to the bedroom corridor and tapped on Celia's door.

'Come in.' Celia was sitting in an armchair in a blue cashmere dressing gown. Her face was white and she'd been crying. 'Fanny says my grandmother's dead.'

'I'm sorry to say it's true.'

'What happened?'

I thought that there were enough lies, without my telling more. So I told her how I'd found Mrs Beedle. She made a whimpering sound, like a hurt puppy. I went towards her and her cold and trembling hand came out of the dressing-gown sleeve and clasped mine.

'You're saying she was killed?'

'I think she must have been.'

'But by whom and why?'

'I don't know.'

'My stepfather. He never liked her.'

'It can't have been. He was at the table when it happened.'

'He paid somebody to do it, then.'

'Miss Mandeville . . . Celia, your grandmother spoke to me just as we were going in to dinner. She said something had occurred and I was to leave dinner early and meet her in the schoolroom. Have you any idea what she meant?'

'No.' I didn't know whether she'd even understood my question. She seemed lost in her own thoughts. 'I think I want to see Grandma. Will you take me to her?'

The footman on duty outside Mrs Beedle's room opened the door for us. Celia stood for a long time looking down at her grandmother, then, rather to my surprise, knelt on the rug beside the bed and bent her head in prayer. Finally she stood up and kissed her on the forehead. She was crying. 'Why would someone do this to a poor old lady?'

'I think she was more than a poor old lady. She didn't like what was happening and was doing her best to stop it.'

'But I don't like it either. Does that mean somebody wants to kill me?'

'I hope not. Just stay quietly in your room today and I'll help you get away tonight, if that's still what you want. They'll have to cancel the ball, I suppose.'

'They won't. My stepfather's been planning this for a long time. He won't let the death of an old lady he hated prevent it.' She took a last look at the figure on the bed and turned away. 'I must go to my mother.'

'I think she may be asleep.'

Her look showed she knew exactly what I meant by that. She seemed to have grown up a lot in the last few minutes. 'I'll wait with her till she wakes up. I can't leave him to tell her.'

We went out and I watched her walking heavily away along the corridor. There were several things I must attend to and the first of them was getting out of my ridiculous dinner dress back into proper clothes. The staircase up to the maids' dormitory was dark and I hesitated there for some time. For all I knew, the killer might have escaped that way, into the maze of servants' quarters. When I got to the landing by the maids' room, a reassuring sound of snoring came from inside. I hesitated for a while, then continued up the narrower staircase to my room. At the door, I thought I heard a rustling noise above me.

'What do you want?' I said into the darkness.

No answer. Probably a pigeon in the roof timbers. I opened the door, hoping that if I had to scream at least it would wake the maids below.

'Is anybody in there?'

The sound of my own voice bouncing back told me that the room was empty. It must have been dawn in the world outside because a little grey light was coming through the window. I took a deep breath and lit the candle. It took three tries because my hand was shaking, but I felt better when its light flickered round the walls.

I struggled out of the dress. It was a small relief to turn to my own clothes, neatly folded on the bed. Then my heart lurched and I started trembling again because I hadn't left them on the bed. I'd left them folded on the chair. And a shawl Betty had loaned me had disappeared.

There was something wrong with the washbowl, too. I was sure I'd emptied it after washing, but now there were a few inches of dirty water in it and my small cake of soap had been moved. Somebody had come into my room and washed. Somebody who needed to wash blood off his hands? I looked at the water. No blood, just soap scum. I knelt, bludgeoned by fear and misery. Not even my room was safe. If somebody had come in and attacked me at that moment, I should not have had the strength or will to do anything about it.

In the end, it was anger that brought me back to my feet. I was sure that the person who'd killed my father was also the murderer of Mrs Beedle. I was under the same roof with him. Wasn't that what I'd wanted all along? I put my own clothes on and went downstairs. The only idea in my mind was to speak to Daniel. I walked round the outside of the wall of the kitchen garden, onto a pathway that I'd sometimes taken with the children to the Greek Pavilion where the musicians were sleeping. It was a fine morning, the sky blue and cloudless. The musicians had been playing until late so I hardly expected to find anybody awake at that hour, but when I came up the last spiral of path somebody was sitting on a bench, looking out at the view over the heath.

'Oh, Daniel.'

'Child?' He was still wearing his evening clothes. I ran to him and poured out the story as if I really were the child he called me.

At some point in the story he must have taken my hand and kept hold of it. 'Have you any idea what it was she wanted to tell you?'

'Something to do with Mr Brighton, I'm sure.'

'And she didn't mention any names?'

'No.'

He said nothing for a long time, holding my hand and looking out at the view.

'Haven't you slept?' I asked.

He shook his head. 'I wish I'd come to find you last night, Liberty. God knows I wanted to, but it seemed an intrusion.'

'Why?'

'Yesterday evening, when you came down the stairs, you were so beautiful, I hardly recognised you—no, that's not complimentary, is it? I mean, you were by far the most beautiful of the ladies there. That young fop who took you in to dinner was clearly entranced and . . .'

'Daniel, that's nonsense.'

'When I looked for you after dinner, you weren't there. Then rumour began to get round that somebody had died and I couldn't help worrying. You'll say that's nonsense too, I suppose.'

'But you must have soon found out it wasn't me?'

'Yes. The word spread that our host's elderly mother-in-law had died suddenly of a heart seizure. I felt like playing a jig when I heard. Not that the bereaved son-in-law would have cared if I had. I asked him whether, in the circumstances, he wished us to continue to play.'

'What did he say?'

'At risk of offending your ears, I shall quote him verbatim: "Damn your eyes, sir, it's only my mother-in-law. I'm paying you, and if I say so, you'll go on fiddling until hell freezes over."'

'I'm sure he knows something about it. Whoever killed her must have been a member of his household or one of his guests.'

Daniel went quiet again. 'Liberty, there is something you should know. I don't think for one moment that it has anything to do with her death, but . . .' He looked embarrassed and miserable. 'My dear, please don't jump to conclusions, but the fact is, Blackstone is here.'

I stared at him. 'What's he doing here?'

'We think he must have contrived to have himself employed among the extra waiters. He collapsed while serving dinner last night.'

If an elderly man had just run up the backstairs and down, he might well collapse. I let go of Daniel's hand. 'Where is he now?'

'Here. Asleep in my bed, as a matter of fact.'

I felt myself going hard as stone. 'Why is he here?'

Daniel looked surprised at my tone. 'I haven't had a chance to ask him yet. He's a very sick man, Liberty. He was hardly conscious when we brought him in here last night.'

'Probably not, seeing as he'd just bludgeoned a poor old lady to death.'

'Child, you can't . . .'

'Don't child me. She needed to tell me something, that was why she wanted to meet in the schoolroom. If she'd discovered Blackstone was here disguised as a waiter—'

'Did she even know the man?'

'To the best of my knowledge, no. But what if she'd found out he wasn't a proper waiter, and had begun to ask what he was doing here . . .'

'That's mere supposition.'

'You're not claiming that he was here simply as a waiter, I hope?'

'I'm not claiming anything.' Daniel was beginning to be annoyed now. 'And no, I don't suppose he was simply acting as a waiter.'

'Then tell me why he's here?'

'Liberty, when he wakes up, I'll ask him, provided he's strong enough.'

'He was strong enough to kill Mrs Beedle. He was strong enough to kill my father.'

I stood up. He tried to take my hand again, but I pulled it away.

'Liberty, please. You can't know—'

'I know he was in Calais when my father was killed. Now he's here and she's dead too. What more do you need?'

'Quite a lot more, if I'm to think him guilty of two murders.'

'Of course, he's more than a friend, isn't he? What was it you said? A Freemason.'

'I promise you that if I find cause to believe he killed your father or that poor old woman, I shall hand him over to the hangman.'

'Well, let's go in there now, wake him up and ask him.'

I made for the door of the pavilion. Daniel jumped up and stood in front of me. 'Later, I promise you—'

'I'm tired of promises. He made me promises when he wanted me to spy for him, and look what . . .'

It came to me that I might be partly to blame for Mrs Beedle's death, if my reports had brought Blackstone there, and my voice choked with tears. I was too angry with Daniel to let him see that, so I turned away and walked quickly down the spiral path and back across the park.

By the time I reached the house, I'd recovered myself enough to face Betty and the children. The schoolroom was still being cleaned, so they'd been allocated a sitting room at the far end of the nursery corridor. The two boys were at the table, listlessly spooning up bread and milk, with broad black bands round the sleeves of their jackets. Henrietta was sobbing on the sofa in bodice and petticoats, while Betty sat in an armchair, hurriedly stitching away at a small black crepe dress. Betty's eyes were red, her cheeks swollen with crying. I knelt on the floor beside her, threaded a needle and started on the dress hem.

Once breakfast was over and Henrietta fitted into her dress they had to be taken to pay their last respects to their grandmother.

We filed into the room and stood in a line by the bed. For a second time I looked down at that stern, wrinkled face under the nightcap. James's hand tightened in mine. Henrietta started sobbing again, loudly and painfully. It was, I think, their first experience of death. As soon as we decently could, we took them back upstairs.

Betty suggested I go up and lie down for a couple of hours. I was reluctant to leave her on her own with them but the effects of a night without sleep were catching up with me and I knew I'd be no use to Celia unless I rested.

I hesitated on the landing outside my room, reluctant to open the door for fear of finding things disturbed again. Fixed to the wall was a wooden ladder that led upwards from the landing. I'd barely noticed it before. Today, for some reason, it seemed different. Sunlight and a waft of fresh air came from higher up. My eyes followed the ladder up to a square of blue sky. There shouldn't have been a square of sky. It had never been there before. A trap door then, left open to the roof.

The ladder was a rough affair. I put my hands on the uprights. What I intended to do wasn't wise, but I was too tired and angry for wisdom. I climbed up and my head came out into the warm sun while my hands felt the chill of the lead roof-covering. I pulled myself through somehow, and ended crouching in a kind of broad trough that ran behind the parapet of the house. After a while I stood upright and looked left and right along the ramparts.

The view was similar in both directions, yards of emptiness then a chimney stack. No sign of anybody. But when my eyes adjusted to the light there was a difference between left and right. Something small was lying at the base of the right-hand chimney stack. It looked like a dishcloth at first, until I recognised the green and grey stripes of the shawl I'd borrowed from Betty. I took a few steps and bent to pick it up.

When it resisted, I tugged harder, thinking it had caught on something. It still wouldn't budge and from behind the chimney-stack came a little noise, between a protest and a moan. There was nothing threatening about the sound, so I went round the chimney stack. The rest of the shawl was wrapped round a woman sitting with her back to the brick-work. She was clinging on to the shawl with her right hand and had the other arm raised, guarding her face, as if she expected to be hit.

'It's all right,' I said. 'I'm not going to hurt you.'

I let go of the shawl. She rocked backwards and let her arm fall, blink-ing up at me. Her face was lined, her grey eyes bewildered. She seemed to be in her late forties. A light came into her eyes as if she thought she knew me, but I was certain I'd never seen her before in my life.

'Are you employed here?' I asked.

She laughed. 'Here? On the roof to scare the crows? Oh yes.'

The words were mad, but the voice wasn't. It was hoarse but fairly cultivated, like an upper servant's.

'It's my shawl,' I said. 'You can keep it if you like, but did you take it from my room?'

'Your room, was it?'

'What's your name?'

I'd intended to say it quite kindly, but it must have sounded harsh because she pulled the ends of the shawl tightly around her.

'No more questions. I've had enough of questions.'

'Well, you can't stay up here all day.'

'I've been up here all night, so I don't see why I can't stay up here all day.'

'All night? When did you . . .?'

She pulled the shawl up right over her head.

'Aren't you—I mean, you must be hungry and thirsty.'

'Thirsty, yes.' It came muffled through the shawl.

'If you'll come down with me, I'll fetch you some water.'

She seemed to consider it, then: 'Did the old lady send you?'

'Yes.' It was true, after a fashion. My tongue was twitching with ques-tions I wanted to ask her, but the first thing was to persuade her down from the roof. I helped her along the roof trough and went first through the trapdoor so that I could guide her down the ladder.

The moment the door of my room shut behind us she collapsed on the chair. I told her to wait, ran down the stairs to the nursery kitchen and came back with a jug of water and a glass. She drank two glassfuls of water straight off, closed her eyes and gave a shudder. It seemed to bring her back to herself because she made an attempt at tidying her hair. 'I look a sight, don't I? I'm sorry I used your good soap.'

'So it was you in my room yesterday?'

She nodded. At least she'd answered a question.

'What were you doing here?'

'The old lady said I was to stay here until she called me.'

'An old lady in black?'

A reluctant nod. She gulped more water. I waited.

'So are you going to take me to her?' she said.

'Do you want me to?' I decided not to tell her at once about Mrs Beedle's death. For all I knew she might have had a hand in it.

'It's not a question of what I want or don't want, is it? I've been passed like a parcel, hand to hand, over the sea and back until I don't know where I am or what I'm doing.'

'Over the sea and back?'

'Over by trickery and back by force. I told the old lady about it. She said she'd look after me, once it was all over. Will she keep her promise, do you think?'

'Why shouldn't she?'

'There was a gentleman promised to look after me too, but he didn't come back.'

My whole body tingled, like lightning in the air. 'A gentleman where?'

'In France.'

I tried hard to keep my voice steady. 'You said he didn't come back. What happened to him?'

'They told me he'd been shot. I don't know what to believe from anyone any more.'

'What was his name?'

'He said he was Mr Lane, but I don't know if it was his real name.'

'It was his real name. He was my father.'

Visions of beautiful ladies and angry husbands fell away. The search for the woman in my father's letter had ended here, in this bleak room.

'Do you know, I thought you had the look of somebody I recognised when I saw you up there. Only I couldn't call it to mind.'

'The old lady, Mrs Beedle, she was killed last night,' I said.

I was past being careful. Her mouth fell open. 'Where?'

'Downstairs in the schoolroom.'

'Is that the room with the horse and the big globe?'

'Yes. How did you know?'

'She took me in there, before she brought me up here. She said I was to come back down when she gave me the signal. She was going to tap on the bottom stair with that stick of hers. I waited. I washed myself and I put on the shawl and I waited. Then I heard a noise from downstairs.'

'Her stick tapping?'

450 | Caro Peacock

'I wasn't sure. I thought I'd better go down, so I did. The door was closed, but I heard her voice from inside, talking to somebody about me.'

'What did she say?'

'It was something like them having no right to bring me there in the first place. Then she said, quite loud, "No, I've no intention of telling you where she is." I didn't wait to hear anything else. I guessed whoever was in there with her was working for the fat devil, so I was away and up the stairs. I couldn't stop in this room in case he made her tell him where I was, so I climbed up the ladder and came out on the roof.'

'Did she sound scared?'

'Not scared, no. Angry.'

I sat down on the bed. We looked at each other, beyond crying.

'Your name's Liberty?'

'Yes.'

'Your father talked to me about you. He said you were kindhearted and he was going to rent a house in London and I could stay with you until I found somewhere else. He said he was going to write to you and let you know.'

'He did, but he was dead by the time I had the letter. I don't even know your name.'

'Martley. Maudie Martley.'

'Please, Mrs Martley, tell me anything else you can about my father.'

She opened her mouth, then closed it again, looking terrified. Somebody was coming up the stairs. A voice called out:

'Miss Lock, would you come down, please.' Betty, sounding alarmed.

'It's all right, but I must go to her,' I whispered. 'Stay here. Sleep in my bed if you're tired.' She still looked terrified. 'Wait for me,' I said. 'Please wait. I'll be back as soon as I can.'

Betty was on her way back downstairs. 'There's a gentleman insists he must speak to you. I've put him in the boys' bedroom.'

She was hot and miserable at this violation of her sanctuary. I went into the bedroom and there was Daniel.

I wanted to run to him with my news, but I didn't trust him over Blackstone. Perhaps I took a few steps towards him and stumbled, because he spread out his arms, as if to catch me.

'Liberty, are you ill? I don't believe you've slept or eaten.'

'I'll do very well.' I made myself stand up straight and his arms fell to his sides.

'Blackstone's woken up. I think you should hear what he has to say.'

I took him by the backstairs into the courtyard and round the wall of the kitchen garden. When we came to the spiral path to the pavilion he offered me his arm, but I shook my head and went in front of him. At the door, he asked me to wait while he went inside, then beckoned me to join him. It was a big shadowy room, with camp beds arranged along both sides. Blackstone was lying flat on his back on one of the beds. His complexion was grey, his eyes closed. He seemed even thinner than I remembered, and older.

'Miss Lane is here,' Daniel told him.

He opened his eyes, focused on me and slowly brought his feet to the floor. He got himself upright and walked to the door, leaning on Daniel's arm. Outside, the two of them waited until I sat down on the stone bench by the wall, then Daniel settled Blackstone next to me and sat on his other side. Blackstone paused for a while with his face to the sun, eyes closed, taking painful-looking breaths.

'I did not kill your father,' he said, eyes still closed. 'I told you that in Dover, but you wouldn't believe me.'

'But you didn't save him either, and you might have,' I said.

His eyes jerked open. 'That is not true. He was dead before I even knew he'd got to Calais. Believe me, if I'd had the slightest idea they would go to such lengths, I'd have found him and warned him.'

'But you knew he hadn't died in a duel. If you were his friend, why didn't you do something, make people investigate?'

His eyes closed again. 'What good would it have done? Only caused a hue and cry that would alert Kilkeel to the fact that I was watching him? Nothing could bring Jacques back. If I failed in my duty to him, it was for a cause that your father would have approved.'

'What was that?' I said.

'Ridding the world of kings.'

'Not by these methods,' Daniel said.

Blackstone pushed himself away from the wall, eyes fierce. 'By what methods, then? By politely asking, Be so good as to go, sir? Please be so kind as to stop fattening yourself and your brood on the wealth of the labouring people. Please be obliging enough to abdicate and let the men you call your subjects grow into free and honest citizens instead of demeaning themselves as your toadies and flatterers. Is that how you'd bring about a republic?' His voice grew in force as he spoke and some colour came back to his face. Daniel looked ill at ease.

'I've never denied my republican opinions, you know that.'

'Oh no, as long as you can sing about them or recite poetry about them or drink toasts over the punchbowl to them, that's well enough. Have you spent time in prison for them?'

'You know very well I haven't.'

'Well, I have.'

'I know. You've suffered for a cause we believe in, and I honour you for it. But I don't understand what you were trying to do this time.'

Blackstone didn't answer Daniel. He sat there, stiff and upright, staring out over the lake.

'I don't understand either,' I said. 'What was the purpose of dishonouring my father's memory to shield people who are just trying to replace a queen with a king? I don't know anything about little Vicky, but I don't see how she could be much worse than this creature they call Mr Brighton.'

'That is the entire point,' Mr Blackstone said. 'As you have observed, Mr Brighton is—even by Hanoverian standards—more than usually stupid. He is greedy, foppish and entirely at the mercy of the schemers and flatterers who surround him. What's more, he is by nature highly unlikely to beget heirs.'

'How can you know that?' I said.

Blackstone and Daniel looked at each other, then at me.

'I think in that respect Blackstone's probably right,' Daniel said.

'Thank you, Suter. In addition, any claim he might have to the throne would be as the grandchild of George IV, one of the unworthiest monarchs ever to infest the throne of England, and of Caroline of Brunswick, who was no better than a whore.'

'Blackstone!' Daniel protested, looking at me.

'If I have offended, I apologise. But I believe my point is made. If so-called Mr Brighton had a legitimate claim to the throne, then he would probably be a monarch so spectacularly bad that even the lazy, over-tolerant people of England would rise up and say "Enough."'

Daniel was looking at him in amazement. 'So you'd found out about this plot and you were concealing it, to make sure this country was saddled with a bad king?' he said.

Mr Blackstone nodded. 'It was a faint hope, I admit. For one thing, I seriously doubt he could ever prove his claim.'

'And for that faint hope, you were prepared to let the world believe that my father died betraying his own principles,' I said. 'It seems to me a poor exchange.'

'No, because there was a larger hope. Even if the Pretender's claim failed in the end, there were some powerful men like Mandeville and Kilkeel supporting it, so it was quite certain to cause a deal of noise in the country. The streets of our cities are already teeming with hungry men, our country towns are full of labourers turned from their jobs and out of their cottages. And our politicians expect them to forget their empty bellies and cry "God save the Queen!" If the people see those same politicians squabbling among themselves whether it's to be Queen Victoria Alexandrina or King Harold on the throne, might not that be the spark that makes them decide to throw off their chains at last?'

'That wasn't worth my father's life,' I said.

Blackstone closed his eyes and didn't answer. He gave a shiver.

'Why in the world did you decide to come here yourself?' Daniel asked. 'You should be at home in bed.' His tone was gentle. I could see that he still respected the man. Blackstone gave a wan smile.

'I needed to see what their next step would be. Spies have proved to be unreliable and expensive.' I must have made some sound of protest because he turned to me. 'I exempt you, Miss Lane. I wish everybody had been as honest in the cause as you have been.'

'I don't care about the cause. All I want to know is who killed my father.'

'I believe Kilkeel was involved,' Blackstone said. 'I don't suppose he pulled the trigger himself, but they were all furious about that woman.'

I looked away from him so that he shouldn't see anything in my eyes. In spite of his weakness, I still didn't trust him.

'Who is she and what happened to her?' Daniel asked.

'I still don't know. I believe they intended her as some kind of witness, though witness to what exactly I've no notion. I had a man trying to find out for me, but he became scared and let me down. That was why it was so important that I should be present last night.'

'Nothing happened,' Daniel said. 'Or rather, a lot happened, but there was no mystery woman suddenly produced from behind a cloak.'

'Something went wrong with their plans yesterday, I'm quite convinced of that,' Blackstone said. 'Mandeville hasn't gone to all this trouble just to give dinner to his friends. He and Kilkeel are still waiting to make their move, and I don't know why. We must find out.'

It infuriated me that, in spite of everything, he was still plotting.

'Did you know Mrs Beedle was murdered here last night?' I said.

Blackstone stared at me. 'I don't even know who Mrs Beedle is.'

'Mandeville's mother-in-law. Did you kill her?'

Daniel started protesting, then stopped when I gave him a look.

'In all my life, I've never killed anybody,' Blackstone said. He looked straight at me, eyes wide open. 'I hope you believe that. I should be sorry to have your bad opinion, Miss Lane.'

His eyes closed. After a while he slid sideways against Daniel. I thought he might have died, but I felt no grief, nothing. Daniel caught my eye and pointed to a couple of young musicians on the far end of the terrace. The three of them managed to take Blackstone back inside. He tried to walk, but his feet scarcely grazed the gravel. At the doorway he turned and looked at me:

'Do you believe me? About your father, at least?'

I thought of what Daniel had said, that in his prime this man could have marched ten thousand people on Whitehall. 'Yes, I believe you.'

I sat on a bench and after a while Daniel came out to me, head down. 'Thank you for saying that, Liberty.'

'He said something I know is true. That makes me inclined to believe him on the rest.'

'What?'

'My father was killed because of the woman. Don't tell Blackstone or anybody else, but that same woman's hiding in my room.'

'Your room! For heaven's sake, Liberty! If you're right, two people have died because of this woman, and you tell me you're hiding her!'

'You must come and speak to her.'

'Please, leave it and come away with me this instant. Mourn your father and let them all play their games and go to hell in their own way. You know now why your father was killed . . .'

'No, I still don't know why my father was killed. I think she does. There's no doubt whatsoever that she's the woman in his letter. In any case, we can't just go and abandon her here.'

'Liberty, just leave it and—'

'While the man who killed my father is living and breathing, no, I will not.'

He sighed and gave me his hand to help me up from the bench. 'If you won't leave it, then I suppose I must help you, though the gods know there probably isn't a man in the world less fit for this sort of business than I am.'

As we walked back to the house I told him what she'd said, as well as I could remember. We went up the backstairs to the maids' landing. He waited there so that I could go up and warn Mrs Martley. To my relief, she was just where I'd left her, asleep in the hard chair, wrapped in Betty's shawl. Her eyes jerked open when I stepped into the room.

'You should have slept on the bed,' I said. 'Are you well enough to talk to somebody? He's a friend of my father's and will do you no harm.'

She nodded reluctantly and I went down to fetch Daniel. I'd worried that his presence would make her even more scared than she was already, but I should have trusted more in his natural kindness and gift for putting people at ease. He made a polite bow to her and introduced himself. 'Mrs Martley, I am sorry indeed to intrude on you. Jacques Lane was a very good friend of mine, and I'd be obliged to you for anything you could tell me about your acquaintance with him.'

'What do you want to know?'

'How did you come to meet him? Was it in Paris?'

She blinked and pushed back a lock of her lank hair. 'Paris, yes.

When I was trying to get away from the fat devil. I don't know his name to this day. He was keeping me shut up in this house in Paris, a servant on watch in the hall day and night. Only, you see, there was one of them liked a drink and one night I looked out and he wasn't there on guard. So I ran down the stairs and out of the door. That was all I could think of, getting away, only I had no more idea of how to get back to England than flying to the moon, and I don't know any French, not a word.'

She stared at Daniel as though her life depended on making him understand.

'And was that when you met him?' he prompted.

'I knew there was a hotel next door with a coachyard and I'd heard English voices there. So I thought if I went to the coachyard and waited I might come across an English family and beg them for pity's sake to take me back with them.'

'When was this?' Daniel said.

'I don't know. I've lost track . . .' She was becoming perturbed again.

'Don't concern yourself about it, then. Did you get to the courtyard?'

'Yes. There was a gentleman there, talking to a horse. I'm sorry, did you want to say something?'

I must have made some movement. My father talked to all animals, from horses to mice. It brought him back to me so vividly that I felt like yelping from hurt. I pressed my lips together and nodded to Mrs Martley to go on.

'He was talking to it in English. He sounded a pleasant man so I plucked up courage and went over to him. I said I was a respectable Englishwoman fallen on hard times and I wanted to get home. No sooner were the words out of my mouth than his hand went to his pocket. "Thank you, sir, only it's not just the money," I said to him. "I've no notion how to get back and I've enemies next door who'll stop me if they find out." I don't know if he believed me then or not. He took me round a corner to one of those places they have in Paris—like a public house only not so cheerful—and ordered us a glass of brandy apiece and I started telling him my story. Even while I was telling it, I thought it sounded so fantastical, he wouldn't believe me. He did, though.'

'Yes,' I said. 'My father always trusted people.'

'It was more than just trusting. He knew the half of it already. And when I got to the bit about the fat devil asking me questions as if I was in the dock at the Old Bailey he started laughing. "It's nothing to laugh at," I told him. "The fat devil kept on at me until I didn't know right from left or black from white, and all about something that happened twenty years ago. He said I must be sure of everything, very sure, because one day I'd have to stand up in the House of Lords in front of all the judges in their robes and wigs and say exactly the same thing.'"

She paused for breath. Daniel poured her a glass of water.

'What did Mr Lane say to that?'

'He said he was sorry for laughing, but it was all a great nonsense and he was sure I shouldn't have to stand up in the House of Lords or anywhere else. Still, he said, it was a very wrong thing that had been done to me and of course he'd take me back to England. He said he was leaving the day after tomorrow and I could travel with him. He jabbered away in French to the man behind the counter and said I could stay there, all meals provided, and he'd come for me early morning, day after tomorrow. "Don't tell anybody," I said to him. I was terrified the fat devil would find me. So he promised not to tell anybody, not even his friends.'

Daniel looked across at me. 'He kept that promise,' he said.

I think it was in his mind, like mine, that my father might have lived if he'd broken it.

She nodded. 'I thought he would. I did as he told me and stayed where I was. The place wasn't much better than a brothel, but he wasn't to know that, and anyway I kept to my room. The morning after next, just as he'd promised, he called for me. He'd taken a couple of seats for us on the stage. There was no sign of the fat devil or his people, though I kept looking around me. It took us the best part of three days to get to Calais. He took two rooms for us at an inn just on the outside of town and went to book tickets on the steam packet. Only it was full up that day so we had to wait until the day after. Couldn't we go on one of the sailing boats instead, I asked him. But he liked the steam packet better, and who was I to argue?'

I got up and walked to the window, trying to keep control of my feelings and not interrupt her story. Of course my father, ever curious for new things, would prefer steam. If he'd been a less modern-minded man, none of it would have happened. He'd have stepped off some sailing boat in Dover, picked up my letter and come running to find me.

'So what happened then?' I said.

'He said he was going for a stroll round the town and that was the last I saw of him. I was feeling ill, from something I'd eaten, so I went to lie down. He didn't come back that evening. In the morning, I knocked on his door and there was no answer. So I thought maybe I'd misunderstood and he meant me to meet him by the steam packet. I was still feeling ill, but I dragged myself all the way to the harbour and there were crowds of people, but no sign of him. I was in a fair ferment by then. I went all the way back to the inn. Well, what with the worry and the disappointment, I was running a fever. For the next few days I was lying there thinking I'd die and that would be an end to my troubles.

Then one morning I woke up, mortally weak but the fever gone, so I decided I'd better get myself down to the docks and try and find somebody else who'd have the Christian charity to pay for my ticket over. Only when I went downstairs with my bag, the owner of the place took hold of my arm and started jabbering away in French. Your father had gone without paying the bill, you see.'

'I'm sorry,' I said. Ridiculous, of course, but she was almost crying with the memory of her distress. I realised that while Maudie Martley was lying weak with fever, I was probably no more than a mile away, enquiring for my father around the hotels of Calais. If he hadn't chosen an inn on the outskirts, I might have found her a month ago.

'Then I heard this voice in English asking what was going on. God help me, it was the fat devil himself. "Well," he says, "you have given us some trouble. We've been looking all over the place for you."'

By sheer mischance the fat man had found her at last, probably quite soon after they'd tried to kidnap me.

'Did you ask him about my father?' I said.

'I was too terrified to ask him anything. His servants dragged me into his carriage, then we drove off. "You've got yourself in serious trouble now," he said to me. "Trying to defraud an innkeeper, not to mention the money you stole from me when you ran off . . ." I told him, God's truth, I hadn't. But he kept on about how I'd deceived and robbed him, and if he told the French police I'd go to prison for a very long time, perhaps even to the guillotine.'

Even the memory of it scared her. Her hand went to her neck.

'They couldn't have done that,' Daniel said.

'He said he was a lawyer, and I heard people calling him milord. Who'd have believed me against him? I was nearly mad with fear and he could see it. In the end he said he wouldn't report me, only I'd have to do exactly what he said. He took me to his hotel and wrote down a long statement that he made me sign. He called in another man to witness it and then he stamped a big seal on it in red wax. He told me that if I ever tried to go back on my word and say I hadn't said it, that would be perjury and I'd be in even worse trouble. I had to promise to go back to England with him and not try to run away again. So I promised. What else could I do?' She looked at Daniel imploringly.

'I dare say in your place anybody would have done the same,' he said. 'So he never mentioned Mr Lane?'

She looked down at her hands. 'Not as such, not to me. No.'

'To somebody else?'

'I think so, yes. It must have been him the fat devil and another gentleman were talking about. But I was under the floorboards, you see.'

'Floorboards?'

'Yes, of the coach. The fat devil said I must go back to England with him, but I'd better make sure nobody saw me or I'd be arrested.'

'And somebody else was in the carriage with him?'

'Not on the journey over, no. It was when we were off the boat on the other side at Dover. Somebody got in the carriage. This new man said to the fat devil, "I still can't find the Martley woman." The fat devil said he could give up troubling himself because they'd found me without his help. The other one asked, "Where is she?" The fat devil gave a thump with his boot, just above my head, and I think he must have pointed downwards because the other gentleman said, "You mean she's dead too?" in a quavery sort of voice. And the fat devil said, "No. One's more than enough. What in the world possessed you, shooting poor Lane?"'

Daniel leaned forward. 'He said that? "Shooting poor Lane"?'

'Yes. And the other one said, sounding very hangdog, "It wasn't my fault. When you sent me that message from Paris, you said we had to find him and her at any cost." The fat devil said, quite sharp, "I didn't tell you to kill anybody," and the other one said, "I didn't mean to. I was just threatening him, trying to get him to tell us what he'd done with her. Then he made a grab for my pistol and it went off." The fat man said, "I've heard half a dozen men attempt that defence in court and I attended the hangings of all six of them." The other one made a sort of gulping sound, then the fat devil said it was more than he deserved, but he'd managed to make it look as if Lane had died in a duel. "So you won't hang this time," he said, "only you'd better get out because I'd rather not be seen with you after what's happened." Soon after that we were on our way.'

# *Chapter Eight*

THE WORLD HAD GONE BLACK. I turned my head away, not looking at Maudie Martley any more, hardly even hearing her through the rushing in my ears. I thought anger would blow my head apart.

Daniel was asking her a question. He sounded shaken too, but his voice was still gentle. 'This other man, did you see him?'

'Not properly. Only a slice of him, through a gap in the boards.'

'Was he young, old, dark, fair?'

'Not old, from his voice. Dark, I think, quite dark.'

'A servant or a gentleman?'

'A gentleman.'

'Would you know him if you saw him again?'

'I think I might.'

'Would you recognise his voice?'

'Yes, his voice more.'

'And the other one, the one you call the fat devil . . .'

'You'll have seen him for yourself, sir. He's in the house here.'

'His name's Kilkeel,' I said. 'Lord Kilkeel. And he brought you here and kept you shut up?'

'Yes. He made me sleep in his dressing room, with his man on a chair by the door. I kept my clothes on, every stitch, except for my shoes.'

'Why did he want you here?' Daniel said.

'I was to talk to some gentlemen. I was to tell them in my own voice what he'd worried out of me in the statement he took in France, not a word different or he'd have me for perjury and I'd be in prison for life.'

'But you didn't?'

'No, because before that the old woman had found me. She just walked into his dressing room yesterday and told the man watching me to get out. She said she knew very well what was happening, but it was treasonable and she wouldn't allow it. She took me and hid me here. Only I was scared, you see. I've been scared so much and for so long that I can't remember a time when I wasn't.'

There was pity in Daniel's eyes. I couldn't feel it yet. I was still too angry. Even though it wasn't her fault, her story had killed my father.

'There will be a time when you are not scared,' he said to her. 'My friend tried to protect you. For his sake, I'll do all that I can.'

She nodded, her eyes fixed on him as if he were a rock in a rough sea.

'Do you feel strong enough to answer some more questions?' he said.

'What?'

'Such as how you came to be in Paris with that man.'

'From trickery, sir. I'm a midwife by profession, to ladies of quality. Ask anyone in London society: nobody will have a bad word to say of Maudie Martley.'

'I'm sure of it. But Paris?'

'A message came for me one day, to go to a certain address in Burlington Gardens and meet a gentleman. I went to the address, a very respectable-looking house. The man who spoke to me said there was an English lady expecting her confinement in Paris who particularly wanted my services. I asked him her name—wondering if it was one of my ladies—and he said it was not in his power to give it. But if I agreed I was to have ten guineas in my hand in advance, all the travelling arranged and paid for, and a further twenty-five guineas when the lady was safely delivered.'

'Were you not suspicious at the secrecy?' Daniel asked.

'It happens sometimes, sir. A lady—for one reason or another—may not wish to have her condition known in London.'

'So you accepted?'

'I said there was a lady I must see through her confinement in the next few days, but after that I was at the other lady's service. I was to send word the moment I was free. So a livery carriage came to collect me and take me all the way to Dover. I was given a ticket for the steam packet and told to look out for a tall coachman with a blue and gold cockade in his hat who would be waiting for me on the French side.'

'And you met this coachman?'

'Yes. He was in a terrible hurry, but I supposed the lady must be near her time and that was the reason. So we got to Paris. The house wasn't as grand as I expected, but then if the lady wanted to be secret perhaps it wasn't surprising. A manservant took me to a room upstairs and I said I'd have a wash and be with the lady directly. I took my hat and cloak off and I washed and I waited. And I waited, and I waited. After a while, I started to worry that the lady might need me and there I was, sitting up there on my own. So I tried the door handle and the door wouldn't open. Bolted on the outside. Only of course I didn't know that at first, I thought it had just stuck, so I started knocking on the door and calling out. Then there were footsteps, the sound of a bolt being drawn back and the fat devil walked in. "What is this?" I said. "The poor lady might be having her baby at this very moment." The fat devil shook his head. He said, quite quietly, "There really is no hurry, Mrs Martley. The baby we're interested in was born twenty years ago."'

Maudie Martley looked terrified remembering it, like a woman seeing a ghost. Even though I'd expected it, I felt myself shivering.

'Did you know what he meant by that?' Daniel asked her.

'Of course I did. The Princess, of course. Poor Princess Charlotte.'

'Were you midwife to the Princess?' I said. That brought me a warning glance from Daniel, but it seemed to be the cue she needed.

'Not midwife, just midwife's helper. My aunt was a midwife, very well thought of, and she was training me up as her assistant. Of course, with the Princess, there were three great doctors there. One of them was Sir Richard Croft, a gentleman that was the best *accoucheur* in London. My aunt often worked with him. Even with great doctors, you see, there are some things that should only be done for a woman by another woman. At the Princess's country home it was, in Surrey.'

'You must have been nervous,' Daniel said.

'Oh, I was at first. Would you believe, the Archbishop of Canterbury and the Lord Chancellor of England and a lot of other gentlemen from the government were waiting in another room. We knew the baby might be king or queen one day, you see. I was nearly fainting from nervousness, but my aunt said a birth was a birth no matter who. I was mostly in a closet to the side of her bedroom, with a fire for heating the water. Of course, I could hear everything. She had a hard time, poor lady. I knew from the sounds that the baby was coming at last and my aunt called to me to bring warm towels. When I went in, one of the doctors was holding him. He and my aunt wrapped him in the warm towels, but it was no use, no use at all. A fine-looking, big boy he was, but blue in the face and dead.' Even twenty years on, she looked as shocked and grieved as if it had happened yesterday.

'And the poor Princess died too,' I said softly.

'Not at once. We thought we were going to save her. She sat up and I was sent down to the kitchen for chicken broth and barley water and she drank some. But then, a few hours later, she died too. Poor Sir Richard was so grieved he shot himself a few months later. But it wasn't his fault, it wasn't anybody's fault. The poor infant suffocated from her being too long in labour. To the highest and lowest it can happen, and it happened to her, poor lady, that's all. And then years later the wicked rumours started. You know what they were, don't you?'

Daniel said sadly, 'That she and the baby were both poisoned by people at court who didn't want to see a child or grandchild of Queen Caroline on the throne.'

'Wicked, wicked rumours. The poor baby was born stone dead and, as for the princess, I carried the broth and the barley water from the kitchen in my own hands and nobody came near them. My aunt and I were angry and scared too, though nobody thought to ask us anything. Anyway, the rumours died down and we thought that was an end of it—until that devil walked into my room in Paris.'

'Did he talk about the poisoning rumour?' Daniel asked.

'Yes, and worse. He said the Princess had been poisoned but the baby hadn't. He said it had been taken away secretly by loyal people who knew its life was in danger from the Princess's enemies at court.'

'What did you say to that?'

'I told him that it was nonsense. I'd seen the poor baby dead. One of the doctors even had to take it downstairs and show it to the Archbishop of Canterbury and the other gentlemen. "Are you saying that the Archbishop of Canterbury's a liar?" I said to him. And he said,

"I've no doubt at all that the Archbishop saw a dead male baby, but I'm sure dead babies are easy enough to come by when you're in the midwife's trade." God help me, I wanted to hit him in the fat, greasy chops.'

Under Daniel's influence, some of her spirit was coming back.

'So what did you do?' Daniel asked.

'I said he should take me back to London, that you couldn't lock people up just like that. He laughed and said it was different in France. He went away and a servant came up with a tray of sandwiches and a pot of tea. Well, I was hungry and thirsty so I ate and drank it all, but I think there must have been something in the tea because I went straight off to sleep and woke up not knowing where I was or what day it was. The fat devil came back with a clerk to take notes. He kept asking me the same questions about that night. Was I sure I remembered right? Had I been paid by anybody to say the baby died? He made me so confused that in the end I didn't know what I remembered and what he'd put into my head. And I had such a thirst on me all the time, they kept bringing me tea and I had to drink it, but I'm sure they were putting things in it. So I started pouring the tea out of the window and drinking washing water from the pitcher instead, and my head cleared and I knew I had to get away from him.'

I turned away, not wanting her to see my tears. It could so nearly have been otherwise—my father landing safely at Dover and meeting me with rescued Maudie in tow.

'So he brought you here to tell anybody who asked that the baby had lived?' Daniel said.

'Yes, sir.'

'And you're quite certain that the baby did not live?'

'As certain as the daylight, sir. And I'll say that to anybody now my mind's clear again, even if they do put me in prison or kill me for it.'

Daniel caught my eye and nodded towards the door.

'You are a woman of spirit, Mrs Martley. Would you excuse us, we must leave you for a while. Miss Lane won't be far away.'

He and I went down together to the landing outside the maids' dormitory. 'Do you believe her?' I asked him.

'I do, poor woman. I can see why your father decided to help her.'

'Lord Kilkeel's guilty of a crime, isn't he? He knows who killed my father and he's done nothing about it.'

'I think what she's told us makes him an accomplice to murder.'

'Then what do we do?'

'I don't know. I'm not even sure that conversation she overheard would amount to proof in a court of law.'

'If we were to go to a magistrate . . .' I said.

'The word of a bereaved daughter, a musician and a woman who would probably be dismissed as mad, against a lord who also happens to be a lawyer? I believe they'd laugh at us.'

'There has to be a way. Even if they laugh at us, I must at least try telling somebody.'

'It occurs to me that there's one gap in the evidence we might fill: getting Mrs Martley to identify Lord Kilkeel as her milord. Is there any way of giving her a sight of him in our presence without his seeing her?'

I tried to think. 'All the house guests will be going in to dinner before the ball. Mr Brighton will be there so I suppose Kilkeel will be too.'

'You seem to know the back ways of this house. Could it be managed?'

'I think so, yes. Possibly while they're all in the hall, before they go in to dinner.'

I thought of Mrs Beedle's door behind the orange tree. Even dead, she was still helping me.

'Can you persuade Mrs Martley, do you think?'

'I'll try,' I said. 'I'm sure she'll be happier if you're there. In the meantime she can stay in my room. I'll tell her to go up on the roof again if she hears anybody coming.'

'I suppose I must go back to my musicians now, or somebody will be asking questions. When shall we meet and where?'

'Six o'clock by the back door. They're dining early because of the ball.'

Once I had seen Daniel on his way, I brewed tea over the oil lamp in the nursery kitchen and found a piece of stale currant cake. It wasn't much, but Mrs Martley seemed grateful.

It was past ten o'clock by then and the children and I settled to our studies as best we could. Twice I left them to their books and ran upstairs to see that Mrs Martley was safe. The first time she was sleeping on the bed, snoring gently. The second she was awake, thirsty for the new pot of tea I brought with me, and prepared to listen to the plan for identifying Lord Kilkeel.

'I'm afraid of being near him. He'll twist my brains again.'

'I'll be there and so will Mr Suter.'

It was the promise of Daniel's presence that won her over in the end, and it was agreed that I should come to fetch her at half past five.

All through the morning I'd been expecting Celia to visit, but by our lunch time at half past two there was no sign of her. After the meal, Betty decided it would be all right to take the children for some air in the garden. We were all promenading sadly between the clipped box hedges of the knot garden when Celia and her brother came towards us. She was wearing a black and grey silk dress and looked as if she hadn't slept, face pale, eyes puffy. Stephen was dressed in black and looked almost as strained as she did. He came quickly towards us.

'Hello, Betty. Good afternoon, Miss Lock. I understand you found my grandmother. It must have been painful for you. I'm truly sorry.'

I murmured something about sympathy for the family's loss.

'Yes, she'll be much missed,' he said. 'Especially by Celia.'

Celia was standing at a short distance, apparently listening to something Betty was saying, but her eyes were on Stephen and me.

'I sense that she'll need your friendship more than ever, Miss Lock. We're both grateful to you.'

I mumbled something, thinking how little gratitude he'd be feeling towards me in a few hours' time, when he found his sister gone. He thanked me again and walked away. Celia was at my side in an instant.

'What were you talking about?'

'Your grandmother.'

'Thank goodness for that. You both looked so serious I was terrified you'd told him about tonight. Oh, Elizabeth, I am so scared.'

'I'm scared too,' I said. 'But my name isn't Elizabeth. It's Liberty.'

I thought I would never see her again after that night and somehow it mattered to say it, although I was not sure that she heard me. She took my hand in hers, hiding it in the folds of her dress, pretending to point out a flower with her other hand.

'I think Stephen guesses something's happening,' she said.

'Yes, I think *my* brother would have guessed if I were going away.'

'But he mustn't know. Don't try to persuade me again because it's no use. I shall leave the ball after the first set,' she said. 'Then I'll go upstairs and change into travelling clothes. I've given Fanny the evening off to watch the dancing. Will you wait for me in my room?'

'Yes.'

'I've written a letter to my mother. It's on the dressing table. Please make sure she gets it tomorrow morning when . . . when I'm gone.'

Tomorrow morning seemed a world away, but I promised.

'I shall see you again, one day. If I can ever help you in any way, I shall. I promise, Elizabeth.' (So she hadn't heard me.) 'Oh, confound the man!' She was looking at somebody over my shoulder.

'What man?'

'One of the guests. I don't even know his name. He was watching us from the terrace when I began talking to you and now he's coming down the steps. I'm in no mood for talking silly politenesses to people.'

She walked quickly away. I turned and saw the man she meant. Today he was elegant in carefully chosen gradations of grey. His ringlets gleamed and bounced in the sun but his expression was stern. He strode up to me.

'Good afternoon, Mr Disraeli,' I said. 'I'm afraid you've just missed Miss Mandeville.'

'I wasn't looking for Miss Mandeville. I was looking for you, Miss Lock.' His eyes were cold and challenging. I gave him look for look.

In spite of his sternness, the strange feeling of fellowship I'd felt for him at dinner flared again. 'And now that you've found me . . .?'

'Now I've found you, I hope we can continue the conversation we were having at dinner. Miss Lock, I asked you if you knew why we'd all been invited here. You didn't answer me. I don't take you for a fool, and I assure you that I am not one myself.'

'I'm grateful for your good opinion.'

He moved close to me. 'But as a friend of the family, you almost certainly did know why our host is taking such pains to launch a Hanoverian by-blow on society. Ah, so you *did* know?'

He must have been watching my expression very closely. I wasn't aware of giving anything away.

'Which of the many twigs of our prolific royal tree does this one hang from, I wonder? The Fitzherberts or one of Clarence's brood? With so many to choose from, you'd think he'd have picked a better specimen.'

'So of no use at all in your political career?' I said, deciding to attack.

'Miss Lock, what is happening here is quite enough to wreck a political career at the outset. I suspect the friend who had me invited of acting from malice. I suppose Mandeville wanted to recruit some of the up-and-coming men to the cause.'

'You being one of the up-and-coming men?'

He nodded. 'Miss Lock, when you and I spoke last night, I sensed something wrong. Now I'm sure of it. What happened to Mrs Beedle?'

I looked down at a butterfly sunning itself on a clump of mignonette. I desperately needed somebody who might believe my story and be in a position to do something about it. Nobody who mattered would listen to me, nor, I feared, to Daniel. His goodness of heart and honesty might be handicaps in the world of the powerful. Mr Disraeli, on the other hand, seemed to have at least a foothold in that world. Whether he was good-hearted and honest I had no way of telling—I rather feared not—and yet I sensed a kind of honour in him. If the butterfly stays where she is when I move my hand, I thought, I shall tell him some of the truth; if she flies, I'll say nothing.

'You spoke to Mrs Beedle just before we went in to dinner. What she had to say to you was urgent. It must have been quite soon after that she suffered her . . . heart seizure?'

He made the last two words into a question. I moved my hand. The butterfly stayed where she was.

'It wasn't a heart seizure,' I said. 'She was struck on the head. My father was killed too, for knowing about Mr Brighton.'

I told him as much of the story as I wanted him to know. It was quite a considerable amount, but there were two names I left out of it: Mr Blackstone and Mrs Martley. I said simply that a friend who knew about my circumstances had helped me get employment as a governess with the Mandevilles.

'As a governess?' he repeated.

'Yes, a governess in rose damask and opals. Borrowed plumes, I fear. Lock's not even my real name. I'm called Liberty Lane.'

I went on with my account. When I finished speaking he stood staring down for a while, fingering a gold seal hanging round his neck.

'This woman, this alleged witness you're not naming, you say the old lady took her away from Kilkeel. Where is she now?'

'Mrs Beedle sent her somewhere safe.'

'And you're not going to tell me where? Do you not trust me?'

'I hardly know you, but I think I trust you on my own account. I can't speak for her, though.'

'Do you believe her story?'

'Yes. Do you believe me?'

He didn't answer at once. Then, 'Yes, Miss Lane. I think I do. It explains something that has been puzzling me since last night.'

'What's that?'

'Why Kilkeel and Mandeville didn't produce their trump card. I think something was intended to happen last night. The stage was set, yet the trumpets never sounded, the clouds never parted and Jupiter never appeared. We were all left looking at each other and the unprepossessing Mr Brighton, wondering why we'd been invited.'

'What will happen now, do you think?'

'I rather suspect that, unless Mandeville manages to produce something tonight, they've missed the tide. Mandeville will lick his wounds and so-called Brighton will be packed back to whatever Continental spa town or lodging house they brought him out of.'

'They've killed two people at least. They've committed treason.'

He quoted: '*Treason doth never prosper: what's the reason?*'

'*For if it prosper, none dare call it treason.*' I finished the quote for him and added, 'But it is treason. Surely somebody could do something?'

'Bring them to trial? You need witnesses for that, not hearsay. As for treason, has Mandeville yet said publicly that he believes Brighton to be the rightful King of England?'

'Not as far as I know, but surely if the government were to ask questions, they'd find evidence,' I said.

'Quite possibly. Then that evidence would have to be tried in court, the whole story would be made public and you may be sure that there'd be the usual assortment of mischief-makers and malcontents who would take to the streets for the rights of poor disinherited King Harold. If you were in government, is that what you'd want?'

'So you can't do anything? Nothing will happen to them?'

He said slowly, 'If I put some of the story around in the right way in the right places, I believe I can get them laughed at.'

'Laughed at!'

'Never underestimate ridicule, Miss Lane. To an ambitious man, it can be more dangerous than bullets.'

'It won't get justice for my father or Mrs Beedle.'

'Justice is a different matter. Believe me, Miss Lane, if I could supply that for you, I'd do it very willingly.'

'Try, at least. Please try.'

He nodded slowly. 'You have a right to ask. What I can do, I shall.'

Up to that point, he'd spoken like a man very conscious of the effect of his words, but that promise was made simply and quietly. I thanked him and turned to go. There was no sign of Betty and the children.

'Where shall I find you in future?' he said.

I hesitated, not wanting to tell him I had neither future nor home. 'You might write to me care of Mr Daniel Suter, addressed to any musical theatre in London. It should find me sooner or later.'

He raised an eyebrow. 'It might be simpler for you to write to me, at the House of Commons.' I could tell he enjoyed saying it.

I went slowly upstairs, not sorry that I'd taken the decision to trust him, but disappointed it had brought me so little. I sat with the children for a while, then went up to wake Mrs Martley, taking her a glass of water and some bread and butter I'd saved from the children's dinner. She was awake already and nervous.

'I couldn't eat it. Not a crumb. The thought of being in the same room as that fat devil turns my stomach over.'

'You won't have to be in the same room. All you need do is look through a crack in the door and confirm that he's the same person.'

I managed to calm her and get her down the backstairs. The house was humming with preparations for the ball. Daniel met us at the back door. He offered Mrs Martley his arm and she clung to it on the cobwebby journey along some seldom-used passageways. Now and then we heard the buzz of social conversation, the occasional muted laugh, a Haydn string quartet.

We turned into the last short passageway leading to the door behind the orange tree. The music and conversation were almost as loud as if we were in the same room. I signed to Daniel to wait with Mrs Martley, then went on ahead and opened the door a few inches. I looked first towards the big fireplace. Sir Herbert was there, sipping his wine and frowning, with Mr Brighton beside him, glowing like a comet in stripes of purple and gold. There was no sign of Lady Mandeville but Celia was standing by her stepfather in her silver and white dress, hair glinting with diamonds, face blank. Kilkeel wasn't with them.

I'd begun to think that he had decided not to come down to dinner when I caught the smell of him. In a room banked with flowers, it was a waft of something foul and brought a vivid and unwanted memory of being close to him in his carriage. My eyes followed the smell and found him just on the other side of the orange tree, in profile to me and so close that I could almost have reached out an arm and touched him. Two men were with him, one with his back to me. The other one, facing me, was Celia's brother.

I closed the door quickly. This was far too close for comfort. Still, we were too far gone to draw back now. I went back to Mrs Martley and Daniel. 'He's quite near. It will only take one glance.'

She clung to Daniel's arm as we went quietly along the passage. We stopped by the door. Even with it closed, Stephen's voice came faintly through.

'. . . asked me how I knew. Well, it was obvious to anybody . . .'

Mrs Martley was trembling, leaning on Daniel. Now or never. I opened the door a few inches. Kilkeel was three-quarter face to us now, unmissable. I wasn't prepared for what happened. She hardly even seemed to glance, then she said loudly, 'It's the same man.' It was almost a scream. If it hadn't been for the noise of the party, it might have drawn attention to us. I put a hand on her shoulder to warn her to be quiet, but she was already falling backwards, fainting into Daniel's arms.

He staggered under the weight of her. I pushed the door shut and ran to help him. We half dragged, half carried her along the passage. After a minute or so she began to recover consciousness.

'It was him.'

'Don't worry about that now,' Daniel said. 'We'll see you safe.'

We managed to get her back to my room. I brought water for her, got her to lie down on the bed and loosened her stays, while Daniel waited on the landing outside. When she seemed calmer, I covered her over with the blanket and went outside to him.

'I blame myself,' he whispered. 'I didn't know it would be such a shock. Simply identifying Kilkeel was too much for her.'

'Daniel, that wasn't her trouble. Just seeing Kilkeel again wouldn't have affected her so strongly. After all, she knew he was here.'

'Well, what was the trouble then? Why are you looking like that?'

'Because it wasn't Kilkeel she meant,' I said.

'Libby, I simply don't understand you.'

In honesty, I scarcely understood myself. In a few minutes the world had turned upside-down again. My mind was moving so fast that I didn't know where it was leading me next. 'I will explain, but later. One of us must stay with her all the time. Could you come back, do you think, after you've played the first set of dances?'

'Why? What will you be doing?'

'Celia Mandeville's eloping. I've promised to help her.' I'd kept her secret. Now I needed Daniel's help and I couldn't hide it from him.

He groaned. 'Leave them to their own problems.'

'She's been kind to me. I owe her this at least.'

I did my best to reassure him, telling him my part in the proceedings would be over as soon as I'd escorted Celia down the back road. He wanted to come with us, but I refused. 'You must stay here with Mrs Martley. Then we have to find some means of getting her away safely.'

'Didn't you mention a horse?'

'I don't think she's capable of riding. We need a vehicle. Perhaps Amos Legge will think of something.'

We settled it that Daniel should rejoin his musicians and play through dinner. After dinner they'd give the first and, he hoped, only performance of *Welcome Home*. He'd direct the orchestra for the first set of dances, then leave them to his deputy again.

Mrs Martley was asleep when I went back inside. Now and then she muttered, 'No, no,' in her sleep. Once she opened her eyes and focused on me. 'It was him. His voice.'

She slept again. After the stable clock had struck nine, Daniel came back. We spoke on the landing. 'I've found a way of moving her,' he said. 'The tenor insists on going back to Windsor tonight. He says another night in the pavilion on a camp bed will ruin his voice. He's a fool, but I said he owed it to the world of music not to take the risk. So he's bribing somebody from the stables to have a vehicle of sorts ready. She'll manage to walk as far as the stableyard, won't she?'

'Yes. By then, I hope Amos Legge will be here with Rancie. We can all go together.' Daniel put his hands to his head and groaned again. 'I know, but I've got to provide for her somehow. I don't suppose Mr Blackstone will be paying livery bills any more.'

I left Daniel on guard over Mrs Martley and ran down the stairs to the bedroom corridor. I knocked softly on Celia's door.

'Come in.' Then, as soon as I took a step inside, 'Where have you been? I thought you weren't coming.'

She was half in and half out of her white and silver dress, hair coming down and cheeks streaked with tears.

'I can't get out of it,' she said. 'It won't let me go.' She put her arms behind her, wrenching at the long row of buttons at the back of the bodice. Little globes popped to the carpet. I started on what remained of the buttons.

'Do stand still.'

But she was almost past reason, tearing at the waistband. Silk ripped apart. She kicked her way out of the muslin petticoat and white kid shoes. 'I think my stepfather suspects something. He kept looking at me.'

The grey dress and a plain petticoat were ready on a chair and I managed to get them on her. She slid her silk-stockinged feet into the shoes we'd chosen, took a few steps and stumbled. 'I can't do it, Elizabeth. I can't do it.'

'Liberty. Do you mean walking or eloping?'

'Both.'

I put my hand on her shoulder and turned her round to make her look at me. 'Celia, I promise you that if you don't go now while you have the chance, you'll be unhappy for the rest of your life.'

The near-brutality in my hand and voice surprised even me.

'But you were the cautious one,' she said. 'You wanted me to talk to my mother or Stephen. I've been thinking, perhaps you were right . . .'

'It's past all that now,' I said. 'You're lucky that there's somebody who loves you waiting for you out there. You must forget everything else.'

She stared into my eyes and saw something that seemed to convince her. 'I'm sorry. I'm ready now. My cloak and bags are in the wardrobe.'

She'd packed two. I kept hold of one of them and gave her the other, then I opened the door and looked out. The corridor was deserted. I led the way at a fast walk to the servants' door. I heard the occasional gasp and the bumping of her bag on the stairs as she followed me, but she managed bravely enough. I took my usual route, down the narrow staircase to the chamber pots and out into the back courtyard. There were people there: a man and a kitchen maid talking. She put the hood of her cloak up and they took no notice of us. I led her across the courtyard and out through the archway. By the time we came to where the carriageway divided for the back road, she was breathing heavily.

'Let me rest, just a little.'

'A minute, no more.' There was still just enough light for anybody to see us. I'd feel happier once we were on the back road with banks and hedges on either side. She put down her bag and drew a long, shuddering breath. The jaunty rhythm of a mazurka came from the house. Lights from the downstairs windows flooded the terrace. 'Ready?'

We walked on, past the old oak where Mrs Beedle had waited for me, its branches black against a darkening sky. At last there were hedges right and left and beaten earth rather than gravel under our feet.

'Another minute, please.'

Before I could answer, a voice sounded a long way behind us.

'Celia? Where are you, Celia?'

Her body turned as stiff as one of the oak branches. 'It's Stephen. My stepfather must have sent him out to look for me.'

'It's some way off,' I said. 'He's probably on the terrace.'

But she was running down the lane, leaving her bag behind. I picked it up and followed at a fast walk.

'Celia?'

Still distant, but a little closer. I could make out her shape ahead of me. Then it lurched and disappeared. She gasped. 'Elizabeth!'

'Stay there, I'm coming.'

She was on the ground, hands round her left ankle.

'What's happened?'

'I can't get up.'

I knelt to give her my shoulder and she managed to get herself upright, but gasped when she tried to put her foot to the ground.

'Then you must hop,' I said, drawing her arm round my shoulder.

'What about the bags?'

'We'll have to leave them.'

We managed fifty yards or so. We couldn't hear her brother calling any more but now the hunt was up and it was only a matter of time before somebody came after us. Then the ground vibrated and the sound of hoofs came out of the darkness below us.

'Oh thank God,' Celia said. 'It's Philip come for me.'

I was less certain. Philip was supposed to be bringing a coach for her, but I could hear no wheels. It was almost completely dark now. The black shape of a horse's head and ears came into sight, then became a horse and rider. Celia's fingers dug into my arm.

'It isn't him.'

I was scared too, thinking that some of Sir Herbert's men had come to cut off our escape. A second horse's head came into view. The horse stopped suddenly, aware of us. A voice reassured it. 'Don't be feared, girl. Nobody's going to hurt you.' Amos Legge's voice.

'Rancie,' I said. 'Rancie girl.'

'Miss Lane, is that you?' He was riding the first horse.

'Yes. Is anybody behind you?'

'Gentleman with a phaeton, just turning it round in a gateway.'

'Philip,' Celia said. 'That's Philip.'

'How far down?' I said.

'Half a mile or so.'

Celia would never walk that far. 'I've a friend here wanting to get to the phaeton,' I said. 'Can you take her up in front of you?'

He reached down and swung Celia in front of his saddle as easily as if she'd been a bag of apples. 'Could you take hold of the other one, miss? She'll likely follow in any case.'

He handed me down Rancie's reins and she and I followed them along the lane. Rancie's head was up and she was sniffing the air. We'd only been going for a minute or two when I saw a circle of light coming up the road: a carriage lamp with a man on foot behind it.

'Philip!' Celia's voice sang out as confident and clear as a blackbird.

'Celia!' A deeper-toned bird called back to her.

When he reached us and the light fell on him I saw a slim and pale-faced man, probably tolerably good-looking but so full of hurry and anxiety it was hard to tell. Celia threw herself off the saddlebow at him and without hesitation he dropped the lamp and caught her in his arms. There was a flurry of 'so scared's and 'darling's and 'safe now'.

'No, you're not safe yet,' I said, bending to pick up the extinguished lamp. 'You're not safe until you're miles away and married.'

The phaeton was visible now, backed into a gateway with its one surviving lamp lit and a groom holding the two horses. Philip carried Celia into it and sat beside her with his arm round her. The groom jumped onto the box and turned the horses. As the phaeton began to move, Celia turned round. 'Elizabeth'—so she still hadn't heard me—'I'll always be grateful to you. I'll send for you when we have a house, I promise.'

'I doubt it very much,' I said. 'On both counts.'

But I said it to the back of the departing phaeton.

Amos Legge slipped off the cob and stood beside me. 'Where we going now, miss?'

'Up to the house.'

Looking back, it hurts me to think I didn't even thank him.

'Give you a leg up on Rancie, if you like. There's a saddle on her.'

'Better not, thank you.'

We both stayed on foot and went slowly up the lane in the dusk, he and the cob leading the way. At a bend, I glanced down to the main road and saw the light of the phaeton speeding through the dark. Somewhere, her conscientious Philip would have a clergyman waiting in a suitably private chapel and whatever happened her name wouldn't be Mandeville any more.

'Mr Legge,' I said into the dusk between us, 'there's something important I want to say to you. If anything happens to me, please keep

Rancie. Or if you can't keep her, find someone who'll treat her well.'

We took another few paces while he considered.

'If it makes your mind easier, yes.'

We went on up the road between clouds of white cow parsley flowers that seemed to glow against the dark hedges. We were almost at the point where the back road joined the carriage drive when Rancie stopped suddenly, raised her head and flared her nostrils.

'What's wrong, Rancie?'

The cob stopped too and whinnied. There were lanterns up ahead, and silhouettes behind. Then voices calling out to us, sharp and angry.

'Who are you? Stop where you are.'

And a sharper voice above the rest, 'Celia, is that you?'

I said softly to Amos Legge, 'Do you have a pistol with you?'

'They don't mean us any harm, miss. It's the other lady they're looking for.'

'Do you have a pistol? If you have, please lend it to me.'

It was a real hope. A man who travelled might carry one to keep off highwaymen.

'No, miss. In any case, there's no call for one.'

The cob was scared by now and wouldn't budge, so we stayed where we were as the lamps came towards us. There were five men. When one of them turned his lamp sideways, I could see that three of them looked like grooms or coachmen, one was the man who called himself Trumper, and the man leading them was Celia's brother, Stephen. His face was furious.

'Turn the light on them,' he snapped at one of the grooms. Then, seeing Amos Legge, 'Who the hell are you? What are you doing here?'

Amos Legge said nothing.

Stephen Mandeville took a step towards him. Legge didn't move an inch. 'I asked you a question.'

When Legge still didn't reply he raised an arm as if to punch him in the face. Legge simply grasped the arm and pushed it aside.

'Take hold of him,' Mandeville said to the grooms.

'Don't touch him,' I said. 'It has nothing to do with him.'

Until then, they'd not been paying me much attention. Now the light came on. 'I've seen her . . .' Trumper began.

'Her friend, the governess,' Stephen said.

'She's not a governess, she's—'

'It doesn't matter who she is. She's just helped my sister run away.'

Trumper yelled something to a groom about running up to the house and bringing back a couple of horses. Stephen rushed towards me. I couldn't see his face but felt the anger burning off him.

'Are you going to kill me too?' I said.

My hand ached for a pistol, a dagger, for anything. He flung me against Rancie's side, and before I could stop him, vaulted into the saddle and snatched the reins. 'Take the other . . .' he yelled.

I'm sure he was calling to Trumper to take the cob and come with him. He jerked sharply on the reins to turn Rancie. She gave him more chance than he deserved. For a moment she simply stood there, surprised by the pain on the bars of her mouth. He cursed her, jerked at the reins again. Her head went up, then up and up until her front hoofs were in the air and the shape of her was towering against the darkness like some horse in a legend landing from the sky. He was thrown off high into the air over my head, flying, then falling like a shot goose. I heard the snatched intake of his second last breath. Second last because, I dare say, he might have rattled a last one as he landed on his head on the hard-packed earth of the road and broke his neck more quickly and cleanly than the hangman would have done.

For another heartbeat Rancie reared up against the sky, then her front hoofs came down to earth with a thud softer than the one Stephen had made when he landed. After that, total silence for a moment, then Trumper and the grooms ran to the dark figure on the ground. His neck was skewed in a way no living man's could be. One of the grooms started swearing. Amos Legge's voice was in my ear. 'Get up on her, miss. You weren't here. You never saw anything.'

'He's dead,' I said.

His hand rested on my shoulder. 'No great loss, I dare say. Up you get.'

I think he must have thrown me up on Rancie, because one moment I was on the ground and the next I was across her back. Amos Legge pushed me upright in the saddle and gave me the reins. 'Go on. Wherever she takes you.'

'But you . . .'

'I'll find you. Now go on, girl.' He slapped a hand on Rancie's hindquarters and she spun round.

'Stop them! The damned horse has killed him.' Trumper's voice, from only a few steps away. The thought that he wanted to kill Rancie in revenge made me dig my heels into her sides. She hit full gallop in a couple of strides and was off into the darkness towards the main carriage drive. My instinct would have been for the back road, but Stephen's body and the grooms were there.

'Stop! Stop her!'

Trumper's voice, behind us and to the left. No hoofbeats, so he was probably following on foot. He might be trying to cut us off as we turned onto the bridge across the ha-ha, and he wasn't far behind. I urged Rancie on. As we hit the gravel of the main drive her pace slackened a little. A man's scream came from behind us. Trumper had come to grief. I supposed he'd forgotten the ha-ha and had fallen into it.

As we rounded the curve of the drive, I drew on the reins to bring Rancie back to a trot, gently I hoped, but she stopped so suddenly that only a handful of mane saved me from going off over her shoulder. Voice shaking, fearing that Trumper would clamber out of the ha-ha and catch up with us, I begged her to go on. Then I saw what was stopping her. There was something blocking the bridge: a carriage.

'Oh Lord, he's coming after us.' A woman's moan of fear came from the carriage. It sounded like Mrs Martley. While I was trying to puzzle it out, another voice from somewhere in the dark behind me.

'Liberty—is that you?' Daniel's voice.

'I'm here,' I said.

'Thank the gods. Where were you? I've been looking for you everywhere.' He came up beside us, caught me as I slid down and started hustling me towards the carriage. Rancie's reins were still in my hand.

'She must come with us,' I said. 'And we must wait for Amos Legge.'

'Legge will look after himself.'

He took the reins from me and tied them to the back of the carriage. I let him guide me. The sheer relief of finding him took away what was left of my strength. He bundled me into the carriage, next to Mrs Martley. There was a man sitting opposite her—presumably the tenor who had been so insistent on getting back to Windsor. The carriage started moving. I looked back at Mandeville Hall, fearful that the doors to the terrace would open and Sir Herbert come rushing out. The doors stayed closed, but all the downstairs windows were blazing with light and incredibly the sounds of a galop drifted out over the park.

'They're still dancing,' I said.

'Last dance in the second set,' said Daniel.

So Celia had left home and Stephen had died in less time than it took to skip through half a dozen dances. When we came to the lodge at the bottom of the drive the great gates were open in case of latecomers to the ball, so we drove straight through. For the next few miles I kept looking back towards Mandeville Hall until its brightly lit windows diminished to candle glimmers, then to nothing.

**I** think Daniel must have told the driver to keep to the back roads in case anybody tried to follow us, because by the time the sky started to grow light we were lurching at walking pace along a rutted lane between hedges. I'd told Daniel the story as we went along. All the time he'd kept hold of my hand.

'Child, I'd have given anything in the world to have spared you that.'

I think I'd shocked Daniel, describing Stephen Mandeville's end. It would have shocked him far more—Daniel being such a civilised man—if I'd tried to share with him the fierce joy I felt when I knew he was dead. That joy had faded now, leaving only an immense weariness.

'Didn't you guess he'd killed my father?' I said to Daniel. 'You must have known why she fainted.' I nodded across at Mrs Martley, asleep with her head against the leather hood. 'She saw him and heard his voice and knew he was the other man in the carriage.'

Daniel nodded.

'You did guess, then. Why didn't you say so?'

'I was concerned at what you might do. I thought if I could take you away to London, put it in the hands of the proper authorities . . .'

'Who'd have done nothing, you know that. He killed his own grandmother too, and they wouldn't have done anything about that either.'

Even now, although justice had been done in my heart, it would not show in the official records. The version put about by Sir Herbert and Kilkeel would be what the world knew. Mrs Beedle died of heart seizure after all and her grandson in a tragic riding accident while nobly trying to rescue his sister from an abductor. What his sister would feel I should probably never hear. I didn't expect to see Celia again. I'd done all I could to save her from the true story about her brother. Now she'd have to do the best she could with the rest of her life. Like me.

'You're convinced he killed Mrs Beedle too?' Daniel said.

'Sure of it. All his future, even his freedom, depended on pleasing his stepfather and making their plot succeed, and she was trying to stop it. Then there was that empty place opposite me at dinner.'

An empty place near the top of a table must be filled. Therefore, the place cards would be moved up and the gap left at the bottom instead. The son of the house had been otherwise employed.

'I wish I'd been with you,' he said.

'There was no time.' I didn't ask the question that was in my mind: 'What would you have done?' We're not allowed revenge any more. It belongs in savage myths and even then usually to men, seldom to women. Yet, remembering Amos Legge's hand resting for a moment on my shoulder, I thought he'd understood. But I'd left him there. He'd given me no choice in the matter.

'We must wait for Amos Legge when we get to Windsor,' I said.

'We're not waiting for anybody,' Daniel said. 'We'll be on the first coach to London. The magistrates there can't all be Sir Herbert's friends.'

'I don't think they can do anything against me now. They have too much to hide.'

'Probably, but I'm not taking the risk.'

I said nothing, not wanting to quarrel with him before I must. As the sun came up, a thin mist rose from the meadows on either side. Rancie, who'd been so quiet, suddenly raised her head and whinnied. Mrs Martley's eyes snapped open. 'Who is it? Who's after us?'

There were hoofbeats coming along the lane behind us at a steady canter. I turned and saw a heavy bay cob. He needed to be heavy because his rider was built like a young oak tree. I stood up and waved. 'Mr Legge. Amos Legge.'

He came up beside us. 'Morning, miss.'

'What happened?'

'Back there, you mean? Couldn't say. Didn't think I was needed, so I went and left them to it. It's taken me a while to catch up because I couldn't puzzle out what way you'd gone, see.' He grinned.

'Mr Legge, what shall you do when we get to Windsor?' My mind was heavy with the thought that we must part there.

'I'll see you and the gentleman on the London coach, then come on up with Rancie. The postboy can take the cob back to the livery stables.'

'Then home to Hereford?'

'No hurry about it, miss. Hereford's not going to run away. Reckon I might see how London suits me for a week or two.'

I felt warmed by that, until a thought struck me. 'We've forgotten the little cat. What will Rancie do without her?'

He smiled and undid the strap of his saddlebag. Two black paws hooked themselves over the edge of the bag and a pair of golden eyes blinked at the light. I looked from them to Amos Legge's grin, then to Daniel's concerned face, thinking that I was not after all so totally alone. True, I had no roof over my head, nothing in my purse and my only close relative was half a world away. Still, I had a horse, a cat and two friends. As for the rest of my revenge, maybe Mr Disraeli would at least half keep his half-promise. I could only hope for that. The walls of Windsor Castle were visible in the distance now, silver against the sun. I supposed little Vicky, if in residence, would be waking soon in her soft bed. In spite of everything, I did not envy her.

# Caro Peacock

'I am so glad that you chose Covent Garden for our meeting,' Caro Peacock told me as she took her seat in the restaurant. 'Some of my next Liberty Lane adventure takes place around here, in Seven Dials, so I have been walking the streets, getting a feel for the area and the distances—the Victorians walked a lot.'

From that moment on, Caro's love of the Victorian age was palpable and, as we talked, she made twenty-first-century London disappear as she told me where the idea for *Death at Dawn* had come from. 'I spent two seasons recently as a National Trust guide at Croft Castle in North Herefordshire. One of the Croft family ancestors, Sir Richard Croft, had been *accoucheur* [obstetrician] to Princess Charlotte, the only legitimate child of George IV. The baby boy was stillborn and the princess died a few hours later. Poor Sir Richard blamed himself—probably wrongly—and shot himself. Afterwards, there were ugly rumours that the princess and baby had been poisoned by enemies at court. Historically, the interesting thing is that if the child had lived, he would have inherited the throne after William IV and there would have been no Victorian age. In fact, Victoria would not even have been born, because with Charlotte dead, all the king's brothers were under orders to marry princesses and beget legitimate heirs. It is one of history's "what-ifs". I added another purely fictional "what-if": what if somebody pretended the baby had lived, had been spirited away, and then returned to claim his throne twenty years later?'

Caro wrote *Death at Dawn* around her work as a guide and as a gardener. 'Authors are like actors, as you know—we have to take several jobs just to keep going!' she admitted, prior to telling me about the activities that support her writing. She no longer acts as a guide, but she does work for two days a week in the garden of a fifteenth-century stately home. 'I'm incredibly lucky, I really am. I work in places that just breathe history. I know all about gardeners taking vegetables to the back door of the big house, because that's what I do. Now the big house has become the conservatory restaurant, but apart from that the setting and the job are just the same.'

What additional research does Caro do to make sure all the historical detail is correct? 'I use the internet, of course, and books, and I have a wonderful CD with maps of the 1830s. This very morning I popped into the London Library where I discovered a wonderful periodical called *John Bull*. Quite a lot of it is almost incomprehensible because it is satirical, but then my attention was grabbed by a full-page advertisement for a gentleman's lodgings, with stabling for three horses. Can you imagine *'What a wonderful* that today? I do love the research. The hardest thing is *world this is to* digging yourself out of it to actually start writing.' *inhabit—I love*

*Death at Dawn* is the first in a series featuring Liberty *being a writer and* Lane and I asked Caro how her heroine took shape? 'I *I am loving having* wanted her to have her roots in the radical tradition so I *adventures with* chose the name Liberty deliberately because I wanted to *Liberty Lane.'* write about a strong, independent woman. Today we view Victorian women as delicate creatures, ruled by men. But it is just not true. Many women travelled and ran businesses—you only have to look at Queen Victoria when she first took the throne. She was only eighteen and yet she had tremendous presence and was nobody's cat's-paw.'

When she is not writing or gardening, Caro Peacock has a real passion for travel. 'My favourite place is the Alps in June—I just love the flowers and the air, and the footpaths are so good that you can walk twenty miles a day. I am an obsessive walker. I also believe that, as you get older, you should take up something new every decade and not so long ago I took up trampolining. But last July I had a bad fall. I was doing a move when I went into a back flip but misjudged it and fell on my neck. I couldn't move it for months and was in a neck brace. My doctor told me, "Never again . . ." but you never know. That's one of the reasons that I look so mysterious in my photograph. To help disguise the neck brace we thought we'd have a bit of fun and add a hint of mystery. Oh, what a wonderful world this is to inhabit—I love being a writer and I am loving having adventures with Liberty Lane. In the next one she investigates the death of a dancer and, of course, Amos Legge and Daniel Suter are on hand to help her—but I'm determined not to marry her off too soon!'

*Jane Eastgate*

Printed and bound by GGP Media GmbH, Pössneck, Germany

601-044 UP0000-1